SHEF
ECHOES THROUGH TIME
- BOOK I -

THE OBSIDIAN STALLION

Anna Charlotte Fox

ISBN - Paperback: 9798325489815

ISBN - Hardcover: 9798325489129

First Edition: June 2024

To K.

My beloved first Arabian mare,
who opened the gates to the enchanting realm of Arabian horses
and their storied past.

Your grace and spirit have galloped through the pages of my imagination,
infusing this tale with the magic and mystery of your lineage.

CONTENTS

PREFACE

From the moment I first opened the pages of Sir Arthur Conan Doyle's stories decades ago, Sherlock Holmes became for me more than a character in a book; he became the gateway to a world of intrigue and intellect - a world I never wanted to leave. The decision to write "The Obsidian Stallion" and begin this series came from a place of deep admiration. A childhood dream came true when Holmes' adventures became part of the public domain.

This series is my homage to the spirit of Doyle's work. While I do not claim to match his literary mastery, I hope to honour the essence of Holmes and Watson in my stories. The stories I have created come from a personal place - they are tales woven with threads of my lifelong fascination with history and the mysteries of the human mind.

As you turn these pages, you will not find reinterpretations of Holmes, but a celebration of the timeless character as Doyle presented him - brilliant, observant and quintessentially British. Set against the backdrop of the Victorian and Edwardian eras, each story resonates with the authenticity and spirit of Holmes' original adventures.

I invite you to join me on this journey, to relive the excitement of Holmes and Watson's escapades, and perhaps to see these beloved characters through the lens of my own experiences and passions. This journey is not just mine, but ours - may you find joy and intrigue in the mysteries we will uncover together.

Thank you for allowing me to share my love of Holmes with you.

PROLOGUE

B eneath the celestial gaze of a crescent moon, the Arabian desert stretched out like an ethereal canvas. Golden sands undulated in gentle waves, interrupted only by the silhouettes of two travellers - father and son - traversing the dunes. Idris Al-Hakim, a master craftsman renowned for his exquisite workmanship, bore the wisdom of ages in his weathered features. The night air whispered secrets of the ancients as they ventured deeper into the heart of the desert.

Idris, his hands as deft with the delicate tools of his trade as they were with the reins of his camel, led the creature with sure command. Beside him, Malik, a youth on the cusp of manhood, rode his camel with wonder in his eyes. "Father," Malik began, breaking the silence, "how do our ancestors find inspiration in such a vast, empty land?"

The desert at night was a realm of paradoxes, both barren and full. Shadows danced across the dunes in the moonlight. The footsteps of the camels and the soft clink of their harnesses mingled with the call of a distant owl, the only sound in the profound silence.

As they ventured deeper into the heart of this timeless landscape, Idris began to speak. "Malik, my son," he began, making sure his words were carried on the wind, "this desert, as endless and eternal as it may seem, is like the canvas of our trade." Suddenly, a distant, eerie wail interrupted his words, hinting at some unseen danger lurking just over the horizon.

Malik listened, his heart open and eager, absorbing his father's wisdom. This journey was more than a journey across the physical sands; it was a passage through the realms of heritage and history, a continuation of the legacy of the Al-Hakim lineage. Idris continued, "Our ancestors, Malik, were craftsmen of great renown, each contributing to the world through his craft. They believed

3

that true mastery lay in the balance between form and function, between the beauty of the object and the purpose it served.

The night grew darker and the stars passed overhead in slow, majestic arcs, each a silent sentinel for the unfolding dialogue between father and son. Idris' voice carried on the cool breeze, his words steeped in the wisdom of generations past. He spoke of the sacred bond between creator and creation, the duty of the craftsman to infuse each piece with integrity and beauty. "To honour the materials we work with," Idris intoned, his eyes reflecting the celestial tapestry above, "is to enrich the world with each creation born of our hands.

As the cool breeze carried his words to Malik, the young man felt a deep connection to their lineage. Yet a sudden chill seemed to creep into the air, a subtle hint of the unpredictable nature of the desert. In the vastness of the desert and the eternal stars above, he saw a reflection of the path he was to follow - a path paved with dedication, skill and the eternal pursuit of excellence, but not without its dangers.

Under the watchful eyes of the crescent moon and the ancient whispering stars, Idris Al-Hakim and his son Malik's journey wove itself through the tapestry of the night, a thread in the grand weave of their family's legacy. The desert, a silent keeper of secrets and dreams, bore witness to this rite of passage, its stark beauty a testament to the passage of time. As the sands shifted beneath their camels' feet, an old era faded, giving way to the dawn of a new age, ripe with promise and untold stories waiting to be told.

⊰⊱

As the moon rose higher, casting a silvery light over the dunes, Idris began to tell Malik stories of their ancestors. "Long ago," he began, his voice soft against the whispering sands, "our ancestors were renowned for their deep understanding of the materials they shaped. As the night deepened, filled with Idris's lessons, a sudden shift in the wind heralded an unforeseen danger.

"Long ago," Idris's voice echoed softly against the backdrop of the whispering sands, "our ancestors were renowned not only for the beauty of their creations, but for their profound understanding of the materials they shaped. Each piece, whether of clay, stone or sand, was a dialogue between the craftsman and the earth.

Malik, his eyes reflecting the starry sky, listened intently, his soul absorbing every word. With each story, he felt the weight and wonder of his heritage - a lineage of skilled craftsmen who had passed their knowledge down through the generations like a sacred torch.

Idris continued, his words flowing like the gentle winds over the dunes. "Consider the sand beneath our feet, Malik. It is both timeless and transient. With patience and skill it can be shaped into glass, clear and strong. Such is the nature of our craft. We must see not only what is before us, but also what could be. We must see the sand not as loose and fleeting grains, but as the clear, solid glass it might one day become.

The desert around them seemed to be listening, the eternal sands a testament to the lessons Idris was imparting. "And just as the desert shapes the landscape," Idris gestured to the vast expanse around them, "so must we shape the materials we work with, guided by respect for their essence and an understanding of their potential."

Feeling the deep connection between the timeless lessons of the desert and the ethos of their craft, Malik found a deeper respect for the materials that had long been the foundation of their family's legacy. He saw in his mind's eye the transformation of raw, unyielding elements into objects of beauty and purpose, each creation a bridge between the past and the future.

Idris, noticing the glimmer of understanding in his son's eyes, smiled gently. "Remember, my son, that each piece we create carries a part of us. It speaks of our commitment to our craft, our respect for the past and our hopes for the future. This is the legacy we inherit, and this is the legacy we will pass on. As I learned from your grandfather, so you will learn from me, and so your children will learn from you.

The night deepened and the stars shone brighter, their celestial glow a canopy of silent witnesses to the sacred transmission of knowledge and wisdom. The desert, with its endless sands and timeless winds, was both classroom and companion, its vastness a constant reminder of the small but significant place they held in the continuum of history.

As the lessons continued, Malik's heart swelled with pride and purpose. He understood that his journey was not simply to follow in his father's footsteps, but to forge his own path, guided by the values and skills he had inherited, but shaped by his own vision and dreams.

Thus, under the watchful eyes of the crescent moon and the ancient stars, the lessons in the dunes forged not only a craftsman, but a guardian of a profound cultural heritage, ready to carry on the legacy of the Al-Hakim family. In the silent symphony of the desert night, the bond between father and son was strengthened, a bond sealed by shared stories, shared wisdom and a shared love of a craft that transcends time.

Idris Al-Hakim and his son Malik began to prepare their campsite for the night as the celestial ballet of stars continued its silent dance across the sky. They sought shelter against a jagged outcrop of ancient rock that jutted out of the soft sand like the spine of the earth. The desert night was falling fast, the air cooling as the last whispers of sunset faded into the deep indigo of dusk, bathing the dunes in an ethereal, otherworldly glow.

Idris dismounted his camel with the practiced ease of one who had spent

THE OBSIDIAN STALLION

many nights under the open sky. "Always remember, my son, that for all its beauty, the desert demands respect and caution," he instructed Malik in a tone seasoned with experience.

With methodical precision he began to unpack their equipment. From the seemingly modest bundles strapped to their camels he extracted woollen blankets, a small portable tent and the necessary tools for a small fire. Each item had its place and purpose, nothing superfluous was carried, for in the desert the weight one carried could mean the difference between endurance and exhaustion.

"First we secure shelter," Idris explained, his hands skilfully assembling the frame of the tent. "The beauty of the desert is matched by its harshness, and the nights can be as cold as the days." Malik watched intently, memorising every move - the way his father spread the canvas, anchored the corners with small sand-filled sacks, and finally arranged the bedding inside.

Next, Idris gathered a handful of dry brush and twigs, sparse gifts from the desert, and arranged them in a cleared space. "Fire is life out here," he said, striking a flint to coax sparks onto a small bundle of dried grass. "It wards off the cold of the night and any predators that might roam the dunes." The tinder caught and the flames began to crackle, casting a warm, flickering light against the stark, shadowed rocks.

Under his father's watchful eye, Malik took lessons in finding scarce firewood and the art of fire-making - skills essential for survival in this vast, untamed landscape. The soft orange glow of the fire illuminated his features, etching them with a look of determined learning.

As the fire grew steadier, Idris turned his attention to preparing a simple meal. From their supplies he produced some flat bread, dried dates and a small pot in which he brewed strong, aromatic tea. "Food need not be elaborate," he remarked, handing Malik a piece of bread. "What matters is that it feeds the body and the mind."

They ate quietly, the silence of the desert enveloping them like a vast, ancient cloak. Above them, the stars shone with a clarity only the desert could provide, each one a story, a history, a silent guardian of the endless sands below.

After their meal, Idris taught Malik the importance of conserving resources, especially water. "In the desert, water is more precious than gold," he explained, showing him how to carefully measure their remaining supply and plan for the next day's needs. Malik took these lessons with the seriousness they demanded, understanding that here, in the heart of the desert, knowledge and prudence were as important as any physical resource.

Eventually, as night sealed them in its cool embrace, Idris taught Malik the art of reading the stars - a navigational skill that had guided desert dwellers for millennia. "The stars are our map and compass," he said, pointing to the constellations that had guided caravans through these shifting sands.

The campsite, now a small bastion of warmth and light against the vast, dark expanse of the desert, was a testament to the skills Idris had passed on. Here, in this elemental solitude, Malik learned not only the practical skills of survival, but also deeper, almost spiritual lessons about respect, resourcefulness and the interconnectedness of life.

As they sat by the fire, the desert around them seemed to listen, a timeless witness to the bond and legacy forged on this starlit night. In the deep silence, filled only with the sounds of the crackling fire and the distant call of a night creature, father and son found a deeper connection - an unspoken understanding that they were part of something greater than themselves, part of the timeless rhythm of the desert.

⸺⸱⸱⸱⸺

Malik wrapped himself in a thick, woven blanket, the fabric still holding the warmth of the day's relentless sun as the embers of the campfire faded to a soft glow. The night had fallen into a deep silence, broken only by the occasional whisper of the wind dancing across the dunes. The stark, infinite beauty of the desert enveloped him, the sky a tapestry of stars, each one a silent sentinel watching over the vast and timeless landscape. In this moment of quiet contemplation, Malik felt the weight of his destiny and the deep connection to the land that had shaped his family's legacy for generations.

After making sure their camp was secure and watching Malik settle down, Idris joined his son by the remains of the fire. "The desert teaches us the impermanence of life and the permanence of legacy," he began, his voice soft but carrying in the crisp night air. "Each grain of sand, a fleeting moment; each crafted artefact, a lasting testament."

Malik, his eyes reflecting the flickering flames, turned to his father, the weight of his future responsibilities pressing lightly on his shoulders. "Father," he ventured, his voice a mixture of awe and uncertainty, "how does one ensure his creations are worthy of the legacy he inherits? How does one build a future that honours the past?"

Idris smiled, the lines around his eyes deepening, a map of years spent under the desert sun. "My son, the creations that last, that truly endure beyond the span of their creator's life, are those made with integrity and passion. You have seen how I work with the materials - be it wood, stone or metal. Each element speaks and the wise craftsman listens. It is a dialogue, Malik, a partnership between the material and the maker."

He pauses, picks up a small handful of sand and lets it slowly trickle through his fingers back onto the floor. "Like these sands, ideas are plentiful and can slip from your grasp. But once you capture one, treat it with respect, shape it with care, and it can become something eternal."

Malik absorbed his father's words, feeling their truth resonate within him. He thought of the pieces his father had made - the intricate inlays on ceremonial chests, the delicate filigree on water jugs, each item not just a thing of beauty but a vessel of function and purpose.

"The responsibility may seem great," Idris continued, reaching out to place a reassuring hand on his son's shoulder, "but remember, you are not merely shaping materials into objects. You are infusing them with your spirit, your vision. That is what makes a true craftsman. Your future creations will be your dialogue with the world, your legacy.

The fire had died down to glowing embers, casting a warm, soothing light. Malik felt a clarity settle over him, like the clear desert sky after a sandstorm. The legacy of craftsmanship wasn't just about preserving tradition; it was about enhancing it, growing it and, most importantly, making it your own. It was about leaving a part of yourself in the work for future generations to see, to touch, to understand.

"Thank you, Father," Malik said, his voice calmer and more confident. "I hope to work not only with my hands, but with my heart, as you taught me."

Idris nodded, pride in his eyes. "And that, Malik, will be your true legacy. More than the objects you create, it will be the heart you put into them that will endure."

As they sat together, the vast desert around them - witness to centuries of shifting sands and changing winds - seemed to agree in silence. The lessons of the night took root in Malik's heart, each one a seed of future possibilities. Here, under the watchful eyes of the stars, a craftsman was not only born, but awakened to the deeper call of his heritage, ready to make his mark on the sands of time.

⊷⊶⊷⊶⊷

The tranquil cocoon of their campsite was abruptly shattered by an ominous shift in the wind. The once gentle breeze grew in ferocity. Idris, his senses honed by decades in the desert, felt a tingle of unease. "Malik, to the tent - quickly!" he ordered, his voice urgent and firm.

The sky, so recently a clear vault dotted with countless stars, began to churn with unsettling speed. The constellations were quickly obscured by a burgeoning mass of dense, churning clouds that swept across the sky with relentless purpose. Idris's eyes, sharpened by decades of navigating the capricious moods of the desert, widened with recognition of the impending danger.

"Malik, to the tent - quickly!" Idris' voice cut through the rising howl of the wind with commanding urgency. His tone left no room for hesitation and Malik, sensing the gravity of the situation, leapt into action, his heart pounding with a sudden surge of adrenaline.

As father and son hunkered down in the modest shelter of their canvas tent, the full wrath of the desert was unleashed outside. The wind grew into a fearsome gale, bringing with it a torrent of sand that pelted the tent with the force of a thousand tiny daggers. The fabric, though sturdy, swayed and strained against the tempestuous assault, the ropes creaking and groaning in protest.

Within the tenuous safety of their shelter, Idris quickly gathered their most essential supplies - waterskins, a small, sturdy lantern and a thick rope. His movements were precise and calculated, each action the result of years of experience and survival instinct honed by countless encounters with nature's wrath.

"Listen carefully, Malik," Idris said, his voice steady despite the chaos raging just beyond the thin edge of the canvas. "A sandstorm of this magnitude can disorientate even the most experienced traveller. We must stay together, and if the tent gives way, hold on to the rope. It will be our lifeline in the blindness of the storm."

Malik nodded, his young face set with determination. His eyes, wide with a mixture of fear and awe, remained fixed on his father, drawing courage from his unyielding composure.

The storm outside grew monstrous, the soundscape a relentless roar that seemed to shake the very ground beneath them. The sand, whipped into a frenzy by the wind, created a dense, abrasive fog that obscured all sight. It was as if the night had been swallowed whole by a ravenous beast, leaving nothing but a swirling, suffocating chaos in its wake.

A sudden chill in the air and a change in the direction of the wind were the first signs. Idris' eyes narrowed as he scanned the horizon. "Malik, something is coming," he muttered. Moments later, a violent gust hit the tent, tearing at the poles. Idris and Malik gripped the rope tightly, the coarse fibres biting into their palms.

"Hold on, Malik! Don't let go!" Idris shouted, his voice barely audible over the roar of the storm. Together they braced themselves against the relentless force of the desert's wrath, their bodies tensed for whatever might come next.

The minutes stretched into what seemed like hours, every second a battle of endurance against the power of the storm. As suddenly as it had begun, the fury of the wind began to subside, the wild howling diminishing to a weary moan that swept across the now eerily silent desert.

As calm returned, Idris and Malik, still clutching the lifeline between them, cautiously emerged from the remains of their battered tent. The landscape around them had completely changed, the familiar contours of the dunes reshaped into unfamiliar patterns by the capricious hands of the storm.

Breathing heavily, their bodies covered in a fine layer of sand, they surveyed the changed world around them - a stark reminder of the desert's power to both create and destroy. Idris placed a hand on Malik's shoulder, a silent gesture of reassurance in the face of nature's overwhelming display.

"This, my son, is the lesson of the desert," Idris murmured, his eyes sweeping over the transformed vista. "In its beauty and fury, it teaches us humility, resilience and respect for forces greater than ourselves."

Together, under the slowly reappearing tapestry of stars, father and son stood amidst the reshaped sands, a testament to their survival and the enduring lessons of the desert. The storm had passed, but its effects would linger in their minds, a profound encounter with the raw and untamed spirit of the vast and mysterious desert.

✦❖✦

Malik and his father, Idris, found themselves caught up in the sudden fury of the desert as relentless sands pounded the landscape. The wind howled, a symphony of chaos that seemed to emanate from a thousand ancient spirits awakened from their slumber. Sharp, unyielding sand swirled around them, a storm of nature's own making, blotting out the moon and stars and plunging the world into a tumultuous darkness. The camels, their eyes wide with primal fear, bucked and writhed against the storm, their plaintive cries swallowed by the ravenous wind.

In the chaos, the camels, those faithful companions of the desert wanderer, faltered. Their eyes, wide with primal fear, reflected the panic of the storm. They bucked and wriggled, struggling against the storm that tore at their hides, their plaintive cries swallowed by the ravenous wind. It was a battle of beasts against the raw elements, a testament to the merciless power of the desert.

Amidst this maelstrom, Malik's grip on his mount tightened, his knuckles white as he clung to the only semblance of stability in the shifting sands. The roar of the storm was deafening, a relentless assault that filled the air with a palpable sense of dread. His heart pounded fiercely, each beating a drum of impending doom as he silently prayed for deliverance from the storm's wrath.

But the desert was not done with its display of savage grandeur. From the heart of the storm emerged a new and fearsome figure - a desert lion, its massive form eerie and terrifying in the swirling sands. Its eyes, fierce and glowing with an unearthly light, fixed on Idris with the cold certainty of a predator. The lion's fur was matted with sand, its powerful muscles rippling beneath its tawny pelt as it prepared to strike.

With a roar that split the night, the lion pounced. Idris, caught off guard, was torn from his camel. The scene was a blur - sand, wind and the terrifying lion all converging. Idris's cry of pain and defiance was almost lost in the storm, a protest against the overwhelming power of nature and beast.

Horrified, Malik could do nothing but watch as his father struggled with the beast. The battle was brutal and primal; man and lion locked in a dance of survival, their forms intermittently visible through the curtains of sand. The lion's claws flashed, its teeth bared in a snarl of rage and hunger, every movement a display of raw, untamed power.

Idris fought back with desperate courage. His hands, those of a craftsman accustomed to shaping the delicate and the durable, now struggled to repel the deadly advances of the desert predator. His movements were a mixture of practiced precision and wild desperation, a fight not only for life but for legacy.

As the storm continued to rage around them, the battle reached its critical climax. The lion, relentless in his charge, seemed an unstoppable force - a creature not only of flesh and blood, but of the desert itself, born of sand and wind and the cruel whims of nature.

Malik, tears streaming down his face, buffeted by wind and sand, felt a helplessness so deep it threatened to engulf him. The sight of his father's struggle, the potential loss of his guiding light and mentor, was more than a threat to his life - it was a threat to the very essence of who he was, the legacy he was destined to inherit.

The fury of battle, the howling of the storm and the roar of the lion merged into a single, overwhelming cacophony - a testament to the desert's savage beauty and brutal power. It was then that Malik understood the true wildness of the world he loved, a world as deadly as it was beautiful, as unforgiving as it was awe-inspiring.

As the battle seemed to reach its tragic conclusion, with Idris faltering under the relentless power of the lion, Malik could only watch in a mixture of awe and despair, his fate and that of his father hanging in the balance of the storm's cruel whims.

⊱✦⊰

Amidst the heightened fury of the desert storm, despair gripped Malik's heart as he watched his father, Idris Al-Hakim, wrestle with the marauding desert lion. The harrowing sight was revealed in fleeting, haunting glimpses as the sand, whipped into a frenzy by the storm's relentless winds, alternately obscured and revealed the tragic struggle. The lion, a formidable embodiment of the merciless spirit of the desert, sunk its claws deep into the fabric of their existence, each tear a brutal reminder of nature's indifference to man's plight. Malik felt the foundations of his world crumble with every passing second, the fragments scattered to the winds.

Malik stood helplessly, the sand stinging his eyes as he witnessed the seemingly inevitable loss of his father, his mentor, his guiding star. Idris' cries of pain, muffled by the roar of the wind, were punctuated by the lion's ferocious growl, each sound a hammer blow to Malik's soul. The young man felt the foundations of his world crumble, each fragment blown away by the storm, leaving him in a maelstrom of hopelessness and despair.

11

As the lion's roar reached a crescendo, signalling his dominance and the seemingly imminent defeat of his father, an extraordinary phenomenon unfolded. From the heart of the storm, where the sands swirled wildest and the winds screamed with the voices of a thousand lost souls, emerged a figure so majestic and unreal that Malik questioned his own senses.

It was a stallion, as if carved from the very essence of the night. His coat shimmered with an obsidian sheen, reflecting the chaotic light of the storm in a spectral display of dark iridescence. The stallion approached silently, in stark contrast to the cacophony around him, moving with a grace that belied the violence of the surrounding storm. His mane and tail billowed like tendrils of smoke, tracing his path through the air with ethereal elegance.

The stallion's eyes burned with a fierce, otherworldly light, twin embers glowing at the heart of the storm, radiating an ancient and formidable power. As the battle between man and beast approached, the air around the stallion seemed to throb with a palpable force, the sand beneath his hooves glowing with an unearthly luminescence.

Without hesitation or fear, the stallion charged the lion, who, sensing the presence of a superior force, faltered in his charge. The lion's roar, once a sound of terrifying dominance, became a whimper of fear. The predator that had embodied the mercilessness of the desert now cowered before the ghostly apparition of the stallion.

In a climactic convergence of forces, as if fate itself had woven its will into the moment, the stallion struck the lion with a force that seemed to resonate with the fundamental energies of the desert. His hooves, glowing with a mystical light, struck the lion's flank with a resounding blow that echoed across the dunes like a cosmic gong, signalling a shift in the very fabric of the unfolding story.

The lion, his body shattered by the force of the stallion's blow, collapsed into the sand, his life force draining away into the land that had given birth to him and now reclaimed him. The desert, always a land of stark contrasts and brutal reckonings, watched in silence as the lion's form was gradually swallowed by the shifting sands, a testament to the impermanence of even the fiercest of lives.

Malik watched in awe and confusion as the stallion turned its piercing gaze upon him and his fallen father. The creature's eyes, deep wells of primal knowledge and ancient magic, seemed to peer directly into his soul, offering not only his father's salvation, but a profound recognition of Malik's own place within the endless cycles of desert lore.

In that moment, with the storm still raging around them, Malik understood that this was no ordinary beast that had come to their aid, but a creature of legend, born from the heart of the desert's deepest mysteries. It was a guardian of the sands, a protector of those who respected and revered the harsh, beautiful wilderness that was their home.

As the stallion slowly turned and disappeared into the swirling sands from whence it had come, Malik felt a profound shift within himself. The despair that had gripped his heart was now mingled with awe and a renewed sense of purpose. The desert had shown its fury, but it had also revealed its magic, giving him a glimpse of the mystical forces that balanced the scales of life and death across its vast, unfathomable expanse.

⊕⊕⊕

The winds of the desert storm slowly subsided, and as the dust began to settle, a poignant and profound scene unfolded beneath the still tumultuous sky. The mythical stallion, his obsidian hide gleaming in the fading light, stood sentinel over the tragic tableau. Idris Al-Hakim lay dying, his lifeblood seeping into the ancient sands that had witnessed countless dramas through the ages. Malik knelt beside his father, grief etching his features as he gripped Idris's hand, the weight of the moment bearing down on him like the relentless desert sun.

Malik, his heart heavy with a grief that seemed to consume the very air around him, knelt beside his father. The sand, stirred into gentle swirls by the dying gusts of the storm, clung to his robes, embracing him as if to draw him into the timeless embrace of the desert. His father's hand, still strong despite the pallor of approaching death, gripped his with a desperation that belied the calm that had settled over his features.

Idris's eyes, once bright with the vigour of life and the joy of creation, now gazed upward with piercing clarity, reflecting the stormy skies above and the profound realisation of his imminent journey beyond the veil of the mortal realm. The sturdy stallion, his presence an ethereal gift bestowed by the mysterious forces of the desert, stood nearby, his breaths visible in the cool air, a rhythmic affirmation of life amidst the encroaching shadow of death.

"Malik, my beloved son," Idris began, his voice a hoarse whisper, but each word carrying the weight of his love and the urgency of his final testament. "The legacy of our ancestors, the art and soul of our people, now rests on your shoulders. Do not let the fear of this moment cloud your vision of your destiny."

He paused, each breath an effort, drawing on the last reserves of his strength. "Create, as we have always created, with honour and reverence for the craft. But more than that, my son, create with the passion that burns in your heart, the same passion that has fuelled the fires of our forges and shaped the destiny of our lineage."

Malik, tears mingling with the desert dust on his cheeks, nodded, his throat tight with emotion. "I will, Father. I will use the tools of our trade with all the skill and wisdom you have given me. I will honour our traditions and forge new paths as you have taught me."

Idris smiled, a faint, fleeting curve of his lips that spoke of pride and indomitable spirit. "Look at the stallion, Malik. Let him be a symbol of the strength and freedom of our spirit. Create in its image the guardians of our heritage - strong, noble, enduring. Let them stand as protectors of the wisdom we cherish, the beauty we create, and the truths we uphold.

With these words, Idris Al-Hakim's grip softened, his hand slowly relaxing as the last vestiges of life faded. His eyes, still fixed on the roiling sky above, seemed to reflect a deep peace, a soul ready to rise on the desert winds to join the ancestors in the realm of eternal sands.

As if sensing the solemnity of the moment, the stallion bowed his great head, his mane falling like a veil of shadow. It was a gesture of respect, of farewell to a soul he had come to lead across the threshold between worlds.

Left in the wake of his father's departure, Malik felt the immensity of his loss, but a new determination stirred within him, fuelled by Idris' last words and the mystical presence of the stallion. He knew that his path was irrevocably set, a path that would require him to combine the traditions of the past with the visions of the future.

As the first light of dawn broke through the clouds, illuminating the desert in shades of gold and crimson, Malik rose. His heart was heavy with loss, but a new resolve had taken root within him. He felt a new sense of responsibility and purpose, ready to honour his father's legacy. His figure, determined yet solemn, stood against the vast expanse of the desert, a testament to his transformation and the enduring spirit of those who call its sands home.

With a final nod, the stallion turned and galloped into the burgeoning light, his form gradually fading into the glow of the new day, leaving Malik to forge his lineage's legacy in the sands of time. In the years to come, the memory of that night, of the storm, the lion and the obsidian stallion, would shape Malik into a legend of his own, a guardian of ancient wisdom and a creator of wonders yet unseen.

For in the desert, where reality and myth dance on the shifting sands, legends are not simply born. They are forged in the fires of trial and tribulation, sculpted by the winds of fate and polished by the sands of time. And Malik Al-Hakim, son of Idris, chosen by the Obsidian Stallion, would rise to meet his destiny, his creations standing as monuments to the power of the human spirit and the legacy of those who came before.

⚜

Malik Al-Hakim stood alone amidst a transformed landscape as the tumultuous echoes of the sandstorm faded, leaving a hushed silence over the vast desert. The first tendrils of dawn stretched across the horizon, painting the endless sand dunes in a cascade of gold and amber, transforming the barren expanse into a sea of glowing warmth. Before him, a simple mound, marked by a single, unassuming stone, stood as a humble memorial - the final testament of his father, Idris Al-Hakim. Idris's life, as rich and intricate as the crafts he created, had been cut short by the unforgiving desert and a savage encounter with a lion, leaving Malik to shoulder the weight of his legacy.

The rawness of the loss gripped Malik's heart, a deep ache that felt as if a vital part of his being had been irrevocably torn away. Yet amidst this deep well of grief, there was a growing sense of responsibility - the weight of his father's legacy settling on his shoulders like a mantle that was both an honour and a burden. It was not a legacy of tangible wealth or widespread fame, but rather one of extraordinary skill, profound wisdom and an unbreakable bond between creator and creation - a profound continuum that Malik was now destined to uphold and advance.

Lost in a reverie of grief and reflection, Malik barely noticed the silent presence watching him from afar. Turning to the sensation of being watched, his eyes widened in a mixture of wonder and recognition as they met the gaze of the obsidian stallion. The magnificent creature that had miraculously emerged from the heart of the storm stood silently, its piercing crimson eyes holding Malik in a steady, almost protective gaze. It was more than a saviour; it was a symbol of the untamed spirit of the desert - of the hidden mysteries and ancient secrets buried beneath the shifting sands, secrets waiting to be unearthed by those brave enough to seek them out.

In this silent communion, a profound understanding passed between man and mythical beast - an unspoken acknowledgement of the arduous journey Malik was about to embark upon. The stallion was not merely a protector of flesh and blood, but a guardian of destiny, embodying the raw, primal essence of the desert and its timeless lore.

With a heavy but determined heart, Malik offered a prayer of gratitude and farewell to the desert and the forces that had spared his life. Then he turned his gaze to the distant oasis that shimmered like a mirage on the horizon, promising a sanctuary for rest and reflection, a place to begin anew. Mounting the camel that had patiently weathered the storm at his side, Malik felt the tangible weight of his father's teachings and the mystical encounter with the stallion solidify into a driving force within him.

As he set off into the vast unknown, the soft glow of dawn illuminating his path, the obsidian stallion remained a watchful figure in the background. Then, as if acknowledging the end of his earthly role, the stallion turned and galloped back into the heart of the desert. Its form gradually blurred into the landscape, shimmering and shifting until it was indistinguishable from the sands and winds of legend.

Malik watched until the stallion was nothing more than a speck against the vast, brightening sky - a final, fleeting glimpse of the extraordinary magic and mystery that had irrevocably changed the course of his life. As the light of day grew stronger, painting the desert once again in vibrant hues of life, Malik knew that the road ahead would be littered with challenges and moments of despair. But he also felt an unshakable conviction that he would not face these trials alone. The spirit of his father, the wisdom imparted by his teachings, and the guidance of the mystical stallion would be with him, invisible yet palpable presences, guiding him to his destiny.

Thus, with each step forward, Malik Al-Hakim embraced his role as the bearer of his family's legacy, ready to forge a future that would honour the past while forging a new vision for generations to come. In the vast, whispering sands of the desert, where reality meets legend and the old dances with the new, Malik's journey was just beginning - a journey that would see him emerge as a guardian of ancient wisdom and a creator of enduring beauty, his own legend woven into the fabric of the desert's endless stories.

ACT I

CHAPTER 1

A DAY AT THE DERBY

U nder the vast expanse of a cerulean sky, devoid of even the faintest wisp of cloud, Epsom Downs stretched out like a verdant sea, its undulating waves of grass swaying gently in the breeze. It was Derby Day, a jewel in the crown of British tradition, and there was a palpable sense of anticipation in the air. A myriad of colours burst from the crowds of spectators, whose attire ranged from the height of fashion to the simple, practical garb of the common man, creating a vibrant tapestry that reflected the diverse social strata that had come to witness this great spectacle.

The scent of freshly cut grass mingled with the earthy aroma of horses and leather to create a distinctive Derby Day bouquet. The tempting smells of roast meat and sweet confectionery wafted from the scattered food stalls, enticing the crowds to indulge in more than just the spectacle of the race.

The Downs were a breathtaking sight. Grandstands packed to the rafters lined the vast expanse, while the rolling Surrey hills provided a picturesque backdrop. The meticulously groomed track looped around the green, ready to thunder with the hoofbeats of the finest horses in the land.

A symphony of excited chatter filled the air as people from all walks of life - aristocrats, merchants, labourers, young and old - gathered, united by the thrill of the race and a shared love of this timeless tradition. Children's laughter rang out, a joyful counterpoint to the buzz of conversation, adding a touch of innocence to the day's festivities.

"Lovely, isn't it, Holmes?" I remarked, my eyes sweeping over the colourful array of humanity. My companion, Sherlock Holmes, stood beside me, his keen eyes taking in the scene with a detached curiosity that revealed his intrigue.

"Quite a panorama, Watson," he replied, a hint of amusement in his voice. "A study in sociology and anthropology presented under the guise of sport."

Indeed, Holmes was never one to simply observe; he analysed, dissected every nuance and detail with the precision of a scholar. And yet, despite his analytical detachment, I knew he appreciated the spectacle for what it was - a celebration of tradition and human endeavour.

As we made our way through the crowd, I couldn't help but be drawn in by the energy that surrounded us. Flags and banners fluttered in the breeze, each bearing the colours and emblems of the jockeys and their patrons. The bookmakers called out the odds from their stands, their voices ringing out like carnival barkers, enticing eager punters to place their bets.

The horses themselves were paragons of equine beauty and power. As they were paraded by their handlers, these majestic animals impressed spectators with their rippling muscles, glossy coats, meticulously braided manes, and flowing plumed tails, fully embodying the image of elite athletes. The sight of these magnificent creatures, so full of potential energy and grace, gave me a deep appreciation for the art of riding.

"Each one is a testament to years of careful breeding and training," I mused aloud as I watched a bay stallion prance slightly, his nerves evident even in his regal bearing.

Holmes nodded, his eyes following a speckled grey. "Indeed, Watson. It is the culmination of generations of knowledge and instinct, honed to a fine point for days like this."

And so, with the sun shining brightly overhead and a gentle breeze tugging at the edges of our coats, Holmes and I continued our leisurely stroll through Epsom Downs. Derby Day, with its rich palette of sights, sounds and smells, promised more than just a race; it was a vibrant celebration of British culture, a tapestry woven from threads of history, tradition and the universal human love of spectacle.

⊷⊷⊱⊰⊰

Among the hustle and bustle at Epsom Downs, my thoughts drifted back to the previous week when an unexpected invitation landed at 221B Baker Street. It was a quiet evening, the kind that often found Holmes and I engrossed in our respective pursuits - he with his chemical experiments and I with my medical journals.

The soft rustling of paper drew my attention to Holmes, who had just received the post. Among the usual assortment of correspondence, a single envelope stood out. It was thick and of high quality, with the unmistakable seal of the Diogenes Club. Holmes' eyes flickered with a momentary spark of interest as he broke the seal and scanned the contents.

"A letter from Mycroft, Watson," he remarked, his tone carrying an undercurrent of curiosity. "It seems he has extended an invitation for us to join him at the derby."

I looked up in surprise. Mycroft Holmes, Sherlock's older brother, was a man of considerable influence and intellect, deeply ensconced in the labyrinthine workings of government. His interests were typically far removed from the frivolities of public spectacle.

"The Derby?" I echoed, rising from my chair to look over Holmes's shoulder at the letter. "This is most unusual. Mycroft never showed much interest in horse racing, did he?"

"Indeed, Watson," Holmes replied, his brow furrowing slightly as he continued to read. "Mycroft's pursuits are generally of a more clandestine nature, involving matters of national importance. For him to invite us to such an event suggests that there may be more at play than meets the eye."

The letter was short and to the point, written in Mycroft's precise and unflinching hand. It invited both Holmes and myself to join him in a private box at the Derby, hinting at the pleasure of our company but offering little in the way of explanation.

"Holmes, do you think this could have anything to do with one of Mycroft's many government affairs?" I ventured, my curiosity piqued. "Or perhaps he has some other motive in mind?"

"Possibly," Holmes mused, folding up the letter and placing it on the mantelpiece. "Mycroft's motives are often layered and complex. However, his invitation suggests that our presence is of particular importance, whether for personal or professional reasons."

And so, with a mixture of curiosity and anticipation, we had accepted the invitation. For me, the prospect of attending the Derby held a certain appeal - a day of excitement and tradition, an opportunity to see the finest horses in the country compete for glory. For Holmes, it was a chance to delve into whatever underlying reasons Mycroft might have for attending.

Now, as we stood amidst the bustling crowd, the memory of Mycroft's enigmatic invitation lent an air of mystery to the day's proceedings. What were the motives behind his uncharacteristic interest in the Derby? And what role were we to play in this grand spectacle?

"Holmes," I said, breaking the silence that had settled between us, "do you have any further thoughts as to why Mycroft has asked us to join him today?"

Holmes' eyes, always sharp and alert, scanned the sea of faces around us. "Mycroft is a master of subtlety, Watson. His reasons will reveal themselves in time. For now, let us enjoy the atmosphere and remain vigilant. The answers we seek may be closer than we think."

With that, we continued our journey through Epsom Downs, the vibrant energy of the Derby drawing us deeper into its embrace. Amidst the pageantry and excitement, the mystery of Mycroft's invitation hung over us, a tantalising thread that promised to be unravelled in the fullness of time.

As Holmes and I continued our leisurely stroll through the bustling grounds of Epsom Downs, the vibrant tapestry of Derby Day unfolded around us in all its colour and bustle. The grandstands stood tall against the azure sky, filled to the brim with eager spectators, while the track itself, a meticulously manicured ribbon of turf, lay in anticipation of the thundering hooves that would soon grace it.

The air was thick with the scent of freshly cut grass, mingled with the earthy aroma of horses and the mouth-watering smells wafting from the food stalls. Vendors hawked their wares with boisterous shouts, adding to a symphony of sounds that included the excited chatter of the crowd, the rustling of racing programmes and the distant strains of a brass band.

"Holmes, isn't it marvellous? Look at the sheer number of people here, all brought together by their love of the sport. It's a magnificent display of unity and tradition," I remarked enthusiastically, pausing to take in the scene before us.

Holmes, his keen eyes darting from one detail to the next, nodded thoughtfully. "Indeed, Watson, a veritable carnival of human behaviour. If only such unity extended beyond these fleeting moments of spectacle."

"Oh, come now, Holmes," I said, smiling. "Don't you see the charm in it all? Families, friends, even strangers coming together to share the excitement of the race. It's quite heartwarming."

"Heartwarming, perhaps," Holmes replied with a touch of sarcasm. "But behind the veneer of camaraderie lies the usual tapestry of human vices. Observe the bookmakers, for example. Behind their smiles lies a ruthless calculation of profit and loss. They are masters at reading the crowd, at sensing the shifting tides of fortune. Their livelihoods depend on their ability to gauge the mood and predict the outcome, a skill not unlike our own deductive methods. And the so-called 'gentlemen' who place the bets, their civility thinly disguising the desperation of their gambling habits."

"You always find the darker side of things, Holmes," I said, slightly deflated.

"Not darker, Watson, merely truer," Holmes replied. "The racecourse is a microcosm of society, a stage on which the same dramas of ambition, envy and deceit are played out. Think of it as a study in anthropology, if you like."

"I suppose you have a point," I said thoughtfully. "Still, there's a certain joy in seeing people so engaged and excited."

"Ah, the eternal optimist," Holmes said with a grin. "It's one of your more endearing qualities, Watson. However, always keep in mind to investigate beyond the superficial. Even the most festive gatherings can conceal the most sinister plots."

As we walked through the crowd, the diversity of the crowd struck me. There were gentlemen in top hats and morning suits, ladies in extravagant dresses and hats adorned with feathers and flowers, and families of more modest means, their children wide-eyed in wonder at the surrounding spectacle. Social classes were temporarily blurred, united by a common love of sport.

As we continued our walk, the excitement around us began to build. The chatter of the crowd grew louder, the calls of the bookmakers more urgent, and the atmosphere seemed to crackle with anticipation. The approaching spectacle of the upcoming race could be sensed by the quickening collective heartbeat of the crowd.

"Holmes, do you feel the increased energy?" I asked, my excitement growing. "The race is approaching, and the crowd is electric with anticipation."

"Indeed, Watson," Holmes replied, his eyes shining with a mixture of curiosity and intensity. "The Derby is a convergence of many elements - sport, society and human nature. Each layer adds to the complexity of the event, and it is within this intricate tapestry that we may find the answers to the day's mysteries."

As we approached the parade ring where the horses were led out for the crowd to admire, the sense of anticipation was almost palpable. The sleek thoroughbreds, their coats gleaming in the sunlight, moved with a grace and power that captivated the crowd. In their bright silks, the jockeys mounted their horses with ease, their focus and determination evident.

"The genuine stars of the show," I murmured, watching a magnificent chestnut stallion prance with nervous energy. "Each horse is a testament to years of breeding, training and dedication. It is a wonder to behold."

Holmes nodded, his eyes fixed on the scene before us. "Yes, Watson, and all that effort, skill and passion converge in a moment of unbridled competition. Quite a spectacle for those who find wonder in such things." He added with a grin, "Personally, I find the human element far more fascinating."

As we made our way through the crowd, the excitement building around us, I couldn't help but feel a sense of wonder at the sheer scale and significance of the event. The Derby was more than just a race; it was a celebration of tradition, a testament to the enduring spirit of competition, and a vivid reflection of the society that had come together to witness it.

With each step, Holmes' observations provided deeper insights into the crowd and the day's significance, setting the stage for the unfolding drama that awaited us. The anticipation was palpable, and as we approached the heart of the action, I knew we were on the cusp of a day filled with intrigue, excitement and perhaps even a touch of mystery.

※※※

Navigating the crowds, Holmes and I made our way to the private boxes, our steps guided by the anticipation of the day's events. The grandeur of the Epsom Downs racecourse became even more apparent as we approached the exclusive seating area, a testament to the prestige and tradition that surrounds the Derby.

As we climbed the steps to our designated box, the view unfolded before us like a grand panorama. The sprawling racecourse stretched out in a green arc, bounded by the packed grandstands and the picturesque Surrey hills in the distance. The buzz of the crowd, the fluttering of bunting and the distant strains of a brass band created an atmosphere that was both exhilarating and sophisticated.

Upon reaching our box, we were greeted by Mycroft Holmes, a solitary figure standing with an air of composed detachment. Dressed in his usual dark suit, he was the epitome of Victorian propriety, his expression inscrutable yet tinged with a hint of satisfaction. Mycroft's presence, as always, exuded an aura of quiet authority, a stark contrast to the animated fervour of the crowd below.

"Sherlock, Watson," Mycroft greeted us with a nod, his voice soft and measured. "Glad you could join me. I trust the journey was uneventful?"

"Indeed, Mycroft," Sherlock replied, his tone equally calm. "The atmosphere here is quite remarkable. One can hardly help but be drawn into the excitement of the day."

"Ah, the Derby," Mycroft mused, his eyes sweeping over the bustling scene. "A convergence of the many facets of society, all united by the spectacle of racing. A fascinating study in human nature, wouldn't you say?"

Holmes' eyes gleamed with a hint of amusement. "Quite so, Mycroft. Although I suspect your reasons for inviting us here go beyond mere sociological observation."

A slight smile played on Mycroft's lips. "You know me too well, Sherlock. But let us enjoy the events of the day. All will be revealed in due course."

With that enigmatic remark, Mycroft motioned for us to take our seats. The private box offered an unparalleled view of the racecourse, the vantage point allowing us to observe the preparations for the main event with a clarity and detail that was both exciting and immersive.

As we settled into our seats, the scene before us was a hive of activity. Jockeys in their bright silks, each colour and pattern representing a different stable, mounted their steeds with practiced ease. The horses, magnificent creatures of muscle and sinew, exuded a nervous energy that reflected the anticipation of the crowd.

Holmes and I watched as the horses were led to the starting line, each one a magnificent specimen of equine athleticism.

"Holmes, look at them! Such grace, such power. Each horse a marvel of breeding and training. The excitement of witnessing them compete, each one striving for glory - it is a spectacle to behold!" I said enthusiastically.

Holmes studied the horses with a clinical eye. "Indeed, Watson. They are impressive creatures, bred for speed and endurance. But beyond their aesthetic qualities, they are merely biological machines, optimised for that very task."

I was surprised at his detachment. "Machines? Holmes, they are not just machines. They have a mind, a personality, a bond with their jockeys. It's not just about physical ability, it's also about heart and courage."

"Heart and courage perhaps, but in the end it comes down to biomechanics and probability. Look at Isinglass, for example," Holmes replied coolly. "Note the symmetry in his gait, the perfect alignment of muscle and bone. His Arabian ancestry gives him an advantage in speed and agility. The outcome of this race, Watson, is more predictable than you think."

"You reduce everything to numbers and calculations, Holmes. Surely there's more to it than that. The unpredictability of the race, the potential for any horse to rise above and claim victory - that is the essence of the sport."

Holmes smiled. "Unpredictability, Watson, is merely a function of incomplete information. Given all the variables - breeding, training, current condition - one can make a fairly accurate prediction. Isinglass has an excellent chance of winning, given his pedigree and current form. The bookmakers' odds reflect this, albeit imperfectly."

"And what about the human element, Holmes? The skill of the jockey, the strategy of the race? Surely these add a layer of complexity that can't be so easily quantified," I challenged.

"True, the role of the jockey is significant. Tommy Loates is renowned for his strategic acumen and his relationship with Isinglass. But even that, Watson, can be analysed. His past performance, his understanding of the course and his ability to gauge the competition all contribute to the overall probability of success," Holmes conceded slightly.

I smiled. "Always the logician, Holmes. Still, I prefer to revel in the beauty and passion of the race. The moment when all that training, all that breeding, culminates in a few glorious minutes on the track - that's something numbers can't fully capture."

Holmes' expression softened. "Perhaps you are right, Watson. There is an art to it, an elegance in the interplay of man and beast. Yet I find satisfaction in the patterns, the predictability. But let us see how today's race unfolds. Sometimes even the most logical of us must allow for a touch of the unexpected.

Mycroft, who had been listening to our conversation with quiet amusement, added: "The Derby is a stage on which many dramas unfold. Everyone involved, from the jockeys to the trainers to the spectators, plays a part in this grand narrative. It is a celebration of tradition, but also a reminder of the relentless pursuit of excellence.

As the final preparations were made, the atmosphere in the grandstands became increasingly charged. The rustling of race programmes, the murmured discussion of odds and favourites and the occasional cheer from an enthusiastic supporter created an almost palpable buzz.

Holmes leaned forward slightly, his attention focused on the scene below. "Observe, Watson. The interplay of emotions, the unspoken tensions, the subtle gestures. Each detail adds to the tapestry of the day."

I followed his gaze, taking in the myriad expressions on the faces of the crowd. There was the focused determination of the jockeys, the anxious excitement of the trainers and the eager anticipation of the spectators. It was a vivid tableau of human endeavour, each element contributing to the rich tapestry of the Derby.

As we waited for the race to begin, Mycroft's presence added an element of suspense to the proceedings. His reserved demeanour and enigmatic hints suggested that the day's events would be more than just a sporting spectacle. There was a deeper narrative at play, one that would be revealed in the fullness of time.

And so, with anticipation building around us and the stage set for the great spectacle, we watched as the final preparations were made. The Derby was about to begin, and with it the promise of excitement, intrigue and perhaps even a touch of mystery.

⊶⊱✶⊰⊷

As we settled into the comfort of Mycroft's private box, the vibrant tapestry of the Derby continued to unfold before us. The grandstand, filled with animated faces and vibrant colours, buzzed with the palpable excitement of the crowd. Below, the racecourse awaited, a stage set for the spectacle to come.

Holmes, ever the keen observer, scanned the scene with his analytical gaze, absorbing every detail. It was a look I had come to recognise, one that signalled a shift from mere observation to profound analysis.

Suddenly, in the midst of the electrifying atmosphere, I noticed a subtle shift in Holmes' focus. His piercing gaze had locked on to something - or someone - in the crowd. His eyes narrowed with an intensity I had rarely seen outside of our most perplexing cases. The world around us seemed to fade away, and for a moment it was as if Holmes and the mysterious figure were the only two people in the stand.

"Holmes, what is it?" I asked urgently, my voice straining to be heard over the roar of the crowd as the winning horse surged across the finish line, its

26

jockey's face a portrait of exultation.

Holmes remained silent, his jaw clenched, his eyes fixed on a distant point in the sea of faces. When he finally turned to me, his expression was a complex mixture of intrigue and unease.

"Watson, have you ever experienced a moment of absolute clarity amidst a maelstrom of chaos, a fleeting connection that defies explanation?"

I followed his gaze, scanning the crowd, trying to locate the source of his fixation. But all I could see was a swirling kaleidoscope of cheering spectators, their faces flushed with excitement, their arms waving in a frenzy of hats, scarves and fluttering betting slips.

"Perhaps it was nothing," Holmes murmured, his voice uncharacteristically hesitant. "Or perhaps it was a glimpse into a mind as sharp and dangerous as a razor's edge, a fleeting connection forged in the crucible of intellect."

"Who was it, Holmes?" I asked, my curiosity piqued by his cryptic words. "Someone you recognised?"

"Not a face, Watson, but a presence," he replied, his eyes scanning the crowd with renewed urgency, as if trying to catch a phantom. "In the briefest of moments, our gazes locked, and I sensed a kindred spirit - a mind capable of unravelling the most intricate of puzzles, of navigating the darkest corners of human nature."

Holmes's words, though enigmatic, carried a weight I had rarely experienced before. His trademark composure, that unshakable facade of detachment, had slipped for the briefest of moments, revealing a flicker of exhilaration mixed with a deep sense of unease.

"What did he look like, this mysterious onlooker?" I inquired, my own interest now thoroughly aroused.

"An elusive figure, Watson, shrouded in shadows and mystery," Holmes replied, his brow furrowed in concentration. "The details of his appearance escape me, but those eyes - they burned with the fire of a formidable intellect, a gaze that both challenged and recognised the depths of my own. It was as if a gauntlet had been thrown down in that fleeting connection, a silent challenge to unravel a mystery yet to be revealed".

The mysterious figure had vanished as quickly as he had appeared, swallowed up by the moving mass of humanity celebrating the end of the race. Yet the brief encounter had clearly left an indelible mark on Holmes, sparking a flicker of intrigue in the depths of his analytical mind.

As the crowd began to disperse, their excitement gradually giving way to satisfied chatter and movement towards the exits, Holmes remained pensive and silent. It was obvious that the day's events had taken on a new dimension for him, one that went beyond the mere excitement of the race.

"Sherlock, could this not be mere coincidence? A mere spectator caught up in the moment?" I ventured, knowing even as I spoke that Holmes' instincts were rarely wrong.

"Perhaps, Watson," he replied, his eyes still scanning the now thinning crowd. "But in our work we have both seen how the most trivial detail can unravel the most intricate mysteries. This may be nothing, or it may be the beginning of something far more complex."

As we made our way out of the private box, the image of this unknown observer lingered in my mind, a puzzle yet to be solved. If there was indeed a deeper narrative intertwined with the day's festivities, I had no doubt that Sherlock Holmes would uncover it. For now, the mystery of the mystery spectator added an intriguing layer to our Derby experience, a reminder that beneath the surface spectacle, deeper currents were always at play.

❂❈❂

The crowd's anticipation reached a fever pitch as the final preparations were made. The rustling of race programmes and the fervent discussion of favourites and underdogs created a buzz that filled the air, a background hum that seemed almost musical. The tension was palpable, an electric charge that coursed through the stands and settled on us all like a tangible presence.

Holmes, though outwardly composed, was clearly preoccupied with the brief but momentous encounter he had experienced. His gaze occasionally drifted back to where the mysterious figure had stood, a flicker of intrigue still evident in his eyes. The enigmatic presence had stirred something in him, a challenge he could not easily dismiss.

The announcer's voice boomed over the public address system, calling for the jockeys to mount. The murmur of the crowd swelled to a roar, a wave of sound that rolled over the stands, filling the room with electric excitement. Holmes leaned forward slightly, his demeanour unchanged but his interest clearly piqued.

"The psychological aspect of this moment is intriguing, Watson. Observe the faces of the jockeys, the crowd, even the horses. Each is a study in concentration and anticipation."

Indeed, as I looked around, I saw a kaleidoscope of emotions. There was the taut face of a jockey, his eyes fixed forward, his jaw set; the eager, slightly anxious expressions of the spectators, their hands clutching the railings; and the tense posture of the horses, their bodies coiled like springs, ready to burst.

Mycroft, who had been quietly watching us, leaned forward slightly. "Sherlock, do you think this race will provide any further insight into our mysterious observer?"

Holmes' eyes remained fixed on the track, but I could feel the wheels of his mind turning. "The race itself may not, Mycroft. However, the reactions of

28

those present, particularly our enigmatic spectator, may prove revealing. We must remain vigilant."

As the announcement was made that the race was about to begin, an electric thrill ran through the crowd. The air was thick with anticipation and every eye was on the track.

Holmes turned to me, his expression a mixture of anticipation and caution. "Keep your eyes open Watson. In a place like this, the most significant events often unfold where you least expect them."

I nodded, feeling a surge of companionship and trust. "I trust your instincts, Holmes. Let's see what the race brings."

The final minutes before the race were a ritual in themselves, a crescendo of sound, movement and emotion that set the stage for the grand spectacle that was the Derby. It was a moment of collective holding of breath, as if all of Epsom Downs was waiting for the same beat to release its pent-up anticipation.

And then, with a suddenness that always seemed to take the breath away, the bell rang, the gates flew open and the Derby began. The crowd erupted, a thunderous applause mingled with shouts and cheers as the thoroughbreds burst onto the track, their hooves thundering in unison, on their way to glory or defeat in the most famous race on the British equestrian calendar.

CHAPTER 2

THE CALM BEFORE THE STORM

A hive of activity, the jockeys' room at Epsom Downs was a cramped space brimming with the nervous anticipation of men about to embark on a great contest. The air was thick with the mixed scents of leather, sweat and the faint, earthy aroma of horses - a distinctive bouquet that embodied the essence of the racecourse. The walls, festooned with racing silks in every conceivable shade, vibrated with the palpable excitement unique to Derby Day.

Tommy Loates stood at his locker, his fingers deftly adjusting the straps of his riding boots. The familiar clink of stirrups and buckles mingled with the indistinct murmur of conversation, creating a symphony of sound that was both chaotic and strangely comforting. His fellow jockeys moved with purposeful urgency, their faces etched with concentration as they prepared for the monumental task ahead.

"Tommy, old boy," a voice called from across the room. It was Johnny Barrett, an experienced jockey with a reputation for both skill and a sharp tongue. "Feeling ready for the big race?"

Tommy looked up and offered a tight smile. "As ready as I can be, Johnny. The Derby is always a test, isn't it?"

Johnny chuckled, a sound that contained both camaraderie and a hint of rivalry. "A test indeed. But it's not just the horses that are being tested today. The crowd out there - they're a spectacle in themselves. All those fine ladies and gentlemen placing their bets and sipping their champagne. They wouldn't last a day in our boots."

A murmur of agreement rippled through the room, punctuated by the occasional laugh. The jockeys, though competitors, shared a bond forged in the crucible of countless races. They understood the pressures and dangers of their profession, and this shared understanding gave rise to a unique camaraderie.

Tommy turned his attention back to his preparations, his thoughts briefly drifting to the grandstands outside. The thought of the throngs of spectators, their faces a blur of expectation and excitement, filled him with a mixture of determination and trepidation. He knew that every ride was a performance, a delicate balance of skill, strategy and sheer willpower.

"Tommy, have you seen Isinglass yet?" another jockey asked, his voice tinged with curiosity. "How does he look?"

"He's in fine form," Tommy replied, his tone betraying the slightest hint of concern. "But there's something different about him today. A restlessness I can't quite put my finger on."

The room fell silent for a moment as the gravity of Tommy's words sank in. Isinglass was no ordinary horse; he was a champion, a marvel of breeding and training with a pedigree that was the envy of the racing world. His performance today would be scrutinised by all, and any deviation from his usual composure would be cause for concern.

"Don't let it get to you, Tommy," Johnny said, his voice calm and reassuring. "Horses can sense our nerves, you know. Just stay calm and focused. Isinglass will do the rest."

Tommy nodded, appreciating the advice. He knew that the bond between horse and jockey was a delicate one, built on mutual trust and understanding. As he finished his preparations, he took a deep breath, steeling himself for the challenges that lay ahead.

The room buzzed with renewed activity as the final touches were made. The jockeys, now fully dressed in their bright silks, exuded an air of quiet determination. They were ready, each one a testament to years of dedication and hard work.

As Tommy made his way to the door, he paused for a moment to take in the scene around him. The jockey room, with its mixture of anticipation and camaraderie, was a microcosm of the larger world outside - a world where triumph and heartbreak went hand in hand.

With a final nod to his fellow jockeys, Tommy stepped out into the corridor, the sounds of the room fading behind him. The race was about to begin and with it the promise of glory, excitement and perhaps even a touch of mystery.

⚜

The hustle and bustle of the jockey's room began to die down as the race approached. Tommy Loates found a quieter corner, away from the jovial banter and clinking of equipment, to concentrate on his horse, Isinglass. The room, once filled with the cacophony of preparation, now seemed to hold its breath in anticipation. The dim light filtered through the small windows, casting a soft glow over the scene.

Isinglass stood patiently in his stall, a magnificent specimen of equine beauty. His coat shone like polished mahogany, every muscle rippling beneath the surface as he shifted his weight. Tommy approached him with the reverence one might show a king, his hands moving deftly as he groomed the horse, checking every inch for signs of strain or injury.

"Easy now, old boy," Tommy murmured, his voice a soothing balm amid the tension. "We've been through this before. Just another race, eh?"

But even as he spoke, Tommy could sense that something was wrong. Isinglass, normally so calm and collected, seemed more agitated than usual. His ears flicked back and forth, and his eyes, normally so calm, had a wild, restless glint in them.

Tommy's brow furrowed in concern as he continued to groom the horse, his mind racing with thoughts of what could be causing this unease. He began to review the pedigree of Isinglass, a horse of exceptional breeding. The Arabian blood coursing through his veins gave him a distinct advantage in speed and agility. Every stride was a testament to generations of careful breeding and training.

"You are a marvel, Isinglass," Tommy said softly, running his hand down the horse's smooth neck. "A true testament to the art of breeding. But today you seem different. What troubles you, my friend?"

As he spoke, Tommy's eyes swept over the horse's tack and equipment, scrutinising every buckle and strap for signs of tampering. The stakes were incredibly high and he knew only too well the lengths to which some would go to ensure victory - or the defeat of a rival. The thought of sabotage gnawed at the edges of his mind, adding to his growing unease.

He checked the girth, the bridle and the bit, his fingers moving with practiced ease but heightened vigilance. Everything seemed in order, but the feeling of foreboding remained. Isinglass's unusual behaviour was not something Tommy could simply dismiss.

"High stakes indeed," Tommy mused aloud, his voice barely above a whisper. "We can't afford any mistakes today, can we, boy?"

The horse responded with a soft nicker, as if it understood the gravity of the situation. Tommy took a deep breath, trying to calm his own nerves as well as Isinglass's. He knew that his own state of mind would inevitably affect the horse, and he needed to be the rock on which Isinglass could rely.

"Remember your lineage, Isinglass," Tommy said, his voice filled with quiet determination. "You are descended from champions, and today we will prove why. Whatever it is that troubles you, we'll face it together."

As he finished his final checks, Tommy took a step back to admire the horse. Isinglass stood tall and proud, a model of strength and grace. Yet beneath the surface there was a flicker of uncertainty - a reminder that even the greatest champions are not immune to the vagaries of fate.

Tommy patted Isinglass gently, his expression resolute. "Let's show them what we're made of, old friend. Today is our day."

With these words, Tommy felt a renewed sense of purpose. He walked back to the hustle and bustle of the jockey room, leaving behind the intimate moment he had shared with Isinglass. The air was still thick with anticipation, but now it carried a sense of quiet determination.

The jockey's room, though a place of preparation, had also become a sanctuary where Tommy could gather his thoughts and steel himself for the race ahead. And as he rejoined his fellow jockeys, he carried with him an unwavering belief in his horse and the hope that together they would rise to the occasion.

The atmosphere in the jockeys' room grew increasingly tense as the minutes ticked by and the start of the Derby drew nearer. The nervous energy was almost palpable and the jockeys, having completed their individual preparations, now gathered in small groups to discuss the race and the formidable challenge that lay ahead.

Tommy Loates, having returned from his moment of reflection with Isinglass, joined a group of his fellow jockeys. The conversation had turned to the upcoming races, a subject that always elicits a mixture of awe and ambition from the riders.

"Quite a crowd out there today," remarked one jockey, leaning against a locker. "You can feel the excitement in the air, can't you?"

"Aye," another jockey nodded. "It's Derby Day, after all. The whole of society is out there - lords and ladies, merchants and labourers, all rubbing shoulders for the love of sport."

"Indeed," said Tommy Loates with a wry smile. "A grand spectacle, to be sure. But let's not forget, gentlemen, that for many of them it is merely a diversion - a chance to place a bet and feel the thrill of risk without ever mounting a horse themselves."

This drew a laugh from a third jockey. "True enough, Tommy. But for us it's more than that. It's the culmination of months, even years, of hard work and dedication. Every race, every training session leads up to this moment."

"Aye, it does," Tommy agreed. "And we have to be at our best, for the sake of our horses and our stables. The Derby is more than just a race; it's a testament to our skill and our bond with these magnificent creatures."

The room fell silent for a moment as the jockeys absorbed Tommy's words, each man lost in his own thoughts. The weight of the day's significance hung heavy in the air, a reminder of the stakes and the glory that awaited the victor.

"So what do you think, lads?" asked the first jockey, breaking the silence. "Does anyone here think they can win all the big races this year?"

A smirk crossed the second jockey's face. "A lofty ambition, that. Winning the Derby is one thing, but winning all the major races? That's another animal altogether."

Tommy took a moment to collect his thoughts, his gaze distant as he recalled his experiences. "True enough. The Derby, the St Leger and the 2000 Guineas - each race is a test of stamina, speed and strategy. To win all three is to achieve a level of excellence that few can boast of.

"Tommy, you've ridden in all three races, haven't you?" asked another jockey, his voice tinged with curiosity. "What do you make of them?"

"Each race presents its own unique challenges," Tommy replied thoughtfully. "The Derby, with its large field and high stakes, is as much a test of nerves as it is of skill. The 2000 Guineas, with its shorter distance, demands speed and quick decisions. And the St Leger, the longest of the three, is a true test of stamina and endurance. To win all three requires not only a great horse, but also a great team and a bit of luck.

"And a bit of Tommy Loates magic, eh?" the first jockey grinned.

Tommy chuckled and shook his head. "There's no magic, just hard work and dedication. And, of course, a horse with the heart and strength to give it everything it's got."

The conversation turned more serious as the jockeys delved deeper into the history and significance of winning the great races. The room, once filled with light-hearted banter, now took on an air of reverence as they discussed the legends of the sport.

"You know," said the second jockey, "one of the first horses to dominate the great races was West Australian in 1853. Since then, only a handful have managed the feat. It's a rare and remarkable achievement."

"Indeed," the third jockey nodded. "West Australian, Gladiateur and Ormonde... each name carries with it a legacy of greatness. To join that list is to be immortalised in the annals of racing history."

"And it's not just the horse," Tommy added thoughtfully. "The jockey, the trainer, the whole team - they all play a vital role. It's a collective effort, a symphony of man and beast striving for perfection.

"It's a reminder of why we do this, isn't it?" mused the first jockey. "The pursuit of greatness, the chance to be part of something bigger than ourselves."

As the discussion continued, the tension in the room seemed to ease slightly, replaced by a sense of camaraderie and shared purpose. Despite their individual ambitions, the jockeys were united by their passion for the sport and their respect for its storied history.

"Well, lads, here's to the race ahead," smiled the second jockey. "May the best horse - and jockey - win."

A murmur of agreement rippled through the group and Tommy felt a renewed sense of determination. The Derby was more than just a race; it was an opportunity to etch their names into the history books, to achieve something truly extraordinary.

As the race approached, the jockeys began to disperse, each man returning to his final preparations. The room was once again buzzing with activity, but now there was a sense of quiet determination, a readiness to face the challenge that lay ahead.

Tommy took a deep breath, his mind focused on the task at hand. The discussion of the great races had reminded him of the stakes, the glory and honour that would come with victory. With Isinglass by his side, he felt ready to face whatever the day might bring.

As he made his way to the door, Tommy glanced back at his fellow jockeys, a silent nod of respect passing between them. They were competitors, yes, but also comrades in the pursuit of greatness.

With that, Tommy stepped out into the corridor, the sounds of the jockeys' room fading behind him. The race was about to begin, and with it the promise of glory, excitement and perhaps even a touch of mystery.

⊸⊷⊱✳⊰⊶⊸

The atmosphere in the jockey room was charged with anticipation, every man aware that the moment of reckoning was at hand. The final adjustments had been made, the last words of encouragement exchanged, and now it was time to lead their horses to the starting line. The transition from the relative sanctuary of the jockeys' room to the cacophony of the racecourse was both a physical and psychological journey.

As the jockeys emerged from the room, the noise of the crowd surged around them, a living entity made up of thousands of voices, each contributing to the collective roar that greeted the sight of the horses. The air was thick with the mingled scents of freshly trampled grass, the tang of sweat and the faint whiff of tobacco smoke. The grandstand, a sea of animated faces, seemed to undulate with excitement, flags and pennants fluttering in the breeze.

Tommy Loates led Isinglass, his mind a storm of thoughts and emotions. The power and grace of the horse beside him was undeniable, but there was an undercurrent of unease that he could not ignore. Isinglass's usual composure was replaced by a restless energy, his ears flicking back and forth, his eyes darting nervously.

As they walked, Tommy's thoughts turned inward. The stakes of the race loomed large in his mind, not just for honour and glory, but as the culmination of years of training and dedication. Every step towards the starting line was a reminder of the immense pressure on his shoulders.

"Calm down, old boy," Tommy murmured to Isinglass, his voice barely audible over the din. "We've faced challenges before, and we've always come through. Trust your training and trust me."

The path to the start line was flanked by spectators, their faces a blur of anticipation and excitement. Tommy's eyes swept over them, taking in the different expressions - hope, fear, exhilaration. He knew that for many, this race was more than a sporting event; it was a moment of collective aspiration, a chance to witness greatness.

As the jockeys approached the starting line, the noise of the crowd seemed to fade, replaced by the tense, focused silence of the competitors. The horses, sensing the impending race, shifted and pranced, their muscles taut with readiness. The atmosphere crackled with electric anticipation, every breath held in collective suspense.

Tommy's internal monologue continued, his mind racing as he tried to calm Isinglass. "This is it, old friend. The moment we've trained for, the moment we've dreamed of. Remember your lineage, your strength, your speed. Today we prove ourselves."

Isinglass snorted softly, as if in response, and Tommy felt a flicker of reassurance. Despite the horse's unusual nervousness, there was still a bond between them, a connection forged through countless hours of training and mutual trust.

⊰••◦❈◦••⊱

The starting gates loomed ahead, a formidable barrier holding back the surging tide of equine energy. The scene was one of controlled chaos, each jockey and horse a study in concentrated tension. The air was thick with the scent of sweat and leather, mingled with the distant aroma of freshly cut grass. The murmur of the crowd was a low hum, punctuated by the occasional shout of encouragement or call from the bookmakers.

Tommy Loates took a moment to check Isinglass' equipment one last time. His fingers moved deftly over the bridle and saddle, making sure everything was in perfect order. But despite the thoroughness of his checks, the feeling of unease remained. Isinglass's eyes, normally so calm and steady, now flickered with a nervous energy that Tommy could not ignore.

"Calm down, boy," Tommy whispered, his voice a soothing balm amid the tension. "We'll get through this together."

37

The jockeys exchanged brief, tense words, the camaraderie of the jockey's room replaced by the competitive edge of the starting line. Each man was acutely aware of the stakes, the danger and the glory that awaited them.

"Ready, Tommy?" called out a fellow jockey, his voice steady despite the palpable tension.

"Ready as I'll ever be," Tommy replied, his tone resolute.

The horses shifted restlessly, their muscles coiled like springs, ready to unleash their power at the first signal. The jockeys, too, were a picture of focused intensity, their eyes fixed on the track ahead, their minds honed to a razor's edge.

<hr />

The final seconds before the race were a study in mounting anticipation. The starting boxes that housed the eager horses seemed to hum with the pent-up energy of the competitors. Every heartbeat was a countdown, every breath a preparation for the explosive start.

Tommy Loates focused all his attention on Isinglass, his hands steady on the reins, his voice a calm murmur of reassurance. "Easy now, old friend. Trust in our training, trust in each other. We are ready."

Isinglass, still showing signs of nervousness, shifted beneath him, his muscles taut and ready to spring forward. Tommy could feel the horse's heart beating in sync with his own, a powerful rhythm that echoed the collective anticipation of the crowd.

The other jockeys were also a picture of intense concentration, their faces masks of determination. The starting gates loomed large, the ultimate test of their skill and endurance just moments away. The roar of the crowd was a distant echo, the world narrowed to the horse beneath him and the track ahead.

The seconds stretched into an eternity, each heartbeat a countdown to the explosive start. Tommy's concentration sharpened, every sense attuned to the moment. Isinglass shifted beneath him, muscles coiled, ready to leap forward.

And then, as if the world held its breath, the launch doors began to open.

CHAPTER 3

SHADOW OVER EPSOM DOWNS

I n the serene expanse of Surrey, amidst rolling greenery stretching endlessly under the early morning sun, stood Wentworth Manor. This grand building, a testament to centuries of British aristocracy, rose majestically against the skyline, its ivy-clad facade whispering tales of bygone eras. It was here, in this sanctuary of historic splendour, that Lord Charles Wentworth, a paragon of refined taste and discerning acumen, resided.

The interior of the mansion was a veritable museum, each room curated with an impeccable eye for beauty and historical significance. The walls were adorned with masterpieces of Renaissance art, the vivid hues of Botticelli and the profound depths of Caravaggio mingling with the soft light filtering through the stained glass windows. Statues of Greco-Roman deities stood guard in the corridors, their marble forms capturing the perfection of human anatomy, every muscle and expression carved with painstaking precision.

On this particular morning, Lord Charles Wentworth stood in the great hall of his ancestral home, the morning light casting a golden glow over the opulent surroundings. The scent of freshly polished wood mingled with the faint scent of roses from the gardens outside, creating an atmosphere of serene elegance. Lord Wentworth, a man in his late prime with charismatic features etched with the thoughtful lines of a deep thinker, surveyed his surroundings with a sense of pride and introspection.

His passion for art and equestrian pursuits was evident in every corner of the estate. The grandeur of the place reflected his refined taste, with every artefact and painting carefully chosen to reflect the legacy of his lineage. As he walked towards the study, his eyes fell on a portrait of Isinglass, his prized thoroughbred. The horse's image, captured with such lifelike precision, seemed to gallop across the canvas, his Arabian lineage evident in the proud arch of his neck and the fire in his eyes.

As he entered his private study, the room where the aroma of aged mahogany and leather-bound books filled the air, creating an almost sacred atmosphere of intellectual pursuit, he was joined by his trusted confidant and curator of his art collection, Adrien d'Arcy. A man of similar tastes, deeply steeped in the arts and understanding of Wentworth's unique perspective on beauty and heritage, Adrien approached with a respectful yet enthusiastic manner.

"Good morning, Lord Wentworth," Adrien began, his tone infused with shared enthusiasm. "Preparations for today are well underway. Isinglass is ready to grace the fields of Epsom."

Lord Wentworth turned, a thoughtful smile playing on his lips. "Indeed, Adrien. Today is not just about the race; it is about celebrating the heritage and beauty that Isinglass represents. In him we see not only power, but the poetry of movement."

Adrien nodded in agreement, his eyes reflecting the same admiration for the magnificent creature. "The crowd will be more than spectators today; they will be witnesses to the artistry you so cherish."

Lord Wentworth's eyes drifted back to the portrait of Isinglass. "It is our privilege, Adrien, to bring such beauty into the world. Whether in the galleries of this mansion or the grandstands of Epsom, today is a celebration not just of speed, but of the sublime."

With a final glance at the artefacts surrounding him, each a bearer of heritage and beauty, Lord Wentworth prepared to leave for the Derby. The significance of the day weighed heavily on him, not just as a competition, but as a testament to the enduring legacy of equestrian excellence and the timeless beauty of Isinglass.

⊶⊷⊷⊷∗⊷⊷⊷⊶

Wentworth's private study, a sanctuary of intellectual pursuit and artistic appreciation, was a room where the aroma of aged mahogany and leather-bound books filled the air. The walls, lined with shelves of ancient tomes and treatises on art, philosophy and equestrian pursuits, bore silent witness to the lord's eclectic interests. At the centre of the room, on a polished oak plinth, stood a particularly striking artefact - an obsidian statuette of a stallion, its surface smooth and cool, whispering the secrets of a civilisation that had mastered the art of beauty and mysticism.

Lord Charles Wentworth, a man in his late prime with charismatic features etched with the thoughtful lines of a deep thinker, stood before the statuette. His gaze, usually one of detached contemplation, now held a mixture of awe and introspection. The statuette, a relic from the ancient sands of Arabia, represented not only an era of splendour, but a lineage that resonated deeply with his own passion for thoroughbred breeding.

As he studied the statuette, Lord Wentworth's mind drifted back to Isinglass, his champion horse. The Arabian lineage of Isinglass was a source of immense pride to him. The bloodline, renowned for its unrivalled speed and endurance, was the result of centuries of careful breeding. The history of Thoroughbreds was a tapestry woven with threads of nobility and excellence, and Isinglass was its crowning jewel.

A sudden shiver ran down his spine, an inexplicable feeling of unease that seemed to emanate from the dark, gleaming stone of the statuette. For a fleeting moment, the shadows in the room seemed to deepen, as if the very air were alive with a foreboding presence. Lord Wentworth shook off the feeling, attributing it to the anticipation of the day's events.

As he turned from the statuette, Adrien d'Arcy, his trusted confidant and curator of his art collection, entered the room. A man of similar tastes and deep interest in the arts, Adrien approached with a respectful yet enthusiastic manner.

"Lord Wentworth," Adrien began, his tone filled with shared enthusiasm, "the preparations for Isinglass are complete. He is ready for the derby."

Lord Wentworth nodded, a thoughtful smile playing on his lips. "Adrien, have you ever considered the significance of Isinglass's Arabian pedigree? It is not just about speed and endurance; it is about the heritage, the centuries of breeding that have culminated in this magnificent creature."

Adrien's eyes brightened with understanding. "Indeed, my lord. The saddle and tack I have made for Isinglass combine the finest elements of Arabian and British tradition. The craftsmanship is a tribute to that heritage."

Lord Wentworth's eyes drifted to a corner of the study where the special saddle and tack Adrien had created were on display. The intricate designs, fine leathers and perfect balance of form and function were a testament to Adrien's skill and dedication.

"In every stitch and every curve, you have honoured this legacy, Adrien," said Lord Wentworth, his voice full of admiration. "Isinglass is not just a horse, he is a living sculpture, a masterpiece in motion. Today, as he races, we celebrate not only his speed, but the poetry of his pedigree and the artistry of your craftsmanship."

Adrien bowed slightly, his pride evident. "Thank you, my lord. It is a privilege to contribute to this celebration of beauty and heritage."

With a final glance at the obsidian statuette, Lord Wentworth felt a sense of calm return. The significance of the day was not just about the race; it was about honouring a legacy, celebrating beauty and witnessing the culmination of centuries of excellence. As he and Adrien prepared to leave for the Derby, the sense of foreboding was replaced by a quiet confidence, a belief in the artistry and legacy they were about to witness.

The morning sun continued its ascent, casting long, golden rays over the manicured lawns and ancient oaks of Wentworth Manor. The tranquillity of the manor was punctuated by the bustling activity of the household staff, each member engaged in the elaborate preparations for the day's momentous event. The stables, normally a place of quiet industry, buzzed with anticipation.

In the courtyard, a gleaming carriage waited, its lacquered surface reflecting the vibrancy of the surrounding gardens. The carriage, adorned with the Wentworth coat of arms, stood as a symbol of the family's long-standing prestige and commitment to excellence. Nearby, stable hands meticulously groomed Isinglass, the champion thoroughbred, his coat gleaming in the morning light.

Adrien d'Arcy oversaw the final preparations with his usual calm efficiency. His keen eye missed nothing, ensuring that every detail was attended to with the utmost care. As he approached the carriage, he found Lord Wentworth standing beside it, an expression of thoughtful determination on his face.

"Isinglass is ready, my lord," Adrien said, his voice steady. "The staff have seen to every detail. It is in top condition for the derby."

Lord Wentworth nodded, his eyes fixed on the magnificent creature. "Today, Adrien, we are not just running a race. The Derby is the culmination of the series of the three most prestigious races in our Empire. It is a test of endurance, skill and thoroughbred spirit. Isinglass must not only win, but exemplify the very essence of excellence."

Adrien's eyes softened with understanding. "Indeed, my lord. This is not just a series of races, it is a legacy. The meticulous preparations reflect our dedication to that legacy. Every aspect, from the training to the craftsmanship of the tack, has been executed with the utmost precision."

Together they watched as the stable hands secured the special saddle and tack to Isinglass. The equipment, crafted by Adrien with an expert blend of Arab and British traditions, was a masterpiece in itself. The fine leather, intricate designs and perfect balance of form and function spoke volumes of Adrien's skill and dedication.

One of the stable hands, a young man called Jack, led Isinglass to the carriage. Jack's partnership with the horse was evident in their seamless interaction, a testament to the mutual respect and trust they had developed over years of training.

As they prepared to leave, Lord Wentworth turned to Adrien. "The stakes are high, Adrien. This is not just about winning; it is about honouring the legacy of our forebears and setting a standard for future generations. Isinglass embodies that legacy, and today we must ensure that it is celebrated in all its glory."

Adrien nodded, his expression one of resolute commitment. "We have done all in our power, my lord. Now it is up to Isinglass and the spirit of excellence that drives him."

With a final glance at the estate, Lord Wentworth stepped into the carriage, followed by Adrien. The journey from the tranquil surroundings of Wentworth Manor to the bustling atmosphere of Epsom Downs was not merely a physical transition, but a passage from the quiet elegance of history to the vibrant present where new legends were being forged.

As the coach rolled down the gravel path, the weight of anticipation settled over them. The grandeur of the mansion faded into the distance, replaced by the growing excitement of the Derby. The stakes were high indeed, but so was their faith in Isinglass and the meticulous preparations that had brought them to this pivotal moment.

⊷⊶⊷⊷⊶⊷

The journey from Wentworth Manor to Epsom Downs was a passage through time and space, from the quiet elegance of history to the vibrant, chaotic energy of the present. As Lord Wentworth's carriage approached the racecourse, the atmosphere was charged with anticipation. The tranquil countryside gave way to a bustling scene, teeming with life and excitement.

Epsom Downs, a vast expanse of green turf, stretched out before them. The grandstands, rising majestically into the sky, were already filled with a diverse crowd. The air buzzed with the hum of animated conversation, the clinking of glasses and the occasional cheer as spectators greeted one another. Flags fluttered in the breeze, their colours a vivid contrast to the clear blue sky, and the scent of freshly cut grass mingled with the earthy aroma of horses and leather.

Stepping out of the carriage, Lord Charles Wentworth was immediately struck by the stark contrast between the quiet dignity of Wentworth Manor and the frenetic energy of the Derby. His presence commanded respect and as he made his way through the crowd, heads turned and whispers followed in his wake. Accompanied by Adrien d'Arcy, his confidant and curator, Wentworth exuded an air of quiet confidence.

"Lord Wentworth, what a pleasure to see you," called Sir Harold Whitaker, a distinguished historian and avid horseman. "I trust Isinglass is in good form?"

"Indeed, Sir Harold," Wentworth replied with a polite nod. "Today promises to be a spectacle of unparalleled excellence."

They continued on their way to the exclusive enclosure reserved for the prominent patrons of the race. As they walked, Lord Wentworth's keen eye took in every detail - the vibrant crowd, the meticulous preparations on the track and the palpable sense of anticipation in the air.

"Lord Wentworth, how nice to see you," greeted Lady Eleanor Pembroke, a noted philanthropist and casual acquaintance. "I hear Isinglass is the favourite this year. Expectations are high."

"Thank you, Lady Eleanor," Wentworth replied, his tone measured and calm. "Isinglass represents not only our hopes, but the culmination of a legacy. Today we honour that legacy."

As they reached the enclosure, the view of the racecourse opened up before them. The vibrant crowd, a mix of aristocracy and commoners, created a tapestry of colour and movement. The stands, filled to capacity, seemed to ripple like a living organism, the collective heartbeat of thousands of spectators echoing the anticipation of the event.

Lord Wentworth paused to take it all in. The Derby was not just a race; it was a celebration of tradition, a gathering of the best and the brightest in the world of thoroughbred racing. The stakes were high, not just for the competitors, but for the legacy of excellence that each one represented.

Standing beside him, Adrien shared the moment of reflection. "The atmosphere is electric, my Lord. The expectations placed upon us are immense, but so is our faith in Isinglass."

Wentworth nodded, his eyes fixed on the track where the horses would soon compete. "Today we are not just participants, we are stewards of a tradition that transcends the mere act of racing. In Isinglass we see the embodiment of that tradition, the living proof of our dedication and passion".

As the final preparations were made, Lord Wentworth felt a sense of calm amidst the chaos. The Derby was more than a race; it was a testament to the enduring spirit of excellence, a celebration of beauty and heritage. And as he stood there, surrounded by the vibrant energy of Epsom Downs, he knew that history was being made.

⊷≪⊱✦⊰≫⊷

The paddock and stable area at Epsom Downs buzzed with a controlled frenzy, a hive of activity as trainers, jockeys and grooms tended to their charges. The anticipation in the air was palpable, each person focused on their task with a unique intensity. In the midst of this bustling scene, Adrien d'Arcy moved with an air of calm precision, his every action deliberate and imbued with a deep care.

Isinglass stood in his stall, his glossy coat shimmering in the soft light. The thoroughbred exuded a quiet strength, his muscles taut with contained energy. Adrien approached him with a gentle touch, his hands moving over the horse's flanks, feeling for any signs of tension or discomfort. His voice, deep and soothing, filled the air between them.

"Easy now, Isinglass," Adrien murmured, his hands continuing their tactile examination. "Today is the day we've been preparing for. You are the epitome of grace and strength, my friend."

Isinglass' ears flicked back and forth in response to the familiar cadence of Adrien's voice. The bond between them was evident in every interaction, a testament to years of mutual trust and respect. Adrien's touch was both clinical and affectionate, his movements reflecting a deep understanding of the horse's needs.

As he inspected the tack and saddle, meticulously crafted to integrate the finest elements of Arabian and British tradition, Adrien's thoughts drifted to the lineage that had produced such an extraordinary creature. The Arabian bloodline, renowned for its speed and endurance, flowed through Isinglass's veins, a legacy of centuries of careful breeding.

"Your ancestors ran across the sands of Arabia, their hooves pounding out a rhythm of endurance and grace," Adrien said softly, more to himself than to the horse. "And here you stand, a testament to that heritage, ready to prove yourself on the grandest stage of all."

The saddle, with its fine leather and intricate designs, was a masterpiece in itself. Adrien's craftsmanship was evident in every stitch, the balance of form and function a reflection of his dedication to honouring the legacy of the Isinglass lineage. He adjusted the straps with practiced ease, making sure everything was in perfect alignment.

Jack, the young stable hand, approached with a quiet reverence, his eyes reflecting the same respect and admiration for Isinglass. "He's ready, Mr d'Arcy," Jack said, his voice tinged with a mixture of excitement and nervousness. "Everything's in place."

Adrien nodded, a quiet smile playing on his lips. "Thank you, Jack. You've done well. Isinglass is in the best shape he can be, and now it is up to him to show the world what he is made of."

As the final preparations were completed, Adrien took a moment to stand back and admire the thoroughbred. Isinglass, with his shimmering coat and taut muscles, was a living sculpture of speed and grace. The bond between them was more than just that of trainer and charge; it was a bond forged through years of dedication, a shared journey towards excellence.

"Today we honour the legacy of your lineage, Isinglass," Adrien said, his voice filled with quiet determination. "You carry with you the spirit of the Arabian sands and the pride of the British tradition. Go forth and show the world the poetry of your movement."

With a final, gentle pat on the horse's neck, Adrien led Isinglass out of the stable, ready for the challenge that awaited them. The atmosphere of anticipation hung heavy in the air, but amid the chaos there was a sense of calm purpose. Today was not just a race; it was a celebration of heritage, craftsmanship and the unbreakable bond between man and horse.

The grandstands and private boxes at Epsom Downs offered a commanding view of the racecourse, a sea of vibrant colour and hustle and bustle. From his vantage point in the exclusive enclosure, Lord Charles Wentworth watched the throngs of spectators, their animated chatter and festive dress creating a tapestry of excitement and anticipation. The air was thick with the aroma of freshly cut grass, mingled with the earthy scent of horses and leather, marking the Derby as an event steeped in tradition and natural beauty.

As Lord Wentworth surveyed the scene, he was approached by Sir Reginald Ashcroft, an old friend and fellow patron of the arts. Sir Reginald's eyes twinkled with excitement as he greeted Wentworth with a firm handshake.

"Charles, my good man," Sir Reginald exclaimed. "The atmosphere here today is positively electric! I trust Isinglass is ready to show his mettle?"

"Indeed, Reginald," Lord Wentworth replied with a measured smile. "Isinglass represents not only the pinnacle of our hopes, but the very essence of equestrian excellence. Today we are witnessing not just a race but a testament to lineage and legacy."

Lady Beatrice Hargreaves, a renowned breeder whose family held a prominent place in the world of thoroughbred racing, joined the conversation. Her presence added an air of sophistication to the gathering. "Lord Wentworth, the expectations are enormous. The Derby, as the final race in the series of the three most important races in our Empire, has a significance that transcends mere competition."

"Quite so, Lady Beatrice," Wentworth agreed, his eyes drifting to the track where preparations were underway. "The Derby is a celebration of tradition and excellence. Each competitor represents years of dedication and the hope of a place in history".

As the conversation continued, Lord Wentworth's thoughts were never far from Isinglass. The thoroughbred, with his shimmering dark bay coat and taut muscles, was more than just a horse to Wentworth. He was a living embodiment of beauty and heritage, a testament to centuries of careful breeding and the art of equine perfection.

His interactions with the other notable figures were punctuated by moments of quiet reflection. Wentworth's appreciation of Isinglass was not merely that of an owner for his prized possession, but that of an artist for his finest masterpiece. The horse's Arabian pedigree, the result of meticulous breeding and training, was a source of deep pride for Wentworth.

"Isinglass is not just a competitor," he said, almost to himself, as he surveyed the track. "He is a living sculpture, a representation of form and function in exquisite harmony. Today's race is a celebration of its beauty and the heritage it represents.

The various dignitaries and patrons, each immersed in their own discussions about the race and its significance, added to the atmosphere of anticipation. As the final race of the series, the Derby carried a weight that was felt by all in attendance. It was a moment when history could be made, when legacies could be forged and celebrated.

From the private box, the view of the track was unparalleled. The stands, filled to capacity, seemed to vibrate with excitement, the collective heartbeat of thousands of spectators echoing the anticipation of the event. The vibrant crowd, a mix of aristocracy and common folk, provided a lively and dynamic backdrop to the proceedings.

As the final preparations for the race were completed, Lord Wentworth felt a sense of calm amidst the excitement. The Derby was more than a race; it was a celebration of excellence, a testament to the enduring spirit of tradition and beauty. And as he stood there, surrounded by the vibrant energy of Epsom Downs, he knew that history was about to be made.

The private box above the grandstand offered a commanding view of the course. The tension was palpable as the crowd's anticipation reached a fever pitch. The vibrant energy of the crowd, the fluttering of flags and the rhythmic buzz of excitement created a symphony of sound that filled the air.

Lord Charles Wentworth stood by the railing, his eyes fixed on the starting line. The horses, each a paragon of strength and grace, were being led to their positions. The atmosphere was electric, yet a disquieting sense of unease nagged at the edges of his consciousness.

Adrien d'Arcy, standing beside him, sensed his unease. "Is everything all right, my lord?" he asked, his voice deep and calm.

Wentworth turned to his trusted confidant, his expression pensive. "Adrien, I cannot shake this feeling of foreboding," he admitted. "It is as if some unseen shadow is looming over this day, casting a pall over the celebrations."

Adrien's brow furrowed in concern. "Isinglass is in perfect condition, my lord. The preparations have been meticulous. Whatever the feeling, we must have faith in our efforts and in Isinglass' abilities."

Wentworth nodded, but the unease remained. His eyes scanned the crowd, the stands filled with thousands of spectators, each a part of the collective anticipation. Yet amidst the vibrant energy, he felt an inexplicable sense of dread, as if some ominous presence lingered just beyond the edges of perception.

The announcer's voice boomed through the megaphone, calling the horses into position. The crowd's excitement reached a crescendo, their cheers and applause echoing across the racecourse. The starting gates loomed ahead, a symbol of the race to come and the culmination of months of preparation and anticipation.

Lord Wentworth's grip on the railing tightened, his knuckles white with tension. "Adrien," he said quietly, "whatever happens today, know that we have done everything in our power to honour the legacy and beauty of Isinglass. He is more than a competitor; he is a testament to our dedication and passion."

Adrien placed a reassuring hand on Wentworth's shoulder. "We are witnessing history today, my lord. Have faith in Isinglass and the legacy he carries."

As the horses took their positions, the weight of anticipation settled over the racecourse. The crowd fell into a hushed silence, their collective breath held in anticipation of the race. Lord Wentworth's heart pounded in his chest, the sense of foreboding growing stronger with each passing moment.

The gates were about to open, the race was about to begin. And as the tension reached its peak, Lord Wentworth sensed an ominous presence, a whisper of impending danger that sent a shiver down his spine. The fate of Isinglass and the culmination of their efforts hung in the balance, on the brink of a moment that could change everything.

The race was about to begin, and in that breathless moment, the sense of foreboding deepened, casting a shadow over the pulsating energy of the Derby. The outcome was uncertain and the stakes had never been higher.

CHAPTER 4

ECHOES OF TRIUMPH AND MYSTERY

T he gunshot echoed through the air, snapping Tommy into razor-sharp focus. Perched on Isinglass in the starting box, he could feel the palpable tension in the air, the anticipation of the crowd manifesting itself in a collective intake of breath. For a fleeting moment, time seemed to stand still, the world on the brink of explosive action. Then, with a thunderous roar that shook the earth beneath them, the gates flung open and the race began.

As Isinglass surged forward, Tommy felt a sudden, uncharacteristic tremor of fear ripple through the horse's powerful frame. It was a momentary hesitation, a flash of uncertainty that threatened to unbalance them both. Isinglass's usual grace seemed to waver, his movements unsteady as he struggled to regain his composure.

"What's the matter, old boy?" Tommy thought, a flicker of concern crossing his mind. "This isn't like you."

Tommy's instincts kicked in instantly. With unmatched reflexes honed by years of experience, he reacted almost instantly. A subtle shift of weight, a gentle but firm squeeze of his knees and a reassuring murmur were all it took to convey his unwavering confidence to Isinglass.

"Easy now, boy, we've got this," Tommy murmured, feeling Isinglass respond to the calm assurance in his voice.

Their deep bond, forged through countless hours of training and mutual trust, allowed Tommy to sense and respond to the horse's needs with a precision that bordered on the miraculous. At the very next gallop, Isinglass began to regain his usual tight control over his movements. The initial flash of fear vanished, replaced by the familiar rhythm of power and precision.

"There you go, lad," Tommy thought as a wave of relief washed over him. "Back to your old self."

Tommy's expert handling ensured that they navigated the initial chaos of the race with the grace of a dancer, each stride a feat of athleticism and determination. The cacophony of hooves, the shouts of the jockeys and the roar of the crowd melded into a symphony of intensity. Amidst the tumult, Tommy's skill shone through. With deft movements, he guided Isinglass through the crowd, a series of subtle shifts of weight and precise tugs on the reins ensuring they navigated the melee with the grace of a dancer.

⚜

Navigating the narrow spaces between the other horses required not only skill but an intimate knowledge of Isinglass's abilities. Tommy guided Isinglass with subtle shifts of weight, precise tugs on the reins and whispered commands that only the horse could hear.

"Easy, easy," Tommy whispered, his voice barely audible over the thundering hooves. "We'll find the gap, just trust me."

His connection with Isinglass was almost telepathic, a bond forged through countless hours of training and mutual trust. He could feel the raw power of the horse beneath him, every muscle coiled and ready to spring, the rhythmic cadence of their movement a testament to their harmony. Together they became one, a seamless blend of man and beast, each attuned to the other's intent.

"This is what you were born for, old friend," Tommy thought, a surge of pride swelling within him. "Every drop of Arabian blood in your veins sings today."

As they moved forward, Tommy couldn't help but think about Isinglass's Arabian pedigree. The horse's bloodline was a tapestry of strength, endurance and grace, traits that had been carefully nurtured and honed over generations. Isinglass's lithe, muscular frame and powerful legs were the physical manifestations of this heritage, and it was these traits that gave him an undeniable edge in the race.

The challenges of the race were many. Tight spaces demanded precision and quick reflexes, while maintaining speed required a delicate balance of strength and control. As they navigated a particularly congested section of the track, Tommy could feel Isinglass's muscles coiling and releasing beneath him, each stride a testament to their shared resilience. The horse's nostrils flared and his breaths came in powerful, rhythmic bursts, a symphony of effort and determination.

At one point, a competitor came dangerously close, threatening to cut them off. With a deft manoeuvre, Tommy shifted his weight and guided Isinglass to

54

the inside, avoiding the potential collision and maintaining their momentum. It was moments like this that underlined the deep bond between them, a bond that transcended the mere mechanics of riding.

"Close," Tommy thought, his heart racing. "But we've faced worse, haven't we, boy?"

The race continued, and with each passing second, Tommy's confidence in Isinglass grew. They surged ahead, their movements synchronised to a degree that bordered on the uncanny. The challenges they faced only served to strengthen their resolve, each obstacle a testament to their teamwork and resilience.

"Good boy," Tommy encouraged, feeling the thrill of their collective effort. "Just a bit further now."

As they approached the final stretch, Tommy could feel the anticipation building, a crescendo of energy and excitement that seemed to permeate the very air around them. The roar of the crowd was a distant echo in his ears as he focused on the task at hand. He and Isinglass were poised for victory, their journey through the race a testament to their unparalleled bond and unyielding determination.

"Keep your head, Tommy," he reminded himself. "This is it. The moment we've worked for."

The race was far from over, but in the midst of the challenges they faced, Tommy and Isinglass had already proved their mettle. Their journey was a celebration of the bond between horse and jockey, a testament to the power of trust, resilience and the relentless pursuit of excellence.

"Let's show them what we're made of, Isinglass," Tommy whispered, a fierce determination in his voice. "Together, we're unstoppable."

In those moments, Tommy knew that they were racing not only against time and their opponents, but also against the limits of their own abilities. And as they continued to surge forward, the finish line drawing ever closer, he felt a profound sense of pride and gratitude for the extraordinary horse beneath him.

Their journey through the race was not just a matter of strategy and speed, but a symphony of shared effort, mutual trust and the indomitable spirit that had brought them to this point. And with every step, Tommy knew that they were not just racing, but creating a legacy that would last long after the race was won.

⁕

The race had reached its climax, the final stretch beckoning with the promise of glory. Tommy felt every sinew of Isinglass's mighty frame beneath him, coiled and ready to unleash the final burst of speed. The initial chaos had given way to a focused intensity, and the competitors were now a blur in his wake.

"This is it, old friend," Tommy thought, his heart pounding in time with Isinglass' powerful strides. "Every challenge, every moment has brought us to this point."

As they approached the final bend, Tommy could feel the tension in the air, the electric anticipation of the crowd palpable. The roar of the crowd was a distant thunder, their collective energy propelling him and Isinglass forward. With a deft manoeuvre, Tommy guided Isinglass to the outside, positioning them perfectly for the final push.

"Now, boy, give it all you've got," Tommy urged, his voice a mixture of encouragement and command.

Isinglass responded with a burst of strength that seemed to draw from the depths of his bloodline. His legs stretched out in perfect synchrony, each hoof striking the turf with the precision of a master craftsman. The gap between them and their nearest rival widened with every stride, the finish line drawing ever closer.

The crowd's reaction was electric, a wave of cheers and applause cascading down the track. Tommy could barely hear his own thoughts over the cacophony, but he didn't need to. His focus was on the task at hand, the bond between him and Isinglass guiding them with almost preternatural precision.

"We've got this," Tommy thought, his chest swelling with a mixture of exhaustion and triumph. "Just a little more and victory will be ours."

With a final, monumental effort, Isinglass crossed the line a full length ahead of his rival. The roar of the crowd was deafening, a symphony of jubilation that matched the elation coursing through Tommy's veins. He could feel the exhaustion setting in, but it was accompanied by an overwhelming sense of triumph.

"Good boy," Tommy whispered, patting Isinglass on the neck as they slowed to a gallop. "You did it. We did it."

As they came to a halt, Adrien ran up to them, his face aglow with pride and joy. He took the reins from Tommy, his movements gentle and affectionate as he led Isinglass away to cool down.

"You were magnificent," Adrien said, his voice filled with genuine admiration. "Both of you."

Tommy dismounted, his legs trembling with fatigue but his heart soaring with the thrill of their victory. He watched as Adrien tended to Isinglass, their bond evident in every careful touch and murmured word.

"Thank you, Adrien," Tommy said, his voice hoarse with emotion. "I couldn't have done it without you."

Adrien looked up, his eyes shining with a mixture of pride and gratitude. "And Isinglass couldn't have done it without you, Tommy. You both made history today."

Tommy nodded, the weight of their achievement settling over him like a warm embrace. The immediate aftermath of the race was a blur of congratulations and celebratory exclamations, but through it all Tommy felt a deep, abiding connection to the extraordinary horse beside him.

As the noise of the crowd began to die down, Tommy and Adrien walked Isinglass to the stables, their steps slow and measured. The bond between them was palpable, a testament to the countless hours of training and the unwavering trust they had built.

In that moment, amidst the thrill of victory and the quiet camaraderie of shared triumph, Tommy felt a deep sense of gratitude. For Isinglass, for Adrien, and for the journey that had brought them to this point. It was a victory that went beyond simply winning a race, a celebration of the indomitable spirit and the power of unwavering dedication.

"Let's get you settled, old boy," Adrien murmured to Isinglass, his voice soft and soothing. "You've earned your rest."

Tommy watched as Adrien led Isinglass into the stables, his heart full of pride and affection. The race was over, but the bond between them would endure, a legacy of trust and triumph that would be remembered for years to come.

In the aftermath of the race, Epsom Downs was transformed into a vibrant tableau of celebration. The air buzzed with excitement and the scents of fine tobacco, spiced wine and trampled grass mingled. As the sun faded to a softer gold, the festive mood persisted, each exclamation of victory and congratulatory handshake adding to the jubilant cacophony.

Lord Charles Wentworth, still contemplative, was soon swept up in the exchange of congratulations. Noblemen clapped him enthusiastically on the back and distinguished ladies smiled in admiration. Every interaction reflected the high regard in which he was held. His triumph with Isinglass had not only won the race, it had cemented his reputation as a patron of excellence.

"Wentworth, a splendid victory!" exclaimed Sir Edward Kingsley, a rotund and jovial figure whose laughter seemed to shake the air. "Isinglass has broken the odds!"

Wentworth nodded politely. "The race was thrilling, Sir Reginald. But more than this victory, I reflect on what it represents - years of dedication by many hands, minds and spirits who dared to dream of triumph."

A murmur of agreement went through the group, and Lady Annabelle Forsythe, a slim woman with sharp features and an even sharper intellect, added: "It is the artistry of it all that captures the imagination, is it not, Lord

Wentworth? The grace of the horse, the precision of the jockey - it is like watching a ballet unfold amidst the thunder of hooves."

"Exquisitely put, Lady Annabelle," Wentworth replied, his eyes reflecting a glimmer of appreciation for her analogy. "It is indeed an art form, one that transcends the mere mechanics of sport and reaches into the realm of the aesthetic, where beauty and performance intertwine to create something truly memorable."

As he navigated these social waters, Adrien d'Arcy remained close at hand, watching Wentworth with an almost protective attitude, ensuring that the conversations did not veer too far into the idle or trivial. Their bond, forged through mutual respect and shared passion, was evident in every glance and unspoken word.

Amidst the sea of well-wishers, Tommy and Adrien briefly joined the celebrations. Tommy, still basking in the afterglow of his triumph, was greeted with hearty congratulations from his fellow jockeys. His face, flushed with the thrill of victory, reflected the pride he felt for Isinglass and the journey they had taken together.

"Tommy, you were extraordinary out there," one of his countrymen exclaimed, clapping him on the back. "You and Isinglass make a formidable team."

"Thank you," Tommy replied, his voice tinged with humility. "It was a team effort, really."

Adrien, ever attentive to Isinglass' needs, excused himself to check the horse's tack and ensure that every detail was attended to. His care and affection for Isinglass was evident in the meticulous attention he paid to every buckle and strap, his hands moving with practiced ease.

"Isinglass deserves the best," Adrien murmured to himself, a smile playing on his lips. "And he'll get nothing less on my watch."

Before they parted ways, Adrien and Tommy shared a brief but meaningful acknowledgement with Lord Wentworth. Their eyes met, and in that moment a silent understanding passed between them - a recognition of the triumph they had achieved together, and the legacy they were building.

"Thank you, my lord," Tommy said, his voice steady with determination. "For believing in us."

"It is I who should thank you, Tommy," Wentworth replied, his tone filled with genuine gratitude. "Your skill and dedication have brought us to this moment. Let us savour it and remember what we have achieved."

With that, Adrien and Tommy returned to their respective duties, leaving Wentworth to reflect on the day's events. The social dynamics of the celebration continued to swirl around him, but in the midst of it all he felt a profound sense of fulfilment. The victory was not just a personal triumph, but a testament to the collective effort and unwavering dedication of everyone involved.

As the sun began its descent, casting long, cool shadows across the verdant grounds of Epsom Downs, the celebrations took on a more subdued tone. The laughter and chatter died down and a sense of quiet satisfaction settled over the gathering.

In those moments, amidst the fading light and the echoing cheers, Wentworth stood as a man who had not only witnessed a moment of perfect beauty, but had helped to create it. The victory of Isinglass was a celebration of excellence, a testament to the power of vision and the indomitable spirit of those who dared to dream.

The legacy of Isinglass and the bond between horse and rider would be remembered not only for their triumphs on the racecourse, but for the beauty and inspiration they inspired. It was a victory that transcended the ephemeral, touched the eternal and left a lasting imprint on the hearts and minds of all who were fortunate enough to witness it.

⊕⊕⊙⊛⊙⊛⊕⊕

As the festive atmosphere at Epsom Downs began to fade, the sun sank lower in the sky, casting long, cool shadows across the green grounds. The air, still humming with the echoes of celebration, gradually settled to a more subdued hum. Feeling the need for a moment of solitude, Lord Charles Wentworth gently withdrew from the remaining social intercourse and made his way to the ancient oak that stood guard near the paddock.

The oak, with its gnarled branches and broad canopy, had seen many such races and celebrations over the years. It was a place of reflection and tranquillity, a stark contrast to the vibrant tableau of the racecourse. Wentworth's footsteps were soft on the trampled grass, his thoughts a tumultuous mix of triumph and contemplation.

He reached the tree and placed a hand on its rough bark, feeling the centuries-old strength beneath his fingertips. He took a deep breath, the cool evening air filling his lungs, and allowed his mind to wander over the events of the day.

"What a day it has been," Wentworth mused, his gaze drifting to the horizon where the sun was a disc of molten gold. "Isinglass has once again proved his mettle, and Tommy's jockeying skills have shone brilliantly. But beyond the immediate victory, what does it all mean?"

The significance of the victory went beyond the race itself. It was a testament to years of dedication, of nurturing talent and potential, of believing in a vision even when the odds seemed insurmountable. Isinglass, with his Arabian pedigree and indomitable spirit, had etched a moment of beauty into the fabric of time - a legacy that Wentworth felt a strong responsibility to preserve.

"Every victory is a fleeting moment of glory," Wentworth reflected. "But it is the legacy we leave behind that lasts. Isinglass has carved his place in history today, and so have all of us who believed in him."

The peace of the setting enveloped him, the rustling of the leaves whispering secrets of the past, the soft chirping of the birds a lullaby to the approaching twilight. Wentworth's thoughts turned introspective as he considered his own place in the tapestry of history. He had always sought to capture beauty in its most fleeting and perfect forms, to celebrate it and ensure it was remembered.

"What is a legacy if not the lasting imprint of our actions, our choices?" he pondered, echoing his earlier conversation with Adrien. "Today, Isinglass' triumph is a moment we are privileged to witness and responsible to preserve."

As he stood, lost in thought, the serenity of the moment was subtly tinged with a sense of foreboding. The shadows were lengthening, casting darker patches across the ground, and a cool breeze rustled the leaves above. Wentworth's thoughts were interrupted by an inexplicable feeling of unease, a sense that he was not entirely alone.

"Strange," he thought, his eyes scanning the surroundings. "It's as if a shadow has fallen over this moment of triumph."

The peacefulness of the oak's shade now seemed to hold an undercurrent of tension. Wentworth could not shake the feeling that something was amiss, a lurking presence that cast a pall over his reflections. The stillness of the air and the gathering darkness seemed to whisper of impending danger, a shadow moving behind the oak, fleeting yet palpable.

"What could it be?" he wondered, his senses heightened. "Is it just the weight of the day's events, or something more sinister?"

As the last rays of sunlight dipped below the horizon, plunging the landscape into a dusky twilight, Wentworth's unease grew. The stillness of the air and the gathering darkness seemed to whisper of impending danger, a shadow moving behind the oak, fleeting yet palpable.

"I must remain vigilant," Wentworth resolved, his mind now alert to the subtle hints of threat. "This moment of triumph must not be marred by unseen threats."

⬦⬦⬦⬦⬦

With a final, lingering glance at the ancient oak, Lord Wentworth turned to make his way back to the paddock, the sense of foreboding clinging to him like a spectre. The serenity of the setting had given way to an undercurrent of suspense, setting the stage for the dramatic events of the next chapter.

In the quiet of the evening, with the triumph of Isinglass still fresh in his mind, Lord Wentworth walked away from the oak, determined to protect the beauty and achievements he had so carefully cultivated. The shadows lengthened, and the narrative subtly hinted at the lurking presence, weaving a thread of anticipation that would carry forward, keeping the reader on the edge of their seat in eager anticipation of the unfolding drama.

As he moved away from the oak, a flicker of movement caught his eye once more - a shadowy figure, just at the edge of his vision. Wentworth paused, his heart pounding as he turned in the direction of the disturbance. The figure was gone, dissolved into the encroaching darkness, but the sense of foreboding remained, a chilling reminder that darkness lurked beneath the gilded veneer of his world.

"Who could it be?" Wentworth mused, the question gnawing at his consciousness. "And what could they possibly want?"

The answers would inevitably come, but for now the suspense hung heavy in the air, a palpable tension that hinted at further revelations. Wentworth resumed his walk, his mind a whirl of thoughts and speculation, the shadowy presence a constant and unwelcome companion as he made his way back to the paddock. The stage was set, the players were in place and the next act of the drama was about to unfold.

CHAPTER 5

A CRY IN THE TWILIGHT

L aughter and celebration filled the air at Epsom Downs on Derby Day, as the jubilant festivities enveloped the venue in a tapestry of triumph and merriment. Isinglass's victory had crowned the day's events, and the crowd, overwhelmed with exhilaration, echoed with cheers and the clinking of glasses. But in the midst of this revelry, a deafening scream cut through the joyous din like a jagged shard of glass, instantly silencing the merriment and plunging the atmosphere into chilling chaos.

I, Dr John Watson, ever the faithful companion of Sherlock Holmes, felt my senses jolt as the scream echoed through the air. Instinctively, I turned to my friend, whose keen eyes had already located the source of the disturbance. The transformation in Holmes was instantaneous; from the genial observer of human folly, he became the razor-sharp detective, every fibre of his being attuned to the unfolding crisis.

"Watson, come quickly!" Holmes commanded, his voice cutting through the growing murmur of the crowd.

We rushed forward, our progress hampered by the crowd of onlookers drawn by the scream. Faces that had been wreathed in smiles moments before now wore expressions of shock and fear. The cacophony of previously joyous sounds had turned into a discordant symphony of gasps, whispers and desperate cries. Every fibre of my being was focused on reaching the source of the scream, my medical training compelling me to offer aid, while Holmes' singular intensity promised swift justice.

Navigating the sea of bodies required a delicate balance of urgency and tact. The smell of spilled wine and crushed grass permeated the air, remnants of overturned glasses and trampled picnics as we pushed through the once-celebratory crowd. The stark contrast between the earlier revelry and the current pandemonium was palpable.

"Make way, please!" I pleaded, my voice calm but urgent. "Let us through!"

Holmes, with his characteristic blend of authority and calm, moved purposefully, his sharp gaze scanning the faces around him for any clue, any sign of unusual behaviour. His presence seemed to divide the crowd, an unspoken recognition of his role as a harbinger of order amid the chaos.

As we approached the grove of ancient oaks, the crowd thickened, drawn by a morbid curiosity. The trees, which had previously provided a tranquil retreat, now loomed menacingly, their shadows lengthening in the fading twilight. The scream had come from this secluded spot, Lord Wentworth's favourite for moments of quiet reflection. My heart pounded in my chest, a mixture of professional duty and personal fear driving me forward.

We finally broke through the last ring of onlookers, our breath taken away by the sight that awaited us. The celebratory atmosphere had been irrevocably shattered, replaced by a scene of grim reality that demanded our immediate attention.

***

The cry had drawn the crowd into a tight, anxious knot around the grove of ancient oaks, their faces pale and their eyes wide with a mixture of horror and curiosity. The once vibrant scene of celebration now stood in stark contrast to the grim reality that lay beneath the spreading branches of the oldest oak. The air, once filled with laughter and music, was now heavy with an oppressive silence, the weight of unspoken fears hanging like a pall over the gathering.

When Holmes and I finally broke through the last ranks of onlookers, our eyes were immediately drawn to the lifeless form sprawled beneath the oak. Lord Charles Wentworth lay there, his body unnaturally contorted, his fine clothes dishevelled and a dark, ominous stain spreading across his chest. The rich tones of his clothing seemed dulled by the approaching twilight, the vivid colours muted by the shadow of death.

Holmes quickly surveyed the scene with the precision of a master detective, his keen eyes scanning every detail. He moved with deliberate grace, his every action measured and purposeful. As he knelt beside the body, I followed suit, my medical instincts urging me to check for signs of life, though I already knew the truth. The stillness of Lord Wentworth's form, the lack of breath, the pallor of his skin, all spoke the unmistakable language of death.

I placed my fingers gently on his neck, feeling for a pulse that I knew was not there. The skin was cool, the stillness beneath my fingertips absolute. "He's gone, Holmes," I confirmed quietly, my voice tinged with the sadness that comes from witnessing the finality of life's departure.

Holmes nodded, his expression one of deep concentration, his mind already shifting into the analytical mode that had earned him his unparalleled reputation. "The wound, Watson," he said quietly, his eyes fixed on the dark mark. "Right through the heart. A precise, calculated blow. This was no random act of violence."

Examining the wound more closely, I noted the nature of the cut - a single, deep penetration, clean and efficient. "Indeed, Holmes. The blade must have been driven in with considerable force and precision. Death would have been instantaneous."

Holmes' gaze shifted to the ground around the body, his eyes narrowing as he took in the scene with a detective's meticulous attention. The grass was disturbed, footprints overlapping in a chaotic pattern, but one set of prints stood out - larger, deeper, suggesting a person of considerable weight or a hasty, forceful movement. He noted the position of the body, the way it lay in relation to the oak, and the scattered leaves that bore bloodstains.

"There are clues here Watson," Holmes murmured almost to himself. "Clues that will speak to us if we have the wit to listen."

His eyes fell on an object lying near Lord Wentworth's body, partially obscured by the leaves. It was an ornate dagger, its blade stained with blood, its hilt intricately carved with exotic designs. Holmes' hand reached out, his touch as soft as a whisper, and lifted the dagger into the fading light.

"The murder weapon," he said, his voice a mixture of fascination and grim determination. "Note the craftsmanship, Watson. This is no ordinary blade. It is of Arabic manufacture, an antique perhaps, passed down through generations. This dagger tells a story, one that is central to the mystery of Lord Wentworth's death."

As I leaned forward to examine the dagger, the intricate details of the hilt became clear - patterns of sinuous vines and mythical creatures, each line and curve a testament to the artistry of a distant culture. "Remarkable, Holmes," I agreed. "But what could such a weapon be doing here, at the Derby, in the hands of a murderer?"

"That, Watson, is the heart of our mystery," Holmes replied, a determined light in his eyes. "This dagger is a key, not only to the act of murder, but to the motives and stories intertwined with it. We must follow its history to uncover the truth behind this heinous crime."

Holmes paused, his brow furrowed as he considered the implications of the dagger's presence. His voice took on a contemplative tone as he continued, "The precision of the wound indicates a calm and controlled hand, Watson. This was not an act of spontaneous violence or a struggle. The killer was in complete control, fully aware of his actions. Such a person would not simply lose or forget a weapon of this nature.

I nodded, understanding the gravity of his conclusions. "So the dagger left here is no accident?"

"Exactly," Holmes confirmed, his eyes narrowing in suspicion. "It was deliberately left here for us to find. The question we have to ask ourselves is why. What message is the murderer trying to convey by leaving such a distinctive and traceable weapon at the scene?"

The weight of his words hung in the air, the implications profound. The game was afoot and the path to justice lay in deciphering the silent messages left in the wake of Lord Wentworth's untimely death.

⊕⊕⊰✳⊱⊕⊕

The oppressive silence that had settled over the scene was abruptly broken by the arrival of Inspector Lestrade and his contingent of policemen. The familiar figure of Lestrade, with his brisk, authoritative stride, cut through the crowd, his presence bringing a semblance of order to the chaos. The murmurs of the onlookers began to die down and the crowd dispersed to allow the Inspector and his men to pass.

"Holmes," Lestrade called out, his tone a mixture of urgency and the ever-present frustration that marked his interactions with Sherlock. "I should have known I'd find you here, already deep in analysis."

Holmes straightened from his crouched position beside Lord Wentworth's body, his keen eyes meeting Lestrade's with a mixture of respect and determination. "Inspector, your timing is impeccable," he replied, his voice calm and steady. "We have a most unusual case on our hands."

Lestrade's eyes fell on the lifeless form of Lord Wentworth, his brow furrowed in recognition of the gravity of the situation. "Lord Wentworth," he murmured, his expression sombre. "An important figure, indeed. What have you discovered so far, Holmes?"

Holmes gestured to the ornate dagger lying in the grass, its blood-stained blade glinting ominously. "This dagger, Inspector," he said, lifting the weapon with a cautious hand. "It is of Arabic manufacture, an antique, possibly passed down through generations. The craftsmanship is exquisite, but more importantly, the nature of the wound suggests a precise, controlled strike. This was not an act of spontaneity".

Lestrade's scepticism was evident in the arch of his brow. "Arab, you say? Seems a stretch, Holmes. We're in Surrey, not the Sahara."

"Yet it is the unexpected pieces of a puzzle that often prove the most illuminating," Holmes replied sharply. "We must look beyond the geographical improbability and consider the historical and cultural significance. Who here in the Derby would possess such a dagger? Who would have the motive to turn such a rare artefact into an instrument of murder?"

66

Lestrade sighed and ran a hand through his hair as he absorbed Holmes' words. "Very well, Holmes. I'll have my men search the crowd. See if anyone is missing such a dagger or if any witnesses have noticed any unusual behaviour."

As Lestrade turned to coordinate with his officers, his voice cutting through the air as he gave instructions to secure the area and begin questioning the guests, Holmes pulled me aside. His eyes were bright with the thrill of the chase, a determined light sparking in their depths.

"Watson," he said, his voice low but charged with energy, "we have before us a case that promises to plumb the depths of human history and emotion. Are you prepared for what we may discover?"

"Always, Holmes," I replied, feeling the familiar thrill of adventure stir within me again. "Lead on."

As Lestrade's men began to control the crowd, directing them away from the immediate area and ensuring that the crime scene remained undisturbed, Holmes and I took a moment to observe the wider surroundings. The ancient oak, with its whispering leaves, seemed to keep a silent vigil over the scene, its branches casting long shadows in the fading light.

Lestrade returned, his expression a mixture of resignation and determination. "Holmes, we'll need to do a thorough search of the area and speak to everyone present. This is a high profile case and the pressure to solve it quickly will be immense."

"Indeed, Inspector," Holmes replied, his tone one of agreement. "We must be meticulous. Every detail, no matter how seemingly insignificant, could hold the key to unlocking this mystery."

With the crime scene now secured and the first steps of the investigation underway, the sense of urgency and purpose was palpable. The first threads of the investigation had been woven and the task now was to follow them with unerring precision. The game was on, and with Sherlock Holmes at the helm, I felt a surge of confidence that justice would be served.

⊷⊶⊱✧⊰⊷⊶

There was a sudden commotion as Adrien d'Arcy and Tommy Loates arrived, attracted by the piercing scream. The two men had been in the stables, meticulously tending to Isinglass, the champion horse, when the harrowing sound had shattered the air. The once orderly stables had fallen eerily silent as Adrien wiped his dye-stained hands on his apron, a cold fear gripping his heart. Now they hurried towards the copse of ancient oaks, their expressions a stark contrast to the earlier jubilation. Adrien's face was a mixture of fear and urgency, his eyes wide with fear and determination.

"Let us through!" Adrien pleaded, his voice cracking with desperation as he pushed through the crowd of onlookers. His urgency was palpable, each step driven by the fear of what he might find.

As Adrien approached the tragic scene, each step felt heavier than the last, as if the weight of his grief and disbelief were physically dragging him down. The atmosphere was suffocating, the silence broken only by the gentle rustle of the leaves on the ancient oak, a whispered elegy for the man who had so often sought solace in its shade. Adrien's heart raced, his breath coming in short, painful gasps as he drew closer to the body of his friend and mentor. The ground beneath his feet seemed to shift and sway, the uneven terrain a physical manifestation of the emotional upheaval that threatened to consume him.

Sherlock Holmes, standing sentinel over the scene, recognised the close relationship these men had with the victim. With a nod to the constables, he allowed them access. "Let them pass," he ordered, his authoritative tone brooking no argument. "You are known to the deceased."

When Adrien finally reached Lord Wentworth's side, the sight of his lifeless form hit him like a sledgehammer to the chest, forcing the air from his lungs with a silent cry of anguish. He fell to his knees, his trembling hands hovering over the still, cold form of the man who had meant so much to him. Lord Wentworth's face, once so full of life and passion, was now a mask of eerie stillness, his vibrant spirit extinguished forever. Adrien's vision blurred, hot tears streaming down his cheeks as he gently touched his friend's hand, desperately searching for some flicker of warmth, some sign that this was all a terrible mistake.

"Charles... no..." Adrien whispered, his voice breaking as he gently touched Lord Wentworth's pale, lifeless hand. How could this have happened? he thought, his mind racing through the possibilities. Only this morning he had spoken of his plans for the future.

But there was no mistaking, no denying the harsh reality that lay before him. Lord Wentworth, his mentor, his confidant, his friend, was gone, and with him a piece of Adrien's own soul. The pain was all-consuming, a physical pain that radiated from his heart to his fingertips, leaving him feeling hollow and lost. In that moment, kneeling beside the man who had shaped so much of his life, Adrien knew that nothing would ever be the same again.

Adrien felt a wave of nausea wash over him as he knelt in the damp grass beside Lord Wentworth's body. The cold of the earth beneath him was a cruel reminder of the warmth and vitality that had been so violently torn from his friend. With trembling hands, he reached out to touch the dark crimson stain that marred the ground, his fingers hovering just above the spot where his friend's life had been so brutally cut short. The metallic scent of the blood mixed with the fresh, green scent of the grass, creating a sickening contrast that made Adrien's stomach churn. He closed his eyes, fighting back the bile that rose in his throat, but the image of Lord Wentworth's lifeless form was seared into his mind, a haunting vision that he knew would never leave him.

A sob tore from Adrien's chest, his shoulders heaving as he struggled to breathe through the crushing weight of his grief. He wanted to scream, to rage against the injustice of it all, but his voice was trapped in his throat, choked by the raw, unbridled emotion that consumed him. When he finally found the strength to speak, his words were barely audible, a broken whisper that seemed to echo in the silence of the clearing. "He was everything to me," Adrien choked out, his voice cracking with the depth of his pain. "Not just a patron, but a true friend, a guiding light in my life. We shared so much, not just a love of history and craftsmanship, but a bond of trust and understanding that I've never known with anyone else."

Tommy stood nearby, his face a mask of shock and grief. He placed a supportive hand on Adrien's shoulder, offering what little comfort he could in the face of such a devastating loss. "I'm here, Adrien," he murmured, his voice calm. "We'll find out who did this."

Holmes, standing beside Adrien, remained silent for a moment, allowing the weight of the young man's grief to settle in the cool evening air. His expression was sombre, his eyes reflecting not only the moonlight but also a deep, unspoken sympathy.

Adrien's grief soon turned to a desperate plea for justice. He looked up at Sherlock Holmes, his eyes red-rimmed and filled with a raw, pleading intensity. "Please, sir," he pleaded, his voice trembling with emotion. "We must find whoever did this. Lord Wentworth was a good man, a kind and generous soul who didn't deserve this fate. I won't rest until his killer is brought to justice."

Holmes knelt beside Adrien, his gaze unwavering. "I will see that justice is done," he said, his voice low but determined. "I give you my word."

A flicker of recognition crossed Adrien's face. "Wait," he said, his voice barely a whisper. "You're Sherlock Holmes? The detective from the papers?"

"Indeed I am," Holmes replied, a slight nod acknowledging the recognition. "And I will do everything in my power to uncover the truth behind this tragedy."

Tommy, though usually composed, found his voice now tinged with a raw edge of grief. "He was more than a patron to us, Mr Holmes. He was a mentor, a guiding light. We cannot leave his death unanswered."

Holmes laid a comforting hand on Tommy's shoulder. "Your loyalty and devotion to Lord Wentworth do you credit. Rest assured, we will find the culprit."

Lestrade, who had been coordinating with his officers, approached the group. His expression was one of professional determination tempered with sympathy. "We will conduct a thorough investigation," he assured Adrien and Tommy. "Every detail will be examined, every witness questioned. We will find the culprit."

Adrien nodded, the weight of his grief momentarily lifted by the promise of action. "Thank you," he said, his voice breaking. "Thank you all."

Holmes rose, his eyes sweeping the scene once more. "The game is afoot," he declared, his voice carrying a note of finality. "And we will not rest until justice is done."

As the constables moved to secure the area and the crowd began to disperse, the sense of purpose among those who remained was palpable. The investigation had begun in earnest, driven by a shared determination to bring justice to Lord Wentworth and to unravel the deeper complexities of the case.

Holmes' solemn vow echoed through the silent room like a clarion call. "We will find those responsible," he declared, his voice filled with unwavering determination. "Justice will be served."

I watched the scene with a mixture of admiration and solemnity. Holmes' words were a beacon of hope amidst the encroaching darkness, lifting the spirits of all who had gathered. The gravity of the situation weighed heavily upon us, but there was a sense of purpose, a collective resolve that bound us together in this quest for justice.

As the evening shadows lengthened and the air grew heavy with an almost palpable tension, I could not help but reflect on the gravity of the task before us. The stage was meticulously set for the next chapter of this unfolding drama. The legacy of Lord Wentworth, the mystery surrounding his untimely demise, and the indomitable determination of my esteemed friend, Sherlock Holmes, heralded a journey deep into the heart of mystery and retribution. It was a path that promised to ensnare and challenge every soul brave enough to tread its intricate and perilous course.

Holmes' keen eyes scanned the darkening scene, his mind no doubt racing through the myriad possibilities. His determination was a palpable force, a beacon guiding us through the gathering darkness. As his loyal companion, I felt a renewed sense of duty and a fierce commitment to help him uncover the truth.

The shadows grew longer, their tendrils stretching out like dark omens, but in the encroaching darkness the light of Holmes' determination shone brightly. The air was thick with the weight of unspoken fears and the promise of revelations yet to come. It was in this charged atmosphere that we prepared to embark on the next phase of our investigation, driven by the promise of justice and the relentless pursuit of truth.

And so, with a final, determined nod to Adrien and Tommy, Holmes turned his full attention to the task at hand. The stage was set, the players were in place and the next act of the drama was about to unfold. It was a journey into the heart of intrigue and justice that would captivate and challenge all who dared to follow, and I, Dr John Watson, was honoured to be at the side of the greatest detective of our time as we ventured into the unknown.

CHAPTER 6

THE OBSIDIAN ENIGMA

A s the echoes of Sherlock Holmes' vow to seek justice faded into the cool evening air, a quiet determination gripped the small group gathered beneath the ancient oak. Adrien d'Arcy, still kneeling beside the lifeless form of Lord Wentworth, slowly rose to his feet. The raw emotion of his plea was now tempered by a steely resolve and his eyes met Holmes's with a renewed sense of purpose.

"Mr Holmes," Adrien began, his voice steady but tinged with lingering sorrow, "allow me to introduce myself formally. My name is Adrien d'Arcy. I am a master craftsman specialising in the finest leatherwork. My workshop has been in my family for generations and I have dedicated my life to perfecting the art of making leather goods of the highest quality."

Holmes nodded, his keen eyes taking in every detail of Adrien's appearance and manner. "Your expertise in craftsmanship is evident, Mr d'Arcy. I have no doubt that your skills are exceptional. But what interests me most is your relationship with Lord Wentworth and your connection to the champion horse, Isinglass."

Adrien's eyes softened as he spoke of his friend and patron. "Lord Wentworth was more than a client to me. He was a mentor, a confidant and a dear friend. Our bond was forged through a shared passion for history and the art of craftsmanship. He entrusted me with the care of Isinglass, not only as his craftsman, but as someone who truly understood the significance of the horse's lineage and the legacy it represented."

He paused, his eyes flickering briefly with the memory of happier times. "Isinglass was not just a racehorse to Lord Wentworth; he was a symbol of excellence and tradition. The care and attention I put into making the bridles, saddles and other tack for Isinglass was a reflection of the deep respect I had for both the horse and his owner."

Holmes listened intently, his analytical mind already piecing together the various threads of the tale. "Your connection with Lord Wentworth and Isinglass is indeed profound, Mr d'Arcy. It is clear that you have a personal interest in uncovering the truth behind this tragedy."

Adrien nodded, his expression resolute. "I do, Mr Holmes. Lord Wentworth saw potential in me and supported my work in a way that went beyond mere patronage. He believed in the value of preserving our heritage through craftsmanship, and he shared that belief with me. Isinglass was a testament to that shared vision, a living link to the past and a beacon of hope for the future.

Holmes' eyes narrowed slightly as he considered Adrien's words. "Your dedication to your craft and your loyalty to Lord Wentworth are commendable, Mr d'Arcy. They will undoubtedly prove invaluable as we delve deeper into this investigation. The more we understand about the connections and motivations surrounding Lord Wentworth, the closer we will come to uncovering the truth."

Adrien's eyes hardened with determination. "I will do whatever it takes to help you, Mr Holmes. Lord Wentworth's memory deserves nothing less than our best efforts to bring his killer to justice."

Holmes nodded in agreement, his sharp mind already formulating the next steps. "Very well, Mr d'Arcy. We will begin by examining the artefacts associated with Lord Wentworth, starting with the obsidian dagger. Your expertise in craftsmanship will be crucial in deciphering the meaning of these items."

With that, the stage was set for the next phase of their investigation. The bond between Adrien and Lord Wentworth, forged through a shared passion for history and artistry, would serve as a guiding light as they navigated the shadows of intrigue and deceit that surrounded the murder. The search for justice had begun in earnest, and with Sherlock Holmes at the helm, there was a renewed sense of hope that the truth would soon be revealed.

⊷⊷⊱✴⊰⊷⊷

As the shadows deepened around us, Sherlock Holmes carefully removed the obsidian dagger from his cloak and handed it to Adrien d'Arcy. The moment seemed to stretch into eternity as the master leatherworker accepted the blade, his hands steady despite the tempest of emotions swirling within him.

Adrien held the dagger up to the fading light, his eyes narrowing as he studied the weapon that had stolen his friend's life. The obsidian blade was flawless, its polished surface reflecting the world around it with an almost unnatural clarity. The razor-sharp edge caught the last rays of the setting sun, glittering with a cold, merciless beauty that sent a shiver down Adrien's spine.

Turning the dagger over in his hands, Adrien's fingers traced the intricate patterns that adorned the hilt. The carvings were unlike anything he had ever seen before, a mesmerising swirl of ancient symbols and flowing lines that spoke of a craftsmanship that was both breathtaking and unsettling. There was a ferocity to the design, a primal energy that seemed to pulse beneath the surface of the dark, gleaming stone.

"This is no ordinary blade," Adrien murmured, his voice low and tinged with a mixture of awe and disgust. "The skill required to create such a piece is immense, but there's something about it that feels... wrong. It lacks the harmony and balance I see in the Obsidian Stallion, the sense of purpose and nobility that Lord Wentworth so admired."

Holmes' eyes narrowed with interest. "The Obsidian Stallion? Are you referring to Isinglass, Lord Wentworth's champion racehorse?"

Adrien shook his head, a wistful smile crossing his lips briefly as he corrected the misunderstanding. "No, Mr Holmes. I am not referring to Isinglass, the flesh and blood who raced to victory today, but to a small obsidian statuette, a stallion, given to Lord Wentworth by his wife when Isinglass was a young foal. This statuette was Lord Wentworth's most treasured possession, his personal lucky charm, deeply cherished beyond its physical form".

He continued, his eyes reflecting the flicker of our lantern as he delved deeper into the tale. "Lady Wentworth gave it to him on a notable wedding anniversary. She knew of his love of history and his deep connection with horses. Lord Wentworth saw it as a talisman, a charm of good fortune and protection, linking him to the storied past of his cherished steeds".

The master craftsman's eyes took on a distant look as he recalled the countless times he had seen Lord Wentworth cradle the statuette in his hands, a look of reverence and awe on his face. "The stallion was exquisitely crafted," Adrien continued, his voice filled with admiration. "Every detail was perfect, from the flowing mane to the powerful muscles beneath the gleaming obsidian surface. It was a true work of art, a testament to the skill and passion of the craftsman who created it."

He turned the dagger in his hands, comparing the two obsidian artefacts in his mind. "The statuette and this dagger are worlds apart," he mused, his brow furrowed in concentration. "Where the stallion is a symbol of beauty, strength and nobility, this blade is a tool of violence and destruction. It's as if they were made by two entirely different hands, with two entirely different purposes."

Holmes, his analytical mind racing, asked another question, his voice low and contemplative against the rustling of the oak leaves. "Do you think, Mr d'Arcy, that the dagger and the statuette were made by the same craftsman?" The question hung in the air, laden with the potential to reveal a deeper connection between the artefacts and the crime.

After a moment of thoughtful consideration, Adrien replied, "After careful consideration, no," he concluded decisively. "These cannot be the work of the same hands. The dagger, for all its craftsmanship, lacks the pure beauty and soul of the statuette. The statuette exudes a harmony with nature, as if it were not so much made as discovered and freed from obsidian by the craftsman. This dagger, however, seems forced upon the material, lacking that unity. The carvings on the statuette flow seamlessly, capturing the essence of the stallion's spirit, whereas the dagger's designs, though intricate, seem almost forced upon the obsidian, lacking the same fluidity and grace."

Adrien's attention then shifted to the swirling colours of the hilt. "Look here," he pointed, indicating the twisted veins of crimson, gold and silver that marred the hilt. "The dagger's hilt is decorated with a stark contrast to the natural golden veins that adorn the obsidian stallion statuette. It's as if the dagger is trying to mimic the essence of the statuette, but introduces a discordant note, an amalgamation of colours that speaks more of conflict than harmony. The veins seem to wriggle within the obsidian, as if capturing the tumultuous energy of its creation rather than the calm power of the stallion. This suggests a different purpose, a darker intent behind its creation.

Sherlock listened intently, his mind whirling with the implications of Adrien's words. "The statuette," he pressed, his voice urgent. "Where is it now? If it meant so much to Lord Wentworth, it may hold the key to understanding his murder."

Adrien's expression became pensive, his brow furrowed as he pondered the question. "Well, Mr Holmes, the statuette always accompanied Lord Wentworth to important events, especially the races. He kept it in a custom-made leather pouch, specially designed to hold such a precious object. I made the pouch myself - of the finest leather, soft yet strong, lined with velvet to protect the statuette".

A momentary pause to allow the weight of his words to sink in before he added, "He would always have it with him, especially on days like today."

Sherlock's response was quick, his mind already racing. "Mr d'Arcy, when you found Lord Wentworth today, did you notice this bag on him?" There was an urgency to his voice that seemed to ripple through the still night air.

Adrien, taken aback by the question, stumbled through his memory. "I... I must admit, Mr Holmes, in the shock of the moment I did not notice. My main concern was for Lord Wentworth himself."

Without missing a beat, Sherlock turned to me, his eyes shining with the sharp gleam of deduction. "Watson, do you remember seeing the bag when we examined the body?"

Thinking quickly, I realised that no such bag had been in evidence. "No, Holmes, there was no bag at the scene - not that I observed."

With this confirmation, Sherlock's demeanour changed; the gears of his mind visibly turning as he pieced together the implications. "That's very worrying. If the bag - and presumably the statuette inside it - was indeed missing, it suggests a premeditated theft, possibly directly linked to the motive for the murder."

Sherlock turned on his heel. "Watson, Mr d'Arcy - back to the scene now. We may have missed clues and every second counts." Without another word he started off, his coat flaring behind him, urgency quickening his steps as we followed.

As we hurried back towards the crime scene, the gravel crunching under our feet in the stillness of the night, the ancient oak receded into the background, a silent witness to the unfolding drama. Sherlock's pace was swift, his figure a darting shadow under the moonlit sky, driven by the urgency of discovery and the relentless pursuit of truth. Our path, though shadowy and uncertain, was marked by a relentless determination to unravel the web of deceit and danger that had claimed Lord Wentworth's life.

As we hurried back to the scene of Lord Wentworth's untimely demise, the night air seemed to thicken with anticipation and an unspoken urgency. The path, lit by the ghostly silver glow of the moon, wound back beneath the ancient oak, its sprawling limbs casting eerie shadows that danced on the ground like ghosts of the past stirring restlessly.

Sherlock Holmes, his cloak billowing slightly behind him, moved with a purpose that was both thrilling and frightening to witness. Adrien d'Arcy, still visibly shaken but buoyed by a newfound sense of purpose, followed close behind, his earlier hesitation replaced by a determination spurred on by Sherlock's infectious determination.

Upon reaching the sombre scene, Sherlock wasted no time. He knelt beside Lord Wentworth's body, which lay beneath the oak as if cradled by history itself. The detective's keen eyes quickly began to reassess the evidence, his every move precise and deliberate.

"Observe carefully, Watson," Sherlock instructed as I approached, my medical bag in hand, though I knew full well that its contents were of no use to us here. "The key to understanding this heinous act lies not only in what is present, but more importantly, in what is absent."

With meticulous care, Sherlock produced a magnifying glass from his pocket and began to examine the area around Lord Wentworth's body. He pointed to the cut marks on the fabric of Lord Wentworth's jacket. The fabric bore a clean, decisive cut, too precise to be anything other than the work of a skilled hand.

"Note the direction and nature of this cut Watson. It suggests a single, swift movement, probably made by someone with considerable expertise in the use of bladed weapons."

His fingers traced the air just above the cut, careful not to contaminate any remaining evidence. "The thief, or assassin, made a calculated decision to cut here, at the strap of the bag which, as Mr d'Arcy informed us, contained the Obsidian Stallion statuette."

Turning his attention to the fatal wound inflicted on Lord Wentworth, Sherlock's expression grew sombre. The wound, a dark, cruel opening in the otherwise impeccable clothing of the deceased, spoke of brutal efficiency.

"And here, the wound itself. Positioned directly over the heart, a blow designed to be instantly fatal. This was no random act of violence, Watson, but a deliberate execution carried out with chilling competence."

Adrien, standing at a distance, watched Sherlock's examination with a mixture of awe and horror. The implications of Sherlock's conclusions were not lost on him, underlining the gravity of the threat they faced.

Sherlock stood abruptly, his eyes scanning the ground around the body. "The assassin probably approached Lord Wentworth under the guise of familiarity or with a distraction. With one hand, he slashed the strap of the bag and almost simultaneously used the ensuing moment of shock or confusion to deliver the fatal blow." He paused, letting the grim scenario sink in. "Such precision indicates not only skill, but a profound coldness of purpose."

I watched as Sherlock's eyes swept over the scene, taking in every detail with an almost preternatural acuity. He knelt down and examined the grass and scattered leaves with his magnifying glass. "Here, Watson," he called, his voice low but intense. "See these faint impressions in the ground? They indicate a struggle, brief but intense."

Sherlock's fingers traced the marks in the earth, his mind clearly racing through the possibilities. "The footprints are irregular, overlapping. But here," he pointed to a deeper, more defined mark, "this indicates a heavier weight bearing down, probably at the moment the killer made his move."

He continued to examine the area with a meticulous eye, noting every detail. "The cuts on the leather straps of the bag," he murmured, "are precise and clean, suggesting the use of a razor-sharp blade. Our murderer is no amateur, Watson. They are highly trained, possibly even a professional killer."

Adrien's breath caught in his throat as he absorbed Sherlock's conclusions. "A professional killer?" he repeated, his voice tinged with disbelief and fear. "But why? Why would someone go to such lengths to murder Lord Wentworth and steal the statuette?"

Sherlock rose to his full height, his eyes shining with a mixture of determination and resolve. "That, Mr d'Arcy, is the question we must answer. But one thing is certain: the stakes are much higher than we first suspected. This is no ordinary crime. We are dealing with a calculated, cold-blooded killer, and the motive behind this act is likely to be as intricate as the craftsmanship of the dagger itself".

The weight of Sherlock's words hung heavily in the air, casting a shadow over the already grim scene. The murder of Lord Wentworth was not merely a crime of passion or opportunity; it was a meticulously planned and executed act, carried out by a professional with a specific purpose in mind.

As we stood under the ancient oak, the reality of our task became starkly apparent. We were not simply seeking justice for a fallen friend; we were unravelling a web of intrigue and danger that extended far beyond the confines of Epsom Downs. The road ahead was fraught with peril, but with Sherlock Holmes leading the way, I felt a renewed sense of determination that we would uncover the truth and bring the perpetrator to justice.

Sherlock's keen eyes scanned the ground one last time, his mind already working out the next steps. "We must proceed with caution, Watson," he said, his voice low and steady. "The game is indeed in progress and we are up against a formidable opponent. But rest assured, we will not rest until justice is done."

With that, we turned our attention back to the body of Lord Wentworth, the gravity of our mission weighing heavily upon us. The clues we had uncovered were only the beginning, and the true depths of the mystery were yet to be revealed. But with each step we took, we drew closer to the truth, driven by an unyielding determination to see justice done.

⊱✧⊰

As we stood under the ancient oak, the weight of recent discoveries bearing down on us, Sherlock Holmes turned to Adrien d'Arcy with a renewed intensity in his gaze.

"Mr d'Arcy," Holmes began, his voice calm and deliberate, "we need to understand the origins of the obsidian statuette. You mentioned it was a gift from Lady Wentworth. Can you tell us more about that?"

Adrien nodded, his expression pensive as he delved into his memories. "The statuette was given to Lord Wentworth by his wife on a notable wedding anniversary. She knew of his love of history and his deep connection with horses. Lady Wentworth presented it as a symbol of their bond and mutual passions."

Holmes' eyes lit up with interest. "And do you know where Lady Wentworth obtained such an exquisite piece?"

Adrien shook his head, a hint of frustration in his voice. "No, Mr Holmes, I never inquired as to its provenance. It was a very personal gift and I respected her privacy. I do know, however, that it came from a distant land, a place where such craftsmanship is revered and passed down through generations. The statuette was said to be part of an ancient tradition, a symbol of strength and protection.

Holmes' mind was clearly racing as he considered the possibilities. "We must speak to Lady Wentworth," he declared. "She may hold the key to understanding the significance of the statuette and its connection to the murder."

Adrien nodded in agreement, his resolve firm. "I will accompany you to the manor. Lady Wentworth will need support at such a difficult time and I can help provide context for any questions you may have."

Holmes nodded briefly, his focus unwavering. "Very well. We will visit the manor first thing in the morning. In the meantime, there are other matters that require our attention."

As the conversation drew to a close, the brisk sound of approaching footsteps pierced the night air. The crunch of gravel underfoot was sharp and insistent, a harbinger of urgency in the otherwise still night. I turned, half expecting to face some new threat, but the figure emerging from the shadowy path was neither stranger nor foe - it was Mycroft Holmes, Sherlock's older brother. His presence here, in the depths of the countryside, away from the corridors of power where he was most at home, signalled a matter of extraordinary gravity.

Mycroft Holmes, always the embodiment of government authority, approached with his usual calm urgency. His silhouette, framed by the moonlit night, carried the weight of matters of state and the burden of knowledge that often seemed to isolate him in his rarefied world. His face, usually an impassive mask, tonight seemed etched with an intensity that spoke of concerns beyond ordinary bureaucratic entanglements.

"Sherlock, Dr Watson," Mycroft acknowledged us with a nod, his voice carrying the crisp, clear tone of one accustomed to command. His gaze then shifted to Adrien, who gave a brief nod of recognition. "Mr d'Arcy."

"Sherlock, a moment of your time," Mycroft continued, his eyes fixed on his brother's with a seriousness that immediately drew Sherlock's full attention. "There are developments in London that have a direct bearing on what has happened here. Developments that suggest the implications of Lord Wentworth's murder go far beyond a mere personal tragedy or criminal act."

The air seemed to thicken with Mycroft's words, adding a layer of foreboding to the already heavy atmosphere. Sherlock's expression, previously marked by the clinical detachment of the investigator, subtly shifted to one of keen alertness to the wider implications his brother was hinting at.

"Mycroft," Sherlock's tone sharpened, "are you suggesting that this is a matter of national security? That this murder is intertwined with the machinations of power and politics on a grand scale?"

"I am," Mycroft confirmed with a slight nod. "It appears that the theft of the Obsidian Stallion statuette may be linked to an international network of agents with interests hostile to the Crown. Your investigation into Lord Wentworth's murder may well unravel threads that lead us into a labyrinth of espionage and geopolitical intrigue."

The gravity of Mycroft's revelation hung like a heavy curtain between us, momentarily drawing a veil over the personal dimensions of the crime to reveal the silhouette of larger, darker machinations.

"This is no ordinary criminal enterprise, Sherlock. The parties involved in this matter are manoeuvring from the shadows. Caution and discretion will be paramount," Mycroft added, his gaze intense, impressing upon us the gravity of the situation.

Sherlock, his mind visibly adjusting to the larger scope of the problem, nodded slowly. "Understood, Mycroft. We will proceed in the knowledge that the stakes are considerably higher than we first suspected."

Turning to me, Sherlock's eyes conveyed a silent message of determination mixed with the thrill of the hunt ahead. "Watson, it seems that our investigation has just expanded into areas that neither of us could have anticipated at the outset."

Mycroft, having delivered his urgent message, seemed ready to leave but paused. "I must return to London immediately. Keep me informed, Sherlock. The implications of this case are likely to reverberate at the highest levels of government."

With that, Mycroft Holmes turned and left as quickly as he had come, his figure soon swallowed up by the night, leaving behind a palpable sense of the enormity of the task ahead.

In the echo of Mycroft's fading footsteps, a shared glance passed between Sherlock, Adrien and myself - a silent acknowledgement of the stakes. Our hunt was no longer for a mere murderer and thief; we now found ourselves pulling at threads that could unravel a conspiracy woven through the shadowy realm of global intrigue.

"The game is indeed afoot," Sherlock murmured, almost to himself, but loud enough for us to hear. "And it is a game played in the shadows, with stakes far beyond what we see."

As the weight of Mycroft's revelation settled on us, Holmes turned his attention back to Adrien d'Arcy with a renewed sense of urgency.

"Mr d'Arcy," Holmes began, his tone both commanding and reassuring, "it is imperative that we proceed with the utmost caution. Until we can speak to Lady Wentworth, I must ask you to look after Isinglass and ensure that Lady Wentworth is looked after."

Adrien nodded, his determination unshakable. "I understand, Mr Holmes. I will see that Isinglass and Lady Wentworth are well looked after. You have my word."

Holmes gave a brief nod of agreement. "Excellent. Watson and I will return to London to follow up on the leads Mycroft has provided. We will visit the manor house first thing in the morning to speak to Lady Wentworth and gather any additional information that may aid our investigation."

Sherlock's gaze softened for a moment as he turned to Adrien. "Your assistance so far has been invaluable, Mr d'Arcy. I have no doubt that your continued support will be vital as we unravel this mystery."

With our immediate tasks outlined, Holmes and I prepared to say goodbye. The night air was cool and crisp, the silence broken only by the occasional rustle of leaves and the distant sounds of the estate settling into the stillness of the night.

As we made our way to the waiting carriage, Holmes' mind was clearly racing with the myriad possibilities and connections that lay ahead. The journey to London promised to be one of contemplation and planning, a prelude to the intense investigation that lay ahead.

Before entering the carriage, Holmes turned to Adrien one last time. "Stay alert, Mr d'Arcy. The threads of this mystery are complex and intertwined. We must be prepared for whatever may come."

Adrien's nod was firm, his determination evident. "I will, Mr Holmes. We will see this through to the end."

With that, Holmes and I climbed into the carriage, the wheels crunching over the gravel as we set off for London. The stage was set, the players were in place, and the next act of the drama was about to unfold. The road ahead was fraught with danger and uncertainty, but with Sherlock Holmes leading the way, there was a renewed sense of hope that justice would prevail and the truth would be revealed.

As the coach carried us away from Epsom Downs and into the night, the ancient oak under which we stood seemed to whisper secrets and stories far older than any of us - a reminder that the dance of power and intrigue is as old as mankind itself. We were but the latest players on this grand stage, and our actions would determine not only the resolution of a personal tragedy, but potentially the fate of far greater designs.

CHAPTER 7

FOG OF INTRIGUE

With the evening chill, a dense mist settled over London, shrouding the city in an air of mystery with its whispers and shadows. The mist clung to every cobblestone and lamppost, reducing the sturdy architecture to mere silhouettes that loomed like ghosts from a bygone era. Gas lamps, struggling against the opalescent fog, cast dim halos of light that barely penetrated the darkness, creating eerie shadows that danced on the wet cobbles.

Sherlock Holmes and I, Dr John Watson, navigated these dimly lit paths through the heart of London's ancient buildings. Our footsteps were muffled, the usual clatter absorbed by the dense air, lending an unnatural stillness to our journey. It was as if we were moving through a world not our own, but the setting for a play of the most gothic and foreboding nature.

"The mist, Watson," Holmes began, his voice resonating deeply as if in tune with the thick air around us, "acts as both veil and revelation. It obscures the familiar, rendering the world as illegible as a smudged palimpsest, yet it also invites the keen observer to look closer, to see what might otherwise be missed."

I listened intently, the weight of my coat feeling heavier in the chilly damp. Around us the gas lamps cast ghostly shadows that flickered on the cobbles like "spectral beings performing a silent ballet".

"In a way," Holmes continued, his eyes piercing the mist as if to reveal its secrets, "this mist is much like the case before us. It shrouds details in obscurity and makes the truth elusive. Yet, paradoxically, it simplifies the landscape, stripping away the superfluous and leaving only the most essential elements for the discerning eye".

The streets of London, usually vibrant and bustling, were now silent, the fog muffling both sound and spirit. The outlines of buildings loomed like great ships in a grey sea, their features blurred and mysterious. The occasional passerby appeared briefly, emerging from the mist only to be swallowed up again by its opacity.

"As we delve deeper into this investigation," Holmes remarked, his silhouette a dark shape against the lighter grey of the fog, "we must be mindful of what is hidden and what is revealed. Much like navigating this fog, we must move forward with caution, yet be prepared to see what emerges when the fog finally lifts."

His words hung in the air, mingling with the mist as if to become part of the very atmosphere of mystery that enveloped the city. The sheer aptitude of Holmes's metaphor struck me - the mist as a symbol of our current endeavour, a physical echo of the layers of intrigue we were about to unravel.

The path wound through some of the oldest parts of London, where buildings stood huddled together as if in community, their histories layered like the fog itself. Here the modern rubbed shoulders with the ancient, creating a tapestry of time felt rather than seen.

"Consider, Watson," Holmes said, gesturing to the obscured shapes of the surrounding architecture, "how the fog distorts and yet defines. It obscures the distance but clarifies the near; it veils the future but illuminates the present. Our perceptions are challenged, forcing us to look, think and deduce with greater care.

As we approached our destination, the governmental heart of the Empire, the fog seemed to thicken, as if aware of the gravity of the place and the conversation that awaited us. The air itself breathed a sense of solemnity, preparing us for the weighty discussions to come with Mycroft Holmes.

The fog, with its dual nature of concealment and revelation, was indeed a fitting metaphor for the intricate realms of international intrigue we were about to navigate - a reminder that clarity emerges from obscurity and that truth, like the heart of this misty London night, often lies in plain sight.

<hr/>

As we continued our deliberate progress through the dense London fog, the architectural grandeur of the governmental heart of the Empire began to materialise before us. The imposing building, a monolith of power and authority, stood as a testament to the might of the British Empire. Its facade, blurred by the mist, conveyed an unspoken gravity that demanded both respect and discretion from those who approached its hallowed halls.

On reaching the colossal bronze doors, carved with intricate reliefs depicting scenes from British history, we were met by a uniformed guard. His face, stern and impassive beneath the brim of his cap, scrutinised us briefly before giving a curt nod, recognising either our faces or the purpose of our visit. He pushed open the doors, which moved with a quiet, well-oiled precision that seemed at odds with their massive size.

The interior was a stark contrast to the obscured world outside. We entered a realm of clarity and light, where the air was still and held an almost palpable weight of solemnity. The corridor was lined with statues of notable figures from the Empire's past, each cast in cold marble, their gaze eternally fixed forward. The floor, a meticulously polished checkerboard of black and white marble tiles, reflected the soft glow of gas lamps hanging from the high ceiling.

We were led through several corridors, each more imposing than the last, the silence broken only by the echo of our footsteps. It was a silence that spoke of secrets and strategies, of decisions that could change the course of nations. Eventually we reached the door to Mycroft Holmes' office, marked by a simple brass plaque bearing his name and title.

The door opened to reveal an office that was both a workspace and a statement of power. The room was large, the walls lined with shelves containing countless leather-bound volumes and documents. Two walls had floor to ceiling windows, though the heavy curtains were drawn, probably a concession to the confidentiality required by Mycroft's work.

Mycroft's desk, a massive affair of dark polished wood, sat squarely in the centre of the room, piled high with papers and artefacts that suggested the global reach of his responsibilities. Behind the desk stood Mycroft Holmes, a figure of imposing intellect and poise. His suit was impeccably tailored, his posture rigidly upright, reflecting the discipline and control he exercised over himself and the information that flowed through this room.

"Sherlock, Dr Watson," Mycroft greeted us, his voice deep and resonant, with an undertone of warmth reserved for those few he truly respected. His eyes, sharp and demanding, assessed us in a single glance, taking in every detail from our damp coats to the expressions on our faces.

"Please, take a seat," he gestured to the chairs in front of his desk, which, like everything else in the room, were of exquisite craftsmanship but designed for function rather than comfort.

As we sat down, Mycroft resumed his position behind his desk, his fingers crossed as he looked at us both. The room, richly decorated with artefacts and symbols of the Empire, seemed to close in slightly, drawing all attention to the man before us. The air was thick with the scent of polished wood and leather, mixed with a faint trace of tobacco - a scent that underlined the seriousness of the discussions within these walls.

"Thank you for coming on such short notice," Mycroft began, his tone formal but with an urgency that suggested the gravity of the situation. "The matter we are about to discuss affects not only national security, but the delicate balance of international relations."

As he spoke, the light from the desk lamp accentuated the subtle lines of strain on his face, marks of the burdens he carried as one of the guardians of the Empire's secrets. The room, a microcosm of the power he wielded, was about to reveal truths that reached far beyond the fog-shrouded streets of London, into the dark and intricate web of global diplomacy and intrigue.

In the opulent confines of Mycroft Holmes' office, the air seemed weighted with the gravity of empire and global intrigue. The room, with its heavy curtains and shelves of state secrets, underlined the seriousness of the matter at hand.

"Sherlock, Dr Watson," Mycroft began, his voice carrying the controlled calm of a seasoned diplomat, yet with an unmistakable undercurrent of urgency. "The murder of Lord Wentworth, while a tragedy in its own right, is only the veneer over a much deeper and potentially more catastrophic situation. We seem to be on the precipice of international turmoil."

Sherlock, leaning forward, his eyes never leaving Mycroft's, nodded slightly to encourage him to continue. I found myself leaning forward as well, the gravity of Mycroft's tone drawing us physically and mentally closer to the web of geopolitical intrigue he was about to unravel.

"The incident at Epsom Downs, marked by the use of an Arabic dagger, is no ordinary crime. It has, whether by calculated design or unfortunate accident, drawn us into a complex web of diplomacy and espionage spanning continents." Mycroft's expression grew solemn, conveying the weight of the geopolitical stakes.

He gestured to a large, detailed map of the world mounted on the wall beside his desk. The expanse of the Ottoman Empire was marked in bold, sprawling script, its reach and strategic importance painfully evident.

"The murder of Lord Wentworth, committed with a weapon steeped in Arab history, sends a precarious signal - one that could be misconstrued as an act of aggression or contempt on our part towards the Arabian Peninsula. Such a misinterpretation, if left unchecked, could ignite a firestorm of diplomatic backlash, destabilising our precarious balance with the Ottomans and, by extension, the entire region".

Sherlock, his mind no doubt piecing together the layers of implications, finally spoke, "The use of the Arabian dagger, then, may not be coincidental, but a calculated element to provoke misunderstanding, or worse, deliberate sabotage."

"Exactly," Mycroft agreed, his eyes narrowing slightly. "Which is why your investigation must tread a path as sharp as the edge of this dagger. We must solve this murder and uncover the true motives behind it, while maintaining the utmost discretion to prevent this from escalating into a full-blown international crisis."

The room, filled with artefacts of empire and the scent of old leather and polished wood, seemed to echo Mycroft's words. Every syllable was a reminder of the burdens borne by those who work in the shadows of power. The stakes were far higher than solving a simple murder; we were now navigating the treacherous waters of international diplomacy, where a single misstep could have catastrophic consequences.

***

Mycroft Holmes leaned back in his chair, the soft creak of the leather punctuating the hushed silence of his meticulously appointed office. The room itself, a testament to his global influence, was lined with books and artefacts of profound geopolitical significance - a fitting setting for the weighty discussion about to unfold. Mycroft's posture, a mixture of contemplation and determination, hinted at the depth of the revelations to come.

"Gentlemen," Mycroft began, his voice measured and resonant, "to fully appreciate the precariousness of our current situation, one must understand the strategic importance of the Arab region within the global political theatre." His hand gestured to the large map of the Middle East and surrounding areas, meticulously pinned to the wall behind him, each country outlined in colours to indicate its political affiliation and current status.

"As you both undoubtedly know, the Ottoman Empire, though waning in power, remains a keystone in the arch of geopolitical stability within the region. Its control of crucial straits such as the Dardanelles and the Bosporus gives it unrivalled strategic importance as the gatekeeper between the Black Sea and the Mediterranean." Mycroft's finger traced the routes on the map, illustrating the vital sea lanes that were lifelines for trade and military movements.

He paused to make sure Sherlock and I were following the thread of his presentation. "This geographical leverage makes the Ottoman Empire, and by extension the Arabian Peninsula, a bedrock upon which much of the European balance of power rests. Our interests, as well as those of other great powers, are deeply rooted in ensuring the stability - and predictability - of this region."

Mycroft's gaze then shifted from the map back to us, his expression sombre. "The murder of Lord Wentworth, carried out with a weapon clearly of Arab origin, introduces a potentially catastrophic variable into this already volatile equation. Should factions within the Ottoman Empire, or indeed rival powers, perceive this as a sanctioned British act of aggression or disrespect, the backlash could be immediate and severe."

Taking a deep breath, he continued: "Imagine, if you will, the domino effect of such a misperception. It could lead to increased militarisation of the Straits, jeopardise our trade routes, and even fuel pro-nationalist movements within the Empire, further destabilising the region. The consequences would reverberate far beyond the borders of the Ottoman Empire, affecting global trade, military alliances and the balance of power in Europe".

Sherlock, who had been listening intently, nodding to the rhythm of Mycroft's narrative, interjected, "So the choice of an Arabic dagger could be seen not just as a personal symbol, but as a wider emblematic message, perhaps intended to provoke such a reaction?"

"Exactly," Mycroft affirmed, tapping his finger on the polished surface of his desk, a gesture that underlined the significance of Sherlock's deduction. "Which is why your investigation must go beyond simply identifying Lord Wentworth's assailant. We must also uncover the wider context of this murder, determine whether outside influences were at play and, if so, their motives."

Leaning forward, Mycroft's eyes locked with ours with an intensity that underlined his next words. "This is not just detective work, gentlemen. This is a delicate dance on the tightrope of diplomacy. Every discovery, every action must be weighed and measured against its potential international repercussions."

The room seemed to close in around us, the walls lined with books bearing silent witness to centuries of similar geopolitical games. The scent of aged paper and the subtle tang of Mycroft's favourite pipe tobacco mingled in the air, creating an atmosphere charged with the weight of history and the urgency of current affairs.

"As you proceed," Mycroft concluded, his voice a low, persuasive cadence, "remember that the stakes are extremely high. This is a game of chess, where the pieces are nations, and the players have the power to dictate peace or plunge regions into conflict. Discretion, as always, will be paramount."

Sherlock and I exchanged a look, a mutual recognition of the gravity of the task before us. The challenge was formidable, weaving through the murky waters of international intrigue, where every piece of evidence could have implications far beyond simply solving a crime. It was a case that would test our acumen, our discretion and perhaps even our understanding of the delicate balance that held the world's powers in check.

❦

The weight of Mycroft's words hung in the air and the room seemed to grow quieter, if that was possible. Just as the gravity of the discussion of the geopolitical stakes settled over us, the door to Mycroft's office opened with a soft, confident creak.

A striking figure entered the room. Dr Amal El-Sharif exuded an effortless grace and an aura of profound intellect. She moved with the poise of a scholar and the subtlety of a seasoned operative. Her eyes, sharp and discerning, scanned the room, taking in every detail with a keen gaze that seemed to absorb the very essence of the room.

"Gentlemen," Mycroft announced, his voice carrying a note of formal introduction, "may I present Dr Amal El-Sharif." He gestured to her with a nod of respect. "Dr El-Sharif is a renowned expert on the history and culture of the Middle East, with an unparalleled understanding of the region's intricate tapestry of traditions, conflicts and alliances. Her knowledge spans centuries, from the ancient civilisations that gave birth to the Arabian Peninsula to the modern geopolitical landscape that shapes its present.

Sherlock and I exchanged a look of recognition. It was clear that we had met Dr El-Sharif before, under different circumstances, and her reputation as a leading authority in her field preceded her.

"Dr El-Sharif," Sherlock greeted her, a hint of warmth running through his typically analytical tone. "It's a pleasure to see you again. Your expertise will no doubt prove invaluable to our investigation."

Dr El-Sharif smiled, her demeanour exuding both confidence and humility. "Mr Holmes, Dr Watson," she acknowledged, her voice rich and melodious, with the faintest hint of an exotic accent. "It is some years since our paths last crossed. I have followed your work with great interest and I am honoured to be able to assist with this investigation."

Mycroft continued, "Dr El-Sharif's expertise extends beyond the realm of science. She is fluent in several Middle Eastern languages and dialects, allowing her to communicate with a level of nuance and understanding that is essential in delicate diplomatic situations. Moreover, her experience in the field, both as a researcher and an operative, has given her an unparalleled ability to decipher cultural cues and navigate the labyrinthine world of Arab politics.

Dr El-Sharif accepted the introduction with a gracious nod, her demeanour exuding a quiet confidence. "Thank you, Mr Holmes," she said. "I believe my knowledge of Arabic history and culture, coupled with my experience in navigating complex diplomatic situations, will prove valuable in solving the mysteries surrounding Lord Wentworth's murder and the missing obsidian statuette."

As she spoke, I couldn't help but be struck by the depth of intelligence in her eyes, a gaze that seemed to penetrate to the very heart of the matter at hand. It was clear that Dr El-Sharif was not merely an academic or an operative, but a formidable intellect in her own right, capable of bringing a unique perspective to our investigation.

Mycroft surveyed the room, his gaze conveying the immense responsibility he was entrusting to each of us. "Given the explosive nature of this investigation, I must remain behind the scenes, pulling the strings from the shadows," he explained. "Dr El-Sharif will be my direct liaison, my eyes and ears on the ground. It is imperative that you keep her informed of every development, no matter how seemingly insignificant. The fate of nations may well depend on the information she relays to me.

Dr El-Sharif took her seat and joined our strategic conclave. The dynamic of our meeting shifted, the room now a crucible of high stakes and sharp intellect. History, diplomacy and investigation were now more intertwined than ever, each of us playing a pivotal role in a narrative that would undoubtedly echo through the annals of the Empire.

Sherlock leaned forward, his eyes meeting Dr El-Sharif's with an intensity that spoke of a shared passion for unravelling complex mysteries. "Your unique combination of academic expertise and practical experience in the field makes you an invaluable addition to our investigation. The historical and cultural context you bring to the table may well prove to be the key to unlocking the mysteries behind Lord Wentworth's murder and the missing obsidian statuette."

Dr El-Sharif met his gaze with equal intellectual engagement, her eyes sparkling with the excitement of the challenge ahead. "Thank you, Mr Holmes," she replied. "I, too, have long admired your work, and the opportunity to work with you on a case of such historical and diplomatic significance is truly exciting."

As the conversation continued, the air in Mycroft's office seemed to crackle with the energy of intellectual engagement and shared purpose. With Dr Amal El-Sharif's unique blend of expertise and experience added to the formidable talents of Sherlock Holmes and Dr John Watson, the investigative team was now better equipped than ever to tackle the complex web of history, politics and crime that lay ahead.

⊶⊷⊹⊱⊰

The atmosphere in Mycroft's office became even more charged as the conversation shifted focus. The room, lined with artefacts and documents of global significance, seemed to vibrate with the weight of the discussion to come. Mycroft, ever the calm observer, gestured for Dr El-Sharif to continue with her insights into the cultural and historical significance of the obsidian artefacts.

Dr El-Sharif, sitting with an air of poised confidence, began to explain, her voice carrying the depth of her scholarly expertise. "The obsidian dagger found at the scene of Lord Wentworth's murder is no ordinary weapon. In Arab culture, obsidian has been revered for centuries, not only for its practical uses, but also for its mystical properties. Obsidian is believed to repel negative energy and protect its wearer. This belief in its protective qualities is ancient, dating back to early Arab civilisations.

Holmes leaned forward, his eyes sharp with curiosity. "You mentioned earlier the symbolic importance of the stallion motif in Arab culture. Could this combination of obsidian and stallion point to a deeper, perhaps ritualistic significance?"

Dr El-Sharif nodded, her gaze steady. "Indeed, Mr Holmes. The stallion, in Arabic tradition, symbolises nobility, strength and freedom. It is not uncommon for such symbols to be intertwined with materials believed to have protective powers. The fact that the statuette is carved from obsidian suggests that it was intended to be more than just an ornamental piece - it was probably seen as a talisman, imbued with both cultural significance and protective symbolism".

Watson, ever the keen observer, interjected, "So the theft of the statuette and the use of an obsidian dagger could suggest that the perpetrator is not just a common criminal, but someone deeply steeped in these cultural beliefs. Someone who understands and perhaps worships the symbolism".

"Exactly," Dr El-Sharif confirmed. "This suggests that the murder and the theft were not impulsive acts but calculated ones, probably driven by a deeper motive. The choice of weapon and the stolen artefact indicate a perpetrator with considerable knowledge of Arab cultural and historical contexts. This knowledge may lead us to identify the suspect and understand his motives.

Holmes' eyes sparkled with the thrill of a complex puzzle. "We must consider all possibilities," he mused. "Could this crime be an attempt to send a message, to upset the delicate balance of power by using these cultural symbols? Or is it a personal vendetta masked by layers of historical and cultural significance?"

Mycroft, listening intently, added: "Given the geopolitical tensions and strategic importance of the Arabian Peninsula, it is also possible that this act is part of a larger plan. An attempt to destabilise relations or provoke a response. Every angle needs to be explored".

Dr El-Sharif continued, "We must also consider the historical context of the obsidian artefacts. As I said, obsidian has been used for centuries in rituals and as a protective material. The stallion statuette, given its symbolism, could have been a gift of great significance, perhaps even a diplomatic gesture. Its theft could therefore be seen as an act of profound disrespect or a strategic move to weaken the morale of the Wentworth lineage".

Holmes, always quick to integrate new information, leaned back in his chair, his mind visibly piecing together the threads of this intricate tapestry. "This investigation," he said, "requires us to look beyond the immediate evidence. We must delve into the cultural and historical contexts, understand the symbolism and decipher the true intent behind these acts."

The room fell into a contemplative silence as each of us processed the layers of complexity that Dr El-Sharif's insights had revealed. The case had been transformed from a straightforward murder and theft into a multi-faceted investigation where history, culture and international diplomacy intertwined in a delicate balance.

As the discussion continued, it became clear that Dr El-Sharif's expertise would be indispensable in navigating the treacherous waters ahead. Her deep understanding of Arab culture and history provided a crucial lens through which to view the crime, offering avenues that Sherlock and I might not have considered.

With a renewed sense of purpose, we prepared for the next steps in our investigation, armed with the knowledge that this case was far more than it appeared on the surface. It was a journey into the depths of history and human motivation, where every clue held the potential to unravel a mystery that spanned continents and centuries.

Holmes, his gaze fixed on Dr El-Sharif, concluded, "Your insights are invaluable, Dr El-Sharif. Together we will navigate this intricate web and uncover the truth. The stakes are indeed high, but with your guidance we are well equipped to meet the challenges ahead.

With that, the stage was set for the next chapter of our investigation, where history, culture and crime intersected in a story that promised to test our intellect and resolve to the limit.

⊕⊱✶⊰⊕

The atmosphere in Mycroft's office grew more intense as he leaned forward, his eyes boring into ours with a mixture of gravity and determination. The room, already thick with the scent of polished wood and old leather, seemed to pulse with the weight of the geopolitical stakes being discussed.

"My dear brother, Dr Watson, Dr El-Sharif," Mycroft began, his voice measured and resonant, "we are not merely investigating a murder and a theft. We are navigating a geopolitical chessboard where nations are the pieces and the stakes are incalculably high."

He gestured to the detailed map on the wall, his finger tracing the fine lines that demarcated countries and empires. "The Arabian Peninsula, as we know, is a region of immense strategic importance. Its stability - or lack of it - has far-reaching implications for the balance of power in Europe and beyond. The murder of Lord Wentworth and the theft of the obsidian statuette, if misinterpreted, could set off a series of events that destabilise that delicate balance."

Sherlock, his face a mask of concentration, nodded. "Every move we make must be precise, calculated. A single misstep could lead to diplomatic fallout or worse."

Dr El-Sharif, her eyes reflecting the gravity of Mycroft's words, added: "The cultural and historical significance of the artefacts involved adds another layer of complexity. We must not only solve the crime, but also ensure that our actions do not exacerbate existing tensions."

Mycroft's gaze hardened, his voice taking on a note of urgency. "Discretion is paramount. The implications of our findings could reverberate through the highest echelons of power. We must tread carefully, like pieces on a chessboard, always anticipating the next move."

Watson, ever the steady presence, voiced the team's collective resolve. "We understand, Mycroft. We will proceed with the utmost caution and precision."

The room fell silent, the weight of the task before us falling like a shroud. Each of us understood that this investigation was more than a quest for justice - it was a mission to preserve the fragile balance of international relations.

Mycroft's eyes softened slightly, a hint of gratitude in his voice. "I have no doubt of your abilities. Together we will navigate these treacherous waters and uncover the truth."

With a final nod of agreement, the team solidified their approach, fully aware of the high stakes involved and the delicate balance that must be maintained.

As the gravity of the situation settled over us, Mycroft rose from his chair and moved with deliberate precision to a nearby cupboard. He removed a small, intricately carved wooden box and handed it to Dr El-Sharif.

"Dr El-Sharif," Mycroft said, his tone solemn, "this box contains copies of communications and treaties relating to our recent interactions with the Ottoman Empire. They may provide context or clues to the more subtle motives behind the murder."

Dr El-Sharif accepted the box with a nod, her fingers brushing over the carvings with a reverence that spoke of her deep respect for historical artefacts. "Thank you, Mr Holmes. This will be useful indeed."

Sherlock, always eager to get on with things, leaned forward. "Our immediate next step must be to visit Lady Wentworth. It is imperative that we understand more about the origins of the obsidian statuette and its significance."

Mycroft nodded, his eyes reflecting a mixture of concern and confidence. "Lady Wentworth may hold the key to understanding the wider context of these events. Her insights may prove invaluable."

Watson, always the voice of calm pragmatism, added: "We must also be prepared for any resistance or reluctance on her part. The shock of her husband's murder and the theft may make her reluctant to share certain details".

Dr El-Sharif, her voice calm and measured, reassured us. "I will ensure that our approach is both respectful and thorough. Lady Wentworth's cooperation is crucial and we must handle this with the utmost sensitivity."

Sherlock, his eyes sharp with determination, concluded, "This investigation requires a delicate balance - a harmony of caution and a relentless pursuit of the truth. We will tread carefully, but we will uncover the secrets that lie hidden."

With the plans in place, we prepared to leave Mycroft's office. The weight of the task before us was clear, but so was our determination. As we stepped out into the misty streets of London, the chill in the air seemed to fade, replaced by a newfound sense of purpose and the warmth of our alliance.

The game, as Sherlock would say, was on. And with our combined expertise and determination, we were ready to face whatever challenges lay ahead.

As we made our way back to Baker Street, the streets of London whispered secrets, every shadow and flicker of light a reminder of the hidden depths we were about to explore. The mist seemed to thicken with each step, reflecting the growing complexity of our investigation and the secrets yet to be uncovered. Arriving at 221B, Sherlock and I settled into the familiar confines of our quarters. The room, with its eclectic mix of Victorian furnishings and Sherlock's scientific paraphernalia, felt like a sanctuary from the chaos of the world outside.

Sherlock, lost in thought, paced slowly by the fireplace, the flames casting a warm glow that danced across his contemplative expression. "Watson," he began, his tone thoughtful, "this case is turning into a maze more complex than we first realised. The interplay of history, culture and international politics is formidable. Every piece of evidence, every testimony we gather must be weighed with precision."

I watched him, noting the intensity of his gaze as it flickered in the firelight. "Indeed, Sherlock," I replied, feeling the weight of our responsibility. "The stakes are unusually high, and the paths we tread are fraught with potential repercussions far beyond the immediate crime."

Sherlock nodded, stopping at his desk to scribble some notes in his ever-present chaotic ledger. "Exactly, Watson. And yet it is in such complexity that the truth often lies. It is our task to unravel it, to shed light on the shadows that cloud the reality of this case. Dr El-Sharif's expertise will be invaluable, not only in matters of cultural significance, but in navigating the delicate nuances of international intrigue.

I poured each of us a glass of brandy, the rich amber liquid glowing in the dim light. Handing one to Sherlock, I ventured, "It seems we are not only detectives in this case, but also diplomats of sorts."

Sherlock chuckled softly and took the glass. "Indeed, my dear Watson. Diplomacy in our case, however, must be handled with the precision of a scalpel. Tomorrow's visit to Lady Wentworth will be telling. We must watch not only what is said, but perhaps more importantly, what is left unsaid."

As we settled into our armchairs, the crackle of the fire a pleasant accompaniment to our contemplative silence, I reflected on the journey ahead. The interweaving of past and present, of cultural heritage and geopolitical manoeuvring, promised a case as complex as it was perilous. But with Sherlock Holmes at my side, and now Dr Amal El-Sharif, I felt a cautious optimism.

"Tomorrow then," Sherlock said, raising his glass slightly, his eyes meeting mine with a spark of unwavering determination. "To uncovering truths, however veiled they may be."

"To truths," I echoed, clinking my glass against his. In the quiet of Baker Street, as the world outside hovered unwittingly on the brink of a potentially seismic shift, we braced ourselves for the revelations to come. Our journey into the heart of this mystery, woven with threads of history and tinged with the shadows of espionage, was just beginning.

CHAPTER 8

ECHOES OF WENTWORTH MANOR

D awn was breaking over the English countryside, painting the sky in shades of pale pink and soft gold. Our carriage rumbled quietly along the narrow, winding road to Wentworth Manor. The events of the previous day were weighing heavily on our minds - the brutal murder, the missing obsidian statuette and the desperate plea of Adrien d'Arcy. Sherlock Holmes, Dr Amal El-Sharif and I sat wrapped in our own thoughts, each pondering the complexities of the case that lay ahead.

The cool morning air whispered through the slightly cracked windows. It carried the fresh, earthy scent of dew-soaked grass and the subtle scent of awakening wildflowers.

The landscape unfolded like a verdant tapestry as we drove, rolling hills dotted with clusters of ancient oak trees and fields adorned with the first blush of spring green. Sheep grazed lazily, their coats dewy and glistening in the first light, and further away a lone heron flew gracefully over a small, mirror-like lake, its surface undisturbed except for the occasional ripple of a rising fish.

Dr El-Sharif, ever observant, leaned slightly towards the window, her eyes reflecting the serene beauty of the scene. "It's remarkable, isn't it?" she remarked, her voice filled with reverence for the landscape. "How dawn can make familiar sights seem almost magical."

"Indeed," Sherlock replied, his eyes still on his notes. "But magic often conceals darker truths, as we saw with the Wentworths."

I nodded and added, "The legacy of the Wentworth family is as complex and layered as this landscape. Any piece of history here could hold a clue to solving the mystery that lies before us."

Sherlock, who had been reviewing his notes, looked up and nodded in agreement. "Indeed, Amal. It is in these quiet moments of beauty that the mind finds clarity," he said, then returned his gaze to the papers in his lap, the cogs of his mind visibly turning as he prepared for the day ahead.

Wentworth Manor materialised through the morning mist, rising like a great ship out of the mist. This majestic estate, meticulously preserved by Lord Charles Wentworth, stood as a testament to his dedication and love of history. His efforts to maintain the grandeur of the estate were matched only by his passion for equestrian pursuits and his deep bond with Adrien, his loyal craftsman and friend.

The manor, an example of Gothic Revival architecture, stood majestically. Its towers and turrets stood out sharply against the bright sky. The ancient stones, bathed in the ethereal glow of dawn, whispered of centuries past. They spoke of a time when the manor stood as a beacon of the Wentworth family's prestige and influence.

The coach rolled to a stop at the grand entrance to the manor. The gravel crunched under the wheels, breaking the morning silence. We got out. The imposing beauty of the place overwhelmed me. The front of Wentworth Manor was a marvel of architectural design. Elaborate stone carvings of mythical creatures and creeping vines adorned it. They spoke of a deep appreciation of nature and the fantastic.

The air was cooler here. The scent of ancient stone mingled with that of the roses that climbed the walls of the mansion. Their blossoms were still closed against the morning chill. As we waited for the doors to open, I noticed a carefully carved shrub. It was in the shape of a horse, positioned near the path to the main door. A botanical tribute to the equestrian passions of the Wentworth lineage.

Sherlock, taking in the surroundings with a critical eye, remarked, "Every detail of this estate speaks of history, Watson. It's not just a home, it's a repository of the family's legacy that has stood the test of time."

Dr El-Sharif nodded and added, "And it's within these walls that we may find the clues to not just a murder, but the preservation or demise of a legacy that has stood the test of time."

As the heavy oak doors of the mansion finally swung open, we were not greeted by a servant but by the cool, dim light of the entrance hall, inviting us into the depths of Wentworth Manor where the echoes of the past waited to tell their tales. Thus began our venture into a day that promised revelations and, with any luck, resolutions to the shadowy intrigues that surrounded the Wentworth family.

We stepped out of the confines of the carriage. The crisp morning air enveloped us. It was laden with the earthy scent of dew-soaked grass and the subtle fragrance of blossoming flowers. Wentworth Manor, in all its Gothic splendour, cast a long and stately shadow over the grounds. These spread out around it like a verdant sea. Meticulously curated gardens punctuated the landscape and spoke of generations of careful stewardship and a deep appreciation of the natural world.

Dr Amal El-Sharif stepped onto the gravel path first. Her eyes were wide with the appreciative gaze of a scholar attuned to cultural nuance. She paused. She took a moment to breathe in the scenery - a tableau vivant of floral abundance and horticultural artistry.

"The gardens are a testament to the Wentworth's allegiance not only to heritage but to beauty," she remarked thoughtfully, her eyes sweeping over the dew-kissed roses that lined the path. Each blossom seemed to catch the first rays of light, transforming ordinary colours into extraordinary hues. The roses ranged from the deepest maroon, through a cascade of pink, to the palest blush, each bouquet arranged to complement and enhance the next.

Sherlock Holmes, ever observant, nodded in agreement, his keen eyes catching the subtle variations in the flora that suggested both wild growth and careful cultivation. "Indeed, Amal," he replied, his voice deep and thoughtful. "Each plant, each sculpture has been chosen with precision, much like the words of a well-crafted poem, to evoke emotion and provoke thought."

As we continued along the path, our attention was drawn to a remarkable topiary - a horse carved from a living shrub, its form so lifelike and dynamic you could almost expect it to break into a gallop. The topiary was not just a display of virtuoso garden craftsmanship, but a symbol that resonated with the Wentworths' renowned passion for equestrian pursuits.

"The choice of a horse," I mused aloud, "is no mere whim. It's a celebration of the Wentworth's equestrian lineage, isn't it?" My question, rhetorical as it was, hung in the cool air, mingled with the morning mist.

Sherlock, walking beside me, looked at the topiary with a discerning eye. "Yes, Watson, and it is also a statement. Such artistry serves as a reminder of the family's enduring legacy and their continuing influence in the realms of nature and culture. It is a statement of identity crafted from the living essence of the earth."

Further along, the path wound past a series of sculptures that seemed to chart the historical and artistic journey of the Wentworth family. One sculpture, a marble maiden draped in Grecian robes, stood beside a small fountain, her expression one of serene contemplation. The sound of water trickling from the fountain provided a soothing soundtrack to our explorations, blending harmoniously with the soft rustle of leaves stirred by a gentle breeze.

Dr El-Sharif stopped to admire the statue. She touched on the symbolism. "In it we see the Wentworth's appreciation of classical beauty. The ideals of balance and harmony are also expressed in their stewardship of the land and their patronage of the arts."

Sherlock nodded, his eyes reflecting a spark of inspiration. "Every element here is interconnected, every piece a testament not only to the family's tastes but to their philosophies and their very souls. This estate is not just a home, but a canvas, a carefully composed masterpiece that reveals its truths only to those who know how to look."

As we approached the grand entrance to the mansion, the full majesty of the estate came into view. The building itself, with its towering columns and sweeping arches, its stone facade softened by climbing ivy and flowering vines, stood as a proud monument to the architectural and aesthetic ideals of a bygone era, yet vibrant with the spirit of those who still call it home.

When we walked up the stone steps of Wentworth Manor, we were entering not just a house, but a legacy, each stone and flower a silent testament to the centuries of life, art and passion that have flourished within and around its walls. The manor, with its storied past and botanical splendour, was waiting to unveil its secrets, as intricate and varied as the patterns of frost on the windows of history.

❧◦❦◦❧

As our footsteps echoed softly on the cobbled path leading from the lush gardens of Wentworth Manor, the silhouette of the stables began to materialise through a delicate morning mist – a structure of such venerable brick and fine wood that it seemed to whisper tales of ages past. The stables, with their deep burgundy brickwork partly covered in ivy, stood like sentinels guarding the precious equine heritage of the Wentworth family. The heavy wooden doors, arched and reinforced with iron hinges, bore the patina of centuries, suggesting a history as rich and storied as the manor itself.

As we entered the stables, the rich scent of hay and leather enveloped us, a warm, earthy aroma that spoke of the generations of prized horses that had been housed within these walls. The interior was a harmonious blend of functionality and aesthetic grace, with rows of polished wooden stalls on either side, each with brass nameplates and fittings that gleamed in the soft light filtering through the tall windows.

At the far end of the stable, tending to a particularly majestic stallion, was Adrien d'Arcy. His rugged appearance contrasted with the smooth, practiced movements with which he tended the horse. There was an elegance to Adrien's movements that reflected his deep intimacy and reverence for the creatures he cared for. This was Adrien d'Arcy, the craftsman responsible for tacking the estate's horses, a man whose life's work was as much a part of the Wentworth legacy as the portraits hanging in the manor's Great Hall.

Sherlock, Dr El-Sharif and I approached quietly, not wanting to frighten the magnificent animal under Adrien's care. The stallion, Isinglass, was a striking sight - a creature of powerful build and noble bearing, with a coat that shimmered like burnished copper in the rays of sunlight. His mane flowed like a cascade of dark silk, and his eyes, intelligent and alert, watched us with quiet curiosity.

As we approached, I stepped forward with compassion in my voice. "Adrien," I began quietly, "how are you holding up? How is Lady Wentworth coping with all this?"

Adrien sat up and wiped his hands on a cloth before greeting me. "Good morning, sirs, madam," he said, his voice rich with the accent of the region, though his tone was heavy with sorrow. "We are... holding. Lady Wentworth is strong, but this has been a terrible blow."

Sherlock, his sharp eyes instantly recognising the horse, made a direct comment. "Isinglass," he said, implicitly introducing the horse to Dr El-Sharif. "He was exceptional in the Derby."

Dr El-Sharif, always eager to embrace new knowledge, stepped forward with an appreciative smile. "He is magnificent, Mr d'Arcy. I must say, the care and passion you put into these animals is evident in every detail here."

Sherlock formally introduced Dr El-Sharif. "Adrien, this is Dr Amal El-Sharif, an expert in Arabic culture who will be assisting us on this case."

Adrien's face softened with pride and a momentary distraction from his grief. "It is a pleasure to meet you, Dr El-Sharif. My interest in Arabian horses and leatherwork runs deep. Isinglass here shows clear signs of the Arabian bloodlines used in his breeding."

Amal nodded, her eyes reflecting admiration. "Yes, I can see that. The elegance and strength are unmistakable. His pedigree must be remarkable."

For a moment, Adrien seemed to forget his grief. "Indeed, Dr El-Sharif. Isinglass carries the bloodline of legends. The Byerley Turk, the Darley Arabian and the Godolphin Arabian. His veins flow with the heritage of the founding stallions, making him a model of Thoroughbred excellence."

Sherlock listened with a certain detachment, his focus on the case. He found the enthusiasm for the horse somewhat annoying. Just then, Isinglass, sensing the detective's presence, approached Sherlock and nudged him gently with his warm nostrils. Surprised, Sherlock looked into the horse's large, soulful eyes.

What happened next was beyond the scope of his usual observations. Sherlock felt a deep, almost raw connection - pure, wordless communication. In Isinglass's eyes he saw deep grief, fear, determination and an unmistakable plea: "Find the murderer of my friend, Lord Wentworth. There is more at stake than you can see. You must help us."

The intensity of the moment left Sherlock momentarily stunned. He realised that this horse knew more about the case than he had previously deduced. It was a rare and humbling moment for the great detective.

Watson noticed the interaction and asked, "Holmes, are you all right? You seem quite taken with Isinglass."

Sherlock, regaining his composure and masking his vulnerability with wit, replied, "Just admiring the horse's... unique perspective, Watson."

As we prepared to leave the stables, Sherlock's mind was a whirl of thoughts. That raw, silent communion with Isinglass had shaken him more than he cared to admit. The horse's plea had been clear and urgent, a reminder that there were layers to this mystery that his intellect alone could not unravel. For once, Holmes found himself contemplating the possibility that some connections transcended logic and reason, reaching into the very essence of life and loyalty. As he left the stables, he decided to honour Isinglass's request and delve deeper into the heart of this intricate and emotional case.

<hr />

As we left the cool, shadowy interior of the stables, Adrien joined us, his presence a silent testament to the gravity of the situation. Our footsteps echoed on the ancient cobbles leading us back to the main building of Wentworth Manor. The morning sun, now higher in the sky, cast a golden glow over the ivy-clad facade, transforming the stony visage into a warm, welcoming sight. The heavy oak doors of the manor stood open, as if inviting us into another chapter of its long and storied history.

Crossing the threshold, we were greeted by the sight of Lady Elizabeth Wentworth. She stood at the foot of a grand staircase, her figure silhouetted against the light streaming through the stained glass windows above. Her presence was both commanding and serene, but her eyes betrayed the depth of her grief.

"Lady Wentworth, please accept our deepest condolences on your tragic loss," I began, stepping forward in a gentle tone. "How are you holding up, and how is the rest of the household faring at this difficult time?"

Lady Elizabeth offered a small, gracious smile, though it did little to hide her grief. "Thank you, Dr Watson. We are managing as best we can. The support of friends and family is a great comfort."

Sherlock stepped forward, his tone respectful and sincere. "Lady Wentworth, your home is a testament to the rich heritage of the Wentworth family. We appreciate you taking the time to meet with us at such a difficult time."

"Your home is indeed magnificent, Lady Wentworth," Dr El-Sharif added, her voice filled with genuine admiration. "The art and history within these walls speak volumes of your family's contributions to art and culture."

Lady Elizabeth nodded, her expression a mixture of pride and melancholy. "Thank you, Dr El-Sharif. Charles had a passion for art and history. He believed in preserving and celebrating our heritage."

Adrien, who had been standing quietly by, looked up and addressed Lady Wentworth. "Milady, it is an honour to be here and to continue to serve the Wentworth legacy. Isinglass and I do our best to uphold the standards set by Lord Wentworth."

Lady Wentworth's eyes softened as she looked at Adrien. "Thank you, Adrien. Your loyalty and dedication means a great deal to all of us."

As we followed Lady Wentworth through the grand hall, our surroundings spoke volumes of the manor's rich history. Portraits of ancestral Wentworths lined the walls, each frame encasing a piece of the past, their expressions captured in oil-painted eternity. The air was a mixture of old wood and lavender, probably from the fresh bouquets that adorned the hall tables.

We paused before a striking portrait of a gentleman on horseback, his auburn hair mirroring Lady Elizabeth's own. "This is Sir Alfred Wentworth, a patron of the arts and a keen rider. Under his guidance in the late 1700s, Wentworth Manor became a cultural beacon in the region."

There was a note of pride in her voice as she spoke of her ancestors, but there was also a wistful quality, as if each word evoked the weight of responsibility to uphold the greatness and goodwill of her lineage. "Sir Alfred was also instrumental in founding several charities in the area, many of which continue to this day," she continued, leading us deeper into the manor.

The house itself was a maze of history, each room a doorway to another era. We passed through the library, where shelves rose up the walls, crammed with leather-bound tomes, their spines gleaming with gold lettering. Beyond, the drawing room opened up, its antique furnishings telling of countless gatherings where discussions of art, politics and philosophy once filled the air.

Lady Elizabeth then led us into a smaller, more intimate study. "This room," she explained, "serves as a private retreat from the demands of estate management and social obligations. It is here that I often contemplate the future of Wentworth Manor, especially in these trying times following my husband's untimely demise."

Sherlock nodded slowly with his usual perceptiveness. "Your devotion to this legacy is truly admirable, Lady Wentworth. It is evident that you honour both the past and the future of your family's legacy."

Lady Elizabeth met his gaze, her eyes reflecting a mixture of determination and melancholy. "Thank you, Mr Holmes. It is not an easy task, especially in the present circumstances. But I am determined to ensure that Wentworth Manor remains a beacon of heritage and culture, true to the vision of my ancestors."

As the tour drew to a close, it was clear that Lady Elizabeth Wentworth was not merely the guardian of a grand estate, but a custodian of history, charged with bridging the gap between a storied past and an uncertain future. Her grace and strength, so eloquently displayed against the backdrop of her ancestral home, left us in no doubt that the mysteries surrounding Wentworth Manor were inextricably linked to the legacy she so passionately sought to preserve.

As Lady Elizabeth Wentworth led us through the vast corridors of Wentworth Manor, the weight of centuries seemed to resonate with every step on the aged oak floor, polished to a soft sheen by the passage of countless soles. The air within these walls, subtly infused with the scent of beeswax and the faint, lingering aroma of sandalwood, spoke of well-preserved antiquity and meticulous care.

Our first stop was the Great Hall, a vast chamber with soaring ceilings supported by ornate columns that rose like the trunks of giant stone trees. Sunlight streamed through the great mullioned windows, casting kaleidoscopic patterns on the floor through the stained glass, each a vivid vignette depicting scenes from the manor's storied past. Lady Elizabeth paused at one such window, pointing to the intricate depiction of a medieval hunt.

"This glass," she began, her voice echoing slightly in the vast room, "dates from the early sixteenth century. It is said to have been commissioned by Gregory Wentworth, the fifth Earl, who was known for his passion for falconry and hunting. Each scene tells a part of the story of our family's deep connection with these lands and the natural bounty they offer".

Next we entered a room that took my breath away - the manor's library. It was a bibliophile's sanctuary, the walls lined from floor to ceiling with leather-bound books, their spines gilt and painted in rich shades of burgundy, navy and forest green. Ladders on rails gave access to the higher shelves, where rare first editions were kept safely out of reach. The air was filled with the musty, comforting smell of old paper and leather, a scent that spoke of wisdom preserved through the ages.

"It was in this very room," Lady Elizabeth said as she gently ran her fingers over the spines of several volumes, "that my great-grandfather, the twelfth Earl, spent his evenings poring over texts of ancient law and philosophy. It is said that he corresponded with some of the most prominent thinkers of his time, and many of their replies are contained in these collections".

As we continued, the atmosphere changed as we entered the Art Gallery, a long hall lit by skylights that revealed an impressive array of paintings and sculptures. The walls were adorned with portraits of Wentworth ancestors, each in gilded frames and each telling a silent story of the era over which they presided. Interspersed with these portraits were landscapes and still lifes, masterful depictions of the verdant countryside surrounding the manor and sumptuous arrangements of fruit and flowers.

Lady Elizabeth paused before a particularly striking portrait of a lady, her expression serene yet enigmatic, dressed in the splendour of the Restoration. "This," she said, "is Lady Marianne Wentworth, noted in our family history for her patronage of the arts and her formidable intellect. She established the first Wentworth art collection, and many of the pieces you see here were commissioned by her".

Each piece in the gallery, Lady Elizabeth explained, was not merely decorative, but had significance either in the historical context of the period in which it was created or in its connection to the family. For example, a small landscape painting by a lesser-known contemporary of Turner's depicted the very lake we could see from the east windows of the house, a favourite picnic spot for generations of Wentworth children.

Our final stop was the conservatory, a crystal palace of glass and iron, home to an astonishing variety of plants from all over the world. The air inside was warm and humid, filled with the rich, earthy scent of clay and the sweet perfume of blooming flowers. Orchids of every imaginable colour clung to bark and stone, and ferns unfurled their fronds beside trickling stone fountains.

"Here," Lady Elizabeth gestured widely, "is where the Wentworths have always felt the lure of the exotic and the beauty of nature most keenly. Every plant here has been carefully selected to thrive in the meticulously maintained conditions, a living testament to the family's commitment to both beauty and scientific curiosity."

As we finished our tour and stepped back into the cooler air of the main hall, it was clear that Wentworth Manor was more than a home. It was a repository of history, a gallery of art, a library of wisdom and a conservatory of natural wonders, each room a chapter in the great story of the Wentworth family. Lady Elizabeth, as the present custodian of this legacy, carried her responsibilities with a grace and dignity as much a part of the estate's heritage as the stone and timber of which it was built.

⚜

The conservatory at Wentworth Manor was a veritable Eden of exotic plants and vibrant flowers. The air was thick with the mingled scents of orchids, ferns and roses, creating a tranquil yet poignant atmosphere. Soft light filtered through the glass panes, casting prismatic reflections on the lush foliage around us.

Lady Elizabeth Wentworth led us to a small seating area amidst the greenery. Sherlock, Adrien, Dr El-Sharif and I settled into the wicker chairs, the setting almost too peaceful for the gravity of our discussion. The delicate balance of beauty and sorrow seemed to reflect Lady Elizabeth's own condition, her grief palpable yet held in check by a stoic dignity.

Sherlock leaned forward, his voice carrying a gentle firmness. "Lady Wentworth, Adrien mentioned that the obsidian stallion statuette was a gift from you to Lord Wentworth when Isinglass was still a foal. Could you tell us more about its origin and significance? It seems that its disappearance may be more than a simple theft - there may be deeper implications tied to its history and symbolism.

Lady Elizabeth sighed softly, her gaze becoming distant as she delved into her memories. "Ah, the statuette," she began, her voice tinged with nostalgia. "It was indeed a treasure like no other, discovered by Sir Reginald Ashcroft, a dear friend and fellow patron of the arts."

She paused, her fingers tracing the intricate carving on the armrest beside her. "It was during one of Charles's expeditions to the Arabian Peninsula - an experience that deepened his appreciation of the region's rich heritage. When I presented the statuette to Charles, it was much more than a gift. It symbolised a guardian spirit, a beacon of good fortune to guide and protect him.

As she spoke, the air around us seemed to thicken with the weight of history and the depth of her personal connection to the statuette. "Charles cherished it deeply, believing it to embody the very ideals he pursued - purity, beauty and the eternal quest for understanding. It was not just an object of art, but a symbol of his deepest beliefs and aspirations."

Sherlock nodded, absorbing her words with a thoughtful frown. "And now, with the statuette missing, it seems that more than just a valuable artefact has been taken from Wentworth Manor. It is as if, with its disappearance, a part of Lord Wentworth's spirit has also been taken."

Dr El-Sharif, who had been listening intently, added: "The symbolism of the statuette, its connection to both Lord Wentworth's personal and philosophical pursuits, suggests that its theft may have deeper implications. It's as if the thief sought not just to possess a valuable object, but to destroy the very legacy that Lord Wentworth sought to preserve."

Lady Elizabeth nodded solemnly, her gaze fixed on a distant point as if imagining the statuette in its rightful place. "Indeed, Dr El-Sharif. The loss of the statuette feels like an ominous portent, as if the shadows that have long lingered on the fringes of our family's legacy are now drawing closer, emboldened by the void its absence has created."

The conversation, layered with history, personal connection and palpable loss, left us thoughtful. The missing obsidian stallion was more than an aesthetic object; it was a key piece in the puzzle of Lord Wentworth's demise and the threats to the Wentworth legacy.

As the conversation lingered on the origins and significance of the missing obsidian stallion statuette, Sherlock Holmes, with his usual penetrating insight, cast a thoughtful glance at Lady Elizabeth Wentworth. The light filtering through the conservatory foliage danced across his sharp features, casting a pensive shadow as he asked his next question.

"Lady Wentworth," Sherlock began, his voice calm but with a palpable curiosity, "you mentioned Sir Reginald Ashcroft in connection with the acquisition of the statuette. May I enquire who he is, and where we might find him?"

Lady Elizabeth seemed to draw strength from the question, her posture straightening slightly. "Sir Reginald is a distinguished figure in London's academic and cultural circles. He is the Director of the Guildhall Museum and has been a close friend of our family for many years. He has an unparalleled knowledge of Middle Eastern artefacts and helped Charles acquire many of the treasures that adorn this house.

Dr El-Sharif's eyes lit up with recognition. "Sir Reginald Ashcroft? I know him well. We have collaborated on several academic papers and symposia on Middle Eastern antiquities. His insights into the region's cultural heritage are profound. Given his connection to the statuette through Lady Wentworth and his professional standing, he could very well offer additional perspectives on the artefact itself - perhaps even clues as to why it might have been targeted by thieves."

Sherlock's eyes narrowed thoughtfully, the gears of his analytical mind visibly turning as he considered this new avenue of investigation. "Most intriguing," he murmured. "It seems a visit to the Guildhall Museum may prove indispensable."

Lady Elizabeth, who had been listening to the exchange with a mixture of anticipation and apprehension, nodded in agreement. "Sir Reginald is a man of impeccable integrity and profound knowledge. If anyone can shed light on the circumstances surrounding the statuette's significance, it is he."

Sensing the urgency and potential breakthrough in our investigation, Dr El-Sharif glanced towards the window where the afternoon light was beginning to fade. "If it pleases the group, we could arrange a visit to the museum at once. I believe Sir Reginald will be there until the evening, supervising the installation of a new exhibit."

Sherlock stood up, his tall frame unfolding with decisive readiness. "Excellent suggestion, Dr El-Sharif. Time, as always, is of the essence. Let us proceed immediately to the Guildhall Museum. With luck and Sir Reginald's cooperation, we may yet unravel this tightly coiled mystery."

With a plan of action in place, we prepared to leave Wentworth Manor. The prospect of meeting Sir Reginald Ashcroft and exploring the corridors of the Guildhall Museum added a new layer of anticipation to our search for answers.

As we emerged from the grand entrance of Wentworth Manor, the late afternoon sun cast a warm golden glow on the ivy-clad walls and towering chimneys, painting a picturesque yet sombre tableau. The meticulously manicured lawns, bordered by neatly clipped hedges, stretched out before us, leading to the waiting carriage. The air was crisp, filled with the faint, sweet scent of blooming roses from the adjacent gardens. The mansion, steeped in history and recent sorrow, seemed to watch over us with a silent, melancholy gaze as we made our way to the gravel path that crunched softly underfoot.

We descended the steps of Wentworth Manor, each of us lost in thought. Holmes walked slightly ahead, his tall, lean figure silhouetted against the backdrop of the mansion. Dr Amal El-Sharif and Adrien d'Arcy flanked him, their expressions reflecting the weight of our recent discoveries. I brought up the rear, my mind preoccupied with the complexities of our investigation.

As we approached the waiting carriage, I noticed Holmes' gaze drifting towards the stables. There, standing with an almost regal stillness, was Isinglass, the magnificent horse whose silent presence seemed to bear witness to the secrets of the manor. For a brief moment, Holmes' piercing eyes locked with the horse's deep, expressive ones. There was an uncanny, unspoken connection, a silent communication that seemed to transcend the usual boundaries of understanding between man and beast.

In that fleeting moment, Holmes felt an inexplicable urge to send a message of reassurance. Without uttering a word, his thoughts reached out to Isinglass: "You can count on me. I will uncover the truth." To his astonishment, the horse's eyes reflected a sense of gratitude, an unspoken acknowledgement that resonated deeply with Holmes. It was as if Isinglass understood the gravity of their mission and trusted Holmes to uncover the truth.

What is this strange connection? Holmes mused, "It was not a calculated gesture, but a subconscious reaction that defied my usual logical precision. Yet it felt inexplicably real, as if this creature and I shared an unspoken bond.

As we continued our walk towards the carriage, I noticed a rare expression of contemplation on Holmes' face. He seemed momentarily lost in thought, reflecting on the unusual connection he had just experienced. It was not a calculated gesture, but a subconscious reaction that defied his usual logical precision. The interaction felt inexplicably real to him, leaving him both puzzled and intrigued by the depth of the moment.

Concerned by Holmes' brief distraction, I inquired, "Are you all right, Holmes? You seemed momentarily lost in thought."

Holmes, masking his confusion with his characteristic wit, replied with a sardonic smile, "Merely contemplating the mysteries of human-animal communication, Watson. It seems that even the most rational of minds can become entangled in the mysterious."

We reached the carriage and, as we settled in, the weight of our mission pressed upon us once more. The carriage doors closed with a final thud, signalling the beginning of the next crucial phase of our investigation. As the wheels of the carriage began to turn, carrying us towards the bustling streets of London and the hallowed halls of the Guildhall Museum, a sense of anticipation and determination filled the air.

Holmes' mind was undoubtedly racing with the myriad possibilities and unanswered questions that lay ahead. The connection with Isinglass, however fleeting, lingered in his mind, adding another layer of mystery to our already complex case. The journey to the Guildhall Museum promised new revelations and challenges, but for now the silent communion with the horse remained an enigmatic prelude to the unfolding drama.

CHAPTER 9

SECRETS OF THE OBSIDIAN GUILD

L ondon's splendour unfolded as the midday sun dispelled the lingering morning mist. The city's venerable buildings, bathed in a golden hue, stood out against the azure sky. Our carriage, carrying Sherlock Holmes, Dr Amal El-Sharif, Adrien d'Arcy and myself, wound its way through the bustling thoroughfares, drawing ever closer to our destination - the Guildhall Museum.

Within the confines of the carriage a lively discourse ensued. Dr Amal El-Sharif, her eyes aglow with anticipation, spoke animatedly of Sir Reginald Ashcroft. "Sir Reginald is a luminary in our field, Sherlock. Although we are not intimately acquainted, I have had the honour of debating him at several academic symposia. His scholarship on Near Eastern artefacts is unparalleled.

Holmes, his gaze fixed on the passing scenery, replied thoughtfully, "It is always beneficial to have an ally of such expertise, especially given the intricacies of our current investigation."

Adrien, who had been quietly absorbing the conversation, leaned forward with a question. "Dr El-Sharif, what can we expect from Sir Reginald? Is he likely to welcome our inquiries, or should we prepare ourselves for a more guarded reception?"

A slight smile played on Dr El-Sharif's lips. "Sir Reginald is a man of deep intellect and boundless curiosity. While he values his privacy, he also understands the importance of collaborative efforts in the pursuit of knowledge. I am confident that he will be receptive to our questions, especially given the urgency of our mission.

As our coach pulled up to the Guildhall Museum, the morning mist had completely cleared, revealing the Gothic Revival façade in all its majestic glory. The museum stood proudly against the early midday sky, its intricate stone carvings and towering spires glistening in the sunlight. Flanked by statues of historical luminaries, the grand entrance beckoned us into a realm where history and knowledge blended seamlessly.

As we stepped out of the carriage, our footsteps echoed along the cobbled path leading to the Grand Entrance. The air was crisp, carrying the fresh scent of dewy grass from the nearby gardens, mingled with the familiar urban aromas of smoke and river mist. The exterior of the museum, with its sturdy Victorian Gothic lines, exuded an aura of timeless reverence.

Holmes, his keen eyes scanning the historic building, seemed to absorb every detail, his mind no doubt cataloguing and connecting threads known only to him. Dr El-Sharif, with her scholarly passion for cultural artefacts, wore an expression of deep enthusiasm, her gaze lingering on the stately presence of the museum. Adrien, more accustomed to the rustic charm of stables than the hallowed halls of museums, seemed suitably impressed by the grandeur surrounding us.

"We are about to cross a threshold that transcends mere geography," Holmes remarked quietly, his voice filled with a reverence befitting the occasion. "The artefacts housed within these walls are not mere relics; they are echoes of the ages, whispers from the past that still resonate with the present."

Dr El-Sharif nodded in agreement, her eyes glowing with scholarly fervour. "Indeed, Sherlock," she replied, her tone reflective. "Places like this are where time converges - where the past meets the present, and where history is not only remembered but kept alive."

Ascending the steps, we entered the museum, greeted by the rich aroma of polished wood and aged parchment. The high ceilings, decorated with frescoes depicting scenes from London's storied past, and the dimly lit corridors lined with display cases of ancient relics, created an atmosphere of awe and timelessness. Each exhibit whispered secrets of bygone eras, inviting us to delve into the rich tapestry of the city's history.

We navigated the museum with a sense of anticipation and purpose, ready to uncover the truths hidden within its venerable walls.

⊷⊶⊷⊶

The museum's imposing oak doors swung open with a solemn creak, revealing a dimly lit foyer. The air inside was redolent with the scent of polished wood and antique paper, an intoxicating bouquet for any lover of history. The cooler temperature and subdued solemnity lent an added grandeur to this venerable repository of knowledge.

Here we were greeted by Sir Reginald Ashcroft, the museum's esteemed director. His figure, framed by the door to his office, was both welcoming and imposing - a man who seemed to carry the weight of history on his shoulders. His face lit up with recognition and warmth when he saw Dr El-Sharif.

"Dr El-Sharif," he exclaimed, extending his hand. "Always a pleasure to see you. Welcome again to the Guildhall Museum."

"Sir Reginald, thank you for seeing us at such short notice," Amal replied, shaking his hand. "Allow me to introduce my esteemed colleagues: Mr Sherlock Holmes, Dr John Watson and Mr Adrien d'Arcy."

As the introductions were made, Sir Reginald's eyes widened slightly in recognition, especially at the mention of Sherlock Holmes. "Mr Holmes," he said, his tone now filled with a mixture of respect and curiosity. "The famous detective of Baker Street. I have read much about your exploits in the newspapers. It is an honour to meet you."

Sherlock bowed his head humbly. "The honour is mine, Sir Reginald. We are most grateful for your time."

With that, we entered this sanctuary of history, led by a man who seemed as much a part of the museum as the artefacts it housed. The morning light continued to spread across London, casting long shadows and illuminating paths, much like our investigation, which sought to uncover truths long shrouded in mystery and darkness.

As we began our journey through the museum's labyrinthine corridors, Adrien's eyes widened with admiration. "This place is incredible," he murmured, his voice filled with awe. "The history, the artefacts - it's like stepping back in time."

Sir Reginald smiled at Adrien's enthusiasm. "Indeed, Mr d'Arcy, every corner of this museum holds a story waiting to be told."

The air pulsed with the essence of bygone eras - a heady mix of aged parchment, worn leather and the pervasive aroma of history. The dark, polished wooden floors creaked softly beneath our feet, whispering echoes of the countless scholars and curators who had walked these halls before us.

⚜

Sir Reginald's office, tucked away in a secluded wing of the museum, was a testament to his esteemed position. Upon entering, I was immediately struck by the profound character of the room. Soaring bookshelves lined the walls, crammed with leather-bound volumes whose spines ranged from deep burgundy to faded gold. Interspersed with these scholarly treasures were artefacts that seemed to span the breadth of human history: Roman coins, Egyptian scarabs, medieval manuscripts and more, each carefully displayed in protective glass cases.

The room itself was dimly lit, with light filtering through the stained glass windows and casting colourful patterns on the Persian rugs that adorned the floor. The air was slightly musty, the smell of decades spent preserving the relics of the past.

Sir Reginald, standing amidst this treasure trove of history, was an artefact himself - a figure from another time, dressed in a tweed suit that seemed as timeless as the objects he curated. His white hair was slicked back from his forehead and his eyes, behind round glasses, flickered with a mixture of warmth and concern as he looked at us.

"Ah, Mr Holmes, Dr Watson, Dr El-Sharif, Mr d'Arcy, please, take a seat," he gestured to a group of leather chairs arranged around a large oak desk cluttered with papers and ancient texts. His voice, rich and sonorous, carried an inflection of both erudition and unease.

As we sat down, Sir Reginald leaned back slightly in his chair, his fingers twisted in thought. "It is not every day that one is visited by such illustrious company," he began, his tone somewhat jovial but underlined by tension. "But I suspect this is no ordinary visit. The matters at hand, I gather, are of a rather serious nature."

"Sir Reginald," Sherlock began, his voice calm and commanding yet respectful, "we come to you driven by a matter of great urgency and delicacy. The obsidian statuette, a piece of considerable historical value and personal significance to Lady Wentworth, has gone missing under the most distressing of circumstances."

Sir Reginald's expression grew solemn, his eyes reflecting a storm of thoughts as he adjusted his spectacles with a slightly trembling hand. "Yes, Mr Holmes, the statuette. A most exquisite and enigmatic artefact; it is indeed deeply disturbing to hear of its disappearance and the tragic events surrounding it."

Leaning back in his chair, surrounded by the high shelves of ancient books and artefacts that seemed to watch over the room like silent sentinels, Sir Reginald clasped his hands together and took a deep breath. "Recently," he continued, his voice taking on a more serious tone, "I was visited by a gentleman with considerable knowledge of Arabic artefacts. His erudition was impressive and his passion for the subject was palpable. However, there was an intensity to his interest that went beyond mere scholarly curiosity".

Adrien leaned forward, his interest piqued. "Did he mention anything specific about the craftsmanship of the statuette, Sir Reginald?"

"He did, Mr d'Arcy," Sir Reginald replied, nodding. "He was particularly fascinated by items made from Arabian obsidian, which, as you may know, is quite rare and of great cultural importance. The gentleman seemed to have an uncanny familiarity with the history and practices of the Obsidian Guild, discussing their techniques and the mystical properties they imbue their creations with a level of detail that was both impressive and somewhat unsettling."

Sherlock nodded slightly, encouraging Sir Reginald to continue. The room seemed to close in on him, listening.

"The gentleman was erudite, his English tinged with an accent that suggested Middle Eastern origins. We had a long discussion about the properties and historical uses of obsidian in Arab culture. He was particularly fascinated by the idea of obsidian artefacts being shaped into animal forms - a detail that now seems eerily relevant to me.

Sherlock's interest grew visibly, his analytical mind parsing every word. "Did this gentleman express why he was drawn to such specific artefacts?" he asked, his tone even but probing.

Sir Reginald paused, his gaze drifting to the window where the light cast long shadows across the floor. "He was speaking of the symbolic significance of these artefacts within certain Arabian legends. According to him, animal figures carved from obsidian were believed to be protective amulets, warding off evil and misfortune. However," Sir Reginald's voice trailed off with a hint of distress, "his fascination seemed to turn to an almost obsessive curiosity. When I informed him that we had none in our collection, his disappointment was palpable, almost... foreboding."

The revelation hung in the air, as thick as the musty tomes that surrounded us. Sherlock's silhouette was rigid, his mind no doubt racing over the implications of this encounter. "And you think, Sir Reginald, that this gentleman's visit might be connected with the theft of the statuette?"

"It is a possibility we cannot afford to ignore," Sir Reginald admitted, his hands unfolding as he leaned forward, a serious frown on his brow. "In retrospect, I realise that my frank discussion of the statuette, albeit in a theoretical sense as it was never part of our collection, may have inadvertently drawn his attention to Lady Wentworth."

"One cannot blame oneself for the actions of others, Sir Reginald," I interjected gently, always the voice of reason and empathy. "Your scholarly sharing of knowledge was done in good faith, not with malice."

Sherlock nodded slowly, his eyes never leaving Sir Reginald's. "Indeed, Watson is right. But now we find ourselves in a web that may well have been woven from such scholarly exchanges. Sir Reginald, can you remember anything else about this gentleman? Any detail could prove vital.

As Sir Reginald pondered, the weight of history seemed to press down on us, the artefacts around us whispering their secrets into the charged silence. This room, a cradle of the past, now held the keys to a mystery that spanned worlds and eras - a mystery that Sherlock Holmes was determined to unravel.

The atmosphere in Sir Reginald Ashcroft's office had grown thick with the gravity of our discussion. The sombre shadows cast by the faint light filtering through the stained glass windows seemed to deepen, reflecting the growing concern on Sir Reginald's venerable face. Leaning back in his well-worn leather chair, he let out a sigh that carried the weight of untold stories and unspoken concerns. The air was filled with the scent of ancient parchment and the slightly acrid smell of burning oil from the lamp on his desk, which flickered as if sympathetic to the current of emotion swirling through the room.

"I must confess," Sir Reginald began, his voice trembling slightly with palpable remorse, "that in my eagerness to share knowledge and perhaps relive the glories of a bygone era through conversation with a fellow enthusiast, I may have inadvertently drawn unwanted attention to the Wentworth's most prized possession."

At this his hands, spotted with age and trembling slightly, clasped together as if to physically hold together his crumbling composure. "To think that my revelations, made in good faith and scholarly camaraderie, could have set in motion such terrible events... It weighs heavily on me, gentlemen, heavily indeed."

Sherlock, his sharp eyes softening slightly in sympathy, remained silent, allowing the gravity of Sir Reginald's self-reproach to hang in the air, acknowledging the depth of his distress. It was a rare sight to see Sherlock so subdued, his usual rapid fire of analytical deduction tempered by the visible turmoil of our host.

Feeling a pang of sympathy for the troubled scholar, I felt compelled to interject. "Sir Reginald," I began, my voice calm and hopefully reassuring, "one cannot be held responsible for the actions of others driven by their own dark motives. They acted out of a love of history and a desire to share its wonders, not a desire to do harm."

Sir Reginald looked up, his eyes, rimmed with the wisdom of years and the weariness of his present concerns, meeting mine. "Thank you, Dr Watson. Your words are comforting, but the heart is not so easily moved from its burdens."

"It is the curse of those who care deeply for the past that they sometimes fear its shadows," I continued, gently urging him to look beyond his self-recrimination. "You have dedicated your life to the preservation and transmission of knowledge, Sir Reginald. It is a noble pursuit, fraught with many dangers, but the benefits to mankind are immeasurable. We must concentrate on correcting the present situation rather than dwelling on what cannot be undone.

Amal, who had been listening intently, added quietly, "Your passion for history is evident, Sir Reginald. It is that passion that will help us find the truth and bring justice."

Sherlock nodded in agreement and added, "Indeed, Sir Reginald, Watson and Dr El-Sharif speak wisely. Our efforts must now be directed towards unravelling this tangled web and ensuring that justice is served. The past, with all its mysteries and complications, also teaches us resilience and the relentless pursuit of truth.

Sir Reginald's eyes, though still clouded with concern, seemed to regain a spark of determination. "You are right, all of you. We must forge ahead with determination. Let us uncover the truth and preserve the legacy we hold dear."

The room seemed to breathe a little easier at these words, as if the walls themselves, lined with volumes filled with centuries of human thought, resonated with the renewed determination now reflected in Sir Reginald's eyes. He straightened slightly, the scholar's innate sense of duty fortifying his bearing.

"Very well," Sir Reginald declared, the newfound determination in his voice, "then let us get on with what needs to be done. I am at your disposal, Mr Holmes, Dr Watson. Let us illuminate this darkness with the tools of our trade: truth, reason and the unflinching pursuit of justice."

Thus reassured and strengthened in our collective resolve, we prepared to delve deeper into the labyrinth of our investigation. Each of us was aware that the road ahead would be fraught with challenges, but we were buoyed by the knowledge that the pursuit of truth was a worthy endeavour, whatever shadows we might encounter along the way.

In the refined atmosphere of Sir Reginald Ashcroft's office, surrounded by the weight of countless artefacts, each whispering its own ancient tale, Sherlock Holmes leaned forward, his keen gaze fixed on the museum director. The morning light filtered through the windows, illuminating the specks of dust dancing around the leather-bound volumes - a silent testament to the age and gravity of the room.

"Sir Reginald," Sherlock began, his voice low but clear, cutting through the quiet tension of the room, "you mentioned that you acquired this distinctive obsidian statuette for Lady Wentworth. Could you reveal where exactly this piece was obtained?"

The room seemed to stand still at the question, the very air charged with anticipation. Sir Reginald, a scholar who had spent a lifetime among such relics, showed a momentary hesitation. His eyes, reflecting a mind that catalogued history with precision, flickered with the recollection of a memory long filed away in the archives of his experience.

"Yes, Mr Holmes," he replied, his voice tinged with scholarly intrigue. "The statuette was acquired through a contact of mine, a merchant in the markets of Constantinople. A fascinating character, this merchant, widely known for his collection of rare and exotic artefacts. It was from his stock that I secured the obsidian statuette, a piece which he claimed was of considerable historical significance".

Sherlock's interest grew visibly, his analytical mind weaving through the threads of this new information. "And is it possible, Sir Reginald, to contact this merchant? Could he provide any further insight into the statuette's provenance or its historical lineage?"

The question hung in the air, a palpable presence in a room filled with artefacts that spoke of centuries past. Sir Reginald's expression changed subtly, a shadow of regret passing fleetingly over his scholarly features. He adjusted his spectacles, a prelude to the delivery of unwelcome news.

"I'm afraid that avenue is closed to us, Mr Holmes," he revealed with a sigh. "The merchant, a man of great knowledge and mystery, died some years ago. His death was noted with some importance in certain circles, but the collection he once possessed was scattered to the winds, sold or claimed by various collectors around the globe."

This revelation seemed to cast a slight shadow over the room, as if the walls themselves were mourning the loss of a key that might have unlocked further depths of their historical treasures. Sherlock, however, showed no sign of discouragement; instead, his mind seemed to race even faster, processing the information, cataloguing it and recalibrating his approach.

"That is most unfortunate," Sherlock replied, his voice calm but thoughtful. "The threads of history are often frayed and tangled, and it seems we have encountered a knot that will not be easily untied."

Sensing the shift in Holmes' thinking, I remarked, "It would seem, then, that we must rely on other clues to unravel this mystery. The past has a way of hiding its secrets, but also of revealing them when least expected."

Sir Reginald nodded in agreement, his manner that of a man at peace with the limitations of his historical pursuits. "Indeed, Dr Watson. And while this particular path has reached its end, the journey of discovery continues. There are always more paths to explore, more relics to study and more stories to understand."

<hr />

Invigorated by our renewed purpose, the air in Sir Reginald Ashcroft's office seemed to hum with the palpable excitement of discovery as we turned our discussion to the enigmatic Obsidian Guild. Sir Reginald, now a shade more composed, retrieved a thick, dust-covered tome from one of the high shelves. The book, bound in leather that was cracked and faded from years of scholarly consultation, made a soft thud as it landed on the cluttered surface of his desk.

"This," Sir Reginald began, his fingers caressing the cover with a reverence reserved for the most sacred texts, "is one of the few comprehensive accounts of the Obsidian Guild, compiled from various sources by scholars of the ancient arts of the Middle East. The Guild was, as one might suspect, no ordinary group of craftsmen. They were artisans of the highest order, revered throughout the Arabian Peninsula and beyond for their unparalleled skill in working with obsidian."

He paused and opened the book to a bookmarked page. "Historical records suggest that the Obsidian Guild was founded during the early Abbasid Caliphate, a period marked by significant advances in science, art and culture. Their creations, often commissioned by royalty and high officials, included intricately carved amulets, ceremonial daggers and statues imbued with protective and mystical properties. One notable example is the Obsidian Falcon of Al-Mansur, a legendary artefact believed to grant its owner invincibility in battle. The influence of the Guild extended far beyond its immediate patrons, shaping the artistic and spiritual landscapes of the regions it touched.

Sherlock, ever the attentive listener, leaned forward, his eyes scanning the text with an intensity that matched the flickering light of the lamp. "Fascinating," he murmured, "and do you think, Sir Reginald, that the statuette acquired for Lady Wentworth might have been a product of such beliefs?"

"Indeed, Mr Holmes," Sir Reginald replied, his voice tinged with a mixture of academic fervour and cautious speculation. "The craftsmanship of the statuette, its intricate detail and the aura it seems to possess, all point to the legendary techniques of the Obsidian Guild. It is said that their creations were not only visually magnificent, but also served as talismans, imbued with properties to guard and protect their owners".

Adrien, his curiosity growing, leaned forward. "Sir Reginald, what exactly were these mystical properties that the Guild attributed to obsidian?"

Dr Amal El-Sharif, whose expertise in Arabic cultural history had been silent but simmering with interest, now spoke. "The use of obsidian in Middle Eastern cultures is well documented, but the Guild's approach was unique. They used not only the physical properties of obsidian, but also its lore. Obsidian is volcanic glass, born from the fire of the earth - transformative, powerful and, to some, sacred.

She walked over to one of the shelves and carefully picked up a piece of raw obsidian, its edges catching the flickering light and casting sharp shadows on the walls. "Note its lustrous, glass-like quality," she said, turning the stone in her hand. "This quality, combined with its characteristic deep, dark colour, has been symbolically associated with the void, with the vastness of the night sky, and with the profound depths of the human psyche."

Returning to her seat, Dr El-Sharif placed the obsidian on the table before us, its presence almost palpable, as if it were a living being participating in our meeting. "Among the Bedouins in particular, obsidian was revered not only for its beauty and sharpness, but also for its properties as a protective amulet. It was often worn by travellers to ward off the evil eye, and by healers for its supposed power to purify negative energy."

Her gaze swept over each of us, making sure we were connected to the narrative thread she was weaving. "So when we consider the obsidian statuette - a meticulously crafted artefact, possibly by the hands of the skilled craftsmen of the Obsidian Guild - we must see it as more than an object of aesthetic or material value. It is potentially a talisman, imbued with layers of cultural and mystical significance that could give it a power highly coveted, perhaps even feared, by those who understand its deeper meanings".

Sherlock, who had been listening intently, his analytical mind absorbing every detail, nodded slowly. "This casts the theft of the statuette in a very different light," he mused aloud. "It suggests motives beyond mere greed or the desire to possess a rare artefact. We may be dealing with someone who seeks or fears the reputed powers of the statuette."

The room fell into a contemplative silence, each of us pondering the implications of our discoveries. The idea that we were dealing with an object of such extraordinary heritage and reputed power added a weighty, almost oppressive dimension to our investigation. It was as if we were no longer simply hunting a thief or murderer, but entering the realm of ancient mystical practices, where the line between the tangible and the ethereal is blurred.

As Sir Reginald carefully closed the ancient tome, the sound seemed to echo around the room, a definitive punctuation of our profound discovery. We were left with the daunting task of navigating not only the physical world in our quest for justice, but perhaps also the unseen forces of a bygone mystical era. The challenge was immense, but with Sherlock Holmes leading our investigation, I felt a cautious optimism that we would indeed unravel the mystery of the obsidian statuette and restore a semblance of order to the chaos that had enveloped the Wentworth legacy.

With the revelations of the Obsidian Guild still in the air like the faint, musty aroma of the old tomes that surrounded us, Sherlock Holmes, his face aglow with the rigour of intellectual pursuit, leaned forward. The flickering light from the antiquated lamp cast elongated shadows across his sharply defined features, lending an almost spectral quality to his pensive expression. Outside, the muted sounds of London - the passing carriages and distant cries of street vendors - faintly permeated the museum's thick oak-panelled walls, a subtle reminder of the bustling world beyond our scholarly enclave.

"Given what Dr El-Sharif has told us about the cultural and mystical significance of obsidian," Sherlock began, his voice a calm, measured timbre that commanded attention, "we must consider the possibility that the theft of the statuette goes beyond mere financial greed or the coveting of a rare artefact."

I listened intently, seated somewhat uncomfortably in a high-backed chair that seemed designed more for aesthetic effect than ergonomic support. Sherlock's ability to weave disparate threads of information into a coherent theory never ceased to fascinate and impress me.

"The fact that the statuette was made by the Obsidian Guild - a collection of craftsmen renowned not only for their craftsmanship but also for their esoteric knowledge - adds a significant layer of complexity to our case," Sherlock continued, his keen eyes scanning the room as if visualising his thoughts in the air around us.

He paused to make sure we understood the gravity of his conclusions. "If we accept the premise that the statuette is indeed imbued with the properties attributed to protective amulets in Arabian lore, as Dr El-Sharif suggests, then it stands to reason that the perpetrator of the theft may have been motivated by a desire to harness these mystical powers."

The thought seemed to hang in the air as thick and ominous as the heavy London fog outside. Sir Reginald, who had resumed his position behind his huge, cluttered desk, wrung his fingers and considered Sherlock's hypothesis.

"It's a chilling thought," Sir Reginald finally replied, his voice tinged with concern. "That someone might seek to possess the statuette, not merely as a collector of rare objects, but as a seeker of its supposed powers."

Dr El-Sharif, her expression pensive, added, "And if that is the case, then we are dealing with an individual who not only appreciates the historical and artistic value of such artefacts, but who may also believe in, or wish to exploit, their esoteric properties."

Sherlock nodded, his eyes narrowing slightly as he considered this. "This hypothesis could also shed light on the unfortunate demise of Lord Wentworth," he suggested. "If the thief - or thieves - believed that Lord Wentworth was aware of the statuette's powers, it may have escalated their motivations from mere theft to eliminating any threat to their possession of the artefact."

The room fell silent as the implications of Sherlock's theory sank in. The very idea that the statuette could be a catalyst for murder added a macabre tinge to the already grim proceedings.

"To think," I mused aloud, "that an object of such beauty and craftsmanship could also be a central figure in such dark dealings is deeply disturbing."

"Yes, Watson," Sherlock agreed, his gaze still fixed on some distant point, as if he were putting the puzzle together in his mind's eye. "It is often the case that the most beautiful of objects can possess the most potent of powers, real or ascribed. Our task now is to unravel the true nature of these powers and the identity of those who seek to wield them."

As the discussion drew to a close, the weight of our newfound knowledge seemed to penetrate the very walls of Sir Reginald's office, imbuing our scientific surroundings with a sense of urgency and danger. The mystery of the obsidian statuette had deepened, branching out into realms of mysticism and malevolence, and as we prepared to leave, it was with a renewed determination to illuminate the dark corners of this most perplexing case.

Sherlock Holmes, his silhouette etched against the windowpane, turned back to us, his gaze intense, signalling that our meeting was far from over.

"Consider, Watson," Sherlock continued, his voice resonating with a clarity that cut through the heavy atmosphere of the room, "the intricate nature of the legends that surround the Obsidian Guild. These artisans were not merely creators of objects; they were weavers of protection, imbued with a deep, almost sacred craftsmanship. The objects they forged were vessels of intent, designed to interact with the cosmos in ways that defy ordinary comprehension".

The room, its walls lined with ancient tomes and artefacts, seemed to echo Sherlock's observation, as if to confirm the gravity of his conclusions. I found myself nodding along, my mind racing to keep up with the unfolding implications.

"Yet here we are," Sherlock continued, his tone tinged with both frustration and fascination, "tasked with grounding these ethereal tales in the harsh soil of reality - a theft and a murder. How do you weigh the ancient belief in the mystical powers of obsidian against the very real, very tangible weight of a life brutally ended, or the loss suffered by Lady Wentworth?"

Dr Amal El-Sharif, her insights keen and informed by her deep understanding of Arab cultural history, added her perspective. "Mr Holmes, the answer may not lie in separating myth from reality, but rather in recognising that these legends represent a palpable truth for the perpetrator. The beliefs surrounding the obsidian's powers likely shaped the motivations behind the crime, making them as consequential and real as the statuette itself."

Sherlock considered her words, a look of recognition crossing his features. "Indeed, Dr El-Sharif," he agreed. "Our challenge, then, is to navigate this confluence where legend and reality merge, to trace the effects not only of the physical theft, but also of the stolen object's supposed mystical attributes."

Sir Reginald, who had been a silent observer, chimed in, his voice calm but thoughtful. "Navigating the overlapping realms of history and mythology is indeed daunting, Mr Holmes. In the pursuit of this case, one treads not only the visible paths laid by clues, but also the obscured trails of human belief and superstition."

⊱•❈•⊰

The discussion seemed to come to a natural pause, and a thoughtful silence fell over the room. It was then that Sir Reginald's expression changed subtly, a flicker of recollection crossing his features. "Ah, before we conclude," he said, rising slowly from his chair, "there is one more item which may aid your investigation."

He moved to a large, cluttered filing cabinet in the corner of the room. After a moment's rummaging, he produced a faded, carefully preserved photograph. "Here," he announced, returning to his desk to present the item to us, "is a photograph of the obsidian statuette, taken just before it was presented to Lady Wentworth. I had almost forgotten it existed.

The photograph, although aged, clearly showed the statuette in remarkable detail. It was an additional piece of the puzzle, a visual link to the object at the centre of our investigation.

"I trust this photograph will serve you well," Sir Reginald said, his voice echoing slightly in the high room. "May it lead you to the answers we seek, and may those answers bring justice and peace to all those affected by this unfortunate series of events."

As Sherlock studied the photograph with keen interest, his expression suddenly changed, a flicker of realisation crossing his sharp features. "Wait," he murmured, holding the photograph up to the light. "There's something here, a detail I hadn't noticed before..."

His voice trailed off as he squinted at the image, the room hushed with anticipation. "Look here," he said, pointing to a particular part of the statuette where the intricate golden veins seemed to converge. "These golden veins, they're not just random natural formations. They seem to resemble an Arabic script or symbol."

Dr El-Sharif and Sir Reginald immediately leaned forward, their eyes fixed on the photograph. Sir Reginald took a powerful magnifying glass from his desk and handed it to Dr El-Sharif. The two renowned experts huddled over the image, studying the intricate pattern of golden veins with intense concentration.

"You're right, Mr Holmes," Dr El-Sharif said, her voice filled with a mixture of excitement and awe. "The way these veins are arranged, it's too deliberate to be an accident. In fact, they resemble an ancient Arabic script."

Sir Reginald peered through the magnifying glass, his brow furrowed in thought. "I agree, but the specific meaning eludes me. The style is reminiscent of early Islamic calligraphy, but the context is unclear."

The two scholars engaged in a rapid exchange of academic theories and historical references, their voices rising with enthusiasm as they debated the possible interpretations of the symbol. Finally, after several minutes of intense discussion, Dr El-Sharif's eyes widened in sudden realisation.

"Of course!" she exclaimed, her voice trembling with the weight of the discovery. "The symbol, seen in this light, is an ancient Arabic representation of 'wisdom'. It was often used in mystical texts and talismanic inscriptions to invoke the power of divine knowledge and understanding."

Sir Reginald nodded slowly, a look of awe and admiration on his face. "Remarkable. The craftsmanship required to weave such a symbol into the very structure of the obsidian is truly astounding. The artisans of the Obsidian Guild were not merely skilled, they were masters of their craft, imbuing their creations with layers of meaning and power."

Sherlock Holmes listened intently, his mind racing with the implications of this revelation. The presence of the 'wisdom' symbol within the statuette added a new dimension to the mystery, suggesting that the obsidian artefact was more than just a work of art - it was a conduit for ancient knowledge and perhaps even supernatural abilities.

As the gravity of the discovery sank in, the atmosphere in the room became electric with anticipation. We knew we were on the verge of solving a mystery that spanned centuries and went to the very heart of human belief and power. The road ahead was sure to be perilous, but armed with this new knowledge, we felt a renewed sense of purpose and determination to follow the trail of the Obsidian Guild wherever it might lead.

❈❖❈

Sir Reginald Ashcroft watched us with a mixture of hope and solemnity, aware that the artefact he had helped to document was now central to a mystery far greater and darker than any of us had anticipated, and that Sherlock's keen observation might just have uncovered a crucial clue.

Sir Reginald's office, with its towering bookshelves and relics of countless cultures, seemed to close in around us, as if the walls themselves wanted to impart their silent wisdom before we left.

Sherlock nodded his approval and turned to us - Dr Amal El-Sharif, Adrien d'Arcy and myself - with a look of determination. "We have much to discuss and analyse," he said, his mind clearly already racing through the implications of our new evidence. "Let us make haste."

We left Sir Reginald's office and walked through the labyrinthine corridors of the Guildhall Museum. The air was rich with the smell of aged paper and the subtle musk of artefacts long kept from the light of day. Each display we passed seemed to whisper secrets of its own, holding stories both glorious and grim within its glass confines. It was as if the entire museum was alive with the echoes of the past, each step we took a ripple across the surface of a deep and still pool of time.

Emerging into the daylight, the city of London greeted us with its usual bustling indifference. The streets were awash with the bustle of commerce and the hurried footsteps of its inhabitants, a stark contrast to the quiet, scholarly sanctuary we had just left. The air was brisk, carrying the faint scent of impending rain, mixed with the ever-present soot and smoke that marked the city's industrial heartbeat.

As we made our way through the crowded streets, Sherlock was pensive, his hands clasped behind his back, his eyes occasionally darting to the passing faces, as if searching for some sign only he could discern. Dr El-Sharif, her expression pensive, seemed to be mentally reviewing every detail of the discussion we had just concluded. Adrien, though less accustomed to the gritty realities of detective work, walked with determination, his youthful energy a stark contrast to the weight of history we carried.

"We must consider every detail, every possibility," Sherlock murmured as we made our way through a particularly busy thoroughfare. "This photograph not only serves as a clue to the physical appearance of the statuette, but may also help us identify the circles in which such items are traded, valued or even stolen."

As we reached the relative quiet of a less frequented side street, I found myself reflecting on the journey ahead. The photograph, a simple piece of paper bearing the image of an artfully crafted object, was now a beacon in our quest – a quest that spanned continents and centuries, touching on the deepest fears and aspirations of humanity. It was a reminder of the power of objects of beauty and mystery, and of the lengths to which individuals will go to possess such power.

As the city bustled around us, we decided to reconvene at Baker Street, where we would meticulously examine the photograph and all the evidence we had gathered. Our aim was to unravel the intricate web of history, myth and crime that had ensnared us. The sense of urgency was palpable, for we were not merely on the trail of a thief, but delving into a deeper, darker mystery that bridged the mundane and the mystical.

Suddenly, a figure emerged from the crowd, its face obscured by a hood, and pressed a folded piece of paper into Sherlock's hand before disappearing as quickly as it had appeared. Sherlock unfolded the note, his eyes widening as he read the hastily scribbled message: "The obsidian holds the key. The secrets of the Guild run deeper than you know. Tread carefully, for you are not the only ones who seek its power."

The words sent a shiver down my spine, and I could see that my companions were similarly affected. The road ahead was uncertain, fraught with hidden dangers and elusive truths, but this new piece of the puzzle only strengthened our resolve. We quickened our pace towards Baker Street, ready to decipher the cryptic warning and face the shadows of the Obsidian Guild head-on, knowing that the stakes had just been raised.

Back at 221B Baker Street, the familiar surroundings of our study brought a sense of focus and determination. Mrs Hudson, ever the attentive housekeeper, had already prepared a pot of tea and some light refreshments, sensing the intensity of our mission.

Sherlock spread the photograph and note out on the table, his eyes bright with the excitement of the hunt. "Watson, Dr El-Sharif, Adrien," he addressed us, "we have before us a challenge beyond the ordinary. The Obsidian Guild, the ancient legends, the mystical properties of the statuette - these are threads in a tapestry that we must unravel with precision and insight."

Dr El-Sharif, her scholarly mind sharp and ready, nodded in agreement. "We must delve deeper into the historical context and legends surrounding obsidian. There may be clues hidden in texts and artefacts that we have yet to uncover."

Adrien, his youthful enthusiasm undiminished, added: "And we must also consider the modern implications. Who would benefit from owning such an artefact today? What circles could it move in?"

I, always the chronicler of our adventures, felt a renewed sense of purpose. "Indeed, Holmes. Let us leave no stone unturned, no clue unexamined. The truth is out there, waiting for us to uncover it."

Sherlock's eyes sparkled with a mixture of determination and excitement. "Then let us begin. The game is afoot, and the shadows of the Obsidian Guild will not remain hidden for long."

As we settled into our respective tasks, the room buzzed with the energy of our collective endeavour. The mysteries of the obsidian statuette, the cryptic message, and the dark legacy of the Obsidian Guild lay before us - an intricate puzzle that only the keenest minds and most fearless hearts could hope to solve.

With each passing moment, we inched closer to the heart of the puzzle, driven by the unyielding spirit of inquiry and relentless pursuit of truth that defines our very being. The journey ahead promised to be perilous, but together we were ready to face whatever challenges and revelations awaited us in the shadows of history and myth.

CHAPTER 10

JOURNEY TO CONSTANTINOPLE

S tepping into the venerable residence at 221B Baker Street, the air was filled with the scent of aged books and the sound of ticking clocks, creating an atmosphere that exuded an intellectual sanctuary. The pervasive scent of tobacco and leather-bound books mingled with the faint aroma of Mrs Hudson's freshly brewed tea. Flickering gas lamps cast a warm golden glow on the rich mahogany furniture, while the soft rustling of papers and the distant ticking of the grandfather clock created a symphony of scholarly pursuit. The room was alive with the subtle creak of the floorboards and the occasional crackle of the fireplace, each sound a testament to the countless mysteries unravelled within these hallowed walls.

We gathered around the fireplace: Sherlock Holmes, Dr Amal El-Sharif, Adrien d'Arcy and myself. The flames flickered and danced, casting an eerie glow that seemed to animate Sherlock's keen, contemplative features. The gloomy weather outside reflected the gravity of our task, weaving together the disparate threads of an investigation that stretched from the shadowy alleys of London to the sun-drenched deserts of Arabia.

Taking my customary seat at Sherlock's side, I couldn't help but reflect on the eclectic nature of our gathering. Dr Amal El-Sharif, with her profound knowledge of Middle Eastern cultures and languages, brought an essential perspective to our deliberations. Her presence added invaluable depth to our understanding of the complexities involved. Adrien d'Arcy, though less experienced in the art of sleuthing, had proved himself to be a diligent and keen observer of human nature. His youthful vigour and insight into the modern machinations of society added a fresh dynamic to our ensemble.

Sherlock stood by the fire, his slender figure outlined by the sporadic bursts of flame, his eyes reflecting a fire not unlike the blaze before him. His face was one of intense concentration, the kind that heralds the weaving of fact into conjecture and conjecture into theory.

"Ladies and gentlemen," Sherlock began, his calm voice cutting through the crackling of the fire, "tonight we find ourselves at a critical juncture in our investigation. The threads we are holding, each a story in itself, are different in their origins but intertwined in their implications."

He paused, letting his words reverberate in the shadowed room, filled with the rich, musty aroma of old wood and the faint, lingering scent of Mrs Hudson's evening tea. The heavy curtains fluttered slightly as a gust of wind challenged the windowpanes, as if nature itself were eager to listen.

"At Epsom Downs, amidst the rejoicing of Isinglass's victory, my attention was drawn not to the cheering crowd but to a singular, penetrating look. A gaze that showed not mere interest, but purpose, fuelled by knowledge and intent as deep as the history it pursued.

Sherlock's hands, those eloquent conductors of his thoughts, gestured subtly, guiding our minds to that moment of discovery. "This glimpse, fleeting as it was, has proved to be a cornerstone of our investigation. For it belongs, we now suspect, to a person who walked the corridors of the British Museum and engaged Sir Reginald Ashcroft in discussions centred on Arabian artefacts, and obsidian in particular."

The room seemed to close in, the walls themselves pressing in as if to capture every syllable Sherlock uttered. The soft ticking of the clock, the whisper of the wind and the occasional creak of wood created a symphony of tension.

"Sir Ashcroft, in his scholarly candour, related how this enigmatic visitor had expressed a deep interest in obsidian artefacts in the shape of animals - a detail that takes on added significance when one considers the obsidian statuette, a relic of considerable mystery and allure, that had been procured for Lady Wentworth from the depths of Constantinople."

As Sherlock paused, his gaze lingered momentarily at the window, as if he could see through the misty streets of London. The gravity of our undertaking seemed all the more palpable. We were not merely chasing a thief or a shadow; we were unravelling a tapestry woven with the threads of history, art and deep-seated intrigue. The room, with its flickering shadows and the timeless ticking of the clock, was a silent witness to the unfolding drama - a drama that promised to delve deep into the annals of history and the complexities of human desire.

In the intimate confines of our sitting room at 221B Baker Street, lit by flickering candlelight casting long shadows across the walls, our discussion delved deeper into the enigmatic puzzle before us. Sherlock Holmes had just laid out the fundamental threads linking the mysterious observer at Epsom Downs to the wider implications of our obsidian statuette case. Now it was time for Dr Amal El-Sharif and Adrien d'Arcy to weave their insights into the tapestry of our investigation.

Dr Amal El-Sharif, whose expertise in Arabic cultures was invaluable, adjusted her glasses thoughtfully before speaking. The soft glow of the fire accentuated the seriousness in her eyes as she began to explain the significance of the artefact in question. Sherlock, ever the keen observer, watched her with a mixture of respect and curiosity, recognising the depth of her knowledge. Adrien, sitting nearby, leaned in closer, his youthful enthusiasm tempered by a growing admiration for Dr El-Sharif's insights. As she spoke, I noticed a subtle exchange of glances between Sherlock and Dr El-Sharif - a silent acknowledgement of the intellectual synergy that had begun to form between them. The room, filled with the warmth of the fire and the shared purpose of our mission, felt charged with a sense of camaraderie and mutual respect.

"The obsidian statuette, while ostensibly a mere object of art, carries with it a profound cultural resonance," she explained, her voice rich with the nuances of her vast knowledge. "Obsidian, especially in Arabic lore, is not just a stone, but a symbol of mystical protection. It is believed to ward off the evil eye and is often associated with the search for truth and clarity."

She paused, letting the weight of her words sink in as the rain outside pattered against the window in a steady, rhythmic symphony. "This statuette, then, is not merely an artefact to be admired for its craftsmanship, but is imbued with a deeper, almost sacred significance. Its disappearance and the obvious interest in our mysterious figure suggest that it is sought not only for its aesthetic or historical value, but perhaps also for its reputed mystical properties".

Adrien d'Arcy, who had been listening intently, leaned forward, the creaking of his chair punctuating the quiet atmosphere. His background in anthropology gave him a unique perspective on the matter, particularly regarding the craftsmanship of the statuette. "Indeed, Dr El-Sharif," he agreed, his youthful face lit by the seriousness of his intrigue. "And when we consider the craftsmanship, it speaks volumes about the time and region from which it came. The intricate carving, the stylistic nuances, all point to a time when art was deeply intertwined with spirituality and symbolism."

His hands gestured animatedly as he spoke, emphasising his points. "The artisan who created this statuette was not just a sculptor, but a bearer of the stories and beliefs of his culture. Through this obsidian he channelled a narrative that was both personal and universal - a narrative of protection, power and perhaps prophecy."

Sherlock nodded thoughtfully, absorbing the insights of Dr El-Sharif and Adrien. "It seems, then, that our investigation is as much about recovering a stolen object as it is about understanding the confluence of history, art and belief that this statuette represents. It is a key, not just to a locked safe somewhere, but to the very essence of a cultural heritage threatened by its disappearance".

The crackling of the fire seemed to echo his words, dramatically underlining the gravity of our quest. Dr El-Sharif nodded in agreement, her expression sombre yet determined. "And so our path forward must be taken with a sensitivity to the cultural ramifications of our actions. We are not merely detectives in this case; we are custodians of a legacy that spans centuries and civilisations."

As the discussion drew to a close, the storm outside began to die down, leaving in its wake a silence that seemed filled with the echoes of our conversation. We sat there, in the dimly lit room of Baker Street, surrounded by the ghosts of past cases and the very real shadows of the one unfolding before us. Each of us was acutely aware that the journey ahead would require not only keen observation and deductive reasoning, but also a profound understanding of the cultural and historical tapestry into which we were now being woven.

As the last echoes of our profound discussion on the cultural and historical significance of the obsidian statuette lingered in the air, a sudden, sharp knock on the door shattered the contemplative silence that had enveloped the room. The sound was unexpected, assertive, and echoed off the walls of 221B Baker Street with an urgency that seemed at odds with the dying thunder of the storm outside. Sherlock, who had been leaning thoughtfully against the mantelpiece, straightened immediately, his piercing eyes narrowing slightly as he gazed at the door with a mixture of curiosity and anticipation.

Before either of us could react, the door swung open with a quiet but firm motion, revealing the imposing figure of Mycroft Holmes. The elder Holmes, typically immersed in the labyrinthine bureaucracy of the British government, appeared before us with his usual impeccable posture and an expression that managed to be both inscrutable and intensely serious. His umbrella, a constant companion, was neatly rolled up at his side, glistening with the remnants of the evening's rain.

"Sherlock, Dr Watson, Dr El-Sharif, Mr d'Arcy," Mycroft announced, his deep voice echoing around the room as he acknowledged each of us in turn. His gaze lingered on each face for a moment, as if imprinting the scene before him in his meticulous mind. Without waiting for an invitation, he stepped into the room, closing the door behind him with a soft click that seemed to seal us off from the rest of the world.

"Mycroft," Sherlock greeted, his tone a rare blend of familial recognition and professional caution. "Your timing, as always, is most... punctual."

Mycroft nodded slightly, his lips curving in what could be interpreted as a wry smile. "Indeed, brother. When it comes to matters of state and international intrigue, timing can be everything." He paused, allowing his words to settle in the air like the thick London fog. "I understand your investigation has uncovered connections that stretch across borders and into the annals of history."

Sherlock's eyes twinkled with an unspoken challenge. "You are well informed, as always. We were just discussing the wider implications of the obsidian statuette's disappearance - implications that seem to resonate with cultural, historical and now, it seems, geopolitical significance."

Mycroft's eyes swept over the assembled group, his analytical mind no doubt cataloguing every detail of our surroundings - the maps unfolded on the table, the hastily scribbled notes, the intensity of our concentration. He moved further into the room, choosing a chair with strategic deliberation, before sitting down with an air of calm authority.

"The geopolitical landscape, Sherlock, is indeed where this puzzle begins to unfold into greater complexity," Mycroft began, his voice taking on the tone of an experienced lecturer imparting vital knowledge. "The obsidian statuette is not simply a stolen relic. It is a nexus of cultural heritage and political power, a symbol whose disappearance could cause far more than scholarly consternation or collector's frustration."

As Mycroft spoke, the room seemed to shrink, the walls closing in as the weight of his revelations grew heavier. He continued, "This artefact has implications that could affect the stability of regions, influence the balance of power and dictate the fate of nations. And it is into this volatile arena that your investigation moves, Sherlock. Not just through the shadowy streets of London, but across the shifting sands of political landscapes fraught with intrigue and danger."

The gravity of Mycroft's words hung between us, a palpable presence that seemed to suck the air out of the room. Dr El-Sharif's expression reflected a newfound understanding of the stakes, while Adrien d'Arcy sat slightly forward, his youthful demeanour overshadowed by the magnitude of the challenges ahead.

Sherlock, always the master of composure, met his brother's gaze with steely determination. "Then let us not shrink from the magnitude of what we face, Mycroft. As the shadows grow longer, so will the reach of our efforts."

As Mycroft nodded in silent agreement, the meeting in the sitting room of 221B Baker Street, under the watchful eyes of the Holmes brothers, transformed from a mere meeting of minds to a council of war, strategising against a backdrop of international espionage and the dark dance of empires. The storm outside may have passed, but within the walls of Baker Street, a far greater tempest was just beginning to brew.

As Mycroft Holmes settled into the ambience of our dimly lit living room, his presence seemed to command the very air around us, drawing the shadows closer as if to listen. The rain had slowed to a gentle patter against the windows of 221B Baker Street, lending a sombre rhythm to the gravity of his revelations.

"Sherlock and esteemed colleagues," Mycroft began, his voice imbued with the gravitas of his position and the weight of his burden, "to fully grasp the intricacies of this case one must understand the wider geopolitical landscape, in particular the current state of the Ottoman Empire."

He paused to ensure that his audience was attuned to the significance of his remarks. "Sultan Abdul Hamid II, the figure at the helm of the empire, sits precariously on a throne beset by internal and external threats. His reign has been marked by a fervent drive towards modernisation, juxtaposed with an autocratic suppression of dissent."

Mycroft's eyes, sharp and calculating, scanned our faces as he painted a portrait of a ruler ensnared by the very reforms he championed. "The Sultan's efforts to fortify his empire - whether through advances in infrastructure or the modernisation of the military - are mirrored by his equally vigorous efforts to crush any opposition. This has led to a state of heightened tension within the empire, a tension exacerbated by the encroaching interests of European powers.

Dr Amal El-Sharif, her interest clearly piqued by the mention of her ancestral lands, leaned forward. Her eyes, reflecting the firelight, were filled with a mixture of concern and curiosity. "And in the midst of these tumultuous currents, Mr Holmes, how does the theft of an obsidian statuette figure into the Sultan's calculations?"

Mycroft nodded, acknowledging her question with a slight tilt of his head. "An astute question, Dr El-Sharif. To the uninitiated, the theft of such an artefact might seem a minor footnote in the grand ledger of international affairs. To Sultan Abdul Hamid II, however, it represents far more. The statuette is not just a cultural relic; it is a symbol of his legitimacy and his claim to be the custodian of history and heritage.

He paused to let the magnitude of this statement sink in. "The disappearance of the statuette coincides with a period of delicate diplomatic negotiations and internal power struggles. For the Sultan, the theft is a potential scandal that could undermine his authority both at home and abroad. It is a vulnerability that could be exploited by his opponents to foment unrest or justify foreign intervention".

Sherlock, who had been listening intently, snapped his fingers and said, "So you are suggesting that the Sultan sees this theft as an existential threat to his rule?"

"Exactly," Mycroft confirmed, his manner sombre. "And it is in this context that he has asked for help. The Sultan's request for your involvement, Sherlock, is born of desperation and a nuanced understanding of your particular skills. He believes that resolving this matter quickly and discreetly could help to stabilise a precarious situation."

Mycroft paused dramatically, letting the significance of his next words sink in. "I have just received a secret communiqué from the Sultan himself. He is aware of the murder of Lord Wentworth and the theft of the obsidian statuette. In his message, he specifically requests your assistance, Sherlock. He did not reveal the full context of his request, but insisted that you and your companions leave for Constantinople with the utmost haste."

The room fell silent, the implications of Mycroft's revelations hanging heavily in the air. This direct invitation from the Sultan was the clue we had been looking for, a clear next target for our investigation. The geopolitical chessboard on which we were now unwitting pawns was one of daunting complexity, each move fraught with potential repercussions.

Adrien d'Arcy, usually the least vocal of us, found his voice, his tone tinged with newfound gravity. "So our pursuit of a thief has become a mission with stakes far higher than any of us anticipated. We are not merely recovering a stolen object; we are potentially securing the stability of an empire."

Mycroft nodded slowly, his expression unreadable. "Indeed, Mr d'Arcy. And as you embark on this journey, remember: the eyes of powers both seen and unseen will be upon you. Discretion as well as valour will be your necessary companions."

Sherlock and his companions exchanged looks of confusion and surprise, pondering the reasons for this personal invitation. What context or deeper machinations lay behind the Sultan's urgent request? The weight of our burden settled on our shoulders, the storm outside a mere whisper compared to the storm we were about to enter. The game was afoot, and its arena was nothing less than the grand, tumultuous stage of empires.

As Mycroft Holmes' revelations about the geopolitical stakes underlying our investigation settled like a thick fog in the room, Sherlock resumed his position by the fire, his contemplative gaze reflecting the dancing flames. The quiet crackle of the fire provided a subtle backdrop to his thoughts as he prepared to delve deeper into the intricate web of international politics that now framed our search for the stolen obsidian statuette.

"The matter at hand," Sherlock began, his voice low and even, drawing us all into the gravity of the situation, "goes beyond the simple recovery of a stolen artefact. This statuette, as Mycroft has explained, is imbued with a significance that transcends its physical form."

He paused, pacing slowly, hands clasped behind his back, each step measured and deliberate. "Consider the position of Sultan Abdul Hamid II, a ruler whose grip on power, though firm, is constantly threatened by both internal strife and the covetous eyes of foreign powers. For him, the theft of such a symbol - a relic of cultural and historical importance - could be seen as a weakening of his authority, a crack in the facade of his imperial command."

Sherlock stopped and looked at us, his eyes sharp and penetrating. "This is not just about the loss of a valuable object. It is about what the object represents: the continuity of a dynasty, the legitimacy of a rule, and the sanctity of a nation's heritage. In the hands of another, especially a foreign entity, it could serve as a powerful propaganda tool or, worse, as a pretext for political or military intervention".

Dr Amal El-Sharif nodded thoughtfully, her keen understanding of Middle Eastern politics adding depth to the discussion. "The region is a tapestry of delicate alliances and simmering conflicts," she added, her voice steady and informed. "The Ottoman Empire is currently a focal point of tension, with various European powers eager to exploit any vulnerability. In this context, the statuette could become a symbol around which internal dissent or external aggression could coalesce".

Adrien d'Arcy, who had been quietly absorbing the complexities of the situation, now interjected with a question that reflected his growing understanding of the stakes. "So the recovery of the statuette is not just a matter of returning a stolen object, but of maintaining a balance of power, of ensuring that this symbol does not become the spark that ignites a larger conflagration?"

"Exactly," Sherlock confirmed with a nod of agreement at Adrien's succinct summary. "Our actions must therefore be guided by an acute awareness of the wider implications. We are not just detectives in this scenario; we are, in effect, diplomats navigating a maze of international intrigue."

The weight of this realisation seemed to settle on each of us, the room charged with a new sense of purpose and danger. Mycroft, who had watched the exchange in silence, now spoke again, his voice resonating with the authority of his governmental position. "I must stress the importance of discretion and tact. The eyes of many will be upon you as you tread this precarious path. The outcome of your endeavours could well affect the diplomatic standing of our own country in relation to the Ottoman Empire and beyond".

By the end of the discussion, the implications of our mission were clearer and more daunting than ever. The obsidian statuette, a mere object to the uninitiated, was now revealed to be the keystone in a complex arch of geopolitical dynamics. Our quest to recover it, set against the backdrop of empires and eras, was a mission with the potential to change the course of history.

In the quiet of Baker Street, with the storm outside reduced to a whisper and the fire casting a warm glow on the thoughtful faces of my companions, I wrote these revelations in my diary. The task before us was monumental, not only in the physical distance we had to cover, but in the intricate dance of diplomacy and detection we were about to undertake. As I laid down my pen, the weight of history, heavy and profound, seemed to echo through the chambers of 221B Baker Street, a reminder of the gravity of the adventure we had embarked upon.

⁖⁘⁜⁘⁖

As the weighty discussions of geopolitical dynamics and the intricate implications of our mission began to settle, Sherlock Holmes shifted our focus to the practical aspects of our upcoming journey to Constantinople. The room, still echoing with the gravity of earlier revelations, gradually transformed into a hive of strategic activity. Maps of Europe and the Ottoman Empire were unfurled across the mahogany surface of the study table, their aged edges slightly curled, reminiscent of ancient scrolls bearing the secrets of the ages.

With the meticulous precision that characterised his methodical mind, Sherlock began to outline the logistics required for our expedition. "Watson," he began, turning to me with a determined tone, "your medical expertise will be indispensable on this journey. The variety of climates and potential dangers we may encounter will require a well-equipped medical kit."

I nodded, already mentally cataloguing the items I would need to collect: anti-toxins, bandages, remedies for common ailments such as dysentery and cholera, and, perhaps more importantly, medicines for conditions prevalent in the regions we would be travelling through. The thought of navigating the varied landscapes, from the bustling streets of London to the exotic bazaars of Constantinople, was both daunting and exhilarating.

Dr Amal El-Sharif, whose knowledge of the customs and languages of the region was invaluable, was tasked with a different kind of preparation. Sherlock nodded respectfully to her, "Dr El-Sharif, if you could prepare a briefing on the cultural etiquette and potential language barriers we might encounter, it would greatly enhance our ability to navigate the social landscapes of Constantinople."

Dr El-Sharif's eyes lit up with an understanding of the importance of her role. "Certainly, Mr Holmes. I will also be reaching out to my academic contacts in the region to provide us with insights and possibly assistance upon our arrival. The nuances of Ottoman etiquette are complex, and navigating them correctly could be crucial to our success".

Adrien d'Arcy, who had been listening intently, was given a role that suited his youthful enthusiasm and keen eye for detail. Sherlock turned to him and said, "Mr d'Arcy, your task will be to manage our logistical needs. From securing our travel arrangements aboard the Orient Express to ensuring we have the necessary visas and paperwork to enter the Ottoman Empire, your attention to detail will be vital."

Adrien, his expression a mixture of determination and awe, nodded firmly. "I will not let you down, Mr Holmes. I'll start tomorrow by contacting the travel agencies and the embassy."

Satisfied with the division of responsibilities, Sherlock turned his attention to the broader strategy. "We must all be aware that our actions in Constantinople will be scrutinised, not only by the Sultan and his court, but probably by other international players with interests in the region. Every step we take must be measured, every decision weighed with the utmost discretion".

The room, filled with the musty smell of old books and the crackling of the fireplace, had been transformed into a strategic command centre. Charts, maps and various documents littered the table, each piece a part of the intricate puzzle we were about to solve.

As the meeting drew to a close, the storm outside had all but subsided, leaving behind a calm that seemed at odds with the storm of activity that had just taken place within the walls of 221B Baker Street. We each retreated to our respective tasks, the air around us charged with a palpable sense of urgency and the weight of the monumental task that lay ahead.

As night fell around us and the soft glow of the gas lamps cast shadows on the walls, I took a moment to record the details of our preparations in my diary. The story I was recording was no ordinary tale; it was the chronicle of a journey that promised to test our limits and perhaps even change the course of history. As I put down my pen, the reality of our undertaking sank deep into my bones, a thrilling yet sobering reminder of the adventure and challenges that awaited us.

⊕≫≈≪⊕

As the hour grew late and the embers in the fireplace at 221B Baker Street began to fade, casting long, flickering shadows across the room, Mycroft Holmes, with his characteristic blend of gravitas and precision, began to outline the details of our impending journey from London to the heart of the Ottoman Empire, Constantinople.

"The arrangements for your journey have been meticulously planned," Mycroft began, his voice calm and confident, reflecting the thoroughness of his preparations. "You will leave London early tomorrow morning by train for Dover. There you will take a ferry across the Channel to Calais."

He paused, reached into the inside pocket of his immaculately tailored coat and produced a small, detailed itinerary, which he handed to Adrien d'Arcy. The young man accepted it with a nod, his eyes scanning the document briefly, noting the precision with which each leg of the journey had been planned.

"On arrival in Calais," Mycroft continued, "you will board the Orient Express. This legendary train will be your setting for most of your journey to Constantinople. It is equipped with every imaginable comfort and convenience to ensure that your journey is not only safe, but enjoyable."

Sherlock, who had been listening intently, now interjected, "The Orient Express, renowned for its luxury and the diversity of its passengers, will also be fertile ground for intelligence gathering. We must be alert to our fellow travellers; alliances and enmities often travel covertly in such close quarters."

Mycroft nodded in agreement. "Indeed, Sherlock. The diplomatic and social intricacies aboard the Orient Express mirror those of the destinations it links. Your journey will be not only a physical traverse, but a navigation through a microcosm of European - and occasionally wider - geopolitics."

Dr Amal El-Sharif, who had been quietly absorbing the logistical details, now spoke up, her voice tinged with a mixture of anticipation and concern. "Given the complexity of our mission and the regions we will be traversing, I assume arrangements have been made for our safety?"

"Most certainly, Dr El-Sharif," Mycroft replied, reassuring her with a slight, confident smile. "While I have faith in your collective ability to deal with unforeseen circumstances, additional precautions have been taken. Discreet security measures will be in place throughout your journey, although they will remain unobtrusive to ensure they do not interfere with your investigation."

As Mycroft outlined the details of our journey, the room seemed to shrink, the walls closing in with the enormity of the task. Maps, timetables and various documents were spread out before us, each piece a fragment of the intricate tapestry of our mission.

"The train will pass through several key cities - Paris, Munich, Vienna and Budapest - before reaching its final stop in Constantinople," Mycroft added, pointing to the marked routes on one of the maps. "Each city is a hub in the complex web of European politics and culture. Your awareness and discretion in these places must be as sharp as your investigative acumen."

Sherlock nodded, his mind already running through the various scenarios and possibilities each location could present. "The journey itself is as much a part of this investigation as the destination. Every interaction, every observation could prove vital."

As Mycroft finished his briefing, the atmosphere in the room was thick with both the gravity of our undertaking and the resolute determination to succeed. The transition from planning to action had been made, the course charted and the roles defined. What lay ahead was a journey not just through the physical landscapes of Europe, but through a maze of cultural, political and historical complexities.

We each took a moment to absorb the final details, the silence in the room a stark contrast to the storm that had raged earlier. Outside, the streets of London were quiet, the city asleep, unaware of the small group of individuals at 221B Baker Street who were about to embark on a journey that could change the course of history.

With a final nod of acknowledgement and a firm handshake, Mycroft took his leave, his silhouette disappearing into the misty London night, leaving behind a room charged with anticipation and the spirit of adventure. As I made my own preparations, packing my medical bag with the tools of my trade and the necessities of travel, I reflected on the journey ahead. The Orient Express awaited, a steel artery running through the heart of Europe, and with it the promise of a mystery as deep and intricate as the cities it connected.

⊷⊶⊷⊶⊷

As the final echoes of Mycroft Holmes' departing footsteps faded into the misty London night, the gravity of his instructions hung heavy in the air of our small meeting at 221B Baker Street. A charged silence enveloped the room, electrified with the anticipation of the monumental journey that lay ahead. It was the kind of stillness that precedes a great adventure, a brief pause that allows the spirit to gather before plunging headlong into the unknown. Our souls hummed with a mixture of exhilaration and trepidation as the magnitude of our impending undertaking sank in, the whirlwind of plans and preparations now crystallising into an inescapable reality.

The fireplace, which had been a vibrant host of crackling flames throughout our discussions, now contained only glowing embers, casting a soft, undulating light that played across the thoughtful faces of my companions. Sherlock Holmes, ever the stoic sentinel in our midst, stood by the window, hands clasped behind his back, watching the obscure dance of the misty streets below. Dr Amal El-Sharif, her features intermittently illuminated by the fading light, pored over a small leather-bound notebook, her brow furrowed in concentration. Adrien d'Arcy, the youngest of us, had taken to pacing a small section of the carpet, his steps quiet but full of the nervous energy of an impending adventure.

In those charged moments, as the reality of our imminent journey from the familiar cobbled streets of London to the exotic and enigmatic city of Constantinople sank in, a frisson of excitement mixed with apprehension coursed through my veins. The enormity of our mission was palpable, a weight not only on our shoulders but on our very souls. We were on the precipice of an adventure that would take us not only across geographical boundaries, but through a labyrinthine web of political intrigue and cultural nuance. Each of us, in our own way, grappled with the thrilling yet daunting prospect of the challenges and revelations that awaited us in the heart of the Ottoman Empire.

The Orient Express, that gleaming marvel of engineering and epitome of the golden age of rail travel, beckoned with the promise of adventure. It was the gateway to a journey that would take us through the heart of Europe, through landscapes steeped in history, where ancient cities, with their towering spires and magnificent domes, whispered tales of empires long gone. Each stop on our route - the glittering lights of Paris, the Gothic grandeur of Munich, the imperial splendour of Vienna, the romantic allure of Budapest - represented not just a change of scenery, but a shift in the historical and political tapestry. We were to be threads ourselves, weaving through this intricate web of alliances and enmities, our every interaction and observation potentially altering the delicate balance of power.

As I sat in the dimly lit sanctuary of 221B Baker Street, which had witnessed countless preludes to adventure, my mind raced with the far-reaching implications of the quest before us. The obsidian statuette, the focal point around which our entire mission revolved, transcended its status as a mere artefact. It was a key, a linchpin in a far-reaching narrative that spanned centuries and civilisations. The ripples of its recovery, I realised, would extend far beyond the hallowed halls of museums and the locked vaults of private collections. This obsidian puzzle held in its glittering depths the very essence of cultural identity and heritage, a tangible link to the stories and struggles of those who came before. In pursuing it, we were not merely chasing an object, but engaging in a dialogue with history itself.

Sherlock, perhaps sensing that the weight of our thoughts needed a break, finally broke the silence. "We stand on the brink of a momentous journey," he said, his voice low but clear, cutting through the thick air of the room. "A journey that will undoubtedly test our limits and challenge our understanding of the world. But it is also a journey that invites us to be part of history - to engage with it, to learn from it, and perhaps to influence its course."

Dr El-Sharif looked up from her notes, her eyes meeting Sherlock's with a determination that matched his own. "Indeed, Mr Holmes. And in doing so, we bear not only the responsibility of solving the immediate mystery before us, but also the duty to treat with care and respect the cultural and historical threads that are interwoven with this case."

Pausing, Adrien added: "It is a daunting task, but one for which I am ready. The lessons to be learned on this journey will be many, I suspect, and I am eager to absorb them".

As the meeting drew to a close and each of us retreated to our respective corners of thought and preparation, I took a moment to record these reflections in my journal. The ink flowed across the pages, capturing not only the plans and details of our upcoming expedition, but also the introspection that such a momentous undertaking would bring.

As I stood there, looking around the room that had become the launching pad for so many of our explorations and adventures, I felt a renewed sense of purpose. This was not just a hunt for a stolen object. It was an exploration of the intersections of history, culture and human ambition - a story in which we were both characters and chroniclers.

As I extinguished the last lamp, leaving the room wrapped in the gentle embrace of London's nocturnal silence, I stepped out into the cool night air. The journey ahead promised challenges and revelations, and as the first light of dawn pierced the horizon, I knew we were ready to meet them.

ACT II

CHAPTER 11

DEPARTURE AT DAWN

A s the first light of dawn appeared, London's skyline transformed into a breathtaking canvas of soft golds and blues. Once more, I found myself at the towering silhouette of Charing Cross Station, that beacon of Victorian engineering and architectural prowess. The air was crisp, carrying the promise of the day's adventures, as I stood alongside Sherlock Holmes, Adrien d'Arcy, and Dr Amal El-Sharif, converging upon the station's grand entrance. Even at this early hour, the station was bustling, a hive of activity where travelers and workers moved in a choreographed dance of departure and arrival.

Holmes, wrapped in his iconic overcoat, his eyes sharp and observant, watched the steam billow from the idling locomotive with a sense of contemplative anticipation. "Remarkable, isn't it, Watson?" he murmured, not turning his gaze from the engine. "A perfect confluence of human ingenuity and ambition."

"Indeed, Holmes," I replied. "The power of steam has revolutionized our world in ways we could scarcely have imagined."

Holmes's eyes gleamed as he continued, "And yet, Watson, it is but a tool— one that can be wielded for both noble and nefarious purposes. The same train that brings us closer to friends and family can also carry a fugitive away from justice. The dichotomy of progress, wouldn't you agree?"

"Indeed, Holmes," I replied, adjusting the strap of my bag. The familiar sense of excitement at the onset of a new adventure bubbled within me, a feeling that had become a cherished constant since my association with Holmes began. I pulled out my notebook, already envisioning the words I would pen to describe this journey—the landscapes, the discoveries, and the inevitable unraveling of mysteries.

Adrien d'Arcy, a man whose life had been irrevocably intertwined with the equine world, appeared slightly out of his element amid the steam and steel of the railway. Yet, his posture betrayed no uncertainty, only a quiet resolve. "This will be an interesting journey," he said, his voice steady. "There is much to uncover, and it touches upon the very essence of my passions and fears."

Holmes interjected with his characteristic sharpness, "Indeed, Mr. d'Arcy. In our pursuit of truth, we must be prepared to face both our passions and our fears. It is often in the crucible of such trials that we find our true mettle."

Dr Amal El-Sharif, her keen intellect and profound knowledge of ancient cultures a vital key to the puzzle we sought to solve, stood with an air of quiet confidence. Her eyes reflected the dawn's light, a mirror to her thoughts on the historical and archaeological significance of our quest. "A voyage through time," she mused softly, "connecting the dots between the past and the present. I look forward to the discoveries we shall make."

The cacophony of the station provided a symphony of life—porters hustling to and fro, the shrill whistles of the conductors, and the murmured conversations of early-morning travelers. The scent of coal and steam mingled with the fresh morning air, creating an atmosphere charged with potential and mystery.

As the train departed, slicing through the awakening city, Holmes turned his gaze towards the Thames, its waters glistening softly in the burgeoning light. "London," he mused aloud, "a city built upon layers of history, each stone a silent witness to the dramas of human endeavor."

"It's as though we've traversed into another world," I remarked, my words tinged with a blend of wonder and nostalgia, as the countryside of Kent unfolded before us. The fields, awash with the golden hue of dawn, stretched endlessly, dotted with grazing sheep and framed by hedgerows and ancient oaks. The quaintness of farmhouses, with smoke curling from their chimneys, offered a stark contrast to the urban tapestry of London.

Holmes, leaning back in his seat, engaged Adrien and Amal in a discussion on the strategic importance of railways in the modern age. "The railroads," he stated, "have transformed the landscape of criminal investigation, allowing both the pursued and the pursuer to vanish into the vastness of the country."

Adrien nodded, adding, "Indeed, Mr. Holmes. And yet, the same railways that offer such anonymity also provide a network of clues, if one knows where to look."

Holmes's eyes gleamed with interest. "Precisely, d'Arcy. The intricate web of rail connections can reveal much to those with a keen eye for detail. Each station, each track, holds its own secrets."

Adrien nodded, adding, "Indeed, Mr. Holmes. And yet, the same railways that offer such anonymity also provide a network of clues, if one knows where to look."

"Holmes's eyes gleamed with interest. 'Precisely, d'Arcy. The intricate web of rail connections can reveal much to those with a keen eye for detail. Each station, each track, holds its own secrets.'"

Adrien then began to share his insights about the historical use of horses in England. "Did you know that horses were once used for towing ships along the canals of London?" he asked. "The process, known as 'towing,' involved horses walking along towpaths, pulling barges laden with goods through the canals. This method was essential for transporting heavy loads and played a vital role in London's economy."Holmes, ever the keen observer, listened with a mix of interest and mild impatience. "Fascinating how beasts of burden have been romanticized. Perhaps next, we shall discuss the noble contributions of mules to civilization," he remarked with a hint of sarcasm, causing Watson to chuckle and Adrien to slightly bristle.

Undeterred, Adrien continued, "It's remarkable to think of the sheer effort and coordination involved. These horses were the backbone of trade, quite literally pulling the weight of commerce."

Dr Amal El-Sharif, her eyes lighting up with curiosity, added, "And yet, their contributions are often overlooked in the grand tapestry of history. It's a testament to the unsung heroes of our past."

Holmes's sharp wit returned, "Indeed, Dr El-Sharif. Much like the detectives of the past who toiled in obscurity while others basked in the glory of solved cases. History, it seems, has a habit of overlooking the laborers in favor of the luminaries."

The journey from London to Dover thus became more than a mere traversal of geography; it was a journey through the layers of history, society, and the human psyche, a fitting prelude to the adventure that lay ahead.

As the train drew to a halt at Dover, the early morning sun had begun its ascent, casting a warm, golden hue over the iconic white cliffs. We disembarked, each of us momentarily caught in a spell of quiet contemplation as we beheld the natural marvel before us. The cliffs of Dover, tall and proud against the brightening sky, served as a poignant reminder of our island nation's storied past—a sentinel at the edge of the English realm.

Holmes, his eyes narrowing as they adjusted to the increased light, observed the bustling activity of the port. The constant motion of people and goods, the shouts of dockworkers mingling with the cries of seagulls, painted a vivid picture of humanity's relentless pursuit of exploration and commerce. "The cliffs," he mused aloud, "provide not only a natural defense but also, for the cunning and unscrupulous, a means of concealment and illicit trade."

I stood beside Holmes, allowing my gaze to wander across the expanse of the English Channel. The vastness of the sea, with its undulating waves shimmering under the sun's early rays, stirred within me thoughts of the countless souls who had traversed these waters—not just merchants and travelers, but soldiers and spies, each with their tales of courage and desperation. "It's remarkable," I reflected, "how these waters have borne witness to both the best and the worst of human endeavors."

Adrien d'Arcy, ever the equestrian, found his thoughts drifting to the horses that had made similar journeys across this channel, bound for wars or trade, their fates intertwined with those of their human companions. The sight of the cliffs evoked in him a sense of respect for the animals' unspoken bravery and resilience, a silent testament to the bonds formed in the face of adversity.

"You know," Adrien began, his voice thoughtful, "during the Roman conquest of Britain, around two millennia ago, Julius Caesar and subsequent Roman invaders brought Arabian horses with them across this very channel. These horses played a crucial role in enhancing the British breeding stock and were integral in the Roman military efforts in Britain."

Holmes raised an eyebrow, his interest piqued. "Arabian horses, you say? I imagine their endurance and agility were highly prized in the legions."

"Indeed," Adrien replied. "The Arabian bloodlines contributed significantly to the development of British horses, improving their speed, stamina, and overall resilience. It's fascinating how these noble creatures have influenced our history."

Dr Amal El-Sharif, her scholarly interests piqued by the historical significance of our surroundings, contemplated the myriad cultures that had come into contact at this crossroads of nations. "These cliffs," she observed, "stand as a monument not only to the natural beauty of our world but also to the complex tapestry of human history that has unfolded at their base."

Holmes's sharp eyes scanned the port, taking in every detail. "Every stone, every grain of sand here holds a story—of trade, of conquest, of survival. And now, we add our own chapter to this ancient narrative."

The activity around the port continued unabated, a testament to the enduring spirit of exploration and commerce. The shouts of dockworkers and the cries of seagulls created a symphony of human endeavor against the backdrop of the majestic cliffs. The air was filled with the scent of salt and sea, a reminder of the ever-present connection between land and water.

Adrien continued, "The Romans valued these horses not just for their physical attributes but for their symbolic significance as well. To bring Arabian horses to Britain was to bring a piece of their empire's heart. These horses, with their unmatched endurance and spirit, were seen as emblems of Rome's power and reach."

"Fascinating," Holmes remarked, a hint of sarcasm in his voice. "The noble beasts carried not just men, but the weight of empires upon their backs. And now, it seems they carry the weight of your admiration, Mr. d'Arcy."

Adrien smiled, undeterred by Holmes's dry wit. "Indeed, Mr. Holmes. There is much to admire in their history and legacy. They have shaped our world in ways both seen and unseen."

Dr El-Sharif added, "The cliffs themselves are witnesses to these transitions, these crossings. They have seen empires rise and fall, cultures intermingle, and histories rewritten. Standing here, one cannot help but feel a profound connection to all those who have come before us."

Holmes nodded, his gaze fixed on the horizon. "Yes, El-Sharif. And as we embark on our own journey, let us remain ever vigilant. For it is not just the past that haunts these shores, but the present as well."

As we stood there, each lost in our own thoughts, it became clear that this journey would be one of both discovery and reflection, a quest that would take us deep into the heart of history and beyond.

As we boarded the steamboat to Calais, the fog began to roll in, shrouding the channel in a cloak of mystery. The air grew colder, and the sea's vast expanse became an indistinct blur. Holmes, leaning against the railing at the bow, peered into the mist, his mind alive with the possibilities it presented.

"Fog," he stated, casting a sideways glance at us, "can be both an ally and an adversary. It conceals and reveals, often at the whim of fate. Many a crime has been cloaked in its embrace, just as many a truth has been unexpectedly unveiled."

Adrien d'Arcy, standing nearby, appeared uneasy. His complexion had paled, and there was a tightness to his lips. "I'm not fond of sea travel," he confessed, gripping the railing. "I've always found it... unsettling."

Holmes turned his keen gaze towards Adrien. "Seasickness, Mr. d'Arcy? A common enough malady, though not one that befalls me. Dr Watson, I trust you have some remedy at hand?"

I observed Adrien with concern. "Seasickness, Adrien?" I asked gently.

He nodded, a faint smile playing at his lips. "Yes, Dr Watson. It's quite embarrassing, really. I've spent my life around horses, but a simple boat ride can undo me."

"Nothing to be embarrassed about," I reassured him, reaching into my medical bag. "Here, this should help." I handed him a small vial. "A bit of ginger and peppermint. It should ease your discomfort."

Adrien took the vial gratefully. "Thank you, Doctor. I feel better already knowing you have a remedy."

As Adrien sipped the concoction, Holmes continued his musing, his voice cutting through the fog like a beacon. "Consider the nature of fog, Watson. It acts as a barrier, yet it is permeable. It hides but does not hold back. In many ways, it is like the human mind, concealing truths until the right moment of revelation."

I wrapped my coat tighter around me as the chill of the sea air cut through the fog. The rhythmic lapping of waves against the hull offered a soothing counterpoint to Holmes's musings. "These waters have been a stage for tales of heroism and treachery, a barrier that has both protected and isolated, depending on the currents of history," I reflected. "Soldiers crossing under the cover of night, secret agents braving these waters with nothing but their wits and resolve. The channel, in its foggy, inscrutable state, seems a fitting metaphor for the mysteries we are pursuing—veiled in shadows, yet undeniably present."

Dr Amal El-Sharif joined our contemplations, her voice thoughtful. "Fog has always held a certain mystique, hasn't it? It blurs the lines between reality and illusion, creating a world where the known and unknown intertwine. It's a reminder that not everything is as it seems, and sometimes, the truth lies just beyond our grasp."

Holmes nodded, his eyes still fixed on the horizon. "Indeed, El-Sharif. It is in these moments of obscurity that we must sharpen our senses, trust in our intellect, and remain ever vigilant. For within the fog lies not just a physical barrier between nations but the metaphorical divide between clarity and confusion, knowledge and ignorance."

Adrien, his nerves somewhat calmed by Watson's remedy, ventured a comment. "It's interesting how the fog, in a way, forces us to rely on our instincts and intuition. Much like navigating through the complexities of life, one must trust the inner compass even when the path ahead is unclear."

Holmes turned to Adrien, his eyes gleaming with a mix of curiosity and amusement. "A perceptive observation, Mr. d'Arcy. Indeed, the fog challenges us to look beyond the obvious and find the hidden truths. Much like the case we are currently entangled in, wouldn't you agree?"

Adrien nodded, his confidence slowly returning. "Absolutely, Mr. Holmes. And I must say, this journey is teaching me much about the nuances of observation and deduction."

Our journey across the channel, amidst the swirling mists and the rhythmic lapping of waves, became a time of introspection and reflection. Each of us, lost in our own thoughts, pondered the broader implications of our quest. For within the fog lay not just the physical barrier between nations but the metaphorical divide between the known and the unknown, the seen and the unseen, that we sought to bridge in our pursuit of truth.

The steamboat's engine droned steadily, a comforting sound in the enveloping mist. The deck beneath our feet vibrated softly with the power of the machine, reminding us of the progress we were making, despite the obscured vision. Holmes, ever the detective, seemed to draw energy from the mystery, his sharp mind probing the hidden depths of the fog, seeking out the secrets it concealed.

In the fog, our roles seemed to take on a new significance. Holmes, the ever-watchful sentinel; Watson, the healer and chronicler; Adrien, the historian of equine legacy; and Dr El-Sharif, the bridge between ancient cultures and our present mission. Together, we formed a fellowship bound by purpose, moving forward through the mists of uncertainty, each step bringing us closer to the truth that lay hidden, waiting to be discovered.

As we disembarked from the steamboat in Calais, the air felt distinctly different, imbued with the essence of the Continent. The transition from the misty English Channel to the vibrant hues of the French countryside was immediate and striking, marking not just a change in geography but in the very atmosphere that surrounded us. The scent of freshly baked baguettes and the distant aroma of strong coffee wafted through the air, mingling with the briny tang of the sea, creating a sensory mosaic that was unmistakably French.

Holmes, ever alert, took in the bustling port with a discerning eye. "Observe, Watson," he said, gesturing subtly towards the dockworkers and travelers. "The rhythms of daily life, though different in detail, are strikingly similar in essence. Humanity's constant dance of order and chaos."

We boarded the train bound for Paris, settling into a comfortable compartment as the engine began its rhythmic chug through the picturesque landscape. The French countryside unfurled before us like a tapestry of living history. Lush vineyards and sprawling fields, bathed in the soft light of the afternoon sun, offered a stark contrast to the pastoral scenes of the English countryside we had left behind.

Leaning closer to the window, my eyes traced the contours of the land. "There's a certain... complexity to this landscape," I mused, my voice tinged with wonder. "Each vineyard, with its myriad vines, reminds me of the intricate cases we've untangled. Each vine, a clue; each row, a narrative leading us closer to the heart of the mystery."

Holmes nodded absently, his mind clearly occupied with thoughts on the case. "Indeed, Watson. The land tells its own story, much like our investigations. Each element, seemingly insignificant, contributes to the whole."

Adrien d'Arcy, seated across from us, leaned forward, his eyes alight with a different kind of excitement. "You know, the traditions of horseback hunting and eventing in both France and England have deep roots and have been a cornerstone of country life for centuries," he began. "In France, these activities were often grand social gatherings, tied to the regal traditions of the nobility. The hunts were as much about social standing and community as they were about the chase."

He paused, a reflective look crossing his features. "In contrast, British fox hunting has always been more focused on the chase itself, the thrill of the pursuit, and the communal aspect of overcoming the challenge together. It's a subtle difference, but it speaks volumes about our respective cultures."

I leaned in, intrigued. "And your family, Adrien? How does your heritage play into this?"

A smile spread across his face. "My family has been involved in equestrian activities in both countries. My great-grandfather was a renowned horseman in France, well-respected in the circles of the nobility. When he moved to England, he brought those traditions with him, blending them with the local customs. It has given me a deep appreciation for the nuances of each tradition and how they enrich our understanding of equestrian culture."

Holmes glanced at Adrien, his eyes narrowing thoughtfully. "An interesting perspective, Mr. d'Arcy. The convergence of these traditions mirrors the blending of clues in our case. Each piece, no matter how seemingly unrelated, adds depth to our understanding."

Dr Amal El-Sharif, who had been quietly absorbing the conversation, spoke up. "It's fascinating how these cultural practices shape our identities and interactions. The way we approach a hunt or an investigation reflects our broader worldview and values."

Holmes nodded, a rare smile tugging at the corners of his mouth. "Indeed, El-Sharif. And it is this very convergence of perspectives that will aid us in unraveling the mysteries before us."

As the train sped through the French countryside, the conversation ebbed and flowed, weaving together tales of history, tradition, and the intricate dance of human endeavor. The landscape outside the window seemed to echo our thoughts, each passing field and vineyard a silent testament to the rich tapestry of life.

Holmes, ever the pragmatist, turned his attention to the practicalities of our journey. "The French gendarmes patrolling the station reminded me of the unique challenges we face in international investigations. The interplay between different judicial systems presents both obstacles and opportunities for an investigator."

He paused, his gaze sharpening. "The French approach, with its emphasis on inquisitorial processes, contrasts sharply with the adversarial system we navigate in England. Navigating these differences will be crucial for effective collaboration across borders."

The rhythm of the train, the soft murmur of conversation, and the ever-changing scenery outside created a sense of anticipation and purpose. We were not just traveling to Paris; we were journeying deeper into the heart of a mystery that promised to challenge us in ways we had yet to imagine.

Adrien gazed out the window, the passing scenery reflecting in his eyes. "The French countryside is so rich in history. Each château, each village, has its own story. It reminds me of the countless times my family participated in grand hunts, the excitement, the camaraderie. In England, it's different, but equally compelling. The thrill of the chase, the community gathering, it's all about the spirit of the hunt."

Dr El-Sharif added, "It's not just the landscape that changes, but the way people interact with it. The traditions, the respect for the land and its history, it's all interconnected."

Holmes, absorbing their reflections, remarked, "And it is in these interconnections that we often find the most valuable clues. Just as in hunting, where understanding the terrain and the habits of the prey is crucial, so too in our investigation, where understanding the cultural and historical context can lead us to the truth."

As the sun dipped lower in the sky, casting long shadows across the landscape, we settled into a comfortable silence, each lost in our own thoughts. The journey ahead was filled with uncertainties, but one thing was clear: together, we would face whatever lay in store, drawing strength from our shared resolve and the bonds we had forged.

The gentle sway of the train, the rhythmic clatter of the tracks, and the warm glow of the setting sun created an almost hypnotic ambiance. Holmes, ever vigilant, continued to make notes and observations, while I recorded our journey, capturing the essence of our experiences and the richness of the conversations that had unfolded.

Adrien, with a newfound sense of calm, leaned back and closed his eyes, no doubt envisioning the hunts of his ancestors and the legacy they had passed down. Dr El-Sharif, always the scholar, perused a book on ancient civilizations, drawing parallels between past and present.

As for me, I felt a deep sense of contentment. We were not just on a physical journey, but a journey of discovery—about ourselves, our histories, and the intricate web of life that connected us all. And with Holmes leading the way, I had no doubt that we would uncover the truths hidden in the shadows, much like the fog lifting to reveal the path ahead.

During the train journey, the rhythmic clatter of wheels on the tracks and the gentle sway of the carriage created a soothing backdrop to our conversation.

Adrien d'Arcy, his eyes reflecting a deep sense of pride, began to share the history of his family and their connection to Hermès.

"My great-grandfather, Étienne d'Arcy, worked closely with Thierry Hermès," Adrien began, his voice imbued with a blend of pride and nostalgia. "Together, they laid the foundations for what would become a legacy of craftsmanship. However, unlike Hermès, Maison d'Arcy remained a small, family-run operation dedicated to bespoke leather goods."

Holmes, always keen on the details, leaned in slightly. "A small operation, yet steeped in tradition. I imagine the precision and care involved in such craftsmanship are unparalleled."

Adrien nodded, his face lighting up. "Indeed. Each piece we create is a labor of love, reflecting our passion for purebred Arabian horses and English thoroughbreds with strong Arabian bloodlines. These horses have unique anatomical differences—Arabian horses, for instance, have one fewer rib and lumbar vertebra compared to other breeds. This affects the design of saddles and other equestrian accessories."

Dr Amal El-Sharif, her scholarly interests piqued, asked, "And how does this anatomical difference influence your craftsmanship?"

Adrien smiled, pleased with the question. "The shape of the saddle must accommodate the distinct curvature of the Arabian horse's back, ensuring both comfort and functionality. The headpieces, too, are designed to fit their finely chiseled bone structure. Each detail is crucial, and understanding these nuances allows us to create pieces that are not only functional but also elegant."

Holmes, with his characteristic curiosity, remarked, "The meticulous attention to detail required in your work is akin to our investigative endeavors. Both demand a profound understanding of the subject and a dedication to uncovering the underlying truths."

Dr El-Sharif then shared her own background, her voice carrying a blend of reflection and pride. "My heritage is rooted in Egypt, yet I also carry the influence of British culture. My family has ties to both Cairo and Britain, which has given me a unique perspective on cultural identity. My ancestors experienced the complexities of life within the British Empire, a history that has shaped my understanding of the world."

I listened, captivated by the depth of her reflections. "It must be fascinating to navigate between such rich cultural histories, El-Sharif. Your dual heritage must provide invaluable insights into our current investigation."

She nodded. "Indeed, Watson. Understanding the intersections of history and culture allows us to approach our quest with a broader perspective. It reminds us that our present is deeply connected to the past."

Adrien, his eyes alight with interest, added, "It's fascinating how the stories of our ancestors shape our present. The craftsmanship passed down through my family is more than a trade; it's a connection to our history and our identity."

The conversation, rich with historical insights and personal revelations, deepened the bonds among us. The landscape outside the window seemed to mirror our thoughts, each passing field and vineyard a silent testament to the rich tapestry of life. The scent of the fertile earth, the sight of the verdant vineyards stretching towards the horizon, and the distant hum of rural life created a serene backdrop for our musings.

⊷⊶⊹⊱⊷⊶

As we approached Paris, the silhouette of the Eiffel Tower, cutting a distinct figure against the setting sun, came into view. Unveiled just four years ago for the 1889 World's Fair, the tower stood as a symbol of the era's boldness and innovation.

Holmes, his gaze fixed on the structure, reflected on the significance of such a monument. "The Industrial Age has reshaped the landscape of civilization in profound ways," he observed, his tone laced with admiration and contemplation.

"The Eiffel Tower is not merely a marvel of modern engineering; it is a testament to human ingenuity and ambition, a beacon heralding the dawn of a new era."

Caught up in the anticipation of our arrival in Paris, I felt a surge of excitement at the prospect of immersing myself in the city's cultural richness. "Paris," I said, my voice filled with enthusiasm, "promises a wealth of experiences. The art, the architecture, the very spirit of the place—it's a veritable feast for the senses."

Adrien d'Arcy, however, brought a personal dimension to our journey through France. "Let me tell you about one of the most famous horses in history, Napoleon Bonaparte's white Arabian, Marengo," he began. "Marengo was bred at the El Naseri stud in Egypt and was known for his incredible endurance and loyalty. He carried Napoleon through significant battles such as Austerlitz and Waterloo."

Dr El-Sharif, her eyes reflecting a deep appreciation for history, added, "Marengo was not just a horse but a symbol of Napoleon's power and reach. After being captured by English forces at the Battle of Waterloo, he lived out his days in England, a living testament to the historical connections between our nations."

Holmes, intrigued, remarked, "A remarkable creature, indeed. It seems that Marengo, much like the Arabian horses you revere, Adrien, played a crucial role in shaping history."

Adrien nodded, his eyes alight with passion. "Absolutely, Mr. Holmes. Marengo's legacy endures, much like the traditions of horseback hunting and eventing that have been a cornerstone of country life in both France and

England. These activities have deep roots, reflecting the cultural and social fabric of our societies."

As the train neared Paris, the conversation flowed seamlessly, weaving together tales of history, tradition, and the intricate dance of human endeavor. The landscape outside the window seemed to echo our thoughts, each passing field and vineyard a silent testament to the rich tapestry of life.

Holmes, ever the pragmatist, turned his attention to the practicalities of our journey. "The French gendarmes patrolling the station reminded me of the unique challenges we face in international investigations. The interplay between different judicial systems presents both obstacles and opportunities for an investigator."

He paused, his gaze sharpening. "The French approach, with its emphasis on inquisitorial processes, contrasts sharply with the adversarial system we navigate in England. Navigating these differences will be crucial for effective collaboration across borders."

The rhythm of the train, the soft murmur of conversation, and the ever-changing scenery outside created a sense of anticipation and purpose. We were not just traveling to Paris; we were journeying deeper into the heart of a mystery that promised to challenge us in ways we had yet to imagine.

Adrien gazed out the window, the passing scenery reflecting in his eyes. "The French countryside is so rich in history. Each château, each village, has its own story. It reminds me of the countless times my family participated in grand hunts, the excitement, the camaraderie. In England, it's different, but equally compelling. The thrill of the chase, the community gathering, it's all about the spirit of the hunt."

Dr El-Sharif added, "It's not just the landscape that changes, but the way people interact with it. The traditions, the respect for the land and its history, it's all interconnected."

Holmes, absorbing their reflections, remarked, "And it is in these interconnections that we often find the most valuable clues. Just as in hunting, where understanding the terrain and the habits of the prey is crucial, so too in our investigation, where understanding the cultural and historical context can lead us to the truth."

As the sun dipped lower in the sky, casting long shadows across the landscape, we settled into a comfortable silence, each lost in our own thoughts. The journey ahead was filled with uncertainties, but one thing was clear: together, we would face whatever lay in store, drawing strength from our shared resolve and the bonds we had forged.

The gentle sway of the train, the rhythmic clatter of the tracks, and the warm glow of the setting sun created an almost hypnotic ambiance. Holmes, ever vigilant, continued to make notes and observations, while I recorded our journey, capturing the essence of our experiences and the richness of the conversations that had unfolded.

Adrien, with a newfound sense of calm, leaned back and closed his eyes, no doubt envisioning the hunts of his ancestors and the legacy they had passed down. Dr El-Sharif, always the scholar, perused a book on ancient civilizations, drawing parallels between past and present.

As for me, I felt a deep sense of contentment. We were not just on a physical journey, but a journey of discovery—about ourselves, our histories, and the intricate web of life that connected us all. And with Holmes leading the way, I had no doubt that we would uncover the truths hidden in the shadows, much like the fog lifting to reveal the path ahead.

The train's whistle echoed through the air as we approached Paris, the City of Light. The sun had dipped below the horizon, casting a golden glow that bathed the urban landscape in an ethereal light. As the train slowed to a halt, the vibrant energy of Paris contrasted sharply with the quiet introspection of our journey.

Stepping onto the platform, we were immediately enveloped by the city's unique blend of sounds and scents—the distant strains of an accordion, the rich aroma of freshly baked bread, and the murmur of conversations in rapid French. Paris was alive, a bustling tapestry of human endeavor and cultural richness.

Holmes, ever the observer, turned his gaze towards the skyline, where the Eiffel Tower stood tall and proud. "The Eiffel Tower," he remarked, his voice tinged with a rare note of admiration, "a marvel of modern engineering. Constructed for the 1889 World's Fair, it stands as a symbol of human ingenuity and the dawn of a new age."

I followed his gaze, marveling at the iron structure that seemed to pierce the sky. "It's remarkable," I said. "A testament to how far we've come and a beacon of the possibilities that lie ahead."

Adrien d'Arcy, ever the romantic, added, "Paris has a way of captivating the soul. The juxtaposition of its historical grandeur with modern innovation creates an ambiance unlike any other city."

Dr Amal El-Sharif, her eyes reflecting the city's lights, spoke thoughtfully. "The history here is palpable. Every street, every building tells a story. It's a reminder that while we forge ahead into the future, we are always connected to the past."

As we navigated the bustling station, the realization that our journey had only just begun settled over us. The mysteries of the Obsidian Guild awaited, and with them, the promise of adventure and discovery.

Holmes, his eyes gleaming with determination, addressed us. "Our time in

Paris is brief. We must board the Orient Express swiftly and continue our journey to Constantinople. The Obsidian Guild's secrets are still shrouded in mystery, and it is up to us to uncover them."

I nodded, feeling the familiar thrill of the chase. "Indeed, Holmes. The game is afoot, and we are ready to pursue it to its end."

Adrien, his earlier nervousness about the sea voyage now a distant memory, stood tall and resolute. "Whatever challenges lie ahead, we face them together. The legacy of the past and the promise of the future guide our steps."

Dr El-Sharif, her scholarly curiosity piqued, added, "Every clue, every piece of history we uncover brings us closer to understanding the full picture. I am ready to delve into the depths of this mystery."

The Orient Express, a symbol of luxury and elegance, awaited us at the station. Its polished carriages gleamed under the station lights, promising a journey of comfort and intrigue. As we boarded, the sumptuous interiors greeted us with rich mahogany panels, plush seating, and an air of opulence, setting the stage for our preparation and anticipation of the challenges ahead.

Holmes, ever the leader, set a brisk pace. "We have much to do and little time to do it in. Let us settle into our compartments and prepare for the tasks ahead. Paris is but a fleeting stop, and the real journey lies ahead."

Holmes, his eyes gleaming with a rare intensity, continued to guide us with unwavering determination. "Our brief passage through Paris is but a waypoint. The true heart of our mission lies ahead in Constantinople."

Adrien, his voice full of renewed confidence, said, "Paris has always been a city of inspiration and innovation. Even in our short stopover, it leaves a mark on our spirits."

Dr El-Sharif, her scholarly demeanor unshaken, added, "Paris is indeed a marvel, but our true quest lies in uncovering the secrets that await us further along our journey. We must stay focused on Constantinople and the mysteries that lie therein."

As the train began to move, the lights of Paris slowly faded into the distance, replaced by the gentle sway of the Orient Express and the promise of new adventures. The vibrancy of Paris had infused us with a sense of purpose and determination. The mysteries that lay ahead were daunting, but with Holmes leading the way, and the strength of our collective resolve, we were prepared to face whatever challenges awaited us.

The Orient Express, with its rich tapestry of history and culture, promised not only to be a vessel for our travels but also a source of endless inspiration. Together, we would navigate its complexities, unravel its secrets, and bring to light the truths hidden in the shadows.

Our adventure from Paris was just beginning, and as we moved through the vibrant city, the sense of anticipation and purpose grew within us. The challenges ahead would test our resolve, but together, we were ready to face whatever came our way, guided by the light of discovery and the spirit of inquiry that had brought us this far.

CHAPTER 12

THROUGH THE GATES OF THE EAST

W ith a gentle lurch, the Orient Express began its journey, leaving behind the grandeur of Paris, now softly bathed in the dawning light. Sherlock Holmes, his eyes pensive and his mind already buzzing with the possibilities of the day, positioned himself comfortably by the window, allowing the changing landscape to occupy his ever-analytical mind.

"The French countryside," Holmes began, his voice a soft baritone that seemed to harmonise with the rhythmic chug of the train, "is much like a well-composed symphony. Every vineyard, every field we pass, meticulously arranged and tended, mirrors the intricate webs of intrigue in which we often find ourselves entangled. The winemaker, with his careful planning and precise execution, is not unlike the detective, sifting through the chaos to find order, meaning in the seemingly mundane".

Sitting opposite Holmes, I was drawn to the poetic serenity of the landscape that unfolded beyond our compartment. The dawn light bathed the world in a soft golden hue, transforming the countryside into a living canvas. The scent of fresh earth and blooming flowers wafted in through the slightly open window, mingling with the rich aroma of the train's polished wood and leather interiors. "There is a profound beauty in the tranquillity of these scenes," I mused aloud, my hand moving almost instinctively to jot down thoughts in my journal. "The rolling hills, the fields bathed in the early morning light - it's as if we've been transported to another realm, far from the misty streets and relentless pace of London."

Holmes nodded, his eyes still fixed on the passing scenery. "Indeed, Watson. There is a certain clarity that comes with distance, a perspective that reveals patterns obscured by the immediacy of city life."

As the train meandered towards Strasbourg, we found ourselves enveloped in a tapestry of conversation, weaving together observations, personal reflections and academic insights. Adrien d'Arcy, whose lineage is deeply rooted in the equestrian and artisanal traditions of France, shared anecdotes about his ancestors, whose legacy is intimately tied to the soil and soul of the French countryside.

"My family," said Adrien with a mixture of reverence and pride, "has always had a deep attachment to the land, to the horses that roam our estates, and to the craftsmanship that is as much a part of our heritage as our name. The vineyards we see, the precise organisation of the fields, all reflect a commitment to excellence, a respect for tradition that guides us like the North Star".

Holmes, always keen to delve into the intricacies of human nature, remarked: "And it is this dedication to tradition, Mr d'Arcy, that often serves as the foundation for great achievement. But it is also a double-edged sword, for it can bind us to the past and blind us to the possibilities of the future. A delicate balance, wouldn't you say?"

He paused, his eyes distant with memory. "I remember a particular saddle my great-grandfather made for a famous French cavalry officer. It was during the Napoleonic Wars. This officer, a trusted aide of Napoleon, relied on this saddle during many campaigns. The craftsmanship was so superior that it became legendary among his peers, a symbol of both functionality and artistry".

Dr Amal El-Sharif, whose keen intellect and vast knowledge of history added depth to our discourse, provided context to the landscape we were passing through. "The regions we pass through," she remarked, her voice carrying the weight of countless stories, "are not only geographical landmarks, but historical touchstones. Every town, every vineyard has played a part in the tapestry of European history, from ancient Gallic settlements to key battlegrounds in wars. The beauty we see is underpinned by a rich, often turbulent history that has shaped the character of this land and its people".

Amal also reflected on the significance of the Orient Express itself. "This train," she remarked, a note of awe in her voice, "is a symbol of luxury and a marvel of engineering, connecting Europe in a way that reflects our intertwined histories. It is a bridge between cultures, just as our conversations weave together the threads of our diverse backgrounds.

The rhythmic clatter of the train on the tracks seemed to synchronise with our heartbeat, a steady pulse propelling us forward. Holmes, ever observant, glanced at his companions. "This train, much like our investigation, is a conduit. It moves us not only through space, but through time and culture, uncovering layers of human experience."

Adrien leaned back, his gaze pensive. "There is a certain romance in travel, especially by train. It allows for reflection, for the soul to wander even as the body remains confined within these walls."

As the Orient Express continued its journey, the dialogue between us - rich with historical nuance, personal insight and the keen observations of Holmes - transformed the journey from Paris to Strasbourg into a journey through time, a contemplation of the human condition and a celebration of the enduring beauty of the French countryside. The landscape, with its verdant fields and meticulously tended vineyards, served as both a backdrop and a catalyst for the deepening bond between us, each bringing our unique perspective to a shared adventure that was only just beginning.

The train's steady progress towards Strasbourg symbolised not only a physical movement across the geography of France, but also a journey into the heart of the mysteries that lay ahead, the landscapes outside our window a metaphor for the layers of history, culture and intrigue we were about to unravel.

Holmes turned to me, his eyes bright with the thrill of the chase. "Watson, notice how the landscape unfolds before us like the pages of a book. Every field, every village, is a chapter in the history of this land. And it is in these stories that we shall find the clues to unravel our own mystery."

⎯⎯⋇⦿⋇⎯⎯

As the Orient Express settled into its rhythm, the morning light illuminating the French countryside, our conversations turned to the many facets of life and history. Adrien d'Arcy, with his characteristic blend of enthusiasm and erudition, picked up where he had left off on our previous journey from London to Dover.

"Continuing our discussion of tugs," Adrien began, his eyes twinkling with the light of shared knowledge, "it is remarkable to consider how indispensable these animals were to the canals of industrial London. Their strength and endurance were the lifeblood of commerce, hauling immense loads along the waterways."

Watson, ever the curious listener, leaned forward. "Yes, Adrien, your insights so far have been quite enlightening. I had never fully appreciated the extent of their contribution to our economy."

Adrien nodded. "Indeed, the canals were the arteries of industrial London, and the horses played a central role. It's a vivid reminder of how closely our progress was intertwined with these noble creatures."

Holmes, seated by the window, allowed a brief smile to touch his lips before his familiar air of detached amusement returned. "Ah, romanticising beasts of burden again, Adrien? You would think these horses were the saviours of the industrial age rather than mere labourers."

Adrien chuckled. "Perhaps it is a romantic notion, Holmes, but it's one based on the reality of their contributions. Without them the pace of industrialisation

165

would have been much slower."

Holmes raised an eyebrow, his voice tinged with sarcasm. "And yet, with the advent of steam power, these draught horses were rendered obsolete. The very Industrial Revolution that they made possible eventually did away with them. Such is the chaotic march of progress.

Dr Amal El-Sharif, ever the scholar, joined the discussion. "The Industrial Revolution brought about profound changes, transforming societies and economies at an unprecedented rate. It was a time of both great progress and significant upheaval, affecting every aspect of life."

Holmes interrupted, his tone sharper. "Indeed, Amal. The steam engine, the so-called 'iron horse', replaced many traditional practices, for better and for worse. It revolutionised transport and industry, but also displaced countless workers and changed the landscape of towns and countryside alike."

As the train wound its way towards Strasbourg, Watson and Adrien found a moment to discuss their favourite places in Paris, the city they had recently left.

"Paris has a charm like no other," said Watson, his eyes reflecting fond memories. "The gardens of Luxembourg, the serene beauty of the Seine at dusk... there's a magic to it."

Adrien smiled, sharing the sentiment. "For me, it's the Marais, with its mix of history and vibrancy. And, of course, the great equestrian statues that dot the city, a nod to its storied past."

Their conversation was briefly interrupted by the breathtaking view of the Rhine, its waters glistening in the morning sun. Seizing the moment, Holmes turned the discussion to the historical significance of their surroundings.

"The Rhine," he gestured towards the window, "is more than a geographical landmark. It's a ribbon of history, a silent observer of the ebb and flow of human ambition and conflict. Through the ages it has been a strategic artery, coveted and contested by empires and nations. Its banks tell tales of alliances forged and battles fought - a fluid testament to the ceaseless struggle for power and dominance".

Inspired by Holmes' reflections and the stirring scenery, Watson found himself pondering the parallels between the river's history and his own quest. "It's fascinating," he mused, his eyes fixed on the flowing waters of the Rhine, "how the course of a river can so closely mirror the course of human events. The Rhine has been a lifeline, a barrier, a battleground - much as the streets of London have been for us. In our quest to unravel mysteries and confront adversaries, we too navigate a landscape marked by conflict and alliance, by shadow and light".

Adrien d'Arcy, intrigued by the architectural discourse, added his own observations. "The Gothic structures, with their soaring spires and stained glass, evoke a sense of awe and reverence. It's a powerful reminder of how beauty and spirituality can be intertwined, how artistry and faith can elevate the human spirit".

Dr Amal El-Sharif, ever the scholar, provided the historical context for the conversation. "The regions we are traversing were once the heart of the Holy Roman Empire, an empire where politics and religion were deeply intertwined. The Gothic cathedrals we admire were not only places of worship, but also symbols of power and prestige. They stood as beacons of divine and earthly authority, reflecting the complex interplay between the sacred and the secular".

The steady rhythm of the train, the passing landscapes and the rich tapestry of conversation in our compartment created a moment suspended in time - a shared journey not only through the heart of Europe but also into the depths of history, thought and the enduring search for meaning that defines the human condition.

As the Orient Express crossed the border from France into Germany, the change in the landscape was both immediate and profound. The train, a silver serpent winding its way through the heart of Europe, carried us into a terrain rich in history and architectural grandeur. The transition from the pastoral elegance of the French countryside to the imposing majesty of German Gothic architecture marked a new chapter in our journey, both literally and figuratively.

Sherlock Holmes, ever observant, was the first to articulate the change. Leaning slightly forward in his seat, his gaze swept over the evolving landscape, capturing every detail. "Observe the pointed arches and intricate facades," he began, his voice carrying the excitement of discovery. "Every building we pass is a testament to the Gothic architecture that flourished here in the Middle Ages. But it's more than just aesthetics. This architectural choice, with its emphasis on verticality and the interplay of light and shadow, reflects the human aspiration towards the divine, towards something transcendent. It's an architectural manifestation of the human condition - a constant striving for heights beyond our reach.

Holmes paused, allowing us to absorb the weight of his words. The train continued its steady progress, skirting the banks of the Rhine, a river that had witnessed centuries of human history.

"The Rhine," Sherlock continued, gesturing towards the window as the mighty river came into view, "is more than a geographical landmark. It's a ribbon of history, a silent observer of the ebb and flow of human ambition and conflict. Through the ages it has been a strategic artery, coveted and contested by empires and nations. Its banks tell tales of alliances forged and battles fought - a fluid testament to the ceaseless struggle for power and dominance".

Inspired by Holmes' reflection and the stirring scenery, I found myself reflecting on the parallels between the river's history and our own aspirations.

"It's fascinating," I mused, my eyes fixed on the flowing waters of the Rhine, "how the course of a river can so closely mirror the course of human events. The Rhine has been a lifeline, a barrier, a battleground - much as the streets of London have been for us. In our quest to unravel mysteries and confront adversaries, we too navigate a landscape marked by conflict and alliance, by shadow and light".

Adrien d'Arcy, intrigued by the architectural discourse, added his own observations. "The Gothic structures, with their soaring spires and stained glass, evoke a sense of awe and reverence. It's a powerful reminder of how beauty and spirituality can be intertwined, how artistry and faith can elevate the human spirit".

Dr Amal El-Sharif, ever the scholar, provided the historical context for the conversation. "The regions we are traversing were once the heart of the Holy Roman Empire, an empire where politics and religion were deeply intertwined. The Gothic cathedrals we admire were not only places of worship, but also symbols of power and prestige. They stood as beacons of divine and earthly authority, reflecting the complex interplay between the sacred and the secular".

Holmes nodded in acknowledgement of her insights, but remained detached from the emotional reverence. "It is remarkable," he said, "how humanity's desire for power and control often manifests itself in such grandiose forms. But beneath the surface, these structures are just another layer in the ever-changing landscape of human ambition".

Sensing an opportunity to delve deeper into history, Adrien told a story about medieval knights and their horses. "In the Middle Ages," he began, "knights relied heavily on their horses, not only for battle, but also for travel and status. Horses were trained for endurance and strength, allowing knights to cross treacherous terrain, much like the Alps we will soon encounter."

Amal added: "Indeed, the symbolism of knights and their horses extends to our current investigation. The horse represents loyalty, strength and strategic advantage, much like the key elements we are trying to uncover in our quest".

As the Orient Express approached Munich, our dialogue deepened, weaving together threads of architecture, history and philosophy. The journey from Strasbourg to Munich had become more than a mere passage through geographical space; it was an intellectual and spiritual pilgrimage through the annals of European culture. The landscape outside our window, with its Gothic spires piercing the sky and the timeless flow of the Rhine, served as both canvas and catalyst for a profound exploration of the many facets of human endeavour.

The steady rhythm of the train, the passing landscapes and the rich tapestry of conversation in our compartment created a moment suspended in time - a shared journey not only through the heart of Europe, but also into the depths of history, thought and the enduring search for meaning that defines the human condition.

As the train rolled into Munich, the majestic silhouette of the Alps began to emerge in the distance, their snow-capped peaks gleaming under the brightening sky. Conversation naturally turned to the formidable mountains and their historical significance.

"The Alps," Holmes remarked, his eyes fixed on the horizon, "have always been both a barrier and a gateway. Their imposing presence has shaped the destinies of countless civilisations, serving as both protection and formidable obstacle."

Adrien nodded, eager to share his knowledge. "Hannibal's crossing of the Alps in 218 BC is one of the most famous examples. Using elephants and horses, he managed to cross the treacherous terrain, outmanoeuvring the Romans and demonstrating the strategic importance of understanding and exploiting the natural landscape."

Dr Amal El-Sharif, always insightful, added: "The Alps have witnessed numerous such crossings, each underlining the resilience and ingenuity required to conquer these natural fortresses. The Roman legions also used specialised breeds of horses, prized for their endurance and agility, to cross these heights".

Reflecting on his own military experience, Watson said: "In Afghanistan, understanding the terrain was vital. Horses were indispensable there, much as they were in Hannibal's time. Their ability to navigate rugged landscapes made them invaluable in both ancient and modern military strategies".

Adrien shared another anecdote about Hannibal's clever use of horses to deceive the Roman army. "Hannibal used decoy fires to trick the Romans into thinking his troops were still encamped while he moved his troops through another pass. The silence and sure-footedness of the horses were crucial to this daring manoeuvre, highlighting the strategic role of the horse in history".

Holmes, with a rare hint of admiration, commented: "Hannibal's tactical genius is indeed commendable. It underlines the importance of adaptability and strategic thinking, qualities that we must employ in our current investigation".

As the train continued its journey towards Munich, the conversation flowed seamlessly from historical reflection to personal anecdote, each adding a layer of depth to our understanding of the landscape and its significance. The Alps, with their towering presence, served as a poignant reminder of the enduring interplay between nature and human ambition.

As we approached Munich, the blend of historical insight and personal reflection had transformed our journey into a tapestry of shared knowledge and experience. The landscape outside, with its breathtaking vistas and historical echoes, was not just a backdrop but a living testament to the resilience and ingenuity of those who had walked it before us.

As the Orient Express left the vibrant city of Munich, the journey to Vienna unfolded like a meticulously crafted symphony, each passing landscape a note in an ever-evolving musical masterpiece. The train, a marvel of engineering and luxury, glided through the Bavarian countryside, approaching the Austrian border. The anticipation in the opulent carriage was palpable, a shared excitement at the cultural and historical riches that lay ahead.

Sherlock Holmes, seated at the window with an air of contemplative concentration, broke the silence as the first distant glimpses of the Alps pierced the horizon. "Think of the Alps," he began, his voice carrying a depth of thought, "not merely as geographical wonders, but as historical sentinels. These mountains have served as both shield and barrier, influencing the tides of human history. They've witnessed the advance of legions, the retreat of empires and the silent passage of countless nameless souls seeking passage or refuge".

Adrien d'Arcy, caught in Holmes' reflection, leaned forward, his gaze following the detective's. "Indeed, Holmes, the Alps are more than mere mountains. They are guardians of history, keepers of secrets. In their shadow countless tales of bravery, tragedy and triumph have unfolded. Their peaks, shrouded in snow and mystery, have dictated the ebb and flow of cultures and commerce for centuries".

Dr Amal El-Sharif, her scholarly mind fascinated by the discussion, added: "And let us not forget the strategic importance of these natural fortresses. The Alps have been a decisive factor in military campaigns, a natural defence that has reshaped the strategies of generals and the borders of nations. Their geological majesty is matched only by their impact on human endeavour, serving as a stark reminder of nature's enduring influence on the course of history".

As the train wound its way through the foothills, I was captivated by the sublime beauty of the alpine landscape. The crisp air, tinged with the faint scent of pine, flowed through the slightly open windows. The distant peaks, adorned with a delicate veil of snow, seemed to whisper ancient secrets to those who listened. "There is a certain transcendence in these landscapes," I remarked, my eyes reflecting the awe-inspiring view. "One cannot look at these towering peaks without feeling a rush of inspiration. It's no wonder that this land gave birth to composers like Mozart and Beethoven. The very air seems imbued with creativity, every breath a muse calling forth the heights of human expression".

The conversation, rich in historical insight and philosophical depth, mirrored the journey itself - a passage through time, nature and the nature of human endeavour. As the Orient Express approached the Austrian border, the silhouette of the Alps looming in the distance, we contemplated the layers of history, culture and artistry that these mountains had witnessed. The train's steady progress towards Vienna symbolised not just a physical journey, but a journey through the annals of European civilisation, where each mountain pass held the echoes of ancient paths trodden by seekers and dreamers, warriors and scholars.

As we approached Vienna, Adrien d'Arcy's eyes lit up with a distinct glow of nostalgia and excitement. "Vienna," he began, "is home to the famous Spanish Riding School and its magnificent Lipizzaner stallions. I remember attending a performance as a child, mesmerised by the grace and precision of these horses. The art of dressage practised there is not just a sport, but a form of high art, cultivated over centuries".

Holmes, ever pragmatic, chimed in with a dry observation. "A magnificent display, no doubt, though one might question the practicality of such traditions in our modern world. A dance of horses, admirable for its beauty, but perhaps a little removed from the necessities of everyday life."

Adrien smiled, unfazed by Holmes' sardonic tone. "True, but these traditions are more than mere performances. They are a testament to our heritage, a living link to our past. The Lipizzaner stallions represent the pinnacle of equestrian breeding and training, embodying centuries of dedication to the craft. I remember the performance vividly. The movements of the horses, synchronised with the music, seemed almost otherworldly. It was a ballet of power and grace, a dance that told a story of discipline, harmony and the deep bond between horse and rider.

Dr Amal El-Sharif added: "The Spanish Riding School is also a symbol of the grandeur of the Austro-Hungarian Empire. It reflects the Empire's investment in culture and the arts, as well as its complex political landscape. Vienna itself is a city where music, art and science flourished, often intertwined with the machinations of power.

Holmes, with a rare hint of admiration, commented: "Indeed, the political manoeuvring within the Austro-Hungarian Empire was akin to a grand game of chess, each move meticulously planned to secure power and influence. Such complexity is not unlike the cases we pursue, where every clue and every action can determine the outcome".

As the train approached Vienna, I told an anecdote about my time in Afghanistan. The memory seemed to cast a shadow over my otherwise cheerful demeanour. "In the rugged terrain of Afghanistan, horses were indispensable. I remember one mission where, despite the harsh conditions, our cavalry units navigated the mountainous terrain with remarkable agility. Their ability to adapt to the environment was crucial, as was the historical significance of horses in crossing difficult terrain such as the Alps. One particular mission stands out - our unit was tasked with reaching a remote village to deliver supplies. The road was treacherous, narrow and winding. We couldn't have done it without the horses. Their sure-footedness and resilience were a testament to their training and our dependence on them.

Adrien nodded in recognition. "Horses have indeed been vital across different terrains and eras. Hannibal's clever use of horses to deceive the Roman army is a prime example. He used decoy fires to trick the Romans into thinking his forces were still encamped while he moved his troops through another pass. The silence and sure-footedness of the horses were crucial to this daring manoeuvre".

As the train continued its journey towards Vienna, the conversation flowed seamlessly from historical reflection to personal anecdote, each adding a layer of depth to our understanding of the landscape and its significance. The anticipation of arriving in Vienna, a city synonymous with musical brilliance and architectural splendour, added a palpable excitement to our conversation.

The promise of walking the same streets as some of the world's greatest composers and artists, of experiencing the cultural heartbeat of a city that had been a crossroads of empires and ideas, lent an air of eager expectation to our journey. As the Orient Express entered Austria, the majestic backdrop of the Alps gave way to softer landscapes, heralding our approach to Vienna. The journey from Munich to Vienna, set against the grandeur of the Alps and enriched by our varied experiences, had been a journey through layers of human history and natural wonder - a prelude to the wonders that awaited us in the heart of Austria.

As the Orient Express pulled out of the imperial grandeur of Vienna and began its journey towards Budapest, the mood among Sherlock Holmes, Adrien d'Arcy, Dr Amal El-Sharif and myself was one of quiet introspection mixed with eager anticipation of the discoveries that lay ahead. The train, a symbol of human ingenuity and a vessel for the curious and bold, steamed through the lush landscapes that were once the heartland of the Austro-Hungarian Empire.

The rhythmic chug of the locomotive seemed to harmonise with the tranquil landscape outside, creating a sense of serene progress. Vibrant green fields stretched to the horizon, punctuated by picturesque villages and the occasional spire of a distant church. The gentle rocking of the carriage lulled us into a contemplative silence, broken only by the occasional murmur of conversation.

Sherlock Holmes, ever the observer, was the first to articulate the thoughts that had been brewing in his mind. His gaze, penetrating and analytical, shifted from the landscape outside to his companions in the luxurious confines of our carriage. "Consider the Austro-Hungarian Empire," he began, his voice carrying the weight of contemplation. "A mosaic of cultures, languages and ethnicities, united under a single crown. Yet beneath the veneer of unity, a web of tensions, loyalties and conflicts simmered, threatening at any moment to unravel the fabric of the empire."

Dr Amal El-Sharif, her interest piqued by Holmes' comparison, leaned forward. "Indeed, Holmes. The Empire was a microcosm of the wider human condition - diverse, complex and often contradictory. Its capitals, Vienna and Budapest, stood as beacons of culture and progress, but the empire was also a battleground for the struggle for identity and autonomy among its myriad peoples."

The carriage fell silent for a moment, each of us lost in thought. The landscape outside began to change, the rolling hills giving way to more rugged terrain as we approached the Hungarian border. The sky, a canvas of soft blues and whites, seemed to reflect the historical weight of the land we were crossing.

Adrien d'Arcy, his gaze pensive, added: "The dual monarchy was an attempt to balance the competing demands of its constituent parts, much as a skilled horseman strives to maintain harmony between rider and horse. But as history has shown us, the balance was precarious, a constant negotiation of power and influence".

Reflecting on the lives of those who lived in the shadow of the Empire, I mused: "Imagine the stories that unfolded within this vast domain. Tales of love and loss, of ambition and despair, set against the backdrop of palaces and peasant huts alike. The empire was a stage on which the drama of human life in all its varied forms was played out.

As the train wound its way through the picturesque landscapes that once bore witness to the complexities of imperial rule, our conversation deepened. We discussed the legacy of the Austro-Hungarian Empire, its contributions to art, music and science, and the nationalist movements that eventually led to its dissolution.

Holmes, always adept at drawing parallels, remarked: "The task of uncovering truths, of solving mysteries, is not unlike navigating the intricate web of alliances and enmities that characterised the Empire. One has to look beyond the surface, to discern the hidden connections and underlying motives that drive events".

Adrien, inspired by the comparison, said: "Equestrian skill, much like political balance, requires a harmonious relationship between rider and horse. The slightest discord can lead to failure. The history of the Empire is a testament to the delicate balance required to maintain such a vast and diverse entity.

The conversation took on a more personal note when I shared a memory from my time in Afghanistan. The rugged terrain outside the window reminded me of the harsh landscapes I had once navigated. "There was a mission where our cavalry units relied heavily on horses to navigate the mountainous regions. The terrain was unforgiving, much like the political landscape of the Austro-Hungarian Empire. The endurance of the horses and our strategic use of them was crucial to our success. It reminds me that understanding and adapting to the terrain, both physical and political, is vital in any endeavour.

Dr El-Sharif, with her characteristic enthusiasm for cultural exchange, added: "Vienna and Budapest, despite their political tensions, have significantly influenced each other's art, cuisine and scientific achievements. The movement of ideas and innovations between these cities has enriched both and created a vibrant cultural landscape that we continue to cherish today".

As Budapest approached, the anticipation in our coach grew. The city, with its storied history and architectural splendour, promised a new chapter in our journey. But the discussions that had taken place among us had given our approach to the Hungarian capital a deeper meaning. Budapest was not just a destination; it was a symbol of the enduring human spirit, of resilience and creativity in the face of adversity.

So the journey from Vienna to Budapest was more than a physical traversal of space. It was an exploration of the human condition, a reflection on the complexities of history and culture, and a testament to the power of dialogue and discovery. As the Orient Express pulled into the station, Sherlock Holmes, Adrien d'Arcy, Dr Amal El-Sharif and I stepped off the train, not just as travellers, but as witnesses to the rich tapestry of human experience that had unfolded along the banks of the Danube.

The setting sun cast a warm glow over Budapest, its golden hues reflecting off the waters of the Danube. The city, vibrant and alive, seemed to welcome us with open arms. The scent of freshly baked pastries wafted through the air, mingled with the distant strains of a violin playing a hauntingly beautiful melody. The sounds, sights and smells of Budapest enveloped us, promising new adventures and discoveries in this historic and culturally rich city.

⊰⊹⊱

As the Orient Express glided out of Budapest, the silhouette of the city's magnificent architecture gradually faded into the Hungarian countryside. The journey from Budapest to Belgrade, a passage that followed the meandering course of the blue Danube, provided a moment of respite and reflection for Sherlock Holmes, Adrien d'Arcy, Dr Amal El-Sharif and myself. The train, a vessel of luxury and history, served as our cocoon as we plunged deeper into the heart of the Balkans.

Holmes, his gaze fixed on the flowing waters of the Danube, began to articulate his thoughts, each word measured and deliberate. "Consider the Danube," he mused, his voice a low murmur against the steady rhythm of the train, "a river that has served as a conduit for ideas, goods and, on occasion, less savoury transactions. Its banks have witnessed the ebb and flow of civilisations, the ambitions of empires and the resilience of the communities that call it home. The river, in its quiet majesty, is a testament to the endurance of nature amidst the vagaries of human endeavour".

The scent of fertile soil and fresh vegetation permeated the air as the landscape outside transformed from urban sprawl to lush, rolling hills. The waters of the Danube glistened in the midday sun, reflecting the vibrant green of the surrounding countryside.

Dr Amal El-Sharif, intrigued by Holmes's philosophical musings, added her perspective, her voice a harmonious blend of curiosity and insight. "The Danube, transcending borders and cultures, is a symbol of connectivity in a region marked by division. It is a reminder of our common humanity, of the thread that binds us together despite the myriad differences that seek to divide us. This river, in its relentless journey to the sea, embodies the indomitable spirit of progress and the perpetual quest for understanding that defines our species".

Adrien d'Arcy, whose family roots are intertwined with the equestrian traditions of France, found a different kind of resonance in the landscape. "The banks of the Danube, with their green expanses and the occasional sight of a lone rider or a herd of horses, speak of a harmony between man and nature that is becoming increasingly rare. It reminds me of the pastoral beauty of my family's estate, of a time when the rhythm of life was dictated not by the machinations of industry but by the more elemental cadences of earth and sky".

The rhythmic clatter of the train on the tracks underscored our reflections, a steady heartbeat carrying us through time and space. Holmes, always an observer of human character and the natural world, saw in the river's journey a metaphor for the adventures we had undertaken. "The Danube," he said, his eyes fixed on the flowing water, "with its calm flow and the occasional tumult of its rapids, mirrors the vicissitudes of our own experiences. Just as the river navigates the landscape, shaping it and being shaped by it, so we navigate the landscape of human affairs, our path alternately smooth and fraught with obstacles. It is a reminder of the enduring beauty of the world and the transient nature of our struggles and triumphs.

Adrien continued in a thoughtful voice. "Did you know that the influence of Ottoman horse breeds significantly shaped the European cavalry? The Danube region played a key role in this exchange. Known for their endurance and agility, Ottoman horses were highly prized and often integrated into European breeding programmes. This cultural and biological exchange enriched the cavalry traditions of many European nations".

Amal leaned forward, her eyes bright with scholarly enthusiasm. "The movement of these horses along the Danube routes facilitated not only military prowess, but also cultural exchange. Techniques of horse breeding, riding and even veterinary practice were shared and refined. It is a testament to the interconnectedness of our histories."

Holmes, keen to draw connections to our journey today, reflected: "The river's role in shaping trade routes and military campaigns is undeniable. Its waters have carried armies, merchants and diplomats. Understanding the geographical and historical context of our journey is crucial. It is this context that often holds the key to unlocking the mysteries that confront us.

As the Orient Express continued its journey towards Belgrade, the conversations became richer, weaving together threads of history, philosophy and personal reflection. The train, with its rhythmic clacking and humming, provided a backdrop to our dialogue, a moving stage on which the drama of intellectual exploration unfolded.

The landscape outside our window shifted from the cultivated fields of Hungary to the rugged, untamed beauty of the Balkans. Towering cliffs and dense forests flanked the river, their shadows dancing on the surface. The air grew cooler, carrying with it the scent of pine and the promise of adventure.

"The Danube," I thought, "is not just a river, it is a lifeline that runs through the heart of Europe. It has seen the rise and fall of empires, the forging of alliances and the march of armies. Much like our journey, it is both a path and a boundary, a source of sustenance and a site of conflict".

By the time the spires and domes of Belgrade came into view, we had crossed not only geographical distances, but the vast expanse of contemplation and comradeship. The journey on the Orient Express, with its luxurious confines and the ever-changing landscapes that unfolded beyond its windows, offered a rare space for reflection, a reminder of the indelible link between the natural world and the labyrinth of human endeavour.

As we stepped off the train in Belgrade, the air was filled with the rich aroma of roasted chestnuts and the distant hum of the bustling city. We were not just travellers moving through space; we were explorers delving into the depths of history and the human spirit, each step bringing us closer to the heart of our shared adventure.

⚜

As the Orient Express pulled out of Belgrade, the landscape began to change, transforming into the rugged terrain of the Balkans. The train, a symbol of human achievement and connectivity, seemed almost to whisper secrets of antiquity as it wound its way through the mountains and valleys that had been silent witnesses to centuries of human history. The journey to Sofia promised not only a change of scenery, but also a deeper exploration of the complexities of human nature and the indomitable spirit of the local people.

The air grew cooler as the train climbed through the mountainous terrain, the scent of pine mingled with the distant aroma of wood smoke from scattered villages. The rhythmic clatter of the train on the tracks provided a soothing backdrop to our reflections.

Sherlock Holmes, his keen eyes observing the changing landscape, struck up a conversation that seemed to echo the mood of the surroundings. "The Balkans," he began, his voice reflective, "present us with a landscape as complex

176

and turbulent as the history it has witnessed. It's a region where the beauty of nature collides with the harsh realities of human conflict, where the struggle for identity and autonomy has painted the hills with the stories of past wars".

I, always sensitive to the human element in our observations, added: "It's remarkable, Holmes, how the resilience of the local population shines through despite the adversity they've faced. Their lives, like the terrain itself, are a testament to the endurance of the human spirit against the elemental forces of nature and the machinations of power. It provides a poignant backdrop against which to contemplate the human condition - a struggle against both the internal and external forces that shape our destiny".

Adrien d'Arcy, whose upbringing had instilled in him an appreciation of the land and its stories, shared his perspective. "Travelling through the Balkans, one cannot help but feel a deep connection to the land and its people. Every mountain, every valley tells a story of survival and resilience. It's a reminder of how our lives are intertwined with the land, how our stories are etched into the very soil we walk on. The raw beauty of this place, with its rugged landscapes, speaks of a primal connection to the earth that modern life often obscures".

As the train climbed steadily through the mountains, we were treated to breathtaking views. Forests covered the slopes, interspersed with clearings where small villages nestled, their red-tiled roofs standing out against the green backdrop. The occasional sound of a distant waterfall reached our ears, adding to the symphony of nature that surrounded us.

Dr Amal El-Sharif, always keen to delve into the historical and cultural layers of our journey, offered an insight into the wider implications of our observations. "The history of the Balkans is a vivid illustration of the complexity of human identity and the often arbitrary nature of borders. The region's turbulent past, marked by shifting allegiances and the struggle for national identity, reflects the unpredictability of human nature that Holmes often speaks of. It's a powerful reminder of how history, culture and geography come together to shape the narrative of a region and its people.

Adrien then told a story that captured our imagination, his voice rich with the cadence of storytelling. "There is a legend in these parts about a horse called Šarac, which belonged to the great Serbian hero Marko Kraljević. Šarac was not just a horse, but a companion, a symbol of strength and loyalty. Together they faced many trials and battles. The story goes that Šarac was so intelligent and loyal that he understood Marko's words and intentions without needing to be commanded. It illustrates the deep bond between man and horse, a bond that transcends mere utility".

As he spoke, the train was passing through a dense forest, the trees casting mottled shadows across the tracks. The play of light and shadow seemed to echo the themes of our conversation, highlighting the contrasts and complexities of the region's history and landscape.

Holmes, though typically aloof, showed a moment of genuine curiosity about the local customs and traditions. "Such stories, though often romanticised, provide valuable insights into the cultural psyche. They reveal the values and aspirations of a people, their reverence for loyalty, courage and camaraderie. Understanding these nuances can often illuminate the underlying motives of our investigations".

The journey from Belgrade to Sofia, set against the rugged terrain of the Balkans, became more than a passage through geographical space; it was an exploration into the heart of human resilience and the complexities that define our shared history. The landscape outside our window, with its untamed beauty and the scars of battles long past, served as a catalyst for exploring themes of conflict, resilience and the ongoing search for identity.

As the train approached Sofia, the conversations that had taken place along the way left a lasting impression on Holmes, Adrien, Amal and myself. We disembarked from the Orient Express not only as travellers who had bridged the physical distance between cities, but also as witnesses to the rich tapestry of human experience that the journey through the Balkans had revealed. The rugged beauty of the landscape, the stories of resilience and survival, and the contemplation of the human condition had enriched our journey with a deeper understanding and a heightened sense of connection to the lands and peoples we had encountered.

The soft light of the approaching evening bathed the landscape in a golden glow, and as we disembarked in Sofia, the city greeted us with its unique blend of history and modernity, promising new adventures and deeper insights into the intricate web of human experience.

As the Orient Express resumed its journey, leaving the vibrant city of Sofia in its wake, Sherlock Holmes, Adrien d'Arcy, Dr Amal El-Sharif and I found ourselves on the final leg of our journey to the legendary city of Constantinople. The anticipation in the luxurious confines of our carriage was palpable, each of us aware that we were not only crossing geographical distances, but also moving through layers of history and culture, drawing ever closer to the mystical allure of the Orient.

The landscape outside was gradually changing, the European sensibilities of Sofia giving way to a terrain that whispered hints of the East. Minarets and mosques began to dot the skyline, and the air seemed to hold the promise of secrets waiting to be revealed. The scent of exotic spices, carried on the gentle breeze, mingled with the crisp mountain air, creating an atmosphere of anticipation.

Sherlock Holmes, his mind always at work, was the first to express his thoughts on our approach to Constantinople. "Think of Constantinople," he began, his eyes reflecting the depth of his thought, "not just as a city, but as a historical crossroads, a meeting point between East and West. Its strategic location has made it a coveted prize for empires, a battleground for ideologies and a melting pot of cultures. The city, with its layers of history, is a testament to the complexity of human civilisation and the intertwining of destiny and ambition".

Dr Amal El-Sharif, whose interest was piqued by Holmes' analysis, added: "Indeed, Constantinople's significance goes beyond the geopolitical. It is a cultural tapestry, woven with threads from Asia, Europe and Africa. The city's architecture, art and even its cuisine reflect a mix of influences that speak of centuries of exchange, conflict and cooperation. It is a living museum, a place where you can trace the ebb and flow of human history.

As the train made its way to Plovdiv, Adrien d'Arcy was captivated by the changing landscape and the historical weight it carried. "Travelling through these lands," he mused, "one cannot help but feel a sense of awe at the resilience of the people and the beauty of their creations. The mosques and minarets that dot the skyline, the bazaars filled with spices and textiles, all speak of a rich heritage that has survived the ravages of time and the ambitions of conquerors."

Drawn to the vibrant life pulsing through the towns and cities we passed, I remarked, "The bazaars of Constantinople, with their kaleidoscope of colours, smells and sounds, are a microcosm of the spirit of the city. They are places of commerce, yes, but also of cultural exchange, where stories are shared and new ones begin. It is here, amidst the bustle of the marketplace, that you can truly feel the heartbeat of the city."

Amal nodded, her eyes bright with excitement. "There is a famous story about an old market in Constantinople, the Kapalıçarşı or Grand Bazaar. Founded in the 15th century, it has been a hub of trade and interaction for centuries, a place where merchants from all over the world came together, bringing with them goods, stories and traditions. It's a living testament to the city's enduring role as a "bridge between worlds".

The journey from Sofia to Constantinople, against the backdrop of the ever-changing landscape, became more than a passage through geographical space; it was a contemplation of the forces that shape history and the human spirit. The conversation in our carriage grew richer, weaving together threads of history, philosophy and personal reflection.

Holmes, ever the strategist, reflected on the city's role in shaping trade routes and military campaigns. "Control of Constantinople has always been a key factor in regional power dynamics," he observed. "The strategic importance of the city cannot be overstated. It has been the prize of countless empires, each seeking to control the gateway between Europe and Asia. This historical context is crucial to understanding the complexities of our current investigation".

As the Orient Express approached its final destination, our conversation deepened, weaving together threads of history, culture and personal reflection. We spoke of Constantinople not just as a place of historical interest, but as a symbol of human endeavour and imagination, a city that had stood at the crossroads of history, witnessing the best and the worst of human nature.

The rhythmic clatter of the train wheels on the tracks became more pronounced as we approached Sirkeci Station. The anticipation among us was palpable, the excitement of entering the ancient city growing with each passing moment.

Holmes, ever the observer, took in the sights and sounds with a rare intensity. The minarets, silhouetted against the setting sun, stood as sentinels of the city's storied past. The muezzin's call to prayer echoed through the narrow streets, mingling with the lively chatter of bazaar merchants. Every sensory detail was a clue, a piece of the great puzzle that was Constantinople.

Adrien, his eyes wide with wonder, took in the bustling life around them. "This city, with its rich tapestry of cultures and histories, is like no other," he said, his voice filled with awe. "It is a testament to human resilience and the ability to adapt and grow."

Amal, ever the historian, reflected on the deeper layers of the city's history. "Constantinople has been a beacon of civilisation, a bridge between worlds," she remarked. "Its history is a testament to the enduring human spirit and the eternal quest for knowledge and understanding."

As we approached Sirkeci Station, the scent of spices and the vibrant colours of the market stalls enveloped us, creating a sensory feast that was both overwhelming and exhilarating. The city was alive with stories, every corner revealing a new chapter in its rich and complex history.

Holmes, his mind always analytical, took in the atmosphere with a keen eye. "This city, Watson, is a confluence of history and destiny," he mused. "It is a place where past and present coexist, where the threads of countless lives are woven into a single, intricate tapestry. Understanding this context is essential to unravelling the mysteries that confront us."

The Orient Express slowed as it pulled into Sirkeci Station, the final stop on our remarkable journey. The train's whistle blew a final, lingering note, signalling the end of one chapter and the beginning of another. The anticipation among us was palpable, each of us eager to enter the city that had been the nexus of our conversations and dreams.

Our journey on the Orient Express had brought us to this fabled city, and as we prepared to disembark, we felt a sense of anticipation and wonder. The city of Constantinople awaited us with all its mysteries and wonders, ready to reveal its secrets to those who dared to explore its depths.

Holmes, ever the strategist, took a deep breath, his eyes scanning the busy station. "Let us not waste a moment," he said, a rare note of excitement in his voice. "Constantinople has much to tell us, and we must be ready to listen."

As the train came to a gentle stop, we gathered our belongings, each of us carrying with us the memories of the journey, the conversations that had enriched our understanding, and the anticipation of the adventures that lay ahead in this city where East meets West. The doors of the Orient Express opened and we stepped into the vibrant, pulsating heart of Constantinople, ready to embark on the next chapter of our adventure.

CHAPTER 13

CROSSROADS OF EMPIRES

Bathed in the gentle touch of the early morning sun, the domes and spires of the ancient city shimmered with a captivating radiance, serving as a picturesque backdrop for the grand arrival of the Orient Express. The air, crisp and tinged with the promise of the day, carried the scents and whispers of a city that has stood at the crossroads of history for millennia. It was here, amidst the mix of sea air and the musky perfume of distant lands, that I stepped off the train, my heart buoyed by a sense of adventure and my mind clouded by the uncertainties that lay ahead.

Beside me, Sherlock Holmes, a figure of unflappable composure, surveyed our surroundings with an inscrutable gaze. His keen eyes, those windows to a mind that had unravelled the most Byzantine of mysteries, seemed to pierce the veneer of the busy station, seeking the unseen, the unspoken.

"Watson," he murmured, "observe the details of our surroundings. Each detail, however insignificant it may seem, adds to the larger tapestry of the scene. The hurried footsteps, the anxious glances - each is a thread that, when woven together, reveals the true nature of the narrative before us".

Dr Amal El-Sharif, a beacon of scholarly elegance amidst the chaos of our arrival, stood with a poise that belied the tumultuous emotions I sensed bubbling beneath her surface - a mixture of anticipation for the journey ahead and a deep-seated connection to the land of her ancestors that we were about to enter. Adrien d'Arcy, whose life had hitherto been confined to the more tangible mysteries of leather and thread, seemed almost overwhelmed by the sensory onslaught, but there was a spark in his eyes that spoke of an insatiable curiosity, a desire to unlock the artistic secrets of this ancient metropolis.

Our quartet, so different in origin but united in purpose, would have continued to stand there, lost in our own reflections, had it not been for the approach of a figure who seemed to command the very air around him. Kâmil Pasha, the Grand Vizier, was a man in whom the past and present of this storied empire seemed to converge - a living testament to the confluence of cultures that Constantinople represented. His attire, a seamless blend of traditional Ottoman dress with the understated elegance of Western fashion, symbolised not only his high office but also the delicate balance between tradition and modernity that he, and indeed the city itself, had to navigate.

"Welcome to Constantinople, Mr Holmes, Dr Watson, Dr El-Sharif and Mr d'Arcy," he intoned, his voice rich with the gravitas of his position but not without warmth. "The Sultan has been awaiting your arrival with great interest." His gaze lingered on each of us in turn, as if trying to gauge from our countenances the measure of our resolve, the depth of our commitment to the task before us.

Sherlock replied with a nod that was both recognition and respect: "Thank you, Kâmil Pasha. We are honoured by the Sultan's attention and are prepared to assist in resolving the matter that has prompted his request." His words, though courteous, carried an undercurrent of determination - a silent vow that no stone would be left unturned, no shadow unexplored in the search for the truth.

Kâmil Pasha's smile, though brief, suggested a depth of understanding, an acknowledgement of the challenges that awaited us in the heart of this empire. "Come," he said, motioning for us to follow. "The city awaits."

And so we set off, away from the relative familiarity of the station and into the heart of Constantinople. As we navigated the crowds, each caught up in the ebb and flow of daily life, my senses were assaulted by the rich tapestry of sights, sounds and smells that the city offered. The air was alive with the shouts of merchants hawking their wares, the melodious call to prayer from nearby minarets and the distant sound of waves lapping against the city's ancient shores.

It was a city of contradictions, where the ancient and the modern, the East and the West, seemed to coexist in a delicate dance of cohabitation. Here, the remnants of Roman aqueducts bore silent witness to the city's ancient past, while the sleek lines of the tram whispered of its aspirations for the future. There, the labyrinthine alleys of the Grand Bazaar beckoned with the promise of untold treasures, a stone's throw away from the stately elegance of European-style boulevards.

As we journeyed deeper into the heart of this enigmatic city, guided by the steady presence of Kâmil Pasha, I was captivated by the stories that every stone, every whisper of the wind seemed to tell. This was Constantinople, the crossroads of the world, where empires had risen and fallen, where history was not only remembered but lived. And as we made our way through its streets, I could not shake the feeling that we were stepping into a story far greater than any we had encountered before - a story that would test the limits of our courage, our intellect and our resolve.

And so, under the watchful eye of Kâmil Pasha, we ventured into the heart of the Empire, unaware of the trials that awaited us, but undaunted in our quest for the truth. For in the end it was not only the mystery of Lord Wentworth's demise that called to us, but the lure of the unknown, the promise of adventure and the relentless pursuit of justice, no matter where it might lead.

As we followed Kâmil Pasha through the busy corridors of Sirkeci Station, his voice, both rich and authoritative, broke the morning silence. "Welcome to Constantinople, Mr Holmes, Dr Watson, Dr El-Sharif and Mr d'Arcy. The Sultan has been awaiting your arrival with great interest." The Grand Vizier's words were steeped in the formalities befitting a man of his station, and yet there was an undercurrent of something else - an indefinable tension that seemed to hover just beneath the surface of his meticulously composed exterior.

Sherlock Holmes, whose powers of observation had solved the most intricate of puzzles, gave nothing away as he met Kâmil Pasha's gaze. His response was measured, his tone respectful but without undue deference. "We are most grateful for the Sultan's invitation and are at his service," he said, his voice betraying none of the keen scrutiny I knew was going on behind those sharp, discerning eyes.

As Holmes' gaze lingered momentarily on the Grand Vizier, I found myself studying Kâmil Pasha more closely. The man before us was an enigma, a figure of considerable power within the Ottoman Empire, tasked with navigating the treacherous waters of court intrigue and political machinations. His attire, an embodiment of the crossroads at which this city stood - a blend of East and West - spoke volumes about the delicate balance he had to maintain. Yet it was not his sartorial choices that caught my attention, but rather the subtle nuances of his demeanour.

There was a rigidity to his posture, a certain stiffness that suggested a man on constant guard. His hands, though clasped loosely in front of him, betrayed a faint trembling, as if the weight of his office, the burden of his responsibility, sought to manifest itself through this tiny betrayal of composure. His eyes, dark and inscrutable, flickered with an intensity that suggested the constant vigilance required to navigate the complexities of his position.

In that moment of quiet observation, I sensed a shared understanding between Holmes and our host - an unspoken acknowledgement of the challenges that lay beneath the veneer of formality and grandeur. Constantinople, for all its splendour and historical significance, was a city on the edge; a nexus of power, ambition and intrigue that demanded the utmost caution and discretion.

Kâmil Pasha, seemingly aware of the scrutiny he was under, offered a polite smile, though it did little to disguise the undercurrent of apprehension that seemed to cling to him. "The Sultan's request, as you will soon discover, is of the most delicate nature. The matters involved are of great concern, not only to the palace but to the Empire as a whole," he remarked, his voice taking on a gravity that underlined the seriousness of our mission.

Holmes, ever the master of diplomacy when the situation demanded it, tilted his head slightly, a gesture of recognition. "We understand the sensitive nature of our task and assure you, Kâmil Pasha, of our utmost discretion and dedication to uncovering the truth," he replied, his words carefully chosen to convey both reassurance and the determination that I knew defined him.

As we continued our journey through the station, towards the exit and the city beyond, I couldn't help but reflect on the journey that had brought us here. Constantinople, with its ancient walls and storied past, stood as a testament to the enduring nature of civilisation, a reminder of the countless stories woven into the fabric of its existence. And yet, as we ventured forth, led by a man who carried the weight of empire on his shoulders, I was acutely aware that we were stepping into a narrative fraught with uncertainty, a story whose conclusion had yet to be written.

The city awaited us, a tapestry of history and mystery beckoning us to unravel its secrets. And as the first rays of sunlight began to illuminate the skyline, casting a golden glow over the domes and minarets that define its silhouette, I felt a stirring of anticipation for the adventure that lay ahead. For in the heart of Constantinople, amidst the echoes of empires past, a new chapter of our own history was about to unfold - a chapter that would test our wits, our courage and our resolve in ways we could scarcely imagine.

⊷⊷⊷⊱⊰⊷⊷⊷

Leaving the confines of Sirkeci station behind us, we ventured into the heart of Constantinople under the leadership of Kâmil Pasha. The city, basking in the incipient glow of dawn, unfolded before us in a tapestry of sights, sounds and smells that defied simple description. It was as if we had stepped into a living mosaic, a place where the threads of history, culture and human endeavour were interwoven to create a tableau pulsating with life.

The streets of Constantinople were alive with the hustle and bustle of daily life. Men and women, dressed in an eclectic mix of clothing ranging from the traditional fez and flowing robes to the more tailored lines of European fashion, moved with purposeful strides. The air was a mélange of languages - Turkish mixed with Greek, Armenian and the lilting cadences of French and English, each adding a unique note to the symphony of the city's voice.

The aroma of freshly baked simit, the Turkish equivalent of a bagel, wafted through the air, mingling with the more exotic scents of spices and herbs that seemed to permeate every corner of the city. Street vendors, their carts laden with an array of goods, from luscious fruits to intricately woven textiles, called out to passers-by, their voices a testament to the vibrant commerce that thrived in these ancient streets.

As we made our way towards the majestic silhouette of the Sultan's Palace, I was struck by the architectural wonders that graced the city. To our left, the imposing structure of the Hagia Sophia stood as a testament to the city's Byzantine past, its massive dome and ornate minarets a symbol of the religious and cultural metamorphosis Constantinople had undergone. Nearby, the elegant spires of the Blue Mosque, with their cascading domes and exquisite tile work, spoke of the artistic and spiritual heritage of the Ottoman Empire.

Our route took us through one of the city's bustling bazaars, a labyrinthine network of alleyways and stalls that seemed to pulse with life. The air here was thick with the scents of spices - cinnamon, saffron and cloves - each adding its own note to the rich tapestry of aromas. The bright colours of textiles, the gleam of metalwork and the delicate beauty of hand-painted ceramics vied for attention, while the cacophony of haggling and commerce filled the air with a music all its own.

It was in this chaotic symphony of sights, sounds and smells that I found myself reflecting on the historical significance of Constantinople. This city, at the crossroads of the world, had witnessed the rise and fall of empires. It had been a beacon for scholars, artists and traders, a gateway between continents and a melting pot of cultures, religions and ideologies. The very stones beneath our feet seemed steeped in the echoes of the past, each telling stories of glory and despair, of conquest and resistance.

As we continued our journey, the grandeur of the city's history unfolded before us. The remains of the Theodosian Walls, once the mightiest fortifications in the medieval world, were a stark reminder of Constantinople's resilience in the face of countless sieges. The Genoese and Venetian quarters, with their distinct architectural styles, spoke of a time when the city was a central hub on the trade routes that linked East and West.

Through the eyes of Dr Amal El-Sharif, whose heritage connects her to this land, I saw not only the physical beauty of Constantinople, but also the depth of its cultural and historical tapestry. Her insights, shared in hushed tones as we navigated the crowded streets, added layers of meaning to the sights and sounds that surrounded us.

As Kâmil Pasha led us ever closer to the heart of the Ottoman Empire, I couldn't help but feel a sense of awe at the complexity and vitality of Constantinople. This was a city that defied easy categorisation, a place where history was not only remembered but lived in the vibrancy of the present.

And so, with every step we took, we delved deeper into the heart of this ancient metropolis, our senses attuned to the myriad stories that whispered from the walls and stones. Constantinople, with its blend of the ancient and the modern, the familiar and the exotic, welcomed us into its embrace, inviting us to uncover the mysteries that lay hidden within its depths.

⁕⁜⁕

As we meandered through the labyrinthine streets of Constantinople, the city unfolded before us its rich tapestry of history and culture, a living museum where every stone and whisper seemed imbued with the essence of empires. Amidst this sensory and historical overload, Dr Amal El-Sharif became an invaluable guide, her knowledge of the region's complexities transforming our journey into a vivid narrative of the past.

"With every step we take, we step on layers of history, each telling a story of conquest, faith and the endless quest for knowledge," she remarked, her eyes sweeping over the ancient cityscape with a mixture of academic fascination and personal awe. "This city, perhaps more than any other, embodies the relentless flow of human endeavour. It's where East meets West, where the lineage of the Byzantine emperors clashed and then merged with the power of the Ottoman sultans".

Her words brought to life the landmarks we passed. The Hagia Sophia, with its massive dome challenging the heavens, was not only an architectural marvel but a symbol of religious transformation - from Christian basilica to Muslim mosque and now museum, testifying to the city's many faiths. The cobbled streets of the Grand Bazaar echo with the footsteps of merchants who, centuries ago, traded silks from China, spices from India and furs from the Russian steppes, making Constantinople a hub in the intricate web of medieval trade routes.

Meanwhile, Adrien d'Arcy, our companion, whose life had hitherto been framed by the more tangible realms of leather and thread, found himself equally captivated by Constantinople's allure. The bazaars, a riot of colours, sounds and smells, were a revelation to him. The intricate patterns of Turkish carpets, the delicate filigree work on silverware and the vibrant mosaics adorning lampshades were not just items for trade, but whispers of a rich artistic heritage that spoke to him on a deep level.

"It's overwhelming and yet utterly fascinating," he confessed, his eyes glowing with inspiration. "Each piece tells a story, a fragment of the craftsman's soul captured in material form. I see not only the beauty in their craft, but the potential to weave these influences into my own work, to pay homage to the heritage of this city through leather and thread."

Sherlock Holmes, ever the sentinel, took in the city's multifaceted personality with a discerning eye. While he shared few of his thoughts, it was evident that he was cataloguing every detail, every nuance of our surroundings. "In a city like this, history often conceals more than it reveals," he mused quietly, his gaze lingering on a seemingly unremarkable alleyway off the main thoroughfare. "Every shadow, every echo of the past could hold the key to unravelling the web of intrigue that has brought us here."

His words served as a stark reminder of our purpose in Constantinople. Amidst the awe-inspiring beauty and intoxicating blend of cultures, there was a mystery that had drawn us from the misty streets of London to the heart of the Ottoman Empire. A mystery that, like the city itself, was shrouded in complexity and fraught with unseen dangers.

As our small group continued its journey through the streets of Constantinople, each of us was lost in our reflections on what the city represented - for the region's historical narrative, for the craftsmanship and artistry that flourished in its markets, and for our investigation, which seemed all the more daunting amidst the grandeur and splendour that surrounded us.

Yet it was precisely this complexity, this intertwining of history, culture and mystery, that gave our task a sense of gravitas. We were not just visitors to this ancient metropolis, but active participants in a story that spanned centuries. A story that, with every step we took, revealed new layers to be explored, new mysteries to be unravelled.

And so, with Dr El-Sharif's insights illuminating the past, Adrien's new-found inspiration drawn from the city's artistic soul, and Holmes' analytical mind dissecting every detail, we delved deeper into the heart of Constantinople. Each of us, in our own way, was drawn to the city's myriad facets, and each of us knew that the days ahead would challenge us in ways we could scarcely imagine. For in the shadows of this crossroads of the world lay secrets - secrets that held the key to the mystery we had travelled so far to solve.

⊷⊷⊱⊰⊱⊰⊶

As our little caravan, led by the imposing figure of Kâmil Pasha, approached the gates of the Sultan's palace, I could not help but feel a sense of trepidation mixed with awe. The palace, a sprawling complex that whispered of the immense power and wealth once concentrated in the hands of the Ottoman sultans, rose before us in all its Byzantine and Islamic architectural splendour. The high walls and ornate gates, adorned with intricate carvings and gilded accents, spoke of an empire where opulence was the norm and every stone was steeped in history.

As we entered the palace grounds, I noticed the curious glances of the finely dressed courtiers and guards who populated the lush courtyards. Their expressions, a mixture of curiosity and caution, served as a silent reminder of the political intrigue that undoubtedly simmered beneath the surface of this magnificent facade. The air was heavy with the scent of exotic flowers from the palace gardens, yet it seemed to carry an undercurrent of tension, as if the very atmosphere was charged with the anticipation of events yet to come.

Kâmil Pasha, ever the diplomat, led us through the opulent corridors with a measured stride, his posture betraying none of the underlying tension that I sensed must plague a man of his position. The grandeur of the Ottoman court was on full display, from the rich tapestries that adorned the walls to the intricate mosaic floors upon which we stepped. Each room we passed seemed to surpass the last in splendour, a testament to the empire's former glory and the Sultan's desire to maintain the trappings of power even in an era of decline.

When we reached a more secluded chamber, decorated with delicate frescoes and sumptuous cushions, Kâmil Pasha gestured for us to sit down. The room, though smaller than the grand halls we had passed through, was no less magnificent, its windows offering breathtaking views of the Bosphorus, a strategic waterway that had long been the lifeblood of Constantinople.

"It is here, within these walls, that you will find yourselves in the heart of the Ottoman Empire," began Kâmil Pasha, his voice taking on a more solemn tone. "The Sultan has placed his trust in your abilities, but I must impress upon you the delicacy of the situation. You find yourselves in a city where alliances are as shifting as the sands, and where every word spoken can carry immeasurable weight."

He paused, letting his words sink in before continuing. "Discretion and cultural sensitivity will be your greatest allies in navigating the complexities of our court. The political climate is... tense, and the Sultan's concerns are not unfounded. There are those within these walls who would not hesitate to use any misstep on your part to their advantage.

The gravity of Kâmil Pasha's words was not lost on us. It was clear that our investigation into the murder of Lord Wentworth and the theft of the obsidian statuette was but one thread in a larger tapestry of intrigue and power struggles. The opulence that surrounded us, while breathtaking, served as a facade for the tensions that bubbled beneath the surface of the Ottoman court.

Sherlock Holmes, who had been quietly observing our surroundings with his characteristic intensity, nodded in agreement. "We understand the need for caution, Kâmil Pasha, and you have our assurance that we will conduct ourselves with the utmost discretion," he said, his voice filled with the confidence of a man who had navigated the treacherous waters of political intrigue before.

As Kâmil Pasha nodded his head in agreement, I couldn't help but feel the weight of the task before us. We were strangers in a land where the rules of the game were dictated by centuries of custom, and where the balance of power was as delicate as the filigree on the palace windows. Our mission, already fraught with danger and mystery, had taken on a new dimension - one that involved not just the solution of a crime, but potentially the fate of an empire.

With Kâmil Pasha's words echoing in our ears, we rose to bid farewell, each of us aware of the challenges that lay ahead. As we made our way back through the palace, the splendour of our surroundings took on a new light, a reminder of the complexity of the world in which we found ourselves. And as the doors closed behind us, sealing us into the heart of the Ottoman Empire, I knew that our journey had only just begun - a journey that would test our wits, our resolve and our ability to tread lightly on the delicate fabric of Ottoman politics.

⊷≎⊹≎⊶

Sitting in the opulent yet secluded chamber, the ambient light casting intricate shadows across the ornate frescoes, Kâmil Pasha's demeanour took on a gravity that underscored the importance of the words he was about to deliver. The afternoon sun, now a fiery ball sinking towards the horizon, bathed the room in a warm glow, lending a sense of solemnity to the moment.

"Your presence in our city comes at a time of delicate balance," Kâmil Pasha began, his voice resonating in the stillness of the chamber. "The Sultan's request for your assistance is not without risk, for you and for us. Your reputation precedes you, but I urge you to proceed with caution. Constantinople is a city of many secrets, some of which prefer to remain undisturbed."

The weight of his words hung in the air, a palpable reminder of the intricate web of politics and intrigue that shrouded the Ottoman Empire. The Grand Vizier's gaze, steely and penetrating, sought ours, as if to impress upon us the gravity of the situation and the importance of discretion in our forthcoming endeavours.

Sherlock Holmes, unflappable as ever, met Kâmil Pasha's gaze with an equanimity that belied the keen intellect that simmered beneath his stoic exterior. "Kâmil Pasha, you have our assurances of discretion," he replied, his voice filled with a determination that was as unwavering as it was calm. "However, you must understand that our commitment to uncovering the truth behind Lord Wentworth's murder and the significance of the obsidian statuette is absolute. We will stop at nothing to bring the perpetrators to justice and shed light on the motives behind these heinous acts."

The air in the room seemed to thicken with tension, a silent battle of wills between the Grand Vizier and Sherlock Holmes. It was a moment that spoke volumes, a testament to the complexities and dangers that lie ahead in our quest for the truth.

Kâmil Pasha, after a moment's reflection, gave a slight nod, an acknowledgement of Holmes' determination. "I expected no less from you, Mr Holmes. The Sultan himself is well aware of your tenacity and skill in such matters. I hope that your actions will serve not only to unravel the mystery at hand, but also to navigate the treacherous waters of our court with the delicacy and finesse that the situation demands."

The Grand Vizier's words were a stark reminder of the dual nature of our task: to solve a murder that had repercussions far beyond the personal tragedy it represented, and to do so in a way that would not upset the fragile balance of the Ottoman political landscape. It was a challenge that would require all of Holmes's deductive powers and our collective ability to tread carefully in an area where every word, every action, could have unforeseen consequences.

As the meeting drew to a close and we rose to say goodbye, I found myself reflecting on the task that lay before us. The opulence of the palace, the beauty of Constantinople, could not hide the undercurrent of danger that ran through the city like a hidden river. We were about to embark on a journey that would take us to the heart of the Ottoman Empire's deepest secrets, where the stakes were as high as they could be.

As we left the chamber, the setting sun cast long shadows across the palace grounds, a reminder that night was fast approaching. And with it, the realisation that our search for the truth had officially begun. In the days to come, we would find ourselves navigating a maze of intrigue and deceit, where every discovery could be a double-edged sword and every ally a potential enemy.

Yet despite the dangers that lay ahead, there was a part of me that relished the challenge, a part that was eager to delve into the mysteries of Constantinople. For in the heart of this ancient city, amidst the whispers of history and the shadows of empires past, lay the answers we sought - answers that would reveal not only the truth behind a murder, but also the intricate tapestry of human ambition and desire that had woven it into being. And so, with Holmes leading the way, we ventured out into the gathering dusk, our spirits resolute, our resolve unshaken, ready to face whatever mysteries awaited us in the days ahead.

⊷⊱⊰⊷

As the sun dipped below the horizon, casting a final brilliant glow over the domes and minarets of Constantinople, I found myself on the balcony of our accommodation within the palace grounds, the cool evening breeze whispering tales of ancient empires and long forgotten intrigues. The day had been one of stark contrasts, from the bustling vitality of the city's streets to the solemn grandeur of the Ottoman court, and as I stood there, looking out over the sprawling metropolis that stretched before me, the enormity of our task began to sink in.

The city of Constantinople, with its intricate tapestry of cultures, religions and histories, was like a living organism, pulsating with the ebb and flow of human endeavour. It was a place where past and present merged, where the ghosts of Byzantine emperors walked hand in hand with the shadows of Ottoman sultans, each leaving their indelible mark on the fabric of the city. The very air seemed saturated with the weight of history, every stone and whisper a testament to the countless stories that had unfolded within its walls.

As I stood there, lost in thought, I could not help but reflect on the daunting task that lay before us. The murder of Lord Wentworth and the theft of the obsidian statuette were not just isolated incidents; they were threads in a larger, more intricate tapestry that spanned continents and centuries. We were not simply investigating a crime; we were delving into the heart of a mystery that touched on the very essence of human ambition, greed and the quest for power.

The realisation that our actions here could have unforeseen consequences on a much larger stage was both exhilarating and terrifying. We were just four individuals - Holmes, Dr El-Sharif, Adrien d'Arcy and myself - caught up in a whirlwind of historical forces and political intrigue that went far beyond our own individual lives. The decisions we made, the clues we uncovered, could potentially alter the course of history, shaping the future of empires and the destiny of nations.

As the night deepened, enveloping the city in a cloak of stars, I found myself contemplating the weight of responsibility that rested on our shoulders. We were not merely seekers of truth; we were actors on a global stage where every move, every discovery had the potential to tip the scales of destiny. The complexity of the city, with its labyrinthine alleyways and hidden secrets, reflected the complexity of the task before us - a task that demanded not only our intellect and courage, but also our humility in the face of the unknown.

Yet despite the daunting nature of our journey, a part of me could not help but feel a sense of purpose, a sense of being part of something far greater than myself. For in the heart of Constantinople, amidst the echoes of empires and the whispers of history, lay the answers we sought - answers that had the power to illuminate the darkest corners of the human soul and reveal the intricate web of connections that bound us all together across time and space.

And so, as I retired for the night, the city spread out before me like a vast, uncharted map, I knew that the days ahead would test us in ways we could scarcely imagine. But I also knew that we were not alone in our quest. The spirits of the past, with their tales of glory and tragedy, of love and betrayal, would be our silent guides, leading us through the maze of history to the truth that awaited us at the end of our journey.

For in the end, it was not just the mystery of Lord Wentworth's murder that called to us; it was the lure of the unknown, the promise of discovery and the relentless pursuit of justice, no matter where it might lead. And as I closed my eyes, the sounds of the city lulling me into a fitful sleep, I knew that our adventure in Constantinople had only just begun - an adventure that would change us forever, binding us to this ancient city and to each other in ways we could not yet comprehend.

CHAPTER 14

THE SULTAN'S CONFIDANT

Stepping into the Sultan's palace from the busy streets of Constantinople felt like entering a different world, where history and power held sway over time. The air, heavy with the scent of jasmine and frankincense, carried the whispers of sultans past, of intrigues woven into the stone and silk that adorned the opulent corridors we now walked.

Our guide, Kâmil Pasha, a man who navigated the treacherous currents of Ottoman politics with an enviable grace, led the way with a manner that combined respect with an undertone of solemnity. It was as if the very act of entering the Sultan's domain required one to shed the outside world and prepare for the gravity of what lay ahead.

The palace servants, silent as ghosts but with eyes that missed no detail, greeted us at the grand entrance - a testament to the Sultan's anticipation of our arrival. Their traditional dress, rich in colour and intricate design, served as a visual reminder of the empire's storied past, a tapestry of cultures and conquests that had culminated in the splendour before us.

Guided through the labyrinthine corridors, each turn revealing a new marvel of architectural beauty or artistic mastery, we were led to our quarters. The rooms assigned to us were a study in understated elegance, spacious and airy, with high windows overlooking the palace's lush gardens. It was here that the weight of the day's events began to lift, replaced by a sense of surreal wonder at the hospitality extended to us.

Fresh clothes, carefully selected to respect the cultural norms and climatic considerations of our host country, awaited us, along with an assortment of refreshments that spoke to the Sultan's desire to make us comfortable. Dates, figs and a variety of nuts were laid out next to jugs of cool, rose-scented water, a refreshing break from the heat of the day.

It was in this moment of quiet respite, as we refreshed ourselves and donned the clothes provided, that the significance of our mission really began to sink in. The Sultan's invitation was not just a request for help; it was an acknowledgement of the gravity of the situation that had brought us to his doorstep. The whispered secrets of the city, the tangled web of intrigue that had claimed Lord Wentworth's life and now engulfed us, seemed to converge within these palace walls.

As we gathered, each lost in our own reflections on the day's revelations and the task ahead, Sherlock Holmes broke the silence with a simple yet profound observation. "Gentlemen and Dr El-Sharif," he began, his voice carrying a weight that demanded attention, "we stand on the threshold of a mystery that spans continents and centuries. The Sultan's confidence in inviting us here speaks not only of his desperation, but of his faith in our ability to navigate the labyrinthine complexities of what we are about to face."

His words, though meant to steel us for the evening ahead, carried an undercurrent of the enormity of the trust placed in us. The private dinner with the Sultan, an encounter that promised to lift the veils of secrecy surrounding our quest, loomed large in our minds as we made our final preparations.

The sun, now a mere whisper on the horizon, cast a golden glow through the windows, bathing the room in a light that seemed to bridge the gap between the mundane and the divine. As we stepped out of our quarters, leaving behind the sanctuary of privacy for the grandeur of the Sultan's private chambers, the air seemed charged with anticipation.

Our journey through the bustling streets of Constantinople, the weight of Kâmil Pasha's warnings and the opulent embrace of the Sultan's palace had been a passage through time, a prelude to the moment that awaited us. We were not merely visitors in a foreign land; we were seekers of truth at the heart of a mystery that promised to challenge everything we knew about power, loyalty and the indelible legacy of history.

<hr/>

As we were ushered into the Sultan's private chambers, a hush fell over our group, a collective gasp at the threshold of the unknown. The chambers, a stark contrast to the opulent grandeur we had traversed to get here, held an intimacy that seemed almost incongruous with the power and majesty of the ruler who now stood before us. The Sultan, dressed in simple but elegant garments that spoke more of a scholar than a ruler, extended his hand in greeting with a grace that belied the power he wielded.

"Mr Holmes, Dr Watson, Dr El-Sharif, Mr d'Arcy, welcome to my humble abode," he began, his voice rich with the timbre of one accustomed to command, yet tempered with a warmth that immediately put us at ease. "I trust your journey here has not been too arduous?"

His question, though casual, carried an undercurrent of genuine concern, a trait unexpected in a figure of his stature. Sherlock Holmes, always the epitome of composure, stepped forward and nodded politely in acknowledgement.

"Your Highness, the journey has been most enlightening, and your city holds wonders that defy adequate description," Holmes replied, his words carefully chosen to convey both respect and a hint of the keen observations he had already made. "We are deeply honoured by your invitation and the opportunity to assist in matters of such gravity."

The Sultan's eyes, deep pools of introspection, flickered with a momentary surprise at Holmes' eloquent address before a gentle smile graced his features. He led us to a seating area overlooking a tranquil garden, illuminated by the soft glow of lanterns, and gestured for us to sit down.

As we settled into the plush divans, the Sultan initiated a conversation that meandered through topics of cultural significance, our impressions of Constantinople and subtle inquiries about our journey so far. It was a dialogue that danced around the periphery of the reason for our summons, but served to further dispel the vestiges of formality that remained between us.

It wasn't until the servants had discreetly withdrawn, leaving us in a cocoon of privacy, that the Sultan's demeanour shifted, the weight of his office evident in the subtle lines that framed his eyes.

"Mr Holmes," he began, his voice now a mere whisper against the backdrop of the night, "I have been informed of your reputation, your unparalleled ability to discern truth from the shadows of deceit. Tell me, what have you uncovered in your investigation into the tragic demise of Lord Wentworth?"

Holmes, his gaze unwavering, met the Sultan's with a level of scrutiny that spoke to the depth of his analytical skills. In a measured tone, devoid of any embellishment, Holmes recounted our findings, the threads of evidence we had begun to weave together, and the shadows that lurked just beyond our current understanding.

As Holmes spoke, I watched the Sultan closely, noting the play of emotions that crossed his face - a landscape of grief, intrigue and an undeniable resilience. It was clear that this matter struck a chord deep within him, threads of a personal nature yet to be revealed.

It was Holmes' next words, however, that seemed to echo with a resonance that shifted the very air around us.

"Your Highness," Holmes said, his voice carrying a conviction that bordered on audacity, "if I may be so bold, it is evident that your interest in this case extends beyond the realms of mere curiosity or concern. There are layers here, intricacies that suggest a connection far more personal than has been disclosed."

The silence that followed was palpable, a tension between disclosure and discretion. The Sultan, taken aback by Holmes's directness, looked at him with a mixture of surprise and dawning respect. Here was a man whose keen intellect and fearless pursuit of the truth had peeled back the veils of secrecy with a precision that commanded admiration.

What followed was a moment of profound revelation, a turning point in our understanding of the case that would redefine the scope of our investigation. The Sultan, realising the futility of obfuscation in the face of Holmes's deductions, began to reveal the depth of his involvement and the personal stakes that lay at the heart of this mystery.

In this intimate setting, under the canopy of a starry sky, the boundaries between ruler and subject blurred, giving way to a frank exchange that would illuminate the path ahead. The Sultan, a man of both power and deep sorrow, had extended his trust, guided by the recognition of a kindred spirit in Holmes - a seeker of truth in a world shrouded in shadow.

⁂

In the wake of Sherlock Holmes's bold yet astute deductions, the atmosphere in the Sultan's chambers changed palpably. What had begun as a formal, albeit cordial, exchange now plumbed the depths of personal vulnerability and hidden truths. The Sultan, visibly moved by Sherlock's display of perspicacity, seemed to make an inner decision before he began to tell a story that would indelibly alter the course of our investigation. It was then that Holmes reached into his coat pocket and pulled out a photograph, carefully unfolding it before presenting it to the Sultan.

"Your Highness," Holmes began, his voice calm and collected, "I believe this photograph may be of some significance to our discussion." He handed the photograph to the Sultan who studied it with a furrowed brow. The picture showed the obsidian statuette that had belonged to Lord Wentworth.

"Mr Holmes, your insights compel me to reveal matters that I have held close to my heart, wrapped in layers of grief and secrecy," the Sultan began, his voice tinged with a melancholy that echoed throughout the chamber. "The tragic demise of Lord Wentworth is not an isolated incident, as you have rightly surmised. My own flesh and blood, my son Zafir, met a strikingly similar fate in the shadow of that very night." The Sultan paused, his eyes lingering on the photograph before him. "This statuette," he continued, his voice heavy with emotion, "is almost identical to the one stolen from my son."

The revelation hit us with the force of a storm, our minds struggling to comprehend the implications of his words. The Sultan, a figure of immense authority, was bound to us by a common quest, a search for justice for a lost son whose end mirrored the tragedy of Lord Wentworth.

"Zafir," the Sultan continued, a distant look in his eyes as if he were imagining the face of his late son, "was not only my heir, but the guardian of my heart. His demise was marked by the same sinister signature - an obsidian blade. But the parallels do not end there. Among Zafir's most treasured possessions was a statuette, an obsidian stallion, a miniature marvel bearing the likeness of his beloved stallion, Muntasir. Since that fateful night, the statuette has disappeared, as if swallowed by the very shadows that took my son's life". The Sultan handed the photograph back to Holmes, his expression one of sad recognition. "The resemblance is undeniable. It is as if these statuettes are keys to a larger, more sinister puzzle."

Holmes accepted the photograph with a nod, a glimmer of understanding in his eyes. "Your Highness, this confirmation strengthens the hypothesis that these obsidian statuettes are more than mere artefacts. They are central to the mystery that links the tragedies of Lord Wentworth and your son."

The room fell into a sombre silence, the weight of the Sultan's grief palpable in the air. It was Dr Amal El-Sharif, her keen intellect and compassionate heart driving her investigation, who broke the silence.

"Your Highness," she ventured gently, "you speak of an obsidian statuette. It brings to mind a conversation I had with Sir Ashcroft of the Guildhall Museum, who hinted at the existence of a group of artisans associated with such artefacts. Could there be a connection with your son's statuette?"

The Sultan looked at Dr El-Sharif with an appraising gaze, as if measuring the depth of her insight. "Dr El-Sharif, what you suggest enters the realm of legend, a narrative I had long relegated to the fanciful tales of yore. However, recent events have forced me to reconsider. The 'Obsidian Guild', as it is known, is rumoured to be a conclave of master craftsmen, their skills passed down through generations, shrouded in mystery. Their legacy, it is said, includes the creation of three sacred statuettes, each imbued with significance beyond mere artistic merit".

Holmes, ever the astute listener, interjected, "Your Highness, might one suspect that these statuettes are connected, part of a larger tapestry that ties into the events surrounding Lord Wentworth and your son?"

The Sultan nodded, a look of resigned acceptance crossing his features. "Indeed, Mr Holmes. The parallels between the events cannot be mere coincidence. The legend of the Obsidian Guild, once a tale I regarded with scepticism, now seems to hold the key to the mysteries we face. The city of Petra, famous for its ancient ruins and hidden secrets, has been mentioned in hushed tones as a place of significance in unravelling the truth behind the statuettes".

The revelation set our minds on fire with possibilities. The connection with Petra, a city that has entered the annals of history as much for its architectural marvels as for its enigmatic past, offered a new direction in our search for answers. The idea that the fates of empires, the legacy of the Obsidian Guild and our own quest for justice were intertwined by the threads of legend and reality was both daunting and invigorating.

As the Sultan shared these insights, a plan began to form in Holmes' mind, the gears of his intellect turning with renewed purpose. The road ahead was fraught with unknowns, but the lure of unravelling a mystery that spanned continents and centuries was an irresistible siren call.

In the heart of the Sultan's chambers, amid stories of personal loss and ancient legends, a new chapter in our investigation was being written. The journey to Petra, with its promise of unlocking the secrets of the Obsidian Guild and the sacred statues, loomed on the horizon. It was a venture into the unknown, a quest that would test our resolve and our intellect, guided by the revelations shared in the intimacy of grief and the common bond of a quest for justice.

⸙⁂⸙

In the wake of the Sultan's revelations, the chamber, once a mere architectural marvel, was transformed into a crucible of shared purpose and resolve. The stories of personal loss, interwoven with the threads of ancient legend, had not only bridged the gap between ruler and seeker, but had also charted the course of our investigation with newfound clarity. It was Sherlock Holmes, his mind a storm of thought and deduction, who broke the contemplative silence that had fallen upon us.

"Your Highness," Sherlock began, his voice steady, a beacon of determination amidst the sea of uncertainty that lay before us, "the narrative you've so graciously shared, coupled with the evidence at hand, points us to Petra. It is there, amidst the pink ruins of a civilisation long gone, that we may find the keys to unlock this labyrinthine mystery".

The Sultan, a figure of immense authority and wisdom, looked at Sherlock with an expression that combined admiration with a gravitas befitting his position. "Mr Holmes, your reputation as a master of deduction is certainly well deserved. The path you propose is fraught with peril, but it is one that must be taken if we are to unearth the truths buried in the sands of time."

Rising from his seat, the Sultan approached Sherlock, extending his hand in a gesture that went beyond the mere formalities of acquaintance. "I will entrust you and your companions to one of my most trusted confidants, a guide who knows the heart of the desert as well as the secrets it holds. Together you will embark on this journey with the full support of my kingdom.

The promise of such a companion, a bridge between the worlds of the Ottoman court and the ancient mysteries we sought to unravel, was a testament to the Sultan's commitment to our cause. It was an alliance forged in the crucible of shared loss and mutual respect, a beacon to guide us through the

200

uncertainties that lay ahead.

As we retired for the night, the grandeur of the palace enveloped us in an almost surreal calm, a rare respite before the storm of our journey ahead. Our rooms, lavish yet with an understated elegance, served as sanctuaries of reflection and preparation.

It was in these quiet moments, as the moon cast its silvery glow through the latticed windows, that the weight of our quest truly settled on my shoulders. The journey to Petra, a venture into the heart of legend and the shadow of unknown peril, loomed large, a daunting challenge that would test the limits of our resolve and intellect.

Yet amidst the apprehension that danced at the edges of my thoughts, there was a thread of exhilaration, a spark ignited by the prospect of delving into mysteries that had eluded the grasp of history. Sherlock, ever the stalwart sentinel against the encroaching shadows of doubt, seemed to sense the unspoken turmoil within me.

"Watson," he said, his voice filled with a quiet confidence that had the power to dispel the darkest of fears, "the journey we are about to embark on is one of unparalleled significance. The roads we travel will be fraught with challenges, yes, but it is in the face of such trials that the true measure of our character will be revealed".

His words, a beacon of certainty in the storm of my thoughts, served to strengthen my resolve. The bond of our friendship, forged in the fires of countless adversities, was a testament to the indomitable spirit that defined us.

As I retired to my chamber, the echoes of our conversation lingered, a symphony of purpose and determination. The night, with its mantle of stars and whispers of destiny, enveloped the palace in a stillness that belied the tumult of the journey ahead. In the silence of that moment I found a sense of peace, a resolute calm before the dawn of our departure.

The journey to Petra, a quest that spanned the gap between legend and reality, awaited us. With the Sultan's confidant as our guide, and the mysteries of the Obsidian Guild beckoning from the sands of time, we stood on the threshold of an adventure that promised to reveal truths long shrouded in the mists of history. Our resolve, strengthened by the revelations shared in the Sultan's chambers, burned brightly, a beacon to guide us through the trials ahead.

⁂

In the sanctity of our guest room, the echoes of the day's revelations echoed within the ornate walls, creating an atmosphere at once contemplative and charged with the gravity of our impending mission. Sherlock Holmes, my companion in countless endeavours that had tested the limits of our intellect and courage, sat opposite me, his silhouette framed by the moonlight that filtered through the window, casting patterns of light and shadow across the room.

The Sultan's revelations, woven with threads of personal tragedy and ancient legend, had laid bare the enormity of the task before us. The disappearance of the obsidian statuette similar to Lord Wentworth's, and the murder of the Sultan's son in circumstances similar to those we were investigating, had intertwined our fates with those of empires and epochs.

Sherlock, always the embodiment of calm deliberation, broke the silence that had enveloped us, his voice a beacon in the contemplative darkness. "Watson," he began, his gaze fixed on the distant horizon where the night sky met the silhouette of the palace, "tonight's revelations have cast a new light on our mission. The threads of this mystery extend far beyond the confines of a mere criminal investigation; they are woven into the very tapestry of history itself."

I nodded, the weight of his words hitting me with a palpable force. "Indeed, Sherlock," I replied, the depth of our partnership allowing me to sense the undercurrents of thought that lay beneath his stoic exterior. "The Sultan's personal torment, the legend of the Obsidian Guild and the enigmatic allure of Petra - it is a confluence of elements that speaks to a mystery of unparalleled complexity."

Sherlock's gaze returned to mine, a spark of that indefatigable spirit that had defined our endeavours glowing in his eyes. "Yet it is in the unravelling of such mysteries, in the face of seemingly insurmountable odds, that we find the true measure of our resolve," he asserted, a statement that was both a reminder of the challenges we had overcome and a rallying cry for the journey that lay ahead.

Our preparations for the trip to Petra, a city as shrouded in legend as the sands that guarded its secrets, occupied our thoughts as we discussed the logistics and potential dangers that lay ahead. The need for discretion, for an understanding of the cultural and historical significance of our destination, was paramount - a fact that Sherlock emphasised with characteristic foresight.

"As we venture into Petra, Watson, we must be mindful of the shadows that history casts on the present," Sherlock mused, his thoughts seemingly traversing the vastness of time and space that separated us from the ancient city. "The legends of the Obsidian Guild, the significance of the statuettes - it's a puzzle that demands not only our deductive skills, but an appreciation for the narratives that have shaped the course of empires."

Our conversation, a mixture of analytical deduction and philosophical musing, served as a testament to the depth of our partnership and the unspoken bond that had guided us through the darkest of mysteries. It was a bond forged in the crucible of shared adversity, a beacon that illuminated the path we were to tread.

As we retired for the night, the silhouette of the palace against the starry sky served as a poignant reminder of the stakes. Our mission, now intertwined with the Sultan's personal torment and the shadowy legend of the Obsidian Guild, transcended the boundaries of mere investigation. It was a quest with the potential to change the very fabric of history, a journey into the heart of a mystery that spanned continents and centuries.

Lying in the silence of my chamber, the events of the day replaying in my mind, I found myself on the brink of sleep, teetering on the edge of dreams that whispered of ancient cities and hidden truths. The journey to Petra loomed large, a beacon calling us into the unknown, guided by the determination that had defined our partnership and the unyielding pursuit of justice that was our creed.

In that moment, as night wrapped its cloak around the palace and the stars bore witness to our determination, I knew that the path we were about to take was more than a search for answers - it was a pilgrimage into the heart of history itself, a journey that would test the limits of our intellect, our courage and the indomitable spirit that bound Sherlock Holmes and John Watson in an unbreakable bond of friendship and shared destiny.

CHAPTER 15

ALLIES IN THE DESERT

Awash in the first light of dawn, the courtyard of the Sultan's palace presented a serene tableau that belied the bustle within its walls. The ancient stones, worn smooth by centuries of footfall, seemed to whisper secrets of ages past, while the meticulously tended gardens offered a riot of colour and fragrance. Amidst this scene, Sherlock Holmes, Dr Amal El-Sharif, Adrien d'Arcy and I gathered, our breaths forming clouds of mist in the crisp morning air. The anticipation of the journey ahead gave the atmosphere an electric charge, a palpable sense of destiny that resonated with the stones beneath our feet.

As we made our final preparations, the courtyard served as a testament to the Sultan's love of the exquisite; every detail, from the intricately carved archways to the meticulously tended flora, spoke of a legacy stretching back through the ages. The soft glow of the morning sun filtered through the arches, casting patterns of light and shadow that danced across the stones, a silent witness to the countless goodbyes this room had witnessed.

Holmes, ever the observer, took in the scene with a contemplative gaze. "It is in places like this, Watson," he mused, "that one feels the weight of history. Every stone, every whisper of the wind through the gardens tells a story. It reminds us that we are but fleeting actors on a stage on which countless dramas have been played out."

I nodded, feeling the truth in his words. "Indeed, Holmes. There is a sense of continuity here, a thread that links the past to the present. It makes one reflect on the transient nature of our own existence."

Holmes' eyes sparkled with a rare intensity. And yet, Watson, it is in this impermanence that we find our purpose. To uncover the truths buried within these stones, to bring light to the shadows, is a task that transcends our fleeting existence and connects us to the eternal quest for knowledge and justice.

I nodded, feeling the truth in his words. "Indeed, Holmes. There is a sense of continuity here, a thread that links the past to the present. It makes one reflect on the transient nature of our own existence."

Our conversation was interrupted by the sound of hooves on cobblestones, a rhythm that spoke of power and grace. Our gazes converged on the entrance, where a figure emerged, commanding yet shrouded in an aura of sorrow that seemed almost tangible. Liyana Sultan, the eldest daughter of Sultan Abdul Hamid II, stood before us, her presence a potent mixture of royal authority and personal tragedy. Beside her, a stallion of such breathtaking beauty that it seemed as if the morning light had been created just to illuminate his form. Muntasir, the legendary Arabian stallion, moved with a majesty that was nothing short of mesmerising, his coat shimmering like polished obsidian in the gentle caress of the sun.

Liyana approached us with a grace that spoke of her noble lineage. Her eyes, dark and expressive, held a depth of emotion that belied her calm exterior. "Gentlemen," she began, her voice steady yet tinged with an undercurrent of sorrow, "it is an honour to join you on this journey. Muntasir and I are ready to face whatever challenges lie ahead."

Holmes bowed his head in acknowledgement, his gaze lingering on the stallion. "Muntasir is a magnificent creature," he remarked. "It is clear that he shares a deep bond with you, one that transcends mere training."

Liyana's expression softened as she looked at Muntasir. "He was my companion through the darkest of times," she said softly. "After the death of my brother Zafir, it was Muntasir who gave me the strength to carry on. Together we honour his memory."

As we watched the couple, Sherlock Holmes, typically reserved in his expressions of admiration, could not hide his intrigue. The detective, who had formed a similarly deep, if unexpected, bond with Isinglass, seemed to recognise a kindred spirit in Muntasir. It was a bond that went beyond a mere appreciation of the animal's physical prowess, hinting at deeper, perhaps mystical ties that bound the souls of humans and these noble creatures.

"Your brother's legacy is in capable hands," Holmes said, his voice uncharacteristically gentle. "And in Muntasir, I see a spirit that mirrors your own resilience and strength."

The courtyard, once a place of quiet anticipation, now buzzed with the energy of new possibilities. Liyana's arrival, with Muntasir at her side, was not just a ceremonial gesture, but a symbolic joining of paths that had previously run parallel. Her expertise and intuitive understanding of the equestrian arts promised to add a new dimension to our quest, bridging cultural gaps and enriching our understanding of the legacy we sought to uncover.

As the Sultan and his Grand Vizier joined us, their expressions a mixture of pride and solemnity, it was clear that the journey we were about to embark on was one of unprecedented significance. The Sultan, a figure of regal authority tempered by the wisdom of his years, spoke in a voice that echoed with both the affection of a father and the command of a ruler.

"My friends," he began, his tone solemn, "you are about to embark on a journey of great importance, one that will test your courage and resolve. My daughter, Liyana, and her faithful companion, Muntasir, will be invaluable to you. Together you will uncover truths long buried in the sands of time."

His words hung in the air, a poignant reminder of the stakes involved. We stood on the threshold of the unknown, our hearts lifted by the anticipation of the adventures that lay ahead and the forging of new alliances that would see us through the trials to come. With Liyana Sultan and Muntasir joining our ranks, the journey to Petra - a voyage into the heart of ancient mysteries and untold dangers - promised not only to unlock the secrets of the Obsidian Guild, but also to reveal the depths of the human spirit and the unbreakable bonds that define our common humanity.

⊕H⊙⊁⊱⊙H⊰

As the soft hues of dawn painted the courtyard in a tapestry of light and shadow, the Sultan, accompanied by his Grand Vizier, approached our assembled group. The air, alive with the anticipation of the day's arrival, seemed to stand still at their arrival. Sultan Abdul Hamid II, a figure of regal authority tempered by the wisdom of his years, wore a face of solemn pride. Beside him, the Grand Vizier, a steadfast pillar of advice and strategy, mirrored the Sultan's sombre yet dignified demeanour.

"My friends," the Sultan began, his voice resonating with both the affection of a father and the command of a ruler, "allow me to introduce my eldest daughter, Liyana." He gestured to the young woman beside Muntasir, her presence a fusion of royal command and personal sorrow. "She has been the guardian and trainer of Muntasir since the tragic death of her brother Zafir."

The introduction, though brief, painted a vivid portrait of Liyana Sultan. At 22, she was on the cusp of womanhood, but her eyes, a mirror to her soul, bore the indelible marks of grief and determination. The loss of her brother, Zafir, was not only a personal tragedy, but a pivotal moment that thrust her into a role that bridged the realms of familial duty and the preservation of a legacy. Her stature, poised and commanding, belied the turmoil of emotion beneath, a testament to her strength and determination to honour her brother's memory.

Liyana's gaze, as it swept over us, lingered with an intensity that spoke of her keen intelligence and discerning nature. Her early exposure to the rich equestrian culture of the Empire was evident in the seamless bond she shared with Muntasir, a bond that transcended the conventional boundaries of trainer and horse. Under her tutelage, Muntasir had not only reached a level of horsemanship of the highest order, but had also become a living symbol of the Empire's proud history and the profound bond between horse and rider.

Her attire, while reflecting her royal lineage, was chosen with a pragmatism that spoke to her active role in the equestrian world. The fabrics, rich yet functional, whispered of a woman who was as comfortable in the saddle as she was in the halls of power, embodying the spirit of progress and tradition that defined her unique position within the royal family of the Ottoman Empire.

As Liyana nodded to acknowledge our group, her demeanour was one of quiet confidence. Despite the initial scepticism that might be expected in such a meeting, it was clear that she was willing to engage with us, to offer her insights and skills in the quest that lay before us. Her intelligence, determination and unparalleled expertise in the equestrian arts promised to be invaluable assets, bridging cultural gaps and adding a layer of depth to our understanding of the mysteries we sought to unravel.

Holmes, his sharp eyes taking in every nuance of Liyana's bearing, spoke with measured respect. "Miss Sultan, your brother's legacy clearly lives on in you and in Muntasir. It is evident that you both possess a strength of spirit and a depth of character that will be indispensable in our journey."

Liyana tilted her head, her expression softening as she looked at Holmes. "Thank you, Mr Holmes. Zafir believed in the pursuit of truth and the uncovering of secrets. In continuing his work, I honour his memory and strive to fulfil his vision."

I too felt compelled to acknowledge the depth of her commitment. "Your dedication is inspiring, Miss Sultan. It is clear that you and Muntasir share a bond that goes beyond the ordinary. Such a bond will undoubtedly help us in our quest".

The Sultan's pride in his daughter was palpable, a father's love intertwined with recognition of her abilities and the challenges she has faced. In Liyana, the Sultan saw not only the legacy of his lineage, but the embodiment of a bridge between the old and the new, a beacon of hope and progress in a world often resistant to change.

Liyana Sultan, in her role as guardian and educator of Muntasir, represented more than the continuation of a family legacy; she was a pioneer, a woman who walked the fine line between respecting the traditions of the empire and pushing for modernity. Her journey, marked by personal and political intrigue, had forged her into a figure of compassion and leadership, qualities that would prove crucial as we embarked on our journey to Petra.

With the introduction of Liyana Sultan, we were presented not only with a new ally in our quest, but a complex character whose depth and resilience mirrored the very mysteries we were trying to unravel. Her relationship with her father, Sultan Abdul Hamid II, and the memory of her brother, Zafir, offered glimpses into the fabric of a family bound by love, duty and a shared commitment to their heritage.

As the Sultan concluded the introduction, the courtyard, once the scene of quiet anticipation in the morning, had been transformed into the setting for the beginning of a new chapter in our adventure. With Liyana Sultan and Muntasir joining our ranks, the road ahead, while fraught with unknown challenges, now held the promise of new insights and the forging of bonds that would transcend the boundaries of time and culture.

Holmes turned his attention back to the Sultan, his expression pensive. "Your Majesty, we are honoured to have your daughter's assistance. Her skills and knowledge will be invaluable."

The Sultan nodded, his gaze steady. "Liyana is a true daughter of the realm. She carries the weight of our history and the hope of our future. I trust that together you will achieve great things."

With these words, the Sultan and the Grand Vizier took their leave, leaving us to finalise our preparations. The air seemed to hum with the promise of the journey ahead, a journey that would test our mettle and reveal secrets long buried in the sands of time. As we stood on the threshold of this new adventure, I could not help but feel a sense of excitement and anticipation, for the path before us was fraught with danger and discovery, and the bonds we forged along the way would shape the course of our destinies.

In the quiet reverence of the morning, the courtyard of the Sultan's palace stood still, witness to a convergence of destinies. The air was crisp, carrying the faint scent of jasmine from the gardens, mingled with the earthy aroma of the ancient stones that paved the ground. The first light of dawn was golden, illuminating the intricately carved arches and casting long shadows that danced across the cobbles.

Sherlock Holmes, standing with an air of contemplative determination, was momentarily transfixed by the sight before him. The majestic stallion Muntasir, under the guardianship of Liyana Sultan, turned his attention to the detective. It was a moment that seemed to suspend time, a silent exchange between man and beast that spoke volumes to those attuned to its gravity.

Holmes, whose life had been dedicated to the pursuit of logic and reason, found himself momentarily caught in Muntasir's gaze. The stallion, a creature of unparalleled beauty and grace, regarded Holmes with a depth of understanding and empathy that defied the natural order. It was as if Muntasir was looking into the very soul of Sherlock Holmes, recognising a kindred spirit in the man before him.

Muntasir's eyes, dark and expressive, shone with an ancient wisdom. The morning light accentuated the lithe contours of his muscular frame, every movement a ballet of strength and elegance. His cloak, a lustrous black that reflected the depths of the night, shone as if woven from the very fabric of the dawn. The silence that enveloped the courtyard was punctuated by the soft rustle of leaves and the distant call of a morning bird, creating a symphony of nature's awakening that framed this extraordinary encounter.

Holmes, for his part, was visibly moved by the encounter. His keen appreciation of the majesty of nature's creatures was well documented, but the connection with Muntasir was of a different order. It was as if the stallion embodied the very essence of the quest they were about to embark upon - a symbol of unity, heritage and the transcendent bond between species. His usually analytical eyes softened, reflecting the profound impact of this silent communion.

Dr Amal El-Sharif and Adrien d'Arcy, standing slightly behind Holmes, watched the exchange with a mixture of awe and understanding. Dr El-Sharif, an expert in the cultural and historical contexts of their journey, recognised the symbolic significance of this connection, while Adrien, ever perceptive, seemed to grasp the emotional undercurrents that bound their group together.

Liyana, feeling the need to articulate the significance of Muntasir's presence, spoke quietly. "Muntasir has been more than a companion to me; he has been a source of strength and comfort. His understanding goes beyond the limits of human language. He seems to instinctively know the burdens we carry and the paths we must tread."

Holmes nodded, his eyes still on the stallion. "Indeed, Miss Sultan. In Muntasir, I see not only a magnificent creature, but a symbol of the resilience and nobility we must embody in our quest. His presence reminds us of the virtues we must uphold - courage, loyalty and the unwavering pursuit of truth.

Watson, moved by the depth of the exchange, added: "It is clear that Muntasir will be an invaluable ally. His strength and spirit are palpable, and his bond with you, Miss Sultan, is a testament to the power of trust and mutual respect".

Dr Amal El-Sharif, eager to contribute to the discussion, remarked: "This bond you share with Muntasir, Miss Sultan, is emblematic of the bonds we seek to understand and preserve. It is through such links that we can bridge the gaps between our cultures and histories".

Adrien d'Arcy, always thoughtful, nodded in agreement. "The journey ahead will test us all, but with Muntasir by our side, we are reminded of the unity and strength that comes from such deep bonds."

Liyana smiled, her eyes shining with a mixture of pride and gratitude.

"Thank you, Dr Watson, Dr El-Sharif and Mr d'Arcy. Muntasir and I are honoured to be part of this journey. Together we will face the challenges that lie ahead, united in purpose and determination.

The courtyard, once a place of quiet anticipation, now buzzed with the energy of new possibilities. The meeting, brief but full of meaning, underscored the themes at the heart of their quest - purity, unity and the enduring power of heritage. Muntasir, through his interactions with Sherlock and the rest of the team, transcended his physical form to become a symbol of these ideals. The bond between Sherlock and Muntasir, forged in the quiet of the Sultan's courtyard, was emblematic of the journey that lay ahead - a journey that promised not only to unravel the mysteries of the Obsidian Stallions, but also to explore the soulful connections that defy explanation and elevate the narrative into a realm of mysticism and deep emotional resonance.

As the first light of dawn continued to illuminate the courtyard, the scene was set for the beginning of their journey. The bonds forged in this sacred space, between man, horse and the ethereal tapestry of destiny, would see them through the trials ahead, illuminating the path with the shared light of understanding and unity.

⊕≫⊰⊱⊱⊕

As the first light of dawn began its ascent, casting a soft golden glow over the opulent courtyards of the Sultan's palace, our group gathered, each member lost in their own thoughts yet united by a common purpose. The air, tinged with the cool of dawn, carried the promise of the journey ahead - a journey that would take us from the grandeur of Constantinople to the ancient mysteries of Petra. This moment of transition, from the known to the unknown, from the safety of the palace to the uncertainties that awaited us in the vast deserts of the Middle East, was marked by a palpable sense of anticipation.

The Grand Vizier, a figure of solemn authority and wisdom, stepped forward, his bearing one of grave duty. His robes, rich with intricate embroidery, whispered softly as he moved, the morning light catching the gold thread and making it shimmer. His eyes, sharp and discerning, surveyed our assembled group before he began to speak.

"We have made arrangements for your journey to Petra," he announced, his voice resonating with the weight of the responsibility he bore. "In Damascus you will find a contact waiting for you - a young Bedouin named Khalid Al-Fahmi. He is well versed in the ways of the desert and will be your guide to the ancient city."

The mention of Khalid Al-Fahmi introduced a new element into our preparations, adding a tangible sense of reality to the adventure that lay ahead. The road to Petra, hitherto a concept shrouded in mystery and fraught with unknown dangers, suddenly seemed all the more real, all the more tangible.

Holmes, his eyes reflecting the burgeoning light, turned to the Grand Vizier with an inquisitive gaze. "Khalid Al-Fahmi," he mused, the name rolling off his tongue with a hint of curiosity. "What more can you tell us about this leader?"

The Grand Vizier nodded, understanding the importance of this introduction. "Khalid, as described, is no ordinary guide. A descendant of the legendary Arabian horse breeders, his life is a testament to the rich equestrian traditions of his Bedouin heritage. The lineage of his family, renowned for breeding the majestic Arabian stallions, positions Khalid as a vital link to the ancient practices that have long defined the Arabian Peninsula.

As the Grand Vizier spoke, I could almost see the vast deserts stretching out before us, the wind whispering secrets through the sands. The image of Khalid, a figure steadfast against the relentless sun, guiding us through the treacherous terrain, began to take shape in my mind. His intimate connection with the desert and its creatures, especially the horses, symbolised a living bridge between the past and present of Arabian equestrian culture.

"Khalid is not just a guardian of tradition," the Grand Vizier continued. "He embodies the delicate balance between preservation and evolution, revering his ancestral heritage while remaining open to modern breeding and racing methods. This adaptability, this willingness to combine the wisdom of the past with the innovations of the present, marks Khalid out as a figure of profound insight and resilience".

Holmes, ever the analytical mind, absorbed this information with great interest. "It seems we are in capable hands," he remarked, a note of approval in his voice.

The Grand Vizier's expression softened slightly, a hint of a smile playing at the corners of his mouth. "His intuitive communication with horses, especially his stallion Al-Zarib, suggests a bond that transcends conventional understanding. It is as if Khalid and his horses share a language of their own, a near-telepathic connection that allows them to perceive each other's thoughts and emotions".

Watson, who had been listening intently, could not help but express his admiration. "Such a bond is rare and precious. It speaks to the depth of his character and the strength of his bond with these noble creatures."

The Grand Vizier nodded his head in agreement. "Indeed. This extraordinary relationship underscores Khalid's role not only as a horseman, but as a steward of a legacy that is both ancient and ever evolving."

The challenges Khalid faced - navigating the tension between historical reverence and the need for progress, confronting cultural misunderstandings and protecting his heritage from external threats - mirrored the broader themes of our journey. His journey from strict guardian of tradition to proactive bridge-builder between cultures promised to enrich our understanding of the complexities at the heart of our quest.

As the Grand Vizier concluded his briefing, the courtyard, once a space of quiet anticipation, was now alive with the energy of imminent departure. The mention of Khalid Al-Fahmi, with his deep ties to the equestrian traditions of the Arabian Peninsula and his role as our guide, served as a reminder of the diverse cultures and histories that our journey would encompass. It reinforced the notion that our quest was not just an investigation into the mysteries of the Obsidian Guild, but an exploration of the connections that bind us to the past and to each other.

Our preparations for departure, informed by this new knowledge, took on a renewed sense of purpose. Each member of our team, from Sherlock Holmes with his analytical skills to Liyana Sultan with her equestrian expertise, understood that the road to Petra would be one of discovery, learning and forging new alliances. With Khalid Al-Fahmi as our guide, we embarked on a journey that would transcend the mere physical distance between Constantinople and Petra and venture into the realms of cultural exchange, mutual respect and the enduring bond between man and horse.

As we prepared to leave the safety of the Sultan's palace, the grandeur of Constantinople fading with each step, our thoughts turned to the desert that awaited us, to the ancient city of Petra and the mysteries buried in its sands. The journey ahead, fraught with unknown challenges and dangers, now seemed imbued with a sense of purpose and anticipation. It was not just a search for answers, but a pilgrimage into the heart of history itself - a journey that promised to reveal the ties that bind us to our past and to each other in ways we have yet to imagine.

⊕⊙⊗⊙⊕

As the first light of dawn pierced the veil of night, casting a soft golden glow over the ancient city of Constantinople, our assembled team, led by the Grand Vizier, embarked on the journey that would mark the beginning of a pivotal chapter in our quest. The air, crisp and laden with the promise of the day ahead, seemed to imbue us with a sense of purpose as we navigated the city's winding streets and made our way to the bustling harbour. The city itself, a tapestry of history and culture, seemed to awaken alongside us, its markets humming with activity and its alleyways whispering tales of yesteryear.

The Grand Vizier, a figure of imposing authority and wisdom, assumed the role of our escort with an air of solemn duty. His presence, both reassuring and commanding, served as a constant reminder of the gravity of our mission and the trust the Sultan had placed in us. As we walked through the city, I couldn't help but be drawn into the vibrant life around us. The sounds of merchants setting up their stalls, the rich aroma of spices filling the air, and the kaleidoscope of colours from the fabrics on display in the bazaar created a vivid backdrop against which our solemn procession moved - a band of travellers bound by a common purpose, set against the living, breathing entity that was Constantinople.

"Dr Watson," Sherlock Holmes intoned softly beside me, his eyes sweeping over the bustling streets, "observe how this city pulsates with life. Every corner, every alleyway is teeming with history and intrigue. Constantinople is a living paradox, where the ancient and the modern coexist in a delicate balance".

His words resonated with me and captured the essence of our surroundings. The city, with its minarets and domes silhouetted against the dawn sky, seemed to whisper the secrets of empires long gone, even as it buzzed with the vibrancy of the present. The air was thick with the scent of exotic spices, mingled with the aroma of freshly baked bread, creating a sensory tapestry that was both intoxicating and invigorating.

Arriving at the port, a sense of anticipation gripped us as we were greeted by the sight of the steamship that would take us across the Mediterranean to Beirut. The ship, a marvel of engineering, stood majestically at the quay, its engines humming softly as if in eager anticipation of the journey ahead. The sight of the steamer, with its promise of adventure beyond the horizon, filled us with a new sense of determination. Here was our link to the unknown, our chariot waiting to take us from the familiar confines of the city to the mysteries that beckoned from the distant sands of Petra.

Liyana Sultan, with Muntasir at her side, stood at the gangway, her eyes reflecting a mixture of sorrow and determination. The morning light caught the sheen of Muntasir's cloak, making it gleam like polished obsidian. Liyana's hand rested lightly on the stallion's neck, her touch a silent promise of loyalty and strength.

"The journey ahead is fraught with peril," Liyana said softly, her voice carrying the weight of her bloodline. "But together we will prevail. Muntasir and I are ready to face whatever challenges lie ahead."

Holmes stepped forward, his keen eyes meeting hers with an understanding that went beyond words. "Your courage and wisdom are invaluable to us, Liyana. Together we will uncover the secrets that lie hidden in the sands of Petra."

As we boarded the steamer, the silhouette of Constantinople began to recede into the distance, its minarets and domes fading into the morning mist. It was a poignant moment, saying goodbye to the city that had been our sanctuary, if only for a short time. As the ship began to cut through the waters of the Mediterranean, the reality of our departure sank in. We were leaving behind the safety and familiarity of the known world to venture into uncharted territory, guided by the promise of discovery and the pursuit of justice.

Within the confines of the steamer, as we settled into the rhythm of the journey, Sherlock Holmes and I found ourselves in quiet reflection. Our partnership, forged in the crucible of countless investigations and shared adversity, had prepared us for this moment. The puzzles we had solved and the challenges we had overcome had brought us to this point, to the threshold of what promised to be our greatest adventure. The bond we shared, deeper than mere friendship, was our beacon in the uncertain waters that lay ahead.

"Liyana's presence adds a new dimension to our quest," Holmes mused, his eyes fixed on the horizon. "Her strength, her determination - they are a testament to the resilience of the human spirit. She, like us, seeks justice and truth, driven by a legacy of love and loss."

I nodded, understanding the depth of his words. "Indeed, Holmes. And with Muntasir by her side, she embodies the unbreakable bond between man and beast, a partnership that will prove invaluable in the trials to come."

Liyana, overhearing our conversation, approached with a serene expression. "Gentlemen, this journey is not only ours, but a tribute to those who have gone before us. The memory of my brother and the legacy of the Obsidian Guild weigh heavily upon us all. We must remain steadfast in our resolve and unwavering in our pursuit.

Her words, spoken with quiet determination, filled us with a renewed sense of purpose. As the chapter of our journey came to a close in Constantinople, the city now but a memory on the distant shore, we looked to the future with a sense of determination. The journey to Petra, a pilgrimage into the heart of ancient legends and hidden truths, had begun. It was a journey that promised not only to unlock the secrets of the Obsidian Guild, but also to explore the depths of our own courage and determination. With every mile that separated us from Constantinople, we moved closer to the heart of the mystery, to the secrets buried in the sands of time, and to the hope of bringing peace to the restless spirits that haunted our dreams.

As the steamer moved steadily towards Beirut, the rhythmic churning of its engines and the gentle lapping of the waves against the hull provided a soothing counterpoint to the tension and anticipation that coursed through our veins. We were on the brink of a great adventure, one that would test the limits of our endurance and the strength of our bonds. And as the first rays of the rising sun bathed the horizon in a golden glow, we felt a sense of unity and purpose that would carry us through the challenges that lay ahead.

CHAPTER 16

TOWARDS THE LEVANTINE MIRAGE

D awn was breaking, a soft golden glow creeping over the horizon as our steamer began to stir, its engines humming a low, expectant tune. The air was crisp, filled with the salty scent of the sea and the faint, lingering aromas of spices from the markets we had left behind. On deck, we watched the silhouette of Constantinople, with its towering minarets and domes, fade into the morning mist. The majestic dome of the Hagia Sophia and the slender minarets of the Blue Mosque, once dominating the skyline, now faded into the whisper of a city bridging two continents, two worlds.

Sherlock Holmes, ever the observer, stood beside me, his eyes narrowing as he took in the view. "Constantinople," he mused, his voice carrying the weight of contemplation, "a city that exists in duality, bridging East and West, ancient and modern. It's a fitting starting point for our journey, Watson. We too are about to cross borders, not just of countries, but of understanding."

I nodded, feeling the weight of his words. "Indeed, Holmes. The very air seems to hum with the echoes of history, every stone and archway a testament to the countless souls who have walked these streets before us."

Holmes turned his piercing gaze to the horizon where the first light of dawn painted the sky in shades of gold and rose. "It is a place where past and present coexist, a mosaic of cultures and eras. As we venture forth, we must carry this awareness with us, for the answers we seek may lie buried in the sands of time."

Liyana Sultan, our companion in this quest, joined us at the railing, her eyes also fixed on the receding city. "Leaving the familiar shores of home," she began, her voice a mixture of determination and nostalgia, "reminds me of the journey I embarked on after my brother's death. Following in his footsteps, carrying on his legacy - it's a daunting path, but one I must tread with courage."

Holmes, his gaze never straying from the horizon, replied, "Courage, Miss Sultan, is not the absence of fear, but the triumph over it. Your journey, like ours, is marked by the shadows of the past and the uncertainty of the future. But it is in facing those shadows that we find our true strength.

Her words, spoken with such earnestness, revealed the weight she carried, the responsibility of a legacy that bound her to both the past and the future. "My brother, Zafir, often spoke of the strength to be found in embracing one's destiny. He believed that our journey through life is marked not only by the paths we choose, but by the courage we show in the face of the unknown."

Holmes looked at her with a rare gentleness in his eyes. "Your brother was a wise man, Liyana. The legacy he left you is a powerful one, and you honour it with your determination and strength."

Beside her stood Muntasir, her stallion, his presence a testament to resilience and fortitude. The horse stood proudly on the deck, unfazed by the rolling waves and unfamiliar surroundings. His sleek, muscular form seemed to absorb the morning light, his eyes scanning the horizon with a calm intensity. Holmes turned his keen gaze to Muntasir, admiration evident in his eyes. "Remarkable," he remarked, "to see such calm and resilience in an animal amidst the chaos of a sea voyage. It is a rare and commendable quality."

Liyana smiled, her hand gently stroking Muntasir's mane. "Muntasir has been my faithful companion through many trials. His spirit is unyielding and his loyalty unwavering. In many ways, he embodies the strength I strive to uphold.

As the steamer crossed the Bosphorus Strait, leaving behind the threshold between East and West, I found myself reflecting on the nature of our journey. The gentle rocking of the ship and the rhythmic sound of the waves created a meditative atmosphere, conducive to introspection. It was a tapestry woven from the threads of ancient history and burgeoning modernity, a narrative that spanned continents and eras.

Holmes's reflections on the dual nature of Constantinople sparked a discussion among us, a dialogue that explored themes of identity and transition. Each of us, in our own way, had crossed boundaries, stepped into realms that challenged our perceptions and beliefs.

Holmes continued in a thoughtful voice. "In every stone and shadow of Constantinople, one can feel the pulse of countless stories, each a thread in the great tapestry of human experience. Our quest will require us to unravel those threads, to seek the truths they conceal."

Liyana's gaze remained fixed on the horizon, her voice soft but determined. "And in doing so, we honour the past while forging our own paths. The legacy of those who have gone before us is not a burden, but a guide, illuminating the way forward."

Leaving Constantinople, then, was more than a physical departure; it was a symbolic crossing into a world full of mysteries and contradictions. It was a journey that promised to test our resolve, forge bonds of friendship and understanding, and uncover truths long buried in the sands of time.

As the silhouette of the city faded away, swallowed by sea and sky, I felt a pang of melancholy for the world we were leaving behind. But this was tempered by the anticipation of the discoveries that awaited us. As the steamer ploughed through the waters of the Mediterranean, I knew that the journey we were about to embark on would change the course of our lives forever.

Constantinople, with its rich tapestry of history and culture, was but the prologue to an adventure that would take us to the heart of ancient lands, to the threshold of untold mysteries. And as the first light of dawn heralded the beginning of our journey, I couldn't help but feel that we were on the threshold of something truly extraordinary.

As our ship ventured deeper into the heart of the Sea of Marmara, the sun's first rays transformed the water into a vast expanse of polished obsidian, a mirror to the awakening sky. The light breeze carried the fresh, salty tang of the sea, mingled with the faint, lingering aromas of spices and exotic flowers from distant shores. The rhythmic hum of the engines and the gentle lapping of the waves against the hull created a serene symphony that was both soothing and exhilarating.

Dr Amal El-Sharif, her eyes reflecting the morning light, stood at the bow, her gaze fixed on the horizon. "The Sea of Marmara," she began, her voice resonating with the weight of history, "has served as a bridge between countries and peoples for millennia. It's a testament to the fluidity of cultural identities, how civilisations have merged and influenced each other across these waters."

Her words sparked a rich exchange between us, a dialogue that delved into the nature of transition and the fluidity of identity. Each word seemed to ripple through the air, much like the waves beneath our ship, connecting us to the ancient stories carried by the sea.

Adrien d'Arcy, with his background in thoroughbred breeding, found a parallel in Dr El-Sharif's discourse. "Much like the confluence of cultures across these waters," he mused, his voice thoughtful yet strained, "the evolution of horse breeding practices in different regions reflects a similar mix of influences. The purest bloodlines often carry the legacy of diverse ancestries, each contributing to the strength and grace of the offspring."

His voice wavered and a pallor crept over his face. The gentle rocking of the steamer, so calm to the rest of us, was wreaking havoc on his constitution. Adrien staggered to the railing, his hand clutching his stomach, and then he succumbed to seasickness, his body lurching uncontrollably over the side.

Watson, ever the doctor, was at his side in an instant. "Steady, Adrien," he said, his voice calm and reassuring. He handed Adrien a small vial of medicine. "This should help ease your discomfort. Breathe deeply and try to focus on the horizon."

Adrien's face was a mask of misery, his usually composed demeanour shattered by the relentless waves. Liyana Sultan, observing Adrien's distress, stepped forward with a look of compassionate concern. Her presence was a beacon of calm amidst the tumult of the sea. She knelt beside him, her voice soft and reassuring. "Adrien, let me tell you a story to distract you from your illness. Have you heard of the legendary mare of the Prophet Mohammed?"

Adrien, though pale and trembling, managed a weak shake of his head.

"She was called Al-Buraq," Liyana began, her voice weaving the ancient tale with a cadence that was almost hypnotic. "A majestic creature, smaller than a mule but taller than a donkey, with wings on her sides. It was said that she carried the Prophet from Mecca to Jerusalem and then ascended to heaven. Her strength, loyalty and resilience are celebrated in our history. She symbolises the journey we must all take, facing our trials with courage and grace.

As she spoke, the rhythm of her words seemed to have a calming effect on Adrien. He closed his eyes, his breathing gradually steadying as he listened to the story of Al-Buraq. The vivid images of the legendary mare soaring gracefully through the night sky seemed to transport him away from his present discomfort.

Sherlock Holmes, who had been quietly watching the scene, turned his attention to Muntasir. The stallion stood proudly on the deck, unperturbed by the rolling waves, his powerful frame exuding an air of calm and strength. The morning light played across his smooth coat, highlighting the rippling muscles beneath. "Muntasir is much like Al-Buraq," Holmes remarked, a note of admiration in his voice. "His calm amidst the chaos of the sea is a testament to his indomitable spirit. It is a rare and admirable quality."

Liyana looked up, a faint smile playing on her lips as she continued to soothe Adrien with her stories. "Yes, Muntasir embodies the qualities I admire most - strength, resilience and an indomitable spirit. He reminds us that no matter what trials we face, we can persevere and prevail".

The themes of transition and identity, so eloquently discussed, became a lens through which we looked at our own backgrounds and the influences that have shaped us. For me, John Watson, it was a reflection on the journey from soldier in Her Majesty's Army to chronicler of the greatest detective of our time. Each identity, each transition, has been a voyage across my own Sea of Marmara, navigating the currents of circumstance and choice.

As our steamer sliced through the waters, leaving behind the crossroads of continents, the conversation between us deepened. The rich, multifaceted dialogue was interwoven with the sounds and scents of the sea, creating an atmosphere of deep introspection. We explored the fluidity of our own identities, the myriad influences that had shaped our beliefs and aspirations. It was a dialogue that went beyond the mere exchange of words; it was a sharing of souls, a mutual discovery of the vast, uncharted territories within ourselves and each other.

Crossing the Sea of Marmara, then, was not merely a physical transition from one landmass to another. It was a metaphysical journey, a passage through the fluid landscapes of identity and culture. It reminded us that, like the waters beneath our ship, our own identities are vast, deep and subject to the ebb and flow of experience and encounter.

As Asia drew closer and the horizon expanded before us, the themes of transition and the fluidity of identity had woven themselves into the fabric of our journey. We were no longer simply travellers crossing a body of water; we were voyagers navigating the intricate tapestry of human experience, bound for lands where the mysteries of the past awaited our discovery.

The Sea of Marmara, with its reflective waters and its role as a bridge between worlds, had taught us a profound lesson. It taught us that the voyage of discovery was not only about uncovering the secrets buried in the ancient sands. It was also about exploring the depths of ourselves, understanding the myriad currents that shaped our thoughts, our dreams and our destinies.

As the steamer continued on its course, the dialogue between us did not fade. It grew richer, imbued with the insights and revelations that had emerged from our crossing. We looked forward to the challenges and mysteries that awaited us, armed with a deeper understanding of ourselves and each other, united in our quest to unravel the mysteries of the Levant.

❧❋❧

The steamer ploughed steadily through the azure expanse of the Aegean, the gentle breeze caressing our faces with a cool touch. The sun was rising, casting a golden glow that danced on the rippling waves. Each island we passed, with its unique silhouette and verdant cliffs, seemed to whisper ancient secrets, tales of gods and heroes, of lost civilisations and enduring legacies.

Dr. Amal El-Sharif, her scholarly demeanour infused with palpable excitement, stood at the bow, her gaze sweeping the horizon. "The Aegean Sea," she began, a deep reverence in her voice, "is a testament to the resilience of nature in the midst of human endeavour. Each island, with its unique topography and history, is a reminder of mankind's ability to adapt and thrive in the most diverse environments."

Her words were a catalyst for a lively discussion among us. The dialogue flowed seamlessly, much like the currents beneath our ship, exploring the dichotomy of isolation and connectivity. The islands, isolated yet part of a greater whole, served as a powerful metaphor for our own journey, for the stories that had brought us together from different paths.

Liyana Sultan, whose bond with her faithful companion Muntasir had become a symbol of the unbreakable bond between man and horse, shared her insights with a serene smile. "These islands," she observed, her voice soft yet resonant, "much like the horses we've come to know and love, embody a remarkable adaptability. Each environment shapes them, yet they retain their essence, their spirit. It's a dance of nature and nurture, of isolation forging strength and connection fostering growth.

Muntasir, standing majestically on the deck beside her, was the embodiment of her words. His coat gleamed in the sunlight, his posture exuding a quiet confidence that was both inspiring and humbling. The horse's calm presence amidst the undulating waves was in stark contrast to Adrien d'Arcy who sat nearby, his face pale and drawn by the lingering effects of seasickness.

Adrien, whose life had been intertwined with the noble lineage of Isinglass, nodded in agreement, though his voice was tinged with fatigue. "Indeed, Liyana. The bond between horse and rider, much like the relationship between these islands and the sea, is built on a foundation of mutual respect and understanding. It's a testament to the bonds formed across different environments, to the unity that comes from diversity".

Adrien's vulnerability, juxtaposed with Muntasir's unwavering strength, created a poignant tableau that would not have escaped the keen eye of Sherlock Holmes. Typically reticent and ensconced in the realm of deduction, Holmes seemed particularly taken with the strategic importance of the islands throughout the ages. "Consider," he mused, his gaze sweeping thoughtfully over the horizon, "the historical significance of these islands. They've served as havens, fortresses and crossroads of civilisations. Their isolation made them defensible, but their location ensured that they remained connected to the wider narrative of human history".

Dr El-Sharif, her eyes glowing with scholarly passion, added: "These islands are living museums of human endeavour, each a microcosm of the wider tapestry of our civilisation. They remind us that isolation and connectivity are two sides of the same coin, both essential to the resilience and adaptability of human societies".

Liyana continued to soothe Adrien with her stories, her voice a melodious balm to his weary spirit. "In Arabian culture," she began, her tone weaving a rich tapestry of imagery, "horses are not merely animals; they are revered companions, symbols of freedom and nobility. The Prophet Mohammed's legendary mare, Al-Buraq, carried him on his night journey, her strength and loyalty a testament to the bond between horse and rider. It is said that "her hooves left no trace on the earth, such was her grace and power".

As she spoke, the rhythm of her words seemed to have a calming effect on Adrien. His breathing steadied and he closed his eyes, letting the tale of Al-Buraq transport him away from his present discomfort. The vivid images of the legendary mare soaring gracefully through the night sky filled the air with a sense of wonder and serenity.

For me, John Watson, the dialogue and reflections were a journey into the depths of our own identities. Each story, each observation was a thread in the intricate tapestry of human experience, weaving together the past and the present, the personal and the universal. The themes of resilience and adaptability, of isolation and connection, resonated deeply, reminding us of the myriad influences that had shaped our lives.

As our steamer continued its journey through the Aegean, the discussions that had animated our group lingered in the air, a rich mix of ideas and reflections. The islands, with their diverse landscapes and storied pasts, offered us a mirror in which to view our own lives, our own journeys. They reminded us that despite the distances that may separate us, we are bound by the common waters of human experience, by the stories that bind us together across time and space.

Sailing the Aegean was more than a physical passage; it was a journey through the layers of our own narratives, a voyage of discovery that brought us closer to understanding the mosaic of human civilisation. And as the islands faded into the distance, their silhouettes a poignant reminder of the world's vast beauty and complexity, we turned our gaze forward, to the Levant and the mysteries that awaited us there. With hearts full of anticipation and minds enriched by the tapestry of stories that had unfolded on these waters, we sailed on, ever closer to the heart of ancient lands and the untold stories that beckoned to us.

⁂

The steamer glided through the narrow straits of the Dardanelles, a shimmering ribbon of water that connects the Aegean to the Sea of Marmara. The early morning light cast a golden glow over the landscape, illuminating the ancient ruins of Troy that lay on the hills, barely visible through the mist. The air was thick with the scent of salt and history, every breath a reminder of the civilisations that had once flourished in this storied region.

Sherlock Holmes, his keen eyes fixed on the distant ruins, broke the contemplative silence that had settled over our group. "Consider Troy," he began, his voice thoughtful and measured, "a city that has captured the imagination of the world for millennia. Not just the events that took place there, but the stories that rose from its ashes - the Iliad, the Odyssey - tales that have shaped our understanding of heroism, loyalty and the fickle nature of the gods."

I added: "And yet, beneath the legends, there was a real city, with real people who lived, loved and lost. It is a poignant reminder of the legacy of human conflict, the cycles of war and peace that have shaped civilisations through the ages."

Holmes nodded, his eyes never leaving the horizon. "Indeed, Watson. The ruins of Troy are a testament to the enduring nature of human endeavour. Every stone, every fragment tells a story of resilience and continuity, of the indomitable spirit that has carried us through the ages."

His words hung in the air as if the very spirits of Achilles and Hector were listening. The sea breeze carried a hint of the wild thyme that grows among the ruins, mingling with the scent of salt and ancient stone.

Liyana Sultan, standing beside him at the rail, nodded thoughtfully. "And yet, beneath the legends," she mused, "there was a real city, with real people who lived, loved and lost. It is a poignant reminder of the legacy of human conflict, the cycles of war and peace that have defined civilisations through the ages."

Her eyes glistened with a mixture of admiration and sorrow as she spoke. The morning sun caught the intricacies of her embroidered cloak, each thread telling its own story of heritage and loss.

Dr Amal El-Sharif, our esteemed scholar of Middle Eastern history, added her voice to the conversation. "Just a few years ago, in 1871, Heinrich Schliemann discovered what is believed to be the ancient city of Troy," she began, her tone filled with scholarly reverence. "His excavations revealed a city long thought to be the stuff of legend, buried under layers of earth and time. Schliemann's work proved that the tales of Homer were not entirely without basis in reality. The city we see today is a testament to the enduring power of these ancient stories.

The mention of Schliemann's discovery sparked a deeper sense of wonder in our group. The ruins of Troy, standing silently on the hills, became more than just stones and relics - they were a tangible link to the epic stories that had shaped our understanding of history and myth.

The sight of Troy and the conversation it sparked seemed to bring us closer together, a shared moment of contemplation on the enduring nature of storytelling and its power to unite disparate cultures. With uncharacteristic candor, Holmes shared a personal anecdote from his university days, a rare glimpse into his life beyond the realm of deduction and logic.

"I remember," he began, a hint of nostalgia softening his usual tone, "a particular professor who challenged us to find the truths hidden in myths. It was a lesson in looking beyond the surface, in understanding that stories, even the most fantastic, are rooted in human experience. It taught me that the pursuit of knowledge is not just about gathering facts, but about seeking the connections that bind us together across time and culture".

His story, tinged with both humour and sadness, served to humanise the detective, revealing a depth of character rarely seen by others. Liyana also found a connection in Holmes' words, relating them to the legacy of her brother Zafir. "Zafir believed in the power of stories," she said softly, a quiet strength in her voice. "In their ability to inspire, to teach, to heal. He saw his work not just as preserving artefacts, but as keeping the stories of the past alive for future generations."

As the narrator of our adventures and a chronicler in my own right, I was deeply moved by this conversation. The ruins of Troy, standing silently on the hills, became a symbol of the enduring power of storytelling, a testament to its ability to bridge the gap between past and present, reality and myth. It was a poignant reminder of the role of stories in understanding our past and shaping our future, connecting us to the common human experience that transcends time and geography.

Meanwhile, Adrien d'Arcy, still recovering from his earlier bout of seasickness, lay on a deckchair nearby, his pale face turned towards the ruins. Watson, ever the diligent physician, hovered nearby, keeping him comfortable and administering small doses of medicine to ease his discomfort. Liyana, demonstrating her compassionate nature, continued to soothe Adrien with stories, her voice a gentle balm to his weary mind.

"The legendary mare of the Prophet Mohammed, Al-Buraq," she began, her tone weaving a rich tapestry of imagery, "carried him on his night journey, her strength and loyalty a testament to the bond between horse and rider. It is said that her hooves left no mark on the earth, such was her grace and power."

Adrien listened, his eyes closed, the rhythm of Liyana's words taking him away from his present discomfort. The vivid images of the legendary mare soaring gracefully through the night sky filled the air with a sense of wonder and serenity.

Holmes, who had observed Muntasir's calm presence on deck, added: "Horses have always had a symbolic depth in literature. The Trojan Horse, for example, a cunning stratagem that led to the fall of Troy, reminds us of the dual nature of trust and deception. Muntasir, with his strength and composure, serves as a symbol of our own journey - a blend of resilience and perseverance".

The morning light glinted off Muntasir's sleek coat, accentuating his powerful muscles as he stood unperturbed by the ship's rocking. His presence exuded a sense of calm strength, a stark contrast to the turbulent waters and the ancient conflicts they evoked.

As the steamer continued its course, leaving the Dardanelles behind, the conversation lingered in the air, a rich tapestry of thoughts and reflections that drew us closer together. We were travellers not only in space but in time, seeking not only the secrets buried in the ancient sands but also the stories that shaped our understanding of the world and ourselves.

The ruins of Troy faded from view, but the impact of our passage through the Dardanelles remained, a poignant reminder of the enduring nature of storytelling and its power to connect us across the ages. It was a moment of reflection that deepened our bonds and strengthened our resolve as we travelled on, ever closer to the heart of the Levant and the mysteries that awaited us there.

As our steamer approached the Levantine coast, the world around us seemed to undergo a subtle transformation. The rugged, imposing mountains of the Anatolian peninsula gradually receded, giving way to the fertile plains of the Levant. The coastline stretched out before us, a tapestry of ancient ports and bustling modern cities, each telling its own story of the civilisations that have flourished and withered in this cradle of humanity. It was as if we were navigating not just geographical space, but the layers of history itself, witnessing the sediment of cultures accumulated over millennia.

Dr Amal El-Sharif, standing by my side on the deck, her eyes scanning the approaching coast, broke the contemplative silence. "The Levant," she began, her voice a mixture of reverence and scholarly excitement, "has been a crossroads of empires, a battleground for conquering armies, and a meeting place for traders and scholars for thousands of years. Each wave of conquerors left behind a layer, adding to the rich mosaic that is the cultural heritage of this land".

Her words prompted us to reflect on the sheer depth of the history that lay before us, a history as turbulent as it was enlightening. Sherlock Holmes, whose keen analytical mind was always searching for patterns and connections, seemed particularly thoughtful. "It is remarkable," he mused, "how this country has witnessed the ebb and flow of human endeavour. The continuity of change, the resilience of this region in the face of conquest and conflict, speaks volumes about the indomitable spirit of humanity".

The coast, with its mix of ancient ruins and modern infrastructure, is a testament to the region's role in the annals of history. The ancient ports, once bustling with merchants from faraway lands, now bordered cities that pulsed with the pulse of contemporary life. Yet despite the march of progress, the past was never far from the surface, its echoes reverberating in the stones of bygone temples and the pathways of ancient markets.

As the conversation progressed, it became increasingly clear that our journey was not just a physical passage to a new destination, but a journey through time, a chance to connect with the layers of history that have shaped the very fabric of the Levant. Dr El-Sharif's insights into the historical significance of the region, combined with Sherlock's reflections on the nature of change, provided a rich backdrop against which we considered our own personal journeys and transformations.

The theme of historical continuity in the midst of change resonated deeply with each of us. It served as a poignant reminder of our own experiences, of the changes we have undergone and the constants that have remained. For me, John Watson, it underlined the profound impact of our adventures on my understanding of the world and myself. The anticipation of setting foot on the Levantine coast, of exploring the ancient lands that had witnessed the dawn of civilisations, filled me with a sense of awe and wonder.

As the coast approached, the group gathered at the bow, each of us lost in thought, yet united by a shared sense of purpose and curiosity. The layers of history before us, the sediment of cultures that had contributed to the rich tapestry of the Levant, beckoned us to explore, to uncover the stories woven into the very landscape of this ancient land.

Liyana Sultan, always the caring presence among us, turned her attention to Adrien d'Arcy. Despite the improvement in his condition, Adrien still wore the pallor of seasickness. Liyana's gentle hands administered sips of water and a cooling cloth to his forehead, her voice soothing as she told tales of Arabian lore.

"Adrien," she began, her voice a soft, melodic cadence, "you are well versed in the lineage and qualities of Arabian horses, but have you ever heard the legend of their origin? The Bedouins believed that Allah created the Arabian horse from the south wind and gave it the power to fly without wings".

Adrien's eyes, though tired, showed a glimmer of interest. "Indeed, Liyana, I was unaware of this particular legend. The Arabs are truly magnificent creatures."

"Yes," Liyana continued, her tone filled with pride and awe, "and their endurance and spirit are unsurpassed. Muntasir, my stallion, embodies that very essence. Look at him, standing so proudly, a symbol of strength and resilience, much like the land we are about to enter.

Muntasir stood tall and steady on the deck, his presence a stark contrast to the rocking of the ship. His calm demeanour in the midst of the open sea was a silent testament to the enduring spirit of the Arabian horse. Sherlock Holmes, who had been watching the scene with great interest, remarked: "Muntasir does indeed embody a remarkable fortitude. His composure amidst the turmoil of the sea is commendable, much like the resilience of the Levant itself".

As the steamer continued on its course, the dialogue between us did not falter. It grew richer, imbued with the insights and revelations that had emerged from our crossing. We looked forward to the challenges and mysteries that awaited us, armed with a deeper understanding of ourselves and each other, united in our quest to unravel the mysteries of the Levant.

Approaching the Levantine coast marked a pivotal moment in our journey, a threshold between the familiar waters of the Mediterranean and the mysteries that awaited us in Beirut and beyond. It was a moment of reflection, anticipation and deep connection with the past. As we stood on the threshold of ancient lands, the continuity of change and the resilience of the human spirit were ever present in our minds, guiding us as we ventured into the heart of the Levant, ready to embrace the challenges and revelations that lay ahead.

With hearts full of anticipation and minds enriched by the tapestry of stories that had unfolded on our journey so far, we sailed on, ever closer to the heart of ancient lands and the untold stories that beckoned to us. The Levantine coast, with its promise of discovery and understanding, awaited our arrival, a new chapter in our ongoing quest for knowledge and insight into the complexities of human history and civilisation.

CHAPTER 17

THE ROAD TO FORGOTTEN STONES

Upon reaching the firm embrace of Beirut's docks, our steamboat's gentle rocking came to an end, signifying the start of a fresh chapter in our adventure. As the gangplank descended, Muntasir, his sleek coat shimmering in the sunlight, was carefully led off the steamboat by Liyana, drawing admiring glances from passers-by. The bustling sights and sounds of Beirut enveloped us - a symphony of voices, the clatter of carriages and the distant, melodious call to prayer. The air, rich with the aroma of spices and the sea, reminded us that we had arrived in a country where history was as tangible as the warm breeze on our faces.

Our reception at the harbour was nothing short of royal. The Ottoman Governor of Beirut, a man whose noble bearing was matched only by the warmth of his welcome, greeted us personally. Dressed in traditional garb that spoke of his stature and the rich cultural tapestry of this land, his presence commanded respect and admiration.

"Welcome to Beirut," he began, his voice imbued with the rich timbre of a seasoned orator, echoing with the resonance of one accustomed to addressing gatherings of great importance. "A city where the echoes of the past meet the whispers of the future."

The Governor, obviously well versed in the affairs of the region and aware of the importance of our mission, offered his assistance with a sincerity that left no room for doubt. "Your journey," he continued, a hint of reverence in his tone, "is one of great importance. It is my honour to assist you in your quest." The depth of his commitment to fostering understanding and cooperation was palpable and resonated with each of us on a deep level.

As we stepped onto the solid ground of Beirut's docks, the gentle rocking of our steamship journey lingered in our minds, a reminder of the distance we had travelled and the adventures yet to come. Dr Amal El-Sharif, her dark eyes sparkling with curiosity and intellect, engaged the Governor in a discussion of the historical significance of Beirut's landmarks. Meanwhile, Adrien d'Arcy's keen eyes took in every detail, his curiosity about the city's culture evident.

The Governor's attention shifted to Sherlock Holmes, who stood with his usual air of calm scrutiny. "Beirut has always been a crossroads of civilisations, a place where ideas and cultures meet. It is this confluence that has given our city its unique character and resilience," the governor explained, gesturing to the city's skyline. Holmes, ever the astute observer, nodded in agreement, his keen eyes reflecting a deep appreciation of the Governor's insights.

Adrien d'Arcy, with a pensive expression on his face, asked about the modern implications of ancient trade routes, his questions prompting the governor to elaborate on Beirut's role in contemporary trade. "Beirut's ports are not just historical relics; they are still vital arteries of trade today," the governor replied, his voice carrying the weight of centuries of mercantile tradition. "Goods from all over the world pass through here, mixing cultures and economies in a dance as old as time."

As we were escorted through the bustling streets of Beirut, the governor took on the role of an erudite guide, recounting tales of Beirut's storied past with an eloquence that brought history to life. He pointed out landmarks that testified to the city's resilience and enduring spirit - the ancient Roman baths, the grand Serail and the vibrant souks that bustled with life and commerce. The juxtaposition of ancient architecture against the backdrop of modern buildings served as a vivid canvas, illustrating the city's remarkable ability to adapt and thrive amidst the ebb and flow of history.

"The Roman Baths," said the Governor, his voice tinged with admiration, "are not just ruins, but a reminder of our city's capacity for luxury and public welfare in antiquity. They are a testament to the engineering prowess of our ancestors." As he spoke, the subtle scent of ancient stone and the cool whisper of shaded corridors seemed to come alive in our minds.

The vibrant souks, with their labyrinthine alleyways and stalls overflowing with goods, captured our senses. The air was fragrant with the scent of jasmine and orange blossom, mingling with the more earthy aromas of spices and freshly baked bread. Merchants shouted in a myriad of languages, hawking wares from the far reaches of the known world. The streets were alive with the chatter of merchants, the laughter of children playing in the narrow alleys, and the solemn chants emanating from the mosques.

Holmes paused to watch a craftsman skilfully weave a rug, his hands moving with practiced precision. "Each thread tells a story," Holmes murmured, his voice barely audible over the din of the market. "The craftsmanship is exquisite, each pattern a testament to centuries of tradition and skill."

Our arrival in Beirut and the warm welcome we received from the Ottoman governor marked the beginning of an extraordinary leg of our journey. As we prepared to continue our journey to Damascus, the experiences of Beirut - the insights shared by the Governor, the vibrant tapestry of life in the souks and the architectural marvels that bridged the ancient and the modern - were indelibly etched in our memories. Beirut, with its rich history and dynamic spirit, had set the stage for the road ahead, a road that promised to take us deeper into the heart of the Levant and the mysteries that awaited us in the ancient city of Damascus.

Reflecting on the day's events, I wrote in my diary: "In Beirut, past and present are not merely juxtaposed; they are woven together in a seamless tapestry that speaks of resilience and perpetual renewal. As we move forward, the lessons of this city will undoubtedly guide our steps".

Holmes, his analytical mind ever at work, reflected on the strategic importance of Beirut's location. "This city," he mused, "is a living testament to the power of geographical and cultural convergence. Its role as a hub of trade and ideas cannot be overstated".

Dr Amal El-Sharif shared her thoughts with the group as we gathered for dinner. "The cultural exchanges that have shaped Beirut are a microcosm of the wider interactions that have shaped our world. It is a reminder of the importance of dialogue and mutual respect in bridging divides."

Liyana, her gaze softening as she strokes Muntasir's sleek coat, added: "In every corner of this city, I see the resilience of the human spirit. Beirut stands as a beacon of hope and continuity amidst the turbulence of history."

Adrien d'Arcy, his voice full of admiration, remarked: "The Governor's stories and the vibrancy of this city have deepened my understanding of our journey. Beirut has provided us with a rich tapestry of knowledge and experience that will surely illuminate our path to Damascus".

As we prepared for the next leg of our journey, the sense of unity and purpose was palpable. The shared experiences in Beirut had not only enriched our understanding of the Levant, but had also strengthened the bonds of community among us. The road to Damascus, though fraught with unknown challenges, was now imbued with a sense of promise and anticipation.

At dawn we would set off in horse-drawn carriages, the ancient road to Damascus stretching out before us. The experiences of Beirut - the vivid sensations, the historical insights and the deepened camaraderie - would guide us as we delved deeper into the heart of the Levant and the mysteries that awaited us.

⊕⊱◦≬◦⊰⊕

The evening before our departure was filled with a profound atmosphere of

233

solemn anticipation, heightened by the imposing grandeur of the Ottoman Governor's residence in Beirut. The setting sun cast long shadows across the opulent courtyard, transforming the marble and mosaic into a shimmering canvas of gold and amber. A light breeze carried the scent of orange blossom, mingled with the aroma of spiced tea that awaited us inside.

Upon entering the governor's study - a room richly decorated with artefacts that spoke eloquently of Beirut's storied past - we were greeted by the sight of a large oak table, its surface bare except for the ancient maps and scrolls that would soon be unfurled. These documents, each a relic of a bygone era, were to serve as our guides on the journey ahead.

The Governor, a man whose demeanour seamlessly blended authority with scholarly intrigue, gestured us towards the table. "This road you are about to travel," he began, his voice resonating with a reverence befitting the tales of adventure, trade and discovery it had witnessed, "is more than a mere passage from one city to another. It is a journey through history, a path trodden by countless souls whose stories have become woven into the very fabric of this land".

As he traced the route from Beirut to Damascus with a slender finger, the Governor pointed out landmarks and sites of historical significance. "Here," he said, pausing at a spot marked by an ancient caravanserai, "merchants from distant lands would gather, their camels laden with silk, spices and tales of the Silk Road. And here," his finger moved to a mountain pass, "armies marched, empires rose and fell, leaving echoes of their glory and despair.

The air in the room was thick with the weight of history, each of the Governor's words a brushstroke in the vivid tapestry of the Levant's past. Sherlock Holmes, whose keen interest in strategic geographies was well known to me, leaned forward, his eyes alight with the spark of intellectual curiosity. "The parallels with the ancient Silk Road are indeed striking," he remarked, his voice carrying an undertone of admiration. "It is a reminder of how such routes served not only as conduits for trade, but also as arteries through which ideas, cultures and innovations flowed, connecting disparate civilisations."

Dr Amal El-Sharif, her intellect and passion for history shining through, added: "The Silk Road was more than a trade route. It was a lifeline for cultural exchange, fostering connections that transcended borders and time. The essence of our journey reflects this spirit of discovery and understanding.

Liyana Sultan, her eyes fixed on the ancient maps, spoke softly: "In these paths, I see the footsteps of my ancestors. Each landmark holds a story, a fragment of the past that we are privileged to uncover. This journey is not just about reaching Damascus; it is about embracing the heritage that has shaped our world".

Adrien d'Arcy, ever inquisitive, asked a question that brought a modern perspective to the discussion. "Governor, how do these ancient routes influence contemporary trade and diplomacy? Do the echoes of the past still resonate in today's geopolitical landscape?"

The Governor nodded thoughtfully, "Indeed, Mr d'Arcy. The ancient routes laid the foundations for the interconnected world we navigate today. The principles of trade, cultural exchange and strategic alliances established centuries ago continue to shape our global interactions. Beirut and Damascus remain central hubs in this intricate network, their relevance enduring through the ages".

As the night wore on, each member of our party found themselves lost in contemplation, the maps and scrolls before us portals to the journey ahead. The room was filled with a hushed reverence, the only sound the gentle rustling of parchment and the soft murmur of our discussions. The glow of the lamplight cast a warm halo over the ancient documents, illuminating the paths we were about to tread.

Reflecting on the evening's discussion, I wrote in my diary: "This preparation is more than a strategic endeavour; it is a communion with history. Every map and every scroll is a testament to the enduring spirit of exploration and the relentless pursuit of knowledge. As we prepare to embark on this journey, we carry with us the weight of countless generations and the promise of new discoveries.

Sherlock Holmes, his analytical mind ever active, mused aloud, "Our journey is a microcosm of the Silk Road itself - an exploration of connections that transcend time and geography. It is a reminder that our quest for understanding is a thread that weaves through the fabric of history, connecting us to those who have gone before and those who will follow."

Dr Amal El-Sharif shared her reflections with the group: "The cultural exchanges that have shaped our world are the very essence of our humanity. As we travel from Beirut to Damascus, we are not just travellers; we are custodians of a legacy, entrusted with the stories and wisdom of the past".

Liyana Sultan, her voice full of quiet strength, added: "With every step we take, we honour the resilience and courage of those who have walked these paths before us. This journey is a tribute to their memory and a testament to the enduring power of heritage".

Adrien d'Arcy, his eyes reflecting a deep sense of purpose, remarked, "The insights we've gained tonight are a beacon for our journey. As we traverse the ancient routes, we do so with a deep respect for the past and a keen anticipation of the future discoveries that await us".

Preparing for our trip to Damascus under the guidance of the Ottoman governor was more than an evening of planning and reflection. It was a communion with the past, a solemn acknowledgment of the road we were about to travel - a road that had witnessed the ebb and flow of civilisations and the indomitable spirit of humanity. As we retired for the night, the Governor's words echoed in our minds, a solemn reminder of the continuity of history and the quest for understanding that lay at the heart of our journey.

At dawn we would set off in horse-drawn carriages, the ancient road to Damascus stretching before us, a promise of discoveries yet to come. But that evening, in the governor's residence, amid the maps and scrolls of ages past, we stood on the threshold of history, ready to embark on a journey that would illuminate the depths of human experience and bind us ever closer in the bonds of community.

As the first light of dawn painted the city of Beirut in shades of gold and amber, we set out on the next leg of our journey. The road to Damascus lay before us, a road not only of geography but of history, stretching into the heart of the Levant. I, Dr John Watson, felt a deep sense of duty to record our passage through this ancient landscape, aware that every mile we travelled was steeped in the stories of countless souls who had travelled before us.

Our transport was a series of horse-drawn carriages, modest in their construction but rich in the promise of a closer connection to the land we sought to understand. As we left Beirut, the din of the city gradually gave way to the quiet whispers of the countryside. The transition was subtle at first, but with each mile the urban landscape receded and was replaced by the green expanse of the Levantine countryside.

The road wound through the fertile plains of the Bekaa Valley, a stretch of land that stretched out like a vast green sea. The earth here was a patchwork of fields and vineyards, each plot a testament to the region's agricultural bounty. The air was filled with the scent of ripening grapes and fresh earth, a perfume that spoke of centuries of cultivation and care. It was in this valley that one could truly grasp the essence of the Levant - a bridge between the desert and the sea, a cradle of civilisations that had risen and fallen on its soil.

"Watson," said Sherlock Holmes as he looked out over the vast fields, his voice filled with a rare softness, "observe how this land breathes history. Every stone and furrowed field carries the weight of millennia, whispering tales of those who have toiled and prospered here. It is a living testament to the endurance of human endeavour.

His words resonated deeply and I found myself marvelling at the profound simplicity of the landscape. "Indeed, Holmes. The Bekaa Valley is like an open book, its pages written by countless hands over time. It is humbling to think of the generations who have walked this path before us.

As we travelled on, the Anti-Lebanon Mountains began to rise on the horizon, their rugged slopes casting long shadows across our path. The contrast between the lushness of the Bekaa Valley and the stark majesty of the mountains was breathtaking, a vivid reminder of the diversity of the Levantine landscape. These mountains, their peaks shrouded in mist, seemed to stand as guardians of history, their slopes bearing the scars of countless battles and the whispers of ancient secrets.

Dr Amal El-Sharif, her eyes reflecting the same awe I felt, spoke softly, "These mountains have seen the rise and fall of empires. They have stood as silent sentinels against the ebb and flow of history, watching over the land and its people. The stories they could tell would fill volumes.

Liyana Sultan, riding gracefully beside Muntasir, added: "And yet, amidst their grandeur, there is a serenity, a timelessness that speaks to the soul. It is as if the mountains themselves are a bridge between heaven and earth, connecting us to something greater than ourselves".

Adrien d'Arcy, ever the inquisitive mind, remarked, "The resonance of history is palpable. It is as if the land itself is remembering, holding the echoes of footsteps long past. Our search is not just for answers, but for a deeper understanding of the human journey".

The beauty of the landscape was not just in its visual splendour, but in the stories it held. Every bend in the road revealed vistas as if painted by divine hands - a monastery perched on a hill, a shepherd tending his flock, a ruin suggesting a once-thriving settlement. These were the scenes that unfolded before us, each a chapter in the continuing story of this land.

As the day progressed, the colours of the sky changed from the clear azure of the morning to the rich golden hues of dusk. The setting sun bathed the landscape in a warm, ethereal light, transforming the ordinary into the sublime. The journey, though physically gruelling, was spiritually uplifting, each mile imbued with a sense of discovery and connection to the land and its history.

Holmes, ever the analyst, pondered the strategic importance of the road and its role in the ebb and flow of empires. "Watson," he mused, his voice carrying the weight of his reflections, "this road we traverse is not merely a passage; it is a thread in the tapestry of history, connecting epochs and empires, each layer adding to the richness of the narrative."

Dr Amal El-Sharif, whose deep knowledge of Middle Eastern culture enriches our understanding, shared insights into the traditions that have shaped the region. "The Levant," she explained, her voice resonating with passion, "is a land of convergence, where East meets West and ancient traditions merge with the pulse of modernity. Every village, every landmark tells a story of resilience and cultural fusion".

Liyana Sultan and Adrien d'Arcy exchanged stories of their own countries, finding common threads in the tapestry of human experience. Liyana, her gaze far away as she recalled her homeland, said, "In every stone and every breath of wind there is a whisper of the past. Our journey is a tribute to the ancestors who have walked these paths, their spirits guiding us to new horizons".

Adrien, always inquisitive, remarked: "The resonance of history is palpable. It is as if the land itself remembers and holds the echoes of footsteps long past. Our quest is not just for answers, but for a deeper understanding of the human journey".

In the midst of my efforts to document our journey, I found myself contemplating the continuity of history - the realisation that we were but fleeting travellers on a road that had borne witness to the march of time. "Holmes," I reflected, "our journey is a bridge between the past and the present, a testament to the enduring spirit of exploration and discovery."

The journey to Damascus was a passage through the heart of the Levant, a journey that transcended mere distance. It was a journey through time, through the layers of history laid down by generations of travellers, traders and conquerors. As we made our way along this ancient road, we were reminded of the enduring spirit of humanity, of our ceaseless quest for understanding and connection. And in those moments, amidst the changing landscapes and shifting colours of the sky, we found ourselves united in a bond of fellowship, woven together by the shared experience of our journey through the tapestry of the Levant.

Muntasir, his sleek coat shimmering in the twilight, added a majestic aura to our procession, his presence a symbol of the unbreakable bond between man and beast. Liyana, riding with grace and confidence, shared a quiet moment with the noble steed, their connection a testament to the harmony between rider and horse. The rhythmic sound of hooves on the ancient road was a reminder of the countless travellers who had made similar journeys, their hopes and dreams echoing through the ages.

As night fell and the first stars began to twinkle in the vast expanse of the sky, we found solace in the company we shared. Around the campfire we shared stories and reflections, each voice adding to the chorus of our collective experience. The warmth of the fire and the camaraderie of friends enveloped us, creating a sanctuary of connection and understanding.

In those quiet moments, Sherlock Holmes, ever the philosopher, offered a final reflection. "Our journey, Watson, is a testament to the resilience of the human spirit. It is a reminder that despite the passage of time and the shifting sands of history, the quest for knowledge and connection remains unbroken. We are but travellers on an endless road, seeking the truths that lie beyond the horizon.

With these words we retired for the night, the echoes of our reflections mingled with the gentle whisper of the Levantine breeze. The road to Damascus awaited us, promising new discoveries and deeper understanding.

And as we lay beneath the canopy of stars, the journey ahead seemed imbued with the promise of enlightenment and the enduring bond of fellowship.

Our journey through the Levantine landscape culminated as we approached the ancient city of Damascus at dusk. The silhouette of the city's venerable walls appeared against the backdrop of a setting sun, painting the sky in shades of fiery orange and deep purple. It was a sight that evoked a sense of timelessness, a gateway between the past and the present, a testament to the continuity of history in this fabled land.

The Ottoman governor of Damascus, having been informed of our imminent arrival by his esteemed counterpart in Beirut, awaited us with a retinue of dignitaries that reflected the city's storied heritage. Their presence, a mixture of traditional dress and the formalities of their station, signalled the importance of our mission and the respect it commanded.

As our carriages pulled up to the governor's palace, the air was filled with the scent of jasmine and the distant sound of the muezzin's call to prayer, a melodic echo that seemed to weave its way through the city's narrow streets and open marketplaces. The palace itself was a marvel of Islamic architecture, its intricate tiling and elegant courtyards a tribute to the artistic and cultural heritage that had flourished under the auspices of Damascus's historic rulers.

"Welcome to Damascus," greeted the Ottoman governor, his voice filled with warmth and hospitality. His words, spoken in the fading light of day, were no mere formality, but an invitation to share in the rich tapestry of experiences the city had to offer. "May your stay here be restful and enlightening," he continued, his tone a mellifluous blend of sincerity and grandeur, capturing the essence of our quest in a single sentence.

The generosity of our welcome spoke volumes, not only of the alliances we had forged along the way, but also of the strategic importance of our mission. As we were ushered into the luxurious quarters of the governor's palace, our spirits were lifted by the thought and care that had gone into our reception. The rooms were decorated with hand-woven carpets and intricate tapestries, each telling a story of the city's craftsmanship and skill. The smell of spiced tea and freshly baked bread wafted through the corridors, inviting us to share in the culinary delights that awaited us.

In Damascus, at the crossroads of history and civilisation, we found ourselves on the threshold of a new chapter in our journey. The city, with its labyrinthine souks filled with the chatter of merchants and the scent of exotic spices, its great mosques standing as beacons of faith and architectural ingenuity, and its storied past etched into every stone and alley, promised a wealth of experiences and revelations.

As night fell over Damascus, the echo of the muezzin's call to prayer lulled us into a contemplative silence. It was a moment that transcended the boundaries of time and space, connecting us to the countless travellers, scholars and seekers of truth who had walked these streets in search of understanding and connection. Lying in the comfort of our rooms, the day's journey a tapestry of memories, we were reminded of the purpose that united us - a quest not merely for the artefacts and remnants of a bygone era, but for the essence of human endeavour that had shaped this land.

Our reflections were as varied as the landscapes we had traversed. Sherlock Holmes, ever the analyst, pondered the intricate web of history and strategy that Damascus represented, a city that had witnessed the rise and fall of empires. "Watson," he remarked, his voice tinged with the gravity of his thoughts, "Damascus is a confluence of the ancient and the eternal. It is a place where history has been written in blood and ink, a city that has seen the birth and death of civilisations".

Dr Amal El-Sharif, with her deep understanding of the region's cultural heritage, spoke of the importance of Damascus as a centre of learning and civilisation. "The Umayyad Mosque," she said, her eyes reflecting a reverence for the past, "is not only a place of worship but a symbol of the city's enduring heritage. It stands as a beacon of knowledge and faith, a testament to the intellectual and spiritual contributions of this great city".

Liyana Sultan and Adrien d'Arcy shared their personal insights, drawing parallels between their own experiences and the stories that had unfolded on our journey. Liyana, her voice soft with contemplation, mused, "Damascus feels like a tapestry woven with threads from every culture and era. It is a city that breathes history, each alley and courtyard whispering tales of times long past."

Adrien, ever the keen observer, added: "It is fascinating to see how Damascus has retained its identity despite the passage of time and the many influences that have shaped it. There is a resilience here, a spirit that endures through the ages".

And I, Dr. John Watson, found myself humbled by the magnitude of our endeavour, the bonds of fellowship that had been forged between us, and the anticipation of the discoveries that lay ahead. "Holmes," I reflected, "our journey has brought us to the heart of the Levant, a place where the echoes of history resonate with every step we take. It is a privilege to walk these streets and be part of this timeless narrative."

In Damascus, under the watchful eyes of history and the guiding light of our common purpose, we knew that our journey was far from over. It was but a continuation of the quest for understanding and connection that had brought us from the shores of Constantinople to the heart of the Levant. And as we rested that night, the sounds and smells of Damascus enveloping us, we were reminded that every step we took was a step towards unlocking the mysteries of human history, a step closer to bridging the gulfs of time and culture that separated us from those who had walked these paths before us.

As I lay in my bed, replaying the events of the day in my mind, I couldn't help but feel a deep sense of gratitude for the journey that had brought us here. The camaraderie we had forged, the insights we had gained and the anticipation of uncovering more secrets in this ancient city filled me with a profound sense of purpose. With the promise of new discoveries the next day, I drifted into a restful slumber, the sounds of Damascus a soothing lullaby that carried me into the realm of dreams.

CHAPTER 18

GUARDIANS OF ANCIENT WISDOM

I n the ancient city of Damascus, the first light of dawn delicately disturbed the ethereal calm that enveloped the streets. The Governor's Palace, silent witness to countless dawns, stood bathed in gold, its intricate mosaics reflecting the dawning rays in a kaleidoscope of colour across the courtyards and marble floors. Here, amidst the echoes of history and the palpable anticipation that hung in the air like a morning mist, we stood on the threshold of a new chapter in our extraordinary journey.

The city slowly awakens, the soft murmur of the morning adhan mingling with the distant sounds of the marketplace as it comes to life. The scent of jasmine and fresh earth wafts through the open windows of our accommodation, a subtle reminder of the enduring beauty and mystery of this land. From our vantage point, the rooftops of Damascus stretch to the horizon, a sea of terracotta and stone cradled by the distant silhouette of the mountains. It is a sight that never fails to stir the soul, a testament to the enduring spirit of this ancient city at the crossroads of civilisations.

Within the walls of the Governor's Palace, the atmosphere is one of readiness. Sherlock Holmes, Dr Amal El-Sharif, Liyana Sultan, Adrien d'Arcy and I, Dr John Watson, gather in the great hall, our minds and spirits united by the common purpose that has brought us to this moment. Liyana stands beside Muntasir, her hand resting gently on the stallion's mane, a picture of serene strength and grace. The room, decorated with artefacts and tapestries that whisper tales of the Levant's storied past, serves as a fitting backdrop for the deliberations and preparations that occupy our minds.

Holmes, always the embodiment of serenity and foresight, surveys the

243

assembled group with a keen eye, reflecting on the meticulous preparations of the previous night. His sharp features, illuminated by the morning light, betray a deep, almost fervent anticipation. "Today we are one step closer to unravelling the mysteries that have led us across continents," he says, his voice carrying the weight of the responsibility we bear. His words, though softly spoken, resonate with the gravity of our mission and inspire a sense of determination in each of us. His eyes, always so full of keen insight, seem to look beyond the room and imagine the challenges and discoveries that lie ahead.

Dr El-Sharif, her passion for the ancient world a beacon that has guided much of our journey, leans forward, her eyes bright with anticipation. "Petra awaits," she muses, her voice tinged with a reverence reserved for the holiest of pilgrimages. "A city carved from the heart of the mountains, holding secrets as old as time itself." Her words evoke the grandeur of Petra, a city where history breathes through every stone and the whispers of the past linger in the air.

Liyana and Adrien, both of whom have found in this quest a connection to their own storied heritage, share a look of understanding. Adrien's eyes, usually so full of scholarly curiosity, now shine with the thrill of discovery. Liyana, always composed, allows herself a rare smile, her thoughts seemingly intertwined with the majestic Muntasir at her side. Her journey, like ours, is one of discovery, not only of the outer world, but of the depths within.

As for me, Dr John Watson, the enormity of what lies ahead fills me with a sense of awe and humility. To stand on the brink of such a discovery, to walk in the footsteps of history, is an honour that words can scarcely describe. I find myself reflecting on the community we have forged, each of us bringing our own strengths and perspectives to this great endeavour.

The stillness of the morning, with its promise of new beginnings, is in stark contrast to the swirl of emotions we are experiencing. Excitement, curiosity, a touch of apprehension - all vying for dominance as we contemplate the journey to Petra, that rose-red city half as old as time itself, which holds within its ancient stones the answers we seek. The scent of freshly brewed coffee mingled with the morning air, adding a comforting familiarity to the moment.

Our preparations are meticulous, every detail checked and rechecked, knowing that the path ahead will test us in ways we can scarcely imagine. Maps, journals and an array of instruments that speak to both the scientific and adventurous nature of our endeavour are carefully packed, ready to be called into service at a moment's notice. Adrien checks the harness on Isinglass, his fingers moving deftly, while Liyana makes sure Muntasir's saddle is securely fastened, her calm demeanour a source of reassurance to us all. The sound of Muntasir's gentle snort and the soft rustle of the saddles adds a sensory richness to our preparations.

As the sun rises, casting its light over the city, we are ready to embark on a journey that will take us not only across the deserts to Petra, but deeper into the heart of the mysteries that have drawn us together. In the quiet of the morning, on the cusp of this new chapter, we are reminded that it is not just the destination that defines us, but the journey itself - the quest for understanding that transcends the boundaries of time and culture, uniting us in a purpose far greater than ourselves.

And so, with the ancient city of Damascus awakening around us, we step out into the day, our hearts buoyed by the promise of discovery and the unbreakable bonds of community that have brought us to this moment. The road to Petra awaits, and with it the next chapter in our extraordinary journey through the sands of time. As we move forward, the first rays of sunlight illuminate our path, casting long, hopeful shadows that stretch before us, a silent promise of the wonders and challenges that lie ahead.

⊷⊱⋇⊰⊶

The serene calm of the Damascus morning, already tinged with the anticipation of the day's unfolding adventure, was suddenly shattered by the rhythmic clatter of hooves on cobblestones. It was a sound that, in its insistence, seemed to herald the arrival of a new chapter in our journey. As the echo of the hooves reverberated through the courtyard of the Governor's Palace, our assembled group turned almost in unison towards the source of the sound, our curiosity piqued by this unexpected yet somehow auspicious interruption.

Emerging from the courtyard, framed by the soaring arches and green expanse of the palace gardens, was a figure who seemed at once out of time and deeply rooted in the essence of this ancient land. Khalid Al-Fahmi, our guide to the secrets hidden in the sands, rode with an ease and grace that spoke of a lifetime spent in communion with the desert and its inhabitants. Beside him, matching his poise with a majestic bearing of his own, was Al-Zarib, his stallion, a creature so radiant in the morning light that it seemed as if the dawn itself had conspired to paint his form in gold.

The scent of jasmine and freshly turned earth hung in the air, mingled with the subtle scent of leather and horseflesh. Khalid's clothes, a mixture of traditional Bedouin dress accented with practical elements suited to the rigours of desert travel, spoke volumes about his life and lineage. His features, weathered by sun and wind, were animated by eyes that held the depths of the desert sky, reflecting a knowledge and wisdom born of the sands. As he approached, dismounting with a fluidity that betrayed no hint of the distance already travelled, his gaze met each of ours in turn, a silent acknowledgment of the journey we were about to undertake together.

"I am Khalid," he began, his voice carrying the warmth of the desert wind, rich with the nuances of a life lived in harmony with the unforgiving beauty of the land. "Guide of the sands and keeper of the secrets long buried beneath them. It is my honour to lead you to Petra, the rose-red city half as old as time itself."

His introduction, though brief, was charged with a significance that resonated deeply within each of us. Here was a man who embodied the rich equestrian traditions of his Bedouin heritage, a descendant of legendary Arabian horse breeders whose lineage had shaped the majestic desert steeds for generations. In Khalid we saw not just a guide, but a vital link to the ancient practices and knowledge that had long coexisted with the shifting sands of the desert.

Al-Zarib, perhaps sensing the significance of the moment, stood beside Khalid with quiet dignity. Adrien and Liyana, both of whom had a deep reverence for the bond between horse and rider, were instantly drawn to the stallion, seeing in his grace a reflection of their own cherished steeds, Isinglass and Muntasir. The connection was palpable, a silent communion that spoke of shared heritage and the timeless dance between man and horse.

Liyana stepped forward, her eyes glowing with admiration. "Your stallion is magnificent," she said, her voice warm with genuine respect. Muntasir, standing proudly by her side, snorted softly, as if acknowledging the presence of another noble steed.

Khalid nodded, his gaze meeting Liyana's with deep understanding. "This is Al-Zarib," he introduced, his voice full of pride. "He has been my companion on many journeys, and his strength and loyalty are unsurpassed."

Adrien, his eyes sparkling with curiosity, approached to study Al-Zarib more closely. "The craftsmanship of his harness and saddle is remarkable," he observed. "The artistry speaks of a long tradition of excellence."

Khalid smiled, his pride evident. "Indeed, these were made by the finest craftsmen of my tribe, each piece crafted with care and precision, handed down through generations."

Holmes, ever the observer, nodded approvingly. "A steed like Al-Zarib is not just a means of transport, but a partner in every sense of the word. He speaks volumes of your lineage, Khalid."

The courtyard, once a quiet haven in the heart of the city, had become the setting for a convergence of paths destined to intertwine. In Khalid and Al-Zarib we found not only companions for the journey ahead, but symbols of the enduring spirit of the desert and its people. Their arrival marked the beginning of a partnership that would guide us through the challenges and wonders of the journey to Petra, a journey that promised to be as much about self-discovery as it was about uncovering the secrets of the past.

As Khalid explained his plans for our departure and the route we would take through the desert, his words were infused with a reverence for the land and its history. "The desert," he explained, "is a teacher of resilience, a keeper of secrets and a witness to the passage of time. To travel its vastness is to walk in the footsteps of those who have gone before us, to share a history as old as the sands themselves".

The morning light bathed the scene in a warm glow, casting long shadows that danced across the cobbles. The air was filled with the gentle rustle of leaves and the distant hum of the city awakening. The atmosphere was charged with a sense of purpose and camaraderie as we stood on the cusp of a journey that would challenge us, change us and ultimately unite us in a quest for understanding that transcends the boundaries of time and culture.

With Khalid and Al-Zarib leading the way, we stepped forward into the day, our hearts and minds open to the mysteries that awaited us in the rose-red city of Petra and beyond. The promise of discovery and the unbreakable bonds of camaraderie sustained us and set the stage for the extraordinary adventures that lay ahead.

As the morning unfolded, bringing with it the promise of revelations yet to be uncovered, we found ourselves gathered in a study room within the Governor's Palace. The room pulsated with the intellectual curiosity and scholarly pursuit that had become the hallmark of our journey. The room, bathed in the soft golden light that filtered through the latticed windows, was a sanctuary of knowledge. Its walls were lined with bookshelves that groaned under the weight of tomes and scrolls, while maps lay unfurled on the broad oak table that dominated the room. Each artefact, each piece of parchment and ink, whispered tales of the desert and its hidden city, setting a tone of solemn anticipation for the task ahead.

The air was thick with the scent of aged paper and the faint aroma of frankincense, a scent that seemed to carry the wisdom of centuries. Outside, the distant murmur of the marketplace mingled with the morning adhan, creating a symphony of sounds that spoke of a city alive with history and tradition.

Khalid stood at the head of the table, his presence commanding yet grounded, a bridge between the world of ancient mystery and the pursuit of modern understanding. His eyes, dark and reflective as the depths of a desert night, scanned the room, taking in the serious faces of our group. Sherlock Holmes, always the embodiment of analytical precision, began the debriefing with a meticulous outline of our case and the investigation that had brought us to the threshold of the desert. His voice, calm and measured, echoed through the room, each word carefully chosen, each sentence a step towards unravelling the mystery before us.

"The secrets of Petra," Holmes concluded, his gaze locked with Khalid's, "may hold the key to unravelling a plot that threatens the very fabric of this land's rich heritage."

Khalid listened intently, his expression a tableau of contemplation and determination, as if every word Holmes spoke was carefully catalogued in the vast library of his mind. His answer, when it came, was imbued with a deep understanding and respect for the lore of his ancestors.

"The mysteries of Petra are many," Khalid admitted, his voice echoing the timeless echo of the desert, "and its history is as layered as the desert sands. The city is not only an architectural wonder, but a testament to the resilience, ingenuity and spirit of those who carved their legacy into the very mountains".

As Khalid spoke, the room seemed to expand, the walls dissolving into the vast expanse of the desert, the maps on the table transforming into a living landscape beneath our fingertips. His insights, steeped in the cultural and historical fabric of Petra and the Bedouin traditions that had survived the relentless passage of time, wove a tapestry that enriched our understanding of the monumental task that lay before us. The dialogue that unfolded between Holmes and Khalid was not just an exchange of information but a meeting of minds, a confluence of perspectives that bridged centuries and cultures.

Holmes, with his unerring instinct for discerning the truth from the clutter of the irrelevant, delved deeper into the heart of the mystery, each question a scalpel peeling away the layers of time to reveal the core of our quest. "What do you think is Petra's greatest secret, Khalid?" Holmes asked, his voice a mixture of curiosity and anticipation.

Khalid, for his part, navigated the complexities of the past with the ease of one who has spent a lifetime studying it, his answers painting a vivid picture of Petra not just as a city of stone, but as a living entity pulsing with the stories of those who have passed through its gates. "Petra's greatest secret," Khalid began, "lies not in its grandeur or its architecture, but in its spirit. It is a city of convergence, where cultures, ideas and peoples met and mingled. It is a testament to human resilience, adaptability and the relentless pursuit of understanding.

The atmosphere in the room was charged with a palpable sense of purpose, as if the very air we breathed was imbued with the determination to uncover the truths hidden within the ancient stones of Petra. The dialogue between Holmes and Khalid, rich in the exchange of cultural and historical insights, became the foundation upon which our understanding of the task at hand was built. It was a moment of profound connection, not just between individuals, but between the past and the present, the known and the unknown.

Liyana added, her voice soft yet determined, "The desert has always been a place of trial, where the true nature of one's character is revealed. I believe Petra will test us in ways we cannot yet foresee."

Adrien nodded in agreement, his eyes reflecting the determination of his own journey. "Indeed, it is not only the destination but the journey that will shape us. The challenges we face will forge bonds stronger than any stone."

As the debriefing drew to a close, the room seemed to contract once more, the walls returning to their solid form, the maps flattening into mere representations of the land they depicted. Yet the sense of expansion, of having covered vast distances in the space of one conversation, remained. We stood on the brink of discovery, our path lit by the wisdom shared between Holmes and Khalid, our spirits lifted by the knowledge that the journey to Petra would be not just a physical trek across the desert, but a journey through the annals of history, guided by the insights of those who had dedicated their lives to the study of its mysteries.

In that moment, as we prepared to leave the sanctuary of the study room and step back into the light of day, we were reminded that the quest for understanding is the noblest of pursuits, a journey that transcends the boundaries of time and culture, uniting us in a common purpose that reflects the very essence of mankind's unquenchable thirst for knowledge. With Khalid as our guide and the spirit of discovery as our compass, we were ready to embark on the next chapter of our adventure, each step bringing us closer to the heart of the mystery that awaited us in the rose-red city of Petra.

In the same study room, now transformed into a veritable crucible of intellectual curiosity, the atmosphere changed palpably as Dr Amal El-Sharif, our esteemed companion whose passion for the ancient civilisations of the Middle East had guided much of our journey, initiated a dialogue that would illuminate the depths of Petra's past as never before. The formalities of debriefing vanished, giving way to an exchange marked by passion and a shared thirst for understanding. The room was filled with a golden light that filtered through the intricate latticework of the windows and cast delicate patterns on the floor. The scent of aged parchment and ink mingled with the faint aroma of jasmine, creating an atmosphere that was both scholarly and almost mystical. Every artefact and piece of parchment seemed to hum with the stories of the past, waiting to be unlocked.

Khalid, embodying the bridge between the ancient and the modern, began to unfold the story of Petra with the reverence of one speaking of a sacred trust. "Petra," he intoned, his voice rich and resonant, "is not just a city, but a testament to human ingenuity, a symphony in stone that resonates with the legacy of those who carved their existence into the mountains themselves." His words painted a vivid picture of the Siq, the narrow gorge flanked by towering cliffs that served as the natural gateway to the city. He described its walls as a canvas for the play of light and shadow, leading to the treasury, Al-Khazneh, whose majestic facade has captured the imagination of travellers for centuries.

Dr El-Sharif, her eyes alight with the fire of intellectual pursuit, leaned forward, her questions cutting to the heart of Petra's mystery. "Tell us about the Nabataeans," she urged, her voice filled with a mixture of curiosity and respect.

"Of the people who harnessed the desert, who carved this city out of the mountains and made the sands bloom." Her question, sharp and carrying the weight of genuine curiosity, sought to peel back the layers of history, to understand the spirit of a people capable of such enduring feats.

Khalid's answer was a journey through time, detailing the rise of the Nabataeans from nomadic tribes to architects of an empire built on trade and innovation. "The Nabateans," he explained, "were masters of the desert, their survival honed by the harshness of their environment. They were merchants and engineers, visionaries who made Petra a centre of trade and culture, a crossroads where East and West met". His descriptions of their ingenious water management systems - cisterns and aqueducts that captured and conserved precious rainfall - were particularly evocative, painting a picture of a civilisation that had truly mastered its harsh environment.

As the dialogue deepened, the room seemed to swell with the presence of the Nabataeans, their aspirations and achievements tangibly woven into the very fabric of Petra's stones. Khalid's narrative, enriched by Dr El-Sharif's probing questions, unfolded the layers of Petra's history, from its heyday as a trading metropolis to its gradual decline, obscured by the shifting sands of time, until its rediscovery by the Western world.

"Their story," Khalid continues, "is one of resilience and adaptability. They took what the desert offered and turned it into a sanctuary of life and culture. Petra stands as a monument to their ingenuity and spirit."

Holmes, ever the consummate detective, leaned forward, his eyes sharp and intent. "The Nabataeans' mastery of their environment is remarkable. It speaks of a level of sophistication and understanding that rivals even our modern achievements. What, then, do you think was the key to their downfall?"

Khalid paused, the weight of his ancestors' history on his shoulders. "The key to their downfall, like that of many great civilisations, was multifaceted. External pressures, economic shifts and perhaps a degree of complacency. But above all, it was the inexorable march of time. Petra, like all things, succumbed to the inevitable tide of change".

I felt a deep connection with the people who had walked the streets of Petra. I spoke, my voice tinged with the gravity of our shared mission: "It is humbling to think of the countless lives, stories and dreams that have been etched into these stones. Every step we take in Petra will be in the footsteps of those who have gone before us, a journey through the annals of history".

Adrien d'Arcy, whose artistic sensibilities were deeply stirred, added: "There is an incomparable beauty in the resilience of Petra, in how its stones seem to sing of the triumph of the human spirit over adversity. I feel privileged to be part of this quest to capture the essence of this ancient city through my art".

Liyana Sultan, her voice full of reverence, expressed her connection to Petra's legacy: "Unlocking the secrets of Petra is not just an academic pursuit; it is a deeply personal journey. It is about understanding where we have come from, to better understand who we are and where we are going".

The exchange between Khalid and Dr El-Sharif, punctuated by interjections from Holmes, myself and the rest of our team, transcended mere academic discourse. It was a manifestation of the universal human quest to connect with our past, to understand the forces that shape civilisations. Khalid's descriptions, enlivened by Dr El-Sharif's insightful questions, painted Petra not just as an archaeological marvel, but as a living chronicle of human resilience, creativity and the indomitable will to carve beauty out of barrenness.

The dialogue on Petra, rich in detail and reverence for the city's heritage, transformed the study room into a portal through time, allowing us to peer into the soul of a civilisation that had thrived in the harshest of environments. It was a reminder that history is not just a collection of dates and events, but a tapestry of human stories, dreams and aspirations that continue to inspire and teach across the millennia.

As the discussion drew to a close, the air seemed charged with a profound sense of connection - to the people who had walked the streets of Petra, to the city itself, and to each other. In that moment, bound by our shared journey of discovery, we were reminded that the pursuit of knowledge is a sacred endeavour, one that bridges cultures, ages and the vast expanse of human experience. With Khalid as our guide and the spirit of the Nabataeans illuminating our path, we stood on the precipice of unlocking the secrets of Petra, ready to continue our quest with renewed purpose and a deeper appreciation for the intricate mosaic of history that awaited us in the rose-red city.

As the day waned, casting long shadows through the barred windows of the Governor's Palace, an evolution unfolded within its ancient walls. The initial barriers of unfamiliarity and caution, natural when disparate souls come together, gradually eroded under the influence of shared experiences and the exchange of stories. The atmosphere was transformed, enlivened by laughter and the warmth of budding camaraderie as we, a collection of individuals brought together by fate and purpose, discovered a unity forged in the pursuit of knowledge and understanding.

The palace, with its myriad rooms and corridors, became the stage for this transformation. From the sun-drenched courtyard, where light danced on the intricate mosaics, to the cool, shaded alcoves that offered respite from the day's heat, each space bore witness to our evolving bonds. The air, once heavy with the anticipation of the unknown, now resonated with the comfort of newfound respect and the promise of collective endeavour.

The courtyard, a lush oasis within the ancient structure, was adorned with vibrant flora that filled the air with the sweet scent of jasmine and citrus. Marble fountains, their water murmuring softly, provided a soothing backdrop to our conversations. The play of light and shadow through the foliage created an almost ethereal atmosphere, inviting introspection and dialogue.

Khalid, our guide and the bridge between our world and the mysteries of Petra, was at the heart of this transformation. His openness in sharing the wealth of his knowledge, coupled with an unmistakable reverence for our mission, began to weave a tapestry of trust and mutual respect between us. It was a respect born not of obligation, but of genuine admiration for the depth of his connection to the desert and its secrets, and a recognition of the courage it takes to share one's heritage with strangers.

As we gathered in the palace's grand salon, a room adorned with artefacts that whispered of ages past, our exchange transcended the mere transfer of information. Stories flowed freely, each a thread in the fabric of our shared human experience. Khalid spoke of the desert, not as a barren wasteland, but as a place of beauty and challenge, where the spirit of resilience and the bond between man and nature are forged in the crucible of survival. His stories, rich with the hues of sunset and the chill of starlit nights, painted the desert as a canvas of infinite possibilities.

He described desert nights when the sky, unpolluted by artificial light, revealed a tapestry of stars so vivid you could almost reach out and touch them. "Each star," Khalid mused, "is a reminder of the countless generations that have gazed upon it, seeking guidance and inspiration. His words transported us to those still nights, the cool sand below, the vast expanse above, and the silence of the desert broken only by the occasional call of a distant creature.

In turn, we shared stories of our own - stories of distant lands and cultures, of personal trials and triumphs. Dr Amal El-Sharif, with her bicultural heritage and deep scholarly insight, offered a unique perspective on the convergence of East and West, on the intricate dance of history and modernity. Her descriptions of the bustling souks of Cairo and the ancient ruins of Thebes were vivid, capturing the essence of these places with an artist's eye for detail.

Sherlock Holmes, with his analytical brilliance, spoke of the never-ending search for truth, of the mysteries hidden in the shadows of the ordinary. He recounted some of our most challenging cases, each one a testament to the complexity and unpredictability of human nature. "Each case," he observed, "is a thread in the vast tapestry of life, each revealing a part of the whole but leaving us with more questions than answers."

And I, Dr John Watson, told stories of courage and camaraderie, of the human capacity for kindness and bravery in the face of adversity. I spoke of the battlefields of Afghanistan, the resilience of soldiers and the enduring spirit of those who fought for something greater than themselves. My stories, though tinged with the pain of loss, were also filled with the hope and strength that emerges in the darkest of times.

Through these exchanges, a profound realisation dawned: despite the vastness of the desert ahead and the mysteries of Petra beckoning, we were united by a common thread - the quest for understanding, for a connection to the past, and the hope that our discoveries might illuminate the future. Khalid's words, spoken with a sincerity that touched every heart, summed up this realisation. "Your dedication to uncovering the truth," he remarked, "honours the spirit of discovery that Petra represents".

As the day gave way to evening and the golden light of sunset bathed the palace in a warm glow, a sense of respect and camaraderie was palpable. It was a respect not only for each other's knowledge and skills, but for the shared vulnerability and strength that comes with embarking on a journey into the unknown. The walls that had once separated us - culturally, linguistically and personally - had begun to crumble, revealing the common ground on which we stood.

The fading light of day cast long shadows that danced across the marble floors, and the scent of evening flowers filled the air, mingling with the aroma of the dinner being prepared. The soft murmur of voices, punctuated by the occasional laugh, created a symphony of camaraderie that echoed within the ancient walls.

In the heart of the Governor's Palace, amidst the echoes of history and the whisper of the desert wind, we found unity in our diversity, a sense of belonging forged in the common pursuit of knowledge and awe of the mysteries that awaited us in Petra. As night fell, transforming the palace into a symphony of shadow and light, we stood together, a band of explorers bound by the indomitable spirit of discovery, ready to face the challenges and wonders that lay ahead, united in our journey towards understanding and respect.

As the sun dipped below the horizon, painting the sky in shades of amber and crimson, the courtyard of the Governor's Palace became a sanctuary of contemplation. The warmth of the day lingered in the air, mingled with the scent of jasmine and the distant buzz of the city as evening fell. There, under the burgeoning stars, we, Sherlock Holmes, Dr Amal El-Sharif, Liyana Sultan, Adrien d'Arcy, Khalid and I, Dr John Watson, gathered in a circle, each of us in the reflective mood that the day's revelations had inspired.

The courtyard, with its gently splashing marble fountains and lush gardens scented with jasmine, seemed to hold us in a timeless embrace, a fitting backdrop for the introspection the day's journey of dialogue and discovery had inspired. The lanterns cast a soft glow, creating a tapestry of light and shadow that danced across the ancient stone walls. Khalid, our guide and the newest member of our assembly, stood with us, his silhouette outlined against the fading light, a symbol of the bridge between worlds that he had become.

The day had been one of profound learning and connection, not only to the land and its history, but to each other. Khalid's introduction and the discussions that followed had opened new vistas of understanding, weaving the threads of our diverse backgrounds and disciplines into a tapestry rich with the promise of discovery. It was a moment of convergence, where the paths of our individual quests intersected, guided by a common purpose and anticipation of the mysteries hidden within the ancient stones of Petra.

"I find myself contemplating not only the journey ahead, but the remarkable journey that has brought us to this moment," I remarked, breaking the comfortable silence that had enveloped us. The air was heavy with the scent of jasmine and the distant calls of nocturnal creatures mingled with the soft gurgle of the fountains. "Today we have gained not only a guide in Khalid, but a new perspective on the mysteries that await us in Petra. It's as if we've been given a key to open doors we never knew existed.

Khalid, his gaze fixed on the distant mountains that shrouded the city's secrets, responded with a thought that summed up the essence of our day's exchange. "The desert," he said, his voice full and resonant with the solemnity of the evening, "teaches us that the journey is as important as the destination. It is on the journey that we find ourselves, that we forge bonds that transcend the sands of time".

His words resonated deeply, echoing the feeling that had quietly taken root in each of our hearts. Indeed, the anticipation of uncovering Petra's secrets was tempered by a deeper appreciation of its historical and cultural significance, a reverence for the land and its people that Khalid had helped to foster. Our dialogue had moved beyond the mere exchange of information to a shared exploration of values, beliefs and the universal quest for knowledge that binds humanity together through the ages.

As we stood in the courtyard, the night enveloping us in its embrace, our reflections on the day and the journey ahead seemed to draw us closer, not only as companions on a shared expedition, but as fellow travellers in the pursuit of understanding. The gentle rustling of the leaves and the soft chorus of night sounds added to the atmosphere of serenity and reflection. The realisation that our journey to Petra, under Khalid's expert guidance, was ready to take its next steps filled us with a sense of purpose and anticipation.

"The road ahead will undoubtedly challenge us, test our resolve and perhaps change us in ways we cannot yet fathom," Holmes remarked, his eyes reflecting the starlight. His voice, usually so measured and precise, carried an uncharacteristic note of wonder. "Yet it is a path we walk not merely as seekers of lost truths, but as custodians of a legacy that transcends our own."

Dr El-Sharif, always passionate about the ancient world, added in a soft but passionate voice: "Petra is more than a destination. It is a testament to human ingenuity and resilience. To walk its streets is to walk through history itself".

The emotion in her eyes reflected the depth of her words, the scholar in her deeply moved by the weight of the historical significance.

Adrien and Liyana, both visibly moved by the day's discussions, exchanged a look of understanding. "The stories of the past are not only in the stones," Liyana said softly, her voice barely above a whisper yet resonating with conviction, "but in the spirits of the people who lived and flourished there." Adrien nodded in agreement, his normally ebullient demeanour tempered by the gravity of the moment.

As the evening wore on and we prepared to retire for the night, the echo of our conversations with Khalid, the laughter shared and the insights gained lingered in the air, a testament to the power of understanding and respect to transcend the boundaries that divide us. In the heart of Damascus, at the crossroads of history and civilisation, we found ourselves united in a quest that promised not only to unravel the mysteries of the past, but to illuminate the paths of our own souls.

The scents of jasmine and the cool night air intertwined, creating a sensory tapestry that grounded us in the present while suggesting the timelessness of our journey. The gentle murmur of the fountains and the distant hum of the city provided a soothing backdrop, enhancing the sense of tranquillity and introspection. The flickering lanterns cast an ethereal glow that made the moment seem almost otherworldly.

So, with the stars as our witnesses and the call of the desert in our hearts, we were ready to embark on a journey that would take us through the sands to the rose-red city of Petra, where the past waited to reveal its long-kept secrets. In that moment, under the vast expanse of the evening sky, we were reminded that the true journey lies not in the destination, but in the connections made, the wisdom shared and the horizons broadened along the way.

CHAPTER 19

OASIS OF SECRETS

S hades of pink and gold adorned the sky as the first rays of dawn emerged. They cast a magical light over the great courtyard outside the Governor's Palace in Damascus. The intricate mosaics shimmered, reflecting the dawning rays in a kaleidoscope of colour, while the air, still cool from the night, began to warm with the promise of day. An air of anticipation and solemnity filled the room as the caravan, meticulously prepared for the arduous journey ahead, stood ready, its camels and supplies casting long shadows on the ancient cobbles. The scene bridged the city's storied past with the mysteries of the desert beyond.

Sherlock Holmes, myself, Dr John Watson, Dr Amal El-Sharif, Liyana Sultan, Adrien d'Arcy and our guide Khalid, along with the caravan crew, including experienced camel handlers and guides, were all present. Mounted on her magnificent stallion, Muntasir, Liyana Sultan cut an impressive figure, embodying both grace and strength. The stallion's dark coat shimmered in the dawn light and his eyes, intelligent and alert, reflected Liyana's own readiness. Beside her sat Khalid on Al-Zarib, his loyal and majestic stallion, a living testament to the bond between man and beast. Al-Zarib's muscular form and calm demeanour spoke volumes about his endurance and strength, qualities that Khalid cherished.

Each member of our assembly was immersed in the final preparations, checking and rechecking supplies, ensuring our communications were in order, and mentally preparing for the journey into the vastness of the Arabian desert. The air was thick with a palpable mixture of excitement and the weight of the unknown that awaited us. The scent of jasmine from the palace gardens mingled with the earthy scent of the desert, creating an intoxicating blend that heightened our senses and our awareness of the moment.

As the light of dawn grew stronger, illuminating the intricate details of the palace's architecture and the rugged faces of our companions, Khalid gathered us for a final briefing. His presence, commanding yet down-to-earth, commanded everyone's attention. Dressed in traditional Bedouin garb that spoke of his deep connection to the desert, Khalid stood as a symbol of the bridge between the world we knew and the ancient sands we were about to cross.

"The desert," Khalid began, his voice resonating with the gravity of our undertaking, "is both a beauty and a beast. It demands respect." His gaze met each of ours in turn, impressing upon us the seriousness of his words. "The journey we are about to undertake will test us not only physically, but also spiritually. The sands do not discriminate between prince and pauper; they teach us humility, resilience and the value of water - the lifeblood of the desert."

His words hung in the air, their truth undeniable. The desert, vast and unforgiving, was a leveler, a place where nature reigned supreme and human frailty was laid bare. Khalid's eyes, dark and reflective like the desert night, held a depth of understanding and respect for the land that we, as newcomers, could only begin to fathom.

Sherlock Holmes, always the embodiment of pragmatism and foresight, nodded in agreement. His sharp features, etched with concentration, softened momentarily as he addressed the group. "Our journey is as much about discovery as it is about survival. Each member of this expedition has been chosen for their unique skills and knowledge. It is imperative that we understand our roles, stay together and support each other."

Holmes' usually analytical voice carried an uncharacteristic warmth, a testament to the respect he had for our companions. His eyes, keen and observant, moved from face to face, measuring the readiness and determination etched into each expression.

The caravan of a dozen camels, laden with supplies, instruments for our research and personal belongings, was a testament to the meticulous planning that had gone into preparing for this journey. The handlers, well versed in the ways of the desert and its creatures, went about their tasks with quiet efficiency, ensuring that the animals were well cared for and ready for the journey ahead. The camels, patient and stoic, bore their burdens with a grace that belied their strength.

As the sun rose, casting a golden glow over the yard, the moment of departure arrived. The air, once cool and crisp in the early morning, began to warm, hinting at the heat that would accompany us as we ventured deeper into the desert. With a final check of our provisions and a nod from Khalid, we mounted our camels, the gentle giants that would carry us across the sands to the rose-red city of Petra.

Leaving Damascus, with the governor's palace receding into the distance, was a moment of profound significance. It marked the beginning of a journey not only through the physical landscapes of the Arabian desert, but through the landscapes of history, culture and the depths of our own minds. The rhythmic pounding of the camels' hooves on the cobbles created a steady, almost hypnotic cadence, a soundtrack to our silent reflections.

As the caravan slowly made its way out of the city, the sounds of civilisation faded away, replaced by the vast, enveloping silence of the desert. The transition was almost palpable, a shift from the familiar to the unknown, from the constraints of society to the boundless freedom of the wilderness. The desert in its infinite expanse stretched out before us, a canvas waiting to be explored, its secrets waiting to be revealed.

Our journey to Petra had begun, a caravan moving through time and space to a place where past and present meet, where the mysteries of an ancient civilisation awaited our arrival. At that moment of departure, under the watchful eye of the dawn, we were no longer mere travellers, but pilgrims on a quest for knowledge, understanding and the secrets hidden beneath the sands. The promise of discovery hung in the air, as palpable as the desert breeze that carried us onward into the unknown.

As our caravan began its slow and deliberate advance beyond the outskirts of Damascus, the transition from the familiar confines of the city to the open expanse of the desert unfolded with a surreal grace. The cacophony of the city's morning activities gradually gave way to a serene silence, punctuated only by the rhythmic plodding of the camels and the occasional command from the shepherds leading them. The vastness of the desert stretched before us, an endless canvas of shifting sands and undulating dunes, painted in shades of amber, gold and deep crimson by the first light of dawn.

Liyana rode gracefully on Muntasir, the stallion's powerful strides reflecting the symbiosis between rider and horse. Khalid guided Al-Zarib with practiced ease, the stallion's regal bearing a testament to their shared history. Both horses moved in unison with the caravan, their presence adding an element of nobility to our humble procession.

The air, crisp in the early hours, carried the scent of the desert - dry with a hint of sagebrush and the distant, almost imperceptible aroma of the wildflowers that dared to bloom in this arid expanse. The sky, a dome of pure azure, promised the unrelenting heat that would soon challenge us, but for the moment it served as a majestic canopy, underscoring the stark beauty of the landscape that stretched endlessly in all directions.

Sherlock Holmes, Dr Amal El-Sharif, Liyana Sultan, Adrien d'Arcy, Khalid, the caravan crew and I, Dr John Watson, found ourselves enveloped in an atmosphere of awe and contemplation. The transition from city to desert was not merely a change of location, but a passage into a realm that seemed to exist outside of time, a place where history and legend intertwined with the shifting sands.

"The desert," I mused aloud, unable to contain my sense of wonder at the landscape unfolding before us, "is both desolate and beautiful, unforgiving and generous. It is hard to believe that such desolation could hold secrets as profound as those of Petra.

Liyana Sultan, gazing towards the horizon, where the earth and sky seemed to meet in an endless embrace, reflected: "The desert teaches us humility. Her reverent voice captured the essence of our journey. In the vastness of the desert, we were but fleeting shadows, ephemeral and insubstantial against the backdrop of time and nature. Yet it was in this realisation of our own insignificance that we found a deeper connection to the land and to each other.

As the caravan moved away from the remnants of civilisation, the landscape began to reveal its secrets. Dunes rose and fell like waves on a petrified ocean, their crests sharp against the sky, their valleys shrouded in shadow. Here and there, rocky outcrops punctuated the sand, sentinels of time. The colours of the desert changed as the sun rose, from the soft pastels of dawn to the vivid ochres and deep russets of midday.

The sense of isolation was palpable, a chilling realisation that beyond the thin line of our caravan there was nothing but the desert and the sky. Yet within this isolation was a profound sense of peace, a tranquillity that transcended the challenges of the terrain and the rigours of the journey. It was as if the desert, in its timeless majesty, had extended an invitation to us, beckoning us to shed the shackles of our past and embark on a journey not only to Petra, but into the depths of our own souls.

Khalid, ever vigilant, guided us with an expertise born of a lifetime spent in communion with the desert. His calm assurance was a beacon, reminding us that we were not alone in this vastness, that the desert, for all its challenges, was a place of life, resilience and beauty. His voice, carrying the wisdom of the sands, offered both guidance and comfort, a steady presence in the face of the unknown.

"Liyana," Khalid called, his voice carrying over the gentle sounds of the caravan, "Muntasir carries you with the grace of the ancient spirits. Remember, the desert listens to our footsteps. It watches us and remembers."

Liyana nodded, her eyes meeting Khalid's in shared understanding. "And we must honour it with every step we take," she replied, her voice soft but firm.

As the day wore on and the caravan plunged deeper into the heart of the desert, the sense of time travel became more tangible. With every step we took, we moved further away from the world we knew, closer to the mysteries that awaited us in Petra. The desert, with its stark beauty and profound silence, was our crucible, testing our resolve, deepening our bonds and preparing us for the wonders that lay beneath the sands.

The sun was rising, its rays intensifying the colours of the desert, making the sands glow with an almost otherworldly brilliance. Every dune, every shadow seemed to whisper tales of ancient caravans and lost civilisations, of secrets buried beneath the shifting sands. And as we moved forward, guided by Khalid's steadfast leadership and the quiet strength of Muntasir and Al-Zarib, we felt the weight of history upon us, a reminder that we were but the latest in a long line of seekers drawn to the desert by its enduring mysteries and timeless beauty.

As we ventured deeper into the heart of the Arabian Desert, the initial thrill of embarking on this great adventure gradually gave way to the stark realisation of the desert's unforgiving nature. The sun, an unrelenting ball of fire in the sky, beat down on us with an intensity that seemed to drain the strength from our limbs. By day, the heat was a palpable force, an almost sentient presence that pressed down on us, sapping our energy with every step. And as night fell, the desert transformed once again, this time into a realm of freezing cold, where the absence of the sun turned the sands into a sea of frost, every grain of sand a tiny shard of ice.

Water, that most precious of commodities, became the focus of our every thought. Every drop was conserved with religious fervour, our rations measured out with meticulous care. Khalid, our guide and the steady hand that steered us through this desert odyssey, reminded us daily of the importance of discipline in water consumption. "The desert does not forgive waste," he would say, his voice a constant reminder of the delicate balance between survival and danger in this vast wilderness.

It was on the third day, with the sun a blazing sentinel overhead, that the desert presented us with its most formidable challenge yet. Without warning, the horizon blurred, the clear lines of dunes and sky merging into a haze of shifting sand. A sandstorm, sudden and ferocious, descended upon us with a fury that seemed almost personal in its intensity. The air filled with a maelstrom of sand and wind, a howling storm that blotted out the sun and turned day into night.

In the midst of the chaos, Sherlock Holmes' voice cut through the tumult, his command clear and forceful. "Trust Khalid! Stay close!" he shouted, his silhouette barely visible through the swirling sand. We huddled together, our camels drawn into a tight circle as we braced ourselves against the storm. Scarves and goggles protected our faces, but the fine, penetrating sand found every crack, every crevice.

Liyana, astride Muntasir, shielded her eyes and followed closely behind Khalid, who led Al-Zarib through the storm with unwavering determination. Their horses, seeming to draw strength from their riders, pressed on through the storm, their silhouettes barely visible through the swirling sand.

"Hold on!" Khalid's voice rang out, a beacon of calm in the chaos. "The storm will pass, but we must persevere!" His words, infused with the wisdom of countless journeys across these unforgiving sands, gave us the strength to persevere.

Khalid, undaunted by the fury of the storm, moved among us, his figure a ghostly presence in the storm. His knowledge of the desert, its capricious moods and sudden dangers became our lifeline. Under his guidance, we fashioned makeshift shelters from the supplies we carried and anchored them against the wind. And there we waited, a small island of life in the raging sea of sand and wind.

It was in those harrowing hours, as we clung to each other and to the hope that the storm would pass, that the true mettle of our team was tested. Dr Amal El-Sharif, her medical skills honed in far less hostile environments, rose to the occasion with a calmness that belied the chaos around us. When one of the caravan's crew was struck by flying debris, her hands were steady and sure as she tended to his injuries with the skill of a seasoned field medic. "We are more capable than we know," she said, her voice a beacon of determination in the darkness.

Adrien d'Arcy, his usual intellectual curiosity heightened by the raw power of nature, assisted Amal with a determination that reflected his resilient spirit. His hands, sharpened by years of meticulous craftsmanship, moved with precision, revealing a deepening respect for an environment that had initially seemed so alien, yet deeply fascinating.

"I never imagined the desert could hold such fury," Adrien remarked, his voice muffled by the scarf covering his face. "It is both terrifying and awe-inspiring."

"Indeed," Dr El-Sharif replied, her eyes scanning the horizon. "This land demands respect and it demands that we adapt and endure."

The storm raged on for what seemed an eternity, a timeless battle between the elements and the indomitable spirit of our small band. And then, as suddenly as it had descended upon us, the storm subsided. The winds calmed, the sands settled and the sun, a pale orb, reclaimed the sky.

As we emerged from our shelters, the desert around us was transformed. Dunes had shifted, landscapes altered, as if the storm had been a great artist, reshaping the canvas of the desert with wild, unbridled strokes. Yet in the midst of this chaos, there was a profound sense of renewal, a reminder that even in its most violent moments, the desert is a place of constant change and endless possibility.

Liyana, brushing the sand from Muntasir's mane, spoke softly to her stallion, her voice full of gratitude. "You have the heart of a lion, Muntasir. Together we will conquer these sands."

Khalid, stroking Al-Zarib's neck, reflected on the bond between man and beast, his eyes scanning the changed landscape with a mixture of awe and respect. "The desert tests us, but it also reveals our strengths," he mused. "We are but temporary guests in this eternal expanse."

The sandstorm, in all its fury and terror, had tested our resilience, our ability to endure and adapt. But more than that, it had brought us closer together, forging bonds of trust and camaraderie that would sustain us for the rest of our journey. For in the heart of the storm, we had discovered not only the strength to survive, but the determination to thrive, to continue our quest for the secrets of Petra, united and undaunted.

In that moment of calm after the storm, we felt a deeper connection to the desert, to each other, and to the ancient mysteries that awaited us. The journey ahead was fraught with uncertainty, but our shared experience had strengthened our spirits. Together we would face whatever challenges lay ahead, our resolve as unyielding as the desert itself.

Sherlock Holmes, his gaze fixed on the horizon, spoke with quiet intensity. "This storm has reminded us of the fragility of our existence and the strength of our resolve. Let it be a harbinger of the challenges we will face and the triumphs we will achieve."

Dr John Watson, I, recorded these thoughts in my diary, the pen moving swiftly across the page. "In the crucible of the desert we have found our mettle tested and our bonds strengthened. The journey to Petra is not only one of discovery, but of transformation. We are no longer mere travellers but pilgrims, seeking not only knowledge but enlightenment".

As the sun began its descent, casting long shadows across the dunes, we prepared to move forward, our hearts steeled by the storm and our spirits buoyed by the promise of the ancient city ahead. The desert, with its endless mysteries and unforgiving nature, had become both our adversary and our teacher, and we, its humble pupils, were ready to continue our quest.

After the tempestuous ordeal of the sandstorm, our caravan sought respite at a campsite, a small oasis of peace under a star-studded sky. The desert, so vicious in its stormy fury, now lay calm and serene, its sands cooling in the embrace of night. The stark contrast between the chaos of the day and the peace of the evening gave our surroundings a surreal quality, as if the desert itself was showing us its dual nature.

We gathered around a crackling fire, its flames casting a warm glow on our tired faces. The blaze seemed to dance with the stars above, a terrestrial reflection of the celestial splendour. The beauty of the desert night sky is unparalleled - untouched by the light pollution of civilisation, it offers a glimpse into infinity, a vast canvas on which the mysteries of the universe are painted in light.

Sherlock Holmes, normally a figure of stoic composure, sat in thoughtful silence, his keen eyes reflecting the firelight as he gazed into the flames. Dr Amal El-Sharif, her medical kit at her side, appeared pensive, perhaps reflecting on the day's events and the resilience of the human spirit in the face of adversity. Liyana Sultan, with Muntasir at her side, Adrien d'Arcy, Khalid and I, Dr John Watson, found ourselves drawn into a circle of camaraderie and reflection, our bonds strengthened by the trials we had endured together.

The air around us was cool, carrying the faint earthy scent of the desert, mixed with the sweet aroma of burning wood. The fire crackled and crackled, filling the air with its warm and inviting sound, occasionally sending sparks soaring into the star-studded sky, where they danced and flickered for a brief moment before gracefully fading into the vastness of the night. This tranquil scene was in stark contrast to the fury of the storm we had recently endured, and we welcomed the peace it offered.

"The desert," Khalid began, his voice resonating with the gravity of his experience, "is a land of contradictions. It can be both a sanctuary and a dangerous ordeal. Today we faced its wrath, yet here we find solace under its vast skies". His words, imbued with the wisdom of someone who has lived his life in communion with the desert, struck a deep chord with us.

Adrien, his intellectual curiosity and empathy heightened by the day's events, looked up at the sky. "Out here, you can't help but think about the big questions," he remarked, his voice a mixture of wonder and thoughtful reflection. "The cosmos above us, the desert around us - it's a reminder of how vast the world really is, and how deeply interconnected our histories and traditions are."

"The desert," added Dr Amal El-Sharif, her tone thoughtful, "with all its trials, also brings us closer to the essence of who we are. Stripped of distractions, we are confronted with our true selves." She glanced at Liyana, who was gently stroking Muntasir's mane, her eyes reflecting the flickering firelight.

Liyana, sensing the shared introspection, nodded. "The desert teaches us humility," she said, her voice tinged with reverence. "In its vastness we are but fleeting shadows, yet in that insignificance we find our deepest connection - to the land, to each other, and to the journey that lies before us."

Sherlock Holmes, ever the seeker of truth, spoke next, his voice calm yet filled with a sense of purpose. "Our search for Petra is more than a journey through the sands. It is a journey through time, a quest to unlock the secrets of an ancient civilisation. Each step we take brings us closer to understanding not only the world around us, but the intricate tapestry of history of which we are all a part."

For me, Dr John Watson, the journey was an opportunity to record the adventure of a lifetime, to capture the essence of our quest and the indomitable spirit of those who dare to venture into the unknown. My pen, ready to record the unfolding story, felt like a link between past and present, a bridge across time.

The night deepened and the fire burned lower, its embers glowing softly in the darkness. Around it we sat in a circle, a community forged in the crucible of the desert. The challenges we had faced, the storm that had tested our resolve, had also served to deepen our bonds. Sharing our reflections, our fears and our hopes, we had laid bare the threads of our common humanity, weaving them into a tapestry of shared purpose.

Khalid, his gaze steady and calm, added: "Petra is not just a destination, but a symbol - a testament to the indomitable spirit of human achievement and perseverance. It stands as a beacon of our ancestors' will to carve beauty and purpose out of the harshest of landscapes. It is a reminder that even in desolation there can be majesty, and in solitude a story that speaks across millennia".

Sherlock Holmes, always the embodiment of pragmatism and foresight, nodded in agreement. "Our journey is as much about discovery as it is about survival. Each member of this expedition has been chosen for their unique skills and knowledge. It is imperative that we understand our roles, stay together and support each other."

As the fire dwindled to embers, casting the last of its warmth into the night, our group, united by the common tapestry of our journey, sat in a companionable silence that spoke volumes. The desert around us, a vast and ancient witness to the passage of time, seemed to embrace us in its eternal, silent vigilance.

The stars above, countless and bright, watched over us, silent sentinels in the vast silence of the desert. The journey to Petra, with all its uncertainties, lay ahead of us, but in this moment, under the star-filled sky, we were united, a band of travellers bound by a quest that was as much about discovering ourselves as it was about uncovering the secrets of the ancient city.

Our thoughts drifted to the ancient city of Petra, now a mere whisper on the horizon, its secrets calling to us through the desert night. The anticipation of what lay ahead filled our hearts with a mixture of excitement and awe, for we were not merely explorers but pilgrims on a sacred quest for knowledge and understanding.

As dawn unfolded its golden hues over the desert horizon, our caravan found itself on the precipice of a momentous occasion - the final camp before reaching the enigmatic city of Petra. The sands around us, now familiar in their undulating stillness, seemed to whisper secrets of the ancient past, as if urging us on. The air itself was thick with anticipation, every breath we took a testament to the culmination of our arduous journey across the Arabian desert.

The camp, a temporary bastion of human endeavour in the midst of the vast wilderness, was buzzing with activity. Tents were pitched with practiced efficiency, camels rested, their heavy loads momentarily lifted, as our team busied themselves with the final preparations for the day ahead. Yet beneath the veneer of activity there was a palpable sense of reflection, a collective introspection that seemed to reflect the profound silence of the desert.

Sherlock Holmes, Dr Amal El-Sharif, Liyana Sultan, Adrien d'Arcy, Khalid and I, Dr John Watson, were each lost in our own thoughts, our minds grappling with the enormity of what lay just over the horizon. Our physical preparations - checking equipment, ensuring adequate water supplies and reviewing maps - were mirrored by a mental fortification, a strengthening of our spirits for the mysteries that awaited us in Petra.

Holmes, his keen intellect ever vigilant, was absorbed in the contemplation of ancient texts and maps, his eyes reflecting the flicker of morning light. The fine lines etched into his face seemed to carry the weight of centuries, as if the knowledge of Petra's secrets lay just beyond his reach. He murmured to himself, piecing together the fragments of history with the precision of a master detective.

Dr El-Sharif, her hands skilfully checking her tactical rucksack, exuded a quiet strength. Her presence was a calming influence, her eyes betraying a depth of understanding and empathy. "The journey to Petra," she mused, "is not only a physical challenge, but a journey into the heart of history, a chance to connect with the souls who once walked these sands."

Liyana Sultan, with her regal bearing, was the epitome of grace and determination. Tending her stallion Muntasir, she whispered words of encouragement to her faithful companion, her voice a soothing melody in the morning air. "We are but temporary guests in this timeless land," she mused, her eyes gazing into the distance. "The desert teaches us patience and humility, and reminds us of our place in the great tapestry of existence."

Adrien d'Arcy, his intellectual curiosity now fully engaged, meticulously checked the archaeological instruments with the precision of a craftsman. His enthusiasm was palpable, reflecting his deep appreciation of the art and history that parallels his own work in the leather trade. "To stand in the presence of Petra," he remarked, "is to step into a living chronicle, a story carved in stone by hands long gone but still whispering their secrets".

Khalid, our stalwart guide, moved with the assurance of someone intimately connected to the desert. His every gesture, whether checking Al-Zarib's course or surveying the horizon, spoke of a lifetime spent navigating the shifting sands. "Petra will reveal her secrets in time," he assured. "Our journey across the sands, the trials we've faced and the bonds we've forged have prepared us for this moment. We stand on the threshold of discovery, not as conquerors, but as humble seekers of wisdom.

As the day wore on and the stars began their nightly vigil, our camp was filled with a sense of quiet anticipation. The conversations of the evening, ripe with reflections on our journey and the revelations it had brought, faded gently into the embrace of the desert night.

Beneath the vast expanse of the night sky, the desert around us lay in a profound silence, broken only by the occasional crackle of dying fire and the distant howl of a desert fox. The air, cool and crisp, carried the scent of sagebrush and the indefinable essence of ancient sands, a balm to our weary spirits. As our camp settled into a meditative silence, each member of our expedition found themselves in a reflective reverie, the glow of the fire illuminating our thoughtful faces.

The atmosphere was charged with a contemplative energy that drew us closer together, not just as fellow travellers on a physical quest, but as companions on a profound journey of discovery. The desert, with its endless vistas and timeless solitude, had become more than a backdrop to our expedition; it had become a crucible, honing our characters and deepening the bonds forged by shared adversity.

In the quiet of the night, the experiences of the past few days cascaded through my mind, a montage of challenges overcome, mysteries pondered and friendships deepened. The sandstorm that had tested our resolve, the serene beauty of the desert under the stars, the anticipation of uncovering Petra's secrets - all these experiences had woven themselves into the fabric of our journey, a tapestry rich with the colours of adventure and the threads of human connection.

Holmes, usually the epitome of logical detachment, now sat in a rare moment of introspection. The firelight played on his sharp features, softening them as his eyes reflected the flickering flames. "The desert," he began, his voice uncharacteristically soft, "strips away the superfluous and leaves us with the essence of our being. Here, amidst these ancient sands, we are but passing figures in a landscape that endures."

Dr El-Sharif added her thoughts: "In these moments of silence, we are reminded of the fragility and strength of the human spirit. The desert tests us, but it also teaches us to find beauty and meaning in the harshest of environments".

Liyana Sultan spoke with a quiet wisdom that resonated deeply. "The desert shares its wisdom with those who listen. It teaches us patience, resilience and the importance of each moment. Muntasir and I have learned much from these sands, for they have shaped us both."

Khalid looked up at the stars and shared his thoughts. "The bond between man and nature is timeless. Al-Zarib and I are but one part of a larger tapestry that stretches back through the ages. The desert reminds us of our place in this world, of the connections that sustain us".

Adrien d'Arcy looked up at the starry sky above. "This journey has deepened my appreciation of the past and its profound influence on the present. The desert, in its quiet grandeur, has revealed to me the continuity of craftsmanship and tradition, the enduring legacy of those who came before us, much like the leatherwork passed down through generations in my own family."

As the fire dwindled to embers, releasing the last of its warmth into the night, our group, united by the common tapestry of our journey, sat in a companionable silence that spoke volumes. The desert around us, a vast and ancient witness to the passage of time, seemed to embrace us, a silent affirmation of the journey we had undertaken together.

In the solitude of my tent, I turned to my diary and recorded the day's events with a fervor driven by the knowledge that we were on the cusp of history. "Our caravan to Petra," I wrote, "has been as much a journey through the landscapes within us as through the desert around us. What awaits us is unknown, but we face it together".

That reflection, penned under the canopy of night, was more than a mere record of our travels; it was an acknowledgement of the transformative power of our journey. The challenges of the desert, the mysteries of the ancient world we were about to explore, the camaraderie that had blossomed among us - these were the elements that had made our expedition a quest not only of historical discovery but of personal revelation.

The dawn that would herald our final approach to Petra was only hours away, but in that moment, under the starry canopy of the desert night, time seemed to stand still. We were on the threshold of discovery, not only of the secrets of the rose-red city, but of the depths within ourselves, revealed through the crucible of our journey.

CHAPTER 20

PETRA'S WHISPERING SANDS

O ur caravan made its final approach to Petra through the Siq, a narrow gorge that serves as a natural gateway to the ancient city, as the first rays of the morning sun broke over the horizon, painting the sky with soft pinks and oranges. The cool desert air carried the scent of ancient stone and sage, offering a gentle respite from the heat. The atmosphere was thick with anticipation, every breath a testament to the culmination of our arduous journey.

The Siq, a marvel of natural beauty and geological wonder, meandered through towering cliffs reaching to the heavens, their surfaces a tapestry of hues - red, orange and purple - that shifted with the light. The path, at times barely wide enough for two people to walk side by side, was flanked on either side by these colossal walls, their sheer size a humbling reminder of the grandeur of nature and our own fleeting presence within it.

Sherlock Holmes, Dr Amal El-Sharif, Liyana Sultan, Adrien d'Arcy, Khalid, myself and the stalwart members of our caravan crew navigated this ancient passageway with a reverence befitting the sanctity of our surroundings. Our voices were hushed when we spoke, as if in recognition of the sacredness of the path we were treading.

Holmes, ever the stoic observer, was visibly moved by the spectacle before us. His sharp eyes traced the contours of the cliffs, taking in the intricate details with the precision of a master detective. In a rare moment of open awe, he remarked: "The genius of man and the majesty of nature, in perfect harmony. His words echoed off the walls of the Siq, a testament to the profound effect this place can have on even the most indomitable of minds.

Liyana Sultan, her eyes glowing with the fire of discovery, added: "Petra is more than just a city; it serves as a gateway to understanding a lost civilisation. Her voice, infused with a deep respect for the ancient Nabataeans who carved their city out of the rock, captured the essence of Petra. "Here, in these stones, we find the echoes of their lives, their dreams and their unwavering determination."

Dr Amal El-Sharif, her academic mind attuned to the subtleties of history, could not contain her admiration. "The Nabataeans," she mused, "were not only architects, but artists, philosophers and engineers. Every carving, every inscription is a dialogue with eternity".

Adrien d'Arcy, his deep appreciation of craftsmanship evident, ran his fingers lightly over the ancient carvings. "You can almost feel the hands that created these wonders," he said, his voice a mixture of wonder and awe. "It's as if the stone itself has a soul."

Khalid, our steadfast guide, his presence a calming anchor on our journey, spoke with quiet authority. "These walls have seen countless generations. They whisper their stories to those who will listen.

As we travelled through the Siq, the natural beauty and architectural marvels carved into the rock were revealed in vivid detail at every turn. The walls bore silent witness to centuries of history, their surfaces etched with the marks of water and wind, the inscriptions of ancient peoples and the delicate carvings of flora and fauna. These were not mere decorations, but a dialogue between the Nabataeans and their environment, a testament to their deep understanding and respect for the natural world that cradled their civilisation.

The shifting shadows cast by the morning light added a mystical quality to our journey, transforming the Siq into a living tapestry of light and dark. The play of shadows on the stone seemed to animate the ancient carvings, giving them a life of their own. It was as if the spirits of Petra's past inhabitants were whispering to us from the walls, guiding our steps and sharing their stories with those who would listen.

Our walk through the Siq was a journey of discovery, not just of the physical remains of a bygone era, but of the intangible essence of Petra. With each step, the anticipation of unlocking the secrets of this ancient city grew, a shared excitement that bound our diverse group together in a singular purpose. Petra awaited us, its secrets shrouded in shadow and stone, ready to reveal its wonders to those who approached with open hearts and minds.

⊕∺⊹∺⊖∺⊕

As we neared the end of the Siq, the narrow gorge that had been our companion on this journey into the heart of Petra, a glimmer of light ahead hinted at the grandeur that awaited us. The path that had snaked through the towering cliffs like a serpent through the desert now promised to reveal its secret. The anticipation in our group was palpable, each step forward resonating with the weight of history and the thrill of discovery.

The air, cool and invigorating, carried the scent of ancient stone and desert sage, a soothing balm after the heat of the previous days. The Siq, a marvel of natural beauty and geological wonder, had enveloped us in its majestic embrace, its towering walls painted in shades of red, orange and purple. The play of light and shadow created an ever-changing tapestry that seemed to pulsate with life.

Then, suddenly, we emerged from the shadows of the Siq into the full glory of the morning light. Before us stood the Treasury, Al-Khazneh, its facade glowing in the warm hues of the rising sun, a sight so majestic and awe-inspiring that it commanded silence. Carved directly into the pink sandstone cliff face, the Treasury was a testament to the ingenuity and artistry of the Nabataeans, its intricate details preserved for millennia.

For a moment, time itself seemed to stand still as we, a group of weary travellers from distant lands, gazed upon the beauty and grandeur of Petra's most iconic structure. Sherlock Holmes, Dr Amal El-Sharif, Liyana Sultan, Adrien d'Arcy, Khalid and I, Dr John Watson, stood in collective awe, united by the shared experience of that moment.

Dr El-Sharif, her eyes reflecting the myriad of colours dancing across the facade of the Treasury, whispered, "It is as if time itself has stood still". Her words, softly spoken, carried the weight of our collective emotion, capturing the surreal nature of standing before such a magnificent and enduring relic of human history.

Holmes, his keen gaze fixed on the intricate carvings, murmured, "The genius of man immortalised in stone. Every detail, every line, a testament to their legacy".

Liyana Sultan, her face illuminated by the golden light, reflected with deep reverence, "Petra is more than just a city; it serves as a gateway to understanding a lost civilisation. Every carving, every stone speaks of human resilience and creativity".

Khalid, our faithful guide, whose knowledge of the desert and its secrets had guided us safely through our journey, observed with a reverence born of deep respect, "Every stone here tells a story, waiting for those patient enough to listen". His gaze, fixed on the facade of the Treasury, spoke of a bond with this land and its history that was both personal and profound.

Adrien d'Arcy, his deep admiration for craftsmanship evident, remarked: "The detail is extraordinary. Each figure, each motif seems to whisper its story to those who care to listen".

The Treasury stood as a sentinel at the entrance to Petra, its elaborate facade a welcome to travellers and a warning of the mysteries that lay within. Columns crowned with capitals of intricate design flanked the entrance, supporting a frieze that hinted at the architectural mastery of its creators. The central figure, a magnificent urn on the pediment, caught the first light of day and seemed to hold within it the essence of Petra's lost stories.

As we approached, the details of the Treasury's facade became clearer - carvings of mythological figures and symbols that spoke of the beliefs of the Nabataeans and their interaction with the myriad cultures that passed through this land. The figures seemed to come alive in the sunlight, each shadow playing on the stone, revealing more of the history etched into the fabric of Petra itself.

The air was filled with the scent of ancient stone and the indefinable essence of a place untouched by time. The silence that enveloped us was not just the absence of sound, but a presence in itself, a stillness that bore witness to the centuries of history that had unfolded in this sacred space.

In that moment, before the Treasury, we were no longer a team of explorers and scholars; we were pilgrims at the altar of human history, humbled by the enduring legacy of those who had come before us. The beauty and significance of the site before us transcended words and left an indelible mark on our souls.

Our journey to Petra, full of challenges and revelations, had brought us to this point, where we stood before the Treasury in a moment of awe and reflection. It was a reminder of the enduring power of the human spirit to create, endure and inspire through the ages. The long shadows of Petra cast by the rising sun were not just shadows of the past, but of our own connection to this timeless place, a bond forged through the shared experience of discovery and wonder.

⊷∻⊱⊰⊱∻⊷

Standing before the Treasury, our spirits alight with a sense of awe and reverence, we ventured deeper into the heart of Petra. The path unfolded before us, leading to the outer areas known as the Street of Facades and the Royal Tombs. The morning sun, now higher in the sky, cast its golden light on the pink stones, bathing the city in a warm, ethereal glow.

The air was thick with the scent of ancient dust and the subtle hint of desert sage, carried on a gentle breeze that whispered through the canyons. The sound of our footsteps on the gravel path was soft, almost reverent, as we made our way across this hallowed ground. Each step took us further into the past, the silent stones around us standing as sentinels of history.

Khalid, our stalwart guide, whose knowledge of Petra seemed as boundless as the desert itself, took on the role of historian, his voice a bridge between the present and the ancient past. "The Nabataeans," he began, pointing to the facades carved into the cliffs, "were master architects and craftsmen. Their ability to carve their city out of the rock is a testament to their ingenuity and spirit".

Liyana Sultan, walking beside Khalid, added: "Their respect for the land and their craftsmanship is evident in every detail. It's as if they were talking to the stone, coaxing it to reveal its secrets.

The Avenue of the Facades, a long row of monumental tombs and houses, stretched out before us. The facades, carved with meticulous detail directly into the sandstone, bore witness to the artistic and architectural prowess of the Nabataeans. Each structure, though eroded by time, retained a distinct beauty, its carvings and columns telling of a civilisation that thrived in this harsh desert landscape.

Adrien, his eyes tracing the intricate carvings that adorned their surfaces, remarked, "The detail is extraordinary," his voice tinged with respect. "Each facade tells a unique story of power, faith and beauty. It's as if the stone itself has come alive to speak of its creators".

Dr Amal El-Sharif, her eyes taking in the majesty of the surroundings, added: "In each carving there is a whisper of the past, a connection to those who lived and breathed in this place."

As we continued our exploration, Khalid led us to the Royal Tombs, a series of grandiose burial chambers carved into the cliffs. Majestic in design and scale, the tombs were a clear declaration of wealth and power, their elaborate facades designed to impress both the living and the gods.

"These were not just tombs, they were declarations of wealth and power," Khalid explained, sweeping his hand across the vista before us. "The Nabataeans believed in making a statement with their architecture, ensuring that their legacy would endure through the ages."

The royal tombs, with their soaring facades and intricate carvings, were a testament to the Nabataeans' ambition and artistic vision. The Urn Tomb, with its massive courtyard and imposing columns, seemed to capture the essence of Petra's grandeur, its facade glowing in the sunlight as if still alive with the spirits of those buried within.

As we walked through these ancient streets, the silence around us was profound, a stark reminder of the city's abandonment and the passage of time. Yet in that silence there was a sense of connection, a thread linking us across the millennia to the people who once walked these paths, lived in these houses and honoured their dead in these tombs.

Exploring Petra was not just a journey through a physical landscape, but a journey through the layers of human history, each stone and carving a page in a story that spanned generations. The beauty of Petra lay not only in its architectural marvels, but in its ability to connect us to the past, to remind us of the enduring nature of human creativity and resilience.

As we paused to take in the view from the royal tombs, the city spread out below us in a panorama of ancient splendour, I, Dr John Watson, felt a profound sense of privilege to be standing in this place. Our exploration of Petra was a journey of discovery, not only of the secrets held within these stone walls, but of the common human heritage that unites us all.

Liyana, her eyes fixed on the panorama before us, spoke softly: "Standing here, I feel the whispers of those who came before us. Their stories, their lives, echo through these stones.

Holmes, ever the keen observer, added: "It is a testament to the resilience of human endeavour. Petra stands as a silent witness to the passage of time and the enduring spirit of humanity".

At that moment we all felt a deep connection to the ancient city and to each other. Our journey through Petra had been transformed from an exploration of physical remains to a deep, spiritual communion with the past. The legacy of the Nabataeans, their artistry and their indomitable spirit were etched not only into the stones of Petra, but into our hearts.

As the sun began its descent behind the pink cliffs of Petra, casting long, ethereal shadows across the ancient city, our team found solace in a campsite carefully chosen for its view of the Treasury. The day's exploration had left us with a profound sense of wonder and an insatiable curiosity about what lay beyond the facades and tombs we had wandered among. As twilight enveloped the landscape, transforming the city into a tableau of shifting light and shadow, we gathered around the campfire, the flickering flames casting a warm glow on our faces and igniting the spark of anticipation for the days ahead.

The Treasury, illuminated by the last rays of the setting sun, stood like a silent sentinel in the distance. Its majestic facade, now softened by the twilight, seemed to guard the secrets of a civilisation long lost in the mists of time. The atmosphere around our campfire was one of thoughtful contemplation, mixed with the excitement of the unknown that awaited us. The air was filled with the scent of burning cedar wood, carrying with it the whispers of ancient legends and the mysteries buried in Petra's stone heart.

Sherlock Holmes, his keen gaze fixed on the Treasury, broke the silence with a thoughtful musing. "What secrets lie within, shielded from the eyes of the world for centuries?" he wondered aloud. His voice, usually full of confidence and certainty, now carried a note of humility in the face of Petra's enduring mystery. Holmes' question hung in the air, echoing the collective curiosity that had brought us to this remote corner of the desert.

Dr Amal El-Sharif, her eyes reflecting the dance of the campfire flames, added her reflections to our evening discourse. "Our journey has brought us to this moment. Petra is more than just a city; it is a gateway to understanding a lost civilisation". Her words, spoken with the conviction of a scholar whose life has been dedicated to the pursuit of knowledge, resonated deeply with each of us. El-Sharif's sentiment captured the essence of our quest - not just to uncover

Petra's physical treasures, but to bridge the gap of time and connect with the souls who once called this city home.

Liyana Sultan, her regal presence commanding attention, gazed thoughtfully at the flames. "In these ruins," she said softly, "we find not only the remains of a city, but the echoes of dreams and aspirations that transcend time. The legacy of the Nabataeans is a testament to our common humanity."

As night fell, our conversation turned to the legends that have long shrouded Petra in mystery. Tales of hidden treasures waiting to be discovered by those brave or foolish enough to seek them out, and ancient curses guarding secrets too powerful for the modern world. These stories, passed down through the generations, seemed all the more real in the ruins of Petra, where every stone and shadow whispered of the past.

Khalid, our guide and custodian of countless tales of the desert and its people, regaled us with tales of explorers and adventurers who had come before us, lured by the promise of Petra's hidden riches. His voice, rich and evocative, painted vivid pictures of daring exploits and an insatiable thirst for discovery. Yet beneath the allure of these legends lay a cautionary tale of respect for the sacredness of the place and the spirits that still dwelt within its walls.

"The desert is a harsh and unforgiving teacher," Khalid said, his voice a mixture of awe and warning. "Many have come here seeking fortune, only to be humbled by the sands and the silent guardians of Petra. It is a place that demands respect, for it is not just stone and sand, but the resting place of dreams and legacies".

As the fire burned down to glowing embers and the stars began their nightly vigil in the clear desert sky, a profound sense of unity enveloped our group. We were no longer a collection of individuals, each pursuing our own scientific or personal ambitions. We had become a community, bound together by the shared experience of standing on the threshold of history, ready to step into the shadows of Petra and embrace the mysteries that awaited us.

The night air, cool and crisp, carried with it the promise of dawn and the continuation of our journey into the heart of Petra. As we retired to our tents, the silhouette of the Treasury against the starry sky served as a silent reminder of the adventure that lay ahead. Our reflections and anticipations, shared around the campfire, had forged a bond that would carry us through the challenges and revelations to come. Petra, with its ancient stones and hidden secrets, had already begun to reveal its true treasure - the enduring power of human curiosity and the unbreakable spirit of discovery.

The campfire crackled softly, its gentle light casting a warm glow on the faces of my companions, each lost in his own thoughts as the night enveloped us in its serene embrace. The silhouette of Petra's ancient structures loomed in the background, their forms mere shadows against the starlit sky, a stark reminder of the day's profound journey through history and human achievement. The air was cool, carrying the faint earthy scent of the desert after dusk, mixed with the aroma of cedar wood burning in our campfire. The only sounds that broke the silence of the night were the occasional whisper of the desert wind and the soft, comforting crackle of the fire.

Around me sat Sherlock Holmes, Dr Amal El-Sharif, Liyana Sultan, Adrien d'Arcy, Khalid and the rest of our intrepid team, each reflecting on the day's discoveries and contemplating the mysteries still hidden within Petra's ancient walls. The atmosphere was one of exhaustion, tinged with the satisfaction of a day well spent and a palpable sense of anticipation for what was yet to come. Despite the weariness that weighed on our bodies, our spirits were lifted by a sense of unity and purpose forged by the challenges and revelations we had shared.

As I, Dr John Watson, sat among my companions, the weight of our journey pressed upon me, not as a burden, but as a profound responsibility to bear witness to the wonders we had uncovered. My journal lay open on my lap, its pages fluttering lightly in the breeze, eager to capture the essence of our expedition. With a sense of solemnity I began to write, my words a testament to the depth of our experience: "Petra, with its shadows and mysteries, has brought us closer than ever. Ahead of us lies the heart of our quest, the search for knowledge that transcends time".

Holmes, his eyes reflecting the firelight, turned to me. "Watson, your dedication to recording our journey is invaluable. Every word you write captures the essence of our discoveries and ensures that the stories of Petra will endure."

Dr Amal El-Sharif, her eyes fixed on the stars above, added: "We are but temporary visitors to this timeless place. Yet through our explorations we breathe life into the ancient stones and awaken the spirits of the past".

Liyana Sultan, her regal presence commanding attention, gazed thoughtfully at the flames. "In these ruins," she said softly, "we find not only the remains of a city, but the echoes of dreams and aspirations that transcend time. The legacy of the Nabataeans is a testament to our common humanity".

Adrien d'Arcy, his passion for craftsmanship and history evident, spoke with a newfound reverence. "Every carving, every stone tells a story. It's as if Petra itself is a living, breathing being, whispering its secrets to those who listen".

Khalid, whose connection to this land runs deep in his veins, gazed into the flames, his eyes reflecting the firelight as he offered a final thought that captured the essence of our shared experience. "In the silence of Petra we find not only the echoes of the past, but the whispers of our own destiny." His words, spoken with the weight of centuries of history and the wisdom of the desert, echoed within each of us, a reminder that our journey was also an inward one, a quest to understand not only the mysteries of Petra, but the mysteries within ourselves.

As the fire dwindled to glowing embers, the night grew deeper and the stars above shone with an intensity that seemed to reflect the depth of our adventure. The silhouette of the Treasury, now barely visible in the darkness, stood as a silent guardian over our camp, its secrets locked in stone, waiting for the dawn to reveal them once more.

The end of this day marked not an end, but a threshold. As we retired to our tents, the desert night embraced us, its vastness a canvas for the dreams and aspirations that filled our hearts. The mysteries of Petra, both revealed and hidden, had deepened our resolve to continue our exploration, to peel back the layers of history and uncover the truths buried beneath centuries of sand and silence.

The bond that united our team, strengthened by the adversity we had faced and the wonders we had witnessed, was a testament to the enduring power of human curiosity and the unquenchable thirst for knowledge. As I closed my diary and surrendered to the embrace of sleep, the words I had written echoed in my mind, a mantra for the journey ahead: "Petra, with its shadows and mysteries, has brought us closer than ever. Ahead lies the heart of our quest, the pursuit of knowledge that transcends time". In the heart of the desert, under the watchful gaze of the stars, our adventure was just beginning.

Act III

CHAPTER 21

VEIL OF THE ANCIENTS

A s the first light of dawn appeared, the jagged horizon emerged and cast a golden glow on the pink stones of Petra. Our team, invigorated by the previous night's revelations and the promise of the day ahead, gathered in the heart of the ancient city. The Treasury, Petra's most iconic facade, stood before us, its intricate carvings and solemn grandeur bathed in the morning light, presenting a stunning tableau that seemed to bridge the gap of time.

The air was crisp, a subtle chill that spoke of the desert's nocturnal slumber now giving way to the warmth of a new day. The stillness of dawn enveloped us, a mystical stillness that seemed to heighten the sense of history and mystery that pervades Petra. It was in this hallowed atmosphere that Sherlock Holmes, Dr Amal El-Sharif, Liyana Sultan, Adrien d'Arcy, Khalid, myself and our dedicated caravan crew set out with a renewed purpose: to uncover the elusive links between this ancient city and the enigmatic Obsidian Guild.

Holmes, ever the embodiment of focus and determination, paused to survey our surroundings with a keen eye, his silhouette a stark contrast against the backdrop of Petra's timeless beauty. "Every stone in Petra could be a key to unlocking the secrets of the Guild," he mused, his voice a low rumble in the morning silence. "Observation and deduction will lead us to our quarry." His words, spoken with the unwavering conviction that I have come to know as his trademark, served as a rallying cry, igniting a spark of excitement in each of us.

The scent of ancient dust, disturbed by our passing footsteps, rose in the cool morning air and mingled with the faint scent of the wild sagebrush that dotted the landscape. It was as if we were waking the city from its slumber, each step a whisper in the great conversation between past and present. The textures underfoot varied from the smooth, worn paths to the crunch of gravel and stone, a tactile reminder of the centuries that had unfolded in this very place.

Our search began in earnest, guided by Holmes' principle of methodical investigation. We ventured off the beaten track and sought out the lesser known ruins and inscriptions hidden in the folds of Petra. Each ruin, each carving was a piece of the puzzle, potentially holding clues to the presence of the Obsidian Guild and the secrets they sought to protect.

Dr El-Sharif, with her extensive knowledge of ancient cultures, led our examination of the inscriptions, her fingers tracing the lines of characters etched into the stone millennia ago. The language of the Nabataeans, once spoken in the bustling markets and great temples of Petra, now stood as a silent testament to the city's storied past. Amal's deep understanding and methodical approach were indispensable, and she often paused to give us insights into the historical significance of the symbols she was deciphering, combining scholarly wisdom with practical guidance.

Liyana Sultan, whose keen interest in the legends and lore of the desert had proved invaluable on our journey, pondered the symbology carved into the rock faces, looking for connections to the stories of the Obsidian Guild woven into the fabric of local myth. Her resilience and adaptability shone through as she manoeuvred through the rough terrain, her insights adding a unique perspective to our findings. She often shared anecdotes from her cultural background that enriched our understanding and lifted our spirits at trying moments.

Adrien d'Arcy, deeply committed to his craft and initially sceptical of the mystical elements of our quest, found himself drawn into the intrigue, his analytical mind piecing together the historical and archaeological evidence with a newfound fervour. His scepticism gradually turned to fascination, and he began to work closely with Holmes, helping to decipher the ancient writings and other clues. His reactions to the harsh beauty of the desert reflected his resilience and adaptability, revealing layers of admiration and respect for the ancient city.

Khalid, our faithful guide, shared his intimate knowledge of Petra's hidden corners, taking us to places that many had overlooked, places where the whispers of the past seemed to resonate most strongly. His deep connection to Petra was evident at every turn, and he often spoke of the city with a reverence that underlined its importance in his life. His guidance was not only practical, but also filled with stories and wisdom passed down through generations, giving us a richer, more nuanced understanding of our surroundings.

As we delved deeper into the heart of Petra, each discovery added a layer of understanding, a step closer to unravelling the mysteries that bound the Obsidian Guild to this ancient city. The sense of anticipation among us grew with each passing hour, a shared conviction that the secrets we sought were within our grasp, waiting to be unlocked.

On this early morning expedition, as the sun rose higher and cast its golden light over the rose-red city, we found ourselves not only as seekers of the secrets of history, but as part of the ongoing story of Petra, a chapter yet unwritten in the saga of the Obsidian Guild. The air, once filled with the scent of ancient dust, now seemed charged with the promise of discovery, a testament to the enduring allure of Petra, the Rose City, and the mysteries it holds.

In the golden light of mid-morning, our journey took us along the lesser-travelled paths of Petra to a secluded area near the High Place of Sacrifice. The landscape around us was a tapestry of natural grandeur and ancient mysticism, where the towering cliffs stood as silent guardians of history, their surfaces etched by the passage of time. The climb was steep, the path winding, with each turn revealing breathtaking vistas - vast expanses of desert punctuated by the rugged beauty of Petra's rose-red stones.

It was here, in this secluded part of the ancient city, far from the well-worn paths trodden by countless tourists, that serendipity guided our steps. As we navigated a narrow passage between two towering cliffs, we encountered an elderly Bedouin man. At first glance he appeared to be a simple hermit, his weathered face bearing the marks of a life lived under the desert sun, his clothes a patchwork of traditional fabrics that spoke of a bygone era. He sat cross-legged at the mouth of a small cave, a kettle brewing over a modest fire, seemingly lost in thought, or perhaps in communion with the spirits of the place.

There was a palpable air of serendipity about our meeting, a sense that this was no mere coincidence, but a moment that was meant to happen. The seclusion of the place, away from the prying eyes and ears of the world, added a profound significance to our meeting. Here stood Sherlock Holmes, Dr Amal El-Sharif, Liyana Sultan, Adrien d'Arcy, Khalid, myself and our caravan crew, face to face with a man who, unbeknownst to us, held the keys to the mysteries we sought to unravel.

As we approached, the elderly Bedouin - later introduced to us as Hakim - looked at us with eyes that seemed to look straight into our souls, as if measuring our worth. His greeting was one of quiet dignity, a nod of recognition that betrayed a lifetime of wisdom. "Many seek the treasures of Petra, few seek its wisdom," he began, his voice a gentle timbre that seemed to harmonise with the whisper of the wind. "The Obsidian Guild is not for the greedy of heart." His words, cryptic yet full of meaning, hinted at the depth of knowledge he possessed, not only of Petra, but of the enigmatic Obsidian Guild and the trials that lay ahead.

Dr El-Sharif, ever the scholar, her curiosity piqued by Hakim's words, responded with thoughtful intensity. "You speak as one who guards not only the past, but the way to understanding it," she observed, recognising in Hakim a fellow guardian of history's secrets. Her words struck a chord, a mutual recognition of the responsibility they each bore - to protect and to reveal the truth when the time was right.

Hakim's knowledge of Petra and the Obsidian Guild quickly revealed his true importance, elevating him from the first impression of a simple hermit to a guardian of ancient secrets. He spoke of the trials that awaited us, not as obstacles, but as gateways to understanding the true essence of Petra and the wisdom it held. His cryptic messages, though shrouded in mystery, were clear in their intent: the path to uncovering the secrets of the Obsidian Guild required more than mere physical exploration; it demanded an openness of heart and mind, a willingness to see beyond the surface.

As we sat with Hakim at the mouth of the cave, the desert landscape stretching out before us, the conversation took on a deeper dimension. Here, in the seclusion of Petra's hidden corners, we were not merely explorers or scholars, but seekers on a journey that transcended the physical boundaries of the ancient city. Hakim, with his intimate knowledge of Petra and its connection to the Obsidian Guild, became our guide, not only through the winding paths of stone and sand, but through the labyrinth of history and myth that shrouded our quest.

Meeting Hakim marked a turning point in our journey, a moment of serendipitous discovery that would shape the course of our exploration. In the shadow of Petra's towering cliffs, we found not just a guardian of the past, but a beacon that would light the way to understanding the true nature of the Rose City and the mysteries it held.

<hr />

As we settled into the intimate niche carved by nature and time, the ambience around us subtly changed. The secluded area, at first just a backdrop for an unexpected encounter, now felt imbued with a deep sense of history and secrets waiting to be revealed. The air itself seemed to thicken with anticipation, charged with the weight of the revelations that were about to unfold.

Hakim, the elderly Bedouin who had so fortuitously crossed our path, looked at us with a depth of solemnity that demanded our undivided attention. The fire crackled softly beside him, casting flickering shadows that danced across the ancient walls, as if the spirits of Petra themselves had gathered to listen.

"The Obsidian Guild," Hakim began, his voice resonating with a gravitas that belied his humble appearance, "has long been the keeper of secrets too powerful, too sacred, to fall into the hands of those who seek them for personal gain." The way he spoke of the Guild, it was as if he were not merely describing an organisation, but invoking the essence of a legacy that transcends time itself.

"I am but a guardian," he continued, "charged with protecting the wisdom and knowledge of the ancients and ensuring that it is passed on only to those who are worthy." His eyes, reflecting the glow of the fire, met each of ours in turn, as if measuring the purity of our intentions.

The revelation of Hakim's true role in the tapestry of Petra's history and the mysteries of the Obsidian Guild was both astonishing and humbling. Here, in our midst, was a man who had dedicated his life to preserving the secrets of a civilisation long gone, but whose echoes still echo through the canyons and cliffs of the Rose City.

"The third statuette," Hakim revealed, "lies hidden within Petra, not by castles or earth, but by the veil of ignorance. Only those who see beyond the stone, who understand the true essence of this place, can hope to find it." His words hung in the air, both a challenge and an invitation. It was as if the statuette was not just an object to be found, but a gateway to a deeper understanding, a test of our resolve and our ability to perceive the unseen.

Liyana, always the reflective soul among us, voiced the sentiment that lingered unspoken in the hearts of our team. "Then our journey is not only one of discovery, but of enlightenment." Her observation, thoughtful and profound, captured the essence of the quest before us. We were not merely seekers of artefacts; we were pilgrims on a journey to uncover the wisdom of the ancients, a journey that required not only keen observation but deep understanding and insight.

The revelation of Hakim's role and the clues he provided about the third statuette deepened the sense of purpose that bound us together. As the guardian of the Obsidian Guild's secrets, Hakim was the bridge between the past and the present, a living testament to Petra's enduring legacy and the knowledge it held.

Our conversation with Hakim, under the canopy of stars and the watchful gaze of Petra's ancient spirits, became a confluence of minds and hearts. Every word, every pause was laden with meaning, weaving a deeper connection between us and the mystical landscape that surrounded us.

As the night deepened and our discussion drew to a close, the air around us seemed to lighten, as if the very atmosphere had been transformed by the exchange. We were no longer mere visitors to Petra; we had been entrusted with a mission that went beyond the search for a hidden statuette. We were seekers of knowledge, chosen to tread the path of enlightenment that the ancients had laid out for us.

In that moment, the secluded niche, the flickering fire and the ancient stones of Petra witnessed the forging of a bond that would guide us through the trials and revelations to come. Hakim's revelation had not only revealed the depth of our quest, it had illuminated the path to understanding the true essence of the Rose City and the secrets it guarded.

In the secluded enclave that had witnessed Hakim's profound revelations, a palpable change had taken place among us. The air, once filled with the hushed whispers of ancient secrets, now vibrated with a renewed sense of purpose and determination. This hidden corner of Petra, far from the prying eyes of the modern world, had become a crossroads not only of our physical journey, but of our collective destiny.

As we sat in a semi-circle around the dwindling fire, the flickering flames casting long shadows against the craggy walls of our secluded alcove, each member of our team seemed to be engaged in deep, introspective reflection. The revelation of our unique role in the unfolding mystery of the Obsidian Guild and the ancient wisdom of Petra had given us a renewed sense of commitment to our quest. It was as if the weight of history and the anticipation of what lay ahead had converged on this moment, forging in each of us a resolve as enduring as the stones of Petra itself.

Adrien, who had begun this journey with a sceptical eye, now looked into the fire with a look of resolute determination. Shadows played across his features as he spoke, his voice calm and filled with newfound conviction. "We stand at the threshold of the unknown, our resolve tested but unbroken," he declared. "Let us prove ourselves worthy of the mysteries that await." His words, spoken with a clarity that belied his deep commitment to craft and tradition, echoed around us, a solemn vow to honour the trust Hakim had placed in us.

Khalid, our stalwart guide, whose connection to Petra ran as deep as the roots of the ancient olive trees that dotted the landscape, nodded in agreement. The firelight illuminated his face, revealing a look of deep connection to the land and its stories. "Petra has always been more than stone and sand to me," he affirmed with unwavering conviction. "It is a keeper of stories, and we are its chosen readers." His words, simple yet profound, resonated with a truth that we all felt deeply. In our quest to uncover the secrets of the Obsidian Guild, we were not only unearthing relics of the past, but also the stories of a civilisation that had flourished in the harsh beauty of the desert.

The atmosphere of our remote gathering was charged with a collective energy that transcended the individual. Each member of our team, from Sherlock Holmes with his analytical brilliance, to Dr Amal El-Sharif with her scholarly insight, Liyana Sultan with her intuitive understanding of lore, and myself, Dr John Watson, chronicler of our extraordinary adventures, found ourselves united by a common purpose. Inspired by Hakim's revelations, we vowed to delve deeper into the mysteries of Petra and the Obsidian Guild, understanding that our quest was not just for the tangible remains of history, but for the wisdom and enlightenment it represented.

As we rose from our gathering, the first light of dawn began to touch the tops of the surrounding cliffs, casting a soft golden glow that seemed to bless our renewed commitment. The secluded niche, once a mere waypoint on our journey, had now become a sacred space, a crucible in which our resolve had been tested and found unyielding.

With the promise of the day ahead, we stepped out of the seclusion of our niche and the vista of Petra unfolded before us in the morning light. The ancient city, with its towering facades and hidden chambers, seemed to beckon with the promise of discoveries yet to be made. Our journey, inspired by the revelations of a keeper of secrets and strengthened by our collective dedication, was about to enter a new chapter. We were no longer mere travellers in a land of stone and sand; we were seekers of wisdom, chosen to unravel the mysteries of the Rose City and the secrets it held. Our quest, rich with the potential for enlightenment, lay before us, a path to be walked with reverence, courage and an unwavering commitment to the pursuit of knowledge that transcends time.

As the first rays of sunlight began to crown the ancient cliffs of Petra with a golden halo, our small assembly, now imbued with a purpose far greater than any we had previously conceived, prepared to leave the secluded enclave that had served as the stage for revelations profound enough to alter the course of our quest. The atmosphere among us was one of contemplative silence, a shared reflection on the weight of the journey ahead, each of us inwardly processing the gravity of Hakim's revelations and the solemn vow we had made.

The ancient city of Petra, now slowly awakening under the tender caresses of dawn, lay majestically before us, its myriad secrets embedded in the rose-red stones that had silently witnessed the ebb and flow of the centuries. The beauty of the scene was almost overwhelming, a timeless testament to human endeavour and the mysteries of the past that still held an irresistible allure.

It was in this moment of quiet introspection, as the vastness of Petra unfolded in the burgeoning light of day, that I, Dr John Watson, felt compelled to capture the essence of our experience and the resolve forged in the crucible of our encounter with Hakim. The words seemed to flow from my pen with a life of their own, as if guided by the invisible hand of destiny:

"As we parted from Hakim, the keeper of secrets, the path ahead seemed both daunting and illuminating. Petra, the Rose City, was not just a relic of the past, but a beacon guiding us to a deeper understanding of history, of the Obsidian Guild, and of ourselves.

The significance of our mission had never been clearer, nor the challenges we were likely to face as we sought to unravel the layers of mystery that shrouded our quest. Yet despite the uncertainties and trials that Hakim's words had foreshadowed, there was a burgeoning sense of anticipation within me, a fervent desire to delve deeper into the secrets that Petra held dear.

The city itself, viewed from our vantage point as we prepared to re-enter its ancient confines, seemed to resonate with a silent invitation, its myriad passageways and hidden niches promising revelations yet to be uncovered. The scent of the desert, rich with the aroma of wild herbs warmed by the rising sun, filled the air, a subtle reminder of the natural beauty that cradled Petra's storied past.

Our team, a diverse collection of individuals, each drawn to this quest by their own unique motivations, now stood united by a common purpose. Sherlock Holmes, with his unparalleled analytical mind; Dr Amal El-Sharif, whose scientific expertise had already proved invaluable; Liyana Sultan, whose intuitive grasp of lore and legend had guided us through many a mystery; Adrien d'Arcy, whose scepticism had gradually given way to a grudging fascination; Khalid, our steadfast guide, whose connection to Petra ran as deep as the roots of the ancient olive tree; and myself, chronicler of our adventures and witness to the extraordinary journey we had embarked upon.

As we descended once more into the heart of Petra, the crisp morning air seemed to bristle with the promise of discovery, each step taking us deeper into the embrace of history. The stones beneath our feet, worn smooth by the passage of countless feet over the millennia, seemed to whisper secrets in a language more felt than heard, urging us on.

The chapter of our quest that had unfolded in the secluded niche, under the watchful gaze of Hakim and the ancient spirits of Petra, was but the prelude to a greater saga yet to be written. Our resolve, tempered by the revelations of the Keeper of the Secrets, would guide us through the trials and tribulations that lay ahead, each challenge a stepping stone on the path to enlightenment.

And so, as we ventured forth, the Rose City beckoning with its myriad secrets, I could not help but feel that we were on the cusp of profound and transformative revelations, that our journey was not merely an exploration of the physical remains of a bygone era, but a pilgrimage in search of wisdom that transcends time. Petra, with its shadows and mysteries, had drawn us into its heart and there was no turning back. Ahead lay the heart of our quest, the pursuit of knowledge that promised to illuminate not only the annals of history but the very essence of our souls.

CHAPTER 22

DESERT'S CRUCIBLE

With a gentle rise, the dawn light painted an ethereal glow over the horizon, adorning the ancient city of Petra. In a secluded enclave, a hidden sanctuary amidst the vast expanse of rose-red cliffs and time-worn stones, our assembly gathered. The air was thick with anticipation, a palpable tension resonating with the heartbeat of the ancient city. The profound silence of Petra at this hour provided a solemn canvas for the trials that lay ahead, transcending time itself.

Among us stood Sherlock Holmes, his face one of quiet determination, his keen eyes reflecting the depth of his thoughts. I, Dr John Watson, stood beside him, a mixture of apprehension and curiosity coursing through my veins. Dr Amal El-Sharif, her scholarly demeanour giving way to an obvious eagerness, glanced around the enclave with an air of reverence. Liyana Sultan, her intuitive gaze taking in the surroundings, exuded a calm readiness, while Adrien d'Arcy, once the sceptic, now wore a look of focused determination. Khalid, our steadfast guide, was a pillar of strength, his connection to Petra evident in every gesture.

At the centre of our semi-circle stood Hakim, the elderly Bedouin who had revealed himself to be much more than he appeared. Dressed in traditional garb that whispered of ages past, he exuded an aura of ancient wisdom, his presence commanding yet serene. The rising sun cast a golden glow on his weathered features, accentuating the deep lines etched by time and the elements, each a testament to a life lived within the embrace of Petra's storied landscape.

With a voice that carried the weight of centuries, Hakim addressed us, his words imbued with a gravity that demanded our full attention. "Before the sun sets on this day, each of you will face a test tailored to the essence of your being. Success lies not in the triumph of the body, but in the enlightenment of the soul. His statement, profound and enigmatic, hung in the air, a solemn decree that set the tone for the challenges that awaited us.

Holmes, always the epitome of serenity, responded with a respectful nod, his voice steady and assured. "We understand the gravity of your request and we stand ready." His answer, though simple, resonated with a depth of commitment that spoke volumes, reflecting the resolve each of us felt as we stood on the threshold of the unknown.

The trials, as Hakim had outlined, were not mere tests of physical endurance, but challenges designed to test the depths of our courage, wisdom and heart. These virtues, deemed essential by the Obsidian Guild, would be our guiding lights, illuminating the path to understanding the secrets that Petra, and the Guild itself, had preserved throughout the annals of time.

As the golden light of dawn continued to spread across the ancient city, transforming the rose-red stones into a tapestry of light and shadow, our enclave felt like a sanctuary, a place set apart from the world where the trials of the spirit would unfold. The air around us, once thick with anticipation, now seemed charged with a sense of purpose, a silent recognition of the journey we were about to undertake.

In this sacred moment, as we stood united in our resolve, Petra itself bore witness to our commitment. The ancient city, with its myriad mysteries and timeless beauty, was not merely the setting for our trials, but an integral part of the journey we had embarked upon - a journey that promised not only to reveal the secrets of the Obsidian Guild, but to illuminate the very essence of our being.

⊷⊹⊱⊰⊹⊷

As we followed the winding path that led us deeper into the heart of Petra, the rising sun began to reveal the hidden contours of the city, painting the ancient sandstone with shades of gold and crimson. Our destination, as revealed by Hakim, was a narrow gorge nestled in the embrace of towering cliffs that seemed to reach for the heavens themselves. Here, the air seemed charged with a palpable sense of anticipation, as if the gorge itself were awaiting the unfolding of an event as ancient as the city's storied past.

The path we were following gradually narrowed, giving way to an abyss that yawned before us, its depths shrouded in shadows that the sun's rays dared not penetrate. Standing on the edge, one could not help but feel dwarfed by the sheer scale of nature's grandeur, the gorge a testament to the inexorable forces that have shaped this land over the ages.

It was here, in front of this awe-inspiring display of natural power, that Hakim turned to us, his gaze settling on Khalid. The normally calm and unflappable demeanour of our guide was now charged with a focused intensity, a reflection of the gravity of the test that awaited him. Hakim's eyes, ancient repositories of wisdom, met Khalid's with a profound solemnity.

"Your heart knows the courage of the ancients," Hakim intoned, his voice echoing softly off the sandstone walls. "Let your feet follow where it leads." His words, though softly spoken, carried the weight of a directive that went beyond mere physical action; they were an invocation of the spirit of courage that resided within Khalid, a call to awaken the courage of his ancestors.

Khalid's response was a whisper, carried by the gentle breeze that wound through the gorge. "For Petra, for my ancestors," he murmured, a vow that seemed to draw strength from the very stones beneath our feet. Then, with a determination that bordered on the sublime, he stepped forward to the edge of the precipice.

The leap that lay before Khalid was more than a physical challenge; it was a leap of faith, a testament to the courage it takes to face the unknown and trust in the unseen. The gorge, with its unfathomable depths and imposing cliffs, was a physical manifestation of the fears and doubts that lie within all of us, the invisible chasms we must cross in our quest for understanding and enlightenment.

As Khalid prepared to take the leap, a hush fell over our group, a collective intake of breath held in suspense. The moment was imbued with a sense of timelessness, as if we were standing at the confluence of past and present, witnesses to a trial that echoed the ancient rites of passage that had tested the mettle of those who had walked these lands before us.

Then, with a grace that belied the enormity of the act, Khalid leapt. His figure, silhouetted against the dawning sky, seemed for a moment to merge with the very essence of Petra, a lone warrior facing the void with unwavering courage. The seconds stretched into eternity as we watched, hearts in our throats, until his landing on the other side was heralded by a triumphant shout, a declaration of victory not only over the abyss, but over the fears that try to hold us back.

Khalid's leap, a physical embodiment of the courage that defines the human spirit, was a poignant reminder of the trials we all face in our quest for understanding and truth. As we cheered his success, our hearts swelled not only with pride for our companion, but with a renewed sense of purpose and determination. The test of courage had been met and overcome, a beacon of hope illuminating the path ahead, guiding us further into the depths of Petra's mysteries and the trials that await us.

After Khalid's triumphant leap - a literal and metaphorical crossing into the realms of courage - our spirits were lifted, each of us silently contemplating the nature of the trials that lay ahead. As we ventured deeper into the heart of Petra, the landscape around us seemed to whisper secrets of ages past, the sandstone cliffs casting long shadows that danced in the morning light.

Our next destination, as guided by Hakim, was a place that seemed untouched by the passage of time. Tucked away in a secluded corner of Petra, hidden from the eyes of the casual wanderer, lay an ancient library - a repository of knowledge that had survived the ravages of time and history. The entrance was modest, almost unremarkable, but as we crossed the threshold the atmosphere inside seemed to change palpably. The air was thick with the scent of ancient parchment, a perfume that spoke of centuries of wisdom and the quest for understanding. The dimly lit interior was lined with shelves reaching up to the vaulted ceiling, each crammed with scrolls and artefacts, the physical embodiment of the intellectual endeavours of a bygone era.

Adrien, whom Hakim had chosen for this task, stepped forward with a sense of purpose and determination. His journey with us had only deepened his intellectual curiosity and analytical mind, which had always been open to understanding the intricate connections within the realms of the unknown. It was this keen intellect and unwavering dedication to uncovering truths that Hakim sought to test in this trial of wisdom.

Standing among the ancient tomes, Hakim turned to Adrien with an expression that was both solemn and expectant. "Wisdom is the light that illuminates the shadows of ignorance," he intoned, his voice echoing softly in the hallowed room. "Find the key within the words and you shall uncover truths unseen." With these words he handed Adrien a scroll, its surface covered in symbols and inscriptions that seemed to blur the line between language and art.

Adrien accepted the scroll with a reverence that spoke of his deep appreciation for the gravity of the task. Carefully unfolding it on a nearby table, he began to study the inscriptions with a concentration that was total and unwavering. "Every symbol, every line, speaks of a legacy intricately woven with history and craftsmanship," he murmured, more to himself than to us. "It's not just knowledge, it's understanding the connection between all things and the craftsmen who made them."

The challenge before Adrien was not simply one of translation or deciphering. It was a quest to bridge the gap between knowledge and wisdom, to see beyond the mere words and grasp the deeper meanings hidden within the text. The scroll, a testament to the legacy of Petra and the Guild, held secrets that were guarded not by locks or keys, but by the willingness of a master's mind to see the connections that bound history, craft and wisdom into a coherent whole.

As we watched Adrien immerse himself in the process, the air around us seemed to grow still, filled with the essence of ancient craftsmanship holding its breath in anticipation of a revelation. The silence was broken only by the soft rustle of the scroll and the faint sound of Adrien's passionate voice as he navigated the labyrinth of symbols and inscriptions.

Time passed unmarked, the outside world fading into insignificance as the trial unfolded. Finally, with a soft exhalation that seemed to echo through the library, Adrien stepped back from the table, a look of realisation dawning on his features. "The wisdom of the ancients," he said, turning to us, "is not locked away in the words they left behind, but in the connections they made - between earth and sky, past and present, craft and wisdom."

At that moment, Adrien had not only unlocked the secrets of the scroll, he had also bridged the gap within himself, between scepticism and faith, knowledge and wisdom. His process, a testament to the power of the intellect guided by an open heart, was a profound reminder that wisdom lies not in the accumulation of facts, but in the understanding of the deeper truths that unite all things.

As we left the library, the light of day seemed somehow richer, the shadows cast by the cliffs less threatening. The Trial of Wisdom had not only illuminated the depths of Adrien's intellect, it had also illuminated the path ahead, leading us further into the mysteries of Petra and the trials that awaited us.

⊷∗⊷

As the day faded into dusk, casting Petra in a cloak of shadows and the last rays of sunlight, our journey took us to the ancient amphitheatre carved into the heart of the city. The natural acoustics of the space whispered the echoes of a bygone era, when the air might have been filled with the sounds of performance and assembly. Now it stood as a silent witness to times gone by, its stones imbued with the history and mysteries of the Rose City.

Liyana Sultan, our companion whose insight and intuition had often served to guide us through the enigmatic twists and turns of our quest, stood at the edge of the amphitheatre, her silhouette framed against the dramatic backdrop of Petra's cliffs. The amphitheatre, carved out of the very rock that held it, felt alive with the presence of those who had once gathered in its embrace, the air thick with the weight of untold stories.

Hakim, whose presence had been both a guiding light and a challenge, turned to Liyana with an expression that carried the gravity of the moment. "The heart's journey is the hardest, for it must choose between equally compelling truths," he began, his voice echoing off the ancient stones. "Your choice will light the way not only for you, but for all who follow." The setting sun cast long shadows across the amphitheatre, the fading light painting the scene with an ethereal quality that seemed to transcend time.

In front of Liyana were two paths, each leading out of the amphitheatre into the gathering twilight. One path led to a garden, green and alive with the soft sounds of flowing water, symbolising the principle of compassion - a nurturing

297

force that heals and renews. The other path led to a monument, stark and imposing, representing the ideals of loyalty and sacrifice - a testament to the enduring strength and steadfastness of the human spirit.

The choice that lay before Liyana was emblematic of the trials of the heart: a choice that required not only introspection, but the courage to accept the consequences of her actions. It was a test that would probe the depths of her character, challenging her to reflect on her values and the principles that guided her.

Standing at the crossroads, the silence of the amphitheatre enveloping her, Liyana closed her eyes and took a moment to connect with the ancient spirits that seemed to permeate the very air. When she spoke, her voice was calm, infused with a conviction that resonated deeply with those who bore witness. "In the heart lies the power to heal, to unite and to transcend. My choice reflects not only my own truth, but the truth that unites us all".

With a determination born of clarity and understanding, Liyana turned towards the garden, her steps deliberate as she walked the path of compassion. Her choice, a declaration of her belief in the power of empathy and understanding, was a testament to her strength of character - a strength that lay not in the might of arms, but in the capacity of the heart to embrace love and compassion, even in the face of adversity.

As the last light of day gave way to the embrace of twilight, the amphitheatre seemed to accept Liyana's decision, its ancient stones a silent testament to the trials and triumphs of those who had come before. Her ordeal, a poignant reminder of the complexity of the human heart and the choices that define us, illuminated not only her path, but the path that lies ahead for all of us.

After Liyana's trial, as we gathered in the quiet of the fading day, there was a sense of unity and purpose that bound us together - a shared understanding that the trials we faced were not merely challenges to be overcome, but lessons to be learned, bringing us ever closer to the truths hidden within Petra's heart and within ourselves.

⁂

As darkness enveloped the ancient city of Petra, its timeless monuments silhouetted against the starry sky, our small gathering reassembled at the campsite, nestled in a quiet niche sheltered from the cool desert night. The trials of the day had left their mark, not as scars, but as indelible impressions on our spirits, weaving the fabric of our resolve with threads of courage, wisdom and heart.

The campfire crackled and danced, casting a warm, welcoming glow that flickered across the faces of my companions, illuminating their features with an almost ethereal light. The flames, in their hypnotic dance, seemed to draw us closer, not only to its warmth, but to each other, as we gathered around the fire in a circle of unity and reflection.

Sherlock Holmes, who had been contemplative since our return, cleared his throat quietly, drawing our attention. The firelight played across his features, accentuating the thoughtful expression that had settled on his face. "Tonight," he began, his voice carrying clearly in the stillness of the night, "we have witnessed and participated in trials that have tested the very essence of our being."

He paused, his eyes sweeping over each of us, as if to silently acknowledge the journey we had made together. "In the courage of Khalid, the wisdom of Adrien, and the heart of Liyana, we see not only their individual strengths, but the mirror of our collective soul," he continued, his words weaving a narrative that connected each trial to the larger tapestry of our quest.

Holmes's reflective monologue, imbued with the insight that was his hallmark, delved into the profound wisdom inherent in Hakim's choices. "Each trial," he reflected, "has been not only a test of personal fortitude, but a lesson in the virtues that bind us together as a team and as seekers of truth. Courage, wisdom, heart - these are not isolated qualities to be admired from afar, but interconnected threads that, when woven together, form the fabric of our collective endeavour".

The flickering light of the campfire, coupled with the canopy of stars overhead, created an atmosphere that was both intimate and infinite, grounding us in the moment while reminding us of the vastness of the universe and the mysteries it holds. Holmes' words, spoken with a measured cadence, seemed to resonate with the very essence of Petra itself, echoing off the ancient stones and into the night.

"Hakim, in his infinite wisdom, has not only tested us, but shown us the way forward, together," Holmes concluded, his gaze settling on the fire before us. "The trials have illuminated the path not with the clarity of daylight but with the subtlety of starlight, guided us not with certainties but with the promise of discovery that lies in understanding ourselves and the bonds that unite us."

As Holmes' monologue drew to a close, a contemplative silence enveloped our group, each of us reflecting inwardly on the words that had been spoken. The realisation that our journey was not just one of physical exploration, but of spiritual and emotional growth, settled over us with a profound sense of clarity. The trials we had faced in Petra, under Hakim's watchful eye, had been designed not to test our individual abilities but to strengthen the bonds of our community, to forge from our diverse strengths a unity of purpose that would guide us through the mysteries that lay ahead.

The night air, cool and fragrant with the scent of desert herbs warmed by the day's sun, whispered secrets of the ancient city, of civilisations that had risen and fallen, of stories etched into the stones themselves. And there, under the stars, beside the crackling fire, we found not only the warmth of the flames, but the warmth of shared purpose and renewed resolve, ready to face the unknown with the knowledge that our journey was about more than the mysteries of the Obsidian Guild - it was about discovering ourselves, the virtues that bind us, and the uncharted territories of the heart and soul that await exploration.

In the deep silence of the night, after the embers of our campfire had died down to a soft, glowing warmth, I found myself sitting on a weathered stone at the edge of our camp, a blank page of my diary open before me. The only sounds to grace the silence were the gentle whisper of the desert wind as it caressed the ancient stones of Petra, and the soft scratching of my pen, a lonely but steadfast companion in the chronicling of our journey.

The moon, a slender crescent, hung low in the star-studded sky, casting a silvery light that illuminated the craggy outlines of the surrounding cliffs. These silent sentinels of stone, which had witnessed the passage of countless ages, now stood as guardians over our small gathering of souls, united in purpose and spirit by the trials we had endured under their timeless gaze.

As I tried to capture the essence of the day's events on the pages of my journal, my mind drifted back to the trials each of my companions had endured. Khalid, with his unwavering courage, had jumped over the abyss that yawned like a mouth of darkness, a physical manifestation of the fears that dwell in the hearts of all men. Adrien, whose journey from sceptic to seeker of truth had led him to decipher the ancient scroll in the secluded library, had illuminated the depths of wisdom hidden in the symbols and inscriptions of a bygone era. And Liyana, standing at the crossroads within the embrace of the amphitheatre, had chosen the path of compassion, a testament to the strength of heart that guides the hand of healing and the bonds of unity.

Each trial, unique in its challenge and profound in its significance, had not only tested the mettle of my companions, but also served to illuminate the interconnected threads of courage, wisdom and heart that form the tapestry of our shared human experience. In their facing and overcoming these trials, I saw reflected not only the virtues of the individual, but the indomitable spirit that unites us, a spirit forged in the crucible of adversity and fortified by the bonds of community.

As I write these reflections, my thoughts turn to the journey ahead. The trials, orchestrated by Hakim with a wisdom that seemed to transcend the ages, had served to prepare us, to sharpen our minds for the challenges and mysteries that lay ahead. In the unity forged by our shared experiences, I found a renewed sense of purpose, a clarity of vision that pierced the veil of uncertainty that had once shrouded our path.

"Today, under the ancient gaze of Petra's guardians, we were tested," I wrote, my pen moving with a certainty born of conviction. "And in our trial we have found not only the measure of our own hearts, but the indomitable spirit that binds us together. A path shrouded in mystery lies before us, but we walk it together, stronger, wiser, and with hearts united in purpose".

Closing my diary, I allowed myself a moment of quiet reflection, gazing out into the vast expanse of the desert night. The stars above, a tapestry of light woven across the fabric of the sky, seemed to echo the interconnectedness of our own journey, a reminder that in the vastness of the universe we are bound together by the common pursuit of understanding, knowledge and truth.

In the silence of that desert night, with the ancient city of Petra slumbering in the shadows, I felt a profound connection to the ages, to the countless souls who had walked these paths before us, each in search of their own truths. And as I retired to my tent, the words I had written in my journal echoed in my heart: a testament to the journey we had taken, the trials we had faced, and the path that lay ahead, shrouded in mystery but illuminated by the collective light of our courage, wisdom and heart.

CHAPTER 23

THE SCROLL OF DESTINY

In the hushed dawn that followed the trials, our intrepid assembly - Sherlock Holmes, Dr Amal El-Sharif, Khalid, Adrien d'Arcy, Liyana Sultan and I, Dr John Watson - gathered in a mysterious and ancient setting. Guided by the venerable Hakim, we navigated Petra's labyrinthine passageways and descended into the heart of the city, where the clamour of the modern world faded into a profound silence, as if time itself held its breath in awe. Our destination was a hidden chamber, a sanctuary that had held the whispers of history for centuries.

The chamber greeted us with an atmosphere thick with the scent of antiquity. The air was a library of aromas - the musk of weathered stone mingled with the faint, lingering essence of the oils that once fueled the lamps now replaced by their modern counterparts. These oil lamps, scattered sparsely throughout the room, cast a soft golden glow on the chamber's contents, creating elongated shadows that danced on the walls with a life of their own. It was as if the shadows themselves were whispering the secrets of the past to those who cared to listen.

Amidst these echoes of the past stood Sherlock Holmes, his face a mask of solemn anticipation. Dr Amal El-Sharif, her keen intellect alight with the prospect of unravelling the mysteries enshrined within these ancient confines, surveyed the chamber with an expert eye, her presence a bridge between the modern pursuit of knowledge and the wisdom of ages past. Khalid, whose lineage was as intertwined with Petra as the roots of the ancient olives that dotted its landscape, wore an expression of reverent determination. His connection to this place, to its stories and secrets, was as much a part of him as the blood that coursed through his veins.

Adrien d'Arcy, the master leatherworker whose fascination with craftsmanship knew no bounds, stood among us, his eyes dancing with anticipation as he took in the artistry that surrounded us. His mind was attuned to the historical and cultural significance of the artefacts, eager to unlock the secrets of the craftsmen who had poured their hearts and souls into their creations. Liyana Sultan added another dimension to our group with her intuitive insights and deep empathy. Her ability to read between the lines of ancient texts and sense the emotions underlying historical narratives would prove invaluable in deciphering the scroll's hidden meanings.

As I took my place among my companions, the weight of the previous day's revelations hung heavily over us all. The trials had not only tested our mettle, they had stripped away the layers of our being, revealing the core of who we truly are. Now, as we stood on the threshold of discovery, the anticipation of what lay within the scroll presented by Hakim filled the chamber with an electric tension.

Hakim, the keeper of untold tales, stepped forward, his age-worn face lit by the soft glow of the lamps. In his hands he held an object of unmistakable significance - a scroll encased in a bronze cylinder, its surface etched with symbols that spoke of a heritage far beyond the comprehension of ordinary men.

With solemn reverence, Hakim handed the scroll to Sherlock Holmes. "This scroll," he began, his voice resonant with the weight of history, "has been guarded through the ages. It tells the storied history of the Obsidian Guild and points to the hidden oasis of Al-Hijr. Its words are a beacon that has guided the Guardians through the generations, but they also whisper of the challenges that have tested the Guild's unity."

The mention of challenges caught my attention, and I was intrigued by the subtle change in Hakim's tone. It was as if the parchment of the scroll itself contained not only the Guild's triumphs, but also the echoes of its struggles. As Holmes carefully unfolded the ancient document, I couldn't help but wonder what tales of conflict and resilience lay hidden within its weathered folds.

Holmes accepted the scroll with a nod of recognition, his hands steady as he carefully unfolded the ancient parchment. The rustle of the scroll echoed through the chamber, bridging the gap between past and present. As our eyes traced the lines of text and intricate illuminations, it became clear that we were being granted a glimpse into the very soul of the Obsidian Guild.

⊷⊶⊷

Adrien leaned over the scroll, his eyes widening in wonder as he studied the intricate symbols and designs. "The craftsmanship is extraordinary," he breathed, his voice filled with awe. "The artisans of the Guild were not mere

304

craftsmen; they were masters of their trade, weaving artistry and sacred purpose into every detail. Look at the way the symbols intertwine with the illuminations - it is a testament to their skill and dedication."

Dr El-Sharif, her analytical mind already at work, pointed to a series of symbols that seemed to dance across the parchment. "These symbols speak of a sacred bond between the Guardians and the Mystic Stallions," she explained, her voice a whisper of awe. "The scroll depicts a covenant forged in the crucible of divine encounters and solemn oaths, a foundation upon which the Guild was built. This historical context is crucial to understanding the significance of our quest and the depth of the Guild's legacy."

As Amal continued to decipher the ancient text, providing historical and cultural insights that enriched our understanding, Khalid nodded in agreement, his eyes glowing with a deep connection to the mysteries that lay before us. "This passage speaks of Al-Hijr, the hidden oasis long whispered of in the stories of my people," he said, his voice carrying the weight of generations. "It is a place of immense power, a sanctuary where the sacred and the profane meet. The scroll confirms what I have always known in my heart - that my heritage is intertwined with the fate of the Obsidian Guild."

Holmes, his mind piecing together the clues with the precision of a surgeon, interjected. "The scroll also alludes to a split within the Guild, a split that gave rise to the Sons of Purity." His words hung in the air, a portent of the darkness that threatened to engulf our quest.

Hakim, his eyes heavy with the weight of history, nodded solemnly. "The Schism was our darkest hour," he began, his voice a low rumble. "The Sons of Purity, blinded by their dogmatic interpretation of purity, strayed from our founding principles. They sought to claim the statuettes, believing that by controlling these sacred relics they could bend the will of the Divine to their own misguided ambitions."

As Hakim told the story of the schism, the chamber seemed to echo with the whispers of the past, a solemn reminder of the dangers that lurk when the pursuit of purity becomes a crusade against diversity and inclusion. The revelation of the Guild's internal strife added a new layer of complexity to our mission and underscored the high stakes we faced.

Holmes, his gaze sharp and focused, turned to Hakim. "The murders of Lord Wentworth and Zafir Sultan, the theft of the statuettes - it's all connected to the Sons of Purity, isn't it?" he asked, his voice a razor's edge of certainty.

Hakim nodded, his eyes reflecting the gravity of the situation. "I fear so," he replied, his voice heavy with the weight of responsibility. "The Sons of Purity have emerged from the shadows, determined to claim the statuettes and remake the Guild in their own twisted image. They believe that by uniting the relics, they can purify the world according to their fanatical ideology."

The revelation hung in the air, a chilling confirmation of the dangers we faced. The scroll, with its cryptic prophecies and warnings, had not only shed light on the past, but also on the present. We were no longer mere seekers of knowledge; we were guardians of a legacy, charged with preventing the Sons of Purity from perverting the Guild's sacred mission.

As we delved deeper into the scroll's contents, the story of the Obsidian Guild's origins began to unfold before our eyes. Hakim, his voice resonating with the weight of history, told the story of Malik, the founder of the Guild.

"In the fifteenth century," Hakim began, his eyes distant as if seeing through the veil of time, "a young man named Malik found himself orphaned in the vast expanse of the Arabian desert. His father, a guardian of ancient horse knowledge, had died, leaving Malik alone and adrift in a world of sand and sun".

The room seemed to hold its breath as Hakim spoke, the flickering light of the lamps casting shadows that danced like ghosts of the past. "In his darkest hour, when all hope seemed lost, Malik was saved by a mystical stallion, black as the night, with eyes that shone like stars. This encounter marked the beginning of Malik's sacred journey, a quest that would lead him to the very heart of the Obsidian Guild's legacy."

Adrien, his eyes wide with wonder, leaned forward, hanging on every word. "And the statuettes?" he asked, his voice a whisper. "How did they come to be?"

Hakim smiled, a smile that held the secrets of the ages. "Over the next fifty years," he continued, "Malik's journey led him to three unique stallions in distant oases, each embodying aspects of the mystic stallion's spirit. In homage to these celestial equines, Malik created three obsidian statuettes, each infused with gold, silver and crimson veins, symbolising the virtues of courage, wisdom and heart".

Dr El-Sharif spoke up, her eyes bright with understanding. "The statuettes were more than mere objects of art," she mused, her voice filled with reverence. "They were talismans, imbued with the essence of the stallions and the sacred purpose of the Guild."

Hakim nodded, his eyes meeting Amal's. "Indeed they were. Malik entrusted these statuettes to the noble families of the oases, thus founding the Obsidian Guild, a brotherhood sworn to protect the legacy of the mystic stallions and the wisdom they embodied."

As the story of Malik's journey unfolded, I could not help but feel a sense of awe at the depth of history that lay before us. The origins of the Obsidian Guild were not just the story of one man's quest, but a testament to the enduring power of legend and the sacred bond between man and horse.

Holmes, his mind always sharp, turned the conversation to the schism that had torn the Guild apart. "The scroll speaks of the Guild's unity, but also of the challenges that have tested it," he observed, his eyes narrowing with sharp intensity. "What were these challenges, and how did they cause the Sons of Purity to stray from the Guild's noble purpose?"

Hakim's face grew sombre, the weight of centuries seeming to settle on his shoulders. "The schism," he began, his voice heavy with the burden of memory, "was born of a single act, an act of unity and peace twisted by the Sons of Purity into a perceived betrayal. But the seeds of discord had been sown long before, in the whispers of dissent and the shadows of suspicion that had begun to grow within the Guild."

The room grew silent, the only sound being the soft crackling of the oil lamps as Hakim continued his tale. "In the seventeenth century, the direct descendants of the mystical stallions, now revered as the ancestors of the British thoroughbred lineage, found their genesis in the sacred oases of the Guild. In an act of ultimate reverence, the Obsidian Guild decided to donate these ancestral stallions to the burgeoning British Empire, intending to embed the sacred bloodlines at the heart of the world's most powerful empire".

Khalid spoke up, his eyes wide with understanding. "It was to be a symbol of peace and unity," he said, his voice filled with a quiet reverence. "A way to forge a bond between the Guild and the Empire, to spread the virtues of the mystic stallions throughout the world."

Hakim nodded, his gaze distant. "Yes, that was the intention. But not all within the guild saw it that way. A faction, led by those who harboured a rigid and dogmatic vision of purity, saw the gift of the stallions as a betrayal, a contamination of the sacred bloodlines."

Liyana interjected, her voice soft but filled with a quiet strength. "They could not see beyond their own narrow vision," she said, her eyes sad. "They could not understand that true purity lies in sharing wisdom, not hoarding it."

Hakim's voice grew heavy with the weight of history. "And so the Sons of Purity broke away from the Guild, denouncing the act of unity as sacrilege. They baptized themselves in opposition to the Guild's noble purpose, twisting the very concept of purity into a weapon of division and hatred."

As the revelation of the origins of the Schism hung in the air, I could feel the weight of centuries pressing down upon us. The Sons of Purity, born of a misguided notion of purity, had torn the Guild apart, setting in motion a chain of events that had brought us to this moment, to the precipice of a battle for the very soul of the Obsidian Guild.

Holmes, his gaze sharp and focused, spoke into the silence. "And now the Sons of Purity seek to claim the statuettes, to twist the Guild's legacy to their own ends. We must stop them, whatever the cost."

Adrien, his voice filled with quiet determination, nodded in agreement. "The statuettes are more than just relics," he said, his hand resting on the scroll. "They are the key to preserving the true purpose of the Guild, to preserving the wisdom and unity that Malik sought to protect."

As we sat there, united in our resolve, I could feel the bonds of our fellowship growing stronger, forged in the crucible of the revelations laid before us. We were no longer mere seekers of knowledge, but guardians of a sacred trust, charged with preserving the legacy of the Obsidian Guild from those who would twist it to their own ends.

Dr El-Sharif, her voice filled with a quiet strength, spoke into the silence. "We must not allow the Sons of Purity to prevail," she said, her gaze meeting each of ours in turn. "We must stand against their twisted vision and protect the true purpose of the Guild, no matter what challenges lie ahead."

And so, with the weight of history on our shoulders and the fire of determination in our hearts, we rose to face the trials that lay before us. The scroll of the Stallions, with its tale of tragedy and triumph, of unity and division, had shown us the true nature of our quest. We were not mere adventurers in search of treasure, but guardians of a legacy, sworn to protect the wisdom and magic of the Obsidian Guild.

※◌⋇◌※

As we prepared to leave the chamber, each of us lost in our own thoughts and reflections, I could not help but feel a sense of awe at the path that lay before us. We were walking in the footsteps of legends, following a trail laid down centuries ago by Malik and the founders of the Guild.

And though the road ahead was fraught with danger and uncertainty, I knew that we would face it together, united in our purpose and strengthened by the bonds of our fellowship. For we were the Guardians of the Obsidian Guild, and our legacy would echo through the ages, a testament to the enduring power of wisdom, courage and unity in the face of darkness.

With the scroll of the Stallions as our guide and the fire of determination in our hearts, we stepped into the waiting embrace of the desert, ready to face whatever trials lay ahead. The Sons of Purity would not prevail, not while we still drew breath. We would stand against them, armed with the wisdom of the ages and the strength of our convictions, and we would emerge victorious, guardians of the Light and protectors of the sacred trust that had been bestowed upon us.

And so our journey continued, into the heart of the desert and into the depths of destiny itself. The legacy of Malik and the Mystic Stallions, the true purpose of the Obsidian Guild, would not be lost to the sands of time. We would carry it forward, a beacon of hope and unity in a world too often divided by fear and mistrust.

For we were the Guardians of the Obsidian Guild, and our story was far from over. The desert awaited us, and with it the final chapter of our quest. And though the road ahead was uncertain, one thing was clear: we would face it together, bound by the unbreakable bonds of fellowship and the sacred duty that had been entrusted to us.

And in the end, when the last battle had been fought and the last secret revealed, we would stand tall, the guardians of the light, the protectors of the legacy of the mystic stallions. For ours was a tale of legend, a tale of courage and sacrifice, of unity and hope in the face of darkness. And it was a tale that would be told for generations to come, a shining beacon of the enduring power of the human spirit.

CHAPTER 24

AMBUSH UNDER THE CRESCENT MOON

awn caressed the ancient city of Petra, casting a golden glow over the landscape, transforming the sandstone cliffs into a canvas of light and shadow. The air was cool and crisp, carrying the scent of the desert - a mixture of dry earth, sun-baked stone and the faint, exotic scent of distant flowers that draw life from the arid expanse. In this moment of serene beauty, as day broke on one of the world's most enduring mysteries, our party stood at the precipice of a journey that would plunge them deep into the heart of legend itself.

Sherlock Holmes, Dr Amal El-Sharif, Khalid, Adrien d'Arcy, Liyana Sultan and I had gathered at the edge of the city, where civilisation's grip eased and the untamed majesty of the desert began. We were a gathering bound not only by the bonds of friendship and camaraderie, but by a common purpose that had been ignited in the shadowy chambers beneath Petra. The revelations of the Obsidian Guild, entrusted to us through the ancient scroll, had intertwined our destinies in a quest that sought not only to uncover the hidden oasis of Al-Hijr, but to safeguard a legacy that bridged the divine and earthly realms.

Our preparations for departure were marked by meticulous attention to detail, a testament to the gravity of our undertaking. Holmes, always the embodiment of quiet determination, checked the supplies and maps with a keen eye, ensuring that nothing essential was overlooked. As he worked, I noticed his gaze lingering on Al-Zarib, Khalid's steadfast equine companion. There was a strange intensity in Holmes' expression, as if he sensed something extraordinary about the horse that eluded the rest of us.

Dr El-Sharif, her brow furrowed in concentration, double-checked the translations of the scroll, her fingers reverently tracing the ancient symbols. Khalid, whose lineage was as much a part of this land as the sand and stone, inspected the camels, his actions deliberate and practiced. His weathered hands moved with the assurance of one who has spent a lifetime reading the subtle signs of the desert. Al-Zarib stood beside him, patient and alert, his presence a comforting constant in our uncertain venture.

Adrien, with his keen understanding of cultural heritage, ensured that our artefacts and tools were safely packed. His eyes gleamed with a mixture of excitement and trepidation as he surveyed our equipment, each item a potential key to unlocking the mysteries that lay ahead. Liyana, her intuitive nature attuned to the energy of the group, offered words of encouragement, her quiet strength a balm to our collective nerves. Her own steed, Muntasir, stood nearby, his noble bearing a reflection of his rider's grace under pressure.

As for me, I found the task of organising our medical supplies a grounding exercise. Every bandage, every vial of medicine was a tangible reminder of the very real dangers we might face. The weight of this responsibility settled on my shoulders, a familiar burden that I carried with the solemnity of a physician who understood all too well the capricious nature of fate in such unforgiving lands.

As we prepared to leave, the silence of dawn was a poignant reflection of the introspection that gripped each of us. The desert stretched before us to the horizon, a vast and untamed wilderness that promised both danger and discovery. It was a landscape that demanded respect, its beauty a veneer that belied the challenges that lurked beneath its shifting sands and towering cliffs.

Yet it was within this vast expanse that our path lay, guided by the ancient wisdom contained within the scroll of the stallion. The hidden oasis of Al-Hijr, shrouded in mystery and guarded by the sands of time, called out across the desert, its secrets a beacon that drew us forth.

As we mounted our horses, I couldn't help but notice Holmes' interaction with Al-Zarib. There was an unspoken communication between them, a subtle exchange that seemed to transcend the usual bond between man and beast. Holmes' hand lingered on Al-Zarib's neck, and for a moment I could have sworn I saw a flicker of understanding between them. It was fleeting, yet profound, and I found myself wondering what role this magnificent creature might play in the adventures that lay ahead.

Nearby, Liyana gracefully mounted Muntasir, the bond between rider and horse evident in their synchronised movements. Muntasir's alert eyes seemed to reflect Liyana's own determination, both ready to face whatever challenges the desert might bring.

With the light of dawn as our herald, we began our journey. The camels, laden with supplies, moved with a grace that belied their size, their footsteps a silent testament to the countless generations that had traversed these sands before us. Al-Zarib and Muntasir, however, moved with a purpose that seemed almost prescient, as if they could sense the gravity of our mission.

As Petra receded into the distance, swallowed up by the vastness of the desert, I felt a sense of awe at the journey ahead. The desert, with its varied vistas, cities lost to time, and landscapes that had cradled civilisations long forgotten, was a testament to the enduring allure of the unknown. The cool morning air carried the whispers of ancient tales, and the shadows that danced across the sand seemed to hold secrets of legends past.

It was a reminder that we were but a single thread in the tapestry of history, embarking on a quest that would unravel the mysteries of the past and perhaps shape the destiny of the future. As we ventured deeper into the heart of the desert, each of us lost in our own thoughts, I couldn't shake the feeling that Al-Zarib and Muntasir's presence was more than mere coincidence. In the subtle way Holmes kept glancing at the horses, especially Al-Zarib, I sensed that my friend too felt the weight of something greater than ourselves guiding our path.

As we left the shadow of Petra's ancient gates, the world around us was transformed into a realm of gold and shadow. Dawn caressed the desert landscape, painting the sandstone cliffs in shades of amber and rose. Our caravan moved steadily into the heart of the desert, guided by the silent sentinel of the rising sun. The air was crisp and cool, carrying the scent of sun-baked stone and distant, hardy desert flowers.

Sherlock Holmes rode at the head of our party, his keen eyes constantly scanning the horizon. The set of his shoulders betrayed a tension that belied his outward calm. Beside him, Dr Amal El-Sharif's brow was furrowed in concentration, her fingers absently tracing the outline of the ancient scroll tucked securely into her saddlebag.

Khalid, our guide, moved with the easy grace of one born to the desert. His eyes, lined by years under the harsh sun, missed nothing as he led us through the shifting dunes. The soft clink of his camel's harness was a soothing counterpoint to the crunch of sand beneath our mounts' feet.

Adrien d'Arcy rode slightly apart, his artist's eye taking in the play of light and shadow across the landscape. His hands, usually so steady when wielding a brush, gripped the reins with a nervous energy that spoke of his awareness of the dangers that might lie ahead.

Liyana Sultan, her face partially obscured by a light shawl to protect her from the sun and sand, rode with quiet determination. Her eyes, dark and alert, were constantly scanning our surroundings, her intuitive nature sensing the undercurrents of tension within our group.

As for me, I found the rhythmic sway of my camel strangely comforting. The weight of my medical bag at my side was a constant reminder of the responsibility I bore, not only as chronicler of our adventures, but as the one charged with keeping us alive and well in this unforgiving land.

The desert stretched before us, a vast canvas of ochre and gold. Waves of heat began to rise from the sand as the sun climbed higher, distorting the distant horizon into a shimmering mirage. The silence was profound, broken only by the soft padding of camel hooves and the occasional cry of a distant bird of prey.

As we travelled deeper into the heart of the desert, each of us lost in our own thoughts, I couldn't shake the feeling that we were being watched. The desert, for all its emptiness, seemed alive with hidden eyes and unseen dangers. The weight of our mission, the secrets we carried and the threats we faced hung heavy in the air, as palpable as the growing heat of the day.

⧉⬦⧉

The ambush came as swift and silent as a desert storm. One moment we were riding through the deepening twilight, the crescent moon casting a pale glow over the dunes. The next, shadows emerged from the darkness and materialised into the menacing forms of the Sons of Purity.

Holmes reacted instantly, his revolver appearing in his hand as if by magic. "Stay together!" he shouted, his voice cutting through the sudden chaos. His eyes, sharp and calculating, took in the scene with remarkable speed. At that moment, I saw not only my friend, but the brilliant detective, his mind working furiously to find a way out of our predicament.

Dr El-Sharif's hand flew to the scroll, her academic curiosity giving way to fierce protectiveness. She wheeled her camel around and placed herself between the attackers and our precious cargo. Her face, usually animated with enthusiasm for ancient mysteries, was now set with grim determination.

Khalid moved like a man born to fight, his years of experience in the harsh desert giving him a fluid grace. "To your left, Watson!" he shouted, his warning allowing me to parry a blow that would surely have crushed me. His eyes blazed with a fury born of seeing his beloved desert used as a stage for violence.

Adrien, caught off guard by the sudden attack, fumbled with his reins for a moment before regaining his composure. His artist's eye, so attuned to detail, now served him well as he called out the positions of our attackers. "There! Behind that dune!" he shouted, pointing to a group attempting to flank us.

Liyana moved with purpose, her intuitive nature allowing her to anticipate the flow of battle. "Behind you, Khalid!" she shouted, just in time for him to dodge another attacker. Her face was a mask of concentration, her every move calculated to keep our group together and protected.

The air, so recently filled with silence, now rang with the clash of steel and the screams of men. The acrid smell of gunpowder mingled with the dust raised by our fighting. The once peaceful desert night had been transformed into a maelstrom of violence and confusion.

I found myself back to back with Holmes, my service revolver in my hand. The familiar weight of it was a comfort, even as the gravity of our situation pressed down on me. The metallic taste of fear filled my mouth, but years of experience both on the battlefield and at Holmes' side steadied my hand.

Our attackers moved with fanatical zeal, their eyes burning with righteous anger. They seemed to care little for their own safety, pressing their attack with a fervour that was both terrifying and pitiful. In the chaos, I caught glimpses of symbols etched into their weapons and clothing - ancient markings that spoke of a twisted interpretation of the Obsidian Guild's teachings.

Despite our best efforts, we were slowly but surely being overpowered. For every attacker we killed, two more seemed to take their place. The desert itself seemed to be conspiring against us, the shifting sands beneath our feet making every move a struggle.

As the battle reached its fever pitch, a cry of pain cut through the chaos. Khalid staggered, a dagger protruding from his side. The sight of his blood, dark against his robes, was a stark reminder of the very real dangers we faced. In that moment, the true cost of our quest became painfully clear.

With Khalid wounded and our defences weakened, the outcome of the battle was no longer in doubt. As our weapons were stripped from us and our hands tied, I met Holmes' eyes. In them I saw not defeat, but steely determination. This battle was lost, but the war was far from over.

The crescent moon, indifferent to our plight, continued its arc across the star-studded sky. As we were led away into the deepening night, the desert wind carried the whispers of ancient secrets, a reminder of the mysteries that had led us here - and the dangers that still lay ahead.

⊶⊷⊹⊱⊰⊹⊶⊷

The aftermath of the ambush left us battered and bruised, marching through the unforgiving desert under the watchful eyes of our captors. The once welcoming expanse of sand and sky now seemed a vast prison, the horizon a distant, unattainable freedom. The air, thick with the acrid smell of gunpowder and sweat, hung heavy around us, a constant reminder of our defeat.

Holmes, his usually immaculate appearance now dishevelled, walked with a measured stride. His eyes, sharp as ever, darted from prisoner to prisoner, cataloguing every detail. I could almost see the cogs of his brilliant mind turning, formulating plans even in our dire circumstances. Occasionally his gaze would flicker to where Al-Zarib had been during the ambush, a strange mixture of concern and intrigue crossing his features.

Dr El-Sharif stumbled slightly, the weight of our capture evident in her slumped shoulders. Yet her fingers never strayed far from the hidden compartment where the scroll was concealed, her academic devotion to

315

knowledge unwavering even now. Her lips moved silently, perhaps reciting passages from the ancient text, finding solace in the very wisdom that had led us into this predicament.

Khalid, his face etched with the pain of his wound, gritted his teeth with every step. The desert sand, once his ally, now seemed to shift treacherously beneath his feet. Yet his eyes burned with a fierce determination, a son of the desert refusing to be broken by its harshness.

Adrien's artist's hands, usually so steady, trembled slightly as he walked. But his gaze remained sharp, taking in the layout of our captors' formation, the position of the sun, any landmark that might prove useful. Even in captivity, his observant nature sought to map our journey, to find a way back to freedom.

Liyana moved with a controlled grace, her steps light despite our gruelling march. Her eyes constantly scanned our group, her empathic nature attuned to the needs of her companions. When Khalid stumbled, she was there in an instant, supporting him with a strength that belied her slender frame.

As for me, the weight of my medical bag, now in the hands of our captors, was a phantom presence at my side. My mind raced with concern for Khalid's wound, calculating the increasing risk of infection with each passing hour in the harsh desert conditions.

The sun beat down mercilessly, turning the world into a shimmering haze of heat. The taste of sand and defeat was bitter on my tongue. But when I met Holmes' gaze, I saw not despair, but a flicker of that familiar, indomitable spirit. Whatever lay ahead, I knew we would face it together.

⊰•———••———•⊱

As the twilight painted the sky in shades of deep purple and burnished gold, the Sons of Purity camp materialised before us like a mirage. The air was rapidly cooling, the heat of the day giving way to the chill of the desert night. The smell of wood smoke and roasting meat wafted towards us, a cruel reminder of the comforts now denied.

Tents of various sizes dotted the landscape, their canvas walls rippling in the evening breeze. Fires blazed at regular intervals, casting long, dancing shadows across the sand. The soft whicker of horses and the low murmur of voices created a tapestry of sound that broke the profound silence of the desert.

As we were led deeper into the camp, each member of our group reacted in their own way to our new surroundings.

Holmes' eyes darted from tent to tent, his keen observation taking in every detail. I noticed his gaze lingering on a corral where several horses were kept, including one that bore a striking resemblance to Al-Zarib. A slight furrow appeared on his forehead, as if he were putting together a jigsaw puzzle that only he could see.

Dr El-Sharif's academic curiosity seemed to be at war with her fear. Her eyes widened as she took in the symbols adorning the tents, her lips moving silently as she translated the ancient writing. Even in captivity, her thirst for knowledge remained unquenched.

Khalid's face was a mask of controlled rage. In the firelight I could see the sheen of sweat on his brow, a testament to the pain he had endured. Yet his eyes burned with defiance, scanning the faces of our captors as if memorising each one.

Adrien, the artist in him unable to be suppressed even now, seemed to drink in the visual spectacle of the camp. His fingers twitched at his sides as if he longed for a pencil to capture the scene. Yet beneath his artist's appreciation, I sensed a keen mind cataloguing escape routes and potential weaknesses in the camp's layout.

Liyana moved with quiet grace, her intuitive nature on high alert. She seemed to sense the ebb and flow of tension in the camp, her body subtly shifting to place herself between perceived threats and her more vulnerable companions.

As for me, my medical instincts were at war with our predicament. My eyes were drawn to the makeshift infirmary tent, noting with professional interest the herbs drying outside and wondering about the medical practices of this desert-dwelling faction.

The largest tent loomed before us, its entrance flanked by guards bearing the twisted symbols of the Sons of Purity. As we were ushered inside, the air was thick with tension and the heavy scent of incense. Whatever fate awaited us, I knew it would be decided here.

❦❧❦

The interior of the tent was a study in contrasts. Rich carpets covered the sandy floor, their intricate patterns barely visible in the flickering light of oil lamps. The air was heavy with the scent of incense and sweat, an acrid mixture that lingered in the throat. Shadows danced across the canvas walls, transforming simple objects into looming, menacing shapes.

At the centre of this tableau stood Rasheed Al-Tariq, his imposing figure bathed in lamplight. His eyes, dark and intense, seemed to burn with an inner fire as they swept over our beleaguered group. When he spoke, his voice was surprisingly melodious, a stark contrast to the harsh ideology he espoused.

"Welcome," he said, the false warmth in his tone sending a shiver down my spine, "to the future of the Obsidian Guild. I am Rasheed Al-Tariq, and you are now guests of the Sons of Purity.

Each member of our group reacted differently to this ominous greeting.

Holmes, his composure unshaken, met Rasheed's gaze with steel in his eyes.

"I'm afraid we must decline your hospitality," he replied, his voice calm and laced with dry wit. "We have pressing engagements elsewhere." Even in captivity, his mind seemed to work, his eyes darting briefly to a tapestry behind Rasheed that bore symbols similar to those on the scroll.

Dr El-Sharif's academic curiosity visibly battled with her fear. Her eyes widened as she took in the symbols adorning the tent, her lips moving silently as if translating. Yet her hand remained protectively close to the hidden scroll, her body tense with the determination to protect our precious cargo.

Despite his wound, Khalid drew himself to his full height. His desert-bred dignity shone through his exhaustion, his eyes meeting Rasheed's with a defiance born of centuries of resilience against those who would claim the desert for their own twisted purposes.

Adrien's artist's eye seemed to take in every detail of the tent and its occupants, his fingers twitching as if longing for a sketchbook. Yet beneath this veneer of artistic interest, I could sense his mind at work, analysing the layout, the positions of the guards, any detail that might aid a possible escape.

Liyana's intuitive nature seemed to be working overtime, her eyes darting from face to face, reading the undercurrents of tension in the room. She positioned herself subtly, ready to move at a moment's notice to protect her companions.

As for me, I found my medical training battling with my instinct for self-preservation. My eyes couldn't help but be drawn to Khalid's wound, assessing its severity and the urgent need for treatment.

Rasheed's laugh, cold and mirthless, drew my attention back to him. "Oh, Mr Holmes," he said, his voice dripping with false sympathy, "I'm afraid you misunderstand. You are not here by choice, but by fate. The scroll you carry, the knowledge you seek - it all leads to this moment. The purification of the Obsidian Guild begins now, and you will all play your part, willingly or not."

As he spoke, I felt a shiver run down my spine. The fanaticism in his eyes, the absolute conviction in his voice - it was clear that we faced a formidable opponent, one who would stop at nothing to achieve his twisted vision.

But even as we stood there, bound and at the mercy of our captors, I knew that our story was far from over. I caught Holmes' eye, and in that shared gaze I saw not defeat, but steely resolve. This battle was lost, but the war for the soul of the Obsidian Guild - and perhaps for the fate of the Hidden Oasis itself - was far from over.

As we were led out of the tent and into the cool night air, the camp around us buzzed with activity. Torches flickered to life, casting long, ominous shadows across the sand. The air was thick with tension, punctuated by the low murmur of voices and the occasional clank of weapons.

In this moment, surrounded by enemies and facing an uncertain future, my thoughts drifted to Al-Zarib. The horse's absence was keenly felt, and I couldn't shake the feeling that his role in our adventure was far from over. Whatever trials lay ahead, I sensed that the magnificent steed would play a pivotal role in the unfolding drama of the Obsidian Guild.

CHAPTER 25

CLASH OF CONVICTIONS

B efore us, the Arabian desert extended endlessly, appearing like a midnight blue ocean beneath a luminous sky filled with countless pulsating stars. The earlier twilight of our capture had long since given way to the velvety embrace of night, bringing with it a chill that seeped into our bones, a stark reminder of the desert's capricious nature. The cool air, laden with the scent of sand and distant flowers, was a welcome respite from the oppressive heat of the day, but it carried with it an underlying tension that set our nerves on edge.

I, Dr John H. Watson, found myself bound alongside my dear friend Sherlock Holmes and our faithful companions, prisoners of the fanatical Sons of Purity. The stars above glittered with cold brilliance, indifferent to our plight, as our captors' camp buzzed with activity. Torches flickered to life, casting long shadows across the sand and illuminating the grim reality of our situation. Although midnight was still hours away, the weight of our situation made every moment seem like an eternity.

As we sat in tense silence, our eyes adjusting to the dim light, I noticed two figures emerging from the central tent. One I recognised as Rasheed Al-Tariq, the man who had introduced himself as the leader of the Sons of Purity. Walking beside him was a younger man whose features bore a striking resemblance to Rasheed's. They approached us with purposeful strides, their silhouettes stark against the flickering torchlight.

Holmes, his eyes glittering with keen observation even in the dim light, leaned towards me. His whisper was barely audible, yet charged with meaning. "Watson, watch the younger man carefully. The set of his jaw, the slope of his shoulders - mirror images of Al-Tariq. But notice the hesitation in his step, the fleeting uncertainty in his eyes. This is more than a family resemblance; it's a study in generational conflict. Al-Tariq's son, no doubt, but one who carries the weight of his father's legacy with ambivalence.

As the pair approached, Rasheed's eyes swept over our group, lingering on Holmes and then, with a flash of recognition, on Liyana. His gaze was penetrating, filled with a fervent intensity that sent a shiver down my spine.

Before Rasheed could speak, Holmes straightened up as much as his shackles would allow, his voice carrying a note of sardonic amusement. "Mr Al-Tariq, I must say I'm a little disappointed. I was hoping for a more challenging conclusion to our investigation, but it seems you've made it all too easy."

Rasheed's reaction was a masterclass in controlled emotion. His eyebrow arched with deliberate slowness, a gesture that spoke volumes about his carefully cultivated composure. Yet beneath this veneer of calm, I detected a flicker of something more volatile - a mixture of surprise, curiosity and perhaps a touch of grudging admiration. When he spoke, his voice was a study in measured neutrality, belied only by the intensity of his gaze. "Enlighten us, Mr Holmes. What exactly has led you to such... intriguing conclusions?"

"Simply this," Holmes replied, his tone crisp and analytical. "I am now satisfied, though admittedly disappointed, that both the murders of Lord Wentworth and Zafir Sultan have been so easily uncovered. You, Mr Al-Tariq, are responsible for Lord Wentworth's death, while your son here," he nodded at the younger man, "is the one who took Zafir's life."

A hush fell over the camp, the weight of Holmes' accusation hanging heavily in the air. Rasheed's face betrayed a flicker of surprise before settling into a mask of amused respect.

"It was not my intention to spoil your investigation so easily, Mr Holmes," Rasheed said, a hint of genuine curiosity in his voice. "How did I give away the solution, I wonder?"

Before Holmes could answer, Adrien and Liyana's voices rang out in unison, filled with pain and anger. Adrien's composure shattered like glass. His body contorted against his bonds, every muscle straining as if physical force alone could undo the truth of Holmes' words. "You soulless monster!" he roared, his voice raw with fear and rage. "Lord Wentworth was more than a good man - he was a visionary, a friend to all who knew him! How could you extinguish such a light?" His words trailed off into a choked sob, the full weight of his loss finally crashing down upon him.

Liyana's reaction was no less intense, but hers was a cold rage that sent shivers down my spine. "Zafir," she began, her voice deep and dangerous, trembling with barely contained rage, "was not just my brother. He was hope itself, a bridge between worlds." Her eyes, when they met Rasheed's, held a promise of retribution that made even our captors shift uneasily. "He dreamed of unity, of progress without loss of identity. And you," her voice cracked, a single tear running down her cheek, "you snuffed out that dream. Mark my words, you will both answer for this betrayal. If not to the law, then to the very sands of this desert you claim to revere."

Rasheed raised a hand, silencing their outbursts with a gesture. "Your pain is... understandable," he said, his tone almost patronising. "But necessary sacrifices must be made for the greater good." He turned back to Holmes, his eyes glittering with interest. "So, Mr Holmes, please enlighten us. How did you reach your conclusion?"

Holmes straightened, his eyes gleaming with intellectual triumph. "Mr Al-Tariq, you asked how you gave away the solution. Allow me to illuminate the path of deduction."

"It began at the Epsom Derby," Holmes began. "A pair of eyes in the crowd, too calculating to be mere spectators. They held a keen intelligence that spoke of a purpose far beyond the excitement of the races."

Rasheed nodded slightly, his eyebrow arching. "Observant. But hardly conclusive."

"Perhaps not," Holmes conceded. "But then there was the visit to Sir Reginald Ashcroft at the Guildhall Museum. A well-educated gentleman with a deep interest in Arabic artefacts, particularly those made of obsidian. Your command of English, tinged with a Middle Eastern accent, your extensive knowledge of the Obsidian Guild - it all painted a picture of a man deeply steeped in ancient traditions."

Rasheed's eyes narrowed. "Many share such interests and knowledge."

"Indeed. But it was the dagger that truly revealed your hand," Holmes continued. "The obsidian blade you carry - exquisite, but ill-suited to its sheath. A replacement, perhaps, for the one left at the scene of Lord Wentworth's murder?"

A flicker of surprise crossed Rasheed's face, quickly covered.

Holmes continued, his tone rising. "The dagger found with Lord Wentworth had been in its sheath for years. Yours is new - a hasty replacement for the one sacrificed to send a message. A bold move, leaving such a distinctive weapon behind."

"Speculation," Rasheed countered, but his hand twitched almost imperceptibly.

"Is it?" Holmes challenged. "The precision of the cut that severed Lord Wentworth's satchel strap, coupled with the fatal blow to his heart - both delivered in a single, fluid motion. It speaks of years of training, Mr Al-Tariq.

You're not just a fanatic. You're an assassin of the highest calibre, your movements honed to deadly perfection.

Rasheed's posture shifted slightly and Holmes jumped at the tell. "Your posture betrays you. The balance of a master assassin, honed by decades of brutal discipline. It's a dance you can't unlearn, even if you try to hide it."

Holmes then turned his piercing gaze to Farid. "And you, young man. Your father may be a master of concealment, but you wear your heart on your sleeve - or rather, around your neck."

Farid's hand moved instinctively to his obsidian locket.

"Recently bestowed, I'd wager," Holmes observed. "An initiation ritual marking you as the heir apparent? But it weighs heavily on you, doesn't it? The burden of expectation, a legacy you're not quite sure you want to carry."

Farid stiffened visibly, his face a mask of conflicting emotions.

Holmes' voice softened. "Your hands are steady, but your eyes betray you. They dart about, seeking reassurance, questioning. Your dagger fits perfectly in its sheath, unlike your father's. You didn't leave it at the scene of Zafir Sultan's murder, did you? An oversight born of nervousness, perhaps? Your first kill, your initiation into your father's world - it didn't go as smoothly as planned."

"You know nothing," Farid spat, his voice shaking.

"On the contrary," Holmes replied softly. "I see a young man struggling with the act of taking a life, even in the service of what you've been taught is a greater cause. It gnaws at you, that doubt. You stand at a crossroads, Farid, between the path laid out for you and the questions that plague your conscience."

Holmes paused, his eyes moving between father and son. "But there is more, isn't there? A deep-seated, primal fear."

He turned back to Rasheed and concentrated on his neck. "Those scars, Mr Al-Tariq - barely visible under your clothes - they tell a fascinating story."

Rasheed's hand moved to his neck, his eyes narrowing.

"The pattern is distinctive," Holmes continued. "A desert lion, I'd wager. You've faced one and lived - a feat unmatched in this generation. The scars themselves aren't serious - little more than deep scratches. But the pattern they form... that's the key."

A flicker of respect crossed Rasheed's face.

"Was it chance that echoed the legend of Idris and Malik Al-Hakim?" Holmes asked. "Or a ritual, the final test to prove oneself worthy to lead the Sons of Purity? A rather extreme way to honour the founder of the Obsidian Guild, wouldn't you say?"

Farid's face paled, his eyes darting between Holmes and his father.

"And you, Farid," Holmes concluded, his tone almost gentle, "carry with you the knowledge that you too may face this trial. A heavy burden, isn't it? Knowing that your father is probably the deadliest fighter to walk these sands in a generation or more. I wonder if you can ever live up to such a standard.

The tension between Rasheed and Farid was palpable, a complex mix of pride, expectation and trepidation that spoke volumes about their relationship and the pressures of their shared heritage.

Holmes stepped back, his voice regaining its sharp edge. "So you see, Mr Al-Tariq, the clues were there for those who knew how to read them. The eyes at the Derby, the visit to the museum, the daggers left behind and hastily replaced, the precision of your kills and the telling details of your son's inner conflict. All pieces of a puzzle that, when put together, paint a clear picture of who you are and what you've done.

Rasheed's lips curled into a cold smile. "Impressive indeed, Mr Holmes. Your reputation does you justice. But tell me, with all your vaunted powers of deduction, can you fathom the true meaning of what we are trying to achieve here?"

<hr />

The clash of ideologies erupted, a battle of wits that would determine not only our fate, but possibly the future of the Obsidian Guild itself. Rasheed's eyes blazed in the flickering torchlight, his voice a mixture of fervour and steel.

"Morality?" he sneered, meeting Holmes's gaze. "We face extinction, Mr Holmes. Our traditions are eroding under the corrupting influence of modernity. We are the last bastion against that degradation."

The camp around us hummed with tense energy, its precise layout a stark contrast to the wild desert beyond - concentric rings of tents, each with its own purpose, radiating from the central command post. This rigid order, set against the untamed landscape, embodied the ideology of the Sons of Purity.

I watched my companions' reactions, each a study in restrained emotion. Liyana's controlled rage, her eyes fixed on Farid. Adrien's analytical gaze, taking in every detail of the camp. Khalid, despite his pain, listening intently, his face a mixture of disgust and sadness.

"You speak of tradition," Khalid interjected, his voice weak but determined, "yet you pervert our heritage. The desert teaches adaptability, not dogma."

Rasheed's eyes flashed dangerously. "This 'adaptability' brings us to the brink of losing our identity. We must stand firm, like the ancient stones."

Holmes, ever calm, countered, "And yet, Mr Al-Tariq, it is the flexible reed that survives the storm, while the rigid stone is worn away."

As Holmes spoke, I noticed that his attention was briefly drawn to Al-Zarib, and there seemed to be a strange connection between them.

Farid, who had been silent, spoke hesitantly. "Father, perhaps there is wisdom in their words..."

"Silence!" Rasheed thundered, making Farid jump. "Think of your destiny, son."

Liyana seized the moment. "Farid," she said softly, "you needn't be bound by your father's choices. True strength lies in embracing diversity."

The debate raged on, each side unyielding. Holmes probed Rasheed's beliefs with surgical precision, while Rasheed responded with unwavering conviction.

"Your quest for purity," Holmes argued, "is built on sand. History shows the folly of such thinking.

Rasheed replied, "And what has progress brought but corruption and decay? We seek to preserve what is pure, to return to honour and tradition.

"A code written in blood," I interjected, unable to remain silent. "At what cost, Rasheed?"

His eyes gleamed dangerously. "In Al-Hijr we will unlock ancient secrets. The convergence of statuettes and scrolls will purify not only bloodlines, but the world itself. You cannot fathom what we seek to accomplish."

As the night wore on, the desert around us seemed to watch with ancient, indifferent eyes - a silent witness to this clash between tradition and progress, purity and diversity. The stakes, we all knew, could not be higher.

Around us, the Sons of Purity stood as silent witnesses, their loyalty to Al-Tariq unwavering, but perhaps untested in the light of such revelations. The air between Holmes and Rasheed was charged, a silent battleground of ideology and wit. The desert, with its timeless vastness, seemed a fitting stage for such a pivotal encounter, its ancient sands a reminder that change is the only true constant.

As the confrontation continued, I noticed Adrien's keen eyes moving around the camp, taking in every detail. His gaze lingered on the weapons carried by our captors, the construction of their tents, the arrangement of their supplies. I could almost see his analytical mind cataloguing every observation, no doubt already formulating plans on how to use this knowledge to our advantage.

Adrien's keen eyes missed nothing. He noted the quality of the leather used in the Sons of Purity's saddles, recognising the craftsmanship of a particular region. The way their weapons were cared for spoke of a rigorous routine, probably enforced by an experienced armourer. Even the arrangement of supplies around the camp told a story of logistics and planning. "Their organisation is impressive," he whispered to me. "But it could also be their weakness. Such a rigid structure leaves little room for adaptation".

The atmosphere in the camp grew increasingly tense as the night wore on. The Sons of Purity moved with a nervous energy, their eyes constantly darting towards us and then back to Rasheed. It was clear that something momentous was brewing. Holmes, ever attuned to the subtlest of cues, straightened almost imperceptibly. "Brace yourself, Watson," he murmured. "I think we're about to reach a turning point."

It was nearing midnight when Rasheed finally came to the point. "I offer you a choice, Mr Holmes," he declared, his voice carrying a note of finality. "Join us in our crusade. Lend your considerable intellect to our cause. Or..." he paused, letting the weight of his words sink in, "be left to the mercy of the desert when we leave for Al-Hijr at dawn."

The ultimatum hung in the air like a mirage, tantalising yet fraught with danger. Holmes' face remained impassive, but I could sense the rapid calculations behind those piercing eyes.

"You have until dawn to decide," Rasheed concluded, turning to leave. "Choose wisely, for your lives and the future of our mission hang in the balance."

As Rasheed and Farid retreated into the darkness, leaving us to ponder our fate, I couldn't help but feel a chill that had nothing to do with the desert night. The sand stretched endlessly around us, a stark reminder of the perilous journey that lay ahead, regardless of our choice.

Our captors, perhaps underestimating our resolve or overconfident in their control, had tied us together at the edge of the camp. This unexpected leniency gave us the opportunity to speak in hushed tones, our words masked by the whisper of the desert wind and the ambient noise of the camp. We seized the opportunity, knowing that our unity was our greatest strength in the face of adversity.

Once alone, our group huddled together, bound but unbowed. Holmes' eyes shone with fierce determination as he whispered, "We must act quickly. Rasheed's offer is a poisoned chalice we cannot accept."

"Agreed," Adrien hissed. "The Obsidian Guild stands for knowledge, not fanaticism."

Khalid, his voice weak but urgent, interjected, "The desert itself may be our salvation. To the east lies our best hope - stable dunes, night-blooming jasmine near the water."

"But your wound, Khalid," I murmured, noticing his labored breathing. "Infection is setting in. We must move quickly."

Liyana's eyes flashed with determination. "Farid is our key. I've seen doubt in him, a longing for understanding. I can reach him."

"Excellent," Holmes nodded. "Sow discord in their ranks. Adrien, while Liyana works on Farid, scout their equipment, their routines. Find weaknesses."

Adrien's fingers twitched as if already mapping the camp. "Their rigid structure - that's a weakness. I'll find the cracks."

"Time is against us," I warned, glancing at the lightning in the sky. "Without supplies, we have hours, not days."

Holmes' mind was visibly racing. "Watson, prioritise Khalid's care. Liyana, prepare to attack Farid at first light. Adrien, gather what intelligence you can. Khalid, save your strength - your desert wisdom may save us all."

We fell silent, each of us absorbing our roles. The air buzzed with tension and possibility. In this moment of crisis, our diverse skills had come together in a single, formidable force. As dawn approached, bringing with it unknown dangers, I felt a surge of hope. Together, we stood a chance against the looming shadows of the Sons of Purity.

Our silent conference was a masterclass in strategic thinking. Holmes, his mind working at lightning speed, sketched out the broad outlines of a plan. Liyana, drawing on her diplomatic experience, suggested ways to exploit the doubts we had sown in Farid's mind. Adrien's knowledge of the camp's layout and equipment proved invaluable in identifying potential escape routes. Khalid, despite his weakened state, provided crucial insights into desert survival techniques. And I found myself contributing medical knowledge, assessing how long we could possibly survive in the harsh conditions without supplies. It was a delicate dance of ideas, each of us building on the suggestions of the others, weaving a plan that gave us a glimmer of hope in our seemingly hopeless situation.

The weight of our predicament fell upon us, yet the bonds of our community remained unbroken, a beacon of hope in the face of the trials that awaited us with the coming dawn. As I lay there, bound and uncertain of our fate, I couldn't help but marvel at the indomitable spirit of my companions. Whatever the dawn might bring, I knew that as long as we faced it together, there was hope.

The desert night enveloped us in its silent embrace, the stars above testifying to our determination in the face of seemingly insurmountable odds. The air seemed to pulse with an otherworldly energy, as if the very sands beneath us were alive with the echoes of ancient mysteries. In these tense moments, under the watchful eyes of our captors and the vast canopy of stars, the stage was set for a confrontation that would not only determine our fate, but perhaps sway the hearts and minds of those caught in the grip of Al-Tariq's fervent but flawed vision.

As the first hints of dawn began to colour the eastern sky, my eyes were drawn once more to Al-Zarib. The magnificent stallion stood alert, his eyes seeming to glow with an intelligence that transcended mere animal instinct. For a moment, I could have sworn I saw a flicker of understanding between the horse and Holmes, a silent communication that spoke of depths yet to be plumbed. Little did I know at the time how crucial this connection would prove to be in the trials that lay ahead.

In the face of our dire circumstances, the bond of our group seemed to strengthen. A subtle nod from Holmes, a reassuring touch from Liyana, a determined look from Adrien - these small gestures spoke volumes. Without words, we communicated our unwavering support for one another. Khalid, despite his pain, managed a faint smile that lifted our spirits. In that moment, I knew that whatever challenges lay ahead, we would face them not as individuals, but as a united front.

As the first light of dawn broke over the horizon, I found myself contemplating the nature of true purity. It was not, I realised, the rigid, unyielding ideal to which Rasheed clung, but something far more profound. True purity lay in the bonds of friendship that bound us together, in the courage to face the unknown, and in the wisdom to recognise the value of all life, regardless of race or creed. In our diverse group - an English detective, a doctor, a diplomat, a craftsman and a desert guide - I saw a purity of purpose and spirit that far surpassed the tarnished ideals of the Sons of Purity. And it was this realisation, this unshakable belief in the strength of our unity, that gave me hope as we faced the trials ahead.

CHAPTER 26

DECEPTIONS IN THE DUNES

As the first pale light of dawn crept across the endless expanse of sand, I found myself in a most precarious situation. Bound and imprisoned in a canvas tent, our small band of companions huddled together, the weight of our predicament hanging heavily in the air. The Sons of Purity camp came to life around us, but there was an ominous stillness, as if the desert itself was holding its breath in anticipation of what was to come.

My dear friend Sherlock Holmes sat cross-legged beside me, his sharp grey eyes fixed on some distant point only he could see. Despite our dire circumstances, I could not help but marvel at his calm demeanour. It was a testament to his iron will that even now, as we faced what could very well be our final hours, he exuded an air of quiet confidence.

"Watson," he said softly, breaking the silence that had reigned since Rasheed Al-Tariq's ultimatum the night before, "I trust you have given some thought to our host's generous offer?"

I detected a hint of sarcasm in his tone and knew immediately that Holmes had no intention of accepting Rasheed's proposal, whatever the consequences.

"Indeed, Holmes," I replied, matching his subdued tone. "Though I confess I see little choice before us but to..."

"We cannot allow ourselves to consider Rasheed's offer, not even for a moment," Holmes interrupted, his voice low but firm. "Our principles, our very lives, depend on our resolve."

Liyana, the brave young woman who had become such an integral part of our adventure, leaned in close. "But surely, Mr Holmes, we must consider all options. Rasheed's threat to abandon us to the desert -"

"Is one we shall overcome, my dear," Holmes assured her, a glimmer of his old fire in his eyes. "I have faced worse odds and emerged victorious. We shall do so again."

I could not help but smile, despite our circumstances. "Holmes always has one last trick up his sleeve," I remarked, more to lift my own spirits than anything else.

As if reading my thoughts, Holmes fixed me with a penetrating gaze. "Your faith in me is not misplaced, old friend," he said quietly. "I have never failed you before, and I will not fail you now."

It was then that Liyana, her voice barely above a whisper, made a suggestion that would set in motion the events to come. "Farid," she breathed, glancing towards the tent flap where Rasheed's son stood guard. "His doubt is our key. If we can reach him, appeal to his humanity, we may find an ally."

Holmes nodded slowly, his eyes narrowing in thought. "An excellent observation, Liyana. Indeed, young Farid may prove to be the chink in Rasheed's armour."

Khalid, the desert guide whose knowledge had proved invaluable throughout our journey, spoke up. "If we are to attempt an escape, we must remember the ways of the desert," he warned. "The dunes to the east will be more stable. And if we can find the night-blooming jasmine, it will lead us to water."

"Capital, Khalid," Holmes exclaimed, his voice still low but filled with renewed vigour. "Your expertise may well save our lives should we find ourselves at the mercy of the sands."

It was Adrien, the master leatherworker, who next contributed to our impromptu war council. "We need to gather more information about their equipment and routines," he suggested. "The more we know, the better our chances of finding a weakness."

Holmes' eyes gleamed with agreement. "Excellent suggestions, all of you," he said, looking around our small group. "Our diverse skills may well be the key to our salvation."

As I watched my friend, I could see the gears of his formidable mind turning, piecing together the fragments of a plan that might yet see us through this ordeal. Although our situation remained dire, I felt a spark of hope ignite in my breast. For if anyone could untangle this seemingly impossible knot, it was Sherlock Holmes.

The desert sun was rising, its heat beginning to penetrate the walls of our canvas prison. But as I looked into the determined faces of my companions, I knew that our resolve would not waver. Whatever trials lay ahead, we would face them together, our spirits unbroken and our minds sharpened by adversity.

Holmes, as if sensing the change in the atmosphere, spoke again. "My friends," he said, his voice carrying the quiet authority that had seen us through countless perils, "we find ourselves in a game of chess with a most formidable opponent. But remember: every piece on the board, no matter how insignificant it may seem, has the potential to change the course of the game. We are not yet beaten.

And with these words we began the delicate task of turning our captivity into liberation, each of us aware that our next moves could determine not only the outcome of our adventure, but the course of our lives.

❦❦❦❦❦

As the scorching desert sun climbed higher in the sky, casting long shadows across our canvas prison, we began the delicate task of putting our hastily conceived plan into action. Liyana, her face a mask of determination tinged with barely concealed fear, approached the tent flap where young Farid stood guard. I could see the weight of her brother's memory etched in the lines of her face, a burden that seemed to grow heavier with each passing moment.

"Farid," she called softly, her voice carrying a tremor I had never heard before. It was a sound that spoke of countless sleepless nights and tearful memories. "Please, I need to talk to you."

For a long moment there was no response, and I feared our gambit had failed before it had even begun. The silence stretched on, broken only by the whisper of sand against canvas and the beating of my own heart. But then, with a rustle of fabric, Farid's silhouette appeared at the entrance to the tent, his posture wary yet curious.

"What do you want?" he demanded, his voice harsh but betraying a hint of curiosity that gave me hope. His eyes, dark and wary, scanned our faces with a mixture of suspicion and something else - perhaps a flicker of doubt?

Liyana glanced at Holmes, who gave an almost imperceptible nod. I marvelled at my friend's ability to convey so much with such a subtle gesture. "Please," Liyana pleaded, her voice thick with emotion, "just a moment of your time. There is something you must know - something that could change everything."

Farid hesitated, his hand resting on the hilt of the curved dagger at his belt. I could see the inner struggle in his features - duty battling with curiosity, suspicion battling with a deep-seated need for understanding. Then, with a muttered curse that sounded more like a prayer, he ducked into the tent.

The atmosphere in our cramped quarters grew thick with tension, each breath seeming to carry the weight of unspoken accusations and desperate hopes. Farid's eyes darted from face to face, a cornered animal seeking escape, before finally settling on Liyana. She took a deep breath, steeling herself for what was to come, and I found myself holding my own breath in anticipation.

333

"Farid," she began, her voice barely above a whisper but carrying the force of a thunderclap in the stillness of the tent, "you are not to blame for my brother's death. Your father - Rasheed - he manipulated you, used you as a pawn in his twisted game. Can't you see that?"

Farid's face contorted in a mixture of anger and confusion, his carefully constructed world visibly shaking at its foundations. "How dare you speak of my father in such a manner?" he spat, but I detected a flicker of doubt in his eyes, a crack in the armour of his convictions.

"I speak only the truth," Liyana continued, her voice growing stronger with each word, fueled by grief and righteous anger. "Your father's ambition knows no bounds. He would sacrifice anyone, even his own son, to achieve his goals. Think, Farid! Has he ever shown you true love, or only approval when you obey his commands?"

For a moment, Farid seemed to waver, his resolve visibly shaken. The hand on his dagger trembled, and I saw a lost boy beneath the hardened exterior. "How can I trust you?" he asked, his voice hoarse with emotion, years of indoctrination fighting a desperate need for connection. "You all speak of justice, but would you - could you ever truly forgive me?"

At this crucial moment, I saw Holmes lean forward, his piercing grey eyes fixed on Farid's face. But before my friend could utter a word, Liyana's composure cracked, her pent-up grief and anger bursting forth like a desert storm.

"Forgive you?" she cried, her voice rising with each word, tears streaming down her face. "You stood by while my brother was murdered! You claim innocence, yet your hands are stained with his blood! Do you know how many nights I've lain awake, seeing his face, hearing his screams? Can you even begin to understand the depth of what you've taken from me?

I winced at the vehemence in her tone and watched as Farid's expression hardened once more. The fragile connection that had been formed shattered in an instant, like a mirage dissipating in the harsh desert sun.

"You think I am so easily swayed?" Farid growled, stepping back, his hand tightening on his weapon. "You underestimate me and the teachings of my father. I have seen through your lies, your manipulations. I will never betray him!"

Holmes tried to intervene, his voice calm and measured, a balm to the heated emotions swirling around us. "Young man, think carefully about the path you choose. Your father's ambitions will only lead to ruin and..."

I watched in horror as our carefully laid plan crumbled before our eyes, each word driving Farid further away from us and deeper into his father's clutches. His gaze swept over our group, his lip curled in contempt, and I saw in that moment not just anger, but fear - fear of the truths we offered and the world they threatened to reveal.

"Did you really think I would abandon my father, my people, for the likes of you?" he spat, each word dripping with contempt. "You are nothing but interlopers, meddlers who seek to destroy all that we have built. I was a fool to even consider your words."

As Farid's face contorted in anger and betrayal, I saw Holmes spring into action with a swiftness that belied his usual calm demeanour. My friend stepped forward and placed himself between Farid and Liyana, his hands raised in a soothing gesture.

"Farid," Holmes said, his voice low and urgent, carrying a note of sincerity I had rarely heard before. "I implore you to listen, not to us, but to your own heart. Your anger is justified, your loyalty admirable, but consider this: true strength lies not in blind obedience, but in the courage to question and to seek the truth."

Farid's hand tightened on his dagger, his knuckles white with tension, but he did not interrupt. Taking this as encouragement, Holmes continued, his grey eyes locked with Farid's.

"I have spent my life seeking the truth, young man, and I will tell you this: the path of righteousness is rarely the easiest. Your father has shaped your world, but he is not infallible. The greatest gift you can give him - and yourself - is to think critically about the choices before you.

For a moment, I dared to hope. Farid's resolve seemed to waver, a flicker of uncertainty crossing his features. But then his eyes hardened again and I knew we had lost him.

"You speak of truth, Mr Holmes," Farid spat, his voice trembling with barely suppressed rage, "yet you conspire to turn me against my own blood with honeyed words and false sympathy. I see through your manipulations. I will not be swayed by your so-called wisdom!"

Holmes took a step back, his shoulders slumping almost imperceptibly. Perhaps only I could see the weight of failure settling on him. When he spoke again, there was a sadness in his voice that struck me.

"Then we have failed not only in our mission, Farid, but in showing you the power of independent thought. I can only hope that one day you will look back on this moment and realise the true path you could have chosen."

Farid's face was a mask of rage and betrayal, years of carefully cultivated loyalty reasserting itself with a vengeance. "Silence!" he roared, his voice echoing off the canvas walls. "I see now that this was nothing but a ruse, a desperate attempt to turn me against my own blood. You speak of manipulation, yet here you are, trying to twist my mind with your eloquent phrases and appeals to emotion."

With a final look of disgust that couldn't quite hide the pain and confusion in his eyes, Farid turned on his heel and stormed out of the tent. The tent flap slammed shut behind him with a finality that seemed to reflect the failure of our desperate gambit.

A heavy silence fell over our group, thick with the weight of shattered hopes and bitter realisations. I turned to Holmes, desperately searching for some glimmer of new strategy forming in his quicksilver mind. But for the first time in our long association, I saw something in my friend's eyes that sent a chill through my soul: uncertainty.

As the desert heat pressed in around us, suffocating in its intensity, I could not shake the feeling that we had not only failed in our attempt to influence Farid, but had somehow played right into Rasheed Al-Tariq's hands. The game, it seemed, was far from over, and I feared that the next move would be one from which we might not recover.

Liyana sank to her knees, her body racked with silent sobs, the full weight of her grief and the enormity of our failure crashing down upon her. Holmes placed a comforting hand on her shoulder, his face a mask of grim determination. And as I looked at my companions, each lost in their own thoughts and fears, I realised that our greatest challenge yet lay ahead - not just to escape our physical bonds, but to find hope in the face of crushing despair.

The heavy silence that had fallen over our small group after Farid's angry departure was shattered by the sudden rustle of the tent flap. I turned, my heart sinking as I saw the imposing figure of Rasheed Al-Tariq framed in the entrance. His eyes, dark and glittering with barely concealed triumph, swept over our faces before settling on Holmes.

"Ah, Mr Holmes," Rasheed's voice was as soft as silk, but I detected the hidden barbs beneath. "Did you really think that swaying Farid would be as simple as appealing to his conscience?"

I glanced at my friend, hoping to see a flicker of his usual confidence, but Holmes' face was a mask of stone. Rasheed's lips curled into a smile that never reached his eyes as he continued.

"You see, Holmes, I know my son. His loyalty is unshakable, forged by years of tutelage. Your attempt to manipulate him was doomed from the start." Rasheed's voice took on a lecturing tone that sent a shiver down my spine. "Farid is not only my son, he is my finest student. And you, unwittingly, have played a crucial role in his development. By challenging him, you tested his loyalty in the best possible way."

At these words I saw Farid enter the tent behind his father. The young man's eyes darted nervously between Holmes and Rasheed, a flicker of doubt and fear visible in his tense posture. For a moment I dared to hope that perhaps our words had not been in vain.

But Rasheed, ever observant, turned to his son with a look of pride that dispelled any such notion. "Farid, you did exactly as I had hoped. By taking on Holmes and standing your ground, you have proven your loyalty beyond doubt. I am proud of you."

The effect of these words on Farid was immediate and profound. His shoulders straightened, his chin lifted and the uncertainty in his eyes was replaced by a fierce devotion that made my heart sink.

Rasheed then turned his attention back to Holmes, his voice taking on a tone of mock admiration. "Your strategic mind is commendable, Holmes, but you fail to consider the human element, the bonds that cannot be broken by mere words. You see only puzzles to be solved, whereas I see people to be commanded."

With methodical precision, Rasheed began to dismantle Holmes's deductions and strategies, pointing out flaws and overestimates that even I, in my long association with the great detective, had failed to notice. It was a masterful display of intellect and cunning that left us all reeling.

When Rasheed had finished revealing to Holmes that he had fully anticipated and even planned their attempt to influence Farid, he turned his piercing gaze on Liyana, who was still in the throes of her emotions. His eyes were like cold steel, cutting through the layers of her resolve.

"Have you told my son that he is not to blame for your brother's death?" Rasheed's voice was a low, threatening whisper. "That it was me, his father, who was responsible? That my son is the innocent victim of my indoctrination? And that you and your father, the Sultan, would surely forgive and redeem my son if he now chose to free you and come with you, abandoning his father's false doctrine?"

Liyana's eyes widened and her breath caught in her throat. Rasheed's words hit her like a hammer, shattering her composure. "You did exactly that, didn't you, Miss Sultan?" Rasheed continued, his eyes moving between Liyana, Sherlock and Farid. "You may have pondered together the question of whether Farid would believe you, Miss Sultan. But that is not the real question that matters. The real question is, do you believe it yourself?"

I saw the flicker of emotion in Liyana's eyes as Rasheed peeled away layer after layer of her carefully constructed facade with a brutal clarity that reflected my dear friend's deductive genius. "And you felt the answer to that question all along, Miss Sultan, but you never allowed it to fully surface, did you? You blatantly lied to yourself and to my son out of a desire to succeed in your plan. You cannot hide your true feelings - you knew you would not forgive Farid even if he risked everything to side with you and free you. You would still make him pay for your brother's murder so that your 'justice' could get what it demands.

Rasheed then looked at Farid, his voice a mixture of severity and a twisted sense of pride. "These gentlemen and lady spoke of their noble values and dismissed our beliefs from their position of moral superiority. But then, when it came time to make the hard choices, they chose to lie to you, deceiving themselves into believing it was for the 'greater good' of their noble values. Tell me, my son, you have watched me all your life. Have you ever seen me lie to anyone, friend or foe, even in the most dire of situations?"

Before Farid could answer, I saw Sherlock's eyes as he considered Rasheed's arguments, struck by the realisation that Rasheed was making a point that Sherlock had not anticipated. The atmosphere was thick with tension and the weight of unspoken truths. Farid's response hung in the air, not because he had been indoctrinated by his father, but because Rasheed had spoken a painful truth about this very point.

Farid's voice, trembling but determined, broke the silence. "No, father. You have never lied. You have always faced the truth, no matter how hard it was." His eyes, filled with a mixture of determination and newfound clarity, met Liyana's. "And because of that, I cannot trust you."

The realisation that their plan had not only failed, but had inadvertently cemented Farid's loyalty to Rasheed, weighed heavily on the team. Rasheed's manipulation had not only tested Farid, it had exposed their own weaknesses and hypocrisies.

Rasheed turned back to Sherlock, a smug satisfaction gleaming in his eyes. "Your attempt to influence my son was not just a failure, Holmes. It was a crucial lesson for him - a final step in his journey to understand the true nature of loyalty and conviction. And for that, I am ironically grateful to you."

With a final, victorious look, Rasheed addressed the group. "Your choice has been made clear by your actions. We will leave soon, leaving you to the judgement of the desert." He turned to Farid and placed a hand on his shoulder. "You have proved yourself, my son. You have shown your true strength and loyalty."

As they left the tent, Farid took one last look at us. In his eyes I saw a mixture of hatred, determination and a flicker of pride at having passed his father's test. The tent flap fell behind them with a finality that seemed to echo the failure of our desperate gambit.

In the suffocating silence that followed, I turned to Holmes, hoping against hope to see some glimmer of a plan forming in his quicksilver mind. But for the first time in our long association, I saw a look in my friend's eyes that chilled me to the bone: defeat.

The desert sun beat down on the canvas of our prison, a merciless reminder of the grim fate that awaited us. As I looked at the faces of my companions, each etched with the dawning realisation of our failure, I could not help but wonder if this was finally to be the final chapter in the adventures of Sherlock Holmes.

CHAPTER 27

DESERT'S FURY UNLEASHED

With dawn spreading its pale tendrils over the Arabian desert, the Sons of Purity diligently packed up their camp. The air was thick with the acrid scent of dying embers and the pungent musk of camels, a potent reminder of our dire circumstances. I, Dr John Watson, watched with a heavy heart as our captors went about their preparations with military precision, their faces set in masks of grim determination.

The Sons paid us little heed, treating us as mere cargo to be transported, our fate sealed by Rasheed's pronouncement the previous evening. Our last desperate attempt to change the course of events had failed, leaving us at the mercy of the unforgiving desert. The gravity of our situation weighed heavily on all of us, a crushing burden that threatened to extinguish the last flickering embers of hope in our hearts.

I looked around at my companions, each bearing the marks of our ordeal. Dr Amal El-Sharif's usually bright eyes were dimmed with fatigue and worry, her shoulders slumped under the weight of our impending doom. Liyana Sultan, despite her noble demeanour, could not quite hide the trembling of her hands as she tried to comfort Adrien d'Arcy, whose own face was a study in barely contained panic. But it was Khalid who worried me most; the infection from his wound was advancing with alarming speed, his skin taking on an unhealthy pallor that spoke of the fever raging within.

Summoning what remained of my optimism, I addressed our beleaguered group, my voice hoarse but determined. "My friends, we must not lose heart. We have faced dire straits before and emerged victorious. Holmes," I said, turning to my dear friend, "surely you have one last stratagem, one last trick up

341

your sleeve? And even if that fails, we still have hope of reaching the oasis."

I watched as a fleeting shadow passed over Holmes' face, a momentary hesitation that sent a chill through my soul.

Unknown to me, within the labyrinthine corridors of Holmes' formidable intellect, a veritable maelstrom of thought raged with unchecked ferocity. "How can I convey this painful truth?" he pondered, his inner voice echoing with the anguish of a man confronted by his own fallibility. "How can I confess that it was my own hubris, my unshakable faith in my powers, that led us to this terrible abyss? The Oasis... nothing but a cruel phantasm of my own invention, borne of despair and that most insidious of sins, pride."

The full weight of his decision descended upon him with the force of a great avalanche. "I chose to hide the truth from them, but did I really fathom the consequences of such a choice?" Holmes' ruminations accelerated, each revelation more excruciating than the last. "The risk, yes, I acknowledged it, but in the depths of my conceit I remained so convinced of my infallible ability to divine a solution, whatever the cost, that I failed to truly contemplate the possibility that my dear friends might actually perish."

A flood of self-recrimination swept over him with pitiless intensity. "I trusted in my ability to protect them, to find a solution, as I always have. But now... oh, what monstrous hubris has taken root in me!" The horror of this revelation threatened to overwhelm his normally unflappable faculties. "It was not just a decision based on values, to sacrifice my companions for some lofty ideal. I deluded myself into believing that I could make this choice without actually endangering their lives, for I, Sherlock Holmes, with my much-vaunted genius, would inevitably be their saviour, as I had always been."

Memories of past triumphs, once a source of quiet pride, now crumbled to dust in the crucible of his mind. "Indeed, always so far... in London, on my own hallowed ground, where I forever had a contingency for every contingency. There was always some soul I could bend to my will, some arcane knowledge I could bring to bear. But here..." His gaze swept across the vast, unforgiving expanse of sand and sky. "Here I am in the heart of Arabia, on Rasheed's native soil. Rasheed, a man capable of defeating me in physical combat, who possesses an intellect as keen as my own, albeit one warped by years of treading a shadowy path."

The stark reality of their predicament hit him with crushing force. "Within the hour, Rasheed and his cohort will be gone. There will be no one left to convince, no mystery left to solve. Nothing but the merciless reality of the desert, ready to claim us all in its deadly embrace."

This realisation hit him with the force of a pugilist's well-aimed punch. "It was not only our escape plan that failed. I, Sherlock Holmes, made a fatal error in my assessment of both the situation and my own abilities." A veritable storm of questions assailed his consciousness. "Would a more accurate assessment have changed my decision? Did my miscalculation condemn my friends to perdition? No," he reminded himself with painful clarity, "by my own cursed ego and arrogance.

The weight of his failure threatened to crush his spirit. Holmes, the great detective, the man who had long prided himself on his powers of logic and keen observation, had been blind to his own most serious flaw. As he steeled himself to speak, to reveal his failings to his trusted companions, he felt the full weight of his choices bearing down on him with inexorable force.

❦❦❦❦❦

When he finally gave voice to his thoughts, they were barely more than a whisper, filled with a depth of despair that I had never before witnessed in my faithful companion.

"Watson, my dear fellow, I... I fear I must confess a grave error of judgement. The oasis of which I spoke... it was but a comforting invention, a false hope which I allowed to persist out of my own cowardice and pride." Holmes' eyes, usually so sharp and alert, now bore the haunted look of a man coming to terms with his own fallibility. "I have failed you all and condemned us to this fate."

The impact of Holmes' words hit us like a physical blow. I watched as the last vestiges of hope drained from the faces of our companions, replaced by a mixture of disbelief, despair and dawning horror. The sight of my dearest friend, the great Sherlock Holmes, consumed by helplessness and shame, was almost more than I could bear. His eyes, usually so penetrating, now darted from face to face, unable to meet our gaze for more than a moment before turning away in an act of sheer despair.

"I have failed them all," echoed Holmes' thoughts, a cacophony of self-recrimination. "Watson, my faithful friend, how could I have led you to this? Amal, Liyana, Adrien, Khalid... each of you trusted me, and I betrayed that trust completely. Even Isinglass... I made a solemn vow to right the wrongs of the Sons of Purity, and now that promise lies shattered, as broken as the hopes I foolishly nurtured.

As Holmes looked away, I caught a glimpse of the maelstrom of emotions that raged within him. His shoulders, normally so straight and proud, now slumped under the weight of his perceived failure. In that moment, I longed to offer some word of comfort, some reassurance that might ease his burden, but words failed me.

"Isinglass," the name echoed in Holmes' mind, a beacon in the darkness of his thoughts. "That magnificent creature... I promised him. He answered me. I felt his spirit."

Holmes' gaze fell on Muntasir, the noble steed tethered alongside our captors' horses, awaiting the imminent departure. The stallion stood tall and

343

proud, a reminder of his unwavering courage during our perilous sea crossing from Constantinople to Beirut. For a fleeting moment I saw a glimmer of something - recognition, perhaps - in Holmes' eyes.

"Muntasir," Holmes thought, "braving his fears on the deck of that steamer, so far from his element. I felt the strength of his heart, almost as if I could read it. And now..."

Then, as if drawn by some unseen force, Holmes' attention shifted to Al-Zarib. The horse stood apart from the others, his bearing one of intense concentration and determination that seemed almost preternatural. As I watched, transfixed, Holmes' eyes met those of Al-Zarib and the world around us seemed to fall away.

A realisation dawned in Holmes' mind. "Al-Zarib... there's something different about him. This focus, this determination... it's beyond anything I've seen before. His gaze is the embodiment of concentration. His eyes seem to demand that I look at them," Holmes thought as he remembered "the big black eyes of Al-Zarib that I've been drawn to more than once in the past few days. His big black..."

The world as he had always known it stopped around Sherlock. All there was for him were Al-Zarib's eyes, and the last word Sherlock was able to form in his mind was "...crimson".

At that moment I witnessed something that defied all rational explanation. Holmes suddenly stopped moving, his body becoming unnaturally still. His gaze, usually so sharp and focused, now seemed distant, fixed on some point beyond our immediate surroundings. I had never seen such an expression on anyone's face, let alone my dear friend's.

Intrigued and alarmed, I followed the direction of Holmes' gaze and my eyes came to rest on Al-Zarib. The magnificent stallion stood as if frozen, his posture mirroring the strange stillness that had gripped Holmes. There was an intensity to the horse's stance that I found difficult to comprehend, a concentration that seemed almost unnatural.

As I studied Al-Zarib more closely, I felt my breath catch in my throat. The horse's eyes, which I had always known to be a deep, unfathomable black, now blazed with a brilliant crimson. I blinked hard, certain that the stress of our ordeal must be affecting my vision. But when I looked again, the crimson remained, seeming to glow with an inner light that both fascinated and terrified me.

Shaken by this inexplicable sight, I turned back to Holmes, hoping to find some reassurance in his rational demeanour. What I saw instead sent a shock through me. Holmes' eyes, those keen instruments of observation that had solved countless mysteries, now glowed with the same eerie crimson as Al-Zarib's. It was as if every vein in his eyes had suddenly burst, flooding them with an unearthly light.

I stood transfixed, my mind reeling as I tried to make sense of what I was witnessing. The world around us seemed to vanish, leaving only the silent, inexplicable communion between man and horse. As the first rays of the sun broke the horizon, bathing the desert in a golden glow, I found myself on the brink of something I could neither understand nor explain.

A new day had dawned, bringing with it phenomena that challenged the very foundations of my understanding. Whatever was happening between Holmes and Al-Zarib, I knew with certainty that our journey had entered realms far beyond my comprehension. As I watched, unable to look away, I felt the stirrings of something that might have been hope, or perhaps simply awe in the face of the unknown.

As the connection solidified, Holmes experienced a profound sense of humility and wonder. The despair that had threatened to consume him moments before now seemed distant and insignificant in the face of this extraordinary communion. He realised that in opening himself to this experience, he had not only found a possible path to their salvation, but had also unlocked a part of himself he never knew existed - a part capable of transcending the limits of human understanding and tapping into a deeper, more profound truth.

⚜

As I watched, transfixed by the unfolding tableau before me, I witnessed a transformation in Holmes that defied rational explanation. His eyes, locked with Al-Zarib's, seemed to glow with an unearthly light. The very air around them seemed to shimmer, as if reality itself were bending to accommodate this extraordinary communion.

Holmes' body remained perfectly still, yet I sensed a profound shift within him. The tension that had been etched into every line of his face only moments before melted away, replaced by an expression of wonder and dawning understanding. It was as if he was seeing the world anew, through eyes not quite his own.

There was a visible change in Al-Zarib as well. The stallion's bearing, already noble and proud, seemed to grow even more majestic. His eyes, which I had always known to be a deep, unfathomable black, now blazed with a brilliant crimson that matched the strange glow in Holmes' gaze.

As I watched this silent exchange, I became aware of a strange sensation, as if I were witnessing something far beyond the bounds of ordinary human experience. Though I could not share in their communion, I could feel the echoes of it reverberating through the very air around us.

Holmes and Al-Zarib stood frozen in their silent dialogue, yet I sensed a flurry of activity between them. It was as if they were exchanging not just

345

thoughts, but entire lifetimes of experience in the span of mere moments.

Through their shared consciousness, Holmes was given a vision of the world as Al-Zarib perceived it. The desert, which to our human eyes appeared as a vast expanse of sand and sky, revealed itself as a living tapestry of scents, sounds and sensations beyond our limited comprehension. Every shift of the wind, every grain of sand carried a story, a history that Al-Zarib could read as easily as Holmes could peruse a newspaper.

In this heightened state of consciousness, the ideologies of the Sons of Purity manifested as a visible miasma, a sickly green aura that clung to our captors like a poisonous shroud. It was a corruption that stood in stark contrast to the harmonious balance of the desert's natural rhythms, a cancer that threatened to spread if left unchecked.

As their minds continued to merge, I saw Holmes' expression shift from wonder to understanding. He was absorbing Al-Zarib's knowledge of the desert, his instincts honed by generations of living in this unforgiving landscape. At the same time, Al-Zarib's eyes seemed to take on a calculating gleam, eerily reminiscent of Holmes at his most analytical.

It became clear that they were forging a plan that combined Al-Zarib's brute strength and intimate knowledge of the terrain with Holmes' strategic brilliance and understanding of human nature. Every detail of the Sons of Purity camp, every strength and weakness of our captors, was catalogued and analysed with a precision that surpassed even Holmes' usual thoroughness.

As this extraordinary exchange continued, I became aware of a change in the atmosphere around us. There seemed to be a palpable energy in the air, as if the very fabric of reality was being reshaped by the force of their combined will.

The other members of our group also seemed to sense that something momentous was happening. Liyana's eyes were wide with a mixture of awe and hope, while Adrien leaned forward, his analytical mind clearly struggling to comprehend what he was witnessing. Even Khalid, weak from his wound, seemed to draw strength from the sight of his beloved Al-Zarib in this transcendent state.

As the moments passed, I found myself holding my breath, aware that I was witnessing something that would change the course of our journey forever. Whatever plan was being forged in this crucible of shared consciousness, I knew it would be unlike anything we had attempted before.

As the crimson glow finally faded from their eyes, I saw in both Holmes and Al-Zarib a new determination, a sense of purpose that seemed to radiate from them like a physical force. The despair that had threatened to consume us all only moments before had been banished, replaced by a determined hope that seemed to defy the laws of nature itself.

As Holmes turned to face us, his eyes now their usual piercing grey, but glowing with an inner fire I had never seen before, I knew our fortunes had changed. Whatever trials lay ahead, we would face them not as a group of desperate prisoners, but as a force united by a bond that transcended the boundaries of species and understanding.

The dawn of a new day had indeed come, bringing with it not only the threat of our imminent doom, but the promise of a salvation beyond anything we could have imagined. As I met Holmes' gaze, I saw in it a reflection of the vast, untamed power of the desert itself, and I knew that our journey had only just begun.

⊕⊙⊗⊙⊕

As I witnessed the extraordinary communion between Holmes and Al-Zarib, my thoughts turned to the nature of the desert that surrounded us. Its vast expanse, stretching to the horizon in every direction, often lulls the unwary traveller into a false sense of security. The seemingly unchanging landscape, with its undulating dunes and cloudless skies, creates an illusion of predictability, a deceptive promise that one can foresee what lies ahead.

But as I had learned on our perilous journey, and as Idris Al-Hakim had taught his son Malik centuries ago, the desert is a realm of sudden and dramatic change. A serene vista can be transformed in moments into a maelstrom of swirling sand and howling wind, a deadly sandstorm materialising as if conjured by some malevolent jinn. It is a harsh reminder of the folly of human hubris, a lesson that even the most seasoned desert dweller must relearn time and again.

It was in this moment of reflection that I witnessed the capricious nature of the desert manifest itself once again, not through a sandstorm of wind and sand, but through the unleashed fury of Al-Zarib.

One of Rasheed's men, a figure of medium stature with the hardened bearing of one long accustomed to the harsh dictates of desert life, approached Al-Zarib with a sense of purpose that belied the mundane nature of his task. His hands, calloused and stained by the trials of countless journeys across the desert, reached out to unhitch the stallion to the caravan that would lead them away from this place of confrontation and revelation. Unaware of the intricate tapestry of destiny he was about to unravel, the guard's actions were mechanical, unaware of the profound connection that had blossomed in the silent communion between Sherlock and the majestic horse.

As the guard's fingers worked to untie the final knot binding Al-Zarib, I again witnessed the extraordinary transformation that had taken place only moments before. The memory of that first inexplicable connection between Holmes and the stallion was still fresh in my mind, and I found myself both prepared for and awed by its recurrence.

Al-Zarib, who had masterfully feigned docility as the guard approached, suddenly underwent a change as dramatic as it was familiar. The stallion's eyes, which moments before had seemed dull with feigned fear, now blazed with that brilliant crimson I had observed earlier. It was as if an inner fire, briefly dormant, had roared back to life in the magnificent beast's soul.

My eyes instinctively darted to Holmes and I saw the same transformation overtake him. As before, the whites of his eyes seemed to dissolve, replaced by a network of pulsing crimson veins that glowed with an otherworldly intensity. The sharp, focused gaze that had returned to his eyes after their initial connection now gave way to that distant, transcendent gaze.

Though I had witnessed this phenomenon only minutes before, its recurrence did not diminish its impact. If anything, the sight of this re-connection only deepened my sense of awe at the profound bond that had formed between man and horse.

The guard, oblivious to the extraordinary events unfolding before him, continued with his task. He was unaware that he was standing on the precipice of a moment that would change the course of our journey forever, a moment that I had glimpsed before and was now seeing come to fruition.

As Al-Zarib's restraints fell away, I saw once again in both Holmes and the stallion that singular purpose, that shared determination that seemed to radiate from them with physical force. The air itself seemed to hum with a now familiar energy, charged with the promise of imminent and dramatic change.

In the span of a heartbeat, Al-Zarib's carefully maintained facade of docility shattered. His demeanour instantly changed from one of apparent submission to a concentrated avatar of the untamed spirit of the desert itself, just as it had when they first bonded. This time, however, I sensed that their shared consciousness was primed for action, ready to unleash the plan they had formulated in their earlier communion.

What followed was a display of power and precision that, despite my foreknowledge, left me breathless...

⊕⊣⊱⊰⊢⊕

The guard, realising too late the folly of his actions, found himself transfixed by Al-Zarib's gaze. Those eyes, which moments before had reflected the serene skies of countless desert nights, now blazed with an intensity that seemed to transcend the mortal plane. I saw in them not merely the fury of a wronged creature, but the accumulated wisdom and power of the Obsidian Guild channelled through this magnificent beast. The crimson glow pulsed with an unearthly rhythm, casting an eerie light on the terrified face of the guard.

Before any of us could draw breath to shout a warning, Al-Zarib struck. The very air seemed to crackle with energy as the stallion's muscular body coiled like a spring. In a blur of movement too swift for the human eye to follow, his hooves, instruments of justice forged by centuries of desert life, crashed down upon the hapless guard. The impact echoed through the camp with a sickening crunch, a sound that would haunt my dreams for years to come. The force behind the blow was both terrifying and awe-inspiring, a perfect fusion of raw power and precise calculation. In the span of a heartbeat, a life was extinguished and the guard crumpled to the ground like a puppet whose strings had been severed. The sand beneath him darkened, stained by the life draining from his broken form.

The peaceful dawn shattered like glass, giving way to a maelstrom of chaos. Al-Zarib's furious charge sent shockwaves through the camp, his every move a declaration of war against those who had dared to restrain him. The stallion moved with a grace that belied his size, each stride covering impossible distances, each turn executed with a fluidity that seemed to defy the laws of physics. His mane and tail flowed behind him like banners of defiance, catching the early morning light and turning him into a living flame that scorched through the ranks of our captors.

I could see in this deadly ballet the influence of Holmes's analytical mind fused with Al-Zarib's raw strength and desert-born cunning. Each devastating blow seemed choreographed with preternatural precision, targeting weaknesses in the Sons of Purity's defences that I hadn't even known existed. Tents collapsed in Al-Zarib's wake, supplies strewn across the sand and men falling like wheat before a scythe.

The air was filled with a cacophony of sounds: the thunderous drumbeat of Al-Zarib's hooves against the earth, the sharp cracks of breaking bones, the terrified screams of the Sons of Purity and the whimpering of those who had fallen but still clung to life. The acrid smell of fear permeated the air, mingling with the metallic taste of blood and the dust kicked up by the frenzy of movement.

The Sons of Purity, caught off guard, found themselves scattered like chaff before the desert wind. Men who had stood confident in their dominion over beast and captive alike now fled in blind panic, their carefully cultivated air of superiority shattered in the face of Al-Zarib's wrath. Some tried to stand their ground, brandishing weapons with trembling hands, but their efforts were futile against the whirlwind of destruction that Al-Zarib had become.

I watched in fascination as a group of guards tried to surround the stallion, hoping to overwhelm him with numbers. Al-Zarib's reaction was swift and brutal. He reared up, his massive form silhouetted against the rising sun, a vision of terrible beauty seared into my memory. As he came down, his front hooves struck with the force of a battering ram, sending two men flying through the air like rag dolls. In the same fluid motion, he turned, his powerful hindquarters lashing out to strike another guard in the chest with a sickening thud.

Throughout this deadly dance, I could see Holmes' influence guiding Al-Zarib's actions. The stallion never wasted a move, never struck without purpose.

He seemed to anticipate his opponents' moves before they made them, always one step ahead, always in the perfect position to wreak maximum havoc.

As I watched this spectacle unfold, I was struck by the realisation that I was witnessing more than just an act of rebellion. This was a statement, a declaration of the indomitable spirit that unites those who fight for a cause greater than themselves. In Al-Zarib's fury, I saw the legacy of the Obsidian Guild manifested, a lineage of protectors rising up to defend the sacred truths they had sworn to uphold.

The onslaught seemed to last both an eternity and only moments. Gradually, the sounds of battle began to fade, replaced by an eerie silence, broken only by the moans of the wounded and the soft whisper of the desert wind. The dust began to settle, revealing a scene of utter devastation. Where once there had been a meticulously organised camp was now a wasteland of broken bodies, smashed equipment and torn canvas.

Al-Zarib stood at the centre of the destruction, his cloak glistening with sweat and stained with the blood of his enemies. His sides bulged with effort, but his bearing remained proud and unbowed. As the crimson glow faded from his eyes, returning them to their natural, unfathomable black, I saw in them a depth of intelligence and purpose that took my breath away.

As I surveyed the aftermath of this extraordinary turn of events, I felt a profound sense of humility wash over me. The desert, in its infinite wisdom, had once again shown us the folly of presumption. Through Al-Zarib, it had unleashed a force as ancient and powerful as the sands themselves, reminding us all that true strength often lies hidden, waiting for the right moment to reveal itself.

In the silence that followed, with the sun now fully up and bathing the scene in golden light, I understood that our journey had been irrevocably changed. We had witnessed a miracle, a fusion of man and beast that had rewritten the rules of what I thought was possible. Whatever challenges lay ahead, I knew we would face them with a newfound respect for the hidden depths that lay within all of us, and a deeper understanding of the profound connections that bound us to this ancient land and to each other.

⁕⁂⁕

As the dust settled on the field of carnage, Al-Zarib stood in regal solitude at the heart of the devastated camp. The Sons of Purity, those zealots who only moments before had exuded an air of invincibility, now lay scattered like so many broken dolls - some lifeless, others moaning in agony, while the more fortunate had managed to escape the Stallion's terrible onslaught.

I watched with a mixture of awe and trepidation as the otherworldly crimson glow faded from Al-Zarib's eyes, leaving behind the inscrutable black orbs I had come to know. The magnificent beast stood tall and calm, his bearing that of a conqueror who need not boast of his victory. My gaze was drawn to Holmes, whose own eyes had also returned to their familiar grey. I could see the Herculean effort behind that furrowed brow as my friend's prodigious intellect grappled with the extraordinary events that had just transpired.

For my part, I found myself quite incapable of speech, a condition that also seemed to affect Dr El-Sharif, Liyana Sultan and Khalid, who was barely clinging to life. It was Adrien who first broke the stunned silence that had fallen over us.

"Look," he shouted, his voice barely above a whisper as he pointed to the centre of the camp, "there is Rasheed and his son."

Following the direction of Adrien's outstretched arm, I saw a tableau that will remain etched in my memory to the day I die. There stood Rasheed Al-Tariq, the once mighty leader of the Sons of Purity, amidst the wreckage of his ambitions. He seemed frozen in place, as immobile as the ancient stone monoliths that dotted the desert landscape. Some distance behind him I saw his son Farid, surrounded by the camels and horses of their caravan. The young man's face was a mask of abject terror, his body trembling like a leaf in a storm as he clutched the reins of a mount, clearly torn between fleeing and rushing to his father's aid.

But it was Rasheed himself who caught my attention. Unlike his son, the elder Al-Tariq showed no outward signs of fear or panic. His stillness was not born of paralysis, but of deep introspection. As I studied his face, I was struck by the notion that he did not see the devastation in front of him, but rather the whole of his life's journey unfolding before his mind's eye.

At that moment, through an inexplicable shift in the ether, I found myself privy to Rasheed Al-Tariq's innermost thoughts. It was as if the veil between minds had been momentarily lifted, allowing me a glimpse into the turbulent psyche of our adversary.

Rasheed, a veteran of countless battles and a strategist of unparalleled acumen, had rarely been outmanoeuvred. On those rare occasions when an enemy had managed to catch him off guard, his iron discipline and lightning reflexes had always served him well, allowing him to adapt and overcome in the blink of an eye. But now, for the first time in his long and bloody career, he found himself completely stymied.

I could feel his confusion, his desperate attempt to regain control of a situation that had spiralled so far beyond his comprehension. He had watched Al-Zarib's rampage with a detachment that bordered on the surreal, unable to reconcile the swift and total annihilation of his forces with any strategy or tactic he had ever encountered.

The image of Al-Zarib's eyes, burning with that eerie crimson fire, seemed seared into Rasheed's consciousness. Some deep, primal part of his being recognised the significance of what he had witnessed, even as his rational mind recoiled from the implications. The legends of Idris and Malik Al-Hakim, stories he had long dismissed as mere folklore, now demanded recognition with a force that shook the very foundations of his beliefs.

As if summoned by Rasheed's thoughts, Al-Zarib turned his majestic head and fixed the man with a gaze that seemed to pierce the very veil of reality. For a breathless moment, crimson met mortal brown, and I felt a profound communication taking place, one that transcended the barriers of species and spoke to the very essence of being.

Then, as suddenly as it had appeared, the crimson glow faded from Al-Zarib's eyes, leaving behind pools of infinite blackness. With a grace that belied his size and the violence he had so recently unleashed, the stallion began to approach Rasheed. His stride was measured, each step deliberate and full of meaning. He came to a halt within inches of the man, their eyes perfectly level.

In that moment of confrontation, I witnessed a transformation in Rasheed Al-Tariq. The haze of disbelief left his eyes, replaced by a clarity that was almost painful to behold. For the first time, he truly saw himself - not as the righteous leader he had long believed himself to be, but as the very embodiment of the desert lion he had once vanquished.

The irony of his situation was not lost on him. The predator that had once been his greatest test, the beast he had conquered to prove his worth, had become his own reflection. In defeating the desert lion, he had ultimately become that which he had sought to destroy.

When Rasheed looked into Al-Zarib's eyes, he found not the hatred or vengeance he might have expected, but a deep sadness tinged with an unrelenting sense of duty. This, he realised, was not an act of personal retribution, but the restoration of a balance long out of whack, the protection of innocents long neglected in the blind pursuit of a misguided ideal.

In that final moment, as Al-Zarib reared up, his massive form silhouetted against the desert sky, I sensed a curious mixture of emotions emanating from Rasheed - horror at the realisation of his folly, acceptance of the inevitability of his fate, and, most surprisingly, a sense of peace. He had finally understood the true nature of the path he had taken and the necessity of its end.

As Al-Zarib's hooves descended, I found myself turning away, unable to witness the final act of this tragedy. The sound that followed - a single, resonant thud - seemed to echo across the desert, marking the end of an era and the beginning of an uncertain future.

When I dared to look again, Rasheed Al-Tariq was gone. Al-Zarib stood over him, his head bowed as if in mourning. There was no triumph in the great stallion's eyes as he lifted them to look at us once more, only a weary acceptance of a duty done.

It was then that I realised we had witnessed something far greater than a mere conflict between man and beast. We had witnessed the closing of a circle, the balancing of cosmic scales, and the passing of a torch from one guardian of the desert to another. As the sun climbed higher in the sky, bathing the scene in golden light, I knew that far from ending, our journey had only just begun.

⊛⊰◦⊱⊛

As the dust of conflict settled over the desolate camp, my attention was drawn to the figure of young Farid Al-Tariq. The boy stood transfixed, his face a study in anguish as he watched the fall of his father. It was clear that the profound understanding and peace that had come to Rasheed in his final moments had been lost on his son. Farid's eyes, wide with horror and disbelief, saw only the brutal demise of a man he had revered not only as a parent, but as the very embodiment of the ideals to which he had dedicated his life.

I watched as a maelstrom of emotions played across Farid's features - shock giving way to grief, then to a burning rage that seemed to consume him from within. With a cry that was half sob, half roar, the young man turned and fled towards the horses tied up at the edge of the camp. In his haste to escape, Farid seemed to shed more than just his physical presence; he abandoned the very beliefs and ideals that had led to this moment of disaster.

As Farid's figure faded into the vast expanse of the desert, a mere silhouette against the brightening sky, I could not help but feel a pang of compassion for the boy. His world had been shattered in the space of a few moments, and the path ahead was fraught with uncertainty and danger.

My contemplation of Farid's fate was abruptly cut short when Al-Zarib, the magnificent animal whose actions had so decisively altered the course of our adventure, turned his attention to Holmes. With a grace that belied his size and the violence he had so recently unleashed, the stallion approached my friend. I watched in amazement as Al-Zarib, with a dexterity and intelligence that seemed almost human, used his teeth to sever the ropes that bound Holmes.

No sooner had Holmes regained his freedom than he sprang into action with his characteristic alacrity. "Watson!" he shouted, his voice sharp with urgency. "Your medical kit - where is it?"

As Holmes worked to free Amal, Adrien and Liyana, I hurried to Khalid's side, my medical instincts overriding all else. Holmes, having located my medical kit amidst the wreckage of the camp, tossed it to me with unerring accuracy. I caught it deftly and immediately set about treating our wounded companion.

Al-Zarib, his role in our liberation complete, moved to stand guard over Khalid. The great stallion lowered his head and touched his velvety muzzle to Khalid's fevered forehead in a gesture of such tender concern that I felt my throat tighten with emotion. It was a poignant reminder of the deep bond that

353

exists between man and beast, a connection that transcends species.

As I worked to treat Khalid's wounds and reduce his raging fever, I was only peripherally aware of the activities of our companions. Holmes, his keen mind always alert to potential dangers, had organised our friends into a scouting party. They moved purposefully through the camp, collecting scattered weapons and searching for any remaining threats.

"Watson," Holmes called to me some time later, "how is our patient?"

I looked up from my duties to see my friend standing over us, his face etched with concern. "He is not out of danger yet," I replied, "but I think the worst is over. With rest and continued care he should make a full recovery."

Holmes nodded, satisfaction evident in his countenance. "Excellent news, old friend. We have secured the camp and tended to those of our former captors who are still clinging to life. They are gathered in the central tent, with enough provisions to see them home, once they are able to travel."

I marvelled at Holmes' capacity for mercy, even in the face of those who had shown us none. It was a testament to the nobility of spirit that lay beneath his often brusque exterior.

As the sun climbed higher in the sky, casting long shadows across the sand, our group reassembled. There was a moment of shared silence as we stood together, the enormity of our ordeal and the miracle of our deliverance settling over us like a cloak.

It was Adrien who finally broke the silence. "I can hardly believe it," he said, his voice choked with awe. "Had I not seen it with my own eyes, I would have thought it all a fever dream."

Liyana nodded, her eyes bright with unshed tears. "We owe our lives to Al-Zarib," she said, reaching out to stroke the stallion's gleaming flank. "And to you, Mr Holmes. Your connection with him is... beyond my understanding, but I am grateful for it."

Holmes, uncharacteristically, seemed at a loss for words. He looked at Al-Zarib, a look of deep respect and something like affection in his eyes. "The debt is mutual, I assure you," he said at last. "We have all been part of something extraordinary here, something that I suspect will take a lifetime to fully comprehend."

As Holmes finished his report, my attention was drawn to a movement on the periphery of our gathering. Muntasir, the noble steed whose unwavering courage had been a source of strength throughout our arduous journey, approached with regal bearing. Liyana had freed him in the chaos that followed Al-Zarib's rebellion, and now he seemed unwilling to stray more than a few paces from her side.

The bond between Liyana and Muntasir was a sight to behold, reminiscent of the deep bond we had witnessed between Al-Zarib and Holmes. As Liyana reached out to stroke Muntasir's proud neck, the stallion's eyes, dark and intelligent, seemed to reflect a depth of understanding that went beyond mere animal instinct.

"Muntasir has been my constant companion through this ordeal," Liyana said, her voice soft with affection. "I fear I would have lost all hope had it not been for his unwavering presence."

Holmes nodded, a rare smile playing at the corners of his mouth. "It would appear, Watson, that we are in the company of not one, but two extraordinary equines. The legends of Arabian horses, it seems, have not been exaggerated in the least."

Indeed, as I watched Muntasir stand proudly beside Liyana, his coat gleaming in the desert sun, I could not help but marvel at the noble spirit that radiated from him. Like Al-Zarib, he seemed to embody the very essence of the desert itself - untamed, majestic and possessed of a wisdom that defied human comprehension.

As we stood there, united in our survival and in the face of the unknown challenges that lay ahead, I felt a sense of purpose and camaraderie such as I had never experienced before. The desert stretched before us, vast and unforgiving, but it no longer seemed an implacable foe. Instead, it was a realm of infinite possibility, a canvas upon which our continuing adventures would be written.

With Khalid now stable enough to travel, we began to prepare for our departure. The journey to Al-Hijr still lay ahead, and with it the promise of answers to the mysteries that had brought us to this point. As I helped Holmes secure our supplies and tend to our mounts, I could not shake the feeling that we were on the cusp of something momentous, a turning point not only in our own lives, but in the very fabric of the world we thought we knew.

As our companions busied themselves with preparations for our imminent departure, I watched Holmes approach the fallen form of Rasheed Al-Tariq. His steps were measured, his bearing solemn as he approached the man who had been both our captor and, in a strange way, the catalyst for the extraordinary events that had transpired.

Holmes stood for a moment in silent contemplation, his piercing grey eyes fixed on Rasheed's lifeless visage. Though he did not speak, I could almost sense the workings of his formidable intellect as he processed the profound implications of all that had happened.

Later he would confide to me the substance of his thoughts at that moment. "It was a strange thing, Watson," he mused, "to stand there and look down upon a man who, only hours before, had been the architect of our possible doom. In that moment I was struck by the fragility of human ambition, the transience of power. Rasheed Al-Tariq, for all his misguided zeal, was a man of extraordinary ability. Yet in a twist of profound irony, he met his end at the hooves of the very essence he believed he was serving - Al-Zarib, the embodiment of the legendary Obsidian Stallion. In those final moments, Rasheed was confronted with the true nature of the purity he had so long sought - not in bloodlines or dogma, but in the incorruptible spirit of a creature who stood as guardian of the desert's delicate balance. It was as if the sands themselves had risen to pass judgement, reminding us all that true nobility lies not in pedigree but in the purity of one's soul and actions.

With characteristic efficiency, Holmes then set about recovering the items that had been the cause of so much strife. From the folds of Rasheed's robes, he pulled out two objects that gleamed with otherworldly beauty in the harsh desert sun - the obsidian statuettes, one veined with gold, the other with silver. Beside them lay the Scroll of the Stallions, its ancient parchment a stark contrast to the glossy black of the statuettes.

As Holmes rejoined our group, I saw a mixture of emotions on the faces of our companions. Relief, certainly, at the recovery of these precious artefacts, but also a palpable sense of the weight of responsibility that came with their possession.

"Adrien," Holmes said, his voice soft as he held out the golden-veined statuette, "I believe this rightfully belongs in your care. Lord Wentworth would have wanted it so."

Adrien's hands trembled slightly as he accepted the statuette, his eyes glistening with unshed tears. "Thank you, Mr Holmes," he whispered, holding the artefact as if it were the most precious thing in the world. "I will guard it with my life, in memory of Lord Wentworth and all he stood for."

Turning to Liyana, Holmes offered the silver-veined statuette. "My lady," he said with a small bow, "your brother's legacy. May it serve as a reminder of his courage and the noble cause for which he gave his life."

Liyana accepted the statuette with grace, though I saw a flash of pain cross her features as she looked at it. "Zafir would be pleased to know that it has been recovered," she said softly, her voice thick with emotion. "I will see that it is returned to its rightful place of honour."

Finally, Holmes turned to Dr El-Sharif, the scroll of the stallions held carefully in his hands. "Dr El-Sharif," he said, "your expertise in matters of history and culture makes you the ideal custodian of this ancient document. I entrust it to your care in the hope that it will guide us faithfully on the final leg of our journey to Al-Hijr."

Amal accepted the scroll with reverence, her eyes shining with scholarly excitement despite the gravity of our situation. "I will study it most carefully, Mr Holmes," she assured him. "With luck, it may indeed lead us to the answers we seek."

As I watched this solemn distribution of artefacts, I was struck by the feeling that we had crossed an invisible threshold. The objects that had been the cause of so much conflict were now reunited, entrusted to those who would use their power for the greater good.

With the statuettes and scroll secured and our preparations complete, we turned as one to face the vast expanse of desert that lay before us. The road to Al-Hijr beckoned, promising revelation and challenge in equal measure. As we mounted our horses - Khalid astride Al-Zarib, Liyana on Muntasir, and the rest of us on our horses freed by the Sons of Purity - I felt a surge of anticipation.

Whatever trials lay ahead, we would face them together, bound by the shared experience of our ordeal and the sacred trust now placed in our hands. The desert stretched endlessly before us, a blank canvas awaiting the next chapter of our extraordinary story.

The sun, now high in the cloudless sky, beat down upon us with merciless intensity. But as we mounted our horses and turned our faces towards the horizon, I felt a thrill of excitement run through me. Whatever lay ahead, whatever trials we might face, we would face them together - man and beast, logic and instinct, united in a common purpose.

And so, with Al-Zarib leading the way, his mighty form a beacon of hope and strength, we set off into the heart of the desert, leaving behind the shattered remnants of the Sons of Purity and the ghosts of our own past doubts. The sands stretched endlessly before us, a blank page awaiting the next chapter of our extraordinary story.

CHAPTER 28

THE DESERT'S EMBRACE

As the merciless sun climbed higher in the cloudless sky, we set out into the heart of the desert, leaving behind the shattered remains of the Sons of Purity camp. The sands stretched endlessly before us, a blank page awaiting the next chapter of our extraordinary story. With Al-Zarib leading the way, his mighty form a beacon of hope and strength, I felt a rush of excitement, tempered by the gravity of our mission.

The distribution of the recovered artefacts had given our group a renewed sense of purpose. Adrien cradled the golden-veined statuette with reverence, while Liyana's grip on the silver-veined twin spoke of both determination and sorrow. Dr El-Sharif clutched the Scroll of the Stallions to her breast, her eyes glowing with scholarly anticipation. As for Holmes, his gaze alternated between the horizon and Al-Zarib, a look of deep respect and something like affection in his eyes.

As we rode, my attention was drawn to Khalid, our faithful guide, who had so recently been on the brink of death. His recovery, nothing short of miraculous, was a testament to both his own resilience and the effectiveness of the desert herbs Amal had provided for his treatment. Though still weak, he sat astride Al-Zarib with a quiet determination that spoke volumes of his indomitable spirit.

"Watson," Holmes called from beside me, "I fear we've only begun to scratch the surface of the mysteries that surround us. The connection between man and beast that we've witnessed... it defies all rational explanation."

I nodded, remembering the extraordinary bond between Holmes and Al-Zarib, and the similar affinity between Liyana and Muntasir. "Indeed, Holmes.

It seems we are in the realm of legend, where the lines between the possible and the impossible are blurred."

As if in response to our conversation, Al-Zarib tossed his magnificent head, his eyes seeming to glow with an intelligence far beyond that of an ordinary horse. Beside us, Muntasir nickered softly and nestled close to Liyana's side as if offering comfort.

The landscape we travelled through was a study in harsh beauty. Dunes of burnished gold stretched to the horizon, their shapes constantly shifting in the desert wind. The air shimmered with heat, carrying the faint scent of sun-baked stone and hardy desert flowers. It was a realm both breathtaking and unforgiving, demanding respect from all who dared to cross its vast expanse.

As the day wore on, I found Holmes deep in conversation with Dr El-Sharif, their heads bent over the ancient scroll. The parchment, brittle and yellowed with age, bore on its surface a tapestry of cryptic symbols and arcane passages that spoke of eras long past. Holmes, his nimble mind always eager for a challenge, traced the intricate patterns with his long fingers, his brow furrowed in concentration.

"Fascinating," I heard him murmur. "The way these symbols interlock... it's not just a text, it's a map. A guide to Al-Hijr, hidden within the very fabric of the scroll itself."

Dr El-Sharif nodded, her eyes bright with excitement. "Yes, and look here," she pointed to a series of recurring glyphs, "these markings correspond to celestial bodies. The ancients used the stars to navigate the desert, and it seems they've encoded that knowledge into the scroll."

Their combined efforts were beginning to bear fruit, slowly unlocking the scroll's secrets and giving us a more precise course to our destination. It was heartening to see the growing camaraderie between Holmes and our companions, each contributing their unique skills and knowledge to our shared quest.

As the sun began its descent towards the horizon, painting the desert in shades of gold and crimson, we set up camp in the lee of a large dune. The evening air brought a chill that belied the oppressive heat of the day, a stark reminder of the dual nature of the desert.

Gathered around our humble campfire, we shared a meal of dried dates and salted meat, our spirits lifted by the progress we had made. Amal, her voice rich with the weight of generations, began to speak of Al-Hijr, the mystical oasis that was our destination.

"It is said," she began, her eyes reflecting the dancing flames, "that Al-Hijr lies at the crossroads of the physical and spiritual realms. A place where the veil between worlds thins and the wisdom of ages past can be gleaned by those who are pure of heart and steadfast in purpose."

As Amal's story unfolded, I noticed a change in our equine companions. Al-Zarib and Muntasir, who usually grazed at the edge of our camp, came closer, their ears pricked forward as if listening intently. The firelight reflected in their eyes, giving them an almost otherworldly appearance.

In that moment, surrounded by the vast, star-studded sky and the endless sea of sand, I felt a profound sense of connection to something greater than myself. Whatever trials lay ahead, I knew we would face them together, bound by the shared experience of our ordeal and the sacred trust now placed in our hands.

As I retired to my bedroll that night, the image of our small band of travellers, dwarfed by the vastness of the desert yet united in purpose, remained with me. We had embarked on a journey that would test not only our physical endurance, but the very foundations of our understanding of the world. And as I drifted off to sleep, lulled by the whisper of the wind over the sand, I could not shake the feeling that we were on the verge of discoveries that would change the course of our lives forever.

As our journey through the vast Arabian desert continued, the dual nature of the land became increasingly apparent, both breathtakingly beautiful and dangerously unforgiving. The air shimmered with an otherworldly energy, distorting the horizon into fantastic shapes. Beneath our feet, the powdery sand ranged from pale gold to deep russet, creating an ever-changing landscape.

Holmes' obsession with the Scroll of the Stallion intensified. I often found him awake in the wee hours, the ancient text illuminated by flickering lamplight, his hawklike profile etched in stark relief as he pored over its secrets.

"Watson," he said one night, his eyes glowing with intellectual fervour, "this scroll is extraordinary. Its cryptography is not mere concealment, but a key to understanding our own journey."

Despite my scepticism, I couldn't deny the scroll's uncanny accuracy in guiding us. It seemed to possess a preternatural awareness of the capricious nature of the desert, leading us unerringly towards Al-Hijr.

Our surroundings reflected the contradictions within our group. By day, the merciless sun sapped our strength, the endless dunes a beautiful but deadly illusion. As night fell, the desert changed. A bone-chilling cold replaced the oppressive heat, while the star-studded sky formed a velvety canopy that seemed within reach.

We gathered around the campfire during these nocturnal hours, finding comfort in the company of others. Amal's stories of her people captured the essence of the desert, while Liyana's insights into the complex political landscape that had shaped her life added depth to our understanding.

The harsh environment stripped away civilised comforts and forced me to confront long-buried aspects of my character. It was both terrifying and exhilarating to be so exposed to the harsh realities of life.

One evening, as we sat around the dying embers, an inexplicable phenomenon occurred. A shimmering apparition appeared on the horizon - a magnificent stallion of starlight and desert wind. Though fleeting, its effect was profound. I turned to Holmes, expecting scepticism, only to find him gazing at the apparition's former location with unprecedented wonder.

"There are more things in heaven and earth, Watson," he muttered. "Perhaps it's time we opened our minds to possibilities beyond pure logic."

As we retired that night, the image of the ghostly stallion lingered. I felt we were drawing ever closer to Al-Hijr and the revelations it promised - revelations that would challenge not only Holmes's rational worldview, but the very foundations of our understanding of reality.

As dawn broke, painting the horizon with amber and gold, Al-Hijr revealed itself in incomparable beauty. The legendary oasis emerged like a mirage from ancient tales, a verdant haven nestled among towering rock formations, in stark contrast to the endless sea of sand we'd traversed.

The air in Al-Hijr had an almost ethereal quality - cooler, fresher, infused with the essence of water and greenery. Palm leaves rustled softly, harmonising with the murmur of hidden streams. The scent of water permeated everything, a sweet, intoxicating scent that spoke of the perseverance of life in the heart of the desert.

At the centre of the oasis, hidden from casual observation, stood an ancient temple of the Obsidian Guild. Carved directly into a colossal rock formation, it bore witness to a time when artisan and acolyte were indistinguishable. Obsidian statues flanked the entrance, their dark surfaces gleaming in the dawn light, reflecting it like trapped starlight.

The façade of the temple bore the mark of a civilisation that had mastered the art of stone and imbued it with deep spiritual meaning. Every line and curve spoke of a reverence for its materials, transforming mere architecture into a sanctuary of mystical power.

Standing at the threshold of this ancient building, we felt the weight of centuries pressing down on us. The air seemed charged with echoes of the past - whispered prayers and chanted incantations from those who'd walked these halls before. This temple was more than a building; it was a bridge spanning the gulf between the temporal and the eternal, a nexus where the physical and spiritual realms touched.

The discovery of Al-Hijr, with its hidden streams and ancient temple, marked more than the culmination of our physical journey. It was a moment of profound revelation, where history, legend and destiny converged. Here, in the heart of the desert, we'd found a place where the veil between worlds thinned, where the sacred and the secular merged, and where a physical journey became a spiritual pilgrimage.

In the cool, fragrant air of the oasis, amidst the timeless beauty of Al-Hijr, we stood on the threshold of long-buried secrets. As Holmes exchanged a meaningful glance with Al-Zarib and Liyana whispered to Muntasir, I felt the weight of our quest settle upon us. We were ready to unlock the secrets hidden in the stone and shadows of the Obsidian Guild's ancient temple, our diverse band of seekers united by a common purpose that transcended individual understanding.

As our footsteps approached the threshold of the temple, the air around us seemed to hum with an ancient energy, as if the very stones beneath our feet were whispering secrets of ages past. It was here, amidst the verdant embrace of Al-Hijr, that we were greeted by a figure who seemed to be both guardian and embodiment of the temple itself. His presence was as much a part of the landscape as the towering rock formations and whispering streams. As he stepped forward into the light, the dawn casting long shadows behind him, he introduced himself in a voice that carried the weight of centuries.

"I am Ammar ibn Nadir," he said, his voice echoing softly in the stillness of the oasis, "keeper of the Temple and guardian of the legacy of the Obsidian Guild. My lineage, direct descendants of Idris and Malik, has safeguarded this sacred trust through the generations, a duty passed from parent to child as seamlessly as the desert sands shift with the wind".

Ammar Ibn Nadir stood before us, clad in robes that shimmered with the colours of the desert - crimson, gold and the deep blue of the twilight sky. His clothes seemed to capture the essence of the landscape that surrounded us, and his eyes, deep and knowing, held the serene calm of the desert night. His presence was commanding, yet imbued with an innate serenity, a reflection of the wisdom and strength that had protected the Guild's legacy through the ages.

As Ammar spoke of the Guild and its storied history, his words wove a rich tapestry that bridged the realms of legend and reality. He told of the mystical stallions at the heart of the Guild's heritage, creatures not of flesh and blood but of spirit and essence, embodiments of the elemental forces that had shaped the world. His tale brought to life the living tapestry of the desert - the fierce hues of dawn, the soothing tones of twilight, and the deep silence that spoke volumes in the stillness of night.

He spoke of cities carved from living rock, of oases emerging like jewels from the desert's embrace, and of the people whose lives were interwoven with the land - people whose resilience, creativity and spirit were a testament to the enduring human capacity to thrive in even the harshest of environments. Through Ammar's words, the story of the Obsidian Guild unfolded, revealing a lineage of craftsmen and mystics who had channelled the very essence of the desert into their work, creating not just structures of stone but sanctuaries of spiritual power.

In sharing these ancient truths, Ammar ibn Nadir offered more than an account of the past; he extended an invitation into the deepest depths of spiritual understanding and connection. His insight into the hearts of those who sought the secrets of the Temple, his unwavering dedication to preserving the Guild's legacy, and his deep connection to the mystical forces embodied by the stallions, all spoke to a character whose life was a testament to the balance between preservation and revelation.

Our interaction with Ammar, beneath the ancient palms of Al-Hijr and in the shadow of the temple's obsidian guardians, became a moment of transformation - a journey through the annals of history and the depths of our own minds. His wisdom, shared in the silence of the oasis, became a key that unlocked not only the secrets of the Guild, but the potential for understanding and growth within us all.

In that moment, as we stood on the threshold of secrets long shrouded in shadow, we were united not only by the common quest that had brought us to Al-Hijr, but by a deeper, more profound unity. Forged in the crucible of revelation and tempered in the waters of the oasis, it was a bond that transcended mere fellowship and approached the cusp of a shared destiny. Ammar ibn Nadir, with his serene presence and profound wisdom, stood as a beacon of ancient knowledge and spiritual insight, guiding us through the final stages of our journey and into the heart of the mystical narrative that had bound our destinies together.

⊱⋅⊶⊷⋅⊰

In the cooling shade of the ancient palm trees of Al-Hijr, under the watchful gaze of the temple's obsidian guardians, our group gathered close to hear the words of Ammar ibn Nadir, the spiritual guardian of the Obsidian Guild's most sacred secrets. Sherlock Holmes, his mind always alight with an insatiable thirst for knowledge, took the lead in our small gathering, his keen eyes fixed on Ammar's with an intensity that reflected the gravity of our quest.

"Sherlock Holmes," Ammar began, addressing him with a nod that acknowledged both his reputation and the role he would play in the unfolding narrative of the Guild. "The mysteries that surround the Obsidian Guild are as numerous as the stars that grace our desert skies at night. Yet they are not insurmountable. They only require the courage to seek and the wisdom to understand."

The air around us seemed to still as Ammar spoke, the soft murmur of the oasis' hidden streams the only sound that dared to break the silence. "This temple," he continued, gesturing to the rock-hewn structure that loomed behind him, "is far more than a mere sanctuary. It is a portal, a threshold between the realms of the physical and the spiritual. Here the veil that separates our world from the divine essence of the Stallions is at its thinnest, allowing those who are prepared to step beyond the limits of mortality and commune with ancient and elemental forces."

Sherlock, his curiosity clearly piqued, leaned closer. "And this ritual you speak of?" he asked, his voice a mixture of scepticism and intrigue. "What is its purpose, and how does it relate to the obsidian statuettes we're to reunite?"

Ammar's eyes, reflecting the depth of his knowledge and the weight of his duty, met Sherlock's. "The Ritual of the Obsidian Stallion is the culmination of our guild's quest for unity with the divine. The three statuettes, each a representation of the Stallion's essence - mind, body and spirit - have been scattered across the lands, separated by time and circumstance. Their reunification within the sacred confines of this temple is essential, for only together do they possess the power to pierce the veil and summon the vision of the Obsidian Stallion himself".

Holmes listened intently, his analytical mind working to reconcile these mystical elements with his rational view of the world. I noticed a flicker of awe in his usually steely eyes, a rare glimpse of wonder that seemed to soften his stern demeanour.

Adrien stepped forward, his eyes revealing the depth of his thought and curiosity. "And what of the alignment of the stars mentioned in the scroll? Does it play a role in the success of the ritual?" His question, rooted in his keen interest in the history and craftsmanship of artefacts, demonstrated his intellectual curiosity and dedication to understanding their cultural significance.

Ammar nodded, a slight smile playing on his lips. "Indeed, Adrien. The alignment of the stars acts as a conduit, amplifying the power of the statuettes and facilitating communion with the divine essence of the stallions. Their keen observation is essential to ensure that the ritual is performed at the precise moment".

As Ammar elaborated on the ritual, detailing the necessary preparations and the roles we each had to play, the scope of our journey expanded beyond the confines of mere physical exploration. We were embarking on a spiritual odyssey, one that promised not only to reveal the secrets of the Obsidian Guild, but also to offer us a glimpse into the very essence of existence.

"The statuettes," Ammar explained, "are not mere artefacts. They are keys - keys that unlock the door to understanding, to communion, and to the power that lies within the harmony of all things. Your quest to reunite them has been a trial, a test of your resolve, your courage, and your ability to see beyond the veil of the mundane.

Sherlock, ever the pragmatist, took in Ammar's words with a thoughtful expression, his mind no doubt racing to piece together the puzzle that lay before us. Yet there was a gleam in his eye that spoke of his willingness to embrace the unknown, to challenge the boundaries of his own staunchly rational worldview.

As the sun began its descent, casting long shadows across the oasis, our group, united by a common sense of purpose and destiny, prepared for the ritual that awaited us. In that moment, under the vast expanse of the desert sky, we stood on the threshold of revelation, ready to step beyond the boundaries of the known world and into the heart of the mystic.

As the sun dipped below the horizon, bathing Al-Hijr in golden light, we stood on the threshold of discovery. The vast desert behind us bore silent witness to our journey, while before us yawned the entrance to the temple, a dark promise carved into living rock. The air itself seemed charged with anticipation, the essence of our quest palpable in every breath.

Ammar ibn Nadir stood sentinel at the entrance, his robes shimmering with the palette of the desert - twilight blue, midday gold and the fiery red of dawn. His eyes met each of ours in turn, conveying the gravity of our impending steps without a word.

The oasis whispered around us, its verdant life a stark contrast to the stoic facade of the temple. Cool, fragrant air caressed our skin, carrying the scent of hidden flowers - nature's own incense for this sacred moment.

As we prepared to enter, I felt the bond between us grow stronger. No longer mere travellers thrown together by circumstance, we had become a community united by a purpose that transcended individual desires. Holmes, his usual scepticism tempered with wonder, stood tall beside me. Adrien's hands, so skilled in craftsmanship, trembled slightly with anticipation. Liyana's regal bearing seemed to soften, her connection to this land and its mysteries evident in her steady gaze. Amal's scholarly excitement was palpable, her mind no doubt racing with the historical significance of this moment.

The entrance to the temple, flanked by obsidian statues that seemed to absorb the fading light, beckoned us forward. As we stepped into the cool shadows, the smooth stone walls pulsated with an energy that defied rational explanation. Holmes ran his hand along the surface, his brow furrowed in concentration.

"Remarkable," he murmured. "The stone itself appears to be alive, Watson."

Deeper we ventured, the light from the entrance gradually giving way to darkness. Amal's steady voice offered comfort, sharing wisdom from her cultural heritage that seemed to calm our collective spirits. Liyana moved with grace through the darkening passage, her adaptability shining through as she faced each new challenge with quiet determination.

It was in this darkness that the true nature of our quest crystallised. We were not merely exploring an ancient sanctuary; we were delving into the very soul of the Obsidian Guild, seeking reunion with the forces that bind all life together. This was a journey beyond the physical, a quest for understanding that touched the very heart of existence.

As Ammar led us forward, the darkness deepened, testing our resolve and our faith. Yet within this shroud of mystery shone a promise - a promise of light, of revelation and of the unity we sought. We were walking a path shrouded in mystery, but it was a path we were destined to walk together, as guardians of a legacy that bridged the past and the future, the earth and the divine.

In this moment, on the cusp of revelation, we understood our journey as a microcosm of humanity's eternal quest - for knowledge, for connection, for the light that shines in the darkness. As we prepared to delve deeper into the hidden depths of the Temple, we carried with us not only the physical artefacts of our quest, but the hope that the secrets of the Obsidian Guild and the mystical Stallions would light a path for all seekers of truth.

Holmes, his voice uncharacteristically soft in the darkness, spoke for us all: "Whatever lies ahead, my friends, we will face it together. For at this moment we are more than individuals - we are the bearers of a sacred trust, the guardians of a wisdom long forgotten by the world outside. Let us proceed with courage, with open minds, and with hearts united in purpose.

And so, with Ammar leading the way, we stepped further into the unknown, each of us transformed by the journey that had brought us here, and each of us ready to face whatever revelations awaited us in the heart of this ancient sanctuary.

CHAPTER 29

RITUAL OF ILLUMINATION

Upon entering the innermost sanctum of the ancient temple of Al-Hijr, I was instantly hit by a deep sensation, causing me to inhale sharply. The very air around us seemed to thicken, heavy with the weight of countless ages and pregnant with anticipation. It was as if the stone walls themselves were alive, breathing with the whispered secrets of millennia.

The vast chamber that greeted us was a marvel of ancient architecture, its dimensions so vast that our small party seemed but an insignificant speck in its cavernous vastness. Flickering torches mounted at intervals along the walls cast a wavering amber light that danced across the intricate carvings that adorned every surface. These carvings, I marvelled, were not mere decoration, but an intricate tapestry of stories and histories, each line and curve etched with exquisite precision.

Holmes, ever the keen observer, moved with measured steps, his hawkish gaze darting from one carving to another. I could almost see the wheels of his formidable intellect turning as he pieced together the narrative unfolding before us.

"Watson," he murmured, his voice barely audible over the hushed atmosphere, "notice how these figures intertwine. See how the stallion motif recurs throughout, always close to human figures. It's as if the entire history of the Obsidian Guild is written on these walls.

Before I could answer, our guide, the enigmatic Ammar ibn Nadir, raised his hand for silence. His eyes, dark and unfathomable as the desert night, swept over our small group. When he spoke, his voice seemed to emanate not only from him, but from the very stones around us, rich and resonant with the echoes of ages past.

"Honoured guests," he intoned, each word weighted with meaning, "you are now standing in the very heart of Al-Hijr, a nexus where the veil between worlds becomes gossamer thin. Here, the legacy of the Obsidian Guild has been preserved for countless generations, waiting for those worthy to receive its profound wisdom".

As Ammar's words echoed through the chamber, I watched the reactions of our companions. Adrien d'Arcy, the master craftsman, stood transfixed, his eyes wide with wonder. His fingers, so skilled in working the leather, twitched at his sides as if longing to trace the intricate patterns carved into the ancient stone. Liyana Sultan, radiant in her regal bearing, stood tall and proud, yet I detected a slight tremor in her hand as it rested on the hilt of her ceremonial dagger.

The atmosphere became increasingly charged as Ammar continued his speech. The air itself seemed to vibrate with unseen energies, thick with the dust of time and redolent with the musty yet strangely invigorating scent of ancient stone. The torches flickered and dimmed in rhythmic pulses, as if responding to some inaudible heartbeat of the earth itself. Their flickering light cast ever-changing shadows across the carved figures, bringing them to life in a mesmerising dance that blurred the lines between past and present.

As our guide spoke of the sacred bond between horse and rider, of the timeless virtues of bravery, loyalty and wisdom, I felt a strange sensation. It was as if the boundaries of time were dissolving, the epochs collapsing into a single, eternal moment. I glanced at Holmes, half expecting to see his usual mask of scientific scepticism, but was startled to find an expression of unbridled wonder that I had rarely seen in all our years of friendship.

"My friends," Ammar concluded, his voice swelling with a power that seemed to shake the very foundations of the temple, "you stand now on the threshold of revelation. The secrets of the Obsidian Guild, long guarded by the sands of time, await your discovery. Prepare yourselves, for the mysteries that lie before you may challenge not only your understanding of the world, but the very essence of your being.

In that moment, as we stood united in purpose despite the different paths that had led us to this place, I felt a thrill of anticipation coursing through my veins. Whatever lay ahead, I knew with unshakable certainty that we were about to embark on the most extraordinary chapter of our lives. As I met Holmes' gaze, I saw in his eyes a reflection of my own thoughts - we were on the verge of a revelation that would forever change the course of history, and perhaps the very fabric of reality itself.

⊷≈⧞⊰⋉⊷⧞≈⊷

As we ventured deeper into the heart of the ancient temple, the air seemed to thicken with the weight of countless centuries. Every step we took echoed with a hushed reverence, as if the stone beneath our feet whispered tales of ages long past. The chamber we entered was a sanctuary of such profound silence that the beating of one's own heart seemed an intrusion upon its solemnity.

In the centre of this sacred space stood an altar, hewn from the same unyielding rock that formed the foundation of the temple. On this altar I beheld a sight that will forever be etched in my memory: three obsidian statuettes, their surfaces veined with metals that caught the flickering torchlight - silver, gold and crimson - each a testament to the virtues of the Obsidian Guild: bravery, loyalty and wisdom.

Ammar Ibn Nadir, our enigmatic leader and keeper of ancient lore, approached the altar with a reverence that had been forged by generations of sacred duty. As he stood before it, a solitary figure silhouetted against the backdrop of history, I felt a palpable shift in the atmosphere, as if the very stones of the temple held their breath in anticipation.

As Ammar began the ritual of reunion, his voice, rich and sonorous, filled the chamber with a chant in a language so ancient it seemed to predate civilisation itself. The sound was primal, a melody that transcended time, weaving through the air like a tangible thread connecting past and present. I glanced at Holmes, half expecting his usual scepticism, but instead found an expression of rapt attention, his keen eyes fixed on the unfolding spectacle.

As Ammar's chant intensified, a transformation of such remarkable nature took place that I could scarcely believe the evidence of my own senses. The obsidian statuettes began to glow, as if awakened from a millennia-long slumber. Their metallic veins pulsed with an inner light, casting an ethereal glow that illuminated the chamber in hues I had never seen before. The air around us vibrated with an unseen energy, charged with a power that seemed to emanate from the very essence of the temple itself.

The auras of the statues, now fully awakened, began to intertwine in a dance of shadow and light. Scenes of breathtaking vividness were painted on the ancient walls: great battles of antiquity, majestic stallions racing across the endless desert sands, sages passing on wisdom through the ages. It was as if the spirits of the legendary steeds of the Obsidian Guild had been summoned, their presence filling the chamber with an overwhelming sense of unity and purpose.

I watched my companions, each of them enthralled by the unfolding miracle. Adrien d'Arcy, the master leatherworker, stood transfixed, his craftsman's eyes wide with wonder. He saw his own journey reflected in the glowing statuettes - a bridge between the legacy of Maison d'Arcy and the innovations of the future. Liyana Sultan, her regal bearing enhanced by the mystical light, seemed to embody the very essence of the equestrian world, her connection to her beloved Muntasir reflected in the tales of the legendary stallions brought to life before us.

Dr El-Sharif, ever the scholar, watched with a keen intellect, her mind no doubt piecing together the historical and cultural significance of what we were witnessing. And Khalid Al-Fahmi, guardian of his heritage, stood as if rooted to the spot, the ritual speaking to the core of his being, a living embodiment of the delicate balance between tradition and progress.

As for Holmes, I saw in his face a transformation I had never seen before. The veil of cool logic that typically shrouded his features had lifted, replaced by an expression of unbridled wonder. It was then that I realised that we were witnessing something beyond the bounds of rational explanation, a truth that even the analytical mind of the great detective could not deny.

As the ritual finally reached its crescendo, the chamber was filled with a sense of completion so profound that it seemed to reverberate through the very fabric of reality. As the vibrations subsided and the unearthly light began to fade, we were left in a silence more eloquent than any words, each of us forever changed by what we had witnessed.

In the aftermath, as we stood together, a diverse group united by this extraordinary experience, I felt a sense of purpose and clarity unlike any I had known before. The Obsidian Guild, with its legacy of unity and virtue, had opened our eyes to the possibilities that lay at the intersection of past and future. We had been given a glimpse of the eternal truths that bound all humanity - bravery, loyalty and wisdom - not as relics of a bygone era, but as guiding lights for the journey ahead.

As I met Holmes' gaze in the fading glow of the statuettes, I knew with unshakable certainty that our adventure, far from over, had only just begun. Whatever challenges lay beyond the walls of this ancient temple, we would face them transformed, bearers of a sacred knowledge that would shape not only our own destinies, but perhaps the course of history itself.

⬦⬥⬦⬥⬦

In the wake of the ritual's crescendo, a silence of such profound intensity descended upon the chamber that I thought I could hear the beating of my own heart. This silence, heavy with the weight of millennia, was not just the absence of sound, but a palpable presence, as if the very air had been transformed into a medium for carrying the whispers of ages past.

It was in this moment of exquisite silence that the chamber began to glow with an unearthly luminescence. The rough-hewn walls, which moments before had been solid and unyielding, now seemed to dissolve before our eyes, giving way to a vista of such breathtaking beauty that I found myself utterly incapable of speech.

Before us stretched an endless expanse of desert, bathed in the silvery glow of a moon that seemed impossibly large and close. The night sky above was a tapestry of stars, so vivid and numerous that they seemed to be moving, weaving patterns of celestial significance. It was a landscape that spoke not of our mundane world, but of a realm where the very fabric of reality was malleable to the whims of higher powers.

From the depths of this ethereal desert emerged three figures, their forms at once solid and spectral. They were stallions of such magnificent bearing that no earthly steed could hope to match them. As they drew closer, their individual characteristics became apparent, each a living embodiment of the virtues we had seen reflected in the obsidian statuettes.

It was at this point that Khalid Al-Fahmi stepped forward, his eyes glowing with a fire of recognition. When he spoke, his voice carried the resonance of countless generations, as if the spirits of his ancestors were speaking through him.

"Behold," he intoned, his words seeming to merge with the vision itself, "Al-Sabah, the light of the dawn.

The stallion he pointed to was a creature of living flame, its coat a deep, pulsating crimson that reminded me of the first rays of sunlight breaking over the horizon. As he moved, trails of fire seemed to follow in his wake, each hoofbeat igniting the very air.

"In him we see the embodiment of bravery," Khalid continued, his voice full of emotion. "He charges headlong into the unknown, fear unknown to his noble heart. Yet his courage is not mere recklessness, but a beacon to guide those who would follow in his footsteps."

My gaze was then drawn to the second stallion, a creature of such ethereal beauty that it seemed to have been fashioned from the moonlight itself.

"This," Khalid said, his tone softening, "is Al-Wafaa, the Silver Heart. In him we see loyalty given form. His strength lies not in brute force, but in the unbreakable bonds he forges. He is the companion who stands firm when all others have fallen.

The third stallion was unlike any creature I had ever seen. Its coat shimmered with a golden glow that seemed to emanate not only from its surface, but from some inner source of light.

"And finally," Khalid's voice, barely above a whisper now, but carrying to every corner of the chamber, "we have Al-Hikmah, the Golden Wisdom. It is the culmination of experience, the quiet strength that comes not from youth and vigour, but from a lifetime of learning and understanding".

As we watched in awe, the three stallions began to move in perfect unison, their individual trails of light intertwining to form a single, radiant path. It was a display of such harmony and grace that I felt tears well up in my eyes.

I glanced at my companions, each lost in their own profound experience of the vision. Holmes, whose rational mind I had so often seen dismiss such mystical occurrences, stood with an expression of pure wonder on his face. For once, his sharp analytical gaze was softened, replaced by a look of childlike awe that I had never seen before.

Adrien d'Arcy, the master craftsman, watched with an intensity that spoke of deep professional admiration. His fingers twitched at his sides as if longing to capture the essence of what he saw in his own creations.

Liyana Sultan stood tall and proud, her eyes shining with unshed tears. At that moment, I saw in her not only the regal bearing of nobility, but the weight of a cultural heritage that stretches back through the ages.

Dr Amal El-Sharif's eyes darted back and forth, her quick mind no doubt cataloguing every detail of the vision, making connections and forming hypotheses even in the face of such an overwhelming mystical display.

As the vision began to fade, the desert and its magnificent inhabitants slowly dissolving back into the solid stone of the chamber walls, I felt a profound sense of loss, as if I had been granted a glimpse of a higher reality and was now being cast back into the mundane world.

But as I looked around at my companions, I realised that something fundamental had changed. We stood not as disparate individuals, but as a unified whole, bound together by the shared experience of something truly transcendent. At that moment I understood that our quest had changed irrevocably. We were no longer merely seeking answers to an ancient mystery, but had become part of that mystery ourselves, charged with carrying the wisdom of the ages into an uncertain future.

As the last echoes of the vision faded, leaving us once more in the dim, torch-lit chamber, I caught Holmes' eye. In that shared glance, I saw a reflection of my own thoughts - whatever challenges lay ahead, we would face them not only with our usual resourcefulness and determination, but with the combined strength of courage, loyalty and wisdom that had been so vividly demonstrated to us. Our journey, I realised, had only just begun.

As we stood contemplating the night's revelations, a soft chirping caught my attention. Muntasir, Liyana's trusty steed, had approached our group, ears pricked forward and nostrils flared as if sensing the lingering traces of magic in the air.

Liyana approached her mount and placed a gentle hand on his neck. "He senses it too," she said, her voice filled with wonder. "The presence of Al-Sabah, Al-Wafaa and Al-Hikmah. It's as if the vision has awakened something in him."

Indeed, as I watched Muntasir more closely, I noticed a change in his bearing. The horse stood taller, his eyes shining with an almost human awareness. As he turned his gaze towards the temple entrance, I could have sworn I saw a flicker of recognition, as if he too had glimpsed the legendary stallions in this mystical vision.

"It seems," Holmes remarked, his tone one of fascination, "that our equine companions are as much a part of this unfolding mystery as we are. Perhaps even more so."

The moment served as a poignant reminder that the legacy of the Obsidian Guild was not merely a human affair, but a testament to the enduring bond between man and horse, a bond that ran far deeper than any of us had previously imagined.

As the ethereal vision of the three stallions faded from our sight, leaving us once more within the confines of the ancient chamber, a profound silence fell upon our company. It was a silence pregnant with meaning, as if the very air around us had been transformed into a medium for silent contemplation. The obsidian statuettes on the altar, which moments before had blazed with otherworldly light, now emitted a soft, pulsating glow reminiscent of a steady heartbeat - a tangible reminder of the mystical experience we had just shared.

I was overcome with emotion; my medical training and years of adventure alongside Holmes had done little to prepare me for the magnitude of what we had witnessed. Looking around at my companions, I saw that each of them was similarly affected, their faces reflecting a mixture of awe, introspection and new-found determination.

It was Adrien d'Arcy who first broke the silence. His voice, usually so calm when discussing his craft, now carried a tremor of emotion that reflected the profound impact of our shared experience.

"By Jove," he began, his eyes still fixed on the gently glowing statuettes, "I confess that when I first embarked on this extraordinary journey, I could not have imagined the depths to which it would challenge and alter my very being. The legacy of the Obsidian Guild, the unity of virtues it espouses - bravery, loyalty, wisdom - these are not mere abstractions, but living truths that I have seen reflected in each of you, my dear companions."

He paused, his hands moving as if caressing an invisible piece of leather. "They are the same principles that have always guided my craft, though I see them now with a clarity I have not possessed before. The essence of our work, whether in leather or in life, lies not in the materials we use, but in the spirit and intention we put into our efforts".

Liyana Sultan spoke next, her regal bearing now tempered with a soft vulnerability I had not observed before. Her words carried the weight of centuries, bridging the gap between her noble lineage and the mystical revelation we shared.

"To stand within these hallowed walls," she said, her voice resonating with emotion, "to bear witness to the unfolding legacy of the Obsidian Guild has been nothing short of a revelation. It has illuminated for me the true nature of the bond between horse and rider, the link between past and present. It is more than tradition - it is the very foundation upon which we must build our future.

Her eyes, bright with unshed tears, met each of ours in turn. "As we carry on this legacy, I am reminded of my own sacred duty as a guardian of the treasures of my culture, a living bridge between the old world and the new. It is a mantle I will wear with both pride and humility, inspired by the unity and strength I have witnessed in all of you.

Dr Amal El-Sharif, ever the scholar, delivered her remarks in a measured tone that did little to disguise the excitement underlying her words.

"Our extraordinary journey," she began, her gaze sweeping over the assembled group, "stands as undeniable proof of the power inherent in unity amidst diversity. The legacy of the Guild, with its emphasis on the synthesis of virtues, serves as a poignant reminder of the strength that lies in our collective endeavour."

She paused, her brow furrowed in thought. "As we face the challenges that undoubtedly await us, it is this unity - this shared commitment to the principles of valour, loyalty and wisdom - that must be our guiding light. As a scholar, and as one who straddles the fine line between two worlds, I am compelled to recognise that our pursuit of knowledge and truth is not merely an academic exercise, but a moral imperative, informed by the virtues so vividly exemplified by the Guild".

It was then that Khalid, his weathered visage a map of the desert itself, spoke. His words carried the weight of ancient wisdom, as if the spirits of his ancestors were speaking through him.

"The path before us," he intoned, his eyes fixed on the softly glowing statuettes, "is not an end, but a new beginning. We are called to carry the legacy of the Obsidian Guild into the world beyond these temple walls. In the unity of the stallions, in the harmony of their virtues, we have glimpsed a reflection of our own latent power - a power that resides not in individual prowess, but in our ability to stand as one, to support and uplift one another".

His gaze, penetrating and filled with an inner fire, met each of ours in turn. "As we venture forth, let us do so with the unflinching courage of Al-Sabah, the unwavering loyalty of Al-Wafaa, and the boundless wisdom of Al-Hikmah guiding our every step."

As Khalid's words faded into the hushed atmosphere of the room, I felt a sense of determination settle over our group like a cloak. It was a shared commitment, unspoken but palpable, to carry on the legacy that had been entrusted to us. The path ahead, though shrouded in uncertainty, now seemed illuminated by the light of our new-found unity and purpose.

I turned to Holmes, curious to see how my friend, so often sceptical of matters beyond the realm of cold logic, had been affected by our shared experience. To my astonishment, I found his piercing grey eyes glowing with a fire I had rarely seen. When he spoke, his voice carried a conviction that sent shivers down my spine.

"My dear friends," he said, sweeping his eyes over our assembled group, "we stand on the threshold of a new chapter in our shared adventure. The mysteries we have witnessed, the truths we have uncovered, have changed the very fabric of our understanding. As we move forward, we do so not merely as individuals bound by circumstance, but as custodians of a legacy that spans the breadth of human history."

He paused, his hand unconsciously moving to rest on the pocket where I knew he kept the golden-veined statuette. "Whatever challenges may lie ahead, whatever forces may array themselves against us, we will meet them with the combined strength of courage, loyalty and wisdom. Our quest, I fear, is far from over - indeed, it may have just begun in earnest."

As Holmes finished, I felt a surge of anticipation run through me. The chamber around us, with its ancient stones and mystical aura, seemed to pulse with the promise of adventures yet to come. We stood together, no longer mere travellers on a common journey, but a unified force, ready to face whatever trials lay ahead with the legacy of the Obsidian Guild as our guide and strength.

In that moment, as the soft glow of the statuettes cast our shadows across the chamber walls, I knew with unshakable certainty that our lives had been irrevocably changed. The path ahead was fraught with danger and uncertainty, but I felt no fear. For in the unity we had forged, in the wisdom we had gained, I saw the dawn of a new era - one in which the ancient virtues of the Obsidian Guild would once again shine as a beacon in a world too often shrouded in darkness.

As we emerged from the depths of the ancient temple into the vast expanse of the Arabian night, I was struck by the profound sense of transformation that had descended upon our small company. The cool desert air, laden with the subtle scent of distant oases and the earthy aroma of sun-baked sand, caressed our faces like a blessing, soothing our spirits after the intense revelations we had experienced within the sacred chambers.

As we emerged from the temple into the cool night air, I noticed Holmes pause, his gaze drawn to Al-Zarib. The magnificent stallion stood apart from our group, his coat gleaming like polished obsidian in the starlight. Holmes approached him with a reverence I had rarely seen my friend display.

"Watson," Holmes called softly, never taking his eyes off Al-Zarib, "come and watch."

I joined Holmes and together we watched as he held out his hand to the horse. Al-Zarib lowered his head and met Holmes' palm with his velvet muzzle. In that moment, I witnessed a profound connection that transcended the boundaries between man and beast. Holmes' eyes, usually sharp with analytical focus, now held a depth of understanding that spoke of secrets shared without words.

"Extraordinary," Holmes murmured, his voice thick with emotion. "In all my years, Watson, I have never met a being quite like Al-Zarib. He possesses an intelligence, a wisdom, that defies all rational explanation."

As if in response to Holmes' words, Al-Zarib's eyes seemed to glow with an inner light reminiscent of the crimson fire we had witnessed during our harrowing escape from the Sons of Purity. It was a powerful reminder of the mystical bond that had formed between my friend and this remarkable creature.

Above us, the heavens stretched out in a tapestry of unimaginable beauty, each star a glittering jewel set against the velvety darkness. The moon, a pale crescent, cast a silvery light over the undulating dunes, creating a landscape that seemed more dreamlike than real. In this ethereal setting, our group - Holmes, Adrien d'Arcy, Liyana Sultan, Dr Amal El-Sharif, Khalid Al-Fahmi and myself - stood in silent communion, bound together by an experience that had irrevocably changed the course of our lives.

It was Holmes who first broke the silence, his piercing grey eyes reflecting the myriad stars above as he spoke. "My dear friends," he began, his voice carrying a note of solemnity I had rarely heard, "we stand here under this canopy of celestial wonders as changed men and women. Our quest, which began as a mere investigation, has led us to truths far more profound than I could ever have anticipated."

He paused, his gaze sweeping over our assembled group. "The legacy of the Obsidian Guild, with its trinity of virtues - bravery, loyalty and wisdom - now resides within each of us. Like the stars that have guided travellers for millennia, these principles will be our guiding light as we navigate the uncertain waters that lie ahead".

Adrien d'Arcy spoke next, his face etched with the gravity of our shared experience. "By Jove," he exclaimed softly, his eyes fixed on the distant horizon, "I confess that when I first embarked on this extraordinary journey, I could not have imagined the depths to which it would transform me. The legacy we have uncovered has given my craft a meaning I could never have imagined".

His hands, those skilful instruments of his trade, moved expressively as he continued. "Every piece I create from now on will be a testament to the enduring bond between horse and rider, a physical manifestation of the virtues we have witnessed. The spirit of the Obsidian Guild will live on in every stitch, every carefully crafted design.

Liyana Sultan, her regal bearing now tempered with a newfound humility, added her voice to the discourse. "Gentlemen," she began, her words carrying the warmth of the desert wind, "and Dr El-Sharif, I stand before you profoundly changed. The unfolding of the legacy of the Obsidian Guild has awakened in me a deeper understanding of my role as guardian of the treasures of my culture."

Her eyes, bright with emotion, met each of ours in turn. "I see now that my duty goes beyond mere preservation. I am called to be a living bridge between worlds, to weave the timeless virtues of courage, loyalty and wisdom into the fabric of our rapidly changing world".

Dr Amal El-Sharif, her scholarly demeanour aglow with intellectual fervour, offered her reflections with measured passion. "Our extraordinary odyssey," she began, her gaze sweeping across the star-studded sky, "has illuminated the paramount importance of unity in diversity. The legacy of the Obsidian Guild, with its emphasis on the harmonious interplay of virtues, serves as a potent reminder of the strength that lies in our collective endeavour."

She paused, her brow furrowed in thought. "As we venture forth to face the challenges that undoubtedly await us, it is this shared commitment to enduring principles that shall be our guiding light. Our pursuit of knowledge and truth is no longer a mere academic exercise, but a moral imperative informed by the timeless wisdom we have discovered."

It was then that Khalid, his weathered visage a living map of the desert itself, spoke. His words carried the weight of ancient wisdom, as if the spirits of his ancestors were speaking through him.

"My friends," he intoned, his eyes fixed on the constellation-studded sky, "our journey does not end with our departure from this sacred place. Rather, it marks the beginning of a new beginning. We have been entrusted with a sacred duty - to carry the legacy of the Obsidian Guild into the world beyond these sands.

His gaze, penetrating and filled with an inner fire, met each of ours in turn. "In the unity of the stallions, in the harmony of their virtues, we have glimpsed a reflection of our own latent strength. Let us go forth with the indomitable courage of Al-Sabah, the unwavering loyalty of Al-Wafaa and the boundless wisdom of Al-Hikmah as our constant companions.

As Khalid's words faded into the stillness of the desert night, I felt a deep sense of purpose settle over our group. We stood together, no longer mere travellers bound by circumstance, but a unified force, custodians of a legacy that spanned the breadth of human history.

I turned to Holmes, curious to see how my friend, so often sceptical of matters beyond the realm of cold logic, had been affected by our shared experience. To my astonishment, I found his piercing grey eyes glowing with a fire I had rarely seen. When he spoke, his voice carried a conviction that sent shivers down my spine.

"My dear Watson," he said, his gaze fixed on the distant horizon, "we stand on the threshold of a new chapter in our adventure together. The mysteries we have witnessed, the truths we have uncovered, have changed the very fabric of our understanding. Whatever challenges may lie ahead, whatever forces may array themselves against us, we will meet them with the combined strength of courage, loyalty and wisdom.

As we turned our faces to the journey ahead, each step charged with the essence of the legacy we had unearthed, I knew with unshakable certainty that our lives had been irrevocably changed. The wisdom of the Obsidian Guild, like the desert itself - vast and timeless beneath the eternal stars - would guide us onward, a beacon of unity and purpose in the ever-unfolding story of our extraordinary lives.

CHAPTER 30

THE DESERT'S PARTING WISDOM

I n the tranquil oasis of Al-Hijr, our small gathering came together for one final evening, as the sun's fading light created a stunning display of amber and rose in the sky. The air was thick with the scent of rare desert flowers and the weight of impending farewells. We sat in a circle on ornate carpets, the flickering light of the campfire casting dancing shadows on our weathered faces.

The mysterious structures of Al-Hijr rose from the sands around us, their weathered facades bearing witness to a civilisation long gone. Ancient ruins and elaborate rock-cut tombs stood silent and watchful, while in the distance the soft whisper of the wind through the sparse vegetation provided a soothing counterpoint to the crackling of the flames.

Holmes, his slender frame silhouetted against the deepening twilight, broke the contemplative silence. "My dear friends," he began, his keen eyes reflecting the firelight, "we stand on the threshold of our return to the world we left behind. Yet I dare say that none of us will cross that threshold unchanged."

A murmur of agreement rippled through our gathering. Khalid, his face etched with the wisdom of the desert, spoke next. "Indeed, Mr Holmes. The sands of Al-Hijr have a way of stripping away disguises and revealing one's true nature. I have guided many through these lands, but never have I witnessed such a profound transformation as I have seen in each of you.

Dr Amal El-Sharif, her scholarly demeanour softened by the intimacy of the moment, nodded thoughtfully. "This journey has bridged worlds for me," she confessed, a note of wonder in her voice. "I came in search of historical truths and found instead a living legacy. The Obsidian Guild is not just a relic of the past, but a beacon for our future."

Adrien d'Arcy, typically reserved, surprised us all with the passion in his voice. "I confess I began this journey as a sceptic," he said, his eyes shining in the firelight. "But the artistry, the craftsmanship that I've seen here in these ancient structures... it's awakened something in me. I feel compelled to carry on this legacy in my own work.

Liyana Sultan, her regal bearing tempered by our shared trials, spoke next. "In honouring my brother's memory, I have discovered strengths within myself that I never knew existed," she said softly. "The wisdom of the Obsidian Guild, so long hidden in this remote oasis, shall guide my path in art and life."

As each of my companions shared their reflections, I, Dr John Watson, found myself overwhelmed by the enormity of the task before me. How could mere words on paper hope to capture the profound changes we had undergone? The secrets we had unlocked in these enigmatic ruins? The bonds we had forged in this hidden oasis city?

Holmes, ever perceptive, seemed to sense my inner turmoil. "Watson, my dear fellow," he said, his voice carrying an unusual warmth, "I have no doubt that your chronicles will do justice to our extraordinary adventures. Your pen has always been able to capture not only the facts, but the essence of our experiences."

As the night deepened and the stars came out in their full desert glory, our conversation flowed like the hidden streams beneath the sands of Al-Hijr. We spoke of the challenges that lay ahead in bringing the wisdom of the Obsidian Guild to a world of steam engines and telegraphs. We shared our hopes and fears for the future, each of us forever changed by the crucible of our journey.

In those final hours, as the ancient oasis city of Al-Hijr stood guard around us, I felt a profound sense of both end and beginning. We were no longer mere travellers or adventurers, but guardians of a sacred trust, charged with carrying the light of ancient wisdom into the dawn of a new era.

As the first hints of dawn began to colour the eastern sky, we fell into a contemplative silence. The weight of our experiences, the transformations we had undergone, and the responsibilities we now carried, fell upon us like a cloak. The journey ahead would be fraught with challenges, but we faced them with the strength born of our shared experiences and the unbreakable bond forged in the crucible of Al-Hijr, this hidden oasis that had revealed to us the secrets of ages past.

❦❦❦❦❦

As the first golden rays of the Arabian sun crept over the horizon, painting the vast expanse of Al-Hijr in shades of amber and rose, our intrepid company began the painstaking task of breaking camp. The dawn air, crisp and laden with the subtle scent of ancient stone and rare desert flowers, heralded not only the birth of a new day, but the beginning of our journey back to the world we had left behind. The cool sand beneath our feet shifted gently with the morning breeze, whispering a farewell in a language only the desert could understand.

My dear friend and compatriot, Sherlock Holmes, ever the paragon of calm and foresight, was overseeing our preparations with his characteristic acumen. His tall, lean figure, silhouetted against the burgeoning light, cut a decisive path through the gentle chaos of our dismantling efforts. Every pack, every piece of equipment came under his scrutinising eye, ensuring that no detail was overlooked in our exodus from this land of ancient mysteries and profound revelations.

As I helped to pack our scientific instruments, I found my eyes constantly drawn to the majestic ruins that surrounded us. The rock-cut tombs and intricately carved facades of Al-Hijr stood sentinel, their weathered surfaces glistening in the early morning light. It struck me then, with a poignancy that took my breath away, that we might be the last eyes to behold this hidden wonder for many years to come.

"I say, Holmes," I ventured, my voice hushed with reverence, "does it not seem a terrible shame to leave such wonders behind? To think that these ancient wonders might once again be swallowed by the sands of time and memory."

Holmes paused in his work, his piercing grey eyes scanning the landscape with an intensity I had rarely seen. "Indeed, Watson," he replied, his voice carrying an unusual note of wistfulness. "But perhaps it is fitting that Al-Hijr should retain its secrets. The world is not yet ready for all that this place might reveal. We carry with us not only the physical evidence of our discoveries, but a profound responsibility to use that knowledge wisely."

Our companions, each absorbed in their own preparations, seemed equally affected by the solemnity of our departure. Adrien d'Arcy, his artistic soul clearly stirred, sketched furiously in his notebook, as if trying to capture every last detail of our surroundings. Dr Amal El-Sharif moved from ruin to ruin, her fingers reverently tracing the ancient stone, her lips moving in silent communion with the past.

Liyana Sultan stood apart, her regal bearing accentuated by the backdrop of the ancient city. As she surveyed the landscape, I thought I could see the weight of her heritage in the set of her shoulders, the pride of her lineage in the lift of her chin. Beside her, Khalid Al-Fahmi, our indefatigable guide, seemed to embody the spirit of the desert itself, his weathered features as timeless as the stones themselves.

As the final packs were secured and the last traces of our camp erased, we gathered for a moment of silent contemplation. The rising sun cast long shadows across the sand, the play of light and dark across the ruins creating an ever-changing tableau of breathtaking beauty. I felt a strange mixture of emotions at that moment - a deep sadness at leaving this place of wonder, coupled with an undeniable excitement for the journey ahead.

Holmes, sensing the mood of our company, spoke words that I shall always carry with me. "My friends," he said, his voice carrying clearly in the still morning air, "we stand at the threshold of two worlds. Behind us is the ancient wisdom of Al-Hijr, before us are the challenges of our modern age. Let us go forth not as mere travellers returning from a sojourn, but as guardians of a sacred trust. The legacy of the Obsidian Guild, the secrets of this hidden oasis, are now ours to preserve and share, with all the responsibility that such knowledge entails.

With these words still ringing in our ears, we mounted our steeds. The horses, sensing the importance of the moment, stood proud and eager, their coats gleaming in the early light. At a signal from Holmes, our little caravan began to move, the soft thunder of hooves on sand marking the start of our journey home.

As we crested the first dune, I turned in my saddle to catch a last glimpse of Al-Hijr. The oasis town seemed to shimmer in the growing heat, its ruins beginning to take on the aspect of a half-remembered dream. Yet I knew, with a certainty that defied rational explanation, that the impact of our time in this mystical place would reverberate through all our future endeavours.

Looking forward once more, I urged my mount to Holmes' side. The road ahead was long and arduous, leading us back to the familiar territories of our former lives. But as I watched the determined set of my friend's jaw, the purposeful stance of our companions, I knew that we would not return as we had come, but as something more - bearers of ancient wisdom, guardians of forgotten knowledge, forever changed by the crucible of Al-Hijr.

⊕⊙⊛⊙⊛

As we began our arduous journey from the mystical oasis of Al-Hijr towards the ancient city of Damascus, the vast expanse of the Arabian desert unfolded before us like a great tawny carpet. The sun, a merciless ball of golden fire, beat down on our little caravan with unrelenting intensity, turning the air itself into a shimmering veil that distorted the horizon.

Our horses, noble beasts of impeccable pedigree, bore the weight of our expedition with stoic endurance. Their hooves, muffled by the soft sand, created a rhythmic cadence that served as a constant reminder of our progress through this seemingly endless landscape. Holmes, ever alert, sat astride his mount with the easy grace of a natural horseman, his keen eyes constantly scanning our surroundings for any sign of danger or point of interest.

As we traversed the rugged terrain, our path took us through a series of small settlements and oases, each a welcome respite from the unforgiving desert. These pockets of life, like miracles of nature rising from the arid earth, offered us not only the chance to replenish our supplies, but also to observe the timeless ways of the desert dwellers.

It was during one such stop, as we rested in the shade of a cluster of date palms, that our conversation turned to the application of the wisdom of the Obsidian Guild in our modern world. Dr Amal El-Sharif, her scholarly mind ever active, asked a question that had clearly been weighing on her mind.

"Gentlemen," she began, her voice carrying the measured tones of an academic, "and Lady Liyana, I find myself pondering how we can best translate the profound teachings of the Obsidian Guild into practical applications for our rapidly changing society. How can we bridge the gap between the timeless wisdom of the ancients and the frenetic pace of our industrial age?"

Holmes, fingers clasped under his chin in his characteristic pose of deep contemplation, was the first to answer. "A most pertinent question, Dr El-Sharif. I believe the key lies not in trying to transplant ancient practices wholesale into our modern world, but rather in distilling the essential principles that underpin them."

Adrien d'Arcy, who had been listening intently, nodded in agreement. "Indeed, Mr Holmes. In my craft, I have often found that the most enduring techniques are those that adapt to new materials and technologies while remaining true to their fundamental principles. Perhaps the same could be said for the wisdom of the Obsidian Guild."

Liyana Sultan, her regal bearing tempered by the informal setting, offered her own insight. "In my experience, the power of art lies in its ability to convey complex ideas in a form that speaks to the heart as well as the mind. Could we not use artistic expression as a means of making the Guild's teachings accessible to a wider audience?"

As our journey continued, these conversations became a constant thread weaving through the fabric of our days. We debated the merits of different approaches, each of us bringing a unique perspective to the challenge of preserving and disseminating the ancient wisdom that had been entrusted to us.

As we approached Damascus, the landscape began to change. The endless sea of sand gave way to more varied terrain, with rocky outcrops and sparse vegetation hinting at the proximity of civilisation. But even as the first signs of the great city appeared on the horizon, I felt a strange sense of loss. The profound solitude of Al-Hijr, with its mystical aura and timeless beauty, had affected us all more deeply than we had realised.

Our arrival in Damascus was a shock to the senses after the vast emptiness of the desert. The bustling streets, filled with the clamour of countless voices and the pungent aromas of spices and human habitation, were in stark contrast to the serene silence we had left behind. As we made our way through the narrow alleys to our lodgings, I watched with interest the reactions of my companions.

Holmes, his face a mask of concentration, seemed to be cataloguing every detail of our new surroundings. Dr El-Sharif's eyes shone with scholarly excitement at the historical treasures that surrounded us. Adrien d'Arcy seemed almost overwhelmed by the riot of colours and textures, his artist's soul clearly stirred by the vibrant life of the city. Liyana Sultan, though clearly at ease in this more familiar setting, wore an expression of wistful nostalgia, as if a part of her remained in the timeless sands of Al-Hijr.

As for me, my thoughts turned to the challenge that lay before us. How were we to preserve the profound truths we had discovered in the desert while navigating the complexities of our modern world? The wisdom of the Obsidian Guild, so clear and resonant in the silence of Al-Hijr, now seemed as elusive as a desert mirage in the face of the frenetic energy of Damascus.

But as I watched my companions, each lost in their own reflections, I felt a surge of hope. If any group was capable of bridging the gap between ancient wisdom and modern life, it was surely this extraordinary collection of minds and talents. With renewed determination, I squared my shoulders and followed Holmes into the heart of Damascus, ready to face whatever challenges lay ahead in this next phase of our remarkable journey. CopyRetry

As the first whistle of the Damascus-Aleppo locomotive pierced the morning air, our little party found itself on the busy platform of Damascus station. The scene before us was one of organised chaos, a stark contrast to the serene solitude we had so recently left behind in the depths of the Arabian desert. The iron beast that would carry us north stood gleaming in the early light, its polished brass fittings shining and great plumes of steam rising from its chimney.

Holmes, ever the keen observer, stood by my side, his hawkish gaze darting from one point of interest to another. "Observe, Watson," he murmured, his voice barely audible over the din of the station, "how quickly mankind adapts to the march of progress. Barely a decade has passed since this railway first carved its way through the ancient lands, and already it seems as natural a part of the landscape as the hills themselves."

I nodded in agreement, my own attention drawn to the fascinating process of loading our equine companions into specially designed wagons. The horses, including Al-Zarib and Muntasir, seemed to regard this novel mode of transport with a mixture of curiosity and trepidation. Adrien d'Arcy, ever mindful of the animals' welfare, watched the proceedings with a wary eye.

"I must confess, Holmes," I said as we boarded our own compartment, "that I am of two minds about this leg of our journey. While I cannot deny the marvels of modern engineering which allow us to traverse in hours what would once have taken days, I fear that we may lose something of the intimacy with the land that our desert sojourn afforded us."

My friend's lips twitched in that subtle smile I had come to know so well. "Ah, but therein lies the crux of our current predicament, does it not? The very challenge we face as we seek to integrate the wisdom of the Obsidian Guild into our rapidly changing world."

As the train began to move, we settled into our seats, joined by Dr El-Sharif and Liyana Sultan. Through the window, the landscape began to unfold before us, a tapestry of increasing greenery that spoke of our gradual return to more hospitable climes. The conversation, like the scenery, flowed with an easy rhythm, punctuated by the steady clickety-clack of wheels on rails.

"It occurs to me," Dr El-Sharif began, her scholarly tone tinged with excitement, "that we are witnessing at first hand the very collision of ancient and modern that we have been discussing. This railway, a marvel of Western engineering, cuts through lands that have seen the rise and fall of countless civilisations. How do we reconcile the wisdom of the ages with the relentless march of progress?"

Liyana, her regal bearing softened by the casual surroundings of our compartment, leaned forward with interest. "Perhaps the answer lies not in reconciliation, but in synthesis," she suggested. "Just as this train allows us to cross great distances while still observing the land we pass through, might we not find a way to bring the essence of ancient wisdom into the modern age?"

Holmes, who had been gazing out of the window with an air of deep contemplation, turned back to the group. "An astute observation, Lady Liyana. It reminds me of a case I once encountered in London, where a series of apparently modern crimes were actually rooted in an ancient vendetta. The solution lay not in dismissing either the old or the new, but in understanding how they were intertwined.

As our journey continued, the landscape outside our window underwent a remarkable transformation. The arid outskirts of Damascus gave way to rolling hills and, eventually, glimpses of the fertile Euphrates valley. With every mile we travelled, the signs of human habitation became more frequent - villages, then towns, each a testament to the inexorable spread of civilisation.

Adrien, who had joined us after making sure the horses were comfortable, surveyed the passing scenery with an artist's eye. "It's remarkable," he mused, "how the land itself seems to tell the story of human progress. From the timeless desert to these cultivated fields, every view speaks of the eternal dance between man and nature."

As we approached Aleppo, our discussions took on a more practical tone. How could we, in our various spheres of influence, become conduits for this great synthesis between ancient wisdom and modern progress? Dr El-Sharif spoke of academic programmes that would bridge cultural and temporal divides.

Liyana envisioned art exhibitions that would bring the spirit of the desert to the great cities of Europe. Adrien envisioned a new line of handicrafts that would combine traditional techniques with contemporary designs.

Throughout, I found myself furiously scribbling notes, determined to capture not just the words but the essence of these transformative ideas. Holmes, I noticed, listened with rapt attention, his keen mind no doubt already formulating strategies for implementing these concepts in our future endeavours.

As the spires and minarets of Aleppo came into view, I was struck by a profound sense of transition. We had begun our journey in the timeless depths of the desert, custodians of an ancient heritage. Now, as we steamed into the heart of one of the oldest continuously inhabited cities in the world, we found ourselves ambassadors of that heritage to the modern world.

The train whistle sounded, signalling our imminent arrival. As we gathered our belongings and prepared to disembark, I caught Holmes' eye. The look we exchanged spoke volumes - of challenges faced and overcome, of mysteries unravelled, and of the great work still ahead. For in bridging the gap between the ancient wisdom of the Obsidian Guild and the relentless progress of our modern world, we had embarked on perhaps our greatest adventure yet.

※◆※◆※

As we left the ancient city of Aleppo, our journey took on a new character, combining the modern convenience of rail travel with the time-honoured tradition of horseback. The Damascus-Aleppo railway, a marvel of engineering that had only recently made its way through these ancient lands, would take us part of the way to Adana. However, the incomplete nature of the railway network meant that we would also have to rely on our equine companions for parts of our journey.

The transition from Syria to Turkey was marked by subtle but noticeable shifts in the cultural landscape. As we crossed the border, I observed with great interest the gradual changes in the architecture, dress and even the cadence of speech of the local population. Holmes, ever attuned to the minutiae of human behaviour, remarked on the fascinating interplay of Syrian and Turkish influences in this liminal space.

"Observe, Watson," he said, his grey eyes alight with intellectual fervour, "how the fabric of society changes with every mile we travel. It is a testament to the fluid nature of human civilisation, forever adapting and evolving, much like the wisdom we seek to preserve."

Our journey was not without its trials. The railway, still in its infancy, was prone to unexpected delays and mechanical breakdowns. On one particularly memorable occasion, our train came to a halt in the middle of a desolate stretch of countryside. As we disembarked to stretch our legs and assess the situation,

Adrien d'Arcy's artistic sensibilities were piqued by the juxtaposition of the mechanical hulk of the steam locomotive and the timeless landscape.

"It is as if two worlds have collided," he mused, sketching furiously in his notebook. "The ancient and the modern, locked in an eternal dance."

The delay, while inconvenient, offered our group an unexpected opportunity to deepen the bonds forged in the crucible of our desert adventure. As we waited for repairs to be made, we gathered under the shade of a solitary acacia tree and shared stories and reflections on our journey so far.

Dr El-Sharif, her scholarly demeanour softened by the intimacy of the moment, spoke of her growing understanding of the teachings of the Obsidian Guild. "It occurs to me," she said, her voice carrying the weight of profound insight, "that the wisdom of the Guild is not unlike this very landscape - unchanging in its essence, yet forever adapting to the forces that shape it."

Liyana Sultan, her regal bearing a stark contrast to our dusty surroundings, nodded in agreement. "Indeed, it is this very adaptability that we must emulate if we are to successfully integrate the teachings of the Guild into our modern world."

As the journey progressed, we became increasingly reliant on our horses. Al-Zarib and Muntasir, the noble steeds that had carried us through the depths of the desert, proved their worth once again as we navigated the rugged terrain beyond the reach of the railway.

It was during one of these rides that we encountered perhaps our greatest challenge on this leg of the journey. A sudden and violent sandstorm descended upon us, reducing visibility to mere inches and threatening to separate our party. It was in this moment of crisis that I witnessed the true depth of the bonds that had formed between us.

Holmes, his usual analytical detachment giving way to decisive action, took charge of the situation. His voice, raised above the howling wind, guided us to shelter in the lee of a large rock formation. Drawing on a lifetime of desert experience, Khalid helped us protect our mounts and secure our belongings against the onslaught of sand and wind.

As we huddled together, waiting out the storm, I was struck by the transformation that had taken place within our group. We were no longer a collection of individuals thrown together by circumstance. We had become a cohesive unit, each member's strengths complementing the others, our shared experiences forging bonds deeper than words could express.

When the storm finally subsided and we emerged from our shelter, the landscape had been transformed. Dunes had shifted, landmarks erased, but our resolve remained unshaken. As we remounted our horses and set off again, I felt a profound sense of unity with my companions.

The rest of the journey to Adana passed without incident, but the effects of our shared ordeal lingered. Our conversations took on a new depth, touching not only on the practicalities of our mission, but on the very nature of wisdom, loyalty and courage - the virtues embodied by the Obsidian Guild.

As the spires and minarets of Adana came into view, I found myself reflecting on the journey so far. We had crossed not only physical borders, but cultural and personal ones as well. The wisdom of the ancients, carried in the artefacts we carried and the knowledge we had gained, had begun to take root in each of us, transforming us in ways both subtle and profound.

Holmes, catching my thoughtful expression, offered a rare smile. "My dear Watson," he said, his voice carrying a warmth I had seldom heard, "I believe this adventure has changed us all. We set out in search of ancient wisdom and in the process discovered truths about ourselves that I, for one, will not soon forget."

As we entered the city of Adana, tired but invigorated by our experiences, I knew with certainty that the bonds forged on this journey would last long after we returned to the familiar streets of London. We had become more than fellow travellers - we were now custodians of a legacy, united in our quest to bridge the ancient and the modern, the East and the West, in a way that would shape not only our own lives, but the very future of human understanding.

⊰⊱⊰⊱

As our intrepid company embarked on the Adana to Konya leg of our odyssey, we found ourselves thrust into the crucible of the relentless march of modernity. The partially completed Baghdad railway, that great iron snake of progress, carried us swiftly across a landscape that seemed to metamorphose with every mile. The juxtaposition of this steel behemoth with the timeless vistas of Anatolia served as a stark reminder of the world to which we were inexorably returning - a world that seemed at once familiar and utterly alien after our sojourn in the mystical realm of Al-Hijr.

From our vantage point in the railway carriage, I, Dr John Watson, watched my companions with keen interest. Every face bore the indelible mark of our desert odyssey, but now seemed touched by a growing anticipation of what lay ahead. Holmes, his hawk-like profile silhouetted against the window, seemed lost in contemplation, his fingers clasped beneath his chin in that familiar pose of deep thought.

"I say, Holmes," I ventured, breaking the contemplative silence that had settled over our compartment, "does it not strike you as remarkable how quickly we have moved from the timeless sands of Al-Hijr to this monument of modern engineering?"

My dear friend turned his penetrating gaze on me, a rare smile playing at the corners of his thin lips. "Indeed, Watson," he replied, his voice carrying that note of quiet enthusiasm that I had come to associate with his most profound observations. "We find ourselves straddling two worlds - one ancient and unchanging, the other in a constant state of flux. It is in reconciling these two realms that I believe we will find the true value of our recent adventures.

Dr Amal El-Sharif, her scholarly demeanour softened by the trials of our journey, leaned forward, her eyes alight with intellectual fervour. "You speak the truth, Mr Holmes," she interjected. "The wisdom we have gleaned from the Obsidian Guild must now be translated into a language that resonates with our rapidly changing world. It is a formidable challenge, but one I believe we are uniquely equipped to meet."

As if to underline the prescience of her words, our train suddenly screeched to a halt with a cacophony of screeching metal and escaping steam. The abrupt cessation of our progress sent a wave of anxiety through our company, a stark reminder that even in this age of technological marvels, we were not immune to the vagaries of fate.

It was in that moment of uncertainty that I witnessed the true measure of our transformation. Where once we might have reacted with alarm or frustration, there was now a calm determination. Liyana Sultan, her regal bearing undiminished by the rigours of our journey, was the first to rise.

"Come," she said, her voice carrying the quiet authority of one born to lead, "let us see what obstacles fate has placed in our path. Perhaps this is just another test of the virtues we have so recently affirmed."

As we disembarked to investigate the cause of our delay, I could not help but marvel at the change in Adrien d'Arcy. The young craftsman, once so focused on the tangible aspects of his art, now moved with a newfound awareness of the world around him. His keen eyes scanned our surroundings, not just for beauty or utility, but for the deeper truths that lay beneath the surface of things.

Our impromptu expedition revealed a section of track rendered impassable by a recent rockslide - a reminder that nature, in its own inimitable way, has little regard for man's grand designs. But rather than regard this as a setback, our company approached the challenge with a vigour born of our shared trials.

Holmes, his analytical mind ever attuned to the practical, quickly devised a plan to clear the debris. "Watson," he called, a gleam of excitement in his grey eyes, "remember our experience in the caves of Al-Hijr. The principles of leverage we employed there may prove most effective in our present predicament."

And so we set to work, each member of our party contributing his unique skills to the task at hand. Khalid Al-Fahmi, drawing on generations of desert wisdom, guided us in reading the lay of the land to prevent further slides. Liyana and Adrien, their strength honed by years of riding, lent their muscles to the effort of moving the larger stones.

As we toiled under the unforgiving Anatolian sun, my thoughts drifted to the imminent conclusion of our journey. The prospect of our audience with the Ottoman Sultan - Liyana's father and the architect of our mission - loomed large in my mind. How would we convey the magnitude of our discoveries? How could we articulate the profound changes we had undergone?

As if sensing the direction of my thoughts, Holmes appeared at my side, his voice low and measured. "Fear not, my dear Watson," he said, placing a reassuring hand on my shoulder. "The Sultan has charged us with solving a riddle, and we have solved it. But I suspect he will find that the solution to his case is but a small part of the wisdom we will impart."

With a final concerted effort, we cleared the last of the debris from the tracks. As we stood back to survey our handiwork, a sense of quiet pride settled over our company. This small victory, achieved through the application of both ancient wisdom and modern ingenuity, seemed to encapsulate the essence of our journey.

As we reboarded the train and resumed our journey towards Konya, I sensed a palpable change in the atmosphere of our carriage. The anticipation that had been building throughout our journey now seemed to crystallise into a shared sense of purpose. We were no longer just returning from an adventure; we were embarking on a new quest - one that would challenge us to bridge the gap between the timeless truths of Al-Hijr and the ever-changing landscape of the modern world.

Liyana, her eyes shining with a mixture of excitement and trepidation, gave voice to our collective thoughts. "As we approach Constantinople and our audience with my father," she said, her eyes sweeping over our assembled company, "I am filled with both pride and humility. We carry with us not just the solution to a mystery, but the key to a wisdom that could reshape the very foundations of our world."

As the sun began to set, painting the Anatolian plains in shades of gold and crimson, I was filled with a profound sense of gratitude for the journey we had undertaken and the companions with whom I had shared it. Whatever challenges awaited us in Constantinople, whatever judgement the Sultan might pass on our efforts, I knew with unshakable certainty that the legacy of the Obsidian Guild would live on through our actions and our words.

With the rhythmic clatter of the train as our constant companion, we pressed on towards Konya, each mile bringing us closer to the culmination of our extraordinary odyssey. As I looked out over the rapidly changing landscape, I could not help but feel that we stood on the threshold of a new era - one in which the ancient wisdom of Al-Hijr might yet illuminate the path of progress and lead humanity towards a future of greater understanding, compassion and unity.

As our train pulled out of the ancient city of Konya, its wheels singing a staccato rhythm on the rails, I was overcome by a strange mixture of emotions. The last leg of our extraordinary odyssey stretched out before us, a mere day's journey in modern terms, yet it seemed to span the breadth of human experience. Our destination, Constantinople, that great nexus of East and West, loomed large in our collective imagination, promising both the comforts of civilisation and the weighty responsibilities that awaited us there.

From my vantage point in our private compartment I watched my dear friend and compatriot Sherlock Holmes, his slender figure silhouetted against the window. His keen grey eyes, normally so focused on the minutiae of our surroundings, now seemed to gaze beyond the passing landscape, fixed on some distant point known only to him.

"I say, Holmes," I ventured, breaking the contemplative silence that had settled between us, "does it not strike you as remarkable how quickly we have moved from the timeless sands of Al-Hijr to this marvel of modern engineering? Why, it seems only yesterday that we set out from this very city by steamer, our hearts heavy with the weight of the Sultan's cargo."

Holmes turned to me, a rare smile playing at the corners of his thin lips. "Indeed, my dear Watson," he replied, his voice carrying that note of quiet enthusiasm I had come to associate with his most profound observations. "Time, it seems, is as malleable as the desert sands we have left behind. Our journey, though measured in weeks, has spanned ages of human experience and wisdom. We return to Constantinople not as we left it, but as beings transformed by the crucible of the desert and the legacy of the Obsidian Guild.

At that moment our companions - Adrien d'Arcy, Dr Amal El-Sharif, Liyana Sultan and Khalid Al-Fahmi - entered our compartment, each bearing the marks of our shared trials and triumphs. The anticipation of our imminent audience with the Sultan, Liyana's father, hung palpably in the air, an unspoken thread connecting us all.

Liyana, her regal bearing tempered by the humility born of our desert sojourn, spoke first. "As we approach Constantinople," she began, her voice carrying the weight of both duty and discovery, "I find myself wondering how to convey the magnitude of our experience to my father. The wisdom of the Obsidian Guild, the trials we have endured - these are not mere facts to be reported, but profound truths that have reshaped the very fabric of our being".

Dr El-Sharif, her scholarly demeanour softened by the bonds of our shared adventure, nodded in agreement. "Indeed," she mused, her dark eyes glowing with intellectual fervour, "we carry not only the solution to the riddle that set us on this path, but a far greater treasure - the key to bridging the gap between ancient wisdom and modern progress. How can we translate the timeless virtues of the desert into the language of diplomacy and statecraft?"

As our train wound its way through the Anatolian countryside, the landscape gradually giving way to more populated regions, our conversation deepened, touching on the myriad ways in which our extraordinary journey had changed us. Adrien d'Arcy, once so focused on the tangible aspects of his craft, now spoke with passion about the spiritual dimensions of creation. Khalid, our steadfast guide through the trials of the desert, reflected on how the wisdom of his ancestors might illuminate the way forward for a world caught between tradition and modernity.

Throughout our conversation, my thoughts kept returning to the monumental task that lay before us. How could we convey to the Sultan the profound truths we had uncovered? The mystery of the obsidian statues and the tragic events that had set us on our quest now seemed but a prelude to the greater revelations we had experienced.

As the day wore on and the sun began its descent towards the western horizon, the first hints of Constantinople's grandeur began to appear. The countryside gave way to the suburbs, then the outskirts of the great city itself. With each passing moment, the anticipation within our group grew more palpable, a taut wire of expectation humming with potential energy.

It was Holmes who finally gave voice to the thoughts that had been swirling in all our minds. "My friends," he said, sweeping his eyes over our assembled company, "as we stand on the threshold of our return to civilisation, let us take a moment to reflect on the journey that has brought us to this point. We set out as individuals, each carrying our own burdens and aspirations. We return as a unified whole, bound by bonds stronger than blood or nation.

He paused, his eyes taking on that faraway look I had come to associate with his deepest insights. "The Sultan has charged us with solving a riddle, and we have solved it. But I suspect he will find that the solution to his case is only a small part of the wisdom we will impart. We carry not only answers, but a vision of a world in which the timeless virtues of the desert might guide the course of empires.

As Holmes spoke, the train began to slow, the screeching of the brakes heralding our arrival at the great terminus of Constantinople. Through the windows we caught our first glimpse of the city - a riot of colour and movement, so at odds with the austere beauty of the desert we had left behind. The minarets of the great mosques pierced the sky, while in the distance the waters of the Bosphorus glittered, a fluid bridge between continents.

As we stepped onto the platform, we were immediately engulfed by the bustle of urban life. The air was thick with the mixed scents of spices, sea air and humanity - a stark contrast to the crisp, clean atmosphere of the desert. But even as we navigated the crowds, I sensed a new steadiness in my companions, a core of inner calm forged in the crucible of our shared experiences.

As we made our way through the streets towards our lodgings, the weight of our impending audience with the Sultan fell on us like a cloak. Each step brought us closer not only to the culmination of our quest, but to a moment that could well shape the course of history. The wisdom of the Obsidian Guild, carried in our hearts and minds, stood ready to illuminate the shadowy corridors of power.

As I looked into the determined faces of my companions, I felt a surge of pride and anticipation. Whatever challenges lay ahead in the labyrinthine world of Ottoman politics, I knew with unshakable certainty that we would face them together, our bonds forged by the desert winds and tempered by common purpose.

As the sun dipped below the horizon, painting the sky in shades of gold and crimson, Constantinople spread before us like a tapestry of possibilities. In that moment, standing on the threshold of our greatest challenge yet, I, Dr John Watson, felt the full weight of my role as chronicler. The story that lay before us promised to be one for the ages, a tale of wisdom rediscovered and a world transformed.

With a shared look of understanding, our company moved forward into the heart of the great city, ready to bring the light of the desert to the seat of empire.

As our caravan wound its way through the labyrinthine streets of Constantinople, the air seemed charged with a palpable sense of anticipation. The cacophony of urban life - a symphony of voices, hoofbeats and the distant call of the muezzin - enveloped us, in stark contrast to the profound silence of the desert we had left behind. It was at this moment of transition that we were greeted by none other than the Grand Vizier Kâmil Pasha himself, his stately figure cutting an imposing silhouette against the backdrop of minarets and domes that defined the city's skyline.

"Gentlemen and my lady," the Grand Vizier intoned, his voice carrying the weight of his august office, "on behalf of His Imperial Majesty, Sultan Abdul Hamid II, I welcome you to Constantinople. I trust your journey has been most illuminating?"

Holmes, ever the master of composure, stepped forward to meet the Vizier's gaze. "Indeed, Your Excellency," he replied, his tone measured yet tinged with a hint of the profound experiences we had shared. "Our expedition has yielded knowledge far beyond our original expectations. We are ready to present our findings to His Imperial Majesty at your earliest convenience."

As we followed the Grand Vizier's lead towards the palace, I could not help but observe the myriad reactions of my companions to our sudden re-immersion in civilisation. Adrien d'Arcy, his artistic soul awakened by our desert sojourn, gazed in wonder at the architectural marvels that surrounded us. His eyes darted from ornate tilework to sweeping arches, his fingers twitching as if longing for pencil and paper to capture the beauty he saw.

Dr Amal El-Sharif, ever the scholar, engaged the Grand Vizier in a discourse on the historical significance of various landmarks we passed. Her words, carefully chosen to convey enthusiasm without revealing the depth of our discoveries, painted a picture of a journey rich in cultural and archaeological significance.

"Your Excellency," she ventured, her voice carrying a note of carefully restrained excitement, "our expedition has given us a unique perspective on the interplay between ancient wisdom and modern governance. I believe His Imperial Majesty will find our observations most pertinent to the challenges facing the Empire in these changing times."

Liyana Sultan, her regal bearing more pronounced now that we stood on the threshold of her ancestral domain, maintained a dignified silence. Yet I could see a storm of emotion in her eyes - anticipation, trepidation and a fierce determination to honour the profound experiences we had shared.

As we approached the palace gates, I noticed a subtle change in the Grand Vizier's demeanour. His eyes, which had surveyed our party with diplomatic neutrality, rested on Liyana Sultan with a mixture of deference and curiosity.

"Your Highness," he addressed her, his tone taking on a formal cadence that belonged to years of courtly etiquette, "it gladdens my heart to see that you have returned safely from your expedition. His Imperial Majesty, your father, has been eagerly awaiting news of your travels."

Liyana, who had maintained a dignified silence throughout our procession, now stepped forward. Her posture, always regal, seemed to change before our eyes. Gone was the travel-worn companion of our desert sojourn; in her place stood a princess of the Ottoman Empire, every inch her father's daughter.

"Grand Vizier Kâmil Pasha," she replied, her voice carrying the weight of her royal heritage, "I thank you for your kind welcome. Our journey has indeed been one of great importance, not only to the Empire, but to the understanding of our common human heritage. I look forward to sharing our discoveries with His Imperial Majesty."

The Grand Vizier's eyebrow arched almost imperceptibly at her words. "Indeed, Your Highness? You speak of matters that sound most profound. May I inquire as to the nature of these... discoveries?"

For a moment I feared Liyana was about to reveal too much, but her answer was a masterclass in diplomatic finesse. "Your Excellency," she began, a subtle smile playing at the corners of her mouth, "our expedition has uncovered truths that bridge the ancient and the modern, the East and the West. However, I believe it would be most fitting for His Imperial Majesty to be the first to hear the full account of our findings."

The Grand Vizier nodded, a look of reluctant admiration flickering across his features. "Very well said, Your Highness. His Imperial Majesty has indeed decreed that he shall be the first to receive your full report." Then he turned to address us all once more. "As I said, His Imperial Majesty eagerly awaits your audience. You will be received tomorrow at the hour of afternoon prayer."

With these words we were ushered into the opulent confines of the palace, a world away from the harsh beauty of the desert that had been our home for so many weeks. Servants appeared as if by magic to escort us to our quarters, their quiet efficiency a testament to the well-oiled machinery of Imperial hospitality.

As I settled into my chambers, the luxury surrounding me seemed almost overwhelming after our spartan existence in the wilderness. The plush carpets, intricately carved furniture and gauzy curtains billowing in the Bosphorus breeze spoke of a refinement that felt almost alien after our recent adventures.

A gentle knock on my door announced the arrival of Holmes, his slender figure silhouetted against the warm glow of the corridor lamps. "Well, Watson," he began, a rare smile playing at the corners of his mouth, "it would appear that the final act of our drama is about to unfold. Tomorrow we shall stand before the Sultan himself and unveil the fruits of our labours."

I nodded, feeling the weight of responsibility settle on my shoulders. "Indeed, Holmes. But how do you begin to convey the magnitude of what we have discovered? The legacy of the Obsidian Guild, the trials we have faced - these are not mere facts to be reported, but profound truths that have reshaped the very fabric of our being."

My dear friend's eyes took on that faraway look I had come to associate with his deepest reflections. "Therein lies our greatest challenge, my dear Watson. We must find a way to translate the timeless wisdom of the desert into the language of statecraft and diplomacy. The Sultan has asked us to solve a riddle, and we have solved it. But I suspect he will find that the solution to his case is but a small part of the wisdom we will impart."

As the night deepened and the sounds of the city faded to a distant murmur, I found myself standing at the window of my chamber, gazing out over the moonlit expanse of Constantinople. The city stretched before me, a tapestry of shadows and silvered domes, so different from the stark beauty of the desert, yet no less profound in its mysteries and potential for discovery.

I glanced back at my open notebook, its pages filled with the hastily scribbled observations of our journey. How could mere words on paper hope to convey the depth of our experiences, the transformations we had undergone? Yet I knew I had to try, for the sake of those who would come after us, seeking the wisdom we had found in this timeless place.

As I prepared to sleep, my mind still reeling from the events of the day, I found myself reflecting on Liyana's transformation. The young woman who had shared our trials in the desert had proven herself to be every inch a princess, navigating the treacherous waters of court politics with a grace that belied her years. It struck me then that perhaps this too was a legacy of our journey - each of us stepping into roles we had not known we could fill, guided by the wisdom we had uncovered in the sands of Al-Hijr.

With a final glance at the city beyond my window, I extinguished the lamp and settled into the unfamiliar comfort of my bed. Tomorrow we would stand before the Sultan, ready to bring the light of the desert to the seat of empire. As sleep finally claimed me, my last conscious thought was of the extraordinary story that lay before us - a story of wisdom rediscovered and a world on the brink of transformation.

Act IV

CHAPTER 31

SEEDS OF CONCORD

T he intricate lattice windows of my chamber in the Sultan's palace allowed the golden rays of dawn to gently wake me from a troubled sleep. The opulence that surrounded me was in stark contrast to the austere beauty of the Arabian desert we had so recently left. The plush silk cushions and intricately woven carpets, splashed with patterns of flora and calligraphy, seemed almost vulgar after weeks spent under the vast, star-studded canopy of the desert sky.

I rose and made my way to the window, marvelling at the view of the Bosphorus, its waters shimmering like polished silver in the early morning light. The minarets of Constantinople's great mosques pierced the sky, their silhouettes a reminder of the rich tapestry of cultures that had shaped this ancient city. How different it all was from the endless sea of sand we had traversed, where the only landmarks were the occasional rocky outcrop or the shimmering mirage of an oasis.

A gentle knock on the door announced the arrival of my dear friend and fellow countryman, Sherlock Holmes. As he entered, I could not help but notice the change in his demeanour. The harsh desert sun had weathered his lean features and there was a new depth to his grey eyes, as if the mysteries we had unravelled in the sands of Al-Hijr had left an indelible mark on his soul.

"Ah, Watson," he said, his voice carrying a hint of the excitement I had come to associate with the culmination of one of his great cases, "I trust you have rested well? We have a day of great importance ahead of us."

"Indeed, Holmes," I replied, gesturing at the sumptuous surroundings. "Though I must confess I am somewhat at odds with this luxury after our time in the desert."

A wry smile played across Holmes' lips. "I understand your feelings, my dear fellow. The desert has a way of stripping away the superfluous, leaving only what is essential. But let us not forget that it is precisely this contrast - between the austere and the opulent, the ancient and the modern - that lies at the heart of our mission here."

As we stood there, looking out over the awakening city, I felt the weight of our impending responsibility settle on my shoulders. We were no longer mere chroniclers and detectives, but emissaries of a profound truth, custodians of an ancient wisdom that had the potential to reshape the very fabric of this troubled region.

Our reverie was interrupted by the arrival of our companions - Dr Amal El-Sharif, Adrien d'Arcy, Liyana Sultan and Khalid Al-Fahmi. Each bore the marks of our journey, not only in their sun-bronzed skin and travel-worn clothes, but in the newfound determination that shone in their eyes.

Liyana, in particular, seemed transformed. The princess who had embarked on our expedition with a mixture of duty and trepidation now stood before us with the quiet strength of one who has faced the crucible and emerged tempered by its fires.

"My friends," she said, her voice soft but full of purpose, "as we prepare to meet my father and share the fruits of our journey, I am struck by how much we have changed. We set out in search of artefacts and returned with something far more precious - a vision of unity that transcends the boundaries of nation and creed."

Amal nodded, her scholarly demeanour softened by the trials we had faced together. "Indeed, Your Highness. The wisdom of the Obsidian Guild is not just a relic of the past, but a beacon for our future. The challenge before us now is to translate that wisdom into a language that diplomats and statesmen can understand and act upon."

Khalid, our steadfast guide, whose deep connection to the desert had been our lifeline throughout the journey, spoke up. His voice, usually reserved for practical matters of survival, now carried a note of reverence. "We have been entrusted with knowledge that has lain dormant in the sands for centuries," he said, his eyes distant as if he could still see the vastness of his beloved desert. "It is our duty to ensure that this wisdom does not fade away like a mirage, but becomes a source of peace for generations to come."

Adrien, the artist whose keen eye had captured the subtle beauties of our journey, added his own reflection. "We have witnessed the merging of legend and reality, past and present," he mused, his fingers unconsciously sketching patterns in the air as if still trying to capture the essence of our experience. "Now we must find a way to paint this vision on the canvas of the future."

As we gathered our thoughts and prepared for the day ahead, I could not help but feel a deep sense of anticipation. The adventures that had brought us to this point - the dangers we had faced, the mysteries we had unravelled - now seemed but a prelude to the true test that awaited us. For in the gilded chambers of power, we would seek to sow the seeds of a peace that could thrive in the harsh soil of centuries of conflict.

With a shared look of determination, we made our way from our chambers, ready to face whatever challenges the day might bring. The game, as Holmes would say, was on - and the stakes had never been higher.

⊷⊶⊹⊱⊰⊹⊷⊶

As we descended the grand marble staircase, its steps worn smooth by centuries of noble feet, we found ourselves ushered into a secluded courtyard nestled in the heart of the palace. The space was a veritable oasis, shielded from the bustle of the city beyond by high walls decorated with intricate mosaics depicting scenes from Ottoman history. A fountain splashed softly in the centre, its waters catching the early morning light and casting dancing reflections on the surrounding colonnade.

A table had been laid under the mottled shade of an ancient olive tree, its gnarled branches a testament to the enduring nature of this land. The meal before us was a sumptuous affair, with delicacies both familiar and exotic arranged on fine porcelain. The aroma of freshly brewed Turkish coffee mingled with the scent of orange blossom, creating an atmosphere that was both invigorating and soothing.

As we took our seats, I could not help but marvel at my companions' transformation. Holmes, usually so restless in the confines of civilisation, seemed almost at peace, his keen grey eyes taking in every detail of our surroundings with quiet appreciation. Liyana, resplendent in attire befitting her royal status, carried herself with a newfound grace that spoke of the trials we had endured together.

"I must say," Adrien began, breaking the contemplative silence that had fallen over our group, "it feels almost surreal to be sitting at such a table after weeks of simple fare under the stars. And yet I find myself missing the simplicity of our desert meals".

Khalid, his weathered features softening into a smile, nodded in agreement. "Indeed, my friend. The desert has a way of distilling life down to its essence. But let us not forget that it is the contrast between such simplicity and the complexity of the world beyond that gives weight to our mission here."

As we ate, the conversation flowed as freely as the coffee poured into the delicate cups. We found ourselves recounting the pivotal moments of our journey - the harrowing escape from the Sons of Purity, the mystical encounter in Al-Hijr and the profound revelations of the Obsidian Guild.

"It occurs to me," said Dr El-Sharif, her scholarly tone tinged with wonder, "that we have been privileged to witness the convergence of myth and reality. The challenge before us now is to translate this experience into terms that can shape the course of nations".

Holmes, who had been listening intently, leaned forward, his elbows on the table. "You touch the heart of our predicament, Doctor," he said, his voice carrying that familiar note of analytical precision. "We have uncovered truths that transcend the boundaries of nation and creed. But we must now present these truths in a manner that will resonate in the halls of power."

Liyana, who had been silent, spoke up, her voice carrying the weight of her royal heritage. "My father, the Sultan, is a man of great wisdom, but he is also bound by the constraints of his position. We must find a way to show him that the path to peace lies not in the machinations of empires, but in the shared wisdom of our common ancestors."

As our meal drew to a close, I reflected on the enormity of the task before us. We had travelled across deserts and unravelled ancient mysteries, but in many ways our greatest challenge was yet to come. For in the opulent chambers of the palace, we would attempt to bridge the gap between the timeless wisdom of the Obsidian Guild and the complex realities of modern statecraft.

The gentle chiming of a distant clock reminded us of the passage of time and the approach of our audience with the Sultan. As we rose from our seats, I caught a glimpse of determination in the eyes of my companions. Whatever doubts or fears we might have harboured were now tempered by a shared sense of purpose.

Nodding to each other, we made our way back into the cool corridors of the palace, our steps echoing on the marble floors. The game, as Holmes would say, was most definitely afoot, and we were ready to play our parts in a drama that could reshape the very fabric of this ancient land.

As we left the tranquil sanctuary of the courtyard, we found ourselves back in the labyrinthine corridors of the Sultan's palace. Our guide, a taciturn functionary whose impassive countenance betrayed nothing of his thoughts, led us through a succession of halls and passageways, each more splendid than the last.

The transition from the sun-drenched courtyard to the cool, shadowy interior of the palace was not unlike our own journey from the harsh clarity of the desert to the labyrinthine world of diplomacy. As we moved through the corridors, I could not help but feel that we were moving not only through space, but through time itself.

We passed through chambers whose walls seemed to whisper of past glories and ancient intrigues. Tapestries of exquisite workmanship adorned the walls, depicting scenes from the long and storied history of the Ottoman Empire. Here, a sultan receiving tribute from distant vassals; there, a great naval battle with galleys locked in mortal combat on a sea of silk and gold thread.

Holmes, ever observant, paused before a glass-fronted cabinet containing a collection of ornate daggers. "Remarkable," he murmured, his keen eyes taking in every detail. "Note the craftsmanship, Watson. These blades speak of a tradition that goes back centuries, perhaps millennia."

As we continued our journey, I found my eyes drawn to the faces of my companions. Liyana, her royal bearing more pronounced with each step, seemed to grow in stature as we approached her father's domain. Khalid, our faithful guide through the desert, now looked somewhat uncomfortable in the midst of such opulence, his hand occasionally wandering to the empty scabbard at his waist where his own blade had once rested.

Dr El-Sharif's eyes lit up with scholarly excitement as we passed a series of ancient texts displayed in recessed niches. "These manuscripts," she whispered, her voice full of reverence, "some of them predate the founding of the Empire itself. What secrets could they hold?"

Adrien, for his part, seemed to be committing every detail to memory, his artist's eye no doubt already composing sketches of the wonders that surrounded us.

As we climbed a grand staircase, its marble steps worn by the passage of countless feet, I found myself reflecting on the weight of history pressing down on us from all sides. We had uncovered truths in the desert that had lain hidden for centuries, and now we sought to bring those truths to bear on the great affairs of empires and nations.

At last we came to a set of imposing doors, their surfaces inlaid with mother-of-pearl and precious stones. Our guide, breaking his silence for the first time, announced in measured tones: "His Imperial Majesty awaits you inside."

As we stood on the threshold of the Sultan's private office, I felt a strange mixture of anticipation and trepidation. We had faced untold dangers in the depths of the desert, unravelled mysteries that had baffled generations, and now we were about to translate those experiences into the language of diplomacy and statecraft.

Sensing my unease, Holmes placed a reassuring hand on my shoulder. "Courage, my dear Watson," he said, his voice low but full of conviction. "We have traversed the trackless wastes and returned with wisdom that may yet change the course of history. Let us now see if we can navigate the equally treacherous waters of Imperial politics."

With a shared look of determination, our small band of adventurers-turned-diplomats squared their shoulders and prepared to cross the final threshold. As the doors swung open, admitting us into the presence of the Sultan, I could not shake the feeling that we were entering not just a room, but the pages of history itself.

As we crossed the threshold into the Sultan's private office, I was immediately struck by the curious juxtaposition of opulence and austerity that characterised the chamber. Rich Persian carpets muffled our footsteps, while intricate calligraphy adorned the walls, interweaving verses from the Koran with historical edicts. The air was heavy with the scent of sandalwood and the gravity of impending affairs of state.

At the far end of the room, behind a magnificent desk of polished ebony inlaid with mother-of-pearl, sat His Imperial Majesty, Sultan Abdul Hamid II. His penetrating gaze, at once regal and penetrating, swept over our party as we entered. To his right stood my friend's brother, Mycroft Holmes, his usual air of omniscience tempered by a barely perceptible tension in his bearing.

"Your Imperial Majesty," Sherlock Holmes intoned, bowing with a grace that belied his usual disdain for such formalities, "we are honoured by your audience."

The Sultan bowed his head in acknowledgement, his eyes lingering on each member of our party in turn. When his gaze fell on his daughter, Liyana, I detected a momentary softening in his expression, a flicker of paternal affection breaking through the mask of imperial stoicism.

"My child," he said, his voice rich with emotion, barely restrained, "you have returned to us."

Liyana stepped forward, every inch the princess despite the rigours of our recent travails. "Father," she replied, her voice steady yet filled with warmth, "I stand before you changed by our journey, yet always your loyal daughter."

For a moment, the weight of protocol seemed to hang in the balance. Then, with a sudden movement that startled even the imperturbable Mycroft, the Sultan rose and embraced his daughter. The reunion, though brief, spoke volumes of the trials we had endured and the bonds that had been tested in the crucible of our adventure.

As father and daughter parted, calm returning to their features, Mycroft cleared his throat discreetly. "Your Majesty," he began, his tone measured and diplomatic, "may I present Dr John Watson and the rest of the expedition: Dr Amal El-Sharif, Mr Adrien d'Arcy and Mr Khalid Al-Fahmi."

Each of us bowed in turn as we were introduced. I could not help but notice the way Mycroft's gaze lingered on each of us, his remarkable intellect no doubt cataloguing every detail of our appearance and demeanour.

"Welcome, all of you," the Sultan said as he resumed his seat. "We have awaited your return with great anticipation. The reports we have received indicate discoveries of profound importance."

"Indeed, Your Majesty," Sherlock replied, stepping forward. "Our expedition has uncovered truths that may well reshape our understanding of the history and future of this region."

I watched as a flicker of intrigue passed between the Sultan and Mycroft at these words. The elder Holmes brother leaned forward slightly, his usual languor giving way to keen interest.

"You speak of weighty matters, Sherlock," Mycroft said, his eyes narrowing. "I trust you have not come to us with mere conjecture or flights of fancy?"

"Brother mine," Sherlock replied, a hint of steel in his voice, "you know me better than that. What we have discovered in the depths of the desert is as concrete as the stones of this very palace, and potentially as significant to the future of this empire."

The Sultan raised his hand, quelling the tension between the Holmes brothers. "Gentlemen," he said, his tone brooking no argument, "let us not be hasty. We have time to consider the details of your discoveries. For now, I would like to hear from each of you a brief account of your journey and your initial impressions of its significance."

As our companions began to recount our adventures, each from their unique perspective, I found myself studying the reactions of the Sultan and Mycroft. I could read in their expressions a complex mixture of scepticism, curiosity and a growing realisation of the gravity of our findings.

The game, as Holmes would say, was indeed afoot. But this was no mere puzzle to be solved in the drawing room of Baker Street. Here, in the heart of the Ottoman Empire, we were about to influence the course of history itself. As I listened to my companions, I silently prayed that the wisdom we had gleaned from the sands of the desert would prove equal to the monumental task that now lay before us.

⊰⊹⊱

As the first accounts of our journey drew to a close, all eyes in the Sultan's opulent office turned to Sherlock Holmes. My friend stood there, his slender figure casting a long shadow over the intricate patterns of the Persian carpet, and I could see in his bearing the familiar intensity that foreshadowed one of his remarkable performances.

"Your Imperial Majesty, Mycroft, esteemed colleagues," Holmes began, his resonant voice filling the room, "our expedition, which began as an investigation into a singular murder and theft in London, has led us to discoveries of such profound significance that they may well reshape the future of this region, if not the world."

Holmes paced slowly, his hands clasped behind his back as he began his narrative. "Our journey began with the murder of Lord Charles Wentworth and the theft of an obsidian statuette from his possession. This statuette, we learned, was one of three, each imbued with great cultural and historical significance."

He paused, allowing the weight of his words to settle on his audience. The Sultan leaned forward, his interest clearly piqued, while Mycroft's eyebrow arched almost imperceptibly.

"Our investigations first took us to Constantinople, where we uncovered the tragic murder of Your Majesty's son, Prince Zafir," Holmes continued, bowing slightly to the Sultan. "The similarities between these two crimes, separated by vast distances yet linked by a common thread, pointed to a conspiracy of considerable scope and ambition."

Holmes then went on to detail our journey into the heart of the Arabian desert, his vivid recollections bringing to life the dangers and wonders we had encountered. He spoke of our time in Petra, where we had uncovered ancient Nabataean inscriptions that hinted at the existence of a secret organisation known as the Obsidian Guild.

"It was in Petra that we faced our first trial," Holmes explained, his eyes taking on a faraway look. "Set by a guardian of ancient wisdom, this test of courage, wisdom and heart proved to be but a prelude to the challenges that awaited us."

With meticulous care, Holmes recounted our capture by the Sons of Purity, a faction of the Obsidian Guild led by the fanatic Rasheed Al-Tariq. He described our harrowing escape, facilitated by the extraordinary bond between himself and Al-Zarib, Khalid's mystical stallion.

"The intervention of Al-Zarib," Holmes said, his voice tinged with a rare note of wonder, "was more than mere chance. It was a manifestation of the very principles we had sought to understand - the deep connection between man, beast and the timeless wisdom of the desert."

As Holmes spoke of our journey to the hidden oasis of Al-Hijr, I noticed that the Sultan and Mycroft exchanged a look of significance. My friend, ever observant, did not miss this silent communication.

"I assure you, gentlemen," he said, addressing their unspoken scepticism, "that what we have witnessed in Al-Hijr defies conventional explanation, yet is as real as the ground on which we stand."

Holmes then described the ritual of reuniting the three obsidian statuettes, each representing one of the Guild's core virtues: courage, wisdom and heart. He spoke of the vision we had shared - the manifestation of three mystical stallions and the ultimate emergence of the Obsidian Stallion itself.

"This vision," Holmes explained, his voice resonating with conviction, "was not merely a collective hallucination, but a glimpse into the very essence of the wisdom the Obsidian Guild has guarded for centuries. It revealed to us a path to unity and understanding that transcends the boundaries of nation, creed and culture.

As he finished, Holmes turned directly to the Sultan. "Your Majesty, what we have uncovered is nothing less than a blueprint for peace - a way to bridge the gap between East and West, between ancient wisdom and modern statecraft. The Obsidian Guild, long hidden from the eyes of the world, holds the key to a future where the peoples of this region can live together in harmony".

The room fell silent as Holmes finished. I glanced around, taking in the varied reactions of our audience. The Sultan sat deep in thought, his brow furrowed as he pondered the implications of Holmes' words. Mycroft, usually so impassive, wore an expression of guarded intrigue.

"Mr Holmes," the Sultan finally said, breaking the silence, "your story is extraordinary, bordering on the fantastic. And yet I sense the ring of truth in your words. What would you have us do with this... wisdom you have uncovered?"

Holmes' reply was immediate and emphatic. "Your Majesty, I propose that we use this knowledge as the basis for a new approach to diplomacy in the region. The principles of the Obsidian Guild - courage, wisdom and heart - could serve as the pillars upon which to build lasting peace and understanding between nations."

As Holmes outlined his vision for a peace summit that would bring together the various factions and interests in the region, I marvelled at my friend's transformation. The cold, analytical detective I had known for so long had become an impassioned advocate for a cause that transcended mere crime-solving.

The scene before me - Holmes gesticulating with uncharacteristic animation, the Sultan and Mycroft engaged in rapid, whispered conversation, and our companions watching with a mixture of hope and trepidation - seemed to encapsulate the enormity of what we had discovered and the monumental task that lay ahead.

As I sat there, witnessing this pivotal moment, I could not help but feel that we were on the threshold of a new era. The wisdom of the Obsidian Guild, long hidden in the sands of the Arabian desert, was about to make its mark on the world stage. And we, by some quirk of fate or divine providence, had been chosen to be its messengers.

As Holmes concluded his remarkable exposition, a profound silence fell over the Sultan's office. The weight of our discoveries and their potential implications seemed to rest upon us all, as palpable as the opulent furnishings that surrounded us. It was the Sultan himself who first broke the silence, his voice carrying the gravity of one who holds the fate of millions in his hands.

"Mr Holmes, Dr Watson and honoured guests," he began, his eyes sweeping over our assembled group, "your story is as extraordinary as it is consequential. We find ourselves at a crossroads in history, where the wisdom of the ancients must somehow be reconciled with the demands of modern statecraft."

Mycroft Holmes, his usual languid demeanour giving way to keen interest, leaned forward in his chair. "Indeed, Your Majesty. The challenge before us is to translate these... mystical experiences into concrete diplomatic initiatives. A delicate task, to say the least."

At this, Dr Amal El-Sharif stepped forward, her scholarly countenance tempered by the fire of conviction I had seen kindled during our desert sojourn. "If I may, Your Majesty," she said, her voice steady despite the august company, "I believe the wisdom of the Obsidian Guild offers us a unique framework for approaching regional diplomacy."

The Sultan nodded, encouraging her to continue. Dr El-Sharif took a deep breath before continuing. "The three virtues embodied by the obsidian statuettes - courage, wisdom and heart - can serve as guiding principles in our negotiations. Courage to confront long-standing conflicts, wisdom to seek innovative solutions, and heart to empathise with all parties involved."

I noticed Mycroft's eyebrow arch slightly at this, a sign I had come to recognise as grudging agreement. "An intriguing suggestion, Dr El-Sharif," he murmured. "But how do we operationalise such abstract concepts in the field of international relations?"

It was then that Khalid, our steadfast guide through the perils of the desert, spoke. His voice, though soft, carried the weight of generations of desert wisdom. "In the desert, survival depends on understanding the delicate balance of all things. Perhaps what we need is not to operationalise these concepts, but to help all parties recognise the interconnectedness of our destinies."

The Sultan nodded thoughtfully, his fingers absently tracing the intricate inlays of his desk. "A profound observation, Mr Al-Fahmi. But how do we translate this understanding into practical policy?"

Holmes, who had listened intently to the exchange, now interjected. "Your Majesty, I believe the key lies in the vision we experienced at Al-Hijr. The manifestation of the Obsidian Stallion was not merely a mystical event, but a powerful symbol of unity born of diversity."

"Explain further, Mr Holmes," the Sultan urged, leaning forward with obvious interest.

"The three stallions we witnessed - Al-Sabah, Al-Wafaa and Al-Hikmah - each represented one of the core virtues. But when they came together, they formed something greater than the sum of their parts. This, I believe, is the model we must follow in our diplomatic efforts.

Adrien d'Arcy, who had been furiously scribbling in his notebook throughout the discussion, looked up. "If I may add, Your Majesty, as an artist I am struck by the power of symbols to convey complex ideas. Perhaps we could use the image of the Obsidian Stallion as a central motif in our peace initiatives, a visual representation of the unity we seek."

Liyana, who had been silent, her royal training evident in her poised demeanour, spoke with quiet authority. "Father, our journey has shown me that the strength of our Empire lies not in its military or economic might, but in its ability to unite diverse peoples under a common purpose. The wisdom of the Obsidian Guild offers us the chance to redefine our role in the region, not as conquerors, but as agents of peace and understanding.

I watched as the Sultan's expression softened at his daughter's words, pride and affection briefly overtaking the mask of imperial stoicism.

Mycroft, ever the pragmatist, brought the discussion back to concrete matters. "These are all admirable sentiments, but we must consider the practical challenges. There are entrenched interests that will resist any change to the status quo. How do we overcome such resistance?"

It was Holmes who answered, his grey eyes glowing with the fire of intellectual challenge. "We must appeal not only to the minds of the leaders, but also to their hearts. The vision we experienced in Al-Hijr was not just a spectacle, but a profound emotional and spiritual experience. If we can find a way to convey even a fraction of that experience to others, we may be able to break through the barriers of cynicism and self-interest."

As the discussion continued, delving into the intricacies of regional politics and the logistics of organising a peace summit, I marvelled at the transformation of my companions. Each of us had been changed by our journey, our perspectives broadened and our convictions deepened. Even Mycroft, usually so aloof from matters of the heart, seemed moved by the passion and sincerity of our group.

The Sultan, having listened intently to all points of view, finally spoke. "My friends," he said, his voice carrying the weight of decision, "what you are proposing is bold, perhaps even audacious. It flies in the face of centuries of conflict and mistrust. And yet I find myself fascinated by the possibility."

He paused, his eyes sweeping the room before settling on Holmes. "Mr Holmes, you and your companions have uncovered a great mystery and returned with wisdom that may yet change the course of history. I am inclined to support your proposal for a peace summit, though the road ahead will undoubtedly be fraught with challenges."

As the meeting drew to a close, I felt a sense of both exhilaration and trepidation. We had taken the first step on a journey that could reshape the future of the region, perhaps even the world. The wisdom of the Obsidian

Guild, long hidden in the sands of the Arabian desert, was about to make its mark on the grand stage of international diplomacy.

As we left the Sultan's office, I caught Holmes' eye. The look we exchanged spoke volumes - of the dangers we had faced, the wonders we had witnessed, and the monumental task that now lay before us. The game, as my friend liked to say, was definitely on, and the stakes had never been higher.

As the initial shock of our revelations wore off, the atmosphere in the Sultan's office changed. The air, once heavy with the weight of ancient mysteries and profound discoveries, now crackled with the energy of purposeful planning. It was Mycroft who first steered our discourse towards more practical considerations.

"Gentlemen and lady," he began, his eyes sweeping over our assembled company before settling on the Sultan, "while the wisdom we have uncovered is undoubtedly profound, we must now consider how to translate these abstract principles into concrete diplomatic action."

The Sultan nodded gravely, his fingers crossed in front of him. "Indeed, Mr Holmes. What do you propose?"

Mycroft rose from his seat, taking on the air of a man accustomed to shaping the destinies of nations. "I propose, Your Majesty, that we convene a peace summit. A gathering of the major powers and factions in the region, where we can present the wisdom of the Obsidian Guild and use it as the basis for a lasting peace."

"An ambitious proposal," the Sultan thought. "But where would such a summit be held? The choice of location could be seen as favouring one faction over another."

At this point Sherlock, who had been uncharacteristically silent, spoke up. "Jerusalem," he said, his voice ringing with certainty. "The city stands at the crossroads of faiths and empires. It is a place of profound significance to all concerned. What better place to bridge the gap between East and West, between ancient wisdom and modern statecraft?"

I saw the Sultan's eyes widen slightly, a flicker of surprise crossing his normally impassive features. "Jerusalem," he repeated, as if testing the weight of the word. "A bold choice, Mr Holmes. The city is a powder keg of competing claims and historical grievances."

"Which is precisely why it is the perfect location, Your Majesty," Sherlock countered. "By choosing Jerusalem, we signal our commitment to addressing even the most intractable of conflicts. The wisdom of the Obsidian Guild teaches us that true strength lies in the unity that comes from diversity. What better place to put this principle into practice?

Dr El-Sharif, her scholarly demeanour animated by obvious excitement, added her voice to the discussion. "If I may, Your Majesty, the historical significance of Jerusalem could serve as a powerful backdrop to our efforts. The city has seen the rise and fall of countless empires, yet it endures. It could serve as a poignant reminder of the transient nature of conflict and the enduring power of unity.

Liyana, who had been listening intently, now spoke with the quiet authority I had come to associate with her royal bearing. "Father, I believe that Mr Holmes and Dr El-Sharif are right. By choosing Jerusalem, we are demonstrating our willingness to face the most difficult issues head on. It sends a powerful message about our intentions and the scope of what we hope to achieve."

The Sultan sat for a moment in silent contemplation, his eyes distant, as if looking beyond the opulent confines of his office to the sun-baked streets of Jerusalem. When he spoke, his voice carried the weight of decision. "Very well. Jerusalem it shall be. But the logistics of such a gathering will be formidable. We must consider security, accommodation, the delicate matter of invitations..."

"If I may, Your Majesty," Mycroft interjected smoothly, "I believe I can be of assistance in these matters. My position affords me certain... resources that might prove useful in organising an event of this magnitude."

As Mycroft began to outline the practical considerations of the summit, my attention was drawn to Holmes. My friend was standing by the window, his slender silhouette framed against the skyline of Constantinople. There was a tension in his bearing that I had rarely seen before, a coiled energy that spoke of the momentous nature of what we were about to undertake.

"Watson," he said softly as I approached, his eyes never leaving the vista before him, "do you realise the magnitude of what we are setting in motion? We came to this land in search of a murderer and a stolen artefact. We return as the architects of a peace that could reshape the world."

I put a hand on his shoulder, feeling the tension in his frame. "Indeed, Holmes. It's a far cry from our usual cases at Baker Street. But if anyone can solve this most complex of puzzles, it is you."

He then turned to me, a rare smile softening his hawkish features. "Not I alone, my dear fellow. This is a challenge that will require all of us, each contributing our unique strengths. The game, as we like to say, is afoot - but it is a game unlike any we have played before."

Our quiet exchange was interrupted by the Sultan's voice, raised in command. "Mr Holmes, Dr Watson, please join us. We have much to discuss regarding the practical arrangements for the summit."

As we rejoined the group, I found myself marvelling at the scene before me.

The Sultan of the Ottoman Empire, the inscrutable Mycroft Holmes, our diverse group of companions - all bent over maps and documents, plotting a course that could change the fate of nations. Khalid's deep knowledge of the tribal dynamics of the region proved invaluable in identifying potential participants. Adrien's artistic sensibilities were called upon to design a symbol for the summit, one that would incorporate the powerful imagery of the obsidian stallion.

Discussions continued well into the evening, the light outside the windows fading as lamps were lit inside the office. As the plans for the Jerusalem Peace Summit took shape, I felt a growing sense of anticipation. We were on the cusp of something truly momentous, a convergence of ancient wisdom and modern diplomacy that could heal centuries of wounds.

As the meeting finally drew to a close, the Sultan rose, his bearing regal despite the lateness of the hour. "My friends," he said, his voice carrying a note of both gravity and hope, "we have embarked on a great endeavour. The road ahead will not be easy, but I believe that with the wisdom of the Obsidian Guild to guide us, we may yet achieve what generations before us could only dream of - true and lasting peace in this troubled land."

With these words we were dismissed, each of us retiring to our quarters to rest and prepare for the monumental task ahead. As I made my way through the torch-lit corridors of the palace, my mind swirling with the events of the day, I could not help but feel that we had crossed a threshold. The adventure that had begun in the dusty streets of London had taken us to the precipice of history, and what lay beyond was a future full of possibility - and danger.

⊶⊹⊱

As the golden hues of sunset gave way to the deep indigo of evening, our little band of adventurers found themselves back in the luxurious confines of our palace quarters. The day's momentous discussions had left us all in a state of deep contemplation, each of us grappling with the enormity of the task that now lay before us.

I stood at the window of my chamber and looked out over the glittering expanse of Constantinople. The city's minarets and domes were silhouetted against the darkening sky, a reminder of the centuries of history that had unfolded within these ancient walls. How strange, I thought, that our quest to solve a murder in London should have brought us to this point, on the verge of reshaping the very fabric of international relations.

A gentle knock on my door woke me from my reverie. "Enter," I called, turning to find Holmes framed in the doorway, his slender figure casting a long shadow across the richly carpeted floor.

"Ah, Watson," he said, his piercing grey eyes taking in my pensive posture by the window, "I see you too are finding sleep elusive this evening."

I nodded and gestured for him to join me. "Indeed, Holmes. My mind is swirling with the events of the day. To think that we, the humble denizens of Baker Street, should find ourselves at the centre of such momentous affairs..."

Holmes stepped to my side, his eyes sweeping over the nocturnal cityscape before us. "It is a far cry from our usual cases, is it not, my dear fellow? And yet, in many ways, it is the culmination of all that we have sought in our years together. The pursuit of truth, the unravelling of mysteries - are these not the very principles that have guided us from the beginning?

As we stood there, contemplating the vast panorama of Constantinople at night, our companions joined us one by one. Adrien d'Arcy entered first, his artist's eye drawn to the play of moonlight on the distant waters of the Bosphorus. Dr El-Sharif followed, her scholarly demeanour softened by the emotional discussions of the day. Khalid Al-Fahmi slipped in quietly, his desert-honed senses alert even in these palatial surroundings. And finally Liyana joined us, her regal bearing tempered by a newfound sense of purpose.

For a long moment we stood in companionable silence, each lost in our own thoughts. It was Liyana who finally broke the silence, her voice soft but full of conviction.

"When we set out on this journey," she began, "I thought I understood the weight of responsibility that came with my royal heritage. But now, standing here with all of you, I realise that true leadership is not about wielding power, but about fostering understanding and unity."

Adrien nodded, his artistic sensibilities clearly stirred by her words. "Indeed, Your Highness. As an artist, I have always sought to capture the essence of beauty and truth in my work. But what we have discovered - the wisdom of the Obsidian Guild, the vision of the Mystic Stallions - it transcends anything I could hope to portray on canvas."

Dr El-Sharif, her eyes alight with scholarly enthusiasm, added her own reflection. "In all my years of study, I never dreamed that I would encounter such a perfect synthesis of historical legacy and contemporary relevance. The principles of the Obsidian Guild offer us a framework not only for regional peace, but for a new understanding of our common human heritage.

Khalid, who had been silent, spoke with the quiet wisdom of one long accustomed to the vastness of the desert. "In the sands of Arabia, one learns to read the subtle signs of the wind and the stars, to navigate by the most delicate of indicators. Perhaps this is what we are called to do now - to guide the great powers of the world with the same delicacy and precision".

As our companions shared their thoughts, I watched Holmes closely. My friend, usually so detached and analytical, seemed moved by the serious reflections of our diverse group. When he finally spoke, there was a depth of emotion in his voice that I had rarely heard before.

"My friends," he said, looking at each of us in turn, "we stand at a crossroads in history. The wisdom we have discovered in the depths of the desert now calls us to action on the world stage. It is a daunting prospect, fraught with danger and uncertainty. And yet I cannot help but feel a sense of, dare I say it, optimism.

I raised an eyebrow at this uncharacteristic display of emotion from my usually stoic friend. "Optimism, Holmes? I would not have thought it your habit to indulge in such emotions."

A wry smile played at the corners of his mouth. "Perhaps, Watson, our adventures have changed me more than I realised. Or perhaps it is simply that the magnitude of our discoveries requires a new approach. Whatever the case, I find myself filled with a strange mixture of anticipation and determination."

As the night deepened around us, our conversation flowed freely, touching on our hopes for the peace summit, our concerns about potential obstacles, and our personal reflections on how far we had come. The bonds forged in the crucible of our desert journey had been strengthened by the day's events, uniting us in a common purpose that transcended our individual backgrounds and motivations.

Finally, as the first signs of dawn began to lighten the eastern sky, we bid each other good night - or rather, good morning. As I prepared for a few hours of much-needed rest, I was filled with a sense of cautious optimism. The challenges ahead were daunting, the stakes unimaginably high. Yet I could not shake the feeling that we - this unlikely band of adventurers, scholars and visionaries - were up to the task.

As I drifted off to sleep, my last conscious thought was of the Obsidian Stallion, that powerful symbol of unity born of diversity. In my mind's eye, I saw him galloping across the sands of time, carrying us all into a bright future with the promise of peace and understanding. The game, as Holmes would say, was definitely afoot - and its outcome would shape the destiny of nations.

CHAPTER 32

JERUSALEM'S SHADOWED HOPE

L eaving behind the historic magnificence of Constantinople, I was amazed by the unexpected turns that had brought our exceptional group together on this incredible adventure. The morning sun, rising over the Bosphorus, cast a golden glow on the water as we set off, its warmth a stark contrast to the chill of anticipation that ran through our group.

Our journey to Jerusalem was to be a curious blend of modern convenience and time-honoured tradition. The newly constructed railway would carry us part of the way, a testament to the inexorable march of progress, while the final leg would see us adopt the time-honoured method of travelling on horseback, a nod to the ancient ways that still held sway in this land of deep-rooted custom.

As we boarded the train, I took a moment to observe my companions, each lost in their own thoughts about the momentous task ahead. Sherlock Holmes, my dear friend and colleague, sat with his piercing grey eyes fixed on the passing landscape, his hawkish profile etched against the window. I could almost see the cogs of his formidable intellect turning, no doubt piecing together the complex puzzle of diplomacy and ancient lore that we were about to solve.

Beside him, Dr Amal El-Sharif pored over a collection of ancient texts, her scholarly brow furrowed in concentration. Her expertise in the history and culture of the region had proved invaluable throughout our journey, and I knew her insights would be crucial in the delicate negotiations ahead.

Adrien d'Arcy, the artist whose keen eye had captured so much of our adventure, sat sketching furiously, his pencil flying across the page as he tried to capture the ever-changing vistas that rolled past our window. His artistic sensibility, I thought, brought a unique perspective to our group, often revealing truths that our more analytical minds might miss.

As the landscape gradually changed from the lush hills of Anatolia to the more arid regions of the Levant, our conversations turned more and more to the task that awaited us in Jerusalem. The weight of our responsibility seemed to grow with each mile that brought us closer to the Holy City.

It was during a stop to water the horses that I truly appreciated the magnificent beasts that had become such an integral part of our party. Al-Zarib, the mystical stallion who had formed an inexplicable bond with Holmes, stood proudly beside Khalid, our steadfast guide. The horse's coat shone like polished obsidian in the harsh sunlight, and his intelligent eyes seemed to hold secrets as old as the desert itself.

Nearby, Liyana Sultan, her regal bearing undimmed by the rigours of our journey, tended to Muntasir. The horse, descended from legendary Arabian bloodlines, moved with a grace that belied its strength. The bond between Liyana and Muntasir was palpable, a silent communication flowing between them that spoke of shared trials and mutual trust.

As we continued our journey, now on horseback, the changing landscape seemed to reflect our own transformation. Gone were the green fields and bustling towns; in their place stretched an endless expanse of sand and stone, broken only by the occasional oasis or ancient ruin. The air seemed charged with the weight of history, each breath filling our lungs with the dust of empires long gone.

Khalid, astride Al-Zarib, led our procession with the easy confidence of one born to the desert. His eyes, sharp as a hawk's, scanned the horizon constantly, alert for any sign of danger. Liyana rode beside him, Muntasir moving in perfect synchrony with Al-Zarib, the two horses a living embodiment of the unity we hoped to achieve in Jerusalem.

As the sun began to set on the last day of our journey, painting the sky in shades of gold and crimson, the distant silhouette of Jerusalem appeared on the horizon. A hush fell over our group as we gazed at the ancient walls, their weathered stones bearing silent witness to centuries of triumph and tragedy.

At that moment, as we gazed upon the Holy City, I felt a strange mixture of awe and trepidation. We had come so far, unearthing secrets long buried by the sands of time, and now we stood on the precipice of a negotiation that could reshape the future of this troubled land. As I glanced at my companions, I saw my own emotions reflected in their eyes - determination, hope and a touch of fear at the monumental task that lay before us.

With a shared nod of understanding, we urged our mounts forward, the clip-clop of hooves on ancient stone a steady rhythm that seemed to echo the beating of our own hearts. Jerusalem awaited, and with it the culmination of our extraordinary quest.

As our little cavalcade approached the gates of Jerusalem, the setting sun cast a golden glow on the ancient walls, transforming the weathered stone into a vision of celestial splendour. The city, perched on its sacred hills, seemed to glow from within, as if the stones themselves were imbued with the reverence of countless pilgrims who had walked this path before us.

Riding at the head of our party, Holmes reined in his mount, his keen grey eyes scanning the imposing fortifications with a mixture of admiration and analytical interest. "Observe, Watson," he murmured, his voice barely audible over the gentle evening breeze, "how the shadows play upon these ancient stones. Every crack, every worn edge tells the story of civilisations past and present."

To our right, Khalid sat astride Al-Zarib, man and beast alike standing as still as statues carved from the very bedrock of the land. The obsidian stallion's coat shimmered in the fading light, his intelligent eyes reflecting the golden glow of the city. Khalid's weathered face wore an expression of deep reverence, his lips moving in silent prayer as he gazed upon the sacred place.

Liyana, mounted on the magnificent Muntasir, rode up beside us. The proud bearing of the Arabian stallion matched that of its rider, both embodying the noble heritage of their ancestral lands. "Even after all my travels," Liyana said softly, her voice filled with wonder, "the sight of Jerusalem never fails to stir my soul.

Dr Amal El-Sharif, her scholarly demeanour momentarily set aside, gazed at the city with bright eyes. "Gentlemen, Your Highness," she began, her voice thick with emotion, "we stand at the gates of a city that has been the crucible of faith and conflict for millennia. The very air we breathe is heavy with the hopes and sorrows of countless generations".

Adrien, who had been frantically sketching the panorama before us, looked up from his work, his artist's eye picking up nuances that even Holmes' penetrating gaze missed. "Look there," he said, pointing to the gates, "look at the crowd. What a tapestry of humanity!"

Indeed, as we approached the city gates, I was struck by the eclectic crowd milling about the entrance. Pilgrims from every corner of the globe, their faces etched with the weariness of long journeys and the anticipation of spiritual fulfilment, mingled with local merchants hawking their wares. The chatter of a dozen languages filled the air, punctuated by the braying of donkeys and the shouts of street vendors.

As we dismounted and prepared to enter the town, I could not help but notice the curious glances being cast our way. Our eclectic group - the hawk-like Holmes, the regal Liyana, the scholarly Amal, the artistic Adrien, the desert-loving Khalid and myself - must have presented a curious sight indeed.

The magnificent forms of Al-Zarib and Muntasir only added to the intrigue, their presence drawing whispers of admiration from the crowd.

"Holmes," I whispered as we led our horses to the gate, "do you not feel it? There's a palpable tension in the air, an undercurrent of... something I can't quite put my finger on."

My friend nodded sagely, his eyes darting from face to face in the crowd. "Indeed, Watson. Jerusalem stands at a crossroads of faith and politics, a nexus of ancient grudges and timeless hopes. We must tread carefully here, for every stone beneath our feet is laden with meaning."

As we passed through the massive gates, the last rays of the setting sun slipped behind the western hills, plunging the narrow streets before us into twilight. The transition was sudden and profound, as if we had stepped from one world into another. The bustle of the crowd seemed muted now, voices hushed as if in deference to the sanctity of the place.

Khalid, leading Al-Zarib with a gentle hand, spoke softly. "Welcome to Al-Quds, the holy city. May our presence here bring light to the shadows that have darkened its streets for too long."

Liyana, walking beside Muntasir, added, "And may the wisdom we have gained on our journey guide us in the delicate task that lies ahead."

As we made our way deeper into the labyrinthine streets of Jerusalem, I felt a chill run down my spine - whether from the cooling evening air or the weight of the task before us, I could not tell. One thing was certain: we had entered a realm where the mundane and the miraculous walked hand in hand, and the fate of nations might well depend on our actions in the days ahead.

<hr />

As our unique procession wound its way through the labyrinthine streets of Jerusalem, I was completely captivated by the kaleidoscope of sights, sounds and smells that assaulted our senses. The narrow streets, their stone walls worn smooth by the passage of countless pilgrims and merchants over the centuries, seemed to close in around us, creating an atmosphere at once intimate and overwhelming.

Our party, led by a contingent of Ottoman cavalry, their polished sabres gleaming in the flickering light of the street lamps, cut a remarkable figure. Holmes led the way, his hawkish profile alert to every nuance of our surroundings. Beside him, Khalid led the magnificent Al-Zarib, the hooves of the obsidian stallion striking sparks from the ancient cobbles. The bond between man and beast was palpable, a silent communication flowing between them that spoke of shared trials and mutual trust.

Liyana rode astride Muntasir, the Arabian stallion's proud bearing matching the regal demeanour of his mistress. The princess's eyes darted from face to face in the crowd, her expression a mixture of curiosity and caution. "Observe, Dr

Watson," she murmured as I fell into step beside her, "how the very air seems charged with anticipation. It is as if the city itself is holding its breath, waiting to see what our presence here will bring."

Indeed, the people of Jerusalem regarded our procession with a mixture of awe and wariness. Faces peered out of shaded doorways and barred windows, their expressions ranging from open curiosity to wary suspicion. The diversity of the population was striking - here a group of Orthodox Jews in their distinctive black garb, there a group of Muslim traders closing up their stalls for the evening, and over there a group of Christian pilgrims, their faces aglow with the fervour of faith.

Dr Amal El-Sharif, walking beside me, seemed to vibrate with barely contained excitement. Her scholarly eyes soaked up every detail of our surroundings, and I could almost see the connections forming in her mind, linking the living, breathing city before us to the ancient texts she had so assiduously studied. "Do you feel it, Dr Watson?" she whispered, her voice thick with emotion. "We walk in the footsteps of prophets and kings, conquerors and saints. Every stone, every archway holds a fragment of history."

Adrien, for his part, seemed almost overwhelmed by the sensory feast before him. His artist's eye darted from scene to scene, his fingers twitching as if longing for pen and paper. "Mon Dieu," he breathed, "what a canvas this city is! The play of light and shadow, the vivid colours of the market stalls, the faces of the people themselves - each one a masterpiece in itself!"

As we moved deeper into the heart of the Old City, we were enveloped by the scents of the marketplace - the pungent aroma of spices, the sweet perfume of ripe fruit, the earthy smell of freshly baked bread. These mingled with the more pungent notes of tanned leather and the musky scent of incense wafting from nearby places of worship, creating an olfactory tapestry as rich and complex as the city's history.

Holmes, ever observant, paused briefly to examine a pile of clay pots outside a pottery workshop. "Notice, Watson," he said, his voice low but intense, "how even the most mundane objects here are imbued with centuries of tradition. The very shape of these vessels has remained unchanged since biblical times."

Our progress was slow, the narrow streets and crowds of curious onlookers demanding a measured pace. This gave me ample opportunity to observe my companions' reactions to our extraordinary surroundings. Khalid, despite his familiarity with the region, seemed to regard the holy city with a mixture of awe and apprehension, his hand never far from Al-Zarib's flank. The horse, for his part, remained remarkably calm amid the bustle and clamour, his intelligent eyes scanning the crowd as if searching for potential threats.

As we neared the end of the winding lane, the road suddenly opened into a wider thoroughfare. Here the full majesty of Jerusalem was revealed - the golden dome of the Dome of the Rock glistening in the last rays of the setting sun, the ancient walls of the Temple Mount rising like a bulwark against time itself.

It was at that moment that I truly understood the enormity of our task. Here, in this city that had been a crucible of faith and conflict for millennia, we were to try to forge a peace that had eluded generations of rulers and diplomats. The weight of history was upon us, as palpable as the stones beneath our feet.

Liyana, as if sensing my thoughts, leaned down from Muntasir's back to place a gentle hand on my shoulder. "Take heart, Dr Watson," she said, her voice soft but full of determination. "We carry with us not only the wisdom of the Obsidian Guild, but the hopes of all who long for peace in this troubled land."

As our procession continued towards our lodgings, I caught Holmes' eye. The look we exchanged spoke volumes - of the dangers we had faced, the wonders we had witnessed, and the monumental task that now lay before us. The game, as my friend used to say, was definitely on, and the stakes had never been higher.

⁂

As the last vestiges of daylight faded from the Jerusalem sky, our extraordinary company finally arrived at our designated quarters. The building, a stone structure of considerable age, stood like a silent sentinel at the junction of three narrow streets, its weathered facade bearing silent witness to the passage of centuries. The soft glow of oil lamps spilled from its windows, a welcoming beacon in the gathering dusk.

Holmes, ever alert, was the first to dismount, his keen eyes scanning our surroundings with habitual caution. "Well, Watson," he murmured as I joined him on the cobbles, "it seems our journey has led us to a most intriguing place. Note the Crusader stonework juxtaposed with distinctly Ottoman ornamentation. A fitting metaphor, perhaps, for the task ahead."

Khalid slid from Al-Zarib's back with the fluid grace of one born to the saddle. The obsidian stallion, far from showing signs of fatigue from our long journey, stood proud and alert, his intelligent eyes reflecting the flickering lamplight. "Peace be upon this house," Khalid intoned softly, running a hand down Al-Zarib's powerful neck. "May it provide us with sanctuary and wisdom in equal measure."

Liyana, still astride the magnificent Muntasir, surveyed our quarters with a regal air. "It is humble, perhaps, compared to the palaces of Constantinople," she observed, "but I sense a certain... gravity about the place. As if the stones themselves are imbued with the weight of history."

As Liyana gracefully dismounted, assisted by the ever-gallant Adrien, I noticed Dr Amal El-Sharif approaching the entrance to the building. Her scholarly enthusiasm, seemingly undimmed by the rigours of our journey, was evident in her eager posture. "Gentlemen, Your Highness," she called back to us, her voice tinged with excitement, "do you see the inscription above the door? It's a fascinating mixture of Arabic and Hebrew, dating from the Mamluk period, if I'm not mistaken."

Before either of us could respond to Amal's observation, the heavy wooden door swung open, revealing a figure silhouetted against the warm light from within. As our eyes adjusted, we recognised the face of our local guide, a man whose lined face spoke of a lifetime of navigating the complex currents of Jerusalem's political and spiritual landscape.

"Welcome, honoured guests," he greeted us, his voice carrying the measured tones of one accustomed to dealing with dignitaries. "Your arrival has been eagerly anticipated. Please come in and refresh yourselves after your long journey."

As we crossed the threshold, the guide's next words stopped us all in our tracks. "I trust your journey was without incident? Excellent. You'll be pleased to know that Ammar ibn Nadir awaits you inside."

A wave of surprise ran through our group at this announcement. Holmes, his eyebrow arched in that characteristic expression of intrigued curiosity, was the first to speak. "Ammar ibn Nadir? Here in Jerusalem? Most unexpected, though not unwelcome. The threads of our adventure, it seems, continue to weave themselves into an ever more intricate tapestry."

Khalid, who had been leading Al-Zarib towards the adjoining stables, turned back at the mention of Ammar's name. "The leader of the Obsidian Guild, here?" he mused, his normally impassive features betraying a mixture of awe and concern. "Truly, the hands of fate guide our steps."

Liyana, who had been in silent conversation with Muntasir, as if to bid the noble steed a temporary farewell, looked up sharply. "Ammar's presence can only mean that our mission here is even more important than we imagined," she said, her voice low but intense.

Adrien, who had been sketching the façade of the building in the fading light, closed his notebook with a snap. "Mon Dieu," he exclaimed, "just when I thought our adventure could not get any more extraordinary! What revelations await us now, I wonder?"

As we entered the cool interior of the building, I marvelled once again at the strange turns our journey had taken. From the fog-shrouded streets of London, to the sun-baked vastness of the Arabian desert, and now to the holy city of Jerusalem, each step had led us deeper into a mystery that seemed to encompass the very fabric of history itself.

Holmes, noticing my thoughtful expression, put a hand on my shoulder. "Brace yourself, my dear Watson," he said, his voice carrying that familiar note of excitement that always preceded our greatest adventures. "I suspect that our reunion with Ammar ibn Nadir will prove to be only the opening gambit in a game of unprecedented stakes."

As our guide led us deeper into the building, to the chamber where Ammar awaited, I felt a strange mixture of anticipation and trepidation. The air seemed charged with potential, as if the atoms around us were aligning themselves for some momentous revelation. Whatever lay ahead, I knew with certainty that it would challenge not only our intellects, but our very understanding of the world and our place in it.

Our guide led us through a labyrinth of cool, stone-walled corridors, the flickering light of oil lamps casting dancing shadows that seemed to whisper ancient secrets. At last we reached a heavy wooden door, its surface decorated with intricate arabesque carvings. With a respectful nod, our guide stepped aside, leaving us to enter of our own accord.

Holmes, always the leader in moments of uncertainty, placed his hand on the weathered wood and pushed. The door swung open with a low groan, revealing a chamber that seemed to exist outside the boundaries of time itself.

The room was circular, its high vaulted ceiling lost in shadow. Dozens of candles cast a warm golden glow across the room, their light reflecting off polished brass and gleaming off the gilded edges of ancient tomes that lined the walls. In the centre of the room, seated on a richly embroidered cushion, was Ammar Ibn Nadir.

The leader of the Obsidian Guild looked up as we entered, his ageless eyes sparkling with a mixture of wisdom and warmth. "Ah, my friends," he said, his voice as rich and soft as aged honey, "how good it is to see you again. Your journey from Al-Hijr has been long, but I trust it has been enlightening."

As we entered the room, I watched my companions' reactions. Holmes, his keen analytical mind always at work, studied Ammar with an intensity that spoke of both respect and curiosity. Liyana, her regal bearing tempered by the familiar presence of our desert guide, stepped forward with a graceful tilt of her head. "Ammar ibn Nadir," she said, her voice warm with genuine affection, "your presence here brings us great comfort. The wisdom of the Obsidian Guild is needed now more than ever."

Khalid, who had been silent since our arrival, now spoke, his voice carrying the reverence of one addressing a revered elder. "Master Ammar," he said, "Al-Zarib sensed your presence even before we entered the building. The bond between the Guild and the noble steeds of the desert remains strong."

Ammar's eyes crinkled with delight. "Indeed, Khalid. The horses are in many ways wiser than we are. They understand truths that we humans often find difficult to grasp." He paused, his eyes sweeping over our group. "And speaking of our equine friends, I trust you are prepared for the ceremonial race that will mark the opening of the summit?"

A wave of surprise ran through our group. Holmes, always quick to grasp new information, leaned forward with interest. "A ceremonial race, you say? Tell us more, Ammar."

Ammar nodded, his expression becoming solemn. "Yes, a race that will symbolise the very essence of what we hope to achieve at this summit. Three horses, each representing a different cultural heritage, will race not against each other, but together, in a display of unity and common purpose."

"Isinglass will be there," Adrien interjected, his eyes bright with anticipation. "I received word just before we left Constantinople. He's being flown in from London especially for the occasion."

"Indeed," Ammar confirmed. "Isinglass, representing the legacy of the Darley Arabs. Muntasir, carrying the blood of the Godolphin Barb. And Al-Zarib, descended from the fierce Byerley Turk. These three bloodlines, once separated, are now brought together in the holy city of Jerusalem. It is a powerful symbol of the unity we seek to foster.

Dr Amal El-Sharif stepped forward, her scholarly enthusiasm barely contained. "Ammar," she began, her voice quivering with excitement, "this race... it echoes the prophecies in the texts we discovered in Al-Hijr, doesn't it? The meeting of the three bloodlines in the City of Peace?"

Ammar's eyes twinkled with agreement. "Your insight serves you well, Amal. Yes, the race is more than a spectacle. It is the physical manifestation of ancient wisdom, a living embodiment of the Obsidian Guild's principles of unity and understanding."

He rose to his feet with fluid grace and moved to a large map of Jerusalem hanging on the wall. His finger traced the lines of the city's ancient streets as he spoke. "The race will wind through the heart of Jerusalem, passing landmarks sacred to all three great faiths. It will be a reminder to all who witness it that our strength lies not in our differences, but in our common humanity."

As Ammar continued to explain the significance of the race and its connection to the wider aims of the Summit, I noticed a change in my companions. Holmes' eyes gleamed with the light of intellectual challenge, no doubt already analysing the diplomatic implications. Liyana and Khalid exchanged a look of shared purpose, their bond with their mounts taking on new meaning. Adrien's hand moved quickly over his sketchbook, capturing the moment in quick, sure strokes.

For my part, I felt a sense of awe at the layers of meaning woven into this event. What had initially appeared to be a simple horse race turned out to be a profound act of symbolism and diplomacy.

Ammar, sensing our growing understanding, nodded in satisfaction. "You are beginning to see, my friends, the true nature of the task before you. The wisdom of the Obsidian Guild is not merely knowledge to be guarded, but a living force to be applied. In this race, and in the summit that follows, you must find a way to bridge the chasms of mistrust and hatred that have divided humanity for too long.

As our meeting continued late into the night, with Ammar sharing more of the ancient wisdom that would guide our efforts, I couldn't help but feel that we were on the brink of something truly momentous. The shadows over Jerusalem, it seemed, were about to be illuminated not only by the light of ancient wisdom and modern diplomacy, but by the thundering hooves of three noble steeds carrying the hope of a united future.

⊰※⊱

As the first light of dawn began to creep over the ancient walls of Jerusalem, our eclectic band gathered in a secluded courtyard of our lodgings. Shielded from prying eyes by high stone walls adorned with climbing vines, the space provided an ideal setting for the crucial planning session that lay ahead.

Holmes, his lean figure silhouetted against the pale morning sky, stood at a makeshift table laden with maps of the city and documents relating to the upcoming summit. His keen grey eyes, alight with intellectual fervor, swept over our assembled group.

"Ladies and gentlemen," he began, his voice crisp in the cool morning air, "we stand at a crossroads of history. The knowledge we have gained and the trials we have faced have all led to this moment. Now, we must find a way to translate the wisdom of the Obsidian Guild into the language of modern diplomacy."

Ammar ibn Nadir, seated cross-legged on a richly embroidered cushion, nodded sagely. "Indeed, Mr. Holmes. The ancient and the modern must find harmony if we are to succeed in our endeavor."

As our discussion progressed, Mycroft Holmes cleared his throat, drawing the group's attention. "There is one more matter of significance we must address - the ceremonial race," he stated, his tone measured and deliberate.

Holmes's eyebrow arched with interest. "Ah yes, the race. A masterstroke of diplomacy, I must say. Uniting the bloodlines of the Darley Arabian, Godolphin Barb, and Byerley Turk in a display of shared heritage and cooperation."

Liyana nodded, her eyes bright with anticipation. "Muntasir and I have been preparing for this moment. It's not just a race, but a symbol of the unity we hope to achieve."

Khalid, usually so stoic, allowed a small smile to cross his features. "Al-Zarib, too, seems to understand the gravity of what lies ahead. His spirit is as fierce as ever, but tempered now with purpose."

Adrien leaned forward, his artist's sensibilities clearly stirred by the symbolism of the event. "And Isinglass will be joining us from London. I can hardly wait to see him again. To think, these three great bloodlines, reunited in the holy city of Jerusalem!"

"Indeed," Ammar interjected, his voice carrying the weight of ancient wisdom. "This race is more than a mere sporting event. It is a living embodiment of the principles the Obsidian Guild has long stood for - unity in diversity, strength through cooperation."

As the group delved into the details of the race - its route through the city, security considerations, and diplomatic implications - I couldn't help but feel a sense of anticipation building. However, a nagging thought pressed at the back of my mind, and I found I could not remain silent.

"Holmes," I ventured, "what of Farid? Surely we must consider him in our preparations. After all he's done, could he not pose a threat to the summit or the race?"

A hush fell over the group at the mention of our former adversary. Holmes's expression grew grave as he exchanged a glance with his brother.

"A pertinent question, Watson," Mycroft replied, his voice low. "Farid is currently in our custody, undergoing extensive debriefing. While he has shown signs of remorse and a willingness to cooperate, we cannot discount the possibility of lingering loyalties or hidden agendas."

Holmes nodded, his fingers steepled beneath his chin in that familiar pose of deep thought. "Indeed. We must remain vigilant. Farid's network, though diminished, may not be entirely dismantled. We would do well to consider potential threats not just from without, but from within."

Liyana, her diplomatic instincts coming to the fore, spoke up. "Perhaps we could use this situation to our advantage. If Farid truly wishes to make amends, his insights could prove invaluable in securing both the summit and the race."

"A bold suggestion," Khalid mused, his hand unconsciously moving to the hilt of his curved dagger. "But one not without merit. The wisdom of the desert teaches us that even the scorpion may prove an ally when crossing the river."

As our planning session continued, we wove considerations of Farid and potential remnants of his network into our strategies. The sun climbed higher in the sky, bathing the courtyard in golden light. Ideas were proposed, debated, refined, and either adopted or discarded. Through it all, I sensed a growing unity of purpose among our diverse band.

Holmes, his eyes gleaming with that familiar light of intellectual challenge, addressed us all. "My friends, we have laid the groundwork for what may prove to be the most significant diplomatic endeavor of our age. The ceremonial race will be our opening gambit in this grand game of peace. The path ahead is fraught with challenges, but I have every confidence that together, we shall prevail."

With those words, we dispersed to our various tasks, each of us carrying a piece of the grand design we had crafted together. As I followed Holmes from the courtyard, I cast one last glance over my shoulder. The morning sun, now high in the sky, cast a golden glow over Jerusalem, as if nature itself were offering its blessing to our endeavors. Whatever challenges lay ahead in the coming days, I knew we would face them not as individuals, but as a united force, bound by shared purpose and the timeless wisdom of the Obsidian Guild.

As the last rays of the setting sun painted the ancient stones of Jerusalem in shades of gold and crimson, our small band of adventurers gathered on the flat roof of our lodgings. The frenetic preparations of the day had given way to a moment of quiet reflection, a brief respite before the storm of diplomacy - and the momentous race - that awaited us the following morning.

Holmes stood on the parapet, his hawkish profile etched against the darkening sky. His keen eyes scanned the city's skyline, taking in the domes, minarets and towers that spoke of Jerusalem's long and turbulent history. "Watson," he murmured as I joined him, "do you feel it? The very air seems charged with the weight of tomorrow's proceedings."

I nodded, words failing me as I contemplated the enormity of our task. The summit before us was no mere political gathering, but a confluence of forces that had shaped the destinies of nations for millennia. And at its heart, the ceremonial race that promised to be both a symbol of unity and a potential flashpoint.

Behind us, our companions were engaged in their own quiet reflections. Liyana sat cross-legged on a colourful kilim rug, her regal bearing tempered by the intimacy of the moment. Her fingers absently traced patterns in the fabric as she gazed out over the city. "Muntasir is restless," she said quietly. "He senses the importance of tomorrow's race. I only hope that our performance will live up to its symbolic significance."

Khalid stood a short distance away, his weathered face turned to the east. The call to prayer rose from a nearby minaret and I saw his lips move in silent supplication. His hand rested on the hilt of his curved dagger, an unconscious gesture that spoke of his readiness to defend our mission against any threat. "Al-Zarib is also eager," he added. "But I worry about security. Such a high-profile event, with so many dignitaries present..."

His words hung in the air, giving voice to a concern we had all harboured. Holmes turned from the parapet, his expression grave. "Indeed, Khalid. The race represents both our greatest opportunity and our most vulnerable moment. We must be vigilant."

Dr Amal El-Sharif sat surrounded by a small fortress of books and scrolls, her scholarly enthusiasm undimmed by the lateness of the hour. "This is extraordinary," she said, looking up from an ancient text. "There are prophecies here that speak of a great gathering in Jerusalem, of three noble steeds uniting the peoples. It's as if our race was foretold centuries ago."

Adrien, his artist's eye captivated by the play of light and shadow across the city, sketched furiously in his notebook. "If only I could capture it," he murmured, more to himself than to us. "The essence of Jerusalem, the spirit that has drawn pilgrims and conquerors for thousands of years. And tomorrow, to see Isinglass again, to see him run alongside Muntasir and Al-Zarib... it will be a sight for the ages".

Ammar Ibn Nadir, the venerable leader of the Obsidian Guild, sat in silent meditation, his eyes closed but his face alert. The wisdom of the ages seemed to emanate from his very being, a tangible reminder of the ancient knowledge that had guided our journey. "The race," he said, opening his eyes, "is but a reflection of the greater race we all run - the race towards understanding and peace. Its outcome will set the tone for the entire summit."

As night fell in earnest, stars began to appear in the velvety sky above, their eternal light a stark contrast to the flickering lamps of the city below. A cool breeze blew in, carrying with it the mixed scents of incense, spices and desert sand.

Then we heard it - the soft nicker of horses from the stables below. Al-Zarib and Muntasir, though not on the roof, seemed to be giving their silent support to our vigil. Khalid smiled at the sound, a rare expression that softened his stern features. "Even now they sense the importance of what we are doing here," he said. "The bond between man and horse, like the wisdom of the Obsidian Guild, transcends the boundaries of time and culture."

Holmes, who had been silent for some time, now addressed our group. "My friends," he began, his voice uncharacteristically soft, "we stand at the precipice of history. Tomorrow's race is more than a spectacle - it is the opening gambit in our quest for peace. We must ensure that every aspect of it, from the security measures to the symbolism of the route, reinforces our message of unity and shared heritage".

He paused, his gaze sweeping over each of us in turn. "Liyana, your grace atop Muntasir will remind all of the nobility of our cause. Khalid, your union with Al-Zarib will demonstrate the power of trust and cooperation. Adrien, your reunion with Isinglass will symbolise the bridging of distances, both physical and cultural.

I felt a lump form in my throat at Holmes' words, touched by this rare display of emotion from my usually stoic companion.

"Together," Holmes continued, "we have travelled from the fog-shrouded streets of London, to the sun-baked sands of the Arabian desert, and now to this most ancient of cities. We have faced dangers beyond imagination, unlocked secrets lost to time and forged bonds stronger than steel. Whatever challenges tomorrow may bring, whether in the race or the negotiations that follow, I have no doubt that we will face them together.

As Holmes finished, a hush fell over our group. The enormity of our task, the weight of history and the hopes of countless souls seemed to be bearing down on us. Yet I felt not despair, but a strange exhilaration. For in that moment, standing under the stars of Jerusalem with this extraordinary company, I knew that we were part of something greater than ourselves.

The night deepened around us, the city below slowly fading into silence. Yet Jerusalem itself seemed alive with possibility, its ancient stones whispering of the countless dramas they had witnessed and the new chapter that was about to unfold.

As we finally retired to our rooms, each lost in our own thoughts of the race and the summit to come, I took one last look at the sleeping city. The challenges ahead were daunting, the risks undeniable. But whatever the future held, I knew that the bonds forged in the crucible of our journey would endure. With that comforting thought, I followed Holmes into the shadowy interior of our lodgings, ready to face whatever the new day might bring, be it on the racetrack or in the chambers of diplomacy.

CHAPTER 33

THE FALCON'S GAMBIT

Sleep had come fitfully, if at all, and it seemed but moments before the first light of dawn began to creep through our windows, heralding the arrival of a day that would shape the course of history. As I rose from my bed, the memory of our rooftop meeting the night before weighed heavily on my mind, its ominous discussions still ringing in my ears.

I found myself drawn to the window of our lodgings, gazing out upon the ancient city of Jerusalem, slowly awakening to what promised to be a day of monumental significance. The view before me was not unlike the one we had seen from the roof, but the morning light gave it a new aspect, at once familiar and strangely altered.

The air was crisp and expectant, carrying not only the familiar scents of spices and incense that had accompanied us throughout our stay, but also the faint whiff of excitement that heralded the approaching ceremonial race. These scents seemed to have intensified overnight, as if the very essence of the ancient city had been distilled by the cool night air.

In the streets below, I could see the subtle signs of preparation. Grooms were leading magnificent steeds to the starting point, their coats gleaming in the early morning light. Workers hurried back and forth, making last-minute adjustments to the course that would wind through the heart of the Holy City. The contrast between this building anticipation and the palpable tension in our quarters was stark indeed.

I turned from the window to watch my companions. Sherlock Holmes, his slender figure silhouetted against the brightening sky, stood at a makeshift desk, poring over a collection of documents with his characteristic intensity. The previous night had etched fresh lines of concern across his hawk-like features, a testament to the gravity of our situation. Yet I could not help but notice that his posture retained the same alertness and concentration that had marked our rooftop vigil.

"Gentlemen and lady," Holmes began, his piercing grey eyes sweeping over our assembled group, "I fear we find ourselves in a position of the utmost delicacy. As the city prepares for a spectacle of unity and hope, dark forces are moving to undermine all that we have striven to achieve. We must not forget the potential threat posed by Farid's remaining allies, as we discussed last night.

He went on to outline his suspicions about Farid's imminent threat, each word falling on us with the weight of leaden shot. As he spoke, I could not help but notice that his gaze occasionally flickered to the window, to the race preparations beyond - a silent acknowledgement of the added complexity our mission now faced.

"We must be vigilant," Holmes continued, his voice low and urgent. "The very event that was supposed to herald a new era of peace may well provide our adversaries with the perfect cover for their nefarious deeds. We must remain vigilant, not only for the success of the race, but for any signs of the dangers we've foreseen. This race embodies our hopes for unity, but we must be prepared for those who would seek to undermine it.

I watched the reactions of our companions as Holmes laid out the dangers before us. Liyana, her regal bearing undimmed by the trials of our journey, straightened her shoulders, a look of steely determination settling on her fine features. "I will not falter in my duty," she declared, "neither as a diplomat nor as a rider. Muntasir and I stand ready to champion the cause of peace, come what may."

Khalid, ever the stoic warrior, merely nodded, his hand unconsciously moving to the hilt of his curved dagger. "Al-Zarib and I will be vigilant," he said simply, though the fire in his eyes spoke volumes of his resolve.

Adrien spoke next, his artist's sensibilities clearly stirred by the gravity of our situation. "To think," he mused, "that our race, which should symbolise the unity of nations, could become a kind of battlefield. But perhaps it is fitting - for is not the road to peace often fraught with danger?

Dr Amal El-Sharif, her scholarly excitement tempered by concern, added her own thoughts. "We must not lose sight of the bigger picture," she urged. "The wisdom of the Obsidian Guild, the very legacy we carry, teaches us that true strength lies in unity. Our race must become a living embodiment of this principle, as we discussed beneath the stars last night."

As our group dispersed to make final preparations, each aware of the dual nature of their roles on this momentous day, I found myself back at Holmes' side. "I say, Holmes," I ventured, "we have faced many dangerous situations in our time, but never have the stakes been so high."

My friend's lips curled into that familiar half-smile I knew so well. "Indeed, Watson," he replied, his eyes bright with the thrill of the intellectual challenge before us. "We stand at the confluence of history and destiny. The game, my dear fellow, is most definitely afoot - and it will be played not merely on the streets of Jerusalem, but on the very soul of this ancient land."

With these words ringing in my ears, I steeled myself for the day ahead, fully aware that the fate of nations could well rest on our actions in the coming hours. As we hurried to make our final preparations, I could not shake the feeling that the coming day would test us in ways we had not yet imagined. The sense of being part of something greater than ourselves, which had so moved us during our rooftop gathering, now drove us forward with renewed purpose and determination.

❈※❈

As the first rays of the morning sun bathed Jerusalem in a golden glow, we hurried from our lodgings, the gravity of our morning briefing weighing heavily on our minds. Our carriage clattered over the ancient cobblestones, its wheels echoing the beating of my own heart as we approached the great edifice that was to host our momentous summit. I could not help but marvel at the transformation that had taken place in the city since our rooftop vigil just hours before.

The usual hustle and bustle of daily life had given way to an atmosphere of anticipation and barely concealed tension. It was as if the air hung with the weight of history in the making. As we walked through the narrow streets, I watched the changing cityscape; the holy sites of three great faiths stood as silent sentinels, while the modern trappings of diplomacy intruded upon the timeless tableau.

"Remember, Watson," Holmes murmured, his piercing grey eyes scanning our surroundings, "Farid's agents could be anywhere. We must remain as vigilant now as we resolved to be at our Dawn Council."

As we arrived at the summit venue, the heightened security was immediately apparent. Stern-faced guards, their uniforms a curious mixture of Ottoman pomp and British military precision, stood at attention at every entrance. Their watchful eyes swept over the arriving delegates and attendees, looking for any hint of threat or deception.

"Observe, Watson," Holmes continued, his keen gaze darting from one vantage point to another, "how security has been stepped up, not only for the summit, but for the race as well. Note the extra patrols along what I believe to be the proposed race route, and the increased scrutiny of all who enter, be they diplomats or stable hands. It seems that our warnings have been heeded."

Indeed, as we made our way into the Great Hall, I witnessed a curious mix of summit delegates and race officials. High-ranking diplomats in their finery rubbed shoulders with grooms with stable dust still clinging to their boots. Excited chatter about the upcoming race seemed to momentarily overshadow the weighty matters of state that had brought us all together.

But beneath this veneer of anticipation, I could sense an undercurrent of tension, not unlike that which had permeated our morning meeting. Furtive glances were exchanged between rival factions, and hushed conversations in countless tongues filled the air with a constant, low hum of activity. It was a powerful reminder of the delicate balance we were striving to achieve, and how easily it could be upset.

Holmes, for his part, seemed to be everywhere at once, his demeanour as focused and alert as it had been during our dawn briefing. His hawkish gaze swept over the assembled crowd, pausing here and there as if to memorise every face, every gesture. I knew he was looking for any sign of Farid or his agents, while also assessing the vulnerabilities that the preparations for the race might have introduced into our security.

"This way, Watson," he said at last, leading me to a quieter corner of the hall. "Our companions are taking their positions, as we discussed. We must do the same if we are to have any hope of averting disaster."

Indeed, as we moved through the crowd, I caught glimpses of our allies hard at work, each embodying the resolve they had shown in our morning council. Dr Amal El-Sharif was already deep in conversation with a group of scholars, her animated gestures suggesting a lively debate on some historical point relevant to our cause. Adrien had set up his easel in a corner, his quick, sure strokes capturing the scene before us in a way that I knew would prove invaluable to our later analysis.

Liyana moved with regal grace among the delegates, her diplomatic skills put to the test as she soothed ruffled feathers and smoothed over potential conflicts. Yet I could not help but notice that her eyes occasionally wandered to the windows, beyond which lay the racecourse where she would soon demonstrate her prowess as a rider. The determination I had seen in her eyes at dawn had not diminished in the least.

Khalid, ever vigilant, had positioned himself near one of the main entrances. His watchful eyes scanned the crowd, his hand never far from the hilt of his curved dagger, just as it had been during our meeting on the roof. I knew that even as he stood guard here, his thoughts were partly with Al-Zarib, ensuring that his trusty steed was prepared for the challenges ahead.

As Holmes and I took up our own position, one that afforded us a full view of the proceedings, I felt a strange mixture of excitement and apprehension settle over me, not unlike the conflicting emotions that had stirred within me at dawn. The summit was reconvening, the race was approaching, and with each passing moment the threads of diplomacy and danger were tightening around us.

"Steel yourself, Watson," muttered Holmes, his eyes never leaving the crowd before us. "We stand on the precipice of either greatness or disaster, as I warned you this morning. The next few hours will determine not only the fate of this summit, but perhaps the very future of this troubled land."

With these ominous words ringing in my ears, I straightened my shoulders and prepared myself for the challenges ahead. The game, as Holmes would say, was definitely afoot, and we were its principal players in this ancient city of prophets and kings.

As the morning wore on and the summit was well underway, Holmes beckoned me with a subtle nod. His grey eyes held that familiar gleam of suppressed excitement that always precedes our plunge into the heart of a mystery. Without a word, we slipped out of the grand halls of the venue and into the labyrinthine streets of Jerusalem's Old City.

Our destination was a small, nondescript café tucked away in a shadowy alleyway off the main thoroughfare. With its faded awning and weathered facade, the establishment seemed to shrink from the gaze of passers-by, as if guarding its secrets. As we entered, the rich aroma of Turkish coffee and the pungent scent of tobacco smoke enveloped us, a fitting atmosphere for clandestine business.

In the far corner, partially hidden by a potted palm tree of dubious health, sat our informant. The man Holmes had referred to only as 'The Falcon' was a study in nervous energy. His fingers drummed an incessant rhythm on the worn tabletop, his eyes darting incessantly around the room.

As we approached, Holmes murmured, "Observe, Watson. Note the man's left cuff, slightly frayed but of fine Egyptian cotton. A former man of means now reduced to dealing in secrets. And the calluses on his right hand - not those of a labourer, but of one accustomed to wielding a pen with frequency and urgency."

We sat down and without preamble The Falcon leaned forward, his voice barely above a whisper. "Mr Holmes, the information I carry comes at great personal risk. Farid's network, though diminished, remains dangerous."

Holmes' eyes narrowed. "Speak plainly, sir. Time is of the essence."

The informant nodded and swallowed hard. "Farid plans to strike during the ceremonial race. His target is not one, but three - the Sultan, the British representative and the leader of the Obsidian Guild. A simultaneous attack designed to throw the summit into chaos and reignite the very conflicts it seeks to resolve."

The words sent a shiver down my spine. The audacity of the plan was breathtaking, the potential for devastation immense. Holmes, however, remained outwardly impassive, though I detected a tightening around his eyes that spoke of the rapid calculations behind that formidable brow.

"The method?" Holmes inquired, his voice deep and determined.

"Poison," the Falcon replied. "Administered through the water served to the dignitaries during the race. Farid has agents positioned among both the serving staff and the spectators."

As our informant continued to reveal the details of Farid's nefarious plan, I marvelled at the web of intrigue that had been woven around us. Here, in this unremarkable café, we were privy to information that could change the course of history.

Holmes listened intently, his fingers tucked under his chin in that characteristic pose of deep contemplation. I could almost see the cogs of his remarkable mind whirring, piecing together disparate pieces of information into a coherent whole.

"The race," Holmes mused, almost to himself, "provides the perfect cover. The crowds, the excitement, the movement of people - all designed to conceal the actions of Farid's agents. Ingenious, in its way."

Turning to me, his eyes alight with the thrill of the chase, Holmes spoke urgently. "Watson, we must act quickly. Farid's plan, born of the bitterness we witnessed in the desert, has reached its deadly maturity. But in its complexity lies our advantage."

As we rose to leave, the gravity of our situation weighed on me like a leaden cloak. The peace that our companions - Amal with her historical insight, Adrien with his artistic vision, Liyana with her diplomatic acumen, and Khalid with his desert-born wisdom - had worked so tirelessly to foster was now hanging by the thinnest of threads.

Holmes paused at the door, his hand on my arm. "The game has entered its most critical phase, my dear Watson. We must now marshal all our resources, all our wits, to outmanoeuvre an enemy driven by vengeance and misguided ideology. The fate of nations rests on our next moves."

With those ominous words ringing in my ears, we plunged back into the bustling streets of Jerusalem, racing against time to thwart Farid's deadly gambit. The ceremonial race, meant to symbolise unity and hope, now loomed as a potential stage for tragedy. It was up to us to ensure that the only victory celebrated that day would be that of peace over discord, of wisdom over hatred.

No sooner had Holmes and I re-entered the grand halls of the summit venue than we were met by the keen gaze of Dr Amal El-Sharif. Her scholarly demeanour was tinged with an air of urgency that spoke volumes about her perception of our serious expressions.

"Dr Watson," she said in hushed tones, falling into step beside me as Holmes walked purposefully ahead, "I see from your face that our fears were not unfounded.

"Indeed, Dr El-Sharif," I replied, matching her low voice. "We must hurry to the Security Command Centre. Every second is precious."

With a nod of understanding, Amal fell into step beside me as we hurried through the ornate corridors. The juxtaposition between the grandeur of the place and the deadly danger we faced was not lost on me. Gilded mirrors and priceless tapestries glided past as we hurried towards our destination, each tick of the grandfather clocks we passed seeming to echo the countdown to potential disaster.

We arrived at an unmarked door, indistinguishable from the others except for the two stern-faced guards flanking it. Upon recognising us, they stepped aside, allowing us to enter a world far removed from the opulence of the venue itself.

⊷⊶⊙⊷⊙⊶

The Security Command Centre was a hive of quiet, concentrated activity. Banks of telegraph machines clattered softly, their coded messages a constant stream of intelligence from around the world. Maps adorned the walls, dotted with pins and flags marking troop movements and political hotspots. At the centre of this organised chaos stood Commander Stanton, a bear of a man whose piercing blue eyes seemed to take in everything at once.

"Commander," I began without preamble, "we have uncovered a plot of the most sinister nature."

Stanton's bushy eyebrows knitted together as he listened intently to our hurried explanation. Amal, her encyclopaedic knowledge of regional politics proving invaluable, provided crucial context about Farid's motivations and potential allies.

"A triple assassination," Stanton muttered, his face grim. "During the ceremonial race, you say? That leaves us little time."

With a series of sharp, precise commands, Stanton set his team in motion. I watched in admiration as the security personnel responded with quiet efficiency, each moving with purpose and determination.

"We need to replace all the water supplies for the dignitaries," Stanton declared. "And every member of the serving staff must be re-checked. Dr El-Sharif, your insight into local customs will be crucial in ensuring that our additional security measures do not cause undue alarm or offence."

Amal nodded, her eyes shining with the gravity of our task. "Of course, Commander. I will also contact Liyana. Her diplomatic acumen will be invaluable in keeping the delegates and spectators calm."

As we worked feverishly to take the necessary precautions, I could not help but feel the weight of time pressing down upon us. Every tick of the clock on the wall seemed to reverberate through the room, a stark reminder of the deadly countdown we faced.

Suddenly, the door burst open to reveal Khalid Al-Fahmi, his desert-honed instincts clearly on high alert. "I've secured the stables," he reported, his voice taut with tension. "But there are whispers among the staff of unrest near the racecourse."

Commander Stanton's eyes narrowed. "The racecourse - of course. Dr Watson, perhaps you and Mr Al-Fahmi should investigate. Your medical expertise could prove vital if we're dealing with unknown poisons."

As Khalid and I prepared to leave, Adrien d'Arcy appeared, his artist's eye having noticed subtle changes in the summit's atmosphere. "I've made some sketches of people whose behaviour seemed... off," he said, offering his notebook. "Perhaps they could be of use?"

Stanton nodded in agreement and took the sketches. "Excellent work, Mr d'Arcy. Your keen eye may have provided us with the faces of our conspirators."

As we dispersed to our assigned tasks, the gravity of our situation weighed heavily upon me. The peace of nations, the lives of key figures, and now the symbolism of the ceremonial race - all hung in the balance. And somewhere in the vast venue, or along the race course, Farid's agents moved unseen, their deadly purpose driving them forward.

The game was on, and the stakes had never been higher. As Khalid and I hurried towards the racecourse, I said a silent prayer that Holmes's unparalleled deductive skills, combined with our combined efforts, would be enough to thwart this most deadly of plots. The fate of the summit, the race and perhaps the very future of this troubled region now rested in our hands.

No sooner had I parted company with Khalid to investigate the race course than my attention was drawn to a commotion near the summit. There, amidst the gathering crowd, I spied the slender figure of Sherlock Holmes in hot pursuit of a cloaked figure that could only be Farid himself. Without hesitation, I plunged into the crowd, determined to aid my friend in this critical pursuit.

As we raced through the ancient streets of Jerusalem, the city unfolded before us like a living tapestry of intertwined history and modernity. The preparations for the race added an extra layer of complexity to our pursuit, with workers hastily erecting stands and hanging banners along the designated route. The juxtaposition of our desperate chase against the backdrop of the upcoming ceremonial race was not lost on me.

"This way, Watson!" Holmes called over his shoulder as we rounded a corner, narrowly avoiding a group of excited spectators who had already gathered for the event. The anticipation of the crowd was palpable, their chatter a stark contrast to the gravity of our mission.

As we sprinted past an ancient archway, I caught a glimpse of the race course stretching out before us. Flags of different nations fluttered in the breeze, and the smell of fresh paint mingled with the timeless aromas of the Old City. For a moment, I marvelled at the grand spectacle that would be this race, were it not for the deadly plot we were trying to foil.

Our pursuit took us through a series of narrow streets where the preparations for the race were less obvious, but the character of the city was on full display. Vendors shouted their wares, their cries mingled with the distant sound of hammering as the final touches were put to the race course.

Suddenly, two burly men - clearly Farid's accomplices - emerged from a shadowy doorway, intent on impeding our progress. Holmes, with a display of his mastery of baritsu, deftly neutralised the first assailant. I had to deal with the second, a brute of a man whose strength was fortunately offset by his lack of finesse.

As I grappled with my opponent, I noticed his attire - the uniform of a race official. "Holmes!" I shouted, "You're disguised as a race official!"

My friend, having dispatched his opponent, nodded grimly. "Indeed, Watson. Farid has positioned his men throughout the event. We must be vigilant."

No sooner had we resumed our pursuit than we encountered another of Farid's agents, this one posing as a spectator. The man, startled by our sudden appearance, reached for a concealed weapon. Holmes, his reactions as quick as ever, disarmed the villain with a well-placed blow.

As we paused to catch our breath, I saw Khalid in the distance, his keen desert-honed senses alert to any threat. He moved purposefully through the crowd, his eyes searching for any sign of danger to the horses or the race preparations.

Not far from him I spied Liyana, her regal bearing evident even as she moved with urgent grace. She seemed to be simultaneously calming a group of agitated spectators and conferring with race officials, her diplomatic skills put to the ultimate test.

"Observe, Watson," Holmes said, his breath coming in controlled gasps, "how our companions balance their duties to the race with our greater mission. It is a delicate dance indeed."

As we prepared to continue our pursuit, the distant whinnying of horses reached our ears. The sound seemed to excite Holmes, a reminder of the stakes for which we played this deadly game.

"Come, Watson," he urged, his eyes glowing with determination. "Farid cannot be far away now. We must end this hunt before the race begins, lest all our efforts be in vain."

Nodding, I fell into step beside my friend, our footsteps echoing off the ancient stones of Jerusalem. The city, with its layers of history and the promise of the ceremonial race, seemed to hold its breath as we ran towards our final confrontation with Farid. The fate of the summit, the race and perhaps the peace of nations hung in the balance as we threaded our way through the labyrinthine streets, ever closer to our quarry.

⊰⊱

Our relentless pursuit led us through a final twist of narrow alleyways and suddenly into a secluded courtyard that seemed to exist outside of time itself. The space, enclosed by weathered stone walls festooned with ancient vines, was dominated by a venerable olive tree, its gnarled trunk bearing silent witness to centuries of Jerusalem's turbulent history. With a start, I realised that we were standing on a section of the race route, the freshly painted markings a stark contrast to the ancient cobblestones.

It was here, in this hidden pocket of antiquity, that we finally cornered Farid Al-Tariq. The man who had been the architect of so much potential chaos stood with his back to the ancient olive tree, his eyes blazing with a mixture of defiance and despair. The weight of history seemed to be bearing down on us all, giving the moment a profound gravity.

As I studied Farid's face, I could not help but remember our encounters in the desert. The passionate young man who had once spoken of his cause with such conviction now seemed torn, his features a battleground of conflicting emotions. His hands clenched and unclenched at his sides, a physical manifestation of the inner struggle raging within him.

Holmes, his slender frame taut from the strain of our pursuit, stepped forward. His grey eyes, sharp as flint, locked onto Farid's face. "It ends here, Farid," he declared, his voice carrying the inexorable weight of justice. "Your plot has been exposed, your agents neutralised. Surrender now and perhaps some good will come of this day."

To my surprise, Holmes' tone softened almost imperceptibly as he continued, "I must confess, young man, that your tactical acumen and resourcefulness were most impressive. It is a pity to see such talents wasted on destructive ends."

Farid's response was a bitter laugh, tinged with the pain of a man driven to extremes by grief and misguided ideology. "Surrender, Mr Holmes? To what end? The injustices that drove me to this point still stand. The blood of my people still cries out for vengeance."

As he spoke, I saw a flash of memory cross Farid's face, a shadow of the boy he once was, standing in awe of his father. "My father," he continued, his voice dropping to a near whisper, "he sacrificed everything for our cause. How can I do less?"

Holmes' expression softened further, a flash of understanding crossing his features. "Revenge, Farid? Or justice? There is a world of difference between the two, as I think you well know. Your father's path led to his downfall. Must you follow in his footsteps?"

Farid's eyes darted to the race markings on the floor, his voice taking on a mocking tone. "And what of this farce? This race that purports to unite what centuries of conflict have torn asunder? It is but a hollow gesture, a beautifully painted facade over a crumbling edifice."

But even as he spoke, I noticed a flicker of doubt in his eyes. The freshly painted lines seemed to draw his gaze, as if they held some hidden meaning that he was only now beginning to perceive.

Before Holmes could answer, Ammar ibn Nadir, the venerable leader of the Obsidian Guild, joined us. His arrival seemed to change the very air of the courtyard, his presence a palpable force of wisdom and authority. "Farid Al-Tariq," Ammar intoned, his voice carrying the weight of time, "you stand at a crossroads, not unlike the one your father faced. The path of vengeance leads only to more bloodshed, more pain. But there is another way."

Farid's eyes widened at the mention of his father, the infamous Rasheed Al-Tariq, whose actions had set in motion the chain of events that had brought us to this moment. I could see the conflict raging within him, the clash between the bitterness that had driven him and the glimmer of hope that Ammar's words offered.

"What other way?" Farid demanded, his voice hoarse with emotion. "My father's legacy, the wrongs done to our people - how can these be addressed by mere words and compromises?"

Ammar stepped closer, his voice soft but firm. "Through understanding, Farid. Through an acknowledgement of past wrongs and a commitment to forge a better future. This race you mock - it is more than a gesture. It is a symbol of what we can achieve if we set aside our differences and strive for unity.

As Ammar spoke, I saw Farid's gaze return to the race markings. His brow was furrowed in concentration, as if he were seeing them for the first time. "The three bloodlines," he murmured, almost to himself, "united in a single purpose..."

Ammar nodded in agreement. "Indeed, Farid. Just as the race brings together different traditions, so can we find common ground. The Obsidian Guild has long taught that true strength lies not in purity of blood, but in unity of purpose and nobility of spirit."

I saw the change in Farid as Ammar's words sank in. The fire in his eyes faded, replaced by a look of deep weariness and perhaps a glimmer of hope. Ammar, sensing the change, pressed his advantage.

"The Obsidian Guild offers you a chance of redemption, Farid. A chance to use your knowledge, your passion, to build instead of destroy. To honour the memory of those lost by creating a future they would be proud of. Throughout our history, many have stood where you stand now, faced with the choice between revenge and reconciliation. Those who have chosen the path of peace have left legacies that endure to this day.

The courtyard fell silent, the ancient stones seeming to hold their breath as Farid wrestled with the choice before him. I glanced at Holmes, seeing in his expression the keen understanding of a man who has witnessed the turning points of history.

Holmes spoke again, his voice soft but searching. "Consider, Farid, the true source of the injustices you are fighting. Are they not born of the very cycle of revenge you seek to perpetuate? Break the cycle and you may yet find the justice you seek."

Farid's gaze swept over our group, lingering for a moment on Liyana. The pain in his eyes was palpable as he spoke directly to her. "Your brother," he began, his voice cracking with emotion, "I... I never meant for it to happen this way. I was blind, consumed by my father's vision. Can you ever forgive me?"

Liyana's answer was measured, her voice steady despite the tears glistening in her eyes. "Forgiveness is a journey, Farid. But it begins with one step. The choice you make now will determine whether that journey can ever begin."

Finally Farid spoke, his voice barely above a whisper. "I... I am so tired of the hate, of the fear. If there really is another way..." He looked up to meet Ammar's gaze. "I will submit to your justice, and I will do what I can to prevent any disruption to the summit and the race. Perhaps... perhaps in this way I can begin to make amends."

As Farid sank to his knees, the tension that had gripped us all seemed to dissipate like the morning mist. Holmes stepped forward, not to restrain, but to offer a hand of support to the now repentant Farid.

"Your agents," Holmes said quietly, "they must be neutralised if we are to ensure the safety of the summit and the race."

Farid nodded, his expression resolute. "I will give you all the information you need. Their locations, their plans - everything. It's the least I can do to atone for my actions."

In that moment, surrounded by the whispered echoes of centuries, I felt I had witnessed not only the resolution of our immediate crisis, but a microcosm of the very peace process we had come to Jerusalem to support. The ancient olive tree stood as a silent testament to the endurance of hope, its gnarled branches reaching for the sky as Farid now reached for a new future.

As we prepared to leave the courtyard, I caught Holmes's eye. The look we exchanged spoke volumes - of the dangers we had faced, the delicate balance we had helped to maintain, and the long road ahead in the pursuit of lasting peace. The race, and the summit it symbolised, could now continue, carrying with it renewed hope for a future in which understanding might triumph over enmity.

Farid's voice broke the silence one last time as we turned to leave. "Mr Holmes," he said, his tone filled with a newfound determination, "there is something you should know. A final piece of the puzzle that may prove crucial to the safety of the summit." And with those words, he began to reveal information that would prove invaluable in the days to come, and mark the true beginning of his journey towards redemption.

As the golden hues of late afternoon bathed Jerusalem in a warm glow, our unlikely group made its way back to the summit. Farid Al-Tariq, now a picture of quiet resignation, walked between Holmes and me, with Ammar ibn Nadir and our other companions close behind. The streets, alive with the hustle and bustle of race preparations, seemed oblivious to the momentous events that had just transpired in this secluded courtyard.

I could not help but watch Farid closely as we walked. His face bore the marks of a man struggling with deep inner turmoil. At times his eyes would dart around, as if searching for some remnant of his former convictions, only to be drawn back to the preparations for the race with a mixture of wonder and regret. It was clear that the symbolism of the race, which he had so recently scoffed at, was now speaking to him in ways he had never before considered.

On arrival we were met by Mycroft Holmes, his normally impassive features betraying a hint of relief at the sight of Farid in our company. With a nod to his brother, Mycroft took charge of our former adversary, his voice low but firm as he spoke. "Mr Al-Tariq, your cooperation is essential. We must ensure that your surrender does not disrupt the delicate preparations for the race. Can we count on your discretion?"

Farid nodded, his eyes downcast but determined. "You have my word, Mr Holmes. I will do everything in my power to undo the damage I have done." As he spoke, I noticed his gaze lingering on a nearby poster depicting the three great bloodlines that would be united in the race. The parallel with his own journey of reconciliation was not lost on him, I thought.

Mycroft, ever the master of statecraft, led Farid into a secluded chamber, his movements swift and purposeful. "Sherlock," he called over his shoulder, "a moment of your time, if you please. We must act quickly to neutralise any remaining threats."

Holmes and I exchanged glances before following Mycroft into the room.

The gravity of the situation was palpable as we gathered around a large oak table, its surface strewn with maps and documents relating to the security of the summit and the race.

"Now, Mr Al-Tariq," Mycroft began, his tone businesslike but not unfriendly, "we need a full accounting of your network. Every agent, every planned disruption. The security of the summit and the symbolic importance of the race hang in the balance."

What followed was an intense debriefing in which Farid revealed names, locations and planned operations. I watched in fascination as Holmes, his sharp mind working at a fever pitch, linked each piece of information to our existing knowledge, forming a comprehensive picture of the threats we still faced. It was a testament to Farid's intelligence and organisational skills that he could provide such detailed information from memory.

"The water supply for the dignitaries' refreshment stations," Farid revealed, his voice heavy with remorse. "We had agents in place to tamper with it during the race. And there are others positioned along the route, disguised as spectators and race officials."

As Farid spoke, I noticed a change in him. The tactical acumen that had made him such a formidable opponent was now being used to our advantage. His eyes, once clouded with doubt, now shone with a newfound sense of purpose.

I watched as Holmes' eyes narrowed, his fingers clenched under his chin in deep thought. "The complexity of the plot is both its strength and its weakness," he mused. "Mycroft, we need to prioritise. The water supply needs to be completely replaced and every member of the racing staff re-vetted immediately."

Mycroft nodded, already scribbling notes and giving quiet orders to his staff. "Agreed. And what about the agents along the track?"

"We'll have to carry out subtle but thorough security checks," Holmes replied. "Watson, your medical expertise could prove invaluable in identifying potential toxins. And we need to warn Khalid and Liyana to be extra vigilant, both for their own safety and that of their mounts."

As the debriefing continued, I marvelled at the efficiency with which the Holmes brothers worked, their minds seemingly in perfect synchronisation as they processed and acted upon Farid's information. It was a dance of intellect and strategy, with the fate of nations hanging in the balance.

Mycroft, his brow furrowed in concentration, turned to one of his aides. "Send a message to Commander Stanton immediately. Security protocols for both the summit and the race need to be updated immediately. Stress the need for discretion - we cannot allow panic to undermine everything we have worked for."

As the aide hurried away, Mycroft fixed his gaze on Farid. "Mr Al-Tariq, your cooperation to date is noted and appreciated. However, I must impress upon you the gravity of your position. The success of this summit, the symbolic power of this race - they represent our best hope for lasting peace in this region. Your continued support could go a long way towards atoning for your past actions.

Farid, his shoulders slumped under the weight of his decisions, nodded solemnly. "I understand, Mr Holmes. I am at your disposal. Whatever I can do to ensure the safety of the summit and the race, I will do. Perhaps... perhaps in this way I can begin to honour my father's memory in a way he never imagined."

As he spoke these words, I saw a flicker of old pain cross Farid's face, quickly replaced by a look of resolute determination. It was clear that he was still struggling with his father's legacy, but now he was trying to redefine it in a way that was consistent with the wisdom of the Obsidian Guild.

As the debriefing drew to a close, I caught Holmes' eye. There was a glimmer of something in his gaze - pride, perhaps, or a deeper understanding of the momentous nature of our task. "Well, Watson," he said quietly, "it seems our work is far from over. The race against time continues, but now we run not only to prevent disaster, but to secure a future of peace."

With these words, we set about our tasks with renewed vigour. The Summit buzzed with quiet but intense activity as security was tightened and final preparations for the race were made. Through it all, I could not shake the feeling that we were on the verge of something truly historic - a convergence of ancient wisdom and modern diplomacy that could reshape the future of this troubled land.

As the sun sank lower in the Jerusalem sky, casting long shadows across the ancient stones, I steeled myself for the challenges ahead. The race, both literally and figuratively, was far from over. But as I watched Farid work tirelessly alongside us, I felt a surge of hope. The very man who had tried to derail our efforts was now working with equal fervour to ensure their success. He was a powerful reminder of the transformative power of understanding and reconciliation, a living embodiment of the unity we sought to achieve through the race itself.

<hr />

As the sun began its descent towards the horizon, casting a warm golden glow over the ancient stones of Jerusalem, news of Farid's foiled plot and subsequent cooperation spread like wildfire across the summit. The grand halls and secluded rooms of our venue buzzed with hushed conversations and furtive glances as delegates and diplomats grappled with the implications of what had almost happened and the remarkable turn of events that followed.

I found myself stationed near one of the main meeting rooms, watching the ebb and flow of reactions with keen interest. It was a strange thing to witness; the very event that had been designed to sow chaos and discord was now, paradoxically, serving to unite the various factions in a shared sense of relief and renewed purpose. Farid's transformation from enemy to ally seemed to strike a chord with many, serving as a living example of the change we all hoped to see.

Liyana Sultan, her regal bearing undiminished by the day's tumultuous events, moved gracefully among the delegates. Her voice, though soft, carried a note of quiet authority that seemed to soothe frayed nerves and calm agitated tempers. "Gentlemen," I heard her say to a group of visibly shaken diplomats, "let us not see this as a near-catastrophe, but as a testament to our collective resilience. The race that awaits us tomorrow is a symbol of our unwavering commitment to peace, despite the forces that would see us divided. Indeed, the very fact that one who sought to divide us is now working towards our common goal is perhaps the most powerful symbol of all".

Her words seemed to have a profound effect and I noticed a visible change in the demeanour of those around her. The tension in their shoulders eased, replaced by a look of determination and, dare I say it, hope.

Not far from Liyana, Dr Amal El-Sharif was engaged in a lively discussion with a group of scholars and historians. Her eyes lit up with scholarly enthusiasm as she drew parallels between the foiled plot, Farid's change of heart and historical attempts to derail peace processes. "Consider," she urged her rapt audience, "how often in our shared history moments of great danger have preceded breakthroughs in understanding. Perhaps this event, Farid's transformation and the race that followed, will be remembered as just such a turning point. He is a living embodiment of the Obsidian Guild's teachings of unity and redemption.

Adrien d'Arcy, his artistic sensibilities clearly stirred by the dramatic turn of events, had set up his easel in a quiet corner. His quick, sure strokes captured the shifting moods of the gathering, creating a visual record that I knew would prove invaluable in the years to come. As I passed, I caught a glimpse of his canvas - a powerful image of diverse hands clasped in unity, with the silhouette of racing horses in the background. In the foreground, I noticed, was a subtle depiction of a figure laying down arms, clearly inspired by Farid's decision to support our cause.

Khalid Al-Fahmi, ever vigilant, had positioned himself near one of the main entrances. His watchful eyes scanned the crowd ceaselessly, but I noticed a new softness in his expression as he watched the gradual melding of factions that had been at odds only hours before. As a group of delegates approached him, eager to discuss the role of Arabian horses in the upcoming race, I saw a rare smile grace his weathered features.

Holmes, for his part, moved through the assembly like a silent sentinel, his keen gaze missing nothing of the diplomatic dance unfolding before us.

"Observe, Watson," he murmured as I fell into step beside him, "how the common experience of danger averted, coupled with the redemption of a former enemy, has united these disparate groups. The race, once a mere symbolic gesture, has now taken on a deeper meaning. It has become a beacon of hope, a tangible representation of their collective aspirations for peace and the power of reconciliation".

Indeed, as I surveyed the room, I could not help but marvel at the transformation. Delegates who had previously viewed each other with thinly veiled suspicion were now talking animatedly about the race ahead. I overheard snippets of conversation about the noble bloodlines of the competing horses, speculation about the outcome and serious discussions about the historical significance of the event. More than once I heard Farid's name mentioned with a mixture of caution and grudging respect.

Not all the reactions were uniformly positive, of course. In one corner, I noticed a group of more conservative delegates engaged in heated whispers, their expressions clouded with doubt. But even they seemed unable to fully resist the tide of cautious optimism sweeping through the assembly.

As the evening wore on, I was filled with a profound sense of the historic nature of the moment. We had averted disaster, yes, but more than that, we had inadvertently created an opportunity for real progress. The race that awaited us the next day was no longer merely ceremonial, but a powerful symbol of resilience, unity and shared hope for a peaceful future.

As the assembly finally began to disperse for the night, the atmosphere was charged with anticipation. Delegates bid each other farewell with warm handshakes and genuine smiles, the shared excitement of the race ahead having bridged divides that had seemed insurmountable just hours before.

As Holmes and I made our way back to our quarters, my friend turned to me with a rare smile. "Well, Watson," he said, his voice tinged with satisfaction, "it seems that by foiling one plot and turning an enemy to our cause, we may have laid the groundwork for a far greater victory. Tomorrow's race promises to be a spectacle not only of equestrian prowess, but of human resilience, the power of redemption and the enduring hope of peace".

With these words echoing in my mind, I retired for the night, aware that we were on the brink of a truly momentous day. The game, as Holmes would say, was very much in hand, and its outcome would reverberate far beyond the ancient walls of Jerusalem. As I drifted off to sleep, I could not help but reflect on the extraordinary journey that had brought us to this point, and the pivotal role that Farid's transformation had played in shaping the events to come.

As the first stars began to twinkle in the velvet sky above Jerusalem, our focus shifted to the critical task of securing both the summit and the race ahead. The gravity of our responsibility weighed heavily on all of us, for we knew that the success of our endeavour could well determine the future of peace in this troubled region.

Holmes, his slender figure silhouetted against the lamplight, stood at the centre of the Security Command Centre, a veritable spider at the heart of an intricate web. His sharp eyes darted from card to card, his agile mind processing and correlating information with a speed that never ceased to amaze me.

"Watson," he called, beckoning me to his side, "we must approach this as a two-pronged operation. The summit and the race, though separate in nature, are inextricably linked in terms of security. A breach in one could spell disaster for both."

I nodded, aware of the delicate balance we were trying to maintain. "What would you have me do, Holmes?"

"Your medical expertise will be invaluable, old friend," he replied. "I need you to oversee the final inspection of all refreshments and medical supplies for both the delegates and the race participants. We cannot rule out the possibility of further poisoning attempts."

As I set about my task with the utmost diligence, I watched our companions apply their unique skills to our common cause. Khalid Al-Fahmi, his desert-honed instincts on high alert, conducted a thorough examination of the stables and the horses' equipment. His intimate knowledge of equine behaviour would surely prove crucial in detecting any signs of tampering or distress among the noble steeds.

Demonstrating her diplomatic acumen, Liyana Sultan moved gracefully among the delegates, her reassuring presence and carefully chosen words helping to maintain an atmosphere of calm amidst the heightened security measures. I marvelled at her ability to reassure even the most nervous of diplomats while conveying the seriousness of our precautions.

Dr Amal El-Sharif had been in charge of vetting the historical and cultural aspects of the race route, ensuring that no detail was overlooked that might provide cover for nefarious activities. Her scholarly attention to detail, combined with her deep understanding of the complex history of the region, made her an invaluable asset to our security efforts.

Adrien d'Arcy, his artist's eye attuned to the finest detail, assisted in the final sweep of the race course. His keen observation had already led to the discovery and neutralisation of several well-concealed potential threats, each one a testament to the ingenuity of our adversaries and the need for our vigilance.

As the night wore on, the tension in the air became palpable. Each security sweep along the course brought moments of heart-stopping anticipation. I found myself holding my breath as our teams meticulously examined every nook and cranny, every shadow and crevice that could hide a hidden danger.

One particularly tense moment came near the centre of the course, when a suspicious package was discovered under a decorative archway. Time seemed to stand still as our bomb disposal experts cautiously approached the object, their movements slow and deliberate in the ghostly glow of portable lights.

Holmes, who had insisted on being present for this critical operation, stood beside me, his face a mask of concentration. "Steady now, Watson," he murmured, his voice barely audible over the pounding of my own heart. "Watch them approach from the side, minimising their exposure..."

After what felt like an eternity, but could not have been more than a few minutes, the all-clear was given. The package, though cleverly disguised, had proved harmless - a decoy, perhaps, or a relic of an earlier, aborted plot.

As dawn approached, casting its first tentative rays over the Holy City, we gathered once more in the Security Command Centre for a final briefing. Holmes, his eyes bright despite the long night, addressed our weary but determined group.

"Ladies and gentlemen," he began, his voice carrying that note of quiet authority that always commands attention, "we have done all that is humanly possible to secure both the summit and the race. But we must not allow ourselves to become complacent. Vigilance, now more than ever, must be our watchword".

As we dispersed to our final positions, I caught Holmes' eye. The look we exchanged spoke volumes - of the dangers we had faced, the challenges that lay ahead, and the profound importance of the day that now lay before us. The game, as my friend liked to say, was very much on, and its outcome would reverberate far beyond the ancient walls of Jerusalem.

With a mixture of trepidation and excitement, I stepped out into the cool morning air, ready to face whatever the new day might bring. The summit awaited, the race was about to begin, and history, I was sure, was about to be made.

⊷⊱◦※◦⊰⊶

As the morning sun climbed higher in the Jerusalem sky, casting long shadows across the ancient stones of the city, the Peace Summit reconvened with a palpable sense of renewed purpose. The great hall, with its vaulted ceilings and ornate tapestries, buzzed with an energy that was at once tense and hopeful. The events of the previous day, coupled with the anticipation of the impending race, had given a new urgency to the proceedings.

I found myself near one of the massive arched windows, which gave me an excellent vantage point from which to observe both the summit and the race preparations beyond. Holmes, ever alert, moved among the delegates with the quiet grace of a hunting cat, his keen eyes missing nothing of the subtle interplay of diplomacy unfolding before us.

Our companions, I noted with no small measure of pride, had blended seamlessly into the delicate machinery of the negotiations. Liyana Sultan, resplendent in her formal attire, was holding court with a group of senior diplomats. Her voice, though soft, carried clearly to where I stood.

"Gentlemen," she said, her tone both firm and conciliatory, "let us consider the race that awaits us. Three horses, each representing a different cultural heritage, will run together, not against each other. Can we not see in this a model for our own efforts here today?"

The diplomats, many of whom had looked at each other with thinly veiled suspicion only hours before, nodded thoughtfully. I saw hands that had been clenched in frustration begin to relax, and brows that had been furrowed in disagreement begin to smooth.

Nearby, Dr Amal El-Sharif was engaged in a lively discussion with a group of historians and cultural attachés. Her eyes lit up with scholarly enthusiasm as she drew parallels between the symbolism of race and historical instances of cultural cooperation.

"Consider," she urged her rapt audience, "how the bloodlines of these noble steeds have intertwined over the centuries, much like our own cultures. The strength of the Arabian, the speed of the English thoroughbred, the endurance of the Barb - each brings its unique qualities to create something greater than the sum of its parts. Is this not what we strive for in our negotiations?

I watched as understanding dawned on their faces, the metaphor striking a chord where dry political rhetoric had failed.

Adrien d'Arcy, his artist's sensibilities clearly stirred by the proceedings, had set up his easel in a quiet corner. His quick, sure strokes captured not only the physical likenesses of the delegates, but something of the spirit of the summit itself. As I passed, I caught a glimpse of his canvas - a powerful image of diverse hands clasped in unity, with the silhouettes of racing horses in the background.

Although not directly involved in the negotiations, Khalid Al-Fahmi provided a calming presence. His quiet dignity and intimate knowledge of the desert and its lore seemed to remind all present of the deep roots of tradition that underpinned their modern deliberations.

As the day wore on, I began to notice a subtle shift in the tenor of the negotiations. Where before there had been entrenched positions and circular arguments, there was now a willingness to seek common ground. Race, and the spirit of unity it represented, had become a touchstone to which delegates returned time and again.

One particularly poignant moment came when a dispute over water rights threatened to derail the talks. It was Holmes who intervened, his incisive mind cutting through the rhetoric to the heart of the matter.

"Gentlemen," he said, his voice carrying clearly through the suddenly hushed

SHERLOCK HOLMES - ECHOES THROUGH TIME

room, "let us consider for a moment the horses that will run tomorrow. Each of them, though of different bloodlines, requires the same basic elements to thrive - first and foremost, water. In ensuring the welfare of these noble creatures for a single race, we have managed to put aside our differences. Surely we can apply the same spirit of cooperation to the greater challenge before us?

The effect of his words was electric. I watched as the disputants, chastened and reflective, returned to their negotiations with renewed vigour and a spirit of compromise.

As the sun began to sink towards the horizon, casting a golden glow over the Holy City, I marvelled at the progress that had been made. Agreements that had seemed impossible only days before were now taking shape, each one a testament to the power of shared purpose and mutual understanding.

Holmes joined me at the window, his keen eyes scanning the race course winding through the ancient streets below. "Well, Watson," he said, a note of satisfaction in his voice, "it seems that our little equine metaphor has proved more powerful than we could have imagined. Tomorrow's race may well be remembered not for its winners, but for the victories achieved here today in its name."

As we stood there, watching the final preparations for the conclusion of the summit and the start of the race, I felt a profound sense of hope. Whatever the future might bring, we had witnessed something truly remarkable - the first fragile tendrils of peace taking root in soil long scarred by conflict.

The game, as Holmes would say, was still on. But now, it seemed, all the players were beginning to realise that victory might come not through domination, but through harmony. As night fell over Jerusalem, I retired to my quarters with a heart full of cautious optimism for the day ahead.

⊰••◦ ❈ ◦••⊱

As the last vestiges of daylight faded from the Jerusalem sky, painting the ancient stones in shades of gold and crimson, Holmes and I found ourselves on the balcony of our lodgings. The frenetic activity of the day had given way to a moment of quiet reflection, a brief respite before the momentous events that awaited us the next day.

Holmes stood on the parapet, his hawklike profile etched against the darkening sky. His keen eyes swept the city's skyline, taking in the domes, minarets and towers that told of Jerusalem's long and turbulent history. "Watson," he murmured as I joined him, "do you feel it? The very air seems charged with the weight of tomorrow's proceedings."

I nodded, words failing me as I contemplated the enormity of what lay before us. The race before us was no mere sporting event, but a confluence of forces that had shaped the destinies of nations for millennia.

"It is curious, is it not," Holmes continued, his voice taking on that

457

thoughtful tone I knew so well, "how the pursuit of justice has brought us to this moment? We came to these lands in search of a murderer, only to find ourselves embroiled in a quest for peace that spans cultures and centuries."

"Indeed, Holmes," I replied, finally finding my voice. "It seems that justice, peace and cultural understanding are more closely linked than we might have imagined. Tomorrow's race is a living embodiment of these principles."

My friend nodded, a rare smile playing at the corners of his mouth. "Exactly, Watson. In the thunder of hooves and the striving of noble steeds, we shall see the very essence of our common humanity reflected. It is a powerful metaphor, one that has already begun to bridge divides that seemed insurmountable only days ago."

As we stood in convivial silence, the sounds of the city below reached us - the call to prayer from a nearby minaret, the distant laughter of children, the soft nickering of horses in their stables. Jerusalem, it seemed, was holding its breath in anticipation of the day to come.

"I confess, Holmes," I said at length, "that I approach tomorrow with a mixture of trepidation and excitement. So much is at stake."

Holmes turned to me, his grey eyes glowing with that fire of intellect I knew so well. "As well it should, my dear fellow. But think how far we have come. The plot foiled, the summit proceeding with renewed vigour, and a symbol of unity ready to capture the imagination of all who witness it. We have good reason to be cautiously optimistic.

As night fell in earnest, stars began to appear in the velvety sky above, their eternal light a stark contrast to the flickering lamps of the city below. A cool breeze blew in, carrying with it the mingled scents of incense, spices and the unmistakable aroma of horses - a potent reminder of the event that awaited us.

From our vantage point, we could see the final preparations for the race taking place. Torches were lit along the course, their flames dancing in the gentle breeze. Grooms were leading magnificent horses to their stables, their coats gleaming in the lamplight. Officials scurried about, checking and rechecking every detail of the forthcoming ceremony.

"Observe, Watson," Holmes said, gesturing to the activity below, "how the preparations for this race mirror our own efforts over the past few days. Every detail attended to, every contingency considered, all in the service of a greater purpose."

I nodded, feeling a surge of pride at the part we had played in bringing this moment to fruition. "It is a great endeavour, Holmes. One that may well shape the future of this troubled land."

As the night deepened around us, the city slowly fading into silence, I felt a profound sense of the significance of the moment. We were on the cusp of something truly remarkable - a convergence of cultures, a bridging of divides, a chance for peace that had seemed all but impossible only a few days before.

Holmes, as if sensing my thoughts, put a hand on my shoulder. "Get some rest, Watson," he said, his voice uncharacteristically gentle. "Tomorrow promises to be a day unlike any other. We will need all our faculties."

With one last glance at the sleeping city, its ancient stones now bathed in starlight, I retired to my quarters. As I lay down, my mind swirling with thoughts of the race to come, I could not shake the feeling that we stood on the threshold of history. Whatever the morrow might bring, I knew that the memory of that night, and the hope it carried, would always be with me.

And so, on the eve of a race that promised to be both spectacle and symbol, Jerusalem slumbered. But in that slumber was the promise of awakening - to a new day, a new understanding, and perhaps, just perhaps, a new era of peace.

CHAPTER 34

THE CELESTIAL CONFLUENCE

Standing on the balcony of our lodgings in Jerusalem, I watched as the first rays of dawn painted the ancient walls, with Sherlock Holmes beside me. The air was crisp and expectant, carrying with it the mingled scents of spice markets awakening and the sweet aroma of freshly baked bread.

"Well, Watson," Holmes remarked, his keen grey eyes scanning the cityscape before us, "it seems that all of Jerusalem is holding its breath in anticipation of today's events."

Indeed, even at this early hour, the streets below were already buzzing with an energy that spoke of more than the usual hustle and bustle of daily life. Vendors were setting up their stalls with added vigour, their colourful wares a testament to the diverse cultures that have called this ancient city home. In the distance we could see the first streams of people making their way to the racecourse, their excited chatter carried to us on the morning breeze.

"It is remarkable, Holmes," I remarked, "how this race has captured the imagination of so many. You can almost feel the tension in the air, a strange mixture of excitement and the weight of diplomatic expectations."

Holmes nodded, a thoughtful expression crossing his angular features. "Indeed, my dear fellow. This is no ordinary sporting event. The outcome of today's race may well affect the delicate balance of our peace negotiations. The symbolism of unity represented by these three horses cannot be overstated."

As we spoke, my mind wandered to Isinglass, the magnificent stallion we had first met at Wentworth Manor, now down from London for this momentous occasion. "I wonder, Holmes," I mused, "what Isinglass thinks of his journey from the green fields of Surrey to the sun-baked stones of Jerusalem?"

A rare smile touched Holmes' lips. "Ah, Watson, always the romantic. But you do raise an interesting point. The journey of Isinglass mirrors our own in many ways - from a singular mystery in London to this grand stage of international diplomacy. It is a testament to the unpredictable nature of fate.

Below us, the city continued to awaken. We watched a group of Ottoman officials, resplendent in their finery, make their way to the racecourse. Not far behind them, a group of Bedouin elders walked with dignified purpose, their traditional robes a stark contrast to the suits of the British diplomats hurrying past.

"Observe, Watson," Holmes said, pointing to the various groups, "how the very fabric of this city seems to be woven from threads of innumerable cultures. Today those threads may well be drawn together in a tapestry of unity."

As the sun rose, casting a warm glow over the domes and minarets of Jerusalem, I couldn't help but feel a deep sense of anticipation. The air hummed with possibility, as if the very stones of the ancient city were aware of the historic significance of the day that lay ahead.

"Come, Watson," Holmes said at last, turning from the balcony. "We must prepare. Today promises to be a day unlike any other, and we must be ready to play our part in this great theatre of diplomacy and sport."

Nodding, I followed Holmes back to our chambers, my mind racing with thoughts of the extraordinary events that were about to unfold. Little did I know then how remarkable this day would prove to be, or how it would challenge not only our diplomatic skills, but our very understanding of the world itself.

<hr>

As Holmes and I made our way to the stables, the morning air was alive with the sounds and smells of pre-race preparations. Grooms bustled about, their arms laden with tack and brushes, while the excited whinnies of the horses punctuated the atmosphere. The energy was palpable, a heady mix of anticipation and nervousness that seemed to infect man and beast alike.

Upon reaching the stall where Isinglass was kept, Holmes paused, his piercing eyes softening in a way I had rarely seen. The magnificent stallion, his coat gleaming like burnished copper in the morning light, turned his head towards us, his intelligent gaze seeming to recognise my friend instantly.

"Ah, Isinglass," muttered Holmes as he approached the horse, "we meet again, old friend. Do you remember our last meeting at Wentworth Manor?"

To my astonishment, Isinglass nickered softly, as if in response. Holmes reached out and gently stroked the horse's neck, and I observed a strange connection between man and beast, a silent communication that transcended the boundaries of species.

"I gave you my word, didn't I?" Holmes continued, his voice deep and intense. "I promised to solve the mystery surrounding Lord Wentworth's death, and I am pleased to report that I have kept that promise. The case has been solved, justice has been done, and you, my noble friend, have played no small part in that solution."

As I watched this extraordinary exchange, I was struck by the depth of emotion in Holmes's normally impassive features. It was as if at that moment he had dropped the mask of the cold, calculating detective and revealed an aspect of his nature that I had rarely glimpsed in our long association.

Our reverie was interrupted by the arrival of Tommy Loates, Isinglass's jockey, a compact man with the weathered features of one who has spent a lifetime in the saddle.

"Mr Holmes, Dr Watson," he greeted us, touching the brim of his cap. "A pleasure to see you both again. I trust you find Isinglass in good health?"

"Indeed, Mr Loates," Holmes replied, quickly regaining his composure. "He seems to have made the journey from London admirably. Pray tell us of his journey."

As Tommy recounted the details of Isinglass' journey, I watched as Holmes' eyes kept returning to the horse, a look of thoughtful contemplation in his eyes. It was clear that my friend was pondering something beyond the mere physical condition of the animal before us.

"And how is he doing in this climate?" I inquired, my medical instincts coming to the fore. "The heat of Jerusalem is a far cry from the cool pastures of Surrey."

"He's adapted remarkably well, Doctor," Tommy assured me. "Isinglass has always been a horse of uncommon intelligence and resilience. I dare say he understands the importance of the task ahead of him."

As our conversation with Tommy continued, I noticed that Holmes had grown quiet, his gaze fixed on Isinglass with an intensity that spoke of deep, private reflection. There was something in his expression that suggested a bond far beyond that of man and horse - a bond that perhaps even Holmes himself did not fully comprehend.

As we finally left the stables, I couldn't help but remark, "I say, Holmes, I've never seen you so... moved by an animal. There's something rather extraordinary about Isinglass, isn't there?"

Holmes was silent for a moment, his brow furrowed in thought. "Watson," he finally replied, his voice barely above a whisper, "there are more things in heaven and earth than our philosophy can dream of. Isinglass... it represents something I cannot yet fully articulate. A bridge, perhaps, between the world of cold, hard facts that I have always inhabited and a realm of deeper, more ineffable truths.

As we made our way back to the gathering crowd, I reflected on Holmes' words. Little did I know that this day would challenge not only Holmes's rational worldview, but also my own understanding of the bonds that can exist between man and beast, and the profound truths that lie at the heart of mystery.

⊕H⊖⊹⊖H⊕

As Holmes and I lingered near the stables, we witnessed a touching reunion between Adrien d'Arcy and Tommy Loates. The two men embraced warmly, their faces aglow with the joy of renewed acquaintance.

"Tommy, old friend!" Adrien exclaimed, his artist's eyes shining with emotion. "How good it is to see you again. It seems an eternity since that fateful day at Epsom Downs."

"Aye, Adrien," Tommy replied, a smile creasing his weathered face. "Dark days those were, but here we are now, on the brink of something truly extraordinary."

As they reminisced about the events that had set us all on this remarkable path, I watched Holmes follow the exchange with keen interest, his keen eyes missing nothing of the interplay between the two men.

The conversation soon turned to the matter at hand, with Tommy expressing surprise at Adrien's decision to ride Isinglass himself in the ceremonial race.

"Are you sure about that, Adrien?" Tommy asked, his tone a mixture of concern and admiration. "It's no mean feat to ride a horse of Isinglass' calibre, especially in a race of such importance."

Adrien's face took on a look of determination. "I've never been more sure of anything, Tommy. There's a connection between Isinglass and me that I can't quite explain. It feels... right, somehow, that I should be the one to ride him in this race."

Tommy nodded, a look of understanding crossing his features. "I can see it in your eyes, boy. Well then, let me give you what advice I can. Isinglass is a horse of rare intelligence and spirit. Trust him and he'll trust you."

As Tommy began to share his insights with Adrien, my attention was drawn to the other horses and their riders. Liyana Sultan was standing with Muntasir, her hand resting gently on the pure black stallion's neck. The bond between them was palpable, a connection forged through shared trials and mutual respect.

Not far away, Khalid Al-Fahmi was engaged in what appeared to be a silent communion with Al-Zarib. The wild desert stallion, usually so restless, stood perfectly still under Khalid's touch, their unity of purpose evident in every line

464

of their posture.

Holmes, I noticed, was watching these interactions with an intensity that spoke of more than mere observation. There was a look in his eyes that I had rarely seen before - a mixture of wonder and something akin to longing.

"Remarkable, is it not, Watson?" he murmured, his eyes never leaving the horses and their human companions. "Observe how each pair moves as one, their very breathing synchronised. It's as if they share a single consciousness."

I nodded, equally moved by the sight. "Indeed, Holmes. It's almost... mystical, if I may use such a term."

The shadow of a smile crossed Holmes' face. "Mystical, Watson? Perhaps. Or perhaps it is simply a deeper understanding of the connections that bind all living things. I find myself... strangely affected by it."

As the final preparations for the race began, there was a palpable tension in the stables. Grooms rushed back and forth, checking and rechecking every piece of equipment. The air buzzed with nervous energy, a stark reminder of the high stakes of the event that was about to unfold.

Adrien, now fully dressed in his racing silks, approached Isinglass one last time before mounting. He leaned his forehead against the horse's and whispered words too low for us to hear. The moment was intensely private, almost sacred in its intimacy.

As we watched this final tableau, Holmes' hand came to rest on my shoulder, a rare gesture of camaraderie from my usually reserved friend.

"Come, Watson," he said, his voice deep and thoughtful. "Let us take our places. I have a feeling that what we are about to witness will challenge everything we think we know about the world and our place in it."

With these ominous words we made our way to the grandstand, leaving behind the charged atmosphere of the stables and moving towards what promised to be one of the most extraordinary events of our lives. Little did I know then how prophetic Holmes' words would prove to be, or how deeply that day would affect us all.

❖❖❖

As Holmes and I made our way to our designated box, the racecourse was a veritable sea of humanity, its stands and enclosures rapidly filling with spectators from every corner of the globe. The air was thick with a babel of languages, from the crisp tones of English aristocrats to the melodious cadences of Arabic and the guttural power of Turkish. It was as if the whole world had descended on this ancient city, drawn by the promise of a spectacle unlike any other.

When we reached our box, Dr Amal El-Sharif was already there, her dark eyes alight with scholarly excitement. She rose to greet us, her traditional robes a stark contrast to the western clothes that dominated the crowd.

"Gentlemen," she said warmly, "is it not extraordinary? To see so many cultures, so many histories, coming together in this place?"

Holmes nodded, his keen gaze sweeping over the assembled crowd. "Indeed, Dr El-Sharif. You could say that this racecourse has become a microcosm of our global society, with all its complexities and potential for conflict and harmony."

As we settled into our seats, I took a moment to survey our surroundings. Our box, while not as grand as the Royal Enclosure, had an excellent view of both the track and the other spectators. There was an almost palpable energy in the air, a mixture of excitement and nervous anticipation that seemed to crackle like static electricity.

My attention was drawn to the Royal Box, where a group of dignitaries had begun to assemble. In the centre sat the Sultan of the Ottoman Empire, his regal bearing unmistakable even at this distance. Beside him I recognised the familiar figure of Mycroft Holmes, his usual air of languid detachment belied by the sharp intelligence in his eyes. Ammar ibn Nadir, leader of the Obsidian Guild, stood a short distance away, his ancient eyes scanning the scene with an inscrutable expression.

"I say, Holmes," I remarked, "it seems that no expense has been spared in terms of security. I count no less than a dozen guards in the immediate vicinity of the royal box alone."

Holmes nodded in agreement. "Your powers of observation are improving every day, Watson. Yes, the security is indeed formidable. Note the plain-clothed men strategically positioned throughout the crowd. Their vigilance is commendable, though I dare say their skills will be tested by the sheer diversity of the gathering."

Dr El-Sharif leaned forward, her voice low but fierce. "Gentlemen, do you fully appreciate the historical significance of what we are about to witness? This is more than just a horse race. It is a symbolic union of East and West, of ancient traditions and modern diplomacy."

"Quite so, Dr El-Sharif," Holmes replied, his grey eyes sharp with interest. "And therein lies both its greatest potential and its greatest danger. The outcome of this race may well determine the success or failure of our peace negotiations."

As we continued our discussion, I couldn't help but notice the subtle changes in Holmes' demeanour. His usual air of detached analysis was tinged with what I might almost have called excitement, had I not known him better. His eyes were constantly scanning, taking in every detail of the scene before us, from the positioning of the guards to the reactions of the crowd.

"Watson," he said suddenly, his voice deep and intense, "there is something in the air today, something beyond the usual excitement of a sporting event. Can you feel it? It's as if the very atmosphere is charged with potential, with the weight of history and the promise of the future."

I nodded, feeling a chill run down my spine despite the warmth of the day. "I feel it too, Holmes. It's as if we are on the brink of something momentous, something that will change the course of history."

As the last of the spectators took their seats and a hush fell over the crowd, I found myself holding my breath in anticipation. Whatever was about to unfold on this ancient racecourse, I knew with absolute certainty that it would be unlike anything we had ever seen before. The stage was set, the players were in position, and the world watched with bated breath as the Celestial Confluence prepared to begin.

⊕HG⊹⊱HG

As the last murmurs of the crowd faded to an expectant silence, the pre-race ritual began. It was a spectacle of such profound cultural significance that I found myself holding my breath, aware that I was witnessing a moment that would go down in the annals of history.

Three venerable elders, each representing a different cultural tradition, stepped onto the track. The British representative, a dignified gentleman with silver hair, carried an oak branch. The Ottoman elder held a jar of water from the Bosphorus, while the Bedouin sheik held a handful of desert sand. They approached the three magnificent horses - Isinglass, Muntasir and Al-Zarib - who stood proudly at the starting line, their coats gleaming in the Jerusalem sun.

"Observe, Watson," Holmes murmured, his eyes bright with interest, "how every gesture, every element of this ceremony carries profound symbolic weight. This is diplomacy at its most primitive - a unity of purpose expressed through shared ritual."

Dr El-Sharif nodded in agreement. "Indeed, Mr Holmes. This ceremony draws on traditions that go back thousands of years. The oak represents strength and endurance in British lore, the water from the Bosphorus symbolises the lifeblood of the Ottoman Empire, and the desert sands embody the very essence of Bedouin culture."

As the elders began to chant in their respective languages, their voices blending in haunting harmony, my medical instincts were aroused. "Fascinating," I remarked, "watching the horses respond to the chanting. Their breathing is synchronised, their muscles relaxed yet alert. It's as if they understand the gravity of the moment."

The ritual reached its crescendo as each elder blessed the horses. Oak leaves were gently brushed across their foreheads, the waters of the Bosphorus were sprinkled along their flanks and the desert sand was scattered at their hooves. It

467

was a moment of breathtaking beauty and profound meaning.

As the elders stepped back, a herald stepped forward to formally introduce the horses and their riders. "Isinglass," he announced, his voice echoing across the silent racecourse, "descendant of the legendary Darley Arabian, ridden by Adrien d'Arcy. The crowd murmured in appreciation as Isinglass pranced forward, his dark coat gleaming like polished mahogany.

"Muntasir," the herald continued, "bearer of the noble bloodline of the Godolphin Barb, ridden by Princess Liyana Sultan." Muntasir stepped forward, his jet-black coat a stark contrast to Liyana's gleaming robes.

"And Al-Zarib," the herald concluded, "the wild child of the Byerley Turk, ridden by Khalid Al-Fahmi." Al-Zarib reared slightly as his name was called, his wild spirit barely contained.

As I watched this majestic scene unfold, I noticed a strange expression on Holmes' face. His eyes had taken on a distant look, as if he saw something beyond the physical realm before us. When he spoke, his voice was so low I could barely hear him.

"Watson," he whispered, "there is something here that defies explanation. I feel... somehow connected to these magnificent creatures. Especially Al-Zarib. It's as if I can feel his thoughts, his very essence. Illogical, I know, and yet..."

Before I could answer, a huge cheer went up from the crowd as the horses took their positions at the starting line. The atmosphere was electric, charged with an almost supernatural energy. Dr El-Sharif leaned forward, her eyes bright with excitement.

"Gentlemen," she said, her voice trembling slightly, "we stand at a crossroads in history. What happens in the next few moments may well determine the future of nations."

As the starting gun was fired, I could feel my heart pounding in my chest. Whatever was about to unfold, I knew with absolute certainty that it would be unlike anything we had ever seen before. The Celestial Confluence was about to begin, and with it a new chapter in the history of mankind.

⊕❂⊕

The crack of the starting pistol split the air, and for a moment the world seemed to hold its breath. Then, as if a dam had burst, the three magnificent steeds burst from their starting positions in an explosion of raw power and grace. The thunder of their hooves against the sun-baked earth filled the air, a primal rhythm that stirred the very soul.

"By Jove!" I exclaimed, leaning forward in my seat. "Did you see that start, Holmes? It was like they were shot out of a cannon!"

Holmes, his keen grey eyes fixed on the unfolding drama, nodded sharply. "Indeed, Watson. Observe how Adrien sits astride Isinglass - his posture is

468

impeccable, allowing the horse maximum freedom of movement while maintaining perfect control. A masterful display of horsemanship".

Dr El-Sharif, her voice tinged with excitement, added her own observations. "And look at Liyana! Her riding style is pure Bedouin - she moves as one with Muntasir, echoing the techniques passed down through generations of desert riders."

As the horses thundered down the first straight, my medical instincts came to the fore. "The physical demands on horse and rider are extraordinary," I remarked. "Look how their breathing is already strained, yet perfectly in sync. It's a testament to their training and the deep bond between horse and rider."

Holmes' eyes narrowed as he analysed the unfolding race. "Khalid is using an interesting strategy with Al-Zarib," he mused. "He's holding the horse back a little, conserving energy for a later push. A risky move, but if timed correctly, it could prove decisive."

As the horses rounded the first bend, the roar of the crowd grew to a deafening crescendo. Dr El-Sharif leaned forward, her scholarly excitement palpable. "Gentlemen, what we're witnessing is more than a race - it's a living embodiment of centuries of equestrian tradition. The way Adrien handles Isinglass echoes the techniques developed by the British cavalry, while Liyana's mastery of Muntasir speaks to the Ottoman legacy of horse breeding and training."

I nodded, mesmerised by the unfolding spectacle. "And Khalid's connection with Al-Zarib - it's almost supernatural. The way they move together, it's as if they share one mind."

At this, I noticed a strange expression pass over Holmes's face. His eyes took on a distant look, as if he saw something beyond the physical realm before us. When he spoke his voice was low, almost a whisper.

"There is something here, Watson, something that defies logical explanation. I feel... a connection, not only with Al-Zarib, but with all three horses. It's as if I can feel their thoughts, their very minds. Illogical, I know, and yet..."

Before I could answer, a collective gasp from the crowd drew our attention back to the race. The horses were entering the back straight and the dynamics of the race were shifting dramatically. Isinglass, with Adrien urging him on, had taken a slight lead. Muntasir, under Liyana's expert guidance, was matching him stride for stride. Al-Zarib, true to Khalid's strategy, held back, but the fire in his eyes spoke of untapped reserves of power.

The tension in the air was palpable, electric. Every eye in the huge crowd was on the three magnificent animals as they thundered around the far turn, their riders locked in a contest that seemed to transcend mere sport.

"Holmes," I breathed, barely daring to take my eyes off the spectacle, "I have a feeling that what we're witnessing here today is going to change... everything."

My friend nodded, his expression a mixture of wonder and analytical intensity. "Indeed, Watson. The confluence of cultures, the merging of past and present, the raw power of nature harnessed by human will - it's all coming together in this moment. And I suspect that the true significance of this race is yet to be revealed.

As the horses entered the stretch, the roar of the crowd reached a fever pitch. The Celestial Confluence was reaching its climax, and with it, I sensed, a new chapter in history was about to be written.

⊹⊱✦⊰⊹

As the horses thundered into the final stretch, an extraordinary phenomenon began to unfold before our eyes. At first I thought it was a trick of the light, a shimmering mirage born of the desert heat. But as I blinked and rubbed my eyes, the vision persisted and intensified.

"Good God, Holmes!" I cried, my voice barely audible over the roar of the crowd. "Do you see it? Around the horses - it's like they're... glowing!"

Holmes, his brow furrowed in concentration, leaned forward, his keen grey eyes fixed on the spectacle. "I see it, Watson. Although I hardly trust my own senses. Each horse seems to be surrounded by a distinct aura of light."

Indeed, as we watched in stunned amazement, ethereal halos of light had manifested around each of the racing steeds. Isinglass was enveloped in a brilliant golden glow, Muntasir in a shimmering silver light and Al-Zarib in a pulsating crimson aura.

Dr El-Sharif, her eyes wide with wonder, grabbed my arm. "It's just as the ancient texts described!" she breathed. "The legendary horses of myth, each carrying the essence of their ancestral spirits. But to see it manifest in our time... it's beyond belief!"

I shook my head, my scientific mind reeling. "This defies any rational explanation," I muttered. "Perhaps it's a mass hallucination, brought on by the excitement and heat?"

Holmes, his face a mask of intense concentration, spoke slowly. "When you have eliminated the impossible, whatever remains, however improbable, must be the truth. We are witnessing something beyond our present scientific understanding, Watson. Yet it is undeniably real."

As we watched, transfixed, the auras surrounding the horses began to change. The different colours began to merge and intertwine, creating a dazzling display of light that seemed to encompass the entire racecourse.

"Look!" cried Dr El-Sharif. "The auras are uniting, just as the horses themselves represent the unity of cultures. It's a physical manifestation of the very peace we seek!"

The crowd had fallen into an awestruck silence, the only sound the thunder of hooves and the collective gasp of thousands of spectators. Even the most sceptical observers could not deny the magical spectacle unfolding before them.

Holmes, his expression inscrutable, seemed lost in thought. When he spoke, his voice was low, as if he were talking to himself rather than to us. "There is a connection here, a bond that transcends the physical. I can feel it, Watson. It's as if the very essence of these magnificent creatures is reaching out, touching something deep within all of us."

I glanced at my friend, startled by this uncharacteristic display of emotion. There was a look in his eyes I had never seen before - a mixture of wonder, confusion and something that looked almost like... longing.

As the horses approached the finish line, now almost indistinguishable in the merged aura of light, there was a collective gasp from the crowd. The radiance had intensified to an almost blinding degree, yet no one could look away from the awe-inspiring sight.

In that moment, as the boundaries between the physical and the mystical blurred before our eyes, I felt a profound sense of witnessing something truly transformative. Whatever the outcome of the race, I knew with certainty that the world would never be the same again.

The Celestial Confluence had lived up to its name, bringing together not just horses and riders, cultures and traditions, but the very fabric of our reality with something greater, something beyond our comprehension. As I looked at Holmes, his face illuminated by the otherworldly light, I saw in his expression a reflection of my own feelings - a mixture of awe, disbelief and the dawning realisation that we stood on the brink of a new understanding of the world and our place in it.

⬦⬦⬦⬦⬦⬦

The final moments of the race unfolded with an intensity that defied description. The three magnificent steeds, now enveloped in a singular, blinding aura of light, thundered towards the finish line with a unity of purpose that seemed to transcend mere competition. The very air crackled with an energy that was at once exhilarating and deeply unsettling.

As they approached the final furlong, it was clear that something truly extraordinary was taking place. Isinglass, Muntasir and Al-Zarib were moving as one, their strides perfectly synchronised, their riders moving in harmony as if choreographed by some unseen hand. The crowd, which had fallen into an awestruck silence, now held its collective breath in anticipation.

In a moment that seemed to stretch into eternity, the three horses crossed the finish line in perfect unison. There was no winner, no loser - just a shared triumph that defied the very notion of competition. As the blinding light that had enveloped the racers began to fade, a stunned silence fell over the assembled

471

crowd.

For a heartbeat, the world stood still. Then, as if a dam had burst, the crowd erupted in a cacophony of cheers, gasps and exclamations of disbelief. The roar was deafening, a primal expression of wonder and joy that seemed to shake the very foundations of Jerusalem.

I turned to Holmes, my medical training struggling against the evidence of my own eyes. "Holmes," I stammered, "what we've just seen... it's impossible! Three horses finishing in perfect synchronisation? The laws of probability alone..."

My friend's face was a study in conflicting emotions - astonishment, confusion and an intense concentration I had seen in our most perplexing cases. "Ah, Watson," he replied, his voice barely audible over the roar of the crowd, "when you have eliminated the impossible, whatever remains, however improbable, must be the truth. We have just seen the impossible become manifest".

Dr El-Sharif, her eyes shining with a mixture of scientific excitement and pure awe, grabbed my arm. "Gentlemen," she exclaimed, "we have just seen myth and reality come together! The ancient texts speak of such unity, but to witness it in our time... it's beyond miraculous!"

As the initial shock wore off, I watched the various reactions ripple through the crowd. Hardened gamblers stood slack-jawed in disbelief, their betting slips forgotten. Diplomats and dignitaries in the Royal Box were engaged in fervent discussion, their usual decorum abandoned in the face of the extraordinary. And everywhere, on faces of every nationality and creed, I saw the same expression of wonder and renewed hope.

Holmes, however, had fallen into one of his deep, contemplative silences. His brow was furrowed, his eyes distant, as if he were perceiving something beyond the physical realm. When he finally spoke, his words were so soft that I had to lean forward to hear them.

"Watson," he murmured, "I fear we stand at a crossroads in history. What we have witnessed today goes beyond mere sport or diplomacy. It touches on something... fundamental. The very nature of reality, perhaps, or the invisible bonds that bind all living things together. I sense that the reverberations of this event will reverberate through the ages."

As I pondered Holmes' words, I felt a chill run down my spine, despite the warmth of the day. Looking out over the cheering crowd, at the three riders now embracing at the finish line, their horses standing proudly beside them, I was struck by a profound sense of witnessing a turning point in human history.

The Celestial Confluence had lived up to its name, bringing together not only horses and riders, cultures and traditions, but perhaps even the very fabric of our reality with something greater, something beyond our current comprehension. As the celebration continued around us, I couldn't shake the feeling that the world had changed irrevocably and that we were privileged to be on the cusp of that change.

⊷⊙⊱⊰⊙⊶

The aftermath of that extraordinary race was a tableau of jubilation and wonder that I shall never forget. The racecourse, so recently the scene of an event that defied explanation, was now teeming with an exuberant crowd, their faces aglow with joy and wonder. The air was alive with excited chatter in a dozen languages, a veritable Babel of celebrations.

At the centre of it all stood the three riders - Adrien, Liyana and Khalid - their faces etched with a mixture of exhilaration and awe. Their mounts, Isinglass, Muntasir and Al-Zarib, stood proudly beside them, their coats still gleaming with a faint, otherworldly sheen.

"Come, Watson," said Holmes, rising from his seat. "Let us join the festivities and perhaps gain some insight from our intrepid horsemen."

As we made our way through the crowd, accompanied by Dr El-Sharif, we witnessed the beginning of the ceremonial wreath laying. It was a spectacle that beautifully encapsulated the spirit of unity that had permeated the entire event.

Three elders - one British, one Ottoman and one Bedouin - approached the riders, each carrying a wreath that spoke to their cultural traditions. The British wreath was made from oak leaves and roses, the Ottoman from olive branches and tulips, and the Bedouin from desert flowers and falcon feathers. With great solemnity they placed these symbols of honour around the necks of the horses, an act that went beyond mere ceremony to become a powerful affirmation of shared respect and understanding.

When we reached the riders, I was struck by the transformation in each of them. Adrien's face lit up with a joy that transcended mere victory, Liyana's regal bearing was softened by an air of profound wonder, and Khalid's usual stoicism had given way to an expression of deep reverence.

"My friends," Holmes addressed them, "you have given us a performance that will be spoken of for generations. Pray, tell us, what was it like to be at the heart of such an extraordinary event?"

Adrien was the first to answer, his voice trembling with emotion. "Mr Holmes, Dr Watson, it was... transcendent. For a moment, Isinglass and I were not two beings, but one. I felt connected not only to him, but to Liyana, to Khalid, to their mounts - to the very essence of horsemanship itself."

Liyana nodded in agreement. "It was as if the spirits of our ancestors were riding with us," she added, her eyes shining. "I felt the weight of history, but also a deep hope for the future."

Khalid, always a man of few words, simply placed his hand on Al-Zarib's neck. "The desert speaks in many ways," he said quietly. "Today it spoke through us."

As we talked, I couldn't help but notice the change in the dynamic among the summit participants who had gathered around us. Diplomats who had previously regarded each other with thinly veiled suspicion now spoke animatedly, their barriers seemingly dissolved by the shared experience of the race.

Dr El-Sharif, her scholarly excitement palpable, turned to Holmes. "Mr Holmes, surely you must see the profound implications of this event for the peace process? The unity shown here today could be a powerful catalyst for understanding and cooperation."

Holmes nodded slowly, his grey eyes distant. "Indeed, Dr El-Sharif. What we have witnessed today goes beyond mere symbolism. It touches on something fundamental about the nature of unity and common purpose." He paused, and I sensed he was holding back a deeper insight. "I suspect," he continued cautiously, "that the full significance of today's events will only become clear in time."

As the celebration continued around us, I found myself marvelling at the transformative power of what we had witnessed. The Celestial Confluence had lived up to its name, bringing together not just horses and riders, but cultures, traditions and perhaps even realms beyond our understanding.

Looking at Holmes, I saw in his expression a mixture of wonder and deep contemplation that mirrored my own feelings. Whatever the future held, I knew with certainty that the world had changed that day and that we were privileged to be on the cusp of that change.

⊕⊙⊰⊱⊙⊕

As the last rays of the setting sun painted the Jerusalem sky in shades of gold and crimson, our small group gathered in the secluded courtyard of our lodgings. The extraordinary events of the day had left us all in a state of contemplative wonder, and I could sense that each of us was eager to share our thoughts on what we had witnessed.

Holmes, his slender figure silhouetted against the deepening twilight, was the first to break the silence. "My friends," he began, his voice carrying that familiar tone of quiet intensity, "I believe we have been privileged to witness an event that will reverberate through the ages. Pray, let us each share our impressions of this most remarkable day."

Adrien, still flushed from the excitement of the race, spoke first. "It was as if time itself stood still," he said, his artist's eyes shining with wonder. "When the auras appeared around the horses, I felt as if I were part of some great cosmic design. Isinglass and I moved as one, but I also felt an inexplicable connection to Liyana, Khalid and their mounts."

Liyana nodded in agreement, her regal bearing softened by the intimacy of our meeting. "Indeed, Adrien. It was as if the spirits of our ancestors rode with us. I felt the weight of centuries of tradition, but also a deep sense of hope for the future.

Khalid, always a man of few words, simply nodded. "The desert speaks in many ways," he said quietly. "Today it spoke through all of us."

Dr El-Sharif, her scientific excitement barely contained, leaned forward eagerly. "The parallels with ancient myths and legends are striking," she exclaimed. "The unity of horse and rider, the manifestation of spiritual energies - these are themes that recur throughout the history of all our cultures. To see them manifest in our time is... well, it's beyond extraordinary."

I found myself nodding along, my scientific mind still grappling with the reality of what we had seen. "I must confess," I admitted, "that I am at a loss to explain the phenomena we have witnessed in terms of any known scientific principles. And yet the evidence of our senses cannot be denied."

Holmes, who had listened intently to each speaker, now turned his penetrating gaze upon us all. "My friends," he said, his voice low but intense, "I believe that what we have witnessed today goes far beyond mere sport or spectacle. The unity shown in this race - not just between horse and rider, but between cultures and traditions - offers us a powerful template for the peace we seek."

He paused, his eyes taking on that faraway look I had come to associate with his deepest insights. "Consider, if you will, how the auras surrounding each horse began as separate entities and yet merged into a single, harmonious whole. Is this not a perfect metaphor for what we hope to achieve at our Summit? A unity that does not erase individual identity, but rather celebrates and strengthens it?

A murmur of agreement ran through our group. Liyana spoke up, her eyes shining with renewed purpose. "Mr Holmes, you speak wisely. If we can carry the spirit of what we have witnessed today into our negotiations, surely we can overcome any obstacle."

As the night deepened around us, our conversation continued, touching on the mystical elements we had witnessed and their possible meanings. Each of us offered our own interpretations, but I sensed that Holmes was holding back something, some deeper understanding that he was not yet ready to share.

Finally, as the first stars began to twinkle in the velvet sky over Jerusalem, Holmes rose. "My friends," he said, his voice full of both satisfaction and anticipation, "we stand on the threshold of a new era. The Celestial Confluence has shown us what is possible when we set aside our differences and strive for true unity. Let us carry that spirit forward as we enter the final phase of our Summit.

As we bid each other goodnight and retired to our quarters, I could not shake the feeling that we had been part of something truly transformative. Whatever challenges lay ahead in the final days of the Summit, I knew that the memory of this extraordinary day would guide and inspire us.

Looking at Holmes as he stood at the window, his profile etched against the night sky, I saw in his expression a mixture of wonder and deep contemplation that mirrored my own feelings. The game, as he would say, was still in progress - but it had taken on dimensions that none of us could have anticipated when we first set out on this remarkable journey.

CHAPTER 35

PEACE SEALED IN STONE

Jerusalem, with its ancient stones, stood bathed in a soft, whispering golden glow as the first light of dawn gently kissed its surface, hinting at the promise of a fresh start. I found myself standing at the window of our lodgings, looking out upon a city slowly awakening to what promised to be a day of monumental significance. The air was crisp and expectant, carrying not only the familiar scents of spices and incense, but also the faint hint of anticipation that heralded the imminent signing of the peace treaty.

In the streets below, I could see the subtle signs of preparation for the historic day ahead. Grooms led magnificent steeds to their appointed places, their coats gleaming in the early morning light. Officials hurried back and forth, making last-minute adjustments to the magnificent decorations that adorned the city's ancient stones. The contrast between this building excitement and the weight of history hanging over us was stark indeed.

I turned from the window to watch my dear friend and colleague, Sherlock Holmes. His slender figure was silhouetted against the brightening sky, his keen grey eyes fixed on a distant point only he could see. Despite our dire circumstances just a few days ago, I could not help but marvel at the calm demeanour that now enveloped him. It was a testament to his iron will that even now, as we stood on the precipice of a moment that would change the course of nations, he exuded an air of quiet confidence.

"Watson," he said softly, breaking the contemplative silence that had reigned since we had risen, "do you remember that night in the desert when all seemed lost? How the sands themselves seemed to conspire against us?"

I nodded, the memory of that harrowing experience still fresh in my mind.

479

"Indeed, Holmes. I doubt I shall ever forget the feeling of utter despair that gripped us then."

"And yet," he continued, a hint of wonder in his voice, "here we stand, not only alive, but on the verge of witnessing a peace that seemed impossible only weeks ago. It is a testament, my dear fellow, to the indomitable spirit of those who seek understanding through conflict.

As Holmes spoke, I could not help but reflect on the remarkable changes I had witnessed in my friend throughout our Arab adventure. The man before me was no longer the cold, calculating machine I had known in London. Our trials in the desert, the bonds we had forged with our companions, and the profound mysteries we had unravelled had awakened in him a deeper appreciation of the human spirit and the complexities of the world beyond the realm of pure logic.

"I must confess, Holmes," I ventured, "that I have noticed a change in you since we began this journey. You seem... dare I say it, more connected to the human element of our endeavours."

A rare smile played on his lips. "Your observations, as always, are astute, Watson. This adventure has indeed forced me to confront aspects of existence that I had previously dismissed as irrelevant to the pursuit of truth. I find myself... humbled by the experience."

As we stood there, the weight of the day's significance descended upon us like a tangible force. In a few short hours, we would witness the signing of a treaty that promised to reshape the political landscape of the Empires. Our actions, our discoveries and the bonds we had forged would play no small part in this historic moment.

"Come, Watson," Holmes said at last, straightening his jacket with a decisive gesture. "The game is afoot and history awaits our presence. Let us go forth and see what the day brings."

With these words we prepared to leave our lodgings for the momentous day that lay ahead. As I followed Holmes out into the corridors of our temporary home, I could not shake the feeling that we were about to witness the dawn of a new era, one shaped by the wisdom of the ancients and the promise of a more harmonious future.

⊰∗⊱

As our carriage clattered over the ancient cobblestones of Jerusalem, the grand edifice of the Hotel Howard loomed before us, its imposing facade a curious blend of Eastern and Western architectural styles. The morning sun glinted off its many windows, giving the building an almost ethereal quality that seemed appropriate to the momentous occasion it was about to host.

Holmes, ever alert, leaned forward in his seat, his keen eyes darting back and forth as he took in every detail of our surroundings. "Observe, Watson," he murmured, his voice low but intense, "the heightened security measures. Note the positioning of the guards, the subtle reinforcements at the entrances. Our colleagues have been thorough in their preparations."

Indeed, as we approached, I could not help but marvel at the intricate web of protection that had been woven around the hotel. Stern-faced guards, their uniforms a curious blend of Ottoman splendour and British military precision, stood at attention at every entrance. Their watchful eyes swept over the arriving dignitaries and attendees, looking for any hint of threat or deception.

As we stepped out of our carriage, a familiar figure caught my eye. It was none other than Farid Al-Tariq, the man who had once been our adversary. Now, however, he was moving purposefully among the staff, helping with the last-minute preparations. The change in his demeanour was remarkable, a living testimony to the power of salvation.

Noticing our arrival, Farid approached, his manner hesitant but determined. "Mr Holmes, Dr Watson," he said, bowing his head in greeting. "I trust you find the arrangements satisfactory?"

Holmes looked at him for a moment, his expression inscrutable. Then, to my surprise, he extended his hand. "Indeed, Mr Al-Tariq," he replied, his tone carrying a note of respect I had seldom heard from him. "Your efforts have not gone unnoticed. It takes a man of considerable character to choose the path of peace over that of vengeance."

A look of deep relief washed over Farid's face as he clasped Holmes' hand. "Your words mean more than you know, Mr Holmes. I only hope that my actions today and in the future will continue to prove worthy of the trust you have placed in me."

As Farid excused himself to attend to his duties, we were greeted by the welcome sight of our companions. Liyana Sultan approached, her regal bearing more pronounced than ever, yet tempered by a warmth that spoke of the trials we had faced together. Khalid Al-Fahmi, his weathered face wrinkled in a rare smile, stood beside her, his posture reflecting both vigilance and a newfound sense of purpose.

Adrien d'Arcy, his artist's eye clearly captivated by the grandeur of our surroundings, sketched furiously in his ever-present notebook. As he looked up to greet us, I noticed a depth in his gaze that had been absent at the start of our journey, a testament to the profound experiences we had shared.

"My friends," Liyana said, her voice carrying the quiet authority of one who has faced great challenges and emerged victorious, "it gladdens my heart to see us all gathered here, on the cusp of a new era of peace."

Khalid nodded solemnly. "Indeed, Your Highness. The road has been long and fraught with danger, but the goal, I believe, will be worth every hardship we have endured."

As we exchanged greetings and brief reflections on the enormity of the day ahead, a hush fell over the assembled crowd. Turning, I saw the imposing figure of Ammar ibn Nadir, leader of the Obsidian Guild, making his way towards the hotel entrance. His presence seemed to command the air around him, drawing all eyes to him and giving an added weight to the proceedings.

Holmes straightened almost imperceptibly, a gesture of respect I had seldom seen him extend to a man. "And so," he murmured, his eyes fixed on the approaching figure of Ammar, "the final players take their places on the board. The game, Watson, enters its most decisive phase."

As we made our way to the Hotel Howard, I could not shake the feeling that we were crossing a threshold, not only in space, but in time. Behind us lay a world of conflict and misunderstanding; ahead, the promise of a new dawn of cooperation and peace. Whatever the day might bring, I knew that the bonds forged on our extraordinary journey would see us through.

━━◦✣◦━━

As the hour of the signing of the treaty drew near, our little party found itself sequestered in a private chamber within the labyrinthine corridors of the Hotel Howard. The room, with its rich tapestries and ornate furnishings, seemed a world away from the bustle and excitement that filled the rest of the building. Here, in this quiet sanctuary, we gathered to share our final thoughts before the momentous event that awaited us.

Holmes stood by the fire, his slender figure silhouetted against the dancing flames, his keen eyes watching each of us in turn. The weight of our shared experiences hung in the air, an almost palpable force that bound us together more securely than any formal alliance.

It was Liyana who broke the contemplative silence, her voice soft yet filled with a newfound conviction. "My friends," she began, her eyes shining with barely contained emotion, "I cannot help but marvel at the journey that has brought us to this point. When we first set out, I saw diplomacy as a game of strategy and cunning. Now I see it as a path to true unity, a means of bridging the chasms that divide nations and hearts."

Khalid, his weathered features softened by a rare smile, nodded in agreement. "Indeed, Your Highness. We have traversed not only the physical landscape of our lands, but the far more treacherous terrain of prejudice and misunderstanding. The wisdom I have gained on this journey is more precious than all the gold in Arabia."

Adrien, who had been sketching absentmindedly in his ever-present notebook, looked up, his artist's eye alight with inspiration. "For my part," he said, his voice full of wonder, "I am overwhelmed by the sheer beauty of what we have witnessed and achieved. The colours of the desert, the intricate patterns of ancient wisdom, the spirit of cooperation we have fostered - all this has

482

inspired in me a desire to create art that speaks to the unity of all peoples".

As each of our companions shared their reflections, I could not help but notice the subtle changes in Holmes' countenance. The cold, analytical mask he so often wore had softened, revealing a depth of feeling I had rarely glimpsed in our long association.

It was at that moment that the door opened, admitting the imposing figure of Mycroft Holmes. His entrance, though silent, seemed to change the very atmosphere of the room. As he took his place beside his brother, I observed a silent exchange between the two - a subtle nod from Mycroft that spoke volumes of approval and, dare I say it, pride.

"Gentlemen, Your Highness," Mycroft began, his voice carrying his usual tone of quiet authority, "I believe we are all aware of the magnitude of what we are about to witness. But before we proceed, there is one among us who can shed light on aspects of our journey that have hitherto remained shrouded in mystery."

At these words, all eyes turned to Ammar ibn Nadir, the venerable leader of the Obsidian Guild. As he rose to speak, I was once again struck by the aura of ancient wisdom that seemed to emanate from his very being.

"My friends," Ammar began, his voice deep and resonant, "the treaty we are about to witness is but the visible peak of a mountain whose base extends far into the shadows of history. The Obsidian Guild has worked tirelessly, often in unseen and unacknowledged ways, to bring about this moment of peace".

What followed was a revelation that visibly moved even the unflappable Sherlock Holmes. Ammar spoke of decades of covert negotiations, of peacekeeping efforts in war-torn lands, and of a network of allies and agents stretching to the far corners of the globe. The scope of the Guild's influence was staggering, its commitment to peace and unity unwavering through centuries of conflict and change.

As Ammar's words filled the room, I felt a deep sense of awe settle over our gathering. We had been part of something far greater than ourselves, a tapestry of history and destiny woven by hands both seen and unseen.

Holmes, his voice uncharacteristically soft, broke the silence that followed Ammar's revelations. "It seems, my friends, that our adventure was but a single thread in a far greater design. Let us go forth and bear witness to the fruition of centuries of effort and sacrifice."

With these words we rose as one, ready to take our places in the great hall where history awaited our presence. As we filed out of the room, I could not shake the feeling that we stood on the threshold of a new era, one shaped by the wisdom of the ages and the hope of a more united future.

As we entered the great hall of the Hotel Howard, I was struck by the sheer grandeur of the scene before us. The room, with its soaring ceilings and gleaming marble floors, seemed a fitting setting for the momentous event that was about to unfold. Sunlight streamed through the huge stained glass windows, casting a kaleidoscope of colour over the assembled dignitaries and lending an almost ethereal quality to the proceedings.

At the far end of the hall stood a large table, its surface covered in rich brocade embroidered with intricate patterns that seamlessly blended British and Ottoman motifs. On this table lay the treaty documents, their pristine pages awaiting the signatures that would usher in a new era of peace and cooperation.

Holmes and I took our places among the observers, our vantage point giving us an unobstructed view of the proceedings. As the official delegations entered, I could not help but marvel at the pageantry on display. British officials in their formal attire stood shoulder to shoulder with Ottoman diplomats in their traditional dress, a visual testament to the union of East and West that this treaty represented.

The signing ceremony began with pomp and circumstance. Each signatory approached the table in turn, their steps measured and deliberate, the weight of history in their every movement. As quill met parchment, I thought I could hear the breath of the nations held in anticipation.

It was then that Ammar Ibn Nadir, the venerable leader of the Obsidian Guild, rose to address the assembly. His presence seemed to command the very air around him, and a hush fell over the hall as he began to speak.

"Esteemed colleagues, honoured guests," he began, his voice resonating with the wisdom of the ages, "we stand today at the culmination of a journey fraught with peril and illuminated by hope. The road that has brought us to this moment has been long and arduous, marked by trials that have tested the very limits of human endurance and understanding".

As Ammar recounted the challenges overcome, my mind drifted back to our harrowing experiences in the desert, the mysteries unravelled and the bonds forged in the crucible of adversity. Each word seemed to echo with the truth of our shared experiences, adding profound weight to the treaty being signed before us.

"The Obsidian Guild," Ammar continued, "has long stood as a silent guardian of history, a keeper of ancient wisdom and a bridge between cultures. Today we see the fruits of centuries of work, as East and West come together, not in conflict, but in a spirit of mutual respect and cooperation".

His words painted a vision of a bright and promising future, where the wisdom of the past would guide the progress of nations. As he spoke of the unifying power of understanding and shared knowledge, I noticed Holmes nodding almost imperceptibly, a rare gesture of agreement from my usually stoic friend.

Ammar concluded his speech with a reference to the ceremonial race that had so captured the city's imagination. "Like the noble steeds that ran as one, transcending the boundaries of breed and origin, so too must we move forward in unity, our diverse strengths combining to create a future greater than any of us could achieve alone."

As the final signatures were affixed to the treaty, I glanced around the room, noting the reactions of our companions. Liyana stood tall, her eyes shining with pride and hope. Khalid's weathered features wore an expression of deep satisfaction, while Adrien seemed lost in thought, his artist's mind no doubt brainstorming ways to capture this historic moment on canvas.

But it was Holmes who most caught my attention. For a brief moment I saw a look cross his face that I had rarely seen in our long association - a mixture of wonder, respect and perhaps even a touch of humility in the face of forces greater than even his formidable intellect could fully comprehend.

As the ceremony drew to a close and the assembled dignitaries broke into applause, I felt a surge of emotion rise in my chest. We had witnessed a true turning point in history, a moment when the tides of conflict gave way to the promise of lasting peace. Whatever the challenges of the future, I knew that the memory of this day would stand as a beacon of hope for generations to come.

As the great hall began to empty, the echoes of the historic ceremony still reverberating off its marble walls, Holmes skilfully led our small party to a secluded alcove. The room, though modest in size, afforded us a degree of privacy that seemed most welcome after the pomp and circumstance of the treaty signing.

"Well, gentlemen, and Your Highness," Holmes began, his keen eyes sweeping over our assembled group, "we have witnessed a moment that will undoubtedly go down in the annals of history. I would be most interested to hear your thoughts on the possible ramifications of today's events."

Liyana was the first to speak, her voice carrying the quiet authority that had become so familiar during our trials together. "Mr Holmes, I believe we have set in motion a chain of events that will reshape the very fabric of international relations. The treaty's provisions for cultural exchange and mutual cooperation are unprecedented in their scope."

Khalid nodded in agreement, his weathered features bearing an expression of cautious optimism. "Indeed, Your Highness. But we must remain vigilant. The road to lasting peace is often fraught with unforeseen obstacles."

As our companions shared their findings, I watched Holmes carefully. His brow was furrowed in that familiar expression of deep thought, his fingers clenched beneath his chin. "Watson," he murmured, his voice so low that only

I could hear, "what do you make of the Ottoman delegate's hesitation before the final signature? A mere fit of nerves or something more significant?"

I confess I had not noticed the detail to which Holmes was referring, but I had long since ceased to be surprised by the depth of his observations. "I couldn't say, Holmes. Although I did notice a certain tension in the British Ambassador's posture throughout the proceedings."

"Exactly, my dear fellow," Holmes replied, a hint of approval in his tone. "The language of diplomacy is often spoken in the most subtle of gestures. I suspect the real negotiations are far from over."

Our hushed exchange was interrupted by the arrival of Mycroft Holmes, his imposing figure somehow managing to be both conspicuous and inconspicuous at the same time. "Brother," he addressed Sherlock, "I trust you find the security arrangements satisfactory?"

"Indeed, Mycroft," Holmes replied, a note of grudging respect in his voice. "Although I did notice the absence of guards on the east corridor. An oversight or a calculated risk?"

The ghost of a smile played across Mycroft's normally impassive features. "Neither, dear brother. A necessary concession to our Ottoman friends, who insisted on maintaining a traditional point of entry for their most honoured guests. Rest assured, the corridor is under the most discreet surveillance."

As the Holmes brothers continued their cryptic exchange, my attention was drawn to Adrien, who was uncharacteristically silent. The artist's gaze was fixed on the great hall beyond our alcove, his eyes shining with a mixture of wonder and inspiration.

"My friends," he said at last, his voice barely above a whisper, "I fear words fail me at this moment. But I vow to capture on canvas the spirit of what we have witnessed here today, so that future generations may understand the magnitude of this achievement."

As we stood there, each lost in our own reflections, I was struck by the profound sense of history that permeated the very air around us. We were not mere observers, but active participants in a moment that would shape the course of nations for years to come.

Mycroft's voice broke through my reverie. "I am pleased to report that all potential threats have been neutralised. The treaty and the peace it represents are secure."

Holmes nodded, a grim look of satisfaction on his face. "Excellent work, brother. It seems our efforts have borne fruit beyond our most optimistic projections."

As we prepared to rejoin the main assembly, I could not help but feel a sense of pride in what we had accomplished. But as I caught Holmes' eye, I saw in his expression a reminder that our work was far from over. The game, as he would say, was still in progress, and the real challenge of maintaining this hard-won peace had only just begun.

⊶⊷⊕⊷⊶

After the momentous signing ceremony, we were ushered into a grand dining room where a luncheon of truly magnificent proportions awaited us. The room was a feast for the senses, its opulent décor rivalled only by the sumptuous spread before us. Long tables groaned under the weight of dishes that represented a harmonious marriage of British and Ottoman cuisine, a gastronomic reflection of the alliance we had come to celebrate.

I watched with no small fascination as diplomats and dignitaries mingled, their conversations a mixture of serious discussion and light-hearted banter. Holmes, ever alert, moved among the guests with the grace of a jungle cat, his keen ears no doubt picking up snippets of conversation that lesser men would have missed.

It was during one such tour of the room that we encountered Farid, his manner markedly different from the brash young man we had first met in the desert. He approached us with hesitant steps, his eyes downcast but his chin held high, the very picture of a man striving to make amends.

"Mr Holmes, Dr Watson," he addressed us, his voice carrying a note of humility that I found most fitting, "I... I wanted to express my deepest gratitude for the opportunity you have given me to be a part of this historic moment. Your capacity for forgiveness is truly remarkable."

Holmes looked at him for a moment, his piercing gaze softening almost imperceptibly. "Mr Al-Tariq," he replied, "it is not forgiveness that has brought you here, but your own courage to choose a better way. Remember that in the days to come."

As Farid walked away, visibly moved by Holmes's words, I caught fragments of a lively discussion between a group of British and Ottoman officials. They spoke with great enthusiasm of future ceremonial races, their words painting vivid pictures of majestic steeds thundering across desert sands and verdant English fields alike, a testament to the enduring power of our shared adventure.

The luncheon reached its climax when the Sultan himself rose to address the gathering. A hush fell over the room, the clinking of cutlery and the murmur of conversation giving way to respectful silence.

"My friends," the Sultan began, his voice carrying to every corner of the vast hall, "today we have not merely signed a treaty, but laid the foundation for a new era of cooperation and mutual understanding. Let the ink with which we have written this agreement be but the first drops in a great river of shared knowledge and prosperity that will flow between our nations for generations to come.

His words touched the hearts of everyone present, and I noticed more than one pair of eyes shining with emotion as he finished his speech. The applause that followed was thunderous, a spontaneous outpouring of hope and optimism for the future we had all helped to shape.

As the applause died down, I was surprised to see Holmes rise to his feet, glass in hand. It was rare indeed for my friend to take centre stage at such gatherings, but there was a quiet authority in his demeanour that commanded the attention of everyone present.

"Ladies and gentlemen," he began, his voice clear and steady, "I am a man of logic and reason, perhaps ill-suited to the task of proposing a toast on such an occasion. But I feel compelled to pay tribute to the extraordinary people whose efforts have brought us to this historic moment".

What followed was a masterful speech in which Holmes paid tribute to each of our companions in turn. He spoke of Liyana's diplomatic acumen, Khalid's unwavering loyalty, Adrien's artistic vision and the wisdom of Ammar ibn Nadir. Even Mycroft was not exempt from his praise, though I thought I detected a hint of good-natured sibling rivalry in Holmes' words.

As he finished his toast and raised his glass, I felt a surge of pride in my dear friend and in the remarkable company with which we had shared this extraordinary adventure. The clink of glasses echoed through the room, a joyous sound that seemed to herald the dawn of a new age of peace and understanding.

In that moment, surrounded by the fruits of our labour and the promise of a brighter future, I knew that whatever challenges lay ahead, the bonds forged in the crucible of our shared trials would endure. The game, as Holmes would say, was far from over, but we had certainly entered a new and exciting phase.

⊷•⦂◦⦂•⊷

As the euphoria of the luncheon began to fade, our little party was drawn to the stables where Isinglass, Muntasir and Al-Zarib awaited. The air was thick with the earthy scent of hay and horseflesh, a stark contrast to the rarefied atmosphere of the treaty signing. Yet as we approached the stalls, I could not help but feel that we were in the presence of beings no less noble than the dignitaries we had left behind.

Adrien was the first to step forward, his artisan's eye drawn irresistibly to Isinglass. The magnificent stallion stood tall and proud, his coat gleaming like burnished copper in the soft light filtering through the stable windows. As Adrien ran a reverent hand along the horse's flank, I saw his fingers trace the powerful muscles with the expertise of one who truly understands the marvel of equine form and function.

"By Jove," he breathed, his voice filled with admiration, "what a paragon of the breed you are, old boy. Your pedigree, your strength... you embody the very best of what the union of Arabian blood and British breeding can achieve.

488

Yesterday's race was only a glimpse of your true potential.

Adrien's hands moved with practiced ease, checking Isinglass for any signs of strain from the previous day's exertions. "You have done your ancestors proud, my friend," he murmured, his tone one of deep respect. "From the Darley Arabs to this day, your bloodline has been a bridge between cultures, a living testament to the power of unity."

As he tended to Isinglass, Adrien's thoughts seemed to drift to the intricate leatherwork of the saddle and bridle he had created for the ceremonial race. "It has been an honour to create equipment worthy of your noble bearing," he said, his fingers tracing the fine tooling of the leather. "May it serve as a symbol of the craftsmanship that can flourish when cultures come together in harmony."

Liyana approached Muntasir, her steps purposeful yet tender. The bond between princess and steed was palpable, a connection forged through shared trials and quiet moments of understanding. As she pressed her forehead to Muntasir's and murmured soft words in Arabic, I thought I could see the very essence of their shared heritage passing between them.

"My faithful friend," Liyana said, her voice carrying a warmth I had rarely heard, "you have carried me through countless dangers and hardships. Your courage has been my strength, your steadfastness my anchor. In you I see the spirit of our people, proud and unyielding, yet capable of such gentleness. Yesterday, you carried me not only across the finish line, but into a new era of understanding.

But it was Khalid's reunion with Al-Zarib that truly touched the heart. Man and beast looked at each other with an understanding that went beyond words, their bond a testament to the deep bonds that can form between disparate beings. Khalid's weathered hand rested on Al-Zarib's neck and I saw in that simple gesture a lifetime of shared experience.

"Al-Zarib," Khalid said, his voice raw with emotion, "you are more than a horse. You are the wind of the desert, the spirit of our ancestors. Through you, I have learned the true meaning of freedom and loyalty. Our race yesterday was not just a test of speed, but a journey towards peace. May Allah bless you all the days of your life.

As I watched this tender exchange, I noticed Holmes standing slightly apart, his keen eyes taking in every detail of the scene before him. His expression, usually so reserved, betrayed a depth of emotion I had rarely seen in our long association.

"You know, Watson," he said at length, his voice deep and thoughtful, "I have often dismissed the notion that animals possess any higher faculties. But as I watch these magnificent creatures, I find myself questioning that assumption. They have played a role in our adventure no less crucial than any human. Their performance in yesterday's race was nothing short of extraordinary.

I nodded in agreement, moved by his uncharacteristic display of emotion. "Indeed, Holmes. In fact, you could say they embody the very spirit of unity we have been striving for. Three distinct breeds, each with its own strengths, working together in perfect harmony on the track and beyond".

"A fitting metaphor for our new-found peace, wouldn't you say?" Holmes mused, a rare smile playing at the corners of his mouth. "East and West, tradition and progress, all finding common ground. Perhaps there is more wisdom in these beasts than in all the treatises and diplomatic cables put together."

As we stood there, surrounded by the quiet strength of our equine companions, I felt a profound sense of accomplishment. The journey that had begun in the fog-shrouded streets of London and taken us across deserts and ancient ruins had brought us here, to this moment of understanding and unity.

The horses, standing proud and tall in their stalls, seemed to embody the very essence of the peace we had worked so hard to achieve. In their noble bearing, I saw the promise of a future where differences are not barriers but strengths to be celebrated.

As we finally left the stables, each lost in our own thoughts, I could not shake the feeling that we had been privileged to witness something truly extraordinary. The bond between man and beast, like the treaty we had come to sign, was a testament to the power of understanding and mutual respect to bridge even the widest of divides. The memory of these magnificent creatures thundering across the finish line in perfect unison would forever stand as a symbol of what we had achieved here in Jerusalem.

As the sun dipped below the ancient walls of Jerusalem, casting long shadows across the city, our small band of adventurers gathered for an intimate dinner in a secluded chamber of the Hotel Howard. The room, with its rich tapestries and softly glowing oil lamps, seemed to exist in a world apart from the hustle and bustle of the day. It was here, in this tranquil sanctuary, that we prepared to bid farewell to those who had become much more than mere companions on our extraordinary journey.

The Sultan himself had graciously arranged this private meal, and as we took our seats at the beautifully laid table, I could not help but marvel at the strange twists of fate that had brought us all together. Holmes, as was his wont, sat at the head of the table, his keen eyes taking in every detail of our assembled company.

As the meal progressed, a bittersweet atmosphere descended upon our gathering. It was Khalid who first broke the contemplative silence, rising to his feet with a grace that belied his years of hard desert life.

"My friends," he began, his voice carrying the weight of deep emotion, "our paths may soon diverge, but the bonds forged in the crucible of our shared trials will never be broken. I return to my people with a renewed sense of purpose, determined to continue the work we have begun here. Through education and cultural exchange, we will build bridges of understanding that span the chasms of ignorance and fear.

Adrien spoke next, his artisan hands cradling a small wooden box. "In honour of our adventure," he said, opening the box to reveal an exquisitely crafted leather bracelet for each of us, "I have created these tokens. Each is emblazoned with the symbols of our journey - the desert sands, the emblem of the Obsidian Guild, and the intertwined lines of our noble steeds. May they serve as a reminder of the beauty that can be created when different cultures come together in harmony.

Liyana rose, her regal bearing tempered by the warmth of genuine affection. "My dear companions," she began, her voice clear and strong, "I stand before you not only as a princess, but as a woman forever changed by our shared experiences. As I assume my new role in the diplomatic corps, I carry with me the lessons of courage, wisdom and unity that each of you has taught me. Together, we have written a new chapter in the annals of history, and I am honoured to continue this work in the halls of power.

As each of our companions spoke, I watched Holmes closely. His expression, usually so reserved, betrayed a depth of emotion I had rarely seen. When he finally rose to speak, the room fell into a hush of anticipation.

"My friends," Holmes began, his voice uncharacteristically soft, "I am a man of logic and reason, perhaps ill-equipped to express the profound effect you have had on my understanding of the world. Yet I am compelled to pay tribute to the extraordinary individuals gathered here. Each of you has contributed not only to the success of our mission, but to a fundamental transformation of my perceptions. For that, I am deeply grateful.

The Sultan and Ammar ibn Nadir, who had remained silent throughout our exchange, now rose to bid us farewell. The Sultan presented each of us with a small, intricately carved box of olive wood, a piece of Jerusalem to carry with us always. Ammar, for his part, presented each of us with a small obsidian stone, polished to a mirror finish.

"Within these stones," Ammar said, his voice resonating with ancient wisdom, "lies the essence of the Obsidian Guild's teachings. May they serve as a reminder of the eternal truths we have discovered together, and guide you in the challenges that lie ahead."

As the evening drew to a close, we exchanged hugs and heartfelt farewells. The air was thick with emotion, each of us aware that we were closing a chapter on one of the most remarkable adventures of our lives.

As we finally said goodbye, I found myself lingering for a moment, remembering the faces of those who had become so dear to us. Sensing my mood, Holmes put a hand on my shoulder.

"Come, Watson," he said gently, "the game is not over. New adventures await us, shaped by the wisdom we have gained here."

As we stepped out into the cool Jerusalem night, the stars twinkling above us like a thousand watchful eyes, I felt a strange mixture of sadness and exhilaration. We had been part of something truly extraordinary, and though our paths might diverge, the bonds forged in this ancient land would endure for all time.

⁂

As the last vestiges of daylight faded from the Jerusalem sky, Holmes, Dr Amal El-Sharif and I found ourselves on the terrace of our lodgings, looking out over the ancient city. The view before us was one of breathtaking beauty: the golden dome of the Dome of the Rock caught the last rays of the setting sun, while minarets and church spires alike stood silhouetted against the deepening twilight. The air was heavy with the scent of jasmine, and the distant call to prayer echoed hauntingly over the rooftops.

Holmes stood on the parapet, his slender figure etched against the darkening sky, his keen eyes scanning the cityscape with an intensity that spoke of deep contemplation. Dr El-Sharif, her scholarly bearing softened by the intimacy of the moment, leaned against a stone pillar, her gaze fixed on the distant horizon. I found myself caught between them, both physically and metaphorically, a bridge between the world of cold logic and that of historical perspective.

"Well, gentlemen," Dr El-Sharif began, breaking the contemplative silence, "I dare say we have witnessed events that will be spoken of for generations to come. Our journey has taken us from the fog-shrouded streets of London to the sun-baked sands of Arabia, and now to this city that has seen empires rise and fall. How do you find yourselves changed by these experiences?"

Holmes turned from the parapet, his expression uncharacteristically pensive. "I confess, Dr El-Sharif, that I find my world view significantly altered. Where once I saw only the cold, hard facts of a case, I now perceive the intricate tapestry of human culture and history that gives context and meaning to those facts. It is... a most disturbing yet illuminating transformation.

I nodded in agreement, feeling compelled to add my own thoughts. "Indeed, the weight of the knowledge we have gained rests heavily on my shoulders. We have been privy to secrets that have shaped the course of nations. The responsibility is enormous.

Dr El-Sharif's eyes gleamed with understanding. "Ah, but therein lies the true test of wisdom, does it not? To know when to speak and when to remain silent, to understand the far-reaching consequences of our actions and words.

We have been given a rare gift, gentlemen, and with it comes a sacred duty."

Holmes, his brow furrowed in thought, spoke again. "You speak truthfully, Doctor. Yet I cannot help but wonder at the historical significance of our achievements. How will future generations look upon this peace we have helped to forge?"

At this Dr El-Sharif's face lit up with scientific enthusiasm. "Mr Holmes, what we have witnessed here is nothing short of monumental. The alliance between the British Empire and the Ottoman Empire, bridging East and West, is unprecedented in modern history. The Obsidian Guild's role in preserving ancient wisdom and promoting understanding between cultures may well be the key to a more harmonious future. Our actions here have set in motion events that will reverberate through the ages.

As she spoke, the last light faded from the sky and Jerusalem was transformed before our eyes. Lamps and candles flickered across the city, creating a tapestry of light that mirrored the starry sky above. The beauty of the scene was breathtaking, a fitting backdrop for the profound nature of our conversation.

We fell into a comfortable silence, each lost in our own reflections. The cool night air carried the whispers of centuries past, and I thought I could hear the echoes of all those who had stood where we now stood, pondering the great questions of existence.

It was Holmes who finally broke the silence, his voice soft but full of conviction. "Whatever the future may hold, my friends, I am grateful to have shared this extraordinary journey with you both. We have seen wonders beyond imagination, unravelled mysteries that have baffled generations, and played our part in shaping the destiny of nations. Let us carry these experiences with us always, a light to guide us through whatever darkness we may yet face.

As we stood there, with the ancient city of Jerusalem spread out before us like a living testament to the endurance of the human spirit and the power of shared wisdom, I felt a profound sense of gratitude and purpose. Whatever challenges lay ahead, I knew that the bonds forged on this remarkable adventure would see us through.

The night deepened around us, the stars spinning above us in their eternal dance, as we three unlikely companions shared this last precious moment in the Holy City. The game, as Holmes would say, was far from over, but we had certainly entered a new and exciting phase.

※

The first light of dawn was but a faint promise on the eastern horizon as Holmes, Dr El-Sharif and I emerged from our lodgings, our valises packed and our hearts heavy with the weight of imminent departure. The ancient stones of Jerusalem, which had borne witness to our extraordinary adventure, now seemed to whisper their farewell as we embarked on our final tour of the awakening city.

The streets, so recently thronged with revelers, were now quiet save for the occasional early riser. Yet there was a palpable sense of change in the air, as if the very foundations of the Holy City had been subtly altered by the events of the past few days. I watched in no small amazement as the traditionally segregated quarters seemed less rigidly defined, as people of different faiths exchanged greetings and small courtesies that would have been unthinkable only a few weeks ago.

"Observe, Watson," Holmes murmured, his keen eyes missing nothing, "how the metaphorical bridges we have helped to build are already manifesting themselves in the everyday interactions of Jerusalem's inhabitants. It is in these small gestures that the true impact of our efforts can be measured.

Dr El-Sharif nodded in agreement, her scholarly gaze bright with appreciation for the historical significance of what we had witnessed. "Indeed, Mr Holmes. We are privileged to witness the first tentative steps towards a new era of understanding and cooperation. It is my fervent hope that future generations will look back on this time as a turning point in the long and often troubled history of this remarkable city".

As we made our way to the station, I found myself remembering every detail of our surroundings: the play of early morning light on the ancient stones, the mingled scents of spices and incense wafting from newly opened shops, the distant call of a muezzin echoing over the rooftops. Each sensation seemed imbued with a poignancy born of the knowledge that we might never experience it in the same way again.

At the station we found a small gathering of those who had become dear to us over the course of our adventure. Liyana, resplendent in her formal attire, stood beside Khalid and Adrien. The Sultan himself had condescended to bid us farewell, his presence a testament to the bonds we had forged. Even Farid was there, his demeanour a strange mixture of humility and new-found determination.

The farewells were brief but heartfelt, each handshake and embrace bearing the weight of shared experiences that defy ordinary description. As we finally boarded our train, I felt a strange tightness in my chest, a physical manifestation of the emotions that threatened to overwhelm me.

From our compartment window we watched Jerusalem fade into the distance. The golden dome of the Dome of the Rock caught the first true rays of the morning sun, shining like a beacon of hope on the horizon. Beside me, Holmes sat in uncharacteristic silence, his eyes fixed on the fading cityscape, while Dr El-Sharif murmured a silent prayer in Arabic.

As the Holy City finally disappeared from view, I found myself reflecting on the extraordinary nature of our Arab adventure. We had unravelled ancient mysteries, forged unlikely alliances and played our part in shaping the course of history. But as the train carried us inexorably towards new horizons, I knew that the true impact of our journey was only beginning to unfold.

"Well, gentlemen," Holmes said at last, breaking the contemplative silence, "it seems we have closed one chapter only to open another. The game, as always, remains in progress."

Dr El-Sharif smiled, her eyes bright with the promise of future discoveries. "Indeed, Mr Holmes. And I, for one, am eager to see where this new chapter takes us."

As for myself, I could only nod in agreement, my heart full of gratitude for the adventures of the past and anticipation for those yet to come. The sands of Arabia might be fading behind us, but the wisdom and friendships we had gained would remain with us forever, a compass to guide us through whatever challenges lay ahead.

Our journey from the sun-baked lands of Arabia to the familiar climes of England was one of gradual but profound change. As our train wound its way through varied landscapes, each mile seemed to bring us further from the realm of ancient mysteries and closer to the world of gas-lit streets and genteel society that we called home.

The early stages of our journey were marked by long stretches of desert, the golden sands stretching to the horizon in an unbroken expanse that evoked memories of our recent adventures. Holmes, usually so taciturn on journeys, found himself moved to make occasional remarks about the changing terrain.

"Observe, Watson," he said as we entered more verdant territory, "how the landscape mirrors our own journey from the unknown to the familiar. Every change in vegetation and topography is a step closer to Baker Street."

Dr El-Sharif, her scholarly mind ever active, provided fascinating commentary on the historical significance of the regions we were passing through. "Gentlemen," she would often begin, her eyes glowing with enthusiasm, "the ground beneath us has witnessed the rise and fall of empires, great migrations and moments of profound cultural exchange."

As we moved north, the arid landscapes gave way to the lush greenery of Europe. The change was gradual but unmistakable, like the slow awakening from a vivid dream. Our conversations, once dominated by tales of Bedouin wisdom and ancient artefacts, began to turn to the practicalities of our return to London society.

"I confess, Holmes," I remarked as we entered more familiar territory, "that I am both eager and reluctant to return to our old haunts. How does one resume a normal life after such extraordinary experiences?"

My friend's lips curled into that familiar half-smile. "My dear Watson, I rather suspect that 'normal' is a term we will have to redefine. Our adventures in Arabia have opened our eyes to a wider world, one that will not be easily forgotten or ignored."

Dr El-Sharif nodded in agreement. "Indeed, gentlemen. We return not as we left, but as custodians of knowledge and understanding that bridges East and West. Our true challenge lies in how we apply these insights to our future endeavours."

As our train finally pulled into the outskirts of London, I felt a strange mixture of emotions. The familiar sights and sounds of the great metropolis were a welcome balm after our long journey, yet I could not shake a lingering sense of nostalgia for the exotic places we had left behind.

The dirty bricks and bustling streets of London came into view, a stark contrast to the sun-bleached stones of Jerusalem. Yet even in this most familiar of settings, I thought I could see echoes of our Arabian adventure - in the faces of people from faraway lands, in the scent of exotic spices wafting from a passing vendor's cart.

As our taxi finally turned into Baker Street, Holmes leaned forward, his keen eyes taking in every detail of our old neighbourhood. "Home at last, Watson," he said, a note of anticipation in his voice. "But I suspect our recent experiences have ensured that even these familiar surroundings will never be quite the same."

Indeed, as we approached the familiar door of 221B, I felt a strange sense of standing on the threshold between two worlds. Behind us were the sun-drenched memories of Arabia, with its ancient mysteries and profound revelations. Ahead of us was the promise of new adventures, shaped by the wisdom we had gained.

With a final shared look of understanding, Holmes, Dr El-Sharif and I stepped out of our taxi, ready to cross that threshold and begin the next chapter of our extraordinary journey. The game, as always, was afoot, and I could not help but wonder what new mysteries awaited us in the familiar yet somehow transformed world of Baker Street.

CHAPTER 36

LEGACY OF THE OBSIDIAN STALLION

As the last vestiges of daylight faded from the London sky, casting long shadows across the familiar confines of 221B Baker Street, a strange sense of dislocation overcame me. The gas lamps flickered to life, their warm glow a stark contrast to the harsh brilliance of the Arabian sun that had so recently scorched our brows. The air, heavy with the familiar scents of tobacco, leather-bound books and chemical experiments, seemed almost alien after weeks of breathing in the spice-laden winds of the desert.

Holmes stood silhouetted against the window, his slender figure a dark outline against the gathering twilight. His keen eyes, which had so recently scanned endless horizons of sand, now darted back and forth over the bustling Baker Street below, as if seeking some echo of our extraordinary adventure in the mundane bustle of London life.

I sat at my desk, my trusty diary open before me, the blank page both an invitation and a challenge. How could mere words hope to capture the magnitude of our recent experiences? The weight of the pen in my hand seemed inadequate to the task of recording the wonders we had witnessed and the dangers we had faced.

Mycroft Holmes, a figure of quiet authority, occupied his brother's favourite armchair, his considerable bulk comfortably settled between the cushions. His eyes, half-closed in contemplation, betrayed a razor-sharp mind, no doubt analysing the far-reaching implications of our Arabian odyssey.

Dr Amal El-Sharif, her graceful form bent in study, moved among the artefacts we had brought back from our journey. Her slender fingers traced the intricate patterns of an Arabian dagger, her touch as reverent as that of a priest handling sacred relics. The look of wonder in her eyes as she examined each piece spoke volumes about the profound impact of our shared adventure.

The silence that hung in the air was heavy with unspoken thoughts and half-formed reflections. It was as if the very walls of our accommodation were struggling to contain the vastness of the experiences we had brought back with us. The ticking of the mantelpiece clock, once a comforting reminder of the orderly progression of London life, now seemed to echo the inexorable march of time across the ancient sands of the desert.

At last it was Holmes who broke the contemplative silence, his voice carrying a depth of emotion I had rarely heard from my friend.

"Well, gentlemen - and my dear Dr El-Sharif - it seems that we have returned from the edge of the known world, only to find that the greatest journey is not behind us, but within us."

His words hung in the air, a challenge and an invitation. As I looked around at my companions, I saw a shared understanding in their eyes. We had been changed, irrevocably and profoundly, by our encounters with the mysteries of the East. The question now before us was not what we had discovered in the sands of Arabia, but what those discoveries had revealed within ourselves.

It was with a sense of both trepidation and anticipation that I dipped my pen into ink, ready to commit to paper the first words of what I knew would be an account unlike any I had written before. For in the shadow of the Obsidian Stallion, we had not only solved a mystery, we had become part of one - a mystery as old as civilisation itself and as enduring as the desert sands.

As the embers in the fireplace cast a warm glow over our little gathering, the weight of our shared experiences fell upon us like a tangible presence. Every face bore the indelible marks of our extraordinary journey, etched in lines of wonder, weariness and new-found wisdom.

Holmes, his fingers tucked under his chin in that familiar pose of deep contemplation, was the first to break the thoughtful silence. "I find," he began, his voice carrying an unusual note of introspection, "that our adventures in Arabia have thrown a new light on the nature of deduction and reason. The mysteries we encountered were not merely puzzles to be solved, but gateways to understanding the profound connections that bind all mankind together."

Mycroft, his considerable bulk shifting slightly in his chair, nodded in agreement. "Indeed, my brother. Our escapade has illuminated the delicate interplay of cultures and empires in a way that no amount of diplomatic dispatches could hope to convey. The repercussions of our discoveries will, I suspect, be felt in the corridors of power for years to come."

Dr El-Sharif, her dark eyes glowing with scientific enthusiasm, leaned forward. "Gentlemen, we have not merely uncovered artefacts and ancient secrets. We have touched the very pulse of history itself. The wisdom of the Obsidian Guild, the legacy of the Al-Hakim family - these are not relics of a bygone era, but living threads in the great tapestry of human knowledge."

As I listened to my companions, I could not help but marvel at the profound change that had come over us all. The Holmes brothers, once so firmly rooted in the cold logic of deduction, now spoke with a newfound appreciation for the intangible and the mystical. Dr El-Sharif, her academic rigour tempered by our shared trials, brought a depth of personal experience to her scientific insights.

And what of me? I, John H. Watson, who had set out as a mere chronicler of the exploits of Sherlock Holmes, now found myself an integral part of a story that spanned centuries and continents. The desert wind seemed to whisper in my ears, carrying with it fragments of memory - the glint of starlight on the blade of a dagger, the thunderous hoofbeats of the obsidian stallion, the weight of ancient wisdom contained in crumbling scrolls.

"Do you remember," I ventured, my voice tinged with a mixture of awe and nostalgia, "that moment in the heart of Petra when we first deciphered the inscriptions that spoke of the Obsidian Guild? It was as if the stones themselves were whispering secrets that had lain dormant for millennia."

Holmes nodded, a rare smile playing at the corners of his mouth. "Indeed, Watson. And what of our encounter with the Sons of Purity in the depths of the desert? I have never seen such a perfect blend of ancient fanaticism and modern cunning. It was a stark reminder that the shadows of the past can reach long into the present.

"For my part," Mycroft interjected, his tone thoughtful, "I find myself reflecting on the delicate balance we have struck between exposing hidden truths and maintaining the stability of nations. Our actions have set wheels within wheels in motion, the full implications of which may not be known for generations."

As we continued to share our reflections, the atmosphere in the room seemed to shift and change, as if the very air around us was infused with the magic and mystery of our Arab adventure. The familiar confines of Baker Street faded away, replaced by vivid memories of sun-baked dunes, ancient ruins and the timeless beauty of the desert night.

It was then that I realised we had been transformed, not just by the events we had witnessed, but by the profound connections we had made - to each other, to the land of Arabia, and to the enduring spirit of human curiosity and resilience. We had set out in search of a mystery and returned with something far greater: a deeper understanding of our place in the vast tapestry of history and culture.

As the night deepened around us, our conversation flowed like a river, carrying us through the twists and turns of our shared odyssey. With each memory, each shared insight, I felt the true legacy of the Obsidian Stallion taking shape - not just in the artefacts we had recovered or the secrets we had uncovered, but in the indelible mark it had left on our very souls.

❦❧

As our conversation lulled, my gaze was drawn to the curious collection of artefacts that now adorned our familiar quarters. Each object, so out of place in the heart of London, seemed to pulse with the essence of our Arab adventure.

On the mantelpiece, gleaming in the flickering firelight, rested the obsidian dagger we had recovered from the sands of the deep desert. Its blade, dark as a moonless night, seemed to absorb the light around it, while the hilt, decorated with intricate gold filigree, spoke of a craft long lost to the mists of time. I remembered with a shudder how this very blade had once been held at Holmes' throat, our lives hanging by a thread.

"A remarkable piece," Dr El-Sharif murmured, her eyes fixed on the dagger. "Not just a weapon, but a symbol of the delicate balance between creation and destruction, between the darkness of ignorance and the light of knowledge."

Beside the dagger lay my own diary, its leather cover scarred by sun and sand, its pages filled with the hasty scribblings of our adventures. Holmes reached out and gently lifted the book, his long fingers caressing its worn spine with an almost reverent touch.

"Your chronicles, my dear Watson," he said, his voice uncharacteristically soft, "are far more than mere records of our escapades. They are a testament to the power of the written word to bridge the gap between worlds, to bring the exotic and the extraordinary into the heart of our staid British society."

But it was the trio of statuettes, each no larger than a man's hand, that caught the eye and dominated the room with their presence. Carved from the same obsidian as the dagger, they depicted three Arabian horses in full gallop, their manes and tails seeming to flow in an invisible wind. One was pierced with veins of gold, another with silver and the third with a deep, rich crimson.

Mycroft, his keen eyes narrowed in thought, gestured to the statuettes. "These, I believe, represent far more than mere objets d'art. They embody the very virtues that have guided our journey - courage, wisdom and heart."

"Indeed," Holmes agreed, rising to stand before the statuettes. "The golden horse, with its proud bearing and fearless stance, certainly represents courage. It reminds me of Al-Zarib's indomitable spirit in the face of danger, and of our own determination in the face of seemingly insurmountable odds."

Dr El-Sharif nodded, her scholarly enthusiasm igniting. "And the silver horse, with its pensive gaze and calm demeanour, must symbolise wisdom. It evokes the ancient knowledge of the Obsidian Guild and the insights we have gained from the sands of time."

"Which leaves the crimson horse," I added, feeling a sudden warmth in my chest, "as the embodiment of heart. For it was not just courage or wisdom that saw us through our trials, but the bonds of friendship and loyalty that grew stronger with each challenge we faced."

A contemplative silence fell over our group as we each reflected on the meaning of these symbols. I found myself wondering how these inanimate objects could so perfectly encapsulate the essence of our journey.

"It is strange," Holmes mused, breaking the silence, "how these artefacts, these symbols of our adventure, seem to bridge the gap between the tangible and the intangible. They are physical reminders of experiences that transcend the material world."

Mycroft, his expression uncharacteristically thoughtful, added: "And perhaps therein lies their true power. They act as anchors, linking the extraordinary to the ordinary, allowing us to carry a bit of that desert magic with us into our everyday lives."

As the night deepened around us, the artefacts seemed to glow with an inner light, as if imbued with the very spirit of Arabia. In their presence, the boundaries between past and present, between the mystical and the mundane, seemed to blur and shift. We had brought back more than mere trinkets from our journey; we had returned with talismans of transformation, physical embodiments of the profound changes wrought in our souls by the legacy of the Obsidian Stallion.

⊕┼❍⊰❋⊱❍┼⊕

As the night wore on, I observed a curious change in my dear friend Sherlock Holmes. His piercing grey eyes, usually so keen and analytical, now took on a distant, almost mystical quality. It was a look I had seen only rarely, in moments of his deepest contemplation. When he finally spoke, his voice carried a weight of introspection I had seldom heard before.

"Watson," he began, his gaze fixed on some unseen point beyond the confines of our room, "I find myself in the curious position of having to re-evaluate the very foundations of my methods and beliefs. Our Arab adventure has shaken my world in ways I could never have anticipated."

I leaned forward, eager to hear more. It was indeed a rare occasion when Holmes spoke so openly of his inner thoughts.

"You see," he continued, "I have always prided myself on my ability to observe, to deduce, to follow the cold trail of logic to its inevitable conclusion. But in the heart of the desert, I have encountered mysteries that defy rational explanation."

Holmes rose and began to pace, his slender figure casting long shadows in the flickering firelight. "Do you remember, Watson, our first encounter with the ancient texts in Petra? I approached them as I would any other cipher,

503

confident in my ability to crack their code. And yet, as the meaning of those mysterious symbols became clear, I felt something stir within me that went beyond mere intellectual satisfaction. It was as if the stones themselves were whispering secrets that echoed in the deepest recesses of my soul.

Mycroft shifted in his chair, his usually impassive face betraying a hint of concern at his brother's uncharacteristic display of emotion. Dr El-Sharif, however, nodded in understanding, her eyes bright with shared wonder.

"And then there was the moment in the Temple of Al-Hijr," Holmes continued, his voice dropping to a near whisper. "As we stood in that ancient chamber, surrounded by the weight of countless centuries, I felt something I can only describe as... a presence. Not a physical entity, you understand, but a sense of connection to something vast and timeless. It was most unsettling and yet strangely exhilarating.

I remembered the moment well, for I too had felt that inexplicable sensation. It was heartening to hear that even Holmes, with his razor-sharp intellect, had not been immune to the mystical atmosphere of the place.

"But perhaps most profound of all," Holmes said, turning to us with an expression of wonder, "was my experience with Al-Zarib and the other horses. I have always thought of animals as creatures of instinct, their actions dictated by observable patterns of behaviour. And yet, in the presence of these magnificent animals, I felt a connection that defied all logical explanation.

His voice took on a tone of awe as he continued. "In Al-Zarib's eyes, I saw a wisdom and understanding that equalled, nay, surpassed that of many men I have encountered. Our wordless communication in moments of danger, the sense of common purpose that guided our actions - these experiences have forced me to confront the possibility that there are forms of intelligence and consciousness beyond human comprehension."

As Holmes fell silent, I found myself marvelling at the profound change that had come over my friend. The man who had once declared that emotion was anathema to clear reasoning now spoke of mystical connections and transcendent experiences with the fervour of a convert.

"My dear Holmes," I ventured, "it seems that our journey has not only broadened your horizons, but opened your heart to new possibilities.

A faint smile played at the corners of Holmes' mouth. "Indeed, Watson. I find that my view of the world has been irrevocably altered. The rigid boundaries I once drew between the rational and the inexplicable have blurred, revealing a universe far more complex and wondrous than I ever imagined."

As the night deepened around us, I reflected on the extraordinary transformation we had all undergone. Holmes's journey from strict rationalist to one who could embrace the mysteries of the unseen world mirrored our collective evolution. We had gone in search of answers and returned with questions that would echo through the rest of our lives.

⊹⊱✿⊰⊹

As the hour grew late and the fire burned low, I found myself drawn to the leather-bound journal that had been my constant companion throughout our Arabian Odyssey. Its pages, now dog-eared and stained with the dust of ancient lands, seemed to pulse with the very essence of our adventures. With a sense of both trepidation and excitement, I opened the book and began to read aloud.

"Gentlemen and my dear Dr El-Sharif," I began, my voice carrying the weight of remembered wonders, "allow me to share with you some fragments of our extraordinary journey as I recorded them in the heat of the moment."

I cleared my throat and read on:

"June 15th - The sands of Petra stretch before us, a sea of gold under an unforgiving sun. Today Holmes deciphered the ancient Nabataean inscriptions, his eyes glowing with a fervour I have rarely seen. As the secrets of the Obsidian Guild unfolded before us, I felt the very air tremble with the weight of history.

I looked up to see my companions leaning forward, their faces rapt with attention. Encouraged, I continued:

"July 3rd - In the heart of the desert we encountered the Sons of Purity. Their blades glittered in the moonlight, their eyes burned with fanatical zeal. But it was not Holmes's razor-sharp wit, nor my steady hand on my revolver, that saved us, but the inexplicable bond between my friend and the magnificent Al-Zarib. Man and beast moved as one, a living embodiment of the unity we sought.

Holmes nodded slowly, his eyes distant with memory. Dr El-Sharif's hand moved to her heart as if to feel the pulse of that fateful night.

"July 20th - The Temple of Al-Hijr looms before us, its ancient stones whispering secrets long forgotten. As we stand on the threshold of revelation, I am struck by the profound nature of our quest. We have sought a statuette and instead found the very key to understanding the intertwined destinies of East and West.

As I closed the diary, a thoughtful silence fell over our gathering. It was Mycroft who broke it, his voice uncharacteristically gentle.

"My dear Dr Watson," he said, "you have captured not only the events of your journey, but its very soul. Your words breathe life into these adventures and allow those of us left behind to share in their wonder."

I felt a surge of pride at his words, but also a deep sense of responsibility. "Thank you, Mycroft," I replied, "but I confess to being somewhat overwhelmed by the task before me. How can I convey the true magnitude of our experience to a wider audience? There are elements of our journey that defy rational explanation, that challenge the very foundations of our understanding

505

of the world.

Holmes, his keen gaze fixed on me, leaned forward. "Herein lies your true challenge, Watson, and your greatest opportunity. You must find a way to bridge the gap between the world we knew and the world we have discovered. Your chronicles have the power to open minds and hearts to new possibilities, to expand the horizons of those who may never set foot beyond our shores."

Dr El-Sharif nodded in agreement. "Indeed, Dr Watson. Your role is not merely to record, but to illuminate. Through your words, the wisdom of the Obsidian Guild and the spirit of Arabia can reach across cultures and generations."

As I pondered her words, I felt the weight of my responsibility fall upon me like a cloak. "I will endeavour," I said slowly, "to craft a narrative that honours the truth of our experience while capturing the imagination of our readers. Perhaps by interweaving the tangible details of our adventure with the more... ineffable elements, I can lead our audience to the very threshold of wonder that we ourselves crossed."

Mycroft raised an eyebrow, a gleam of approval in his eyes. "A delicate balance, to be sure, but one I believe you are uniquely qualified to strike."

As the night deepened around us, I found myself filled with a sense of purpose and anticipation. The chronicle I would write would be more than a mere tale of adventure; it would be a bridge between worlds, a testament to the enduring power of friendship, and a call to all who read it to look beyond the boundaries of the known and embrace the infinite possibilities that lie in the realm of the extraordinary.

With renewed determination, I picked up my pen, ready to begin the monumental task of translating our desert odyssey into words that would resonate through the ages. The legacy of the Obsidian Stallion, I vowed, would gallop from the pages of my tale and into the hearts and minds of all who dared to dream of worlds beyond their own.

⊰⊱⊰⊱⊰⊱

As the night wore on, Mycroft Holmes shifted in his chair, his considerable bulk settling into a posture of deep contemplation. The flickering firelight cast shadows across his face, accentuating the keen intelligence that lurked behind his hooded eyes. When he finally spoke, his voice carried the measured tones of one accustomed to moving the levers of empire.

"Gentlemen and my dear Dr El-Sharif," he began, his gaze sweeping over our small gathering, "while your adventure has indeed been extraordinary on a personal level, I feel compelled to illuminate its far-reaching implications on the grand chessboard of international relations."

I leaned forward, eager to hear Mycroft's insights. For all his indolence, Sherlock's older brother possessed an unparalleled understanding of the intricate dance of global politics.

"Our Empire," Mycroft continued, "has long viewed the Ottoman Empire through a lens of suspicion and thinly veiled contempt. But your experience and the alliances you have forged offer us an unprecedented opportunity to rewrite the history of East-West relations."

Holmes nodded slowly, his eyes narrowing in thought. "You speak of a fundamental shift in diplomatic strategy, my brother?"

"Indeed," Mycroft replied, a rare smile playing at the corners of his mouth. "Imagine, if you will, a new approach to our dealings with the East. One based not on conquest and subjugation, but on mutual respect and shared knowledge. The wisdom of the Obsidian Guild, the legacy of the Al-Hakim family - these are not mere curiosities to be locked away in our museums, but living traditions that could inform and enrich our own society".

Dr El-Sharif's eyes lit up with excitement at Mycroft's words. "Such an approach could revolutionise not only diplomacy but also science," she exclaimed. "The exchange of ideas, the blending of Eastern and Western philosophies - the possibilities are endless!"

Mycroft held up a warning hand. "Let us not be carried away by enthusiasm, my dear Doctor. The road ahead is full of challenges. There are those in the highest echelons of power, both in London and Constantinople, who would view such a change with alarm. They cling to the old ways, fearful of any change that might upset the delicate balance of power".

I felt a shiver run down my spine at Mycroft's words, remembering all too well the dangers we had faced from those who feared the truths we had uncovered. "Surely," I ventured, "the benefits of such cooperation far outweigh the risks?"

"In the long run, no doubt," Mycroft agreed. "But we must proceed with caution. The knowledge you brought back from Arabia is as powerful as it is profound. In the wrong hands it could be used to foment unrest, to manipulate ancient enmities for modern gain."

Holmes, who had been listening intently, spoke up. "You're hinting at deeper currents, Mycroft. What are you not telling us?"

Mycroft's expression grew serious. "There are... rumblings, shall we say? Whispers of a growing movement that seeks to exploit the mystical elements of our eastern territories for nefarious purposes. They cloak themselves in the language of tradition and purity, but their aims are far from noble."

A heavy silence fell over the room as we all considered the implications of Mycroft's words. It was clear that our adventure, far from being over, had only opened the door to even greater challenges.

"What would you have us do, Mycroft?" Holmes asked, his voice carrying a note of determination that I knew only too well.

"For now, vigilance is our watchword," Mycroft replied. "Continue your work, all of you. Share your knowledge, but do so wisely. Build bridges between our cultures, but be wary of those who would burn them. The game, as you like to say, my brother, is most definitely in progress."

As Mycroft's words hung in the air, I felt a strange mixture of apprehension and excitement. We had returned from Arabia changed men, bearers of ancient wisdom and profound insight. But it was clear that our true test was yet to come. The legacy of the Obsidian Stallion, it seemed, would gallop far beyond the deserts of Arabia, shaping the future of nations.

With a shared look of understanding, we silently rededicated ourselves to the path ahead, ready to face whatever challenges the future might bring, armed with the wisdom of the East and the determination of the West.

⊷⊶⊹⊱⊰⊹⊶⊷

As the night deepened and the fire cast dancing shadows on the walls of our Baker Street sanctuary, Dr Amal El-Sharif leaned forward, her eyes alight with a fervour I had come to associate with the most passionate of scholars. The adventures we had shared had clearly kindled a flame of intellectual curiosity that promised to burn for years to come.

"Gentlemen," she began, her voice carrying the lilting cadence of her native Arabic, softened by years of Oxford elocution, "our journey has been not merely one of personal discovery, but a veritable revolution in our understanding of history itself. The implications of our findings are, I dare say, nothing short of extraordinary."

Holmes, his keen grey eyes fixed on our learned companion, nodded in encouragement. "Pray enlighten us, Dr El-Sharif. How do you intend to pursue these revelations in the hallowed halls of academia?"

A smile played across Dr El-Sharif's lips as she replied, "My dear Mr Holmes, the path before us is as vast and varied as the Arabian sands themselves. First and foremost, I intend to undertake a comprehensive study of the texts we discovered in the Temple of Al-Hijr. Their insights into the ancient wisdom of the Obsidian Guild could reshape our entire understanding of early civilisations and their knowledge of the natural world".

Mycroft, ever the pragmatist, raised an eyebrow. "And how, pray tell, do you intend to present such revolutionary findings to a scientific community that may be... less than receptive to challenges to established doctrine?"

Dr El-Sharif's expression became serious. "A most pertinent question, Mr Holmes. I suggest a multi-pronged approach. First, a series of carefully curated publications in respected journals, presenting our discoveries within the framework of existing historical narratives. At the same time, I will organise a series of lectures and symposia, bringing together forward-thinking scholars

508

from East and West.

I found myself nodding in appreciation of her strategic approach. "A most prudent plan, Dr El-Sharif. But surely you do not intend to undertake this monumental task alone?"

Her eyes sparkled with enthusiasm as she replied, "Indeed not, Dr Watson. I have already begun correspondence with colleagues at Al-Azhar University in Cairo and the Sorbonne in Paris. There is talk of a joint expedition to further explore the sites we have uncovered. Imagine, gentlemen, a joint effort bringing together the best minds of Europe and the Middle East, working in harmony to unlock the secrets of our shared past!

Holmes leaned back in his chair, a look of quiet approval on his face. "Your vision is both ambitious and admirable, Doctor. But tell me, how do you see these academic endeavours affecting the wider world beyond the ivory tower?"

Dr El-Sharif's expression grew pensive. "Therein lies the real challenge, Mr Holmes. Our discoveries have the potential to bridge the gap between East and West in ways previously unimagined. By demonstrating the interconnectedness of our histories, the common wellsprings of our knowledge, we can foster a new era of cultural understanding and cooperation."

Mycroft, who had been listening intently, spoke up. "A noble aim, to be sure. But one must tread carefully in such matters. The political implications of rewriting history are not to be underestimated."

"Indeed, Mr Holmes," Dr El-Sharif agreed. "Which is why I suggest that we work closely with diplomatic channels, including yourself, to ensure that our findings are presented in a manner that promotes unity rather than discord. The legacy of the Obsidian Stallion must serve as a force for enlightenment, not division."

As I listened to Dr El-Sharif outline her grand vision, I could not help but feel a sense of awe at the far-reaching consequences of our Arab adventure. What had begun as a simple investigation had blossomed into a quest for knowledge that promised to reshape the very foundations of historical understanding.

"And what of the more... esoteric aspects of our discoveries?" I ventured, thinking of the unexplained phenomena we had witnessed in the depths of the desert.

Dr El-Sharif's eyes twinkled with a mixture of mischief and scientific eagerness. "Ah, Dr Watson, here lies perhaps the most exciting frontier of all. I intend to establish a new field of study, one that bridges the gap between empirical science and the ancient wisdom traditions of the East. We are on the verge of unlocking secrets that have lain dormant for millennia!

As the night wore on, our discussion ranged far and wide, touching on topics as diverse as archaeoastronomy, comparative mythology and the hidden properties of desert flora. Through it all, I marvelled at the transformation of our little band of adventurers into the vanguard of a new age of discovery.

As we finally retired for the night, my head spinning with visions of great expeditions and revolutionary discoveries, I could not help but feel that the true legacy of the Obsidian Stallion was only beginning to unfold. The sands of Arabia had given up their secrets, setting us on a path that would lead to the very frontiers of human knowledge.

·÷·≈·÷·≈·

As the night wore on, our discussion turned to the wider implications of our Arabian Odyssey. The fire was low, casting a warm, intimate glow over our little gathering, and I could not help feeling that we were engaged in a conversation that might well shape the course of history.

"Gentlemen and my dear Dr El-Sharif," Mycroft began, his voice carrying the weight of one who has long studied the intricacies of international relations, "I find myself pondering the potential impact of our adventures on the delicate balance between the British Empire and the Ottoman Empire."

Holmes, his fingers tucked under his chin in that familiar pose of deep contemplation, nodded slowly. "Indeed, my brother. Our experiences have shed new light on a culture long viewed through a lens of suspicion and misunderstanding. Might we not be on the cusp of a great shift in perception?"

Dr El-Sharif leaned forward, her eyes bright with enthusiasm. "Exactly, Mr Holmes! Consider, if you will, the reaction of the public when they learn of the profound wisdom we have encountered in the heart of the desert. The legacy of the Obsidian Guild, the ancient knowledge preserved in the sands of Arabia - these are not relics of a primitive past, but living traditions that could enrich our own society immeasurably."

I found myself nodding in agreement. "It is true," I ventured, "that the common perception of the Middle East in our English society is woefully limited. The average Londoner's understanding hardly extends beyond tales of camels and bazaars, with perhaps a dash of 'Arabian Nights' fantasy thrown in for good measure."

Mycroft's brow furrowed in thought. "A point well made, Dr Watson. And therein lies both our greatest challenge and our greatest opportunity. How might we go about reshaping these entrenched perceptions?"

"Through cultural exchange, surely," Holmes interjected, his eyes bright with the excitement of a new intellectual pursuit. "Imagine, if you will, exhibitions of Arab art and artefacts in our museums, not as curiosities of a foreign land, but as evidence of a shared human heritage."

Dr El-Sharif clapped her hands with delight. "Yes! And beyond that, exchanges of scholars and students. Let the young minds of Britain and the Ottoman Empire learn side by side, discovering the similarities that unite us rather than the differences that divide us."

"A noble vision," Mycroft mused, "but one that will require delicate handling. There are those in both realms who would view such exchanges with suspicion, fearing a dilution of their own cultural identity."

I felt compelled to speak up. "But surely, Mycroft, the benefits far outweigh the risks? In my own experience, direct interaction with the people of Arabia - from Bedouin guides to scholars of ancient texts - has shattered my own preconceptions and replaced them with genuine understanding."

Holmes nodded in agreement. "Well said, Watson. It is through personal connections that the greatest advances in understanding are made. Perhaps we may even see the day when English gentlemen take up the study of Arabic with the same enthusiasm they now reserve for Latin and Greek."

"And conversely," Dr El-Sharif added, "when Ottoman scholars delve into the works of Shakespeare and Milton with equal fervour. The cross-fertilisation of ideas could lead to a renaissance of thought unparalleled since the days of ancient Alexandria".

As our discussion continued, touching on everything from diplomatic initiatives to educational reform, I marvelled at the far-reaching consequences of our desert adventure. What had begun as a simple investigation had blossomed into a vision for a new era of cultural understanding and cooperation.

"Of course," Mycroft warned as night fell, "we must be prepared for resistance. Change, especially on such a grand scale, is never embraced without a struggle."

"True," Holmes agreed, "but is that not all the more reason to persevere? After all, nothing less than the future of East-West relations is at stake.

As we finally retired for the night, my mind swirling with visions of a world transformed by mutual understanding and respect, I could not help but feel a profound sense of gratitude for the journey that had brought us to this point. The legacy of the Obsidian Stallion, it seemed, would gallop far beyond the deserts of Arabia, carrying with it the promise of a more enlightened and connected world.

With a final glance at the artefacts that now adorned our rooms at Baker Street - silent witnesses to our extraordinary adventure - I made my way to my chamber, eager for the dawn and the new chapter it would bring in our continuing quest for knowledge and understanding.

As the first light of dawn began to creep through the windows of 221B Baker Street, casting long shadows across the familiar confines of our living room, a contemplative silence fell over our small gathering. The weight of our shared experiences in Arabia seemed to press down upon us, demanding recognition of how profoundly we had been changed by our extraordinary adventure.

It was Holmes who first broke the silence, his piercing grey eyes sweeping over each of us in turn. "My friends," he began, his voice uncharacteristically soft, "I believe we stand at a crossroads, not only in the grand tapestry of history, but in our own personal journeys. Perhaps it would be appropriate for each of us to share our thoughts on the road ahead."

Mycroft shifted in his chair, his considerable bulk settling into a posture of quiet dignity. "For my part," he intoned, "I find myself compelled to reassess the foundations of our diplomatic approach to the East. The wisdom we have encountered, the alliances we have forged - these cannot be allowed to wither on the vine of bureaucratic indifference. I intend to use my influence to foster a new era of understanding between our two great empires.

Dr El-Sharif, her eyes bright with scholarly fervour, leaned forward. "And I, gentlemen, see before me a lifetime of study and exploration. The secrets we have uncovered are but the tip of a vast iceberg of knowledge. I will dedicate myself to bridging the gap between Eastern and Western scholarship, to creating a synthesis of understanding that honours both traditions."

As I listened to my companions, I felt a surge of admiration for their noble aspirations. When it was my turn to speak, I found the words flowing with surprising ease. "As for me," I declared, "I am more committed than ever to recording our adventures. But more than that, I feel a calling to use my medical expertise to explore the healing traditions we encountered in Arabia. There is much our modern medicine could learn from the ancient wisdom of the desert."

Holmes nodded in agreement, a rare smile playing at the corners of his mouth. "Well said, my dear Watson. As for me, I find that our journey has awakened in me a hunger for knowledge that extends far beyond the realm of crime and deduction. I intend to delve deeper into the mystical traditions of the East, to seek an understanding of those aspects of existence that defy mere logic."

As we shared our intentions, my thoughts turned to our other companions, now scattered to the winds. "I wonder," I wondered aloud, "what paths our other friends have chosen in the wake of our shared odyssey."

"Ah," Holmes said, his eyes taking on that distant look that told me he was accessing his vast mental archives, "I received word from our dear Liyana only yesterday. She writes that she has accepted a diplomatic post in Constantinople, dedicated to promoting cultural exchange between our nations. And Khalid, I believe, has returned to the desert, not as a mere guide, but as a guardian of the ancient sites we have uncovered."

"And what about Adrien?" I inquired, remembering the young artist's passion for capturing the beauty of the Arabian landscape.

"Adrien," Holmes replied with a smile, "has embarked on a most ambitious project. He wants to create a series of paintings that will bring the wonders of

Arabia to the salons of Europe. A noble undertaking, to be sure, and one that may do more to change perceptions than a thousand dry treatises.

As we fell into a companionable silence, each lost in our own thoughts of the future, I could not help but marvel at the transformative power of our shared adventure. We had set out in search of a mystery and returned with a mission that would shape the rest of our lives.

The first rays of sunlight now streamed through the windows, illuminating the artefacts of our journey that adorned the room. The obsidian dagger gleamed on the mantelpiece, a testament to the dangers we had faced. The statuettes of the three horses stood proudly on the bookshelf, symbols of the virtues that had guided us. And there, on my desk, lay my trusty diary, ready to record the next chapter in our continuing quest for knowledge and understanding.

As I gazed upon these tokens of our adventure, I felt a surge of anticipation for the journey yet to come. The legacy of the Obsidian Stallion, I realised, was not just a story to be told, but a call to action, a challenge to each of us to carry forward the spirit of discovery and unity that we had found in the heart of the Arabian desert.

With a shared look of determination, we rose to face the new day, each of us ready to embark on our individual quests, yet bound together by the unbreakable bonds forged in the crucible of our extraordinary adventure.

<hr />

As the first light of dawn began to fade and the familiar sounds of Baker Street came to life outside our windows, I found myself alone with Holmes by the dying embers of the fire. Mycroft had taken his leave, his considerable frame moving with surprising grace as he made his way to the corridors of power where his influence was most felt. Dr El-Sharif had retired to the guest quarters, her mind no doubt swirling with plans for future expeditions and scholarly pursuits.

Holmes sat in his usual chair, his slender figure silhouetted against the faint glow of the fireplace. I took my usual place opposite him, feeling the comforting weight of our shared history settle around us like a well-worn cloak. For a long moment we sat in companionable silence, each lost in our own reflections on the extraordinary journey that had brought us to this point.

It was Holmes who finally broke the silence, his voice carrying a note of introspection I had rarely heard before. "I am at a loss, Watson," he began, his eyes fixed on the glowing embers. "Our adventures in Arabia have shaken the very foundations of my worldview. I, who have always prided myself on cold logic and empirical deduction, now find myself grappling with experiences that defy rational explanation."

I leaned forward, sensing the rare vulnerability in my friend's words.

"Perhaps, Holmes," I ventured, "it is not a matter of abandoning reason, but of expanding its boundaries. Our journey has shown us that there are truths beyond the reach of mere logic, truths to be felt as well as deduced."

A faint smile played at the corners of Holmes' mouth. "Well said, my dear fellow. It seems that your role as chronicler has sharpened your philosophical acumen." His expression became pensive. "Do you remember that moment in the heart of the desert when we stood under a canopy of stars so vast and brilliant that it seemed to mock our petty human concerns?"

I nodded, the memory washing over me with startling clarity. "Indeed, Holmes. I remember thinking that we were but a speck of dust in the grand tapestry of the universe and yet, paradoxically, our actions carried a weight and significance beyond measure."

"Exactly, Watson," Holmes replied, his eyes glowing with the fervour of shared understanding. "It was then that I began to understand the true nature of our quest. We were not merely trying to solve a mystery, but to unravel the very fabric of human connection across time and culture."

As we talked, the first rays of sunlight began to creep through the windows, casting long shadows across the room. We spoke of the dangers we had faced, the allies we had made and the profound truths we had uncovered. With each shared memory, I felt the bonds of our friendship deepen and strengthen.

"You know, Watson," Holmes said at length, his voice taking on a tone of rare affection, "I have often thought of you as my Boswell, faithfully recording our adventures for posterity. But our journey through Arabia has shown me that you are far more than a mere chronicler. You are my compass, my moral beacon in a world that often confuses my analytical mind".

Deeply moved by his words, I struggled to find an adequate response. "And you, Holmes," I finally managed, "have been my guiding star, leading me to wonders I could scarcely have imagined. Our partnership has been the great adventure of my life."

As a new day dawned outside our windows, I felt a deep sense of gratitude for the journey we had shared and the challenges that lay ahead. The legacy of the Obsidian Stallion had changed us both, deepening our friendship and broadening our understanding of the world and our place in it.

Holmes rose and moved to the window, his tall frame silhouetted against the morning light. "Come, Watson," he said, a note of anticipation in his voice. "The game is on again. There are still mysteries to be solved, truths to be uncovered. And I can think of no one I would rather have by my side as we face the challenges that lie ahead."

As I joined him at the window, looking out at the bustling streets of London, I felt a surge of excitement for the adventures that lay ahead. Our journey to Arabia may have come to an end, but the true legacy of the Obsidian Stallion was only beginning to unfold. With Holmes by my side, I knew we would continue to push the boundaries of knowledge and understanding, paving the way for a future where the wisdom of East and West could be united in harmony.

⁘

As the morning sun climbed higher in the London sky, casting its golden light over the familiar confines of our Baker Street lodgings, Holmes and I found ourselves once again poring over the artefacts and documents we had brought back from our Arabian odyssey. The excitement of our homecoming had given way to a contemplative mood as we grappled with the myriad questions that still lingered in the wake of our extraordinary adventure.

"You know, Watson," Holmes mused, his long fingers tracing the intricate patterns on the obsidian dagger, "for all that we have uncovered, I cannot help but feel that we have only scratched the surface of the Obsidian Guild's secrets."

I nodded in agreement, my mind wandering back to the ancient chambers of Petra and the whispered legends of Al-Hijr. "Indeed, Holmes. The influence of the Guild seems to extend far beyond the borders of Arabia. One wonders how deep its roots really run."

Holmes' eyes gleamed with that familiar spark of intellectual curiosity. "Exactly, my dear fellow. Consider the evidence we have found of Guild outposts in lands as distant as India and China. What knowledge might be hidden in these distant corners of the Empire?"

As we discussed the tantalising hints of the Guild's global reach, I found myself recalling a curious passage from one of the ancient texts we had discovered. "Holmes," I ventured, "do you remember the cryptic mention of a 'Jade Pavilion' in the scrolls of Al-Hijr? Could it be that the influence of the Obsidian Guild extends as far as the Far East?"

My friend's eyes narrowed in thought. "An astute observation, Watson. The intersection of the Silk Road and the ancient sea routes could well have served as conduits for the Guild's teachings. One can only imagine the synthesis of wisdom that might have taken place at such a crossroads of civilisation."

Our conversation meandered through a maze of possibilities, each speculation leading to new avenues of inquiry. We considered the true extent of the Guild's alchemical knowledge, the possible existence of other mystical artefacts similar to the obsidian statuettes, and the tantalising hints of lost cities hidden in the depths of the Arabian Desert.

"And what about the prophecies, Holmes?" I asked, remembering the enigmatic verses that had guided our search. "Surely we have not seen the last of their influence on world affairs?"

Holmes nodded gravely. "Indeed, Watson. The wheels set in motion by our discovery of the Obsidian Stallion will continue to turn long after we are gone.

I suspect that future generations will grapple with the legacy of the Guild in ways we can scarcely imagine."

As we continued our discussion, I could not help but feel a sense of both excitement and trepidation at the thought of the mysteries that still lay unsolved. The desert, it seemed, had not yet revealed all its secrets.

"You know, Watson," Holmes said at length, with a familiar gleam in his eye, "I have received a most intriguing communication from an old acquaintance in Cairo. It seems that strange occurrences have been reported in the vicinity of the Great Pyramid, occurrences which bear a striking resemblance to certain phenomena we have encountered in Arabia."

I felt a familiar thrill of anticipation run through me. "Surely, Holmes, you don't think..."

"I think, my dear Watson," he interjected, a smile playing at the corners of his mouth, "that the game is far from over. The sands of time have more secrets to yield, and I can think of no one I would rather have by my side as we unravel them."

As I looked out the window at the bustling streets of London, my thoughts wandered to the sun-baked dunes of Arabia. The Obsidian Stallion, though now far from our sight, still seemed to gallop through the corridors of my imagination, carrying with it the promise of adventures yet to come.

At that moment, I knew with certainty that our journey was far from over. The legacy of the Obsidian Guild, with its ancient wisdom and enduring mysteries, would continue to shape our path. And as I turned back to Holmes and saw the fire of curiosity burning brightly in his eyes, I felt a surge of gratitude for the extraordinary partnership that had brought us to this point and would, I was certain, carry us forward into new realms of discovery and wonder.

As the day wore on, our little party reassembled in the familiar confines of our Baker Street lodgings. The afternoon sun cast long shadows across the room, illuminating the curious collection of artefacts that now adorned our quarters - silent witnesses to the extraordinary adventure from which we had so recently returned.

Holmes stood by the fireplace, his slender figure silhouetted against the flickering flames, while Mycroft occupied the armchair usually reserved for clients. Dr El-Sharif and I completed the circle, each of us lost in contemplation of the profound truths we had uncovered in the heart of the Arabian desert.

It was Mycroft who broke the thoughtful silence, his voice carrying the weight of one accustomed to pondering the great machinations of empire. "Gentlemen - and my dear Dr El-Sharif - I am struck by the sheer magnitude of what we have discovered. The Obsidian Guild, it seems, represents far more than a mere secret society. It stands as a testament to the interconnectedness of human civilisation itself.

Holmes nodded, his keen eyes glowing with intellectual fervour. "Indeed, my brother. Our journey has revealed to us a tapestry of history far richer and more complex than we could have imagined. The threads of Eastern and Western thought, so long considered separate and distinct, are in fact intricately interwoven."

"Exactly," Dr El-Sharif interjected, her voice carrying the passion of a true scholar. "Consider, if you will, the great libraries of Baghdad and Alexandria, the philosophical exchanges along the Silk Road, the blending of medical traditions in Andalusia. The Obsidian Guild, I believe, has long stood as the silent guardian of this shared heritage, preserving knowledge that transcends the arbitrary boundaries of nation and creed."

As I listened to my companions, I felt a profound sense of wonder at the vast expanse of human history laid bare before us. "It occurs to me," I ventured, "that our modern notion of East and West as separate spheres may be a relatively recent construct. The wisdom we encountered in Arabia speaks to a deeper unity, a common source of human understanding."

Mycroft leaned forward, his considerable bulk shifting as he warmed to the subject. "An astute observation, Dr Watson. And one that has significant implications for the future of international relations. If we can only recognise this common heritage, might we not forge a new era of understanding between our peoples?"

Holmes, fingers clasped under his chin in that familiar pose of deep contemplation, spoke slowly. "The Obsidian Guild, in its centuries-long mission to preserve knowledge, has shown us a way forward. It is a path that requires us to look beyond the superficial differences of culture and custom to recognise the fundamental truths that unite us all."

"But surely," I interjected, "such a shift in perspective is a monumental challenge. How can we hope to overcome centuries of misunderstanding and conflict?"

Dr El-Sharif's eyes shone with conviction as she replied. "Through education, Dr Watson. Through the patient work of scholars and diplomats, artists and writers. We must strive to build bridges of understanding, to illuminate the connections that have always existed between East and West."

As our discussion continued, touching on topics ranging from comparative mythology to the common roots of scientific inquiry, I marvelled at the transformative power of our Arabic odyssey. We had set out in search of a mystery and returned with a mission that promised to reshape the very foundations of how we view the world and our place in it.

The Legacy of the Obsidian Stallion, I realised, was not just a story to be told, but a call to action. It challenged us to become guardians of knowledge ourselves, to promote understanding and unity in a world too often divided by fear and ignorance.

As the sun began to set, casting a warm glow over our gathering, Holmes rose and walked to the window. His gaze swept over the bustling streets of London, but I knew his mind's eye was fixed on distant horizons. "The game, my friends," he said softly, "has taken on dimensions we could scarcely have imagined. Our task now is to carry on the torch of understanding, to illuminate the paths that unite us all."

With these words we fell into a contemplative silence, each of us pondering the monumental task that lay before us. The Obsidian Guild had preserved the wisdom of the ages through countless trials and tribulations. Now it was up to us to ensure that this legacy of unity and understanding flourished in the modern world, bridging the gap between East and West and fostering a future of shared knowledge and mutual respect.

As I looked at the faces of my companions, I felt a surge of pride and determination. Whatever challenges lay ahead, I knew that the bonds forged in the crucible of our Arab adventure would see us through. The legacy of the Obsidian Stallion would gallop on, carrying with it the promise of a more enlightened and connected world.

❦

As the day drew to a close, we found ourselves once more gathered around the fireplace in the familiar confines of 221B Baker Street. The dancing flames cast flickering shadows across the room, illuminating the curious collection of artefacts that now adorned our quarters - silent testaments to the extraordinary adventure from which we had so recently returned.

Holmes stood before the fire, his slender figure silhouetted against the warm glow, while Mycroft occupied his usual armchair with his usual air of quiet authority. Dr El-Sharif and I completed our little circle, each of us lost in contemplation of the journey that had brought us to this moment.

With a grace that belied his usual brusqueness, Holmes raised a glass of fine brandy, his keen eyes sweeping over our little group. "My friends," he began, his voice carrying a depth of emotion I had rarely heard from him, "I find myself at a loss for words - a most unusual circumstance, I'm sure you'll agree."

A gentle ripple of laughter broke the solemnity of the moment, and I saw a rare smile play across my friend's features.

"We set out," Holmes continued, "in search of a mystery, and found ourselves embroiled in an adventure that has reshaped our understanding of the world and our place in it. Each of you has played a vital role in this extraordinary odyssey, and I feel compelled to acknowledge your contributions.

He turned to his brother first. "Mycroft, your strategic mind and unparalleled knowledge of international affairs have been invaluable. You have shown us

518

how the echoes of ancient wisdom can echo through the corridors of modern power."

Mycroft tilted his head in acknowledgement, a look of quiet pride in his eyes.

"Dr El-Sharif," Holmes continued, "your scholarly insights and deep understanding of Eastern culture have been our guiding light. You have bridged the gap between past and present, East and West, with grace and wisdom."

The good doctor's eyes shone with gratitude and a hint of tears as she raised her glass in return.

"And Watson," Holmes said, turning to me with a warmth that touched my very soul, "my faithful friend and chronicler. Your steadfast companionship, moral compass and keen observations have, as always, been the foundation upon which our adventures have been built. Your growth during this journey has been a wonder to behold.

I felt a lump form in my throat, overwhelmed by the depth of feeling in Holmes' words.

"To each of you," Holmes concluded, raising his glass, "and to the extraordinary legacy of the Obsidian Stallion. May the wisdom we have uncovered light our way forward, and may we continue to unravel the mysteries that bind us all."

As we drank to Holmes' toast, I felt a profound sense of accomplishment, tinged with the exhilarating promise of adventures yet to come. The fire crackled in the grate, its warmth seeming to embrace us all, much as the heat of the Arabian sun had done in what now felt like another lifetime.

I set down my glass and allowed my eyes to wander over the curious collection of artefacts that now adorned our living room. The obsidian dagger glinted in the firelight, a reminder of the dangers we had faced. The statuettes of the three horses stood proudly on the mantelpiece, embodying the virtues of courage, wisdom and heart that had guided us through our trials.

And there, on my desk, lay my trusty diary, its pages filled with the chronicle of our extraordinary journey. I knew that the task of translating our adventures into a narrative worthy of public consumption lay ahead of me, a challenge both daunting and exhilarating.

As the night deepened around us, our conversation flowed like a river, carrying us through the twists and turns of our shared odyssey. With each memory, each shared insight, I felt the true legacy of the Obsidian Stallion taking shape - not just in the artefacts we had recovered or the secrets we had uncovered, but in the indelible mark it had left on our very souls.

We had set out as individuals, each with our own motivations and perspectives, and returned as a unified whole, bound together by the threads of an adventure that had transcended the boundaries of culture, time and understanding. The wisdom of the East and the rationality of the West had merged within us, creating a new paradigm of knowledge and empathy.

As I looked into the faces of my companions, I saw in them the promise of a future where the artificial divisions between cultures could be bridged, where ancient wisdom and modern insight could coexist in harmony. The legacy of the Obsidian Stallion, I realised, was not an end, but a beginning - a call to action that would shape the rest of our lives, and perhaps the course of history itself.

With a shared look of understanding, we silently rededicated ourselves to the path ahead. The game, as Holmes would say, was definitely afoot, and I knew with unwavering certainty that wherever that path might lead, we would face it together, armed with the wisdom of the ages and the unbreakable bonds of friendship forged in the crucible of our Arab adventure.

As the fire burned low and the first hints of dawn crept through the windows of Baker Street, I felt a sense of profound gratitude wash over me. Whatever the future might hold, I knew that the legacy of the Obsidian Stallion would gallop on, carrying with it the promise of a more enlightened and connected world.

⊰•❈•⊱

As the first light of dawn began to creep through the windows of 221B Baker Street, our little gathering slowly dispersed. Mycroft, with a nod of quiet understanding to his brother, took his leave, no doubt to return to the labyrinthine corridors of power where his influence was felt most keenly. Dr El-Sharif, her eyes bright with the promise of future discoveries, bid us a warm farewell, her mind already turning to the academic pursuits that awaited her.

Holmes and I were alone again, the familiar silence of our shared quarters settling around us like a comfortable old coat. My friend stood at the window, his slender silhouette framed by the growing light, his keen gaze fixed on the awakening streets of London. I sat down at my desk, drawn by an irresistible urge to commit my final thoughts to paper while the embers of our extraordinary adventure still burned brightly in my mind.

With a sense of awe, I opened my diary to a fresh page, the crisp parchment seeming to await my pen with eager anticipation. As I began to write, the words flowed with a life of their own, capturing the essence of our journey and its profound impact on us all.

"In the fading shadows of night," I wrote, "as London comes to life around us, I find myself reflecting on the remarkable odyssey from which we have so recently returned. Our search for the Obsidian Stallion has taken us not only across continents, but across the very boundaries of understanding that so often separate East from West, past from present, known from unknown.

"We set out in search of a mystery and returned with a mission that promises to reshape the very foundations of how we view the world and our place within it. The legacy of the Obsidian Guild, with its ancient wisdom and timeless truths, now resides within us, a sacred trust that we must nurture and share with a world too often blinded by prejudice and misunderstanding.

"As I look at the curious artefacts that now adorn our quarters - the obsidian dagger, the statuettes of the three horses, the weathered scrolls of Al-Hijr - I am struck by how these physical remnants of our adventure pale in comparison to the transformative power of the knowledge and insights we have gained. We have been changed, irrevocably and profoundly, by our encounters with the mysteries of the East.

"And yet I cannot shake off the feeling that our journey is far from over. The sands of Arabia, though now distant, still seem to whisper of secrets yet to be revealed, of truths waiting to be revealed. The obsidian stallion, though no longer visible to our eyes, gallops on through the corridors of our imaginations, carrying with it the promise of adventures yet to come".

As I put down my pen, I felt a strange change in the atmosphere of the room. The familiar confines of Baker Street seemed to fade away, replaced by a sense of vast open spaces and endless possibilities. I turned to share this feeling with Holmes, only to find that he had silently left the room, leaving me alone with my thoughts and the whispered echoes of our Arabian Odyssey.

I rose from my desk and walked to the window, gazing out at the bustling streets of London. But in my mind's eye I saw not the grey buildings and misty alleyways of our great metropolis, but the sun-baked dunes and ancient stones of the desert. The legacy of the Obsidian Stallion, I realised, had taken root within us, ready to blossom in ways we had yet to imagine.

As I stood there, between the world we had left behind and the future that lay before us, I felt a profound sense of anticipation. Whatever challenges lay ahead, whatever mysteries awaited our discovery, I knew that the wisdom we had gained and the bonds we had forged would truly guide us.

With one last glance at the room that had witnessed the beginning and end of so many of our adventures, I turned away from the window, ready to face whatever the new day might bring. The game, as Holmes would say, was definitely on, and I could not help but feel that our greatest adventure was yet to come.

EPILOGUE

From the gas-lit confines of 221B Baker Street, the narrative effortlessly transitioned to the vast Arabian desert. Beneath a sky aglow with the fiery hues of twilight, the sands of time whispered tales of ancient civilisations, forgotten empires and the enduring mysteries that lay hidden beneath the sun-scorched surface.

The sun, a molten orb sinking towards the horizon, cast long shadows that stretched across the undulating dunes like the fingers of a forgotten god. The sky, once a canvas of azure blue, was transformed into a breathtaking spectacle of colour - fiery oranges bled into deep purples, while streaks of crimson and gold danced among wisps of lavender and rose. The sand, an endless sea of gold, shimmered and shifted in the fading light, its surface etched with the delicate tracery of windblown patterns.

A profound silence hung in the air, broken only by the soft sigh of the desert wind as it danced across the dunes, carrying with it the whispers of countless stories. The scent of warm sand mingled with the subtle scent of distant oases, creating a unique and evocative aroma that spoke of both aridity and the tenacious grip of life.

In this timeless landscape, where the boundaries between past, present and future blurred into a seamless continuum, the echoes of the adventures of Sherlock Holmes and his companions resonated with a subtle yet profound presence. Their pursuit of the Obsidian Stallion had left an indelible mark not only on their own lives, but on the fabric of history itself, weaving a new thread into the intricate tapestry of human experience.

The desert, a silent witness to the rise and fall of empires, held within its embrace the secrets of countless generations. It was a place of both challenge and solace, where the harsh realities of survival coexisted with the ethereal beauty of nature. And within its vast expanse, the mysteries of the past continued to beckon, inviting explorers and seekers of knowledge to unravel its riddles and uncover the hidden truths that lay buried beneath the sands of time.

As the sun dipped below the horizon, casting its last golden rays over the undulating dunes, the narrative gaze followed its descent, settling on a solitary figure silhouetted against the fiery sky. There, amidst the endless expanse of sand, stood the Obsidian Stallion, a creature of both myth and reality. His presence echoed the characters' journey and served as a powerful symbol of the Al-Hakim family's enduring legacy. The stallion's lineage lived on in the three legendary Arabian sires - The Byerley Turk, The Darley Arabian and The Godolphin Arabian - whose descendants became the foundation of the British thoroughbred lineage, a testament to the enduring link between the desert and the wider world.

The stallion's coat, as dark as the night sky above, shimmered with an almost ethereal sheen, reflecting the fading light like a polished obsidian mirror. His mane, a cascade of midnight silk, flowed and rippled in the gentle desert breeze, while his tail, long and full, trailed behind him like a banner of shadows. Its eyes, deep pools of liquid darkness, held a wisdom born of generations past, reflecting the countless sunrises and sunsets it had witnessed throughout its long and storied life.

With every graceful movement, the stallion embodied the spirit of the desert itself - a creature of power and grace, perfectly adapted to its harsh yet beautiful environment. His hooves, strong and sure-footed, left barely a mark on the shifting sands as he moved with effortless ease across the dunes, his presence a testament to the enduring connection between the natural world and the legacy of those who have walked this land before.

The stallion's existence was inextricably linked to the Al-Hakim family, his lineage stretching back generations to the time of Idris, the master who first tamed his ancestors. With a deep respect for the materials he worked with and an unwavering commitment to creating objects of beauty and functionality, Idris had instilled in his descendants a profound appreciation of the natural world and the importance of honouring the legacy of those who came before.

The stallion, like the desert itself, had witnessed the rise and fall of empires, the triumphs and tragedies of countless lives. He had seen the caravans of traders travelling the ancient spice routes, the armies of conquerors marching across the sands, and the nomadic tribes seeking sustenance in the unforgiving landscape. And through it all, it had remained a symbol of resilience, strength and the enduring spirit of the desert.

As the stars began to appear in the darkening sky, casting their silvery light on the solitary figure of the stallion, his symbolism resonated with the broader themes of history. He embodied the mysteries of the desert and the secrets of the past, his presence a reminder that there were countless riddles still waiting to be unravelled beneath the sands of time. It represented the strength and resilience of the human spirit, echoing the determination of the characters to overcome adversity and leave their mark on the world. And it symbolised the deep connection between humans and the natural world, a connection that transcends time and culture, reminding us of our place in the grand tapestry of life.

Standing alone in the vast expanse of the desert, the Obsidian Stallion was more than a magnificent creature; it was a living embodiment of heritage, connection and the enduring mysteries of the past. Her presence served as a reminder that the characters' journey, though seemingly complete, had left an indelible mark on the world, and that the quest for knowledge, understanding and connection would continue to inspire generations to come.

As the narrative lens widened to encompass the vast expanse of the Arabian Desert, echoes of the past echoed through the shifting sands and timeworn stones. This arid landscape, seemingly desolate and unchanging, held within its embrace the stories of countless generations, the rise and fall of empires and the enduring legacy of civilisations that had left their indelible mark on the world.

Under the starry skies, the spirits of ancient peoples whispered through the ruins of once-great cities, their voices carried on the desert wind. The Nabataeans, masters of trade and engineering, had carved their magnificent city of Petra into the pink cliffs, a testament to their ingenuity and artistic skill. Their intricate network of water channels and cisterns, a marvel of hydraulic engineering, had transformed the arid landscape into a thriving oasis, a testament to their harmonious relationship with nature.

Further south, amidst the haunting beauty of Al-Hijr, also known as Mada'in Saleh, the echoes of the Thamud people echoed through the monumental tombs and dwellings carved into the sandstone cliffs. Their enigmatic rock art and inscriptions, a window into their beliefs and way of life, spoke of a deep connection to the land and a reverence for the mysteries of the desert.

These ancient civilisations, along with countless others that have risen and fallen in the desert's embrace, have left behind a rich tapestry of cultural heritage - a legacy of traditions, beliefs and artistic expressions that continue to inspire and inform the present day. From the intricate geometric patterns that adorn Bedouin textiles to the haunting melodies of traditional music, the cultural echoes of the past echoed through the lives of those who called the desert home.

The characters' journey, intertwined with the hunt for the Obsidian Stallion and the unravelling of the Obsidian Guild's secrets, had brought them face to face with this rich history and cultural heritage. Their exploration of Petra and Al-Hijr, their encounters with individuals who embodied the spirit of the desert, and their discovery of the Guild's role in preserving knowledge and protecting historical treasures had deepened their understanding of the interconnectedness of past and present.

The Obsidian Guild, with its centuries-old legacy of preserving knowledge and promoting cultural exchange, had played a vital role in ensuring that the echoes of the past continued to resonate in the present. Its efforts to protect archaeological sites, preserve ancient texts and promote understanding between different cultures had contributed to a greater appreciation of the rich history and cultural heritage of the Arabian Desert.

As the stars twinkled above the silent expanse of sand, the desert stood as a testament to the enduring power of human connection and the legacy of those who came before. The echoes of the past, carried on the desert wind and etched into the timeworn stones, served as a reminder that the characters' journey, though seemingly over, had left an indelible mark on the world, and that the pursuit of knowledge, understanding and connection would continue to inspire generations to come.

***

Yet for all that had been revealed, the Arabian Desert remained a realm of enduring mystery, its sands hiding secrets that had eluded explorers and scholars for millennia. Beneath the star-studded canopy of the night sky, the desert whispered tales of lost civilisations, forgotten languages and unexplained phenomena that continued to capture the imagination and fuel the quest for knowledge. The reunited obsidian statuettes, now safely guarded by the Obsidian Guild, served as a reminder of the power of ancient artefacts to shape the course of history and the lives of those who sought to unlock their secrets.

The whispers of the wind carried hints of ancient cities swallowed by the shifting sands, their very existence known only through fragmented legends and tantalising glimpses in weathered texts. Forgotten languages, etched on crumbling stone tablets or whispered in the hushed tones of nomadic tribes, held the keys to unlocking the secrets of the past, their meanings tantalisingly out of reach. And amidst the vast expanse of dunes and rocky outcrops, unexplained phenomena - mirages shimmering on the horizon, strange patterns etched into the desert floor, and tales of mythical creatures roaming the desolate landscape - added to the aura of mystery and intrigue that had captivated explorers for centuries.

The characters' journey, though filled with remarkable discoveries and profound insights, had only scratched the surface of what remained unknown. The obsidian stallion, a symbol of the desert's enduring mysteries, served as a constant reminder that the quest for knowledge and understanding was an ongoing process that required both humility and unwavering determination.

The importance of curiosity, exploration and the pursuit of knowledge remained paramount in unravelling the mysteries of the past and shedding light on the complexities of the human experience. Archaeological research, historical investigation and scientific inquiry served as essential tools in this endeavour, with each new discovery adding another piece to the intricate puzzle of the desert's history and cultural heritage.

The Obsidian Guild, with its unwavering commitment to preserving knowledge and promoting cultural exchange, has played a vital role in this ongoing quest. Its efforts to support research, protect archaeological sites and promote understanding between different cultures have served as a beacon of hope, lighting the way to a future where the mysteries of the past can be unravelled and the common heritage of mankind can be celebrated.

The enduring mysteries of the desert resonated deeply with Sherlock Holmes and Dr John Watson, whose own insatiable curiosity and relentless pursuit of the truth reflected the spirit of exploration that had drawn countless others to this enigmatic landscape. Their experiences in the desert had not only broadened their understanding of the world, but had also ignited a passion for uncovering the unknown and a deep appreciation of the complexities of history and culture.

As they returned to their lives in London, the echoes of the desert's mysteries would continue to inspire them, fueling their desire to seek out new challenges, solve complex puzzles and expand their knowledge. The Arabian Desert, with its timeless landscapes and enduring mysteries, had left an indelible mark on their souls, a reminder that the quest for knowledge and understanding was a journey without end, promising both challenge and the exhilarating thrill of discovery.

⬦⬦⬦⬦⬦

As the desert wind whispered through the ancient sands, carrying with it the echoes of countless stories, the narrative shifted once again to focus on the enduring legacy of the characters' journey and the continuation of their quest for knowledge and understanding. Their adventures, though seemingly over, had left an indelible mark on the world, inspiring others to seek truth, to embrace curiosity and to strive to make a positive impact on the world around them.

With his unparalleled intellect and unwavering dedication to justice, Sherlock Holmes had not only solved intricate mysteries, but also illuminated the path to a more just and equitable society. His analytical mind and relentless pursuit of the truth served as a beacon of hope, inspiring others to question assumptions, to challenge the status quo, and to seek knowledge with an open mind and a discerning heart.

Dr John Watson, the ever-faithful companion and chronicler of their adventures, had not only provided invaluable support and medical expertise, but also served as a moral compass, reminding Holmes and others of the human cost of their actions and the importance of compassion and empathy. His unwavering loyalty and ability to see the good in others served as a testament to the enduring power of friendship and the importance of human connection.

With a centuries-old legacy of preserving knowledge and promoting cultural exchange, the Obsidian Guild continues to play a vital role in preserving the past and shaping the future. Their dedication to protecting archaeological sites, supporting research and fostering understanding between cultures ensured that the echoes of ancient civilisations would continue to reverberate through the ages, inspiring future generations to explore, learn and connect with the rich tapestry of human history.

And beyond the immediate circle of characters, countless individuals, inspired by their example, embarked on their own journeys of discovery and positive change. Archaeologists delved deeper into the mysteries of the desert, uncovering lost cities and forgotten languages. Historians pieced together the fragments of the past, shedding light on the lives and legacies of those who came before. And ordinary people, touched by the stories of the characters, embraced curiosity, sought knowledge and strove to make a difference in their own communities and the wider world.

The story did not really end with the setting of the desert sun; it continued through the ongoing efforts of those who dared to dream, to explore and to seek a deeper understanding of the world and their place in it. The legacy of the characters lived on in the hearts and minds of those they inspired, ensuring that the spirit of curiosity, the pursuit of truth and the desire to make a positive difference would endure for generations to come.

As the stars twinkled above the silent expanse of the desert, casting their silvery light on the undulating dunes, the Obsidian Stallion, a symbol of the mystery and enduring spirit of the desert, turned and disappeared into the darkness. His departure, like the end of a chapter in a much larger story, left a sense of both closure and anticipation, a reminder that the journey of discovery was never truly over. For those who dared to dream and explore, the desert, like the future itself, held infinite possibilities waiting to be unlocked under the starry sky.

ABOUT THE AUTHOR

Anna Charlotte Fox has emerged as a fresh and compelling voice in the world of Sherlock Holmes fiction. With 'The Obsidian Stallion', she embarks on an ambitious seven-book series entitled 'Sherlock Holmes - Echoes Through Time', which will captivate readers from 2024. Anna's journey into the literary world is rooted in her deep admiration for Sir Arthur Conan Doyle's iconic detective, Sherlock Holmes.

From a young age, Anna was captivated by the misty streets of Victorian London and the complex mysteries that only Holmes could solve. This fascination blossomed into a lifelong passion, guiding her academic pursuits in history and literature. Anna's deep-seated love of historical narrative and the mysteries of the human mind has become the cornerstone of her writing, allowing her to weave intricate tales that pay homage to Doyle's masterpieces while infusing them with her unique perspective and voice.

Anna's approach to 'The Obsidian Stallion' and the subsequent novels in the series is a testament to her respect and reverence for the original works. She strives not to reinvent Holmes, but to celebrate the character in his quintessential form - brilliant, observant and undeniably British. Set against the rich tapestry of the Victorian and Edwardian eras, her stories aim to capture the authenticity and spirit of Holmes' original adventures.

Beyond her literary pursuits, Anna is an avid equestrian and a keen historian, passions that deeply influence her writing. Her stories are infused with a love of the equestrian world and a keen insight into the historical context that shapes her characters' adventures. Anna's commitment to historical accuracy and her ability to create compelling, character-driven stories make her a remarkable addition to the Sherlock Holmes literary tradition.

As 'The Obsidian Stallion' marks Anna's debut in the world of Sherlock Holmes fiction, she invites readers to join her on a journey of intrigue and intellect. Through her series, Anna hopes to share her love of Holmes with a new generation of readers, offering them the thrill of the chase and the joy of solving mysteries alongside literature's most beloved detective.

Thank you for taking this journey with Anna C. Fox. May the mysteries of 'The Obsidian Stallion' and the 'Sherlock Holmes - Echoes Through Time' series bring you as much joy and intrigue as they have brought to their creator.

ABOUT THE SERIES

Embark on an unparalleled literary adventure with 'Sherlock Holmes - Echoes Through Time', a seven-book series meticulously crafted by the talented Anna Charlotte Fox. This ambitious collection invites readers to walk the misty streets of Victorian London and beyond alongside literature's most beloved detective, Sherlock Holmes, and his faithful companion, Dr John Watson.

More than a series, 'Sherlock Holmes - Echoes Through Time' is an odyssey that redefines the legacy of Sherlock Holmes and Dr John Watson for a new era. Each novel intricately layers mystery over history, challenging the intellect and stirring the spirit. Anna Charlotte Fox masterfully pays homage to Sir Arthur Conan Doyle's creations while charting a course through unexplored territories of the human heart and the annals of time.

I.   The Obsidian Stallion (1893) - Unravel the mystery of the legendary Obsidian Stallion, a symbol of power and knowledge that draws Holmes and Watson into a web of ancient secrets and global intrigue.

II. The Trojan Veil (1889) - Holmes and Watson face a challenge that takes them to the heart of Paris, where a veil shrouded in myth and a mysterious perfume hold the key to preventing a catastrophic conflict.

III. The Byzantine Flame (1898) - In the shadow of Byzantium's lost glory, a rekindled flame leads the duo on a hunt for a relic that could illuminate the world or plunge it into darkness.

IV. The Blighted Crosses (1901) - A series of cryptic crimes across Europe leads Holmes and Watson down a path that intersects with historical mysteries and a conspiracy that threatens the very foundation of the British Empire.

V.   The Thames Serpent (1906) - The murky waters of the Thames hide a secret as old as London itself, leading Holmes and Watson on an investigation where myth and reality converge.

VI. The Abyss Within (1911) - Delve into the depths of the human psyche as Holmes and Watson confront a nemesis whose machinations reveal the darkness that lies in the heart of man.

VII. The Sunken Echoes (1912) - A haunting melody from the depths of the ocean leads the detective duo on their final journey where lost civilisations and timeless mysteries await.

Each story blends historical richness with the enduring intrigue of Sherlock Holmes. Readers will meet historical figures and delve into Viking history and technological breakthroughs. The inclusion of prominent intellectuals and inventors adds depth and authenticity to the narrative, enhancing the historical context and intellectual challenge.

The series explores the intersection of science, the supernatural and advanced technology. Mechanical monsters, ancient manuscripts and cryptic runes challenge the boundaries of reality and reason, creating a compelling narrative where scientific discovery and mystical elements coexist. Through personal stories intertwined with ancient legends, the novels emphasise the forging of bonds that transcend time. Characters from different backgrounds and eras work together to reveal the enduring power of the human spirit in the face of history's darkest mysteries.

Holmes confronts ethical dilemmas and existential questions as he grapples with the overwhelming power and destructive potential of atomic energy and the societal implications of his discoveries. These themes challenge Holmes' understanding of justice and responsibility, adding layers of complexity to the narrative and prompting readers to reflect on profound philosophical questions. Each book presents formidable adversaries who challenge Holmes' intellect and resolve, creating compelling conflicts that drive the narrative forward. The adversaries' diverse motivations and methods add intrigue and suspense, keeping readers on the edge of their seats.

Join Holmes and Watson as they navigate the echoes of the past, unravelling the threads of history to shed light on long-buried truths. With 'Sherlock Holmes: Echoes Through Time', Anna C. Fox invites you to witness the evolution of legends, the forging of bonds that transcend time, and the unveiling of a world where the past is never truly forgotten. Prepare to be captivated as each book in the series is a key to unlocking the mysteries of history, the intricacies of the human condition, and the enduring appeal of Sherlock Holmes.

Made in United States
Orlando, FL
29 June 2025